THE COLLECTED

JOSEPH CONRAD

THE COLLECTED
TALES OF
JOSEPH
CONRAD

Edited and with an Introduction by
SAMUEL HYNES

THE ECCO PRESS

The Ecco Press
100 West Broad Street
Hopewell, New Jersey 08525

Published simultaneously in Canada by
Penguin Books Canada Ltd., Ontario
Printed in the United States of America

Library of Congress Cataloging-in-Publication Data

Conrad, Joseph, 1857–1924.
The collected tales of Joseph Conrad
Includes bibliographical references.
1. Hynes, Samuel Lynn. I. Title
PR6005.04A6 1991   823',912   91-27115
ISBN 0-88001-287-0 (v. III)
ISBN 0-88001-288-9 (v. IV)
ISBN 0-88001-439-3 (combined paperback)

Designed by Janet Tingey
The text of this book is set in Simoncini Garamond
9 8 7 6 5 4 3 2 1
FIRST ECCO PAPERBACK EDITION

TABLE OF CONTENTS

A CONRAD CHRONOLOGY

For fuller details, see the chronology in Norman Page's *Conrad Companion* (1986), or Norman Sherry's excellent brief biography, *Conrad* (1972). The dates of Conrad's books given here are of the first printing, whether the American or the English edition.

1857   Dec. 3rd. Conrad born Jósef Teodor Konrad Korzeniowski, at Berdichev, then in the Russian Ukraine, the son of Apollo Korzeniowski and his wife Eva.

1861   Oct. 21st. Apollo Korzeniowski arrested by Russian police for underground political activities in support of Polish nationalism.

1862   May 9th. Family is exiled to Vologda, in northern Russia.

1865   April 18th. Eva dies of tuberculosis.

1867   Father and son allowed to return to Poland—first to Lvov and then to Cracow.

1869   May 23rd. Apollo Korzeniowski dies. Conrad becomes the ward of his uncle.

1874   Oct. 13th. Conrad leaves Poland for Marseilles, to seek a career in the French merchant service.

1875   Makes three voyages to the West Indies, the last two as a crew
–76   member.

1877   Engages in arms-smuggling to Spain, gambling, perhaps an un-
–78   happy love affair. Attempts suicide.

1878   Travels to England for first time; joins British merchant service.

1878   Voyages, mainly to Far East: to Sydney (1878 and 1880), to
–89   Bangkok (1881–1882), to Madras (1883), to Singapore (1885),
        to Java (1887). Qualifies as second mate (1880), first mate (1884),
        master (1886).
1886   Becomes British subject. Writes first story, "The Black Mate."
1889   September. Begins *Almayer's Folly*, his first novel.
1890   May 10th. Sails for Belgian Congo to take command of river
        steamer.
1891   Two voyages to Australia on clipper *Torrens*, as chief officer.
–93
1894   Last nautical berth, as first officer on *Adowa* (which never leaves
        moorings in Rouen harbor).
        October. *Almayer's Folly* is accepted for publication.
1895   *Almayer's Folly* published.
1896   March 24th. Marries Jessie George and settles in the south of
        England. *An Outcast of the Islands* published.
1898   First son, Borys, born. *Tales of Unrest* published.
1899   Collaborates with Ford Madox Hueffer (later Ford Madox
–02   Ford) on two novels: *The Inheritors* (published 1901) and *Ro-
        mance* (published 1903).
1900   *Lord Jim*.
1902   *Typhoon* (N.Y.); *Youth: A Narrative; and Two Other Stories*.
1903   *Typhoon, and Other Stories* (London).
1904   *Nostromo*.
1906   Second son, John, born. Working visits to Montpellier, France.
        The Mirror of the Sea.
1907   Working visits to Montpellier and Geneva. *The Secret Agent*.
1908   *A Set of Six*.
1910   Serious breakdown in health.
1911   *Under Western Eyes*.
1912   *A Personal Record. 'Twixt Land and Sea*.
1913   *Chance*, Conrad's first best-seller.
1914   Visits Poland with family. First World War begins. Return to
        England difficult. July 25th.
1915   *Victory. Within the Tides*.
1917   *The Shadow-Line*.
1919   *The Arrow of Gold*.
1920   *The Rescue* (a novel begun in 1896).

THE ART OF TELLING
An Introduction to Conrad's Tales

TALE is a term that Conrad used frequently but inconsistently in the titles and subtitles of his works. Among his novels *The Nigger of the Narcissus* is "A Tale of the Sea," *Nostromo* is "A Tale of the Seaboard," *Victory* "An Island Tale," *The Secret Agent* "A Simple Tale"; *Lord Jim* and *Chance* are both "Tales." The term also appears among the shorter pieces, either as a collective book-title (*Tales of Unrest, Tales of Hearsay*), or as a subtitle (*Within the Tides* and *'Twixt Land and Sea* are both "Tales"), or attached to individual stories; in his last collection is one story that Conrad, no doubt tired of inventing titles, called simply "A Tale."

What common element can one find among such various fictions? Certainly there is no defining length: *Nostromo* is a novel of some 200,000 words, while "A Tale" comes to only about 6,000. Nor is there a common kind of action—some are adventures, some aren't; nor a common tone—Conrad's irony comes and goes. Perhaps what they shared in Conrad's own mind was simply the quality of being told; by calling his novels and stories *tales* Conrad was claiming his place in a tradition, among the storytellers.

I have appropriated *tale* as a collective name for the longer stories, a kind he found particularly congenial to his gifts. He described this favorite form in a letter he wrote to his editor at *Blackwood's Magazine* when he was finishing his longest long story, "The End of the Tether":

> I want to give you an idea of how the figure works. Upon the episodes, after all, the effect of reality depends and as to me I depend upon the reader *looking back* upon my story as a whole. This is why I prefer the form which needs for its development 30000 words or so.

Here Conrad specifies a length (unusually long for a story), but he also specifies a method: this kind of story will be told in many episodes, and will be comprehended by the reader retrospectively—not as a continually unfolding action but completed and entire, the way stories live in memory.

Perhaps because he began writing relatively late in his life, after a career as a merchant seaman on remote waters of the earth, Conrad found in memory a natural narrative model. More than most novelists he could draw directly on what he had done or seen or heard about out there: he had lived another life, in a world that was full of tales. In his "Author's Notes" he makes this point again and again: " 'Youth,' " he says, is "a record of experience"; " 'Heart of Darkness' is experience, too"; the pages of "The End of the Tether" are "the product of experience"; Captain MacWhirr in "Typhoon" is "perfectly authentic."

But even while Conrad was claiming the authority of direct experience for his tales, he was undermining that authority: if "Heart of Darkness" was experience, it yet had "a tonality of its own ... like another art altogether"; "Typhoon" might be "a bit of a sea yarn," but it was shaped "to bring out its deeper significance"; MacWhirr was authentic, but he never existed. "None of them are stories of experience in the absolute sense of the word." Two contrary systems of validation were being appealed to: experience and art, the tale and its telling, the testimony of the man of action and the words of the conscious artist.

These opposing systems marked Conrad's sense of himself as a writer from the beginning of his literary career. He put them into the opening paragraph of his autobiographical *A Personal Record*, where he describes the writing of his first novel, as though he had to establish his double identity at once in order to tell his own story. "Books may be written in all sorts of places," the paragraph begins:

> Verbal inspiration may enter the berth of a mariner onboard a ship frozen fast in a river in the middle of a town; and since saints are supposed to look benignantly on humble believers, I indulge in the pleasant fancy that the shade of old Flaubert ... might have hovered with amused interest over the decks of a 2,000 ton steamer called the *Adowa*, on board of which, gripped by the inclement winter alongside a quay in Rouen, the tenth chapter of "Almayer's Folly" was begun.

The scene is pure Experience: Rouen in winter, the icy river, the ship (name and tonnage specified) frozen at the quay. But above the scene hovers Art—the shade of Flaubert, "a sort of literary, saint-like hermit."

In the writing of the tales, experience and art made their conflicting demands, stretching Conrad between fact and invention, between clarity and obscurity, between plain, sea-going words and literary rhetoric, in a struggle that left him exhausted, often ill, in despair. The tracks of his struggle are everywhere in the tales: in the intricacies of narration, the nervous reluctance to march to a resolution, the instabilities of language, the shadows that fall across the brightest scenes.

And in the tellers. Those to whom Conrad gave identities are much like himself: mature men with memories of lives spent at sea in exotic places. They call their remembered stories mere "sea yarns" and "artless tales," but what they do is not artless; their function is not to tell a tale, but to complicate it by probing at the moral, psychological, and ontological issues within it. In his most fully invented form this teller has a name and a story of his own: he is Marlow in "Heart of Darkness" (and in "Youth," *Lord Jim* and *Chance*). In other tales—"Falk," "Freya of the Seven Isles"—he is nameless, but is essentially the same ironic witness. Sometimes he tells his tale to men like himself—a few old sailors on the deck of a moored ship, or a circle of cronies at a riverside inn. But even when neither the teller nor his audience is defined, the voice of the tale is much the same: the voice of a wise and ironic man, made skeptical by experience.

This is even true of the one tale that seems to stand outside the customary Conrad frame. "The Duel" is set in early nineteenth-century France, and concerns a quarrel between two French Army officers; it has nothing to do with the sea, or the Far East, and it owes nothing to Conrad's past life (unless one accepts the story, now generally rejected, that he fought a duel as a young man). Like many other writers of his time (Thomas Hardy was one), Conrad was drawn to the legend of Napoleon and found in it the modern European epic and the last romantic wars. But he filtered his Napoleonic tale through the ironic sensibility of a worn, ironic general, made *honor* an ironic term, and gave to the long contention in the story an ironic, even comic, ending. To resolve an *affaire d'honneur* with two middle-aged generals hunting each other in a wood, neither wounding the other, is entirely Conradian. And so is the tone of the telling.

Conrad's tale-teller is a man who sees more than the person whose tale he relates, whether that person is a young girl, or an innocent old man, or himself when young. We see what he sees, and what we see is the tale's reality. That seen reality is the first principle of Conrad's art. In his preface to *The Nigger of the Narcissus*, his first and most theoretical essay on his own work, he described his intentions in this way:

> My task which I am trying to achieve is, by the power of the written word to make you hear, to make you feel—it is, before all, to make you *see*. That—and no more, and it is everything.

This seems straightforward enough: it is the credo of a realistic writer, concerned to make the physical world sensible to his reader, because that is all there is.

The world Conrad wrote about set him special problems in the accomplishment of that task. His men do work that we his readers have never done, or even seen others doing: they command sailing ships, they confront typhoons, they are becalmed and shipwrecked, they navigate uncharted rivers. Work—the daily work by which men earn their bread—is not ordinarily at the center of English fiction; nobody works in the novels of Jane Austen, or Henry James, or Virginia Woolf. But in Conrad, work is crucial: what men do is what they are, and how they do it—not success or failure, but fidelity to the task—is a measure of their human value, and a source of their identity. "I don't like work," Marlow remarks,

> —no man does—but I like what is in the work,—the chance to find yourself. Your own reality—for yourself, not for others—what no other man can ever know. They can only see the mere show, and never can tell what it really means.

The places where the work is done are also a problem for the realist. Conrad's geography is spacious and exotic: the Malay Straits, the Congo, the China Sea, the islands of Indonesia. This is the world of romance; Conrad took as his task to make it as actual as the English Channel or the Pool of London. He accomplished that task by packing his tales with exact particulars—the cast-iron lamp posts of a Malay town, the snags and islands in the Congo, the homely furnishings of Captain Hermann's *Diana*—densely and sharply observed, as though Conrad had only just left the scene.

There is more than realism in his seeing, though. Look, for example, at Marlow's arrival at the Company station:

I came upon a boiler wallowing in the grass, then found a path leading up the hill. It turned aside for the boulders, and also for an undersized railway-truck lying there on its back with its wheels in the air. One was off. The thing looked as dead as the carcass of some animal. I came upon more pieces of decaying machinery, a stack of rusty nails. To the left a clump of trees made a shady spot, where dark things seemed to stir feebly. I blinked, the path was steep.

What we see here is the derelict rubbish of progress, but we see it with strange, surreal eyes—the boiler *wallowing*, the railway-truck like a dead animal, machinery invested with life and death. *Real* life and death are hidden in the shadows at the edge of our vision, where dark things air. Later on we will identify them as the dying black victims of the Company's enterprise; here they are only things, as the truck is a thing. Seeing fails us, reality will not reveal the whole of its cruel truth.

This sense of the limits of perception is a constant in Conrad. Near at hand, his phenomenal world is clearly seen; but in the distance, at the edge of vision, things blur. Conrad makes us see, all right; but what we see is mysterious, uncertain, unknowable, because that is the way Conrad saw the world. He put that sense of mystery into his *Nigger* preface too, where he wrote of "the aim of art, which, like life itself, is inspiring, difficult—obscured by mists."

"Heart of Darkness" is Conrad's most profound and disquieting expression of this obscured reality. It begins and ends in the chiaroscuro of a Thames-side nightfall, and within that frame it proceeds through shadow, night, fog, and inscrutable jungle, into the heart of the tale—a narrative progress through darkness to darkness. Darkness is physical here, but it is more than that; it is a metaphor for everything that Marlow cannot understand about the hearts that he encounters: the hearts of other white men, the hearts of Africans, Kurtz's heart, the heart of Africa itself. This is not because of any inadequacy in him—Marlow is Conrad's most acute observer—but simply because the world denies humankind's need for meaning, for understanding.

In such a world of mystery, how can one tell a tale? Marlow, in the midst of trying to tell his listeners about the mysterious Kurtz, bursts out that one can't:

No, it is impossible; it is impossible to convey the life-sensation of any given epoch of one's existence—that which makes its truth, its meaning—

its subtle and penetrating essence. It is impossible. We live, as we dream—alone. . . .

If Marlow is right, then these are impossible tales; for they do what he says can't be done—they convey life-sensations, and such truths and meanings as life offers. But they also convey Conrad's sense of limits, and the greatest limitation of all, the loneliness that is the price of being human. Conrad's characters live and dream alone: Renouard on his island, Whalley imprisoned in his blindness, Falk haunted by his past, Kurtz in his private darkness, are all lonely, isolated men.

And what about women? Critics have sometimes treated Conrad's novels as adventure stories with all-male casts, in the tradition of Haggard and Henty. This view is wrong, but one can see how it came about. For there aren't many women in Conrad's tales, and the roles they play are restricted and defined by the man's world in which they live. For this fact there are possible biographical explanations. Conrad was not at ease with women, and didn't appear to know much about them. His mother died when he was seven, and he did not marry until he was thirty-eight. He spent most of the years between—the years from which the tales mainly come—at sea in the company of men. As in the life, so in the art: he chose tales with mostly men in them, and narrators who have no women in their lives—who don't *know* women, but only *witness* them, as disturbing motives in the lives of other men. Conrad felt their disturbing power, too, and admitted that he was most comfortable with a tale that had no women at all in it. Just after he completed "Freya of the Seven Isles," he wrote to his friend Edward Garnett:

> I daresay *Freya* is pretty rotten. On the other hand the *Secret Sharer*, between you and me, is *it*. Eh? No damned tricks with girls there. Eh? Every word fits and there's not a single uncertain note.

Nevertheless, women are important in the tales. But not as agents: in Conrad's world of work they have no active part. "They—the women I mean—are out of it," Marlow says, "—should be out of it. We must help them stay in that beautiful world of their own, lest ours gets worse." And that is how we see them—Hermann's niece in "Falk," Felicia Moorsom in "The Planter of Malata," Freya in "Freya of the Seven Isles," Alice Jacobus in "A Smile of Fortune"—all remote, mysterious, larger than life, not so much women as idealized effigies of women.

Hermann's niece (she has no name in the tale) "could have stood for an allegoric statue of Earth"; Miss Moorsom is "a condescending and strong-headed goddess"; Freya is "like a feminine and martial statue"; Alice Jacobus is "like a figure in a tapestry." Amid the turmoil of men's lives they seem scarcely to move or speak; yet they energize the actions of the man around them. Their appeal is not sexual attraction, exactly; rather it is the appeal of that other, beautiful world of their own, in which a woman is a temptation and a responsibility, but is also a refuge from the world of action.

One woman in the tales is an apparent exception. Marlow sees her at the point of his greatest penetration into the Congo darkness—"a wild and gorgeous apparition of a woman" on the river's bank.

> She walked with measured steps, draped in striped and fringed cloths, treading the earth proudly, with a slight jingle and flash of barbarous ornaments. She carried her head high; her hair was done in the shape of a helmet; she had brass leggings to the knee, brass wire gauntlets to the elbow, a crimson spot on her tawny cheek, innumerable necklaces of glass beads on her neck; bizarre things, charms, gifts of witch-men, that hung about her, glittered and trembled at every step. She must have had the value of several elephant tusks upon her. She was savage and superb, wild-eyed and magnificent; there was something ominous and stately in her deliberate progress. And in the hush that had fallen suddenly upon the whole sorrowful land, the immense wilderness, the colossal body of the fecund and mysterious life seemed to look at her, pensive, as though it had been looking at the image of its own tenebrous and passionate soul.

Many elements in Conrad's imagination come together in this brilliant, mysterious figure: his romanticism, his imperialism, his nervous ambivalence toward women, his assumptions about race. Like his other strong women, this savage is monumental; if, like the others, she is a kind of allegorical effigy, it is an effigy of raw female sexuality, wild and passionate, like a force in nature. Yet her destiny is not different from the others: her power fails before the power of the white men she faces and she is left to grieve in darkness, as back in Europe her mirror-opposite, Kurtz's Intended, grieves.

Darkness is an appropriate setting for most of Conrad's women: they belong to the world of mystery, of questions without answers, in which the tales exist. Their relations with men are one of the contrarieties of life that cause the world's disquiet. But not the only one. Conrad saw other conflicts in his world—conflicts in political thought, in the economics of imperialism, in philosophy, in psychology—all crucial in human life, each with its obscurities and contradictions to mislead and hamper human desires.

The perception of these conflicts doesn't amount to a philosophy: Conrad couldn't be said to have one. His ideas about life, when he put them into discursive prose, were as inconsistent and contradictory as the lives of his characters. He could be blackly solipsistic in his letters to his friend Cunninghame Graham, and yet in another place argue the solidarity of all humanity. He could assert the high purpose of art, yet doubt that one consciousness could ever reach another. He could say that life was tragic, and then say that it was mechanistic and meaningless (and even say both in the same letter).

Conrad could not philosophize consistently, but he could do something more valuable, and more disquieting: he could be faithful in his fiction to his sense of the world and men's place in it. "The part of the inexplicable should be allowed for," he wrote in *A Personal Record*, "in the appraising of the conduct of men in a world where no explanation is final." There is a tolerant skepticism in this remark, by which Conrad seemed to live his life. There is also an aesthetic implicit in it, by which a man might write a possible kind of impossible tale.

THE COLLECTED TALES OF
JOSEPH CONRAD

HEART OF DARKNESS

· I ·

T H E *Nellie,* a cruising yawl, swung to her anchor without a flutter of the sails, and was at rest. The flood had made, the wind was nearly calm, and being bound down the river, the only thing for it was to come to and wait for the turn of the tide.

The sea-reach of the Thames stretched before us like the beginning of an interminable waterway. In the offing the sea and the sky were welded together without a joint, and in the luminous space the tanned sails of the barges drifting up with the tide seemed to stand still in red clusters of canvas sharply peaked, with gleams of varnished sprits. A haze rested on the low shores that ran out to sea in vanishing flatness. The air was dark above Gravesend, and farther back still seemed condensed into a mournful gloom, brooding motionless over the biggest, and the greatest, town on earth.

The Director of Companies was our captain and our host. We four affectionately watched his back as he stood in the bows looking to seaward. On the whole river there was nothing that looked half so nautical. He resembled a pilot, which to a seaman is trustworthiness personified. It was difficult to realize his work was not out there in the luminous estuary, but behind him, within the brooding gloom.

Between us there was, as I have already said somewhere, the bond of the sea. Besides holding our hearts together through long periods of separation, it had the effect of making us tolerant of each other's yarns—and even convictions. The Lawyer—the best of old fellows—had, because of his many years and many virtues, the only cushion on deck, and was lying on the only rug. The Accountant had

brought out already a box of dominoes, and was toying architecturally
with the bones. Marlow sat cross-legged right aft, leaning against the
mizzen-mast. He had sunken cheeks, a yellow complexion, a straight
back, an ascetic aspect, and, with his arms dropped, the palms of
hands outwards, resembled an idol. The Director, satisfied the anchor
had good hold, made his way aft and sat down amongst us. We exchanged a few words lazily. Afterwards there was silence on board the
yacht. For some reason or other we did not begin that game of dominoes. We felt meditative, and fit for nothing but placid staring. The
day was ending in a serenity of still and exquisite brilliance. The water
shone pacifically; the sky, without a speck, was a benign immensity of
unstained light; the very mist on the Essex marshes was like a gauzy
and radiant fabric, hung from the wooded rises inland, and draping
the low shores in diaphanous folds. Only the gloom to the west, brooding over the upper reaches, became more sombre every minute, as if an-
gered by the approach of the sun.

And at last, in its curved and imperceptible fall, the sun sank low,
and from glowing white changed to a dull red without rays and without heat, as if about to go out suddenly, stricken to death by the touch
of that gloom brooding over a crowd of men.

Forthwith a change came over the waters, and the serenity became
less brilliant but more profound. The old river in its broad reach
rested unruffled at the decline of day, after ages of good service done
to the race that peopled its banks, spread out in the tranquil dignity
of a waterway leading to the uttermost ends of the earth. We looked
at the venerable stream not in the vivid flush of a short day that comes
and departs for ever, but in the august light of abiding memories. And
indeed nothing is easier for a man who has, as the phrase goes, "followed the sea" with reverence and affection, than to evoke the great
spirit of the past upon the lower reaches of the Thames. The tidal
current runs to and fro in its unceasing service, crowded with memories of men and ships it had borne to the rest of home or the battles
of the sea. It had known and served all the men of whom the nation
is proud, from Sir Francis Drake to Sir John Franklin, knights all,
titled and untitled—the great knights-errant of the sea. It had borne
all the ships whose names are like jewels flashing in the night of time,
from the *Golden Hind* returning with her round flanks full of treasure,

to be visited by the Queen's Highness and thus pass out of the gigantic tale, to the *Erebus* and *Terror*, bound on other conquests—and that never returned. It had known the ships and the men. They had sailed from Deptford, from Greenwich, from Erith—the adventurers and the settlers; kings' ships and the ships of men on 'Change; captains, admirals, the dark "interlopers" of the Eastern trade, and the commissioned "generals" of East India fleets. Hunters for gold or pursuers of fame, they all had gone out on that stream, bearing the sword, and often the torch, messengers of the might within the land, bearers of a spark from the sacred fire. What greatness had not floated on the ebb of that river into the mystery of an unknown earth! . . . The dreams of men, the seed of commonwealths, the germs of empires.

The sun set; the dusk fell on the stream, and lights began to appear along the shore. The Chapman lighthouse, a three-legged thing erect on a mud-flat, shone strongly. Lights of ships moved in the fairway—a great stir of lights going up and going down. And farther west on the upper reaches the place of the monstrous town was still marked ominously on the sky, a brooding gloom in sunshine, a lurid glare under the stars.

"And this also," said Marlow suddenly, "has been one of the dark places on the earth."

He was the only man of us who still "followed the sea." The worst that could be said of him was that he did not represent his class. He was a seaman, but he was a wanderer, too, while most seamen lead, if one may so express it, a sedentary life. Their minds are of the stay-at-home order, and their home is always with them—the ship; and so is their country—the sea. One ship is very much like another, and the sea is always the same. In the immutability of their surroundings the foreign shores, the foreign faces, the changing immensity of life, glide past, veiled not by a sense of mystery but by a slightly disdainful ignorance; for there is nothing mysterious to a seaman unless it be the sea itself, which is the mistress of his existence and as inscrutable as Destiny. For the rest, after his hours of work, a casual stroll or a casual spree on shore suffices to unfold for him the secret of a whole continent, and generally he finds the secret not worth knowing. The yarns of seamen have a direct simplicity, the whole meaning of which lies within the shell of a cracked nut. But Marlow was not typical (if his propensity to spin yarns be excepted), and to him the meaning of an episode was not inside like a kernel but outside, enveloping the tale which brought it out only as a glow brings out a haze, in the likeness of one of these misty halos that sometimes are made visible by the spectral illumination of moonshine.

His remark did not seem at all surprising. It was just like Marlow. It was accepted in silence. No one took the trouble to grunt even; and presently he said, very slow—

"I was thinking of very old times, when the Romans first came here, nineteen hundred years ago—the other day. . . . Light came out of this river since—you say Knights? Yes; but it is like a running blaze on a plain, like a flash of lightning in the clouds. We live in the flicker—may it last as long as the old earth keeps rolling! But darkness was here yesterday. Imagine the feelings of a commander of a fine—what d'ye call 'em?—trireme in the Mediterranean, ordered suddenly to the north; run overland across the Gauls in a hurry; put in charge of one of these craft the legionaries—a wonderful lot of handy men they must have been, too—used to build, apparently by the hundred, in a month or two, if we may believe what we read. Imagine him here—the very end of the world, a sea the colour of lead, a sky the colour of smoke, a kind of ship about as rigid as a concertina—and going up this river with stores, or orders, or what you like. Sandbanks, marshes, forests, savages—precious little to eat fit for a civilized man, nothing but Thames water to drink. No Falernian wine here, no going ashore. Here and there a military camp lost in a wilderness, like a needle in a bundle of hay—cold, fog, tempests, disease, exile, and death,—death skulking in the air, in the water, in the bush. They must have been dying like flies here. Oh, yes—he did it. Did it very well, too, no doubt, and without thinking much about it either, except afterwards to brag of what he had gone through in his time, perhaps. They were men enough to face the darkness. And perhaps he was cheered by keeping his eye on a chance of promotion to the fleet at Ravenna by and by, if he had good friends in Rome and survived the awful climate. Or think of a decent young citizen in a toga—perhaps too much dice, you know—coming out here in the train of some prefect, or tax-gatherer, or trader even, to mend his fortunes. Land in a swamp, march through the woods, and in some inland post feel the savagery, the utter savagery, had closed round him—all that mysterious life of the wilderness that stirs in the forest, in the jungles, in the hearts of wild men. There's no initiation either into such mysteries. He has to live in the midst of the incomprehensible, which is also detestable. And it has a fascination, too, that goes to work upon him. The fascination of the abomination—you know, imagine the growing regrets, the longing to escape, the powerless disgust, the surrender, the hate."

He paused.

"Mind," he began again, lifting one arm from the elbow, the palm of the hand outwards, so that, with his legs folded before him, he had the pose of a Buddha preaching in European clothes and without a lotus-flower—"Mind, none of us would feel exactly like this. What saves us is efficiency—the devotion to efficiency. But these chaps were not much account, really. They were no colonists; their administration was merely a squeeze, and nothing more, I suspect. They were conquerors, and for that you want only brute force—nothing to boast of, when you have it, since your strength is just an accident arising from the weakness of others. They grabbed what they could get for the sake of what was to be got. It was just robbery with violence, aggravated murder on a great scale, and men going at it blind—as is very proper for those who tackle a darkness. The conquest of the earth, which mostly means the taking it away from those who have a different complexion or slightly flatter noses than ourselves, is not a pretty thing when you look into it too much. What redeems it is the idea only. An idea at the back of it; not a sentimental pretence but an idea; and an unselfish belief in the idea—something you can set up, and bow down before, and offer a sacrifice to. . . ."

He broke off. Flames glided in the river, small green flames, red flames, white flames, pursuing, overtaking, joining, crossing each other—then separating slowly or hastily. The traffic of the great city went on in the deepening night upon the sleepless river. We looked on, waiting patiently—there was nothing else to do till the end of the flood; but it was only after a long silence, when he said, in a hesitating voice, "I suppose you fellows remember I did once turn fresh-water sailor for a bit," that we knew we were fated, before the ebb began to run, to hear about one of Marlow's inconclusive experiences.

"I don't want to bother you much with what happened to me personally," he began, showing in this remark the weakness of many tellers of tales who seem so often unaware of what their audience would best like to hear; "yet to understand the effect of it on me you ought to know how I got out there, what I saw, how I went up that river to the place where I first met the poor chap. It was the farthest point of navigation and the culminating point of my experience. It seemed somehow to throw a kind of light on everything about me—and into my thoughts. It was sombre enough, too—and pitiful—not extraordinary in any way—not very clear either. No, not very clear. And yet it seemed to throw a kind of light.

"I had then, as you remember, just returned to London after a lot of Indian Ocean, Pacific, China Seas—a regular dose of the East—six years or so, and I was loafing about, hindering you fellows in your work and invading your homes, just as though I had got a heavenly mission to civilize you. It was very fine for a time, but after a bit I did get tired of resting. Then I began to look for a ship—I should think the hardest work on earth. But the ships wouldn't even look at me. And I got tired of that game, too.

"Now when I was a little chap I had a passion for maps. I would look for hours at South America, or Africa, or Australia, and lose myself in all the glories of exploration. At that time there were many blank spaces on the earth, and when I saw one that looked particularly inviting on a map (but they all look that) I would put my finger on it and say, When I grow up I will go there. The North Pole was one of these places, I remember. Well, I haven't been there yet, and shall not try now. The glamour's off. Other places were scattered about the Equator, and in every sort of latitude all over the two hemispheres. I have been in some of them, and . . . well, we won't talk about that. But there was one yet—the biggest, the most blank, so to speak—that I had a hankering after.

"True, by this time it was not a blank space any more. It had got filled since my boyhood with rivers and lakes and names. It had ceased to be a blank space of delightful mystery—a white patch for a boy to dream gloriously over. It had become a place of darkness. But there was in it one river especially, a mighty big river, that you could see on the map, resembling an immense snake uncoiled, with its head in the sea, its body at rest curving afar over a vast country, and its tail lost in the depths of the land. And as I looked at the map of it in a shop-window, it fascinated me as a snake would a bird—a silly little bird. Then I remembered there was a big concern, a Company for trade on that river. Dash it all! I thought to myself, they can't trade without using some kind of craft on that lot of fresh water—steamboats! Why shouldn't I try to get charge of one? I went on along Fleet Street, but could not shake off the idea. The snake had charmed me.

"You understand it was a Continental concern, that Trading society; but I have a lot of relations living on the Continent, because it's cheap and not so nasty as it looks, they say.

"I am sorry to own I began to worry them. This was already a fresh departure for me. I was not used to get things that way, you know. I always went my own road and on my own legs where I had a mind to go. I wouldn't have believed it of myself; but, then—you see—I felt somehow I must get there by hook or by crook. So I worried them. The men said 'My dear fellow,' and did nothing. Then—would you believe it?—I tried the women. I, Charlie Marlow, set the women to work—to get a job. Heavens! Well, you see, the notion drove me. I had an aunt, a dear enthusiastic soul. She wrote: 'It will be delightful. I am ready to do anything, anything for you. It is a glorious idea. I know the wife of a very high personage in the Administration, and also a man who has lots of influence with,' etc., etc. She was determined to make no end of fuss to get me appointed skipper of a river steamboat, if such was my fancy.

"I got my appointment—of course; and I got it very quick. It appears the Company had received news that one of their captains had been killed in a scuffle with the natives. This was my chance, and it made me the more anxious to go. It was only months and months afterwards, when I made the attempt to recover what was left of the body, that I heard the original quarrel arose from a misunderstanding about some hens. Yes, two black hens. Fresleven—that was the fellow's name, a Dane—thought himself wronged somehow in the bargain, so he went ashore and started to hammer the chief of the village with a stick. Oh, it didn't surprise me in the least to hear this, and at the same time to be told that Fresleven was the gentlest, quietest creature that ever walked on two legs. No doubt he was; but he had been a couple of years already out there engaged in the noble cause, you know, and he probably felt the need at last of asserting his self-respect in some way. Therefore he whacked the old nigger mercilessly, while a big crowd of his people watched him, thunderstruck, till some man—I was told the chief's son—in desperation at hearing the old chap yell, made a tentative jab with a spear at the white man—and of course it went quite easy between the shoulder-blades. Then the whole population cleared into the forest, expecting all kinds of calamities to happen, while, in the other hand, the steamer Fresleven commanded left also in a bad panic, in charge of the engineer, I believe. Afterwards nobody seemed to trouble much about Fresleven's remains, till I got out and stepped into his shoes. I couldn't let it rest, though; but when an opportunity offered at last to meet my predecessor, the grass growing through his ribs was tall enough to hide his bones. They were all there. The supernatural being had not been touched after he fell. And the village was deserted, the huts gaped black, rotting, all askew within the fallen enclosures. A calamity had come to it, sure enough. The people had vanished. Mad terror had scattered them, men, women, and children, through the bush, and they had never returned. What became of the hens I don't know either. I should think the cause of progress got them, anyhow. However, through this glorious affair I got my appointment, before I had fairly begun to hope for it.

"I flew around like mad to get ready, and before forty-eight hours I was crossing the Channel to show myself to my employers, and sign the contract. In a very few hours I arrived in a city that always makes me think of a whited sepulchre. Prejudice no doubt. I had no difficulty in finding the Company's offices. It was the biggest thing in the town, and everybody I met was full of it. They were going to run an oversea empire, and make no end of coin by trade.

"A narrow and deserted street in deep shadow, high houses, innumerable windows with venetian blinds, a dead silence, grass sprouting between the stones, imposing carriage archways right and left, immense double doors standing ponderously ajar. I slipped through one of these cracks, went up a swept and ungarnished staircase, as arid as a desert, and opened the first door I came to. Two women, one fat and the other slim, sat on straw-bottomed chairs, knitting black wool. The slim one got up and walked straight at me—still knitting with down-cast eyes—and only just as I began to think of getting out of her way, as you would for a somnambulist, stood still, and looked up. Her dress was as plain as an umbrella-cover, and she turned round without a word and preceded me into a waiting-room. I gave my name, and looked about. Deal table in the middle, plain chairs all round the walls, on one end a large shining map, marked with all the colours of a rainbow. There was a vast amount of red—good to see at any time, because one knows that some real work is done in there, a deuce of a lot of blue, a little green, smears of orange, and, on the East Coast, a purple patch, to show where the jolly pioneers of progress drink the jolly lager-beer. However, I wasn't going into any of these. I was going into the yellow. Dead in the centre. And the river was there—fascinating—deadly—like a snake. Ough! A door opened, a white-haired secretarial head, but wearing a compassionate expression, appeared, and a skinny forefinger beckoned me into the sanctuary. Its light was dim, and a heavy writing-desk squatted in the middle. From behind that structure came out an impression of pale plumpness in a frock-coat. The great man himself. He was five feet six, I should judge, and had his grip on the handle-end of ever so many millions. He shook hands, I fancy, murmured vaguely, was satisfied with my French. *Bon voyage.*

"In about forty-five seconds I found myself again in the waiting-room with the compassionate secretary, who, full of desolation and sympathy, made me sign some document. I believe I undertook amongst other things not to disclose any trade secrets. Well, I am not going to.

"I began to feel slightly uneasy. You know I am not used to such ceremonies, and there was something ominous in the atmosphere. It was just as though I had been let into some conspiracy—I don't know—something not quite right; and I was glad to get out. In the outer room the two women knitted black wool feverishly. People were arriving, and the younger one was walking back and forth introducing them. The old one sat on her chair. Her flat cloth slippers were propped up on a foot-warmer, and a cat reposed on her lap. She wore a starched white affair on her head, had a wart on one cheek, and silver-rimmed spectacles hung on the tip of her nose. She glanced at me above the glasses. The swift and indifferent placidity of that look troubled me. Two youths with foolish and cheery countenances were being piloted over, and she threw at them the same quick glance of unconcerned wisdom. She seemed to know all about them and about me, too. An eerie feeling came over me. She seemed uncanny and fateful. Often far away there I thought of these two, guarding the door of Darkness, knitting black wool as for a warm pall, one introducing, introducing continuously to the unknown, the other scrutinizing the cheery and foolish faces with unconcerned old eyes. *Ave!* Old knitter of black wool. *Morituri te salutant.* Not many of those she looked at ever saw her again—not half, by a long way.

"There was yet a visit to the doctor. 'A simple formality,' assured me the secretary, with an air of taking an immense part in all my sorrows. Accordingly a young chap wearing his hat over the left eyebrow, some clerk I suppose,—there must have been clerks in the business, though the house was as still as a house in a city of the dead—came from somewhere up-stairs, and led me forth. He was shabby and careless, with ink-stains on the sleeves of his jacket, and his cravat was large and billowy, under a chin shaped like the toe of an old boot. It was a little too early for the doctor, so I proposed a drink, and thereupon he developed a vein of joviality. As we sat over our vermuths he glorified the Company's business, and by and by I expressed casually my surprise at him not going out there. He became very cool and collected all at once. 'I am not such a fool as I look, quoth Plato to his disciples,' he said sententiously, emptied his glass with great resolution, and we rose.

"The old doctor felt my pulse, evidently thinking of something else the while. 'Good, good for there,' he mumbled, and then with a certain eagerness asked me whether I would let him measure my head. Rather surprised, I said Yes, when he produced a thing like calipers and got the dimensions back and front and every way, taking notes carefully. He was an unshaven little man in a threadbare coat like a gaberdine, with his feet in slippers, and I thought him a harmless fool. 'I always ask leave, in the interests of science, to measure the crania of those going out there,' he said. 'And when they come back, too?' I asked. 'Oh, I never see them,' he remarked; 'and, moreover, the changes take place inside, you know.' He smiled, as if at some quiet joke. 'So you are going out there. Famous. Interesting, too.' He gave

me a searching glance, and made another note. 'Ever any ma—
your family?' he asked, in a matter-of-fact tone. I felt very a in
'Is that question in the interests of science, too?' 'It would b
said, without taking notice of my irritation, 'interesting for scienc
watch the mental changes of individuals, on the spot, but . . .' '
you an alienist?' I interrupted. 'Every doctor should be—a little,' a
swered that original, imperturbably. 'I have a little theory which you
Messieurs who go out there must help me to prove. This is my share
in the advantages my country shall reap from the possession of such
a magnificent dependency. The mere wealth I leave to others. Pardon
my questions, but you are the first Englishman coming under my observation . . .' I hastened to assure him I was not in the least typical.
'If I were,' said I, 'I wouldn't be talking like this with you.' 'What you
say is rather profound, and probably erroneous,' he said, with a laugh.
'Avoid irritation more than exposure to the sun. Adieu. How do you
English say, eh? Good-bye. Ah! Good-bye. Adieu. In the tropics one
must before everything keep calm.' . . . He lifted a warning forefinger. . . . *'Du calme, du calme. Adieu.'*

"One thing more remained to do—say good-bye to my excellent
aunt. I found her triumphant. I had a cup of tea—the last decent cup
of tea for many days—and in a room that most soothingly looked just
as you would expect a lady's drawing-room to look, we had a long
quiet chat by the fireside. In the course of these confidences it became
quite plain to me I had been represented to the wife of the high digni-
tary, and goodness knows to how many more people besides, as an
exceptional and gifted creature—a piece of good fortune for the Company—a man you don't get hold of every day. Good heavens! and I
was going to take charge of a two-penny-half-penny river-steamboat
with a penny whistle attached! It appeared, however, I was also one of
the Workers, with a capital—you know. Something like an emissary of
light, something like a lower sort of apostle. There had been a lot of such
rot let loose in print and talk just about that time, and the excellent
woman, living right in the rush of all that humbug, got carried off her
feet. She talked about 'weaning those ignorant millions from their horrid
ways,' till upon my word, she made me quite uncomfortable. I ventured
to hint that the Company was run for profit.

"'You forget, dear Charlie, that the labourer is worthy of his hire,' d, brightly. It's queer how out of touch with truth women are. They live in a world of their own, and there has never been anything like it, and never can be. It is too beautiful altogether, and if they were to set it up it would go to pieces before the first sunset. Some confounded fact we men have been living contentedly with ever since the day of creation would start up and knock the whole thing over.

"After this I got embraced, told to wear flannel, be sure to write often, and so on—and I left. In the street—I don't know why—a queer feeling came to me that I was an impostor. Odd thing that I, who used to clear out for any part of the world at twenty-four hours' notice, with less thought than most men give to the crossing of a street, had a moment—I won't say of hesitation, but of startled pause, before this commonplace affair. The best way I can explain it to you is by saying that, for a second or two, I felt as though, instead of going to the centre of a continent, I were about to set off for the centre of the earth.

"I left in a French steamer, and she called in every blamed port they have out there, for, as far as I could see, the sole purpose of landing soldiers and custom-house officers. I watched the coast. Watching a coast as it slips by the ship is like thinking about an enigma. There it is before you—smiling, frowning, inviting, grand, mean, insipid, or savage, and always mute with an air of whispering, Come and find out. This one was almost featureless, as if still in the making, with an aspect of monotonous grimness. The edge of a colossal jungle, so dark-green as to be almost black, fringed with white surf, ran straight, like a ruled line, far, far away along a blue sea whose glitter was blurred by a creeping mist. The sun was fierce, the land seemed to glisten and drip with steam. Here and there grayish-whitish specks showed up clustered inside the white surf, with a flag flying above them perhaps. Settlements some centuries old, and still no bigger than pin-heads on the untouched expanse of their background. We pounded along, stopped, landed soldiers; went on, landed custom-house clerks to levy toll in what looked like a God-forsaken wilderness, with a tin shed and a flag-pole lost in it; landed more soldiers—to take care of the custom-house clerks, presumably. Some, I heard, got drowned in the surf; but whether they did or not, nobody seemed particularly to care. They were just flung out there, and on we went. Every day the coast looked the same, as though we had not moved; but we passed various places—trading places—with names like Gran' Bassam, Little Popo; names that seemed to belong to some sordid farce acted in front of a sinister back-cloth. The idleness of a passenger, my isolation amongst all these men with whom I had no point of contact, the oily and languid sea, the uniform sombreness of the coast, seemed to keep me away from the truth of things, within the toil of a mournful and senseless delusion. The voice of the surf heard now and then was a positive pleasure, like the speech of a brother. It was something natural, that had its reason, that had a meaning. Now and then a boat from the shore gave one a momentary contact with reality. It was paddled by black fellows. You could see from afar the white of their eyeballs glistening. They shouted, sang; their bodies streamed with perspiration; they had faces like grotesque masks—these chaps; but they had bone, muscle, a wild vitality, an intense energy of movement, that was as natural and true as the surf along their coast. They wanted no excuse for being there. They were a great comfort to look at. For a time I would feel I belonged still to a world of straightforward facts; but the feeling would not last long. Something would turn up to scare it away. Once, I remember, we came upon a man-of-war anchored off the coast. There wasn't even a shed there, and she was shelling the bush. It appears the French had one of their wars going on thereabouts. Her ensign dropped limp like a rag; the muzzles of the long six-inch guns stuck out all over the low hull; the greasy, slimy swell swung her up lazily and let her down, swaying her thin masts. In the empty immensity of earth, sky, and water, there she was, incomprehensible, firing into a continent. Pop, would go one of the six-inch guns; a small flame would dart and vanish, a little white smoke would disappear, a tiny projectile would give a feeble screech—and nothing happened. Nothing could happen. There was a touch of insanity in the proceeding, a sense of lugubrious drollery in the sight; and it was not dissipated by somebody on board assuring me earnestly there was a camp of natives—he called them enemies!—hidden out of sight somewhere.

"We gave her her letters (I heard the men in that lonely ship were dying of fever at the rate of three a day) and went on. We called at some more places with farcical names, where the merry dance of death and trade goes on in a still and earthy atmosphere as of an overheated catacomb; all along the formless coast bordered by dangerous surf, as if Nature herself had tried to ward off intruders; in and out of rivers, streams of death in life, whose banks were rotting into mud, whose waters, thickened into slime, invaded the contorted mangroves, that seemed to writhe at us in the extremity of an impotent despair. Nowhere did we stop long enough to get a particularized impression, but the general sense of vague and oppressive wonder grew upon me. It was like a weary pilgrimage amongst hints for nightmares.

"It was upward of thirty days before I saw the mouth of the big river. We anchored off the seat of the government. But my work would not begin till some two hundred miles farther on. So as soon as I could I made a start for a place thirty miles higher up.

"I had my passage on a little sea-going steamer. Her captain was a Swede, and knowing me for a seaman, invited me on the bridge. He was a young man, lean, fair, and morose, with lanky hair and a shuffling gait. As we left the miserable little wharf, he tossed his head contemptuously at the shore. 'Been living there?' he asked. I said, 'Yes.' 'Fine lot these government chaps—are they not?' he went on, speaking English with great precision and considerable bitterness. 'It is funny what some people will do for a few francs a month. I wonder what becomes of that kind when it goes up country?' I said to him I expected to see that soon. 'So-o-o!' he exclaimed. He shuffled athwart, keeping one eye ahead vigilantly. 'Don't be too sure,' he continued. 'The other day I took up a man who hanged himself on the road. He was a Swede, too.' 'Hanged himself! Why, in God's name?' I cried. He kept on looking out watchfully. 'Who knows? The sun too much for him, or the country perhaps.'

"At last we opened a reach. A rocky cliff appeared, mounds of turned-up earth by the shore, houses on a hill, others with iron roofs, amongst a waste of excavations, or hanging to the declivity. A continuous noise of the rapids above hovered over this scene of inhabited devastation. A lot of people, mostly black and naked, moved about like ants. A jetty projected into the river. A blinding sunlight drowned all this at times in a sudden recrudescence of glare. 'There's your Company's station,' said the Swede, pointing to three wooden barrack-like structures on the rocky slope. 'I will send your things up. Four boxes did you say? So. Farewell.'

"I came upon a boiler wallowing in the grass, then found a path leading up the hill. It turned aside for the boulders, and also for an undersized railway-truck lying there on its back with its wheels in the air. One was off. The thing looked as dead as the carcass of some animal. I came upon more pieces of decaying machinery, a stack of rusty nails. To the left a clump of trees made a shady spot, where dark things seemed to stir feebly. I blinked, the path was steep. A horn tooted to the right, and I saw the black people run. A heavy and dull detonation shook the ground, a puff of smoke came out of the cliff, and that was all. No change appeared on the face of the rock. They were building a railway. The cliff was not in the way or anything; but this objectless blasting was all the work going on.

"A slight clinking behind me made me turn my head. Six black men advanced in a file, toiling up the path. They walked erect and slow, balancing small baskets full of earth on their heads, and the clink kept time with their footsteps. Black rags were wound round their loins, and the short ends behind waggled to and fro like tails. I could see every rib, the joints of their limbs were like knots in a rope; each had an iron collar on his neck, and all were connected together with a chain whose bights swung between them, rhythmically clinking. Another report from the cliff made me think suddenly of that ship of war I had seen firing into a continent. It was the same kind of ominous voice; but these men could by no stretch of the imagination be called enemies. They were called criminals, and the outraged law, like the bursting shells, had come to them, an insoluble mystery from the sea. All their meagre breasts panted together, the violently dilated nostrils quivered, the eyes stared stonily up-hill. They passed me within six inches, without a glance, with that complete, deathlike indifference of unhappy savages. Behind this raw matter one of the reclaimed, the product of the new forces at work, strolled despondently, carrying a rifle by its middle. He had a uniform jacket with one button off, and seeing a white man on the path, hoisted his weapon to his shoulder with alacrity. This was simple prudence, white men being so much alike at a distance that he could not tell who I might be. He was speedily reassured, and with a large, white, rascally grin, and a glance at his charge, seemed to take me into partnership in his exalted trust. After all, I also was a part of the great cause of these high and just proceedings.

"Instead of going up, I turned and descended to the left. My idea was to let that chain-gang get out of sight before I climbed the hill. You know I am not particularly tender; I've had to strike and to fend off. I've had to resist and to attack sometimes—that's only one way of resisting—without counting the exact cost, according to the demands of such sort of life as I had blundered into. I've seen the devil of violence, and the devil of greed, and the devil of hot desire; but, by all the stars! these were strong, lusty, red-eyed devils, that swayed and drove men—men, I tell you. But as I stood on this hillside, I foresaw that in the blinding sunshine of that land I would become acquainted with a flabby, pretending, weak-eyed devil of a rapacious and pitiless folly. How insidious he could be, too, I was only to find out several months later and a thousand miles farther. For a moment I stood appalled, as though by a warning. Finally I descended the hill, obliquely, towards the trees I had seen.

"I avoided a vast artificial hole somebody had been digging on the slope, the purpose of which I found it impossible to divine. It wasn't a quarry or a sandpit, anyhow. It was just a hole. It might have been connected with the philanthropic desire of giving the criminals something to do. I don't know. Then I nearly fell into a very narrow ravine, almost no more than a scar in the hillside. I discovered that a lot of imported drainage-pipes for the settlement had been tumbled in there. There wasn't one that was not broken. It was a wanton smash-up. At last I got under the trees. My purpose was to stroll into the shade for a moment; but no sooner within than it seemed to me I had stepped into the gloomy circle of some Inferno. The rapids were near, and an uninterrupted, uniform, headlong, rushing noise filled the mournful stillness of the grove, where not a breath stirred, not a leaf moved, with a mysterious sound—as though the tearing pace of the launched earth had suddenly become audible.

"Black shapes crouched, lay, sat between the trees leaning against the trunks, clinging to the earth, half coming out, half effaced within the dim light, in all the attitudes of pain, abandonment, and despair. Another mine on the cliff went off, followed by a slight shudder of the soil under my feet. The work was going on. The work! And this was the place where some of the helpers had withdrawn to die.

"They were dying slowly—it was very clear. They were not enemies, they were not criminals, they were nothing earthly now—nothing but black shadows of disease and starvation, lying confusedly in the greenish gloom. Brought from all the recesses of the coast in all the legality of time contracts, lost in uncongenial surroundings, fed on unfamiliar food, they sickened, became inefficient, and were then allowed to crawl away and rest. These moribund shapes were free as air—and nearly as thin. I began to distinguish the gleam of the eyes under the trees. Then, glancing down, I saw a face near my hand. The black bones reclined at full length with one shoulder against the tree, and slowly the eyelids rose and the sunken eyes looked up at me, enormous and vacant, a kind of blind, white flicker in the depths of the orbs, which died out slowly. The man seemed young—almost a boy—but you know with them it's hard to tell. I found nothing else to do but to offer him one of my good Swede's ship's biscuits I had in my pocket. The fingers closed slowly on it and held—there was no other movement and no other glance. He had tied a bit of white worsted round his neck—Why? Where did he get it? Was it a badge—an ornament—a charm—a propitiatory act? Was there any idea at all connected with it? It looked startling round his black neck, this bit of white thread from beyond the seas.

"Near the same tree two more bundles of acute angles sat with their legs drawn up. One, with his chin propped on his knees, stared at nothing, in an intolerable and appalling manner: his brother phantom rested its forehead, as if overcome with a great weariness; and all about others were scattered in every pose of contorted collapse, as in some picture of a massacre or a pestilence. While I stood horror-struck, one of these creatures rose to his hands and knees, and went off on all-fours towards the river to drink. He lapped out of his hand, then sat up in the sunlight, crossing his shins in front of him, and after a time let his woolly head fall on his breastbone.

"I didn't want any more loitering in the shade, and I made haste towards the station. When near the buildings I met a white man, in such an unexpected elegance of get-up that in the first moment I took him for a sort of vision. I saw a high starched collar, white cuffs, a light alpaca jacket, snowy trousers, a clean necktie, and varnished boots. No hat. Hair parted, brushed, oiled, under a green-lined parasol held in a big white hand. He was amazing, and had a penholder behind his ear.

"I shook hands with this miracle, and I learned he was the Company's chief accountant, and that all the book-keeping was done at this station. He had come out for a moment, he said, 'to get a breath of fresh air.' The expression sounded wonderfully odd, with its suggestion of sedentary desk-life. I wouldn't have mentioned the fellow to you at all, only it was from his lips that I first heard the name of the man who is so indissolubly connected with the memories of that time. Moreover, I respected the fellow. Yes; I respected his collars, his vast cuffs, his brushed hair. His appearance was certainly that of a hairdresser's dummy; but in the great demoralization of the land he kept up his appearance. That's backbone. His starched collars and got-up shirt-fronts were achievements of character. He had been out nearly three years; and, later, I could not help asking him how he managed to sport such linen. He had just the faintest blush, and said modestly, 'I've been teaching one of the native women about the station. It was difficult. She had a distaste for the work.' Thus this man had verily accomplished something. And he was devoted to his books, which were in apple-pie order.

"Everything else in the station was in a muddle,—heads, things, buildings. Strings of dusty niggers with splay feet arrived and departed; a stream of manufactured goods, rubbishy cottons, beads, and brass-wire set into the depths of darkness, and in return came a precious trickle of ivory.

"I had to wait in the station for ten days—an eternity. I lived in a hut in the yard, but to be out of the chaos I would sometimes get into the accountant's office. It was built of horizontal planks, and so badly put together that, as he bent over his high desk, he was barred from neck to heels with narrow strips of sunlight. There was no need to open the big shutter to see. It was hot there, too; big flies buzzed fiendishly, and did not sting, but stabbed. I sat generally on the floor, while, of faultless appearance (and even slightly scented), perching on a high stool, he wrote, he wrote. Sometimes he stood up for exercise. When a truckle-bed with a sick man (some invalid agent from up-country) was put in there, he exhibited a gentle annoyance. 'The groans of this sick person,' he said, 'distract my attention. And without that it is extremely difficult to guard against clerical errors in this climate.'

"One day he remarked, without lifting his head, 'In the interior you will no doubt meet Mr. Kurtz.' On my asking who Mr. Kurtz was, he said he was a first-class agent; and seeing my disappointment at this information, he added slowly, laying down his pen, 'He is a very remarkable person.' Further questions elicited from him that Mr. Kurtz was at present in charge of a trading post, a very important one, in the true ivory-country, at 'the very bottom of there. Sends in as much ivory as all the others put together . . .' He began to write again. The sick man was too ill to groan. The flies buzzed in a great peace.

"Suddenly there was a growing murmur of voices and a great tramping of feet. A caravan had come in. A violent babble of uncouth sounds burst out on the other side of the planks. All the carriers were speaking together, and in the midst of the uproar the lamentable voice of the chief agent was heard 'giving it up' tearfully for the twentieth time that day. . . . He rose slowly. 'What a frightful row,' he said. He crossed the room gently to look at the sick man, and returning, said to me, 'He does not hear.' 'What! Dead?' I asked, startled. 'No, not yet,' he answered, with great composure. Then, alluding with a toss of the head to the tumult in the station-yard, 'When one has got to make correct entries, one comes to hate those savages—hate them to the death.' He remained thoughtful for a moment. 'When you see Mr. Kurtz,' he went on, 'tell him from me that everything here'—he glanced at the desk—'is very satisfactory. I don't like to write to him—with those messengers of ours you never know who may get hold of your letter—at that Central Station.' He stared at me for a moment with his mild, bulging eyes. 'Oh, he will go far, very far,' he began again. 'He will be a somebody in the Administration before long. They, above—the Council in Europe, you know—mean him to be.'

"He turned to his work. The noise outside had ceased, and presently in going out I stopped at the door. In the steady buzz of flies the homeward-bound agent was lying flushed and insensible; the other, bent over his books, was making correct entries of perfectly correct transactions; and fifty feet below the doorstep I could see the still tree-tops of the grove of death.

"Next day I left that station at last, with a caravan of sixty men, for a two-hundred-mile tramp.

"No use telling you much about that. Paths, paths, everywhere; a stamped-in network of paths spreading over the empty land, through long grass, through burnt grass, through thickets, down and up chilly ravines, up and down stony hills ablaze with heat; and a solitude, a solitude, nobody, not a hut. The population had cleared out a long time ago. Well, if a lot of mysterious niggers armed with all kinds of fearful weapons suddenly took to travelling on the road between Deal and Gravesend, catching the yokels right and left to carry heavy loads for them, I fancy every farm and cottage thereabouts would get empty very soon. Only here the dwellings were gone, too. Still I passed through several abandoned villages. There's something pathetically childish in the ruins of grass walls. Day after day, with the stamp and shuffle of sixty pair of bare feet behind me, each pair under a 60-lb. load. Camp, cook, sleep, strike camp, march. Now and then a carrier dead in harness, at rest in the long grass near the path, with an empty water-gourd and his long staff lying by his side. A great silence around and above. Perhaps on some quiet night the tremor of far-off drums, sinking, swelling, a tremor vast, faint; a sound weird, appealing, suggestive, and wild—and perhaps with as profound a meaning as the sound of bells in a Christian country. Once a white man in an unbuttoned uniform, camping on the path with an armed escort of lank Zanzibaris, very hospitable and festive—not to say drunk. Was looking after the upkeep of the road, he declared. Can't say I saw any road or any upkeep, unless the body of a middle-aged negro, with a bullet-hole in the forehead, upon which I absolutely stumbled three miles farther on, may be considered as a permanent improvement. I had a white companion, too, not a bad chap, but rather too fleshy and with the exasperating habit of fainting on the hot hillsides, miles away from the least bit of shade and water. Annoying, you know, to hold your own coat like a parasol over a man's head while he is coming-to. I couldn't help asking him once what he meant by coming there at all. 'To make money, of course. What do you think?' he said, scornfully. Then he got fever, and had to be carried in a hammock slung under a pole. As he weighed sixteen stone I had no end of rows with the carriers. They jibbed, ran away, sneaked off with their loads in the night—quite a mutiny. So, one evening, I made a speech in English with gestures, not one of which was lost to the sixty pairs of eyes before me, and the next morning I started the hammock off in front all right. An hour afterwards I came upon the whole concern wrecked in a bush—man, hammock, groans, blankets, horrors. The heavy pole had skinned his poor nose. He was very anxious for me to kill somebody, but there wasn't the shadow of a carrier near. I remembered the old doctor—'It would be interesting for science to watch the mental changes of individuals, on the spot.' I felt I was becoming scientifically interesting. However, all that is to no purpose. On the fifteenth day I came in sight of the big river again, and hobbled into the Central Station. It was on a back water surrounded by scrub and forest, with a pretty border of smelly mud on one side, and on the three others enclosed by a crazy fence of rushes. A neglected gap was all the gate it had, and the first glance at the place was enough to let you see the flabby devil was running that show. White men with long staves in their hands appeared languidly from amongst the buildings, strolling up to take a look at me, and then retired out of sight somewhere. One of them, a stout, excitable chap with black moustaches, informed me with great volubility and many digressions, as soon as I told him who I was, that my steamer was at the bottom of the river. I was thunderstruck. What, how, why? Oh, it was 'all right.' The 'manager himself' was there. All quite correct. 'Everybody had behaved splendidly! splendidly!'—'you must,' he said in agitation, 'go and see the general manager at once. He is waiting!'

"I did not see the real significance of that wreck at once. I fancy I see it now, but I am not sure—not at all. Certainly the affair was too stupid—when I think of it—to be altogether natural. Still . . . But at the moment it presented itself simply as a confounded nuisance. The steamer was sunk. They had started two days before in a sudden hurry up the river with the manager on board, in charge of some volunteer skipper, and before they had been out three hours they tore the bottom out of her on stones, and she sank near the south bank. I asked myself what I was to do there, now my boat was lost. As a matter of fact, I had plenty to do in fishing my command out of the river. I had to set about it the very next day. That, and the repairs when I brought the pieces to the station, took some months.

"My first interview with the manager was curious. He did not ask me to sit down after my twenty-mile walk that morning. He was com-

monplace in complexion, in feature, in manners, and in voice. He was
of middle size and of ordinary build. His eyes, of the usual blue, were
perhaps remarkably cold, and he certainly could make his glance fall
on one as trenchant and heavy as an axe. But even at these times the
rest of his person seemed to disclaim the intention. Otherwise there
was only an indefinable, faint expression of his lips, something
stealthy—a smile—not a smile—I remember it, but I can't explain. It
was unconscious, this smile was, though just after he had said something it got intensified for an instant. It came at the end of his speeches
like a seal applied on the words to make the meaning of the commonest phrase appear absolutely inscrutable. He was a common
trader, from his youth up employed in these parts—nothing more. He
was obeyed, yet he inspired neither love nor fear, nor even respect.
He inspired uneasiness. That was it! Uneasiness. Not a definite mistrust—just uneasiness—nothing more. You have no idea how effective
such a . . . a . . . faculty can be. He had no genius for organizing, for
initiative, or for order even. That was evident in such things as the
deplorable state of the station. He had no learning, and no intelligence. His position had come to him—why? Perhaps because he was
never ill . . . He had served three terms of three years out there . . .
Because triumphant health in the general rout of constitutions is a
kind of power in itself. When he went home on leave he rioted on a
large scale—pompously. Jack ashore—with a difference—in externals
only. This one could gather from his casual talk. He originated nothing, he could keep the routine going—that's all. But he was great. He
was great by this little thing that it was impossible to tell what could
control such a man. He never gave that secret away. Perhaps there
was nothing within him. Such a suspicion made one pause—for out
there there were no external checks. Once when various tropical dis-
eases had laid low almost every 'agent' in the station, he was heard to
say, 'Men who come out here should have no entrails.' He sealed the
utterance with that smile of his, as though it had been a door opening
into a darkness he had in his keeping. You fancied you had seen
things—but the seal was on. When annoyed at meal-times by the constant quarrels of the white men about precedence, he ordered an immense round table to be made, for which a special house had to be
built. This was the station's mess-room. Where he sat was the first

place—the rest were nowhere. One felt this to be his unalterable conviction. He was neither civil nor uncivil. He was quiet. He allowed his 'boy'—an overfed young negro from the coast—to treat the white men, under his very eyes, with provoking insolence.

"He began to speak as soon as he saw me. I had been very long on the road. He could not wait. Had to start without me. The up-river stations had to be relieved. There had been so many delays already that he did not know who was dead and who was alive, and how they got on—and so on, and so on. He paid no attention to my explanations, and, playing with a stick of sealing-wax, repeated several times that the situation was 'very grave, very grave.' There were rumours that a very important station was in jeopardy, and its chief, Mr. Kurtz, was ill. Hoped it was not true. Mr. Kurtz was . . . I felt weary and irritable. Hang Kurtz, I thought. I interrupted him by saying I had heard of Mr. Kurtz on the coast. 'Ah! So they talk of him down there,' he murmured to himself. Then he began again, assuring me Mr. Kurtz was the best agent he had, an exceptional man, of the greatest importance to the Company; therefore I could understand his anxiety. He was, he said, 'very, very uneasy.' Certainly he fidgeted on his chair a good deal, exclaimed, 'Ah, Mr. Kurtz!' broke the stick of sealing-wax and seemed dumfounded by the accident. Next thing he wanted to know 'how long it would take to' . . . I interrupted him again. Being hungry, you know, and kept on my feet too, I was getting savage. 'How can I tell?' I said. 'I haven't even seen the wreck yet—some months, no doubt.' All this talk seemed to me so futile. 'Some months,' he said. 'Well, let us say three months before we can make a start. Yes. That ought to do the affair.' I flung out of his hut (he lived all alone in a clay hut with a sort of verandah) muttering to myself my opinion of him. He was a chattering idiot. Afterwards I took it back when it was borne in upon me startlingly with what extreme nicety he had estimated the time requisite for the 'affair.'

"I went to work the next day, turning, so to speak, my back on that station. In that way only it seemed to me I could keep my hold on the redeeming facts of life. Still, one must look about sometimes; and then I saw this station, these men strolling aimlessly about in the sunshine of the yard. I asked myself sometimes what it all meant. They wandered here and there with their absurd long staves in their hands, like a lot of faithless pilgrims bewitched inside a rotten fence. The word 'ivory' rang in the air, was whispered, was sighed. You would think they were praying to it. A taint of imbecile rapacity blew through it all, like a whiff from some corpse. By Jove! I've never seen anything so unreal in my life. And outside, the silent wilderness surrounding this cleared speck on the earth struck me as something great and invincible, like evil or truth, waiting patiently for the passing away of this fantastic invasion.

"Oh, these months! Well, never mind. Various things happened. One evening a grass shed full of calico, cotton prints, beads, and I don't know what else, burst into a blaze so suddenly that you would have thought the earth had opened to let an avenging fire consume all that trash. I was smoking my pipe quietly by my dismantled steamer, and saw them all cutting capers in the light, with their arms lifted high, when the stout man with moustaches came tearing down to the river, a tin pail in his hand, assured me that everybody was 'behaving splendidly, splendidly,' dipped about a quart of water and tore back again. I noticed there was a hole in the bottom of his pail.

"I strolled up. There was no hurry. You see the thing had gone off like a box of matches. It had been hopeless from the very first. The flame had leaped high, driven everybody back, lighted up everything—and collapsed. The shed was already a heap of embers glowing fiercely. A nigger was being beaten near by. They said he had caused the fire in some way; be that as it may, he was screeching most horribly. I saw him, later, for several days, sitting in a bit of shade looking very sick and trying to recover himself: afterwards he arose and went out—and the wilderness without a sound took him into its bosom again. As I approached the glow from the dark I found myself at the back of two men, talking. I heard the name of Kurtz pronounced, then the words, 'take advantage of this unfortunate accident.' One of the men was the manager. I wished him a good evening. 'Did you ever see anything like it—eh? it is incredible,' he said, and walked off. The other man remained. He was a first-class agent, young, gentlemanly, a bit reserved, with a forked little beard and a hooked nose. He was stand-offish with the other agents, and they on their side said he was the manager's spy upon them. As to me, I had hardly ever spoken to him before. We got into talk, and by and by we strolled away from the hissing ruins. Then he asked me to his room, which was in the main building of the station. He struck a match, and I perceived that this young aristocrat had not only a silver-mounted dressing-case but also a whole candle all to himself. Just at that time the manager was the only man supposed to have any right to candles. Native mats covered the clay walls; a collection of spears, assegais, shields, knives was hung up in trophies. The business intrusted to this fellow was the making of bricks—so I had been informed; but there wasn't a fragment of a brick anywhere in the station, and he had been there more than a year—waiting. It seems he could not make bricks without something, I don't know what—straw maybe. Anyways, it could not be found there, and as it was not likely to be sent from Europe, it did not appear clear to me what he was waiting for. An act of special creation perhaps. However, they were all waiting—all the sixteen or twenty pilgrims of them—for something; and upon my word it did not seem an uncongenial occupation, from the way they took it, though the only thing that ever came to them was disease—as far as I could see. They beguiled the time by backbiting and intriguing against each other in a foolish kind of way. There was an air of plotting about that station, but nothing came of it, of course. It was as unreal as everything else—as the philanthropic pretence of the whole concern, as their talk, as their government, as their show of work. The only real feeling was a desire to get appointed to a trading-post where ivory was to be had, so that they could earn percentages. They intrigued and slandered and hated each other only on that account,—but as to effectually lifting a little finger—oh, no. By heavens! there is something after all in the world allowing one man to steal a horse while another must not look at a halter. Steal a horse straight out. Very well. He has done it. Perhaps he can ride. But there is a way of looking at a halter that would provoke the most charitable of saints into a kick.

"I had no idea why he wanted to be sociable, but as we chatted in there it suddenly occurred to me the fellow was trying to get at something—in fact, pumping me. He alluded constantly to Europe, to the people I was supposed to know there—putting leading questions as to my acquaintances in the sepulchral city, and so on. His little eyes glittered like mica discs—with curiosity—though he tried to keep up a bit of superciliousness. At first I was astonished, but very soon I became awfully curious to see what he would find out from me. I couldn't possibly imagine what I had in me to make it worth his while. It was very pretty to see how he baffled himself, for in truth my body was full only of chills, and my head had nothing in it but that wretched steamboat business. It was evident he took me for a perfectly shameless prevaricator. At last he got angry, and, to conceal a movement of furious annoyance, he yawned. I rose. Then I noticed a small sketch in oils, on a panel, representing a woman, draped and blindfolded, carrying a lighted torch. The background was sombre—almost black. The movement of the woman was stately, and the effect of the torch-light on the face was sinister.

"It arrested me, and he stood by civilly, holding an empty half-pint champagne bottle (medical comforts) with the candle stuck in it. To my question he said Mr. Kurtz had painted this—in this very station more than a year ago—while waiting for means to go to his trading-post. 'Tell me, pray,' said I, 'who is this Mr. Kurtz?'

"'The chief of the Inner Station,' he answered in a short tone, looking away. 'Much obliged,' I said, laughing. 'And you are the brick-maker of the Central Station. Everyone knows that.' He was silent for a while. 'He is a prodigy,' he said at last. 'He is an emissary of pity, and science, and progress, and devil knows what else. We want,' he began to declaim suddenly, 'for the guidance of the cause intrusted to us by Europe, so to speak, higher intelligence, wide sympathies, a singleness of purpose.' 'Who says that?' I asked. 'Lots of them,' he replied. 'Some even write that; and so *he* comes here, a special being, as you ought to know.' 'Why ought I to know?' I interrupted, really surprised. He paid no attention. 'Yes. To-day he is chief of the best station, next year he will be assistant-manager, two years more and . . . but I daresay you know what he will be in two years' time. You are of the new gang—the gang of virtue. The same people who sent him specially also recommended you. Oh, don't say no. I've my own eyes to trust.' Light dawned upon me. My dear aunt's influential acquaintances were producing an unexpected effect upon that young man. I nearly burst into a laugh. 'Do you read the Company's confidential correspondence?' I asked. He hadn't a word to say. It was great fun. 'When Mr. Kurtz,' I continued, severely, 'is General Manager, you won't have the opportunity.'

"He blew the candle out suddenly, and we went outside. The moon had risen. Black figures strolled about listlessly, pouring water on the glow, whence proceeded a sound of hissing; steam ascended in the moonlight, the beaten nigger groaned somewhere. 'What a row the brute makes!' said the indefatigable man with the moustaches, appearing near us. 'Serve him right. Transgression—punishment—bang! Pitiless, pitiless. That's the only way. This will prevent all conflagrations for the future. I was just telling the manager . . .' He noticed my companion, and became crestfallen all at once. 'Not in bed, yet,' he said, with a kind of servile heartiness; 'it's so natural. Ha! Danger—agitation.' He vanished. I went on to the river-side, and the other followed me. I heard a scathing murmur at my ear, 'Heap of muffs—go to.' The pilgrims could be seen in knots gesticulating, discussing. Several had still their staves in their hands. I verily believe they took these sticks to bed with them. Beyond the fence the forest stood up spectrally in the moonlight, and through the dim stir, through the faint sounds of that lamentable courtyard, the silence of the land went home to one's very heart—its mystery, its greatness, the amazing reality of its concealed life. The hurt nigger moaned feebly somewhere near by, and then fetched a deep sigh that made me mend my pace away from there. I felt a hand introducing itself under my arm. 'My dear sir,' said the fellow, 'I don't want to be misunderstood, and especially by you, who will see Mr. Kurtz long before I can have that pleasure. I wouldn't like him to get a false idea of my disposition. . . .'

"I let him run on, this papier-maché Mephistopheles, and it seemed to me that if I tried I could poke my forefinger through him, and would find nothing inside but a little loose dirt, maybe. He, don't you see, had been planning to be assistant-manager by and by under the present man, and I could see that the coming of that Kurtz had upset them both not a little. He talked precipitately, and I did not try to stop him. I had my shoulders against the wreck of my steamer, hauled up on the slope like a carcass of some big river animal. The smell of mud, of primeval mud, by Jove! was in my nostrils, the high stillness of primeval forest was before my eyes; there were shiny patches on the black creek. The moon had spread over everything a thin layer of silver—over the rank grass, over the mud, upon the wall of matted vegetation standing higher than the wall of a temple, over the great river I could see through a sombre gap glittering, glittering, as it flowed broadly by without a murmur. All this was great, expectant, mute, while the man jabbered about himself. I wondered whether the stillness on the face of the immensity looking at us two were meant as an appeal or as a menace. What were we who had strayed in here? Could we handle that dumb thing, or would it handle us? I felt how big, how confoundedly big, was that thing that couldn't talk, and perhaps was deaf as well. What was in there? I could see a little ivory coming out from there, and I had heard Mr. Kurtz was in there. I had heard enough about it, too—God knows! Yet somehow it didn't bring any image with it—no more than if I had been told an angel or a fiend was in there. I believed it in the same way one of you might believe there are inhabitants in the planet Mars. I knew once a Scotch sail-maker who was certain, dead sure, there were people in Mars. If you asked him for some idea how they looked and behaved, he would get shy and mutter something about 'walking on all-fours.' If you as much as smiled, he would—though a man of sixty—offer to fight you. I would not have gone so far as to fight for Kurtz, but I went for him near enough to a lie. You know I hate, detest, and can't bear a lie, not because I am straighter than the rest of us, but simply because it appalls me. There is a taint of death, a flavour of mortality in lies—which is exactly what I hate and detest in the world—what I want to forget. It makes me miserable and sick, like biting something rotten would do. Temperament, I suppose. Well, I went near enough to it by letting the young fool there believe anything he liked to imagine as to my influence in Europe. I became in an instant as much of a pretence as the rest of the bewitched pilgrims. This simply because I had a notion it somehow would be of help to that Kurtz whom at the time I did not see—you understand. He was just a word for me. I did not see the man in the name any more than you do. Do you see him? Do you see the story? Do you see anything? It seems to me I am trying to tell you a dream—making a vain attempt, because no relation of a dream can convey the dream-sensation, that commingling of absurdity, surprise, and bewilderment in a tremor of struggling re-volt, that notion of being captured by the incredible which is of the very essence of dreams. . . ."

He was silent for a while.

". . . No, it is impossible; it is impossible to convey the life-sensation of any given epoch of one's existence—that which makes its truth, its meaning—its subtle and penetrating essence. It is impossible. We live, as we dream—alone. . . ."

He paused again as if reflecting, then added—

"Of course in this you fellows see more than I could then. You see me, whom you know. . . ."

It had become so pitch dark that we listeners could hardly see one another. For a long time already he, sitting apart, had been no more to us than a voice. There was not a word from anybody. The others might have been asleep, but I was awake. I listened, I listened on the watch for the sentence, for the word, that would give me the clue to the faint uneasiness inspired by this narrative that seemed to shape itself without human lips in the heavy night-air of the river.

". . . Yes—I let him run on," Marlow began again, "and think what he pleased about the powers that were behind me. I did! And there was nothing behind me! There was nothing but that wretched, old, mangled steamboat I was leaning against, while he talked fluently about 'the necessity for every man to get on.' 'And when one comes out here, you conceive, it is not to gaze at the moon.' Mr. Kurtz was a 'universal genius,' but even a genius would find it easier to work with 'adequate tools—intelligent men.' He did not make bricks—why, there was a physical impossibility in the way—as I was well aware; and if he did secretarial work for the manager, it was because 'no sensible man rejects wantonly the confidence of his superiors.' Did I see it? I saw it. What more did I want? What I really wanted was rivets, by heaven! Rivets. To get on with the work—to stop the hole. Rivets I wanted. There were cases of them down at the coast—cases—piled up—burst—split! You kicked a loose rivet at every second step in that station yard on the hillside. Rivets had rolled into the grove of death. You could fill your pockets with rivets for the trouble of stooping down—and there wasn't one rivet to be found where it was wanted. We had plates that would do, but nothing to fasten them with. And every week the messenger, a lone negro, letter-bag on shoulder and staff in hand, left our station for the coast. And several times a week a coast caravan came in with trade goods—ghastly glazed calico that made you shudder only to look at it, glass beads value about a penny a quart, confounded spotted cotton handkerchiefs. And no rivets. Three carriers could have brought all that was wanted to set that steamboat afloat.

"He was becoming confidential now, but I fancy my unresponsive attitude must have exasperated him at last, for he judged it necessary to inform me he feared neither God nor devil, let alone any mere man. I said I could see that very well, but what I wanted was a certain quantity of rivets—and rivets were what really Mr. Kurtz wanted, if he had only known it. Now letters went to the coast every week. . . . 'My dear sir,' he cried, 'I write from dictation.' I demanded rivets. There was a way—for an intelligent man. He changed his manner; became very cold, and suddenly began to talk about a hippopotamus; wondered whether sleeping on board the steamer (I stuck to my salvage night and day) I wasn't disturbed. There was an old hippo that had the bad habit of getting out on the bank and roaming at night over the station grounds. The pilgrims used to turn out in a body and empty every rifle they could lay hands on at him. Some even had sat up o' nights for him. All this energy was wasted, though. 'That animal has a charmed life,' he said; 'but you can say this only of brutes in this country. No man—you apprehend me?—no man here bears a charmed life.' He stood there for a moment in the moonlight with his delicate hooked nose set a little askew, and his mica eyes glittering without a wink, then, with a curt Good-night, he strode off. I could see he was disturbed and considerably puzzled, which made me feel more hopeful than I had been for days. It was a great comfort to turn from that chap to my influential friend, the battered, twisted, ruined, tin-pot steamboat. I clambered on board. She rang under my feet like an empty Huntley & Palmer biscuit-tin kicked along a gutter; she was nothing so solid in make, and rather less pretty in shape, but I had expended enough hard work on her to make me love her. No influential friend would have served me better. She had given me a chance to come out a bit—to find out what I could do. No, I don't like work. I had rather laze about and think of all the fine things that can be done. I don't like work—no man does—but I like what is in the work,—the chance to find yourself. Your own reality—for yourself, not for others—what no other man can ever know. They can only see the mere show, and never can tell what it really means.

"I was not surprised to see somebody sitting aft, on the deck, with his legs dangling over the mud. You see I rather chummed with the few mechanics there were in that station, whom the other pilgrims naturally despised—on account of their imperfect manners, I suppose. This was the foreman—a boiler-maker by trade—a good worker. He was a lank, bony, yellow-faced man, with big intense eyes. His aspect was worried, and his head was as bald as the palm of my hand; but his hair in falling seemed to have stuck to his chin, and had prospered in the new locality, for his beard hung down to his waist. He was a widower with six young children (he had left them in charge of a sister of his to come out there), and the passion of his life was pigeon-flying. He was an enthusiast and a connoisseur. He would rave about pigeons. After work hours he used sometimes to come over from his hut for a talk about his children and his pigeons; at work, when he had to crawl in the mud under the bottom of the steamboat, he would tie up that beard of his in a kind of white serviette he brought for the purpose. It had loops to go over his ears. In the evening he could be seen squatted on the bank rinsing that wrapper in the creek with great care, then spreading it solemnly on a bush to dry.

"I slapped him on the back and shouted 'We shall have rivets!' He scrambled to his feet exclaiming 'No! Rivets!' as though he couldn't believe his ears. Then in a low voice, 'You . . . eh?' I don't know why we behaved like lunatics. I put my finger to the side of my nose and nodded mysteriously. 'Good for you!' he cried, snapped his fingers above his head, lifting one foot. I tried a jig. We capered on the iron deck. A frightful clatter came out of that hulk, and the virgin forest on the other bank of the creek sent it back in a thundering roll upon the sleeping station. It must have made some of the pilgrims sit up in their hovels. A dark figure obscured the lighted doorway of the manager's hut, vanished, then, a second or so after, the doorway itself vanished, too. We stopped, and the silence driven away by the stamping of our feet flowed back again from the recesses of the land. The great wall of vegetation, an exuberant and entangled mass of trunks, branches, leaves, boughs, festoons, motionless in the moonlight, was like a rioting invasion of soundless life, a rolling wave of plants, piled up, crested, ready to topple over the creek, to sweep every little man of us out of his little existence. And it moved not. A deadened burst of mighty splashes and snorts reached us from afar, as though an ichthyosaurus had been taking a bath of glitter in the great river. 'After all,' said the boiler-maker in a reasonable tone, 'why shouldn't we get the rivets?' Why not, indeed! I did not know of any reason why we shouldn't. 'They'll come in three weeks,' I said, confidently.

"But they didn't. Instead of rivets there came an invasion, an infliction, a visitation. It came in sections during the next three weeks, each section headed by a donkey carrying a white man in new clothes and tan shoes, bowing from that elevation right and left to the impressed pilgrims. A quarrelsome band of footsore sulky niggers trod on the heels of the donkey; a lot of tents, camp-stools, tin boxes, white cases, brown bales would be shot down in the courtyard, and the air of mystery would deepen a little over the muddle of the station. Five such installments came, with their absurd air of disorderly flight with the loot of innumerable outfit shops and provision stores, that, one would think, they were lugging, after a raid, into the wilderness of equitable division. It was an inextricable mess of things decent in themselves but that human folly made look like the spoils of thieving.

"This devoted band called itself the Eldorado Exploring Expedition, and I believe they were sworn to secrecy. Their talk, however, was the talk of sordid buccaneers: it was reckless without hardihood, greedy without audacity, and cruel without courage; there was not an atom of foresight or of serious intention in the whole batch of them, and they did not seem aware these things are wanted for the work of the world. To tear treasure out of the bowels of the land was their desire, with no more moral purpose at the back of it than there is in burglars breaking into a safe. Who paid the expenses of the noble enterprise I don't know; but the uncle of our manager was leader of that lot.

"In exterior he resembled a butcher in a poor neighborhood, and his eyes had a look of sleepy cunning. He carried his fat paunch with ostentation on his short legs, and during the time his gang infested the station spoke to no one but his nephew. You could see these two roaming about all day long with their heads close together in an everlasting confab.

"I had given up worrying myself about the rivets. One's capacity for that kind of folly is more limited than you would suppose. I said

Hang!—and let things slide. I had plenty of time for meditation, and now and then I would give some thought to Kurtz. I wasn't very interested in him. No. Still, I was curious to see whether this man, who had come out equipped with moral ideas of some sort, would climb to the top after all and how he would set about his work when there."

· II ·

"One evening as I was lying flat on the deck of my steamboat, I heard voices approaching—and there were the nephew and the uncle strolling along the bank. I laid my head on my arm again, and had nearly lost myself in a doze, when somebody said in my ear, as it were: 'I am as harmless as a little child, but I don't like to be dictated to. Am I the manager—or am I not? I was ordered to send him there. It's incredible.' . . . I became aware that the two were standing on the shore alongside the forepart of the steamboat, just below my head. I did not move; it did not occur to me to move: I was sleepy. 'It *is* unpleasant,' grunted the uncle. 'He has asked the Administration to be sent there,' said the other, 'with the idea of showing what he could do; and I was instructed accordingly. Look at the influence that man must have. Is it not frightful?' They both agreed it was frightful, then made several bizarre remarks: 'Make rain and fine weather—one man—the Council—by the nose'—bits of absurd sentences that got the better of my drowsiness, so that I had pretty near the whole of my wits about me when the uncle said, 'The climate may do away with this difficulty for you. Is he alone there?' 'Yes,' answered the manager; 'he sent his assistant down the river with a note to me in these terms: "Clear this poor devil out of the country, and don't bother sending more of that sort. I had rather be alone than have the kind of men you can dispose of with me." It was more than a year ago. Can you imagine such impudence!' 'Anything since then?' asked the other, hoarsely. 'Ivory,' jerked the nephew; 'lots of it—prime sort— lots—most annoying, from him.' 'And with that?' questioned the heavy rumble. 'Invoice,' was the reply fired out, so to speak. Then silence. They had been talking about Kurtz.

"I was broad awake by this time, but, lying perfectly at ease, remained still, having no inducement to change my position. 'How did that ivory come all this way?' growled the elder man, who seemed very vexed. The other explained that it had come with a fleet of canoes in charge of an English half-caste clerk Kurtz had with him; that Kurtz had apparently intended to return himself, the station being by that time bare of goods and stores, but after coming three hundred miles, had suddenly decided to go back, which he started to do alone in a small dugout with four paddlers, leaving the half-caste to continue down the river with the ivory. The two fellows there seemed astounded at anybody attempting such a thing. They were at a loss for an adequate motive. As to me, I seemed to see Kurtz for the first time. It was a distinct glimpse: the dugout, four paddling savages, and the lone white man turning his back suddenly on the headquarters, on relief, on thoughts of home—perhaps; setting his face towards the depths of the wilderness, towards his empty and desolate station. I did not know the motive. Perhaps he was just simply a fine fellow who stuck to his work for its own sake. His name, you understand, had not been pronounced once. He was 'that man.' The half-caste, who, as far as I could see, had conducted a difficult trip with great prudence and pluck, was invariably alluded to as 'that scoundrel.' The 'scoundrel' had reported that the 'man' had been very ill—had recovered imperfectly. . . . The two below me moved away then a few paces, and strolled back and forth at some little distance. I heard: 'Military post—doctor—two hundred miles—quite alone now—unavoidable delays—nine months—no news—strange rumours.' They approached again, just as the manager was saying, 'No one, as far as I know, unless a species of wandering trader—a pestilential fellow, snapping ivory from the natives.' Who was it they were talking about now? I gathered in snatches that this was some man supposed to be in Kurtz's district, and of whom the manager did not approve. 'We will not be free from unfair competition till one of these fellows is hanged for an example,' he said. 'Certainly,' grunted the other; 'get him hanged! Why not? Anything—anything can be done in this country. That's what I say; nobody here, you understand, *here,* can endanger your position. And why? You stand the climate—you outlast them all. The danger is in Europe; but there before I left I took care to—' They moved off and whispered, then their voices rose again. 'The extraordinary series of delays is not my fault. I did my best.' The fat man sighed. 'Very sad.'

'And the pestiferous absurdity of his talk,' continued the other; 'he bothered me enough when he was here. "Each station should be like a beacon on the road towards better things, a centre for trade of course, but also for humanizing, improving, instructing." Conceive you—that ass! And he wants to be manager! No, it's—' Here he got choked by excessive indignation, and I lifted my head the least bit. I was surprised to see how near they were—right under me. I could have spat upon their hats. They were looking on the ground, absorbed in thought. The manager was switching his leg with a slender twig: his sagacious relative lifted his head. 'You have been well since you came out this time?' he asked. The other gave a start. 'Who? I? Oh! Like a charm—like a charm. But the rest—oh, my goodness! All sick. They die so quick, too, that I haven't the time to send them out of the country—it's incredible!' 'H'm. Just so,' grunted the uncle. 'Ah! my boy, trust to this—I say, trust to this.' I saw him extend his short flipper of an arm for a gesture that took in the forest, the creek, the mud, the river,—seemed to beckon with a dishonouring flourish before the sunlit face of the land a treacherous appeal to the lurking death, to the hidden evil, to the profound darkness of its heart. It was so startling that I leaped to my feet and looked back at the edge of the forest, as though I had expected an answer of some sort to that black display of confidence. You know the foolish notions that come to one sometimes. The high stillness confronted these two figures with its ominous patience, waiting for the passing away of a fantastic invasion.

"They swore aloud together—out of sheer fright, I believe—then pretending not to know anything of my existence, turned back to the station. The sun was low; and leaning forward side by side, they seemed to be tugging painfully uphill their two ridiculous shadows of unequal length, that trailed behind them slowly over the tall grass without bending a single blade.

"In a few days the Eldorado Expedition went into the patient wilderness, that closed upon it as the sea closes over a diver. Long afterwards the news came that all the donkeys were dead. I know nothing as to the fate of the less valuable animals. They, no doubt, like the rest of us, found what they deserved. I did not inquire. I was then rather excited at the prospect of meeting Kurtz very soon. When I say very soon I mean it comparatively. It was just two months from the day we left the creek when we came to the bank below Kurtz's station.

"Going up that river was like travelling back to the earliest beginnings of the world, when vegetation rioted on the earth and the big trees were kings. An empty stream, a great silence, an impenetrable forest. The air was warm, thick, heavy, sluggish. There was no joy in the brilliance of sunshine. The long stretches of the waterway ran on, deserted, into the gloom of overshadowed distances. On silvery sandbanks hippos and alligators sunned themselves side by side. The broadening waters flowed through a mob of wooded islands; you lost your way on that river as you would in a desert, and butted all day long against shoals, trying to find the channel, till you thought yourself bewitched and cut off for ever from everything you had known once—somewhere—far away—in another existence perhaps. There were moments when one's past came back to one, as it will sometimes when you have not a moment to spare to yourself; but it came in the shape of an unrestful and noisy dream, remembered with wonder amongst the overwhelming realities of this strange world of plants, and water, and silence. And this stillness of life did not in the least resemble a peace. It was the stillness of an implacable force brooding over an inscrutable intention. It looked at you with a vengeful aspect. I got used to it afterwards; I did not see it any more; I had no time. I had to keep guessing at the channel; I had to discern, mostly by inspiration, the signs of hidden banks; I watched for sunken stones; I was learning to clap my teeth smartly before my heart flew out, when I shaved by a fluke some infernal sly old snag that would have ripped the life out of the tin-pot steamboat and drowned all the pilgrims; I had to keep a look-out for the signs of dead wood we could cut up in the night for next day's steaming. When you have to attend to things of that sort, to the mere incidents of the surface, the reality—the reality, I tell you—fades. The inner truth is hidden—luckily, luckily. But I felt it all the same; I felt often its mysterious stillness watching me at my monkey tricks, just as it watches you fellows performing on your respective tight-ropes for—what is it? half-a-crown a tumble—"

"Try to be civil, Marlow," growled a voice, and I knew there was at least one listener awake besides myself.

"I beg your pardon. I forgot the heartache which makes up the rest of the price. And indeed what does the price matter, if the trick be well done? You do your tricks very well. And I didn't do badly either, since I managed not to sink that steamboat on my first trip. It's a wonder to me yet. Imagine a blindfolded man set to drive a van over a bad road. I sweated and shivered over that business considerably, I can tell you. After all, for a seaman, to scrape the bottom of the thing that's supposed to float all the time under his care is the unpardonable sin. No one may know of it, but you never forget the thump—eh? A blow on the very heart. You remember it, you dream of it, you wake up at night and think of it—years after—and go hot and cold all over. I don't pretend to say that steamboat floated all the time. More than once she had to wade for a bit, with twenty cannibals splashing around and pushing. We had enlisted some of these chaps on the way for a crew. Fine fellows—cannibals—in their place. They were men one could work with, and I am grateful to them. And, after all, they did not eat each other before my face: they had brought along a provision of hippo-meat which went rotten, and made the mystery of the wilderness stink in my nostrils. Phoo! I can sniff it now. I had the manager on board and three or four pilgrims with their staves—all complete. Sometimes we came upon a station close by the bank, clinging to the skirts of the unknown, and the white men rushing out of a tumbledown hovel, with great gestures of joy and surprise and welcome, seemed very strange—had the appearance of being held there captive by a spell. The word ivory would ring in the air for a while—and on we went again into the silence, along empty reaches, round the still bends, between the high walls of our winding way, reverberating in hollow claps the ponderous beat of the stern-wheel. Trees, trees, millions of trees, massive, immense, running up high; and at their foot, hugging the bank against the stream, crept the little begrimed steamboat, like a sluggish beetle crawling on the floor of a lofty portico. It made you feel very small, very lost, and yet it was not altogether depressing, that feeling. After all, if you were small, the grimy beetle crawled on—which was just what you wanted it to do. Where the pilgrims imagined it crawled to I don't know. To some place where they expected to get something, I bet! For me it crawled towards Kurtz—exclusively; but when the steam-pipes started leaking we crawled very slow. The reaches opened before us and closed behind, as if the forest had stepped leisurely across the water to bar the way for our return. We penetrated deeper and deeper into the heart of darkness. It was very quiet there. At night sometimes the roll of drums behind the curtain of trees would run up the river and remain sustained faintly, as if hovering in the air high over our heads, till the first break of day. Whether it meant war, peace, or prayer we could not tell. The dawns were heralded by the descent of a chill stillness; the wood-cutters slept, their fires burned low; the snapping of a twig would make you start. We were wanderers on a prehistoric earth, on an earth that wore the aspect of an unknown planet. We could have fancied ourselves the first of men taking possession of an accursed inheritance, to be subdued at the cost of profound anguish and of excessive toil. But suddenly, as we struggled round a bend, there would be a glimpse of rush walls, of peaked grass-roofs, a burst of yells, a whirl of black limbs, a mass of hands clapping, of feet stamping, of bodies swaying, of eyes rolling, under the droop of heavy and motionless foliage. The steamer toiled along slowly on the edge of a black and incomprehensible frenzy. The prehistoric man was cursing us, praying to us, welcoming us—who could tell? We were cut off from the comprehension of our surroundings; we glided past like phantoms, wondering and secretly appalled, as sane men would be before an enthusiastic outbreak in a madhouse. We could not understand because we were too far and could not remember, because we were travelling in the night of first ages, of those ages that are gone, leaving hardly a sign—and no memories.

"The earth seemed unearthly. We are accustomed to look upon the shackled form of a conquered monster, but there—there you could look at a thing monstrous and free. It was unearthly, and the men were— No, they were not inhuman. Well, you know, that was the worst of it—this suspicion of their not being inhuman. It would come slowly to one. They howled and leaped, and spun, and made horrid faces; but what thrilled you was just the thought of their humanity—like yours—the thought of your remote kinship with this wild and passionate uproar. Ugly. Yes, it was ugly enough; but if you were man enough you would admit to yourself that there was in you just the faintest trace of a response to the terrible frankness of that noise, a

dim suspicion of there being a meaning in it which you—you so remote from the night of first ages—could comprehend. And why not?
The mind of man is capable of anything—because everything is in it,
all the past as well as all the future. What was there after all? Joy,
fear, sorrow, devotion, valour, rage—who can tell?—but truth—truth
stripped of its cloak of time. Let the fool gape and shudder—the man
knows, and can look on without a wink. But he must at least be as
much of a man as these on the shore. He must meet that truth with
his own true stuff—with his own inborn strength. Principles won't do.
Acquisitions, clothes, pretty rags—rags that would fly off at the first
good shake. No; you want a deliberate belief. An appeal to me in this
fiendish row—is there? Very well; I hear; I admit, but I have a voice,
too, and for good or evil mine is the speech that cannot be silenced.
Of course, a fool, what with sheer fright and fine sentiments, is always
safe. Who's that grunting? You wonder I didn't go ashore for a howl
and a dance? Well, no—I didn't. Fine sentiments, you say? Fine sentiments, be hanged! I had no time. I had to mess about with white-lead
and strips of woollen blanket helping to put bandages on those leaky
steam-pipes—I tell you. I had to watch the steering, and circumvent
those snags, and get the tin-pot along by hook or by crook. There was
surface-truth enough in these things to save a wiser man. And between
whiles I had to look after the savage who was fireman. He was an
improved specimen; he could fire up a vertical boiler. He was there
below me, and, upon my word, to look at him was as edifying as
seeing a dog in a parody of breeches and a feather hat, walking on his
hind-legs. A few months of training had done for that really fine chap.
He squinted at the steam-gauge and at the water-gauge with an evident
effort of intrepidity—and he had filed teeth, too, the poor devil, and
the wool of his pate shaved into queer patterns, and three ornamental
scars on each of his cheeks. He ought to have been clapping his hands
and stamping his feet on the bank, instead of which he was hard at
work, a thrall to strange witchcraft, full of improving knowledge. He
was useful because he had been instructed; and what he knew was
this—that should the water in that transparent thing disappear, the
evil spirit inside the boiler would get angry through the greatness of
his thirst, and take a terrible vengeance. So he sweated and fired up
and watched the glass fearfully (with an impromptu charm, made of

rags, tied to his arm, and a piece of polished bone, as big as a watch, stuck flatways through his lower lip), while the wooded banks slipped past us slowly, the short noise was left behind, the interminable miles of silence—and we crept on, towards Kurtz. But the snags were thick, the water was treacherous and shallow, the boiler seemed indeed to have a sulky devil in it, and thus neither that fireman nor I had any time to peer into our creepy thoughts.

"Some fifty miles below the Inner Station we came upon a hut of reeds, an inclined and melancholy pole, with the unrecognizable tatters of what had been a flag of some sort flying from it, and a neatly stacked wood-pile. This was unexpected. We came to the bank, and on the stack of firewood found a flat piece of board with some faded pencil-writing on it. When deciphered it said: 'Wood for you. Hurry up. Approach cautiously.' There was a signature, but it was illegible—not Kurtz—a much longer word. 'Hurry up.' Where? Up the river? 'Approach cautiously.' We had not done so. But the warning could not have been meant for the place where it could be only found after approach. Something was wrong above. But what—and how much? That was the question. We commented adversely upon the imbecility of that telegraphic style. The bush around said nothing, and would not let us look very far, either. A torn curtain of red twill hung in the doorway of the hut, and flapped sadly in our faces. The dwelling was dismantled; but we could see a white man had lived there not very long ago. There remained a rude table—a plank on two posts; a heap of rubbish reposed in a dark corner, and by the door I picked up a book. It had lost its covers, and the pages had been thumbed into a state of extremely dirty softness; but the back had been lovingly stitched afresh with white cotton thread, which looked clean yet. It was an extraordinary find. Its title was, *An Inquiry into Some Points of Seamanship,* by a man Towser, Towson—some such name—Master in his Majesty's Navy. The matter looked dreary reading enough, with illustrative diagrams and repulsive tables of figures, and the copy was sixty years old. I handled this amazing antiquity with the greatest possible tenderness, lest it should dissolve in my hands. Within, Towson or Towser was inquiring earnestly into the breaking strain of ships' chains and tackle, and other such matters. Not a very enthralling book; but at the first glance you could see there a singleness of intention, an honest concern for the right way of going to work, which made these humble pages, thought out so many years ago, luminous with another than a professional light. The simple old sailor, with his talk of chains and purchases, made me forget the jungle and the pilgrims in a delicious sensation of having come upon something unmistakably real. Such a book being there was wonderful enough; but still more astounding were the notes pencilled in the margin, and plainly referring to the text. I couldn't believe my eyes! They were in cipher! Yes, it looked like cipher. Fancy a man lugging with him a book of that description into this nowhere and studying it—and making notes—in cipher at that! It was an extravagant mystery.

"I had been dimly aware for some time of a worrying noise, and when I lifted my eyes I saw the wood-pile was gone, and the manager, aided by all the pilgrims, was shouting at me from the river-side. I slipped the book into my pocket. I assure you to leave off reading was like tearing myself away from the shelter of an old and solid friendship.

"I started the lame engine ahead. 'It must be this miserable trader—this intruder,' exclaimed the manager, looking back malevolently at the place we had left. 'He must be English,' I said. 'It will not save him from getting into trouble if he is not careful,' muttered the manager darkly. I observed with assumed innocence that no man was safe from trouble in this world.

"The current was more rapid now, the steamer seemed at her last gasp, the stern-wheel flopped languidly, and I caught myself listening on tiptoe for the next beat of the boat, for in sober truth I expected the wretched thing to give up every moment. It was like watching the last flickers of a life. But still we crawled. Sometimes I would pick out a tree a little way ahead to measure our progress towards Kurtz by, but I lost it invariably before we got abreast. To keep the eyes so long on one thing was too much for human patience. The manager displayed a beautiful resignation. I fretted and fumed and took to arguing with myself whether or no I would talk openly with Kurtz; but before I could come to any conclusion it occurred to me that my speech or my silence, indeed any action of mine, would be a mere futility. What did it matter what any one knew or ignored? What did it matter who was manager? One gets sometimes such a flash of insight. The essentials of this affair lay deep under the surface, beyond my reach, and beyond my power of meddling.

"Towards the evening of the second day we judged ourselves about eight miles from Kurtz's station. I wanted to push on; but the manager looked grave, and told me the navigation up there was so dangerous that it would be advisable, the sun being very low already, to wait where we were till next morning. Moreover, he pointed out that if the warning to approach cautiously were to be followed, we must approach in daylight—not at dusk, or in the dark. This was sensible enough. Eight miles meant nearly three hours' steaming for us, and I could also see suspicious ripples at the upper end of the reach. Nevertheless, I was annoyed beyond expression at the delay, and most unreasonably, too, since one night more could not matter much after so many months. As we had plenty of wood, and caution was the word, I brought up in the middle of the stream. The reach was narrow, straight, with high sides like a railway cutting. The dusk came gliding into it long before the sun had set. The current ran smooth and swift, but a dumb immobility sat on the banks. The living trees, lashed together by the creepers and every living bush of the undergrowth, might have been changed into stone, even to the slenderest twig, to the lightest leaf. It was not sleep—it seemed unnatural, like a state of trance. Not the faintest sound of any kind could be heard. You looked on amazed, and began to suspect yourself of being deaf—then the night came suddenly, and struck you blind as well. About three in the morning some large fish leaped, and the loud splash made me jump as though a gun had been fired. When the sun rose there was a white fog, very warm and clammy, and more blinding than the night. It did not shift or drive; it was just there, standing all round you like something solid. At eight or nine, perhaps, it lifted as a shutter lifts. We had a glimpse of the towering multitude of trees, of the immense matted jungle, with the blazing little ball of the sun hanging over it—all perfectly still—and then the white shutter came down again, smoothly, as if sliding in greased grooves. I ordered the chain, which we had begun to heave in, to be paid out again. Before it stopped running with a muffled rattle, a cry, a very loud cry, as of infinite desolation, soared slowly in the opaque air. It ceased. A complaining clamour, modulated in savage discords, filled our ears. The sheer unexpectedness of it made my hair stir under my cap. I don't know how it struck the others: to me it seemed as though the mist itself had screamed, so suddenly, and apparently from all sides at once, did this tumultuous and mournful uproar arise. It culminated in a hurried outbreak of almost intolerably excessive shrieking, which stopped short, leaving us stiffened in a variety of silly attitudes, and obstinately listening to the nearly as appalling and excessive silence. 'Good God! What is the meaning—' stammered at my elbow one of the pilgrims,—a little fat man, with sandy hair and red whiskers, who wore side-spring boots, and pink pyjamas tucked into his socks. Two others remained open-mouthed a whole minute, then dashed into the little cabin, to rush out incontinently and stand darting scared glances, with Winchesters at 'ready' in their hands. What we could see was just the steamer we were on, her outlines blurred as though she had been on the point of dissolving, and a misty strip of water, perhaps two feet broad, around her—and that was all. The rest of the world was nowhere, as far as our eyes and ears were concerned. Just nowhere. Gone, disappeared; swept off without leaving a whisper or a shadow behind.

"I went forward, and ordered the chain to be hauled in short, so as to be ready to trip the anchor and move the steamboat at once if necessary. 'Will they attack?' whispered an awed voice. 'We will be all butchered in this fog,' murmured another. The faces twitched with the strain, the hands trembled slightly, the eyes forgot to wink. It was very curious to see the contrast of expressions of the white men and of the black fellows of our crew, who were as much strangers to that part of the river as we, though their homes were only eight hundred miles away. The whites, of course greatly discomposed, had besides a curious look of being painfully shocked by such an outrageous row. The others had an alert, naturally interested expression; but their faces were essentially quiet, even those of the one or two who grinned as they hauled at the chain. Several exchanged short, grunting phrases, which seemed to settle the matter to their satisfaction. Their headman, a young, broad-chested black, severely draped in dark-blue fringed cloths, with fierce nostrils and his hair all done up artfully in oily ringlets, stood near me. 'Aha!' I said, just for good fellowship's sake. 'Catch 'im,' he snapped, with a bloodshot widening of his eyes and a flash of sharp teeth—'catch 'im. Give 'im to us.' 'To you, eh?' I asked; 'what would you do with them?' 'Eat 'im!' he said, curtly, and, leaning his elbow on the rail, looked out into the fog in a dignified and profoundly pensive attitude. I would no doubt have been properly horrified, had it not occurred to me that he and his chaps must be very hungry: that they must have been growing increasingly hungry for at least this month past. They had been engaged for six months (I don't think a single one of them had any clear idea of time, as we at the end of countless ages have. They still belonged to the beginnings of time—had no inherited experience to teach them as it were), and of course, as long as there was a piece of paper written over in accordance with some farcical law or other made down the river, it didn't enter anybody's head to trouble how they would live. Certainly they had brought with them some rotten hippo-meat, which couldn't have lasted very long, anyway, even if the pilgrims hadn't, in the midst of a shocking hullabaloo, thrown a considerable quantity of it overboard. It looked like a high-handed proceeding: but it was really a case of legitimate self-defence. You can't breathe dead hippo waking, sleeping, and eating, and at the same time keep your precarious grip on existence. Besides that, they had given them every week three pieces of brass wire, each about nine inches long; and the theory was they were to buy their provisions with that currency in river-side villages. You can see how *that* worked. There were either no villages, or the people were hostile, or the director, who like the rest of us fed out of tins, with an occasional old he-goat thrown in, didn't want to stop the steamer for some more or less recondite reason. So, unless they swallowed the wire itself, or made loops of it to snare the fishes with, I don't see what good their extravagant salary could be to them. I must say it was paid with a regularity worthy of a large and honourable trading company. For the rest, the only thing to eat—though it didn't look eatable in the least—I saw in their possession was a few lumps of some stuff like half-cooked dough, of a dirty lavender colour, they kept wrapped in leaves, and now and then swallowed a piece of, but so small that it seemed done more for the looks of the thing than for any serious purpose of sustenance. Why in the name of all the gnawing devils of hunger they didn't go for us—they were thirty to five—and have a good tuck-in for once, amazes me now when I think of it.

They were big powerful men, with not much capacity to weigh the consequences, with courage, with strength, even yet, though their skins were no longer glossy and their muscles no longer hard. And I saw that something restraining, one of those human secrets that baffle probability, had come into play there. I looked at them with a swift quickening of interest—not because it occurred to me I might be eaten by them before very long, though I own to you that just then I per- ceived—in a new light, as it were—how unwholesome the pilgrims looked, and I hoped, yes I positively hoped, that my aspect was not so—what shall I say?—so—unappetizing: a touch of fantastic vanity which fitted well with the dream-sensation that pervaded all my days at that time. Perhaps I had a little fever, too. One can't live with one's finger everlastingly on one's pulse. I had often 'a little fever,' or a little touch of other things—the playful paw-strokes of the wilderness, the preliminary trifling before the more serious onslaught which came in due course. Yes; I looked at them as you would on any human being, with a curiosity of their impulses, motives, capacities, weaknesses, when brought to the test of an inexorable physical necessity. Restraint! What possible restraint? Was it superstition, disgust, patience, fear—or some kind of primitive honour? No fear can stand up to hunger, no patience can wear it out, disgust simply does not exist where hunger is; and as to superstition, beliefs, and what you may call principles, they are less than chaff in a breeze. Don't you know the devilry of lingering starvation, its exasperating torment, its black thoughts, its sombre and brooding ferocity? Well, I do. It takes a man all his inborn strength to fight hunger properly. It's really easier to face bereavement, dishonour, and the perdition of one's soul—than this kind of prolonged hunger. Sad, but true. And these chaps, too, had no earthly reason for any kind of scruple. Restraint! I would just as soon have expected restraint from a hyena prowling amongst the corpses of a battlefield. But there was the fact facing me—the fact dazzling, to be seen, like the foam on the depths of the sea, like a ripple on an unfathomable enigma, a mystery greater—when I thought of it—than the curious, inexplicable note of desperate grief in this savage clamour that had swept by us on the river-bank, behind the blind whiteness of the fog.

"Two pilgrims were quarrelling in hurried whispers as to which bank. 'Left.' 'No, no; how can you? Right, right, of course.' 'It is very serious,' said the manager's voice behind me; 'I would be desolated if anything should happen to Mr. Kurtz before we came up.' I looked at him, and had not the slightest doubt he was sincere. He was just the kind of man who would wish to preserve appearances. That was his restraint. But when he muttered something about going on at once, I did not even take the trouble to answer him. I knew, and he knew, that it was impossible. Were we to let go our hold of the bottom, we would be absolutely in the air—in space. We wouldn't be able to tell where we were going to—whether up or down stream, or across—till we fetched against one bank or the other,—and then we wouldn't know at first which it was. Of course I made no move. I had no mind for a smash-up. You couldn't imagine a more deadly place for a ship-wreck. Whether drowned at once or not, we were sure to perish speedily in one way or another. 'I authorize you to take all the risks,' he said, after a short silence. 'I refuse to take any,' I said, shortly; which was just the answer he expected, though its tone might have surprised him. 'Well, I must defer to your judgment. You are captain,' he said, with marked civility. I turned my shoulder to him in sign of my appreciation, and looked into the fog. How long would it last? It was the most hopeless look-out. The approach to this Kurtz grubbing for ivory in the wretched bush was beset by as many dangers as though he had been an enchanted princess sleeping in a fabulous castle. 'Will they attack, do you think?' asked the manager, in a confidential tone.

"I did not think they would attack, for several obvious reasons. The thick fog was one. If they left the bank in their canoes they would get lost in it, as we would be if we attempted to move. Still, I had also judged the jungle of both banks quite impenetrable—and yet eyes were in it, eyes that had seen us. The river-side bushes were certainly very thick; but the undergrowth behind was evidently penetrable. However, during the short lift I had seen no canoes anywhere in the reach—certainly not abreast of the steamer. But what made the idea of attack inconceivable to me was the nature of the noise—of the cries we had heard. They had not the fierce character boding immediate hostile intention. Unexpected, wild, and violent as they had been, they had given me an irresistible impression of sorrow. The glimpse of the steamboat had for some reason filled those savages with unrestrained grief. The danger, if any, I expounded, was from our proximity to a great human passion let loose. Even extreme grief may ultimately vent itself in violence—but more generally takes the form of apathy. . . .

"You should have seen the pilgrims stare! They had no heart to grin, or even to revile me: but I believe they thought me gone mad—with fright, maybe. I delivered a regular lecture. My dear boys, it was no good bothering. Keep a look-out? Well, you may guess I watched the fog for the signs of lifting as a cat watches a mouse; but for anything else our eyes were of no more use to us than if we had been buried miles deep in a heap of cotton-wool. It felt like it, too—choking, warm, stifling. Besides, all I said, though it sounded extravagant, was absolutely true to fact. What we afterwards alluded to as an attack was really an attempt at repulse. The action was very far from being aggressive—it was not even defensive, in the usual sense: it was undertaken under the stress of desperation, and in its essence was purely protective.

"It developed itself, I should say, two hours after the fog lifted, and its commencement was at a spot, roughly speaking, about a mile and a half below Kurtz's station. We had just floundered and flopped round a bend, when I saw an islet, a mere grassy hummock of bright green, in the middle of the stream. It was the only thing of the kind; but as we opened the reach more, I perceived it was the head of a long sandbank, or rather of a chain of shallow patches stretching down the middle of the river. They were discoloured, just awash, and the whole lot was seen just under the water, exactly as a man's backbone is seen running down the middle of his back under the skin. Now, as far as I did see, I could go to the right or to the left of this. I didn't know either channel, of course. The banks looked pretty well alike, the depth appeared the same; but as I had been informed the station was on the west side, I naturally headed for the western passage.

"No sooner had we fairly entered it than I became aware it was much narrower than I had supposed. To the left of us there was the long uninterrupted shoal, and to the right a high, steep bank heavily overgrown with bushes. Above the bush the trees stood in serried ranks. The twigs overhung the current thickly, and from distance to distance a large limb of some tree projected rigidly over the stream. It was then well on in the afternoon, the face of the forest was gloomy, and a broad strip of shadow had already fallen on the water. In this shadow we steamed up—very slowly, as you may imagine. I sheered her well inshore—the water being deepest near the bank, as the sounding-pole informed me.

"One of my hungry and forbearing friends was sounding in the bows just below me. This steamboat was exactly like a decked scow. On the deck, there were two little teak-wood houses, with doors and windows. The boiler was in the fore-end, and the machinery right astern. Over the whole there was a light roof, supported on stanchions. The funnel projected through that roof, and in front of the funnel a small cabin built of light planks served for a pilot-house. It contained a couch, two camp-stools, a loaded Martini-Henry leaning in one cor-- ner, a tiny table, and the steering-wheel. It had a wide door in front and a broad shutter at each side. All these were always thrown open, of course. I spent my days perched up there on the extreme fore-end of that roof, before the door. At night I slept, or tried to, on the couch. An athletic black belonging to some coast tribe, and educated by my poor predecessor, was the helmsman. He sported a pair of brass earrings, wore a blue cloth wrapper from the waist to the ankles, and thought all the world of himself. He was the most unstable kind of fool I had ever seen. He steered with no end of a swagger while you were by; but if he lost sight of you, he became instantly the prey of an abject funk, and would let that cripple of a steamboat get the upper hand of him in a minute.

"I was looking down at the sounding-pole, and feeling much an- noyed to see at each try a little more of it stick out of that river, when I saw my poleman give up the business suddenly, and stretch himself flat on the deck, without even taking the trouble to haul his pole in. He kept hold on it though, and it trailed in the water. At the same time the fireman, whom I could also see below me, sat down abruptly before his furnace and ducked his head. I was amazed. Then I had to look at the river mighty quick, because there was a snag in the fairway. Sticks, little sticks, were flying about—thick: they were whizzing be- fore my nose, dropping below me, striking behind me against my pilot- house. All this time the river, the shore, the woods, were very quiet—perfectly quiet. I could only hear the heavy splashing thump of the stern-wheel and the patter of these things. We cleared the snag clumsily. Arrows, by Jove! We were being shot at! I stepped in quickly to close the shutter on the land-side. That fool-helmsman, his hands on the spokes, was lifting his knees high, stamping his feet, champing his mouth, like a reined-in horse. Confound him! And we were staggering within ten feet of the bank. I had to lean right out to swing the heavy shutter, and I saw a face amongst the leaves on the level with my own, looking at me very fierce and steady; and then suddenly, as though a veil had been removed from my eyes, I made out, deep in the tangled gloom, naked breasts, arms, legs, glaring eyes,—the bush was swarming with human limbs in movement, glistening, of bronze colour. The twigs shook, swayed, and rustled, the arrows flew out of them, and then the shutter came to. 'Steer her straight,' I said to the helmsman. He held his head rigid, face forward; but his eyes rolled, he kept on lifting and setting down his feet gently, his mouth foamed a little. 'Keep quiet!' I said in a fury. I might just as well have ordered a tree not to sway in the wind. I darted out. Below me there was a great scuffle of feet on the iron deck; confused exclamations; a voice screamed, 'Can you turn back?' I caught sight of a V-shaped ripple on the water ahead. What? Another snag! A fusillade burst out under my feet. The pilgrims had opened with their Winchesters, and were simply squirting lead into that bush. A deuce of a lot of smoke came up and drove slowly forward. I swore at it. Now I couldn't see the ripple or the snag either. I stood in the doorway, peering, and the arrows came in swarms. They might have been poisoned, but they looked as though they wouldn't kill a cat. The bush began to howl. Our wood-cutters raised a warlike whoop; the report of a rifle just at my back deafened me. I glanced over my shoulder, and the pilot-house was yet full of noise and smoke when I made a dash at the wheel. The fool-nigger had dropped everything, to throw the shutter open and let off that Martini-Henry. He stood before the wide opening, glaring, and I yelled at him to come back, while I straightened the sudden twist out of that steamboat. There was no room to turn even if I had wanted to, the snag was somewhere very near ahead in that confounded smoke, there was no time to lose, so I just crowded her into the bank—right into the bank, where I knew the water was deep.

"We tore slowly along the overhanging bushes in a whirl of broken twigs and flying leaves. The fusillade below stopped short, as I had foreseen it would when the squirts got empty. I threw my head back to a glinting whizz that traversed the pilot-house, in at one shutter-hole and out at the other. Looking past that mad helmsman, who was shaking the empty rifle and yelling at the shore, I saw vague forms of men running bent double, leaping, gliding, distinct, incomplete, evanescent. Something big appeared in the air before the shutter, the rifle went overboard, and the man stepped back swiftly, looked at me over his shoulder in an extraordinary, profound, familiar manner, and fell upon my feet. The side of his head hit the wheel twice, and the end of what appeared a long cane clattered round and knocked over a little camp-stool. It looked as though after wrenching that thing from somebody ashore he had lost his balance in the effort. The thin smoke had blown away, we were clear of the snag, and looking ahead I could see that in another hundred yards or so I would be free to sheer off, away from the bank; but my feet felt so very warm and wet that I had to look down. The man had rolled on his back and stared straight up at me; both his hands clutched that cane. It was the shaft of a spear that, either thrown or lunged through the opening, had caught him in the side just below the ribs; the blade had gone in out of sight, after making a frightful gash; my shoes were full; a pool of blood lay very still, gleaming dark-red under the wheel; his eyes shone with an amazing lustre. The fusillade burst out again. He looked at me anxiously, gripping the spear like something precious, with an air of being afraid I would try to take it away from him. I had to make an effort to free my eyes from his gaze and attend to the steering. With one hand I felt above my head for the line of the steam whistle, and jerked out screech after screech hurriedly. The tumult of angry and warlike yells was checked instantly, and then from the depths of the woods went out such a tremulous and prolonged wail of mournful fear and utter despair as may be imagined to follow the flight of the last hope from the earth. There was a great commotion in the bush; the shower of arrows stopped, a few dropping shots rang out sharply—then silence, in which the languid beat of the stern-wheel came plainly to my ears. I put the helm hard a-starboard at the moment when the pilgrim in pink pyjamas, very hot and agitated, appeared in the doorway. 'The manager sends me—' he began in an official tone, and stopped short. 'Good God!' he said, glaring at the wounded man.

"We two whites stood over him, and his lustrous and inquiring glance enveloped us both. I declare it looked as though he would presently put to us some question in an understandable language; but he died without uttering a sound, without moving a limb, without twitching a muscle. Only in the very last moment, as though in response to some sign we could not see, to some whisper we could not hear, he frowned heavily, and that frown gave to his black death-mask an inconceivably sombre, brooding, and menacing expression. The lustre of inquiring glance faded swiftly into vacant glassiness. 'Can you steer?' I asked the agent eagerly. He looked very dubious; but I made a grab at his arm, and he understood at once I meant him to steer whether or no. To tell you the truth, I was morbidly anxious to change my shoes and socks. 'He is dead,' murmured the fellow, immensely impressed. 'No doubt about it,' said I, tugging like mad at the shoe-laces. 'And by the way, I suppose Mr. Kurtz is dead as well by this time.'

"For the moment that was the dominant thought. There was a sense of extreme disappointment, as though I had found out I had been striving after something altogether without a substance. I couldn't have been more disgusted if I had travelled all this way for the sole purpose of talking with Mr. Kurtz. Talking with . . . I flung one shoe overboard, and became aware that that was exactly what I had been looking forward to—a talk with Kurtz. I made the strange discovery that I had never imagined him as doing, you know, but as discoursing. I didn't say to myself, 'Now I will never see him,' or 'Now I will never shake him by the hand,' but 'Now I will never hear him.' The man presented himself as a voice. Not of course that I did not connect him with some sort of action. Hadn't I been told in all the tones of jealousy and admiration that he had collected, bartered, swindled, or stolen more ivory than all the other agents together? That was not the point. The point was in his being a gifted creature, and that of all his gifts the one that stood out preëminently, that carried with it a sense of real presence, was his ability to talk, his words—the gift of expression, the bewildering, the illuminating, the most exalted and the most contemptible, the pulsating stream of light, or the deceitful flow from the heart of an impenetrable darkness.

"The other shoe went flying unto the devil-god of that river. I thought, By Jove! it's all over. We are too late; he has vanished—the gift has vanished, by means of some spear, arrow, or club. I will never hear that chap speak after all,—and my sorrow had a startling extravagance of emotion, even such as I had noticed in the howling sorrow of these savages in the bush. I couldn't have felt more of lonely desolation somehow, had I been robbed of a belief or had missed my destiny in life. . . . Why do you sigh in this beastly way, somebody? Absurd? Well, absurd. Good Lord! mustn't a man ever— Here, give me some tobacco." . . .

There was a pause of profound stillness, then a match flared, and Marlow's lean face appeared, worn, hollow, with downward folds and dropped eyelids, with an aspect of concentrated attention; and as he took vigorous draws at his pipe, it seemed to retreat and advance out of the night in the regular flicker of the tiny flame. The match went out.

"Absurd!" he cried. "This is the worst of trying to tell. . . . Here you all are, each moored with two good addresses, like a hulk with two anchors, a butcher round one corner, a policeman round another, excellent appetites, and temperature normal—you hear—normal from year's end to year's end. And you say, Absurd! Absurd be—exploded! Absurd! My dear boys, what can you expect from a man who out of sheer nervousness had just flung overboard a pair of new shoes! Now I think of it, it is amazing I did not shed tears. I am, upon the whole, proud of my fortitude. I was cut to the quick at the idea of having lost the inestimable privilege of listening to the gifted Kurtz. Of course I was wrong. The privilege was waiting for me. Oh, yes, I heard more than enough. And I was right, too. A voice. He was very little more than a voice. And I heard—him—it—this voice—other voices—all of them were so little more than voices—and the memory of that time itself lingers around me, impalpable, like a dying vibration of one immense jabber, silly, atrocious, sordid, savage, or simply mean, without any kind of sense. Voices, voices—even the girl herself—now—"

He was silent for a long time.

"I laid the ghost of his gifts at last with a lie," he began, suddenly. "Girl! What? Did I mention a girl? Oh, she is out of it—completely. They—the women I mean—are out of it—should be out of it. We must help them to stay in that beautiful world of their own, lest ours gets worse. Oh, she had to be out of it. You should have heard the disinterred body of Mr. Kurtz saying, 'My Intended.' You would have perceived directly then how completely she was out of it. And the lofty frontal bone of Mr. Kurtz! They say the hair goes on growing sometimes, but this—ah—specimen, was impressively bald. The wilderness had patted him on the head, and, behold, it was like a ball—an ivory ball; it had caressed him, and—lo!—he had withered; it had taken him, loved him, embraced him, got into his veins, consumed his flesh, and sealed his soul to its own by the inconceivable ceremonies of some devilish initiation. He was its spoiled and pampered favourite. Ivory? I should think so. Heaps of it, stacks of it. The old mud shanty was bursting with it. You would think there was not a single tusk left either above or below the ground in the whole country. 'Mostly fossil,' the manager had remarked, disparagingly. It was no more fossil than I am; but they call it fossil when it is dug up. It appears these niggers do bury the tusks sometimes—but evidently they couldn't bury this parcel deep enough to save the gifted Mr. Kurtz from his fate. We filled the steamboat with it, and had to pile a lot on the deck. Thus he could see and enjoy as long as he could see, because the appreciation of this favour had remained with him to the last. You should have heard him say, 'My ivory.' Oh yes, I heard him. 'My Intended, my ivory, my station, my river, my—' everything belonged to him. It made me hold my breath in expectation of hearing the wilderness burst into a prodigious peal of laughter that would shake the fixed stars in their places. Everything belonged to him—but that was a trifle. The thing was to know what he belonged to, how many powers of darkness claimed him for their own. That was the reflection that made you creepy all over. It was impossible—it was not good for one either—trying to imagine. He had taken a high seat amongst the devils of the land—I mean literally. You can't understand. How could you?—with solid pavement under your feet, surrounded by kind neighbours ready to cheer you or to fall on you, stepping delicately between the butcher and the policeman, in the holy terror of scandal and gallows and lunatic asylums—how can you imagine what particular region of the first ages a man's untrammelled feet may take him into by the way of solitude—utter solitude without a policeman—by the way of silence—utter silence, where no warning voice of a kind neighbour can be heard whispering of public opinion? These little things make all the great difference. When they are gone you just fall back upon your own innate strength, upon your own capacity for faithfulness. Of course you may be too much of a fool to go wrong—too dull even to know you are being assaulted by the powers of darkness. I take it, no fool ever made a bargain for his soul with the devil: the fool is too much of a fool, or the devil too much of a devil—I don't know which. Or you may be such a thunderingly exalted creature as to be altogether deaf and blind to anything but heavenly sights and sounds. Then the earth for you is only a standing place—and whether to be like this is your loss or your gain I won't pretend to say. But most of us are neither one nor the other. The earth for us is a place to live in, where we must put up with sights, with sounds, with smells, too, by Jove!—breathe dead hippo, so to speak, and not be contaminated. And there, don't you see? your strength comes in, the faith in your ability for the digging of unostentatious holes to bury the stuff in—your power of devotion, not to yourself, but to an obscure, back-breaking business. And that's difficult enough. Mind, I am not trying to excuse or even explain—I am trying to account to myself for—for—Mr. Kurtz—for the shade of Mr. Kurtz. This initiated wraith from the back of Nowhere honoured me with its amazing confidence before it vanished altogether. This was because it could speak English to me. The original Kurtz had been educated partly in England, and—as he was good enough to say himself—his sympathies were in the right place. His mother was half-English, his father was half-French. All Europe contributed to the making of Kurtz; and by and by I learned that, most appropriately, the International Society for the Suppression of Savage Customs had intrusted him with the making of a report, for its future guidance. And he had written it, too. I've seen it. I've read it. It was eloquent, vibrating with eloquence, but too high-strung, I think. Seventeen pages of close writing he had found time for! But this must have been before his—let us say—nerves, went wrong, and caused him to preside at certain midnight dances ending with unspeakable rites, which—as far as I reluctantly gathered from what I heard at various times—were offered up to him—do you understand?—to Mr. Kurtz himself. But it was a beautiful piece of writing. The opening paragraph, however, in the light of later information, strikes me now as ominous. He began with the argument that we whites, from the point of development we had arrived at, 'must necessarily appear to them [savages] in the nature of supernatural beings—we approach them with the might as of a deity,' and so on, and so on. 'By the simple exercise of our will we can exert a power for good practically unbounded,' etc. etc. From that point he soared and took me with him. The peroration was magnificent, though difficult to remember, you know. It gave me the notion of an exotic Immensity ruled by an august Benevolence. It made me tingle with enthusiasm. This was the unbounded power of eloquence—of words—of burning noble words. There were no practical hints to interrupt the magic current of phrases, unless a kind of note at the foot of the last page, scrawled evidently much later, in an unsteady hand, may be regarded as the exposition of a method. It was very simple, and at the end of that moving appeal to every altruistic sentiment it blazed at you, luminous and terrifying, like a flash of lightning in a serene sky: 'Exterminate all the brutes!' The curious part was that he had apparently forgotten all about that valuable postscriptum, because, later on, when he in a sense came to himself, he repeatedly entreated me to take good care of 'my pamphlet' (he called it), as it was sure to have in the future a good influence upon his career. I had full information about all these things, and, besides, as it turned out, I was to have the care of his memory. I've done enough for it to give me the indisputable right to lay it, if I choose, for an everlasting rest in the dust-bin of progress, amongst all the sweepings and, figuratively speaking, all the dead cats of civilization. But then, you see, I can't choose. He won't be forgotten. Whatever he was, he was not common. He had the power to charm or frighten rudimentary souls into an aggravated witch-dance in his honour; he could also fill the small souls of the pilgrims with bitter misgivings: he had one devoted friend at least, and he had conquered one soul in the world that was neither rudimentary nor tainted with self-seeking. No; I can't forget him, though I am not prepared to affirm the fellow was exactly worth the life we lost in getting to him. I missed my late helmsman awfully,—I missed him even while his body was still lying in the pilot-house. Perhaps you will think it passing strange this regret for a savage who was no more account than a grain of sand in a black Sahara. Well, don't you see, he had done something, he had steered; for months I had him at my back—a help—an instrument. It was a kind of partnership. He steered for me—I had to look after him, I worried about his deficiencies, and thus a subtle bond had been created, of which I only became aware when it was suddenly broken. And the intimate profundity of that look he gave me when he received his hurt remains to this day in my memory—like a claim of distant kinship affirmed in a supreme moment.

"Poor fool! If he had only left that shutter alone. He had no restraint, no restraint—just like Kurtz—a tree swayed by the wind. As soon as I had put on a dry pair of slippers, I dragged him out, after first jerking the spear out of his side, which operation I confess I performed with my eyes shut tight. His heels leaped together over the little door-step; his shoulders were pressed to my breast; I hugged him from behind desperately. Oh! he was heavy, heavy; heavier than any man on earth, I should imagine. Then without more ado I tipped him overboard. The current snatched him as though he had been a wisp of grass, and I saw the body roll over twice before I lost sight of it for ever. All the pilgrims and the manager were then congregated on the awning-deck about the pilot-house, chattering at each other like a flock of excited magpies, and there was a scandalized murmur at my heartless promptitude. What they wanted to keep that body hanging about for I can't guess. Embalm it, maybe. But I had also heard another, and a very ominous, murmur on the deck below. My friends the wood-cutters were likewise scandalized, and with a better show of reason—though I admit that the reason itself was quite inadmissible. Oh, quite! I had made up my mind that if my late helmsman was to be eaten, the fishes alone should have him. He had been a very second-rate helmsman while alive, but now he was dead he might have become a first-class temptation, and possibly cause some startling trouble. Besides, I was anxious to take the wheel, the man in pink pyjamas showing himself a hopeless duffer at the business.

"This I did directly the simple funeral was over. We were going half-speed, keeping right in the middle of the stream, and I listened to the talk about me. They had given up on Kurtz, they had given up the station; Kurtz was dead, and the station had been burnt—and so on—and so on. The red-haired pilgrim was beside himself with the thought that at least this poor Kurtz had been properly avenged. 'Say! We must have made a glorious slaughter of them in the bush. Eh? What do you think? Say?' He positively danced, the bloodthirsty little gingery beggar. And he had nearly fainted when he saw the wounded man! I could not help saying, 'You made a glorious lot of smoke, anyhow.' I had seen, from the way the tops of the bushes rustled and flew, that almost all the shots had gone too high. You can't hit anything unless you take aim and fire from the shoulder; but these chaps fired from the hip with their eyes shut. The retreat, I maintained—and I was right—was caused by the screeching of the steam-whistle. Upon this they forgot Kurtz, and began to howl at me with indignant protests.

"The manager stood by the wheel murmuring confidentially about the necessity of getting well away down the river before dark at all events, when I saw in the distance a clearing on the river-side and the outlines of some sort of building. 'What's this?' I asked. He clapped his hands in wonder. 'The station!' he cried. I edged in at once, still going half-speed.

"Through my glasses I saw the slope of a hill interspersed with rare trees and perfectly free from undergrowth. A long decaying building on the summit was half buried in the high grass; the large holes in the peaked roof gaped black from afar; the jungle and the woods made a background. There was no enclosure or fence of any kind; but there had been one apparently, for near the house half-a-dozen slim posts remained in a row, roughly trimmed, and with their upper ends ornamented with round carved balls. The rails, or whatever there had been between, had disappeared. Of course the forest surrounded all that. The river-bank was clear, and on the water-side I saw a white man under a hat like a cart-wheel beckoning persistently with his whole arm. Examining the edge of the forest above and below, I was almost certain I could see movements—human forms gliding here and there. I steamed past prudently, then stopped the engines and let her drift down. The man on the shore began to shout, urging us to land. 'We have been attacked,' screamed the manager. 'I know—I know. It's all right,' yelled back the other, as cheerful as you please. 'Come along. It's all right. I am glad.'

"His aspect reminded me of something I had seen—something funny I had seen somewhere. As I manœuvred to get alongside, I was asking myself, 'What does this fellow look like?' Suddenly I got it. He looked like a harlequin. His clothes had been made of some stuff that was brown holland probably, but it was covered with patches all over, with bright patches, blue, red, and yellow,—patches on the back, patches on the front, patches on elbows, on knees; coloured binding around his jacket, scarlet edging at the bottom of his trousers; and the sunshine made him look extremely gay and wonderfully neat withal, because you could see how beautifully all this patching had been done. A beardless, boyish face, very fair, no features to speak of, nose peeling, little blue eyes, smiles and frowns chasing each other over that open countenance like sunshine and shadow on a wind-swept plain. 'Look out, captain!' he cried; 'there's a snag lodged in here last night.' What! Another snag? I confess I swore shamefully. I had nearly holed my cripple, to finish off that charming trip. The harlequin on the bank turned his little pug-nose up to me. 'You English?' he asked, all smiles. 'Are you?' I shouted from the wheel. The smiles vanished, and he shook his head as if sorry for my disappointment. Then he brightened up. 'Never mind!' he cried, encouragingly. 'Are we in time?' I asked. 'He is up there,' he replied, with a toss of the head up the hill, and becoming gloomy all of a sudden. His face was like the autumn sky, overcast one moment and bright the next.

"When the manager, escorted by the pilgrims, all of them armed to the teeth, had gone to the house this chap came on board. 'I say, I don't like this. These natives are in the bush,' I said. He assured me earnestly it was all right. 'They are simple people,' he added; 'well, I am glad you came. It took me all my time to keep them off.' 'But you said it was all right,' I cried. 'Oh, they meant no harm,' he said; and as I stared he corrected himself, 'Not exactly.' Then vivaciously, 'My faith, your pilot-house wants a clean-up!' In the next breath he advised me to keep enough steam on the boiler to blow the whistle in case of any trouble. 'One good screech will do more for you than all your rifles. They are simple people,' he repeated. He rattled away at such a rate he quite overwhelmed me. He seemed to be trying to make up for lots of silence, and actually hinted, laughing, that such was the case. 'Don't you talk with Mr. Kurtz?' I said. 'You don't talk with that man—you listen to him,' he exclaimed with severe exaltation. 'But now—' He waved his arm, and in the twinkling of an eye was in the uttermost depths of despondency. In a moment he came up again with a jump, possessed himself of both my hands, shook them continuously, while he gabbled: 'Brother sailor . . . honour . . . pleasure . . . delight . . . introduce myself . . . Russian . . . son of an arch-priest . . . Government of Tambov . . . What? Tobacco! English tobacco; the excellent English tobacco! Now, that's brotherly. Smoke? Where's a sailor that does not smoke?"

"The pipe soothed him, and gradually I made out he had run away from school, had gone to sea in a Russian ship; ran away again; served some time in English ships; was now reconciled with the arch-priest. He made a point of that. 'But when one is young one must see things, gather experience, ideas; enlarge the mind.' 'Here!' I interrupted. 'You can never tell! Here I met Mr. Kurtz,' he said, youthfully solemn and reproachful. I held my tongue after that. It appears he had persuaded a Dutch trading-house on the coast to fit him out with stores and goods, and had started for the interior with a light heart, and no more idea of what would happen to him than a baby. He had been wandering about that river for nearly two years alone, cut off from everybody and everything. 'I am not so young as I look. I am twenty-five,' he said. 'At first old Van Shuyten would tell me to go to the devil,' he narrated with keen enjoyment; 'but I stuck to him, and talked and talked, till at last he got afraid I would talk the hind-leg off his favourite dog, so he gave me some cheap things and a few guns, and told me he hoped he would never see my face again. Good old Dutchman, Van Shuyten. I've sent him one small lot of ivory a year ago, so that he can't call me a little thief when I get back. I hope he got it. And for the rest I don't care. I had some wood stacked for you. That was my old house. Did you see?'

"I gave him Towson's book. He made as though he would kiss me, but restrained himself. 'The only book I had left, and I thought I had lost it,' he said, looking at it ecstatically. 'So many accidents happen to a man going about alone, you know. Canoes get upset sometimes—and sometimes you've got to clear out so quick when the people get angry.' He thumbed the pages. 'You made notes in Russian?' I asked. He nodded. 'I thought they were written in cipher,' I said.

He laughed, then became serious. 'I had lots of trouble to keep these people off,' he said. 'Did they want to kill you?' I asked. 'Oh, no!' he cried, and checked himself. 'Why did they attack us?' I pursued. He hesitated, then said shamefacedly, 'They don't want him to go.' 'Don't they?' I said, curiously. He nodded a nod full of mystery and wisdom. 'I tell you,' he cried, 'this man has enlarged my mind.' He opened his arms wide, staring at me with his little blue eyes that were perfectly round."

· III ·

"I looked at him, lost in astonishment. There he was before me, in motley, as though he had absconded from a troupe of mimes, enthusiastic, fabulous. His very existence was improbable, inexplicable, and altogether bewildering. He was an insoluble problem. It was inconceivable how he had existed, how he had succeeded in getting so far, how he had managed to remain—why he did not instantly disappear. 'I went a little farther,' he said, 'then still a little farther—till I had gone so far that I don't know how I'll ever get back. Never mind. Plenty time. I can manage. You take Kurtz away quick—quick—I tell you.' The glamour of youth enveloped his particoloured rags, his destitution, his loneliness, the essential desolation of his futile wanderings. For months—for years—his life hadn't been worth a day's purchase; and there he was gallantly, thoughtlessly alive, to all appearance indestructible solely by the virtue of his few years and of his unreflecting audacity. I was seduced into something like admiration—like envy. Glamour urged him on, glamour kept him unscathed. He surely wanted nothing from the wilderness but space to breathe in and to push on through. His need was to exist, and to move onwards at the greatest possible risk, and with a maximum of privation. If the absolutely pure, uncalculating, unpractical spirit of adventure had ever ruled a human being, it ruled this be-patched youth. I almost envied him the possession of this modest and clear flame. It seemed to have consumed all thought of self so completely, that even while he was talking to you, you forgot that it was he—the man before your eyes—who had gone through these things. I did not envy him his devotion to Kurtz, though. He had not meditated over it. It came to him, and he accepted it with a sort of eager fatalism. I must say that to me it appeared about the most dangerous thing in every way he had come upon so far.

"They had come together unavoidably, like two ships becalmed near each other, and lay rubbing sides at last. I suppose Kurtz wanted an audience, because on a certain occasion, when encamped in the forest, they had talked all night, or more probably Kurtz had talked. 'We talked of everything,' he said, quite transported at the recollection. 'I forgot there was such a thing as sleep. The night did not seem to last an hour. Everything! Everything! . . . Of love, too.' 'Ah, he talked to you of love!' I said, much amused. 'It isn't what you think,' he cried, almost passionately. 'It was in general. He made me see things— things.'

"He threw his arms up. We were on the deck at the time, and the headman of my wood-cutters, lounging near by, turned upon him his heavy and glittering eyes. I looked around, and I don't know why, but I assure you that never, never before, did this land, this river, this jungle, the very arch of this blazing sky, appear to me so hopeless and so dark, so impenetrable to human thought, so pitiless to human weakness. 'And, ever since, you have been with him, of course?' I said.

"On the contrary. It appears their intercourse had been very much broken by various causes. He had, as he informed me proudly, managed to nurse Kurtz through two illnesses (he alluded to it as you would to some risky feat), but as a rule Kurtz wandered alone, far in the depths of the forest. 'Very often coming to this station, I had to wait days and days before he would turn up,' he said. 'Ah, it was worth waiting for!—sometimes.' 'What was he doing? exploring or what?' I asked. 'Oh, yes, of course'; he had discovered lots of villages, a lake, too—he did not know exactly in what direction; it was dangerous to inquire too much—but mostly his expeditions had been for ivory. 'But he had no goods to trade with by that time,' I objected. 'There's a good lot of cartridges left even yet,' he answered, looking away. 'To speak plainly, he raided the country,' I said. He nodded. 'Not alone, surely!' He muttered something about the villages round that lake. 'Kurtz got the tribe to follow him, did he?' I suggested. He fidgeted a little. 'They adored him,' he said. The tone of these words was so extraordinary that I looked at him searchingly. It was curious to see his mingled eagerness and reluctance to speak of Kurtz. The man filled his life, occupied his thoughts, swayed his emotions. 'What can you expect?' he burst out; 'he came to them with thunder and lightning, you know—and they had never seen anything like it—and very terrible. He could be very terrible. You can't judge Mr. Kurtz as you would an ordinary man. No, no, no! Now—just to give you an idea—I don't mind telling you, he wanted to shoot me, too, one day—but I don't judge him.' 'Shoot you!' I cried. 'What for?' 'Well, I had a small lot of ivory the chief of that village near my house gave me. You see I used to shoot game for them. Well, he wanted it, and wouldn't hear reason. He declared he would shoot me unless I gave him the ivory and then cleared out of the country, because he could do so, and had a fancy for it, and there was nothing on earth to prevent him killing whom he jolly well pleased. And it was true, too. I gave him the ivory. What did I care! But I didn't clear out. No, no. I couldn't leave him. I had to be careful, of course, till we got friendly again for a time. He had his second illness then. Afterwards I had to keep out of the way; but I didn't mind. He was living for the most part in those villages on the lake. When he came down to the river, sometimes he would take to me, and sometimes it was better for me to be careful. This man suffered too much. He hated all this, and somehow he couldn't get away. When I had a chance I begged him to try and leave while there was time; I offered to go back with him. And he would say yes, and then he would remain; go off on another ivory hunt; disappear for weeks; forget himself amongst these people—forget himself—you know.' 'Why! he's mad,' I said. He protested indignantly. Mr. Kurtz couldn't be mad. If I had heard him talk, only two days ago, I wouldn't dare hint at such a thing. . . . I had taken up my binoculars while we talked, and was looking at the shore, sweeping the limit of the forest at each side and at the back of the house. The consciousness of there being people in that bush, so silent, so quiet—as silent and quiet as the ruined house on the hill—made me uneasy. There was no sign on the face of nature of this amazing tale that was not so much told as suggested to me in desolate exclamations, completed by shrugs, in interrupted phrases, in hints ending in deep sighs. The woods were unmoved, like a mask—heavy, like the closed door of a prison—they looked with their air of hidden knowledge, of patient expectation, of unapproachable silence. The Russian was explaining to me that it was only lately that Mr. Kurtz had come down to the river, bringing along with him all the fighting men of that lake tribe. He had been absent for several months—getting himself adored, I suppose—and had come down unexpectedly, with the intention to all appearance of making a raid either across the river or down stream. Evidently the appetite for more ivory had got the better of the—what shall I say?—less material aspirations. However he had got much worse suddenly. 'I heard he was lying helpless, and so I came up—took my chance,' said the Russian. 'Oh, he is bad, very bad.' I directed my glass to the house. There were no signs of life, but there was the ruined roof, the long mud wall peeping above the grass, with three little square window-holes, no two of the same size; all this brought within reach of my hand, as it were. And then I made a brusque movement, and one of the remaining posts of that vanished fence leaped up in the field of my glass. You remember I told you I had been struck at the distance by certain attempts at ornamentation, rather remarkable in the ruinous aspect of the place. Now I had suddenly a nearer view, and its first result was to make me throw my head back as if before a blow. Then I went carefully from post to post with my glass, and I saw my mistake. These round knobs were not ornamental but symbolic; they were expressive and puzzling, striking and disturbing—food for thought and also for vultures if there had been any looking down from the sky; but at all events for such ants as were industrious enough to ascend the pole. They would have been even more impressive, those heads on the stakes, if their faces had not been turned to the house. Only one, the first I had made out, was facing my way. I was not so shocked as you may think. The start back I had given was really nothing but a movement of surprise. I had expected to see a knob of wood there, you know. I returned deliberately to the first I had seen—and there it was, black, dried, sunken, with closed eyelids,—a head that seemed to sleep at the top of that pole, and, with the shrunken dry lips showing a narrow white line of the teeth, was smiling, too, smiling continuously at some endless and jocose dream of that eternal slumber.

"I am not disclosing any trade secrets. In fact, the manager said afterwards that Mr. Kurtz's methods had ruined the district. I have no opinion on that point, but I want you clearly to understand that there was nothing exactly profitable in these heads being there. They only showed that Mr. Kurtz lacked restraint in the gratification of his various lusts, that there was something wanting in him—some small matter which, when the pressing need arose, could not be found under his magnificent eloquence. Whether he knew of this deficiency himself I can't say. I think the knowledge came to him at last—only at the very last. But the wilderness had found him out early, and had taken on him a terrible vengeance for the fantastic invasion. I think it had whispered to him things about himself which he did not know, things of which he had no conception till he took counsel with this great solitude—and the whisper had proved irresistibly fascinating. It echoed loudly within him because he was hollow at the core. . . . I put down the glass, and the head that had appeared near enough to be spoken to seemed at once to have leaped away from me into inaccessible distance.

"The admirer of Mr. Kurtz was a bit crestfallen. In a hurried, indistinct voice he began to assure me he had not dared to take these—say, symbols—down. He was not afraid of the natives; they would not stir till Mr. Kurtz gave the word. His ascendancy was extraordinary. The camps of these people surrounded the place, and the chiefs came every day to see him. They would crawl. . . . 'I don't want to know anything of the ceremonies used when approaching Mr. Kurtz,' I shouted. Curious, this feeling that came over me that such details would be more intolerable than those heads drying on the stakes under Mr. Kurtz's windows. After all, that was only a savage sight, while I seemed at one bound to have been transported into some lightless region of subtle horrors, where pure, uncomplicated savagery was a positive relief, being something that had a right to exist—obviously—in the sunshine. The young man looked at me with surprise. I suppose it did not occur to him that Mr. Kurtz was no idol of mine. He forgot I hadn't heard any of these splendid monologues on, what was it? on love, justice, conduct of life—or what not. If it had come to crawling before Mr. Kurtz, he crawled as much as the veriest savage of them all. I had no idea of the conditions, he said: these heads were the heads of rebels. I shocked him excessively by laughing. Rebels! What would be the next definition I was to hear? There had been enemies, criminals, workers—and these were rebels. Those rebellious heads looked very subdued to me on their sticks. 'You don't know how such a life tries a man like Kurtz,' cried Kurtz's last disciple. 'Well, and you?' I said. 'I! I! I am a simple man. I have no great thoughts. I want nothing from anybody. How can you compare me to. . . ?' His feelings were too much for speech, and suddenly he broke down. 'I don't understand,' he groaned. 'I've been doing my best to keep him alive, and that's enough. I had no hand in all this. I have no abilities. There hasn't been a drop of medicine or a mouthful of invalid food for months here. He was shamefully abandoned. A man like this, with such ideas. Shamefully! Shamefully! I—I—haven't slept for the last ten nights . . .'

"His voice lost itself in the calm of the evening. The long shadows of the forest had slipped down hill while we talked, had gone far beyond the ruined hovel, beyond the symbolic row of stakes. All this was in the gloom, while we down there were yet in the sunshine, and the stretch of the river abreast of the clearing glittered in a still and dazzling splendour, with a murky and overshadowed bend above and below. Not a living soul was seen on the shore. The bushes did not rustle.

"Suddenly round the corner of the house a group of men appeared, as though they had come up from the ground. They waded waist-deep in the grass, in a compact body, bearing an improvised stretcher in their midst. Instantly, in the emptiness of the landscape, a cry arose whose shrillness pierced the still air like a sharp arrow flying straight to the very heart of the land; and, as if by enchantment, streams of human beings—of naked human beings—with spears in their hands, with bows, with shields, with wild glances and savage movements, were poured into the clearing by the dark-faced and pensive forest. The bushes shook, the grass swayed for a time, and then everything stood still in attentive immobility.

"'Now, if he does not say the right thing to them we are all done for,' said the Russian at my elbow. The knot of men with the stretcher had stopped, too, halfway to the steamer, as if petrified. I saw the man on the stretcher sit up, lank and with an uplifted arm, above the shoulders of the bearers. 'Let us hope that the man who can talk so well of love in general will find some particular reason to spare us this time,' I said. I resented bitterly the absurd danger of our situation, as if to be at the mercy of that atrocious phantom had been a dishonouring necessity. I could not hear a sound, but through my glasses I saw the thin arm extended commandingly, the lower jaw moving, the eyes of that apparition shining darkly far in its bony head that nodded with grotesque jerks. Kurtz—Kurtz—that means short in German—don't it? Well, the name was as true as everything else in his life—and death. He looked at least seven feet long. His covering had fallen off, and his body emerged from it pitiful and appalling as from a winding-sheet. I could see the cage of his ribs all astir, the bones of his arm waving. It was as though an animated image of death carved out of old ivory had been shaking its hand with menaces at a motionless crowd of men made of dark and glittering bronze. I saw him open his mouth wide—it gave him a weirdly voracious aspect, as though he had wanted to swallow all the air, all the earth, all the men before him. A deep voice reached me faintly. He must have been shouting. He fell back suddenly. The stretcher shook as the bearers staggered forward again, and almost at the same time I noticed that the crowd of savages was vanishing without any perceptible movement of retreat, as if the forest that had ejected these beings so suddenly had drawn them in again as the breath is drawn in a long aspiration.

"Some of the pilgrims behind the stretcher carried his arms—two shot-guns, a heavy rifle, and a light revolver-carbine—the thunderbolts of that pitiful Jupiter. The manager bent over him murmuring as he walked beside his head. They laid him down in one of the little cabins—just a room for a bedplace and a camp-stool or two, you know. We had brought his belated correspondence, and a lot of torn envelopes and open letters littered his bed. His hand roamed feebly amongst these papers. I was struck by the fire of his eyes and the composed languor of his expression. It was not so much the exhaustion of disease. He did not seem in pain. This shadow looked satiated and calm, as though for the moment it had had its fill of all the emotions.

"He rustled one of the letters, and looking straight in my face said, 'I am glad!' Somebody had been writing to him about me. These special recommendations were turning up again. The volume of tone he emitted without effort, almost without the trouble of moving his lips, amazed me. A voice! a voice! It was grave, profound, vibrating, while the man did not seem capable of a whisper. However, he had enough strength in him—factitious no doubt—to very nearly make an end of us, as you shall hear directly.

"The manager appeared silently in the doorway; I stepped out at once and he drew the curtain after me. The Russian, eyed curiously by the pilgrims, was staring at the shore. I followed the direction of his glance.

"Dark human shapes could be made out in the distance, flitting indistinctly against the gloomy border of the forest, and near the river two bronze figures, leaning on tall spears, stood in the sunlight under fantastic head-dresses of spotted skins, warlike and still in statuesque repose. And from right to left along the lighted shore moved a wild and gorgeous apparition of a woman.

"She walked with measured steps, draped in striped and fringed cloths, treading the earth proudly, with a slight jingle and flash of barbarous ornaments. She carried her head high; her hair was done in the shape of a helmet; she had brass leggings to the knee, brass wire gauntlets to the elbow, a crimson spot on her tawny cheek, innumerable necklaces of glass beads on her neck; bizarre things, charms, gifts of witch-men, that hung about her, glittered and trembled at every step. She must have had the value of several elephant tusks upon her. She was savage and superb, wild-eyed and magnificent; there was something ominous and stately in her deliberate progress. And in the hush that had fallen suddenly upon the whole sorrowful land, the immense wilderness, the colossal body of the fecund and mysterious life seemed to look at her, pensive, as though it had been looking at the image of its own tenebrous and passionate soul.

"She came abreast of the steamer, stood still, and faced us. Her long shadow fell to the water's edge. Her face had a tragic and fierce aspect of wild sorrow and of dumb pain mingled with the fear of some struggling, half-shaped resolve. She stood looking at us without a stir, and like the wilderness itself, with an air of brooding over an inscrutable purpose. A whole minute passed, and then she made a step forward. There was a low jingle, a glint of yellow metal, a sway of fringed draperies, and she stopped as if her heart had failed her. The young fellow by my side growled. The pilgrims murmured at my back. She looked at us all as if her life had depended upon the unswerving steadiness of her glance. Suddenly she opened her bared arms and threw them up rigid above her head, as though in an uncontrollable desire to touch the sky, and at the same time the swift shadows darted out on the earth, swept around on the river, gathering the steamer into a shadowy embrace. A formidable silence hung over the scene.

"She turned away slowly, walked on, following the bank, and passed into the bushes to the left. Once only her eyes gleamed back at us in the dusk of the thickets before she disappeared.

"'If she had offered to come aboard I really think I would have tried to shoot her,' said the man of patches, nervously. 'I have been risking my life every day for the last fortnight to keep her out of the house. She got in one day and kicked up a row about those miserable rags I picked up in the storeroom to mend my clothes with. I wasn't decent. At least it must have been that, for she talked like a fury to Kurtz for an hour, pointing at me now and then. I don't understand the dialect of this tribe. Luckily for me, I fancy Kurtz felt too ill that day to care, or there would have been mischief. I don't understand. . . . No—it's too much for me. Ah, well, it's all over now.'

"At this moment I heard Kurtz's deep voice behind the curtain: 'Save me!—save the ivory, you mean. Don't tell me. Save *me!* Why, I've had to save you. You are interrupting my plans now. Sick! Sick! Not so sick as you would like to believe. Never mind. I'll carry my ideas out yet—I will return. I'll show you what can be done. You with your little peddling notions—you are interfering with me. I will return. I. . . .'

"The manager came out. He did me the honour to take me under the arm and lead me aside. 'He is very low, very low,' he said. He considered it necessary to sigh, but neglected to be consistently sorrowful. 'We have done all we could for him—haven't we? But there is no disguising the fact, Mr. Kurtz has done more harm than good to the Company. He did not see the time was not ripe for vigorous action. Cautiously, cautiously—that's my principle. We must be cautious yet. The district is closed to us for a time. Deplorable! Upon the whole, the trade will suffer. I don't deny there is a remarkable quantity of ivory—mostly fossil. We must save it, at all events—but look how precarious the position is—and why? Because the method is unsound.'

'Do you,' said I, looking at the shore, 'call it "unsound method?"'
'Without doubt,' he exclaimed loudly. 'Don't you?' . . . 'No method
at all,' I murmured after a while. 'Exactly,' he exulted. 'I anticipated
this. Shows a complete want of judgment. It is my duty to point it out
in the proper quarter.' 'Oh,' said I, 'that fellow—what's his
name?—the brickmaker, will make a readable report for you.' He appeared confounded for a moment. It seemed to me I had never
breathed an atmosphere so vile, and I turned mentally to Kurtz for
relief—positively for relief. 'Nevertheless I think Mr. Kurtz is a remarkable man,' I said with emphasis. He started, dropped on me a
cold heavy glance, said very quietly, 'He *was*,' and turned his back on
me. My hour of favour was over; I found myself lumped along with
Kurtz as a partisan of methods for which the time was not ripe: I
was unsound! Ah! but it was something to have at least a choice of
nightmares.

"I had turned to the wilderness really, not to Mr. Kurtz, who, I was
ready to admit, was as good as buried. And for a moment it seemed
to me as if I also were buried in a vast grave full of unspeakable
secrets. I felt an intolerable weight oppressing my breast, the smell of
the damp earth, the unseen presence of victorious corruption, the
darkness of an impenetrable night. . . . The Russian tapped me on the
shoulder. I heard him mumbling and stammering something about
'brother seaman—couldn't conceal—knowledge of matters that would
affect Mr. Kurtz's reputation.' I waited. For him evidently Mr. Kurtz
was not in his grave; I suspect that for him Mr. Kurtz was one of the
immortals. 'Well!' said I at last, 'speak out. As it happens, I am Mr.
Kurtz's friend—in a way.'

"He stated with a good deal of formality that had we not been 'of
the same profession,' he would have kept the matter to himself without
regard to consequences. 'He suspected there was an active ill will towards him on the part of these white men that—' 'You are right,' I
said, remembering a certain conversation I had overheard. 'The manager thinks you ought to be hanged.' He showed a concern at this
intelligence which amused me at first. 'I had better get out of the way
quietly,' he said, earnestly. 'I can do no more for Kurtz now, and they
would soon find some excuse. What's to stop them? There's a military
post three hundred miles from here.' 'Well, upon my word,' said I,

'perhaps you had better go if you have any friends amongst the savages near by.' 'Plenty,' he said. 'They are simply people—and I want nothing, you know.' He stood biting his lip, then: 'I don't want any harm to happen to these whites here, but of course I was thinking of Mr. Kurtz's reputation—but you are a brother seaman and—' 'All right,' said I, after a time. 'Mr. Kurtz's reputation is safe with me.' I did not know how truly I spoke.

"He informed me, lowering his voice, that it was Kurtz who had ordered the attack to be made on the steamer. 'He hated sometimes the idea of being taken away—and then again. . . . But I don't understand these matters. I am a simple man. He thought it would scare you away—that you would give it up, thinking him dead. I could not stop him. Oh, I had an awful time of it this last month.' 'Very well,' I said. 'He is all right now.' 'Ye-e-es,' he muttered, not very convinced apparently. 'Thanks,' said I; 'I shall keep my eyes open.' 'But quiet—eh?' he urged, anxiously. 'It would be awful for his reputation if anybody here—' I promised a complete discretion with great gravity. 'I have a canoe and three black fellows waiting not very far. I am off. Could you give me a few Martini-Henry cartridges?' I could, and did, with proper secrecy. He helped himself, with a wink at me, to a handful of my tobacco. 'Between sailors—you know—good English tobacco.' At the door of the pilot-house he turned round—'I say, haven't you a pair of shoes you could spare?' He raised one leg. 'Look.' The soles were tied with knotted strings sandal-wise under his bare feet. I rooted out an old pair, at which he looked with admiration before tucking it under his left arm. One of his pockets (bright red) was bulging with cartridges, from the other (dark blue) peeped 'Towson's Inquiry,' etc., etc. He seemed to think himself excellently well equipped for a renewed encounter with the wilderness. 'Ah! I'll never, never meet such a man again. You ought to have heard him recite poetry—his own, too, it was, he told me. Poetry!' He rolled his eyes at the recollection of these delights. 'Oh, he enlarged my mind!' 'Good-bye,' said I. He shook hands and vanished in the night. Sometimes I ask myself whether I had ever really seen him—whether it was possible to meet such a phenomenon! . . .

"When I woke up shortly after midnight his warning came to my mind with its hint of danger that seemed, in the starred darkness, real enough to make me get up for the purpose of having a look round.

On the hill a big fire burned, illuminating fitfully a crooked corner of the station-house. One of the agents with a picket of a few of our blacks, armed for the purpose, was keeping guard over the ivory; but deep within the forest, red gleams that wavered, that seemed to sink and rise from the ground amongst confused columnar shapes of intense blackness, showed the exact position of the camp where Mr. Kurtz's adorers were keeping their uneasy vigil. The monotonous beating of a big drum filled the air with muffled shocks and a lingering vibration. A steady droning sound of many men chanting each to himself some weird incantation came out from the black, flat wall of the woods as the humming of bees comes out of a hive, and had a strange narcotic effect upon my half-awake senses. I believe I dozed off leaning over the rail, till an abrupt burst of yells, an overwhelming outbreak of a pent-up and mysterious frenzy, woke me up in a bewildered wonder. It was cut short all at once, and the low droning went on with an effect of audible and soothing silence. I glanced casually into the little cabin. A light was burning within, but Mr. Kurtz was not there.

"I think I would have raised an outcry if I had believed my eyes. But I didn't believe them at first—the thing seemed so impossible. The fact is I was completely unnerved by a sheer blank fright, pure abstract terror, unconnected with any distinct shape of physical danger. What made this emotion so overpowering was—how shall I define it?—the moral shock I received, as if something altogether monstrous, intolerable to thought and odious to the soul, had been thrust upon me unexpectedly. This lasted of course the merest fraction of a second, and then the usual sense of commonplace, deadly danger, the possibility of a sudden onslaught and massacre, or something of the kind, which I saw impending, was positively welcome and composing. It pacified me, in fact, so much, that I did not raise an alarm.

"There was an agent buttoned up inside an ulster and sleeping on a chair on deck within three feet of me. The yells had not awakened him; he snored very slightly; I left him to his slumbers and leaped ashore. I did not betray Mr. Kurtz—it was ordered I should never betray him—it was written I should be loyal to the nightmare of my choice. I was anxious to deal with this shadow by myself alone,—and to this day I don't know why I was so jealous of sharing with any one the peculiar blackness of that experience.

"As soon as I got on the bank I saw a trail—a broad trail through the grass. I remember the exultation with which I said to myself, 'He can't walk—he is crawling on all-fours—I've got him.' The grass was wet with dew. I strode rapidly with clenched fists. I fancy I had some vague notion of falling upon him and giving him a drubbing. I don't know. I had some imbecile thoughts. The knitting old woman with the cat obtruded herself upon my memory as a most improper person to be sitting at the other end of such an affair. I saw a row of pilgrims squirting lead in the air out of Winchesters held to the hip. I thought I would never get back to the steamer, and imagined myself living alone and unarmed in the woods to an advanced age. Such silly things—you know. And I remember I confounded the beat of the drum with the beating of my heart, and was pleased at its calm regularity.

"I kept to the track though—then stopped to listen. The night was very clear; a dark blue space, sparkling with dew and starlight, in which black things stood very still. I thought I could see a kind of motion ahead of me. I was strangely cocksure of everything that night. I actually left the track and ran in a wide semicircle (I verily believe chuckling to myself) so as to get in front of that stir, of that motion I had seen—if indeed I had seen anything. I was circumventing Kurtz as though it had been a boyish game.

"I came upon him, and, if he had not heard me coming, I would have fallen over him, too, but he got up in time. He rose, unsteady, long, pale, indistinct, like a vapour exhaled by the earth, and swayed slightly, misty and silent before me; while at my back the fires loomed between the trees, and the murmur of many voices issued from the forest. I had cut him off cleverly; but when actually confronting him I seemed to come to my senses, I saw the danger in its right proportion. It was by no means over yet. Suppose he began to shout? Though he could hardly stand, there was still plenty of vigour in his voice. 'Go away—hide yourself,' he said, in that profound tone. It was very awful. I glanced back. We were within thirty yards from the nearest fire. A black figure stood up, strode on long black legs, waving long black arms, across the glow. It had horns—antelope horns, I think—on its head. Some sorcerer, some witch-man, no doubt: it looked fiend-like enough. 'Do you know what you are doing?' I whispered. 'Perfectly,' he answered, raising his voice for that single word: it sounded to me far off and yet loud, like a hail through a speaking-trumpet. If he makes a row we are lost, I thought to myself. This clearly was not a case for fisticuffs, even apart from the very natural aversion I had to beat that Shadow—this wandering and tormented thing. 'You will be lost,' I said—'utterly lost.' One gets sometimes such a flash of inspiration, you know. I did say the right thing, though indeed he could not have been more irretrievably lost than he was at this very moment, when the foundations of our intimacy were being laid—to endure—to endure—even to the end—even beyond.

"'I had immense plans,' he muttered irresolutely. 'Yes,' said I; 'but if you try to shout I'll smash your head with—' There was not a stick or a stone near. 'I will throttle you for good,' I corrected myself. 'I was on the threshold of great things,' he pleaded, in a voice of longing, with a wistfulness of tone that made my blood run cold. 'And now for this stupid scoundrel—' 'Your success in Europe is assured in any case,' I affirmed, steadily. I did not want to have the throttling of him, you understand—and indeed it would have been very little use for any practical purpose. I tried to break the spell—the heavy, mute spell of the wilderness—that seemed to draw him to its pitiless breast by the awakening of forgotten and brutal instincts, by the memory of gratified and monstrous passions. This alone, I was convinced, had driven him out to the edge of the forest, to the bush, towards the gleam of fires, the throb of drums, the drone of weird incantations; this alone had beguiled his unlawful soul beyond the bounds of permitted aspirations. And, don't you see, the terror of the position was not in being knocked on the head—though I had a very lively sense of that danger, too—but in this, that I had to deal with a being to whom I could not appeal in the name of anything high or low. I had, even like the niggers, to invoke him—himself—his own exalted and incredible degradation. There was nothing either above or below him, and I knew it. He had kicked himself loose of the earth. Confound the man! he had kicked the very earth to pieces. He was alone, and I before him did not know whether I stood on the ground or floated in the air. I've been telling you what we said—repeating the phrases we pronounced—but what's the good? They were common everyday words—the familiar, vague sounds exchanged on every waking day of life. But what of that? They had behind them, to my mind, the terrific suggestiveness of words heard in dreams, of phrases spoken in night-mares. Soul! If anybody had ever struggled with a soul, I am the man. And I wasn't arguing with a lunatic either. Believe me or not, his intelligence was perfectly clear—concentrated, it is true, upon himself with horrible intensity, yet clear; and therein was my only chance—barring, of course, the killing him there and then, which wasn't so good, on account of unavoidable noise. But his soul was mad. Being alone in the wilderness, it had looked within itself, and, by heavens! I tell you, it had gone mad. I had—for my sins, I sup-pose—to go through the ordeal of looking into it myself. No elo-quence could have been so withering to one's belief in mankind as his final burst of sincerity. He struggled with himself, too. I saw it,—I heard it. I saw the inconceivable mystery of a soul that knew no re-straint, no faith, and no fear, yet struggling blindly with itself. I kept my head pretty well; but when I had him at last stretched on the couch, I wiped my forehead, while my legs shook under me as though I had carried half a ton on my back down that hill. And yet I had only supported him, his bony arm clasped round my neck—and he was not much heavier than a child.

"When next day we left at noon, the crowd, of whose presence behind the curtain of trees I had been acutely conscious all the time, flowed out of the woods again, filled the clearing, covered the slope with a mass of naked, breathing, quivering, bronze bodies. I steamed up a bit, then swung downstream, and two thousand eyes followed the evolutions of the splashing, thumping, fierce river-demon beating the water with its terrible tail and breathing black smoke into the air. In front of the first rank, along the river, three men, plastered with bright red earth from head to foot, strutted to and fro restlessly. When we came abreast again, they faced the river, stamped their feet, nod-ded their horned heads, swayed their scarlet bodies; they shook to-wards the fierce river-demon a bunch of black feathers, a mangy skin with a pendent tail—something that looked like a dried gourd; they shouted periodically together strings of amazing words that resembled no sounds of human language; and the deep murmurs of the crowd, interrupted suddenly, were like the responses of some satanic litany.

"We had carried Kurtz into the pilot-house: there was more air there. Lying on the couch, he stared through the open shutter. There was an eddy in the mass of human bodies, and the woman with helmeted head and tawny cheeks rushed out to the very brink of the stream. She put out her hands, shouted something, and all that wild mob took up the shout in a roaring chorus of articulated, rapid, breathless utterance.

"'Do you understand this?' I asked.

"He kept on looking out past me with fiery, longing eyes, with a mingled expression of wistfulness and hate. He made no answer, but I saw a smile, a smile of indefinable meaning, appear on his colourless lips that a moment after twitched convulsively. 'Do I not?' he said slowly, gasping, as if the words had been torn out of him by a supernatural power.

"I pulled the string of the whistle, and did this because I saw the pilgrims on deck getting out their rifles with an air of anticipating a jolly lark. At the sudden screech there was a movement of abject terror through that wedged mass of bodies. 'Don't! don't you frighten them away,' cried someone on deck disconsolately. I pulled the string time after time. They broke and ran, they leaped, they crouched, they swerved, they dodged the flying terror of the sound. The three red chaps had fallen flat, face down on the shore, as though they had been shot dead. Only the barbarous and superb woman did not so much as flinch, and stretched tragically her bare arms after us over the sombre and glittering river.

"And then that imbecile crowd down on the deck started their little fun, and I could see nothing more for smoke.

"The brown current ran swiftly out of the heart of darkness, bearing us down towards the sea with twice the speed of our upward progress; and Kurtz's life was running swiftly, too, ebbing, ebbing out of his heart into the sea of inexorable time. The manager was very placid, he had no vital anxieties now, he took us both in with a comprehensive and satisfied glance: the 'affair' had come off as well as could be wished. I saw the time approaching when I would be left alone of the party of 'unsound method.' The pilgrims looked upon me with disfavour. I was, so to speak, numbered with the dead. It is strange how

I accepted this unforeseen partnership, this choice of nightmares forced upon me in the tenebrous land invaded by these mean and greedy phantoms.

"Kurtz discoursed. A voice! a voice! It rang deep to the very last. It survived his strength to hide in the magnificent folds of eloquence the barren darkness of his heart. Oh, he struggled! he struggled! The wastes of his weary brain were haunted by shadowy images now—images of wealth and fame revolving obsequiously round his unextinguishable gift of noble and lofty expression. My Intended, my station, my career, my ideas—these were the subjects for the occasional utterances of elevated sentiments. The shade of the original Kurtz frequented the bedside of the hollow sham, whose fate it was to be buried presently in the mould of primeval earth. But both the diabolic love and the unearthly hate of the mysteries it had penetrated fought for the possession of that soul satiated with primitive emotions, avid of lying fame, of sham distinction, of all the appearances of success and power.

"Sometimes he was contemptibly childish. He desired to have kings meet him at railway-stations on his return from some ghastly Nowhere, where he intended to accomplish great things. 'You show them you have in you something that is really profitable, and then there will be no limits to the recognition of your ability,' he would say. 'Of course you must take care of the motives—right motives—always.' The long reaches that were like one and the same reach, monotonous bends that were exactly alike, slipped past the steamer with their multitude of secular trees looking patiently after this grimy fragment of another world, the forerunner of change, of conquest, of trade, of massacres, of blessings. I looked ahead—piloting. 'Close the shutter,' said Kurtz suddenly one day; 'I can't bear to look at this.' I did so. There was a silence. 'Oh, but I will wring your heart yet!' he cried at the invisible wilderness.

"We broke down—as I had expected—and had to lie up for repairs at the head of an island. This delay was the first thing that shook Kurtz's confidence. One morning he gave me a packet of papers and a photograph—the lot tied together with a shoe-string. 'Keep this for me,' he said. 'This noxious fool' (meaning the manager) 'is capable of prying into my boxes when I am not looking.' In the afternoon I saw him. He was lying on his back with closed eyes, and I withdrew quietly, but I heard him mutter, 'Live rightly, die, die . . .' I listened. There was nothing more. Was he rehearsing some speech in his sleep, or was it a fragment of a phrase from some newspaper article? He had been writing for the papers and meant to do so again, 'for the furthering of my ideas. It's a duty.'

"His was an impenetrable darkness. I looked at him as you peer down at a man who is lying at the bottom of a precipice where the sun never shines. But I had not much time to give him, because I was helping the engine-driver to take to pieces the leaky cylinders, to straighten a bent connecting-rod, and in other such matters. I lived in an infernal mess of rust, filings, nuts, bolts, spanners, hammers, ratchet-drills—things I abominate, because I don't get on with them. I tended the little forge we fortunately had aboard; I toiled wearily in a wretched scrap-heap—unless I had the shakes too bad to stand.

"One evening coming in with a candle I was startled to hear him say a little tremulously, 'I am lying here in the dark waiting for death.' The light was within a foot of his eyes. I forced myself to murmur, 'Oh, nonsense!' and stood over him as if transfixed.

"Anything approaching the change that came over his features I have never seen before, and hope never to see again. Oh, I wasn't touched. I was fascinated. It was as though a veil had been rent. I saw on that ivory face the expression of sombre pride, of ruthless power, of craven terror—of an intense and hopeless despair. Did he live his life again in every detail of desire, temptation, and surrender during that supreme moment of complete knowledge? He cried in a whisper at some image, at some vision—he cried out twice, a cry that was no more than a breath—

"'The horror! The horror!'

"I blew the candle out and left the cabin. The pilgrims were dining in the mess-room, and I took my place opposite the manager, who lifted his eyes to give me a questioning glance, which I successfully ignored. He leaned back, serene, with that peculiar smile of his sealing the unexpressed depths of his meanness. A continuous shower of small flies streamed upon the lamp, upon the cloth, upon our hands and faces. Suddenly the manager's boy put his insolent black head in the doorway, and said in a tone of scathing contempt—

"'Mistah Kurtz—he dead.'

"All the pilgrims rushed out to see. I remained, and went on with my dinner. I believe I was considered brutally callous. However, I did not eat much. There was a lamp in there—light, don't you know—and outside it was so beastly, beastly dark. I went no more near the remarkable man who had pronounced a judgment upon the adventures of his soul on this earth. The voice was gone. What else had been there? But I am of course aware that next day the pilgrims buried something in a muddy hole.

"And then they very nearly buried me.

"However, as you see, I did not go to join Kurtz there and then. I did not. I remained to dream the nightmare out to the end, and to show my loyalty to Kurtz once more. Destiny. My destiny! Droll thing life is—that mysterious arrangement of merciless logic for a futile purpose. The most you can hope from it is some knowledge of yourself—that comes too late—a crop of unextinguishable regrets. I have wrestled with death. It is the most exciting contest you can imagine. It takes place in an impalpable grayness, with nothing underfoot, with nothing around, without spectators, without clamour, without glory, without the great desire of victory, without the great fear of defeat, in a sickly atmosphere of tepid scepticism, without much belief in your own right, and still less in that of your adversary. If such is the form of ultimate wisdom, then life is a greater riddle than some of think it to be. I was within a hair's breadth of the last opportunity for pronouncement, and I found with humiliation that probably I would have nothing to say. This is the reason why I affirm that Kurtz was a remarkable man. He had something to say. He said it. Since I had peeped over the edge myself, I understand better the meaning of his stare, that could not see the flame of the candle, but was wide enough to embrace the whole universe, piercing enough to penetrate all the hearts that beat in the darkness. He had summed up—he had judged. 'The horror!' He was a remarkable man. After all, this was the expression of some sort of belief; it had candour, it had conviction, it had a vibrating note of revolt in its whisper, it had the appalling face of a glimpsed truth—the strange commingling of desire and hate. And it is not my own extremity I remember best—a vision of grayness without form filled with physical pain, and a careless contempt for the evanescence of all things—even of this pain itself. No! It is his extremity that I seem to have lived through. True, he had made that last stride, he had stepped over the edge, while I had been permitted to draw back my hesitating foot. And perhaps in this is the whole difference; perhaps all the wisdom, and all truth, and all sincerity, are just compressed into that inappreciable moment of time in which we step over the threshold of the invisible. Perhaps! I like to think my summing-up would not have been a word of careless contempt. Better his cry—much better. It was an affirmation, a moral victory paid for by innumerable defeats, by abominable terrors, by abominable satisfactions. But it was a victory! That is why I have remained loyal to Kurtz to the last, and even beyond, when a long time after I heard once more, not his own voice, but the echo of his magnificent eloquence thrown to me from a soul as translucently pure as a cliff of crystal.

"No, they did not bury me, though there is a period of time which I remember mistily, with a shuddering wonder, like a passage through some inconceivable world that had no hope in it and no desire. I found myself back in the sepulchral city resenting the sight of people hurrying through the streets to filch a little money from each other, to devour their infamous cookery, to gulp their unwholesome beer, to dream their insignificant and silly dreams. They trespassed upon my thoughts. They were intruders whose knowledge of life was to me an irritating pretence, because I felt so sure they could not possibly know the things I knew. Their bearing, which was simply the bearing of commonplace individuals going about their business in the assurance of perfect safety, was offensive to me like the outrageous flauntings of folly in the face of a danger it is unable to comprehend. I had no particular desire to enlighten them, but I had some difficulty in restraining myself from laughing in their faces, so full of stupid importance. I daresay I was not very well at that time. I tottered about the streets—there were various affairs to settle—grinning bitterly at perfectly respectable persons. I admit my behaviour was inexcusable, but then my temperature was seldom normal in these days. My dear aunt's endeavours to 'nurse up my strength' seemed altogether beside the mark. It was not my strength that wanted nursing, it was my imagination that wanted soothing. I kept the bundle of papers given me by

Kurtz, not knowing exactly what to do with it. His mother had died lately, watched over, as I was told, by his Intended. A clean-shaved man, with an official manner and wearing gold-rimmed spectacles, called on me one day and made inquiries, at first circuitous, afterwards suavely pressing, about what he was pleased to denominate certain 'documents.' I was not surprised, because I had had two rows with the manager on the subject out there. I had refused to give up the smallest scrap out of that package, and I took the same attitude with the spectacled man. He became darkly menacing at last, and with much heat argued that the Company had the right to every bit of information about its 'territories.' And said he, 'Mr. Kurtz's knowledge of unexplored regions must have been necessarily extensive and peculiar—owing to his great abilities and to the deplorable circumstances in which he had been placed: therefore—' I assured him Mr. Kurtz's knowledge, however extensive, did not bear upon the problems of commerce or administration. He invoked then the name of science. 'It would be an incalculable loss if,' etc., etc. I offered him the report on the 'Suppression of Savage Customs,' with the postscriptum torn off. He took it up eagerly, but ended by sniffing at it with an air of contempt. 'This is not what we had a right to expect,' he remarked. 'Expect nothing else,' I said. 'There are only private letters.' He withdrew upon some threat of legal proceedings, and I saw him no more; but another fellow, calling himself Kurtz's cousin, appeared two days later, and was anxious to hear all the details about his dear relative's last moments. Incidentally he gave me to understand that Kurtz had been essentially a great musician. 'There was the making of an immense success,' said the man, who was an organist, I believe, with lank gray hair flowing over a greasy coat-collar. I had no reason to doubt his statement; and to this day I am unable to say what was Kurtz's profession, whether he ever had any—which was the greatest of his talents. I had taken him for a painter who wrote for the papers, or else for a journalist who could paint—but even the cousin (who took snuff during the interview) could not tell me what he had been—exactly. He was a universal genius—on that point I agreed with the old chap, who thereupon blew his nose noisily into a large cotton handkerchief and withdrew in senile agitation, bearing off some family letters and memoranda without importance. Ultimately a journalist anxious to know something of the fate of his 'dear colleague' turned up. This visitor informed me Kurtz's proper sphere ought to have been politics 'on the popular side.' He had furry straight eyebrows, bristly hair cropped short, an eye-glass on a broad ribbon, and, becoming expansive, confessed his opinion that Kurtz really couldn't write a bit—'but heavens! how that man could talk. He electrified large meetings. He had faith—don't you see?—he had the faith. He could get himself to believe anything—anything. He would have been a splendid leader of an extreme party.' 'What party?' I asked. 'Any party,' answered the other. 'He was an—an—extremist.' Did I not think so? I assented. Did I know, he asked, with a sudden flash of curiosity, 'what it was that had induced him to go out there?' 'Yes,' said I, and forthwith handed him the famous Report for publication, if he thought fit. He glanced through it hurriedly, mumbling all the time, judged 'it would do,' and took himself off with this plunder.

"Thus I was left at last with a slim packet of letters and the girl's portrait. She struck me as beautiful—I mean she had a beautiful expression. I know that the sunlight can be made to lie, too, yet one felt that no manipulation of light and pose could have conveyed the delicate shade of truthfulness upon those features. She seemed ready to listen without mental reservation, without suspicion, without a thought for herself. I concluded I would go and give her back her portrait and those letters myself. Curiosity? Yes; and also some other feeling perhaps. All that had been Kurtz's had passed out of my hands: his soul, his body, his station, his plans, his ivory, his career. There remained only his memory and his Intended—and I wanted to give that up, too, to the past, in a way—to surrender personally all that remained of him with me to that oblivion which is the last word of our common fate. I don't defend myself. I had no clear perception of what it was I really wanted. Perhaps it was an impulse of unconscious loyalty, or the fulfilment of one of those ironic necessities that lurk in the facts of human existence. I don't know. I can't tell. But I went.

"I thought his memory was like the other memories of the dead that accumulate in every man's life—a vague impress on the brain of shadows that had fallen on it in their swift and final passage; but before the high and ponderous door, between the tall houses of a street as still and decorous as a well-kept alley in a cemetery, I had a vision of him on the stretcher, opening his mouth voraciously, as if to devour all the earth with all its mankind. He lived then before me; he lived as much as he had ever lived—a shadow insatiable of splendid appearances, of frightful realities; a shadow darker than the shadow of the night, and draped nobly in the folds of a gorgeous eloquence. The vision seemed to enter the house with me—the stretcher, the phantom-bearers, the wild crowd of obedient worshippers, the gloom of the forests, the glitter of the reach between the murky bends, the beat of the drum, regular and muffled like the beating of a heart—the heart of a conquering darkness. It was a moment of triumph for the wilderness, an invading and vengeful rush which, it seemed to me, I would have to keep back alone for the salvation of another soul. And the memory of what I had heard him say afar there, with the horned shapes stirring at my back, in the glow of fires, within the patient woods, those broken phrases came back to me, were heard again in their ominous and terrifying simplicity. I remembered his abject pleading, his abject threats, the colossal scale of his vile desires, the meanness, the torment, the tempestuous anguish of his soul. And later on I seemed to see his collected languid manner, when he said one day, 'This lot of ivory now is really mine. The Company did not pay for it. I collected it myself at a very great personal risk. I am afraid they will try to claim it as theirs though. H'm. It is a difficult case. What do you think I ought to do—resist? Eh? I want no more than justice.' . . . He wanted no more than justice—no more than justice. I rang the bell before a mahogany door on the first floor, and while I waited he seemed to stare at me out of the glassy panel—stare with that wide and immense stare embracing, condemning, loathing all the universe. I seemed to hear the whispered cry, 'The horror! The horror!'

"The dusk was falling. I had to wait in a lofty drawing-room with three long windows from floor to ceiling that were like three luminous and bedraped columns. The bent gilt legs and backs of the furniture shone in indistinct curves. The tall marble fireplace had a cold and monumental whiteness. A grand piano stood massively in a corner; with dark gleams on the flat surfaces like a sombre and polished sarcophagus. A high door opened—closed. I rose.

"She came forward, all in black, with a pale head, floating towards me in the dusk. She was in mourning. It was more than a year since his death, more than a year since the news came; she seemed as though she would remember and mourn for ever. She took both my hands in hers and murmured, 'I had heard you were coming.' I noticed she was not very young—I mean not girlish. She had a mature capacity for fidelity, for belief, for suffering. The room seemed to have grown darker, as if all the sad light of the cloudy evening had taken refuge on her forehead. This fair hair, this pale visage, this pure brow, seemed surrounded by an ashy halo from which the dark eyes looked out at me. Their glance was guileless, profound, confident, and trustful. She carried her sorrowful head as though she were proud of that sorrow, as though she would say, I—I alone know how to mourn for him as he deserves. But while we were still shaking hands, such a look of awful desolation came upon her face that I perceived she was one of those creatures that are not the playthings of Time. For her he had died only yesterday. And, by Jove! the impression was so powerful that for me, too, he seemed to have died only yesterday—nay, this very minute. I saw her and him in the same instant of time—his death and her sorrow—I saw her sorrow in the very moment of his death. Do you understand? I saw them together—I heard them together. She had said, with a deep catch of the breath, 'I have survived' while my strained ears seemed to hear distinctly, mingled with her tone of despairing regret, the summing up whisper of his eternal condemnation. I asked myself what I was doing there, with a sensation of panic in my heart as though I had blundered into a place of cruel and absurd mysteries not fit for a human being to behold. She motioned me to a chair. We sat down. I laid the packet gently on the little table, and she put her hand over it.... 'You knew him well,' she murmured, after a moment of mourning silence.

"'Intimacy grows quickly out there,' I said. 'I knew him as well as it is possible for one man to know another.'

"'And you admired him,' she said. 'It was impossible to know him and not to admire him. Was it?'

"'He was a remarkable man,' I said, unsteadily. Then before the appealing fixity of her gaze, that seemed to watch for more words on my lips, I went on, 'It was impossible not to—'

"'Love him,' she finished eagerly, silencing me into an appalled dumbness. 'How true! how true! But when you think that no one knew him so well as I! I had all his noble confidence. I knew him best.'

"'You knew him best,' I repeated. And perhaps she did. But with every word spoken the room was growing darker, and only her forehead, smooth and white, remained illumined by the unextinguishable light of belief and love.

"'You were his friend,' she went on. 'His friend,' she repeated, a little louder. 'You must have been, if he had given you this, and sent you to me. I feel I can speak to you—and oh! I must speak. I want you—you who have heard his last words—to know I have been worthy of him. . . . It is not pride. . . . Yes! I am proud to know I understood him better than any one on earth—he told me so himself. And since his mother died I have had no one—no one—to—to—'

"I listened. The darkness deepened. I was not even sure whether he had given me the right bundle. I rather suspect he wanted me to take care of another batch of papers which, after his death, I saw the manager examining under the lamp. And the girl talked, easing her pain in the certitude of my sympathy; she talked as thirsty men drink. I had heard that her engagement with Kurtz had been disapproved by her people. He wasn't rich enough or something. And indeed I don't know whether he had not been a pauper all his life. He had given me some reason to infer that it was his impatience of comparative poverty that drove him out there.

"'. . . Who was not his friend who had heard him speak once?' she was saying. 'He drew men towards him by what was best in them.' She looked at me with intensity. 'It is the gift of the great,' she went on, and the sound of her low voice seemed to have the accompaniment of all the other sounds, full of mystery, desolation, and sorrow, I had ever heard—the ripple of the river, the soughing of the trees swayed by the wind, the murmurs of the crowds, the faint ring of incomprehensible words cried from afar, the whisper of a voice speaking from beyond the threshold of an eternal darkness. 'But you have heard him! You know!' she cried.

"'Yes, I know,' I said with something like despair in my heart, but bowing my head before the faith that was in her, before that great and saving illusion that shone with an unearthly glow in the darkness, in the triumphant darkness from which I could not have defended her—from which I could not even defend myself.

"'What a loss to me—to us!'—she corrected herself with beautiful generosity; then added in a murmur, 'To the world.' By the last gleams of twilight I could see the glitter of her eyes, full of tears—of tears that would not fall.

"'I have been very happy—very fortunate—very proud,' she went on. 'Too fortunate. Too happy for a little while. And now I am unhappy for—for life.'

"She stood up; her fair hair seemed to catch all the remaining light in a glimmer of gold. I rose, too.

"'And of all this,' she went on, mournfully, 'of all his promise, and of all his greatness, of his generous mind, of his noble heart, nothing remains—nothing but a memory. You and I—'

"'We shall always remember him,' I said, hastily.

"'No!' she cried. 'It is impossible that all this should be lost—that such a life should be sacrificed to leave nothing—but sorrow. You know what vast plans he had. I knew of them, too—I could not perhaps understand—but others knew of them. Something must remain. His words, at least, have not died.'

"'His words will remain,' I said.

"'And his example,' she whispered to herself. 'Men looked up to him—his goodness shone in every act. His example—'

"'True,' I said; 'his example, too. Yes, his example. I forgot that.'

"'But I do not. I cannot—I cannot believe—not yet. I cannot believe that I shall never see him again, that nobody will see him again, never, never, never.'

"She put out her arms as if after a retreating figure, stretching them black and with clasped pale hands across the fading and narrow sheen of the window. Never see him! I saw him clearly enough then. I shall see this eloquent phantom as long as I live, and I shall see her, too, a tragic and familiar Shade, resembling in this gesture another one, tragic also, and bedecked with powerless charms, stretching bare brown arms over the glitter of the infernal stream, the stream of darkness. She said suddenly very low, 'He died as he lived.'

"'His end,' said I, with dull anger stirring in me, 'was in every way worthy of his life.'

"'And I was not with him,' she murmured. My anger subsided before a feeling of infinite pity.

"'Everything that could be done—' I mumbled.

"'Ah, but I believed in him more than any one on earth—more than his own mother, more than—himself. He needed me! Me! I would have treasured every sigh, every word, every sign, every glance.'

"I felt like a chill grip on my chest. 'Don't,' I said, in a muffled voice.

"'Forgive me. I—I—have mourned so long in silence—in silence. . . . You were with him—to the last? I think of his loneliness. Nobody near to understand him as I would have understood. Perhaps no one to hear. . . .'

"'To the very end,' I said, shakily. 'I heard his very last words. . . .' I stopped in a fright.

"'Repeat them,' she murmured in a heart-broken tone. 'I want—I want—something—something—to—to live with.'

"I was on the point of crying at her, 'Don't you hear them?' The dusk was repeating them in a persistent whisper all around us, in a whisper that seemed to swell menacingly like the first whisper of a rising wind. 'The horror! the horror!'

"'His last word—to live with,' she insisted. 'Don't you understand I loved him—I loved him—I loved him!'

"I pulled myself together and spoke slowly.

"'The last word he pronounced was—your name.'

"I heard a light sigh and then my heart stood still, stopped dead short by an exulting and terrible cry, by the cry of inconceivable triumph and of unspeakable pain. 'I knew it—I was sure!' . . . She knew. She was sure. I heard her weeping; she had hidden her face in her hands. It seemed to me that the house would collapse before I could escape, that the heavens would fall upon my head. But nothing happened. The heavens do not fall for such a trifle. Would they have fallen, I wonder, if I had rendered Kurtz that justice which was his due? Hadn't he said he wanted only justice? But I couldn't. I could not tell her. It would have been too dark—too dark altogether. . . ."

Marlow ceased, and sat apart, indistinct and silent, in the pose of a meditating Buddha. Nobody moved for a time. "We have lost the first of the ebb," said the Director, suddenly. I raised my head. The offing was barred by a black bank of clouds, and the tranquil waterway leading to the uttermost ends of the earth flowed sombre under an overcast sky—seemed to lead into the heart of an immense darkness.

TYPHOON

· I ·

CAPTAIN MacWHIRR, of the steamer *Nan-Shan,* had a physiognomy that, in the order of material appearances, was the exact
counterpart of his mind: it presented no marked characteristics of
firmness or stupidity; it had no pronounced characteristics whatever;
it was simply ordinary, irresponsive, and unruffled.

The only thing his aspect might have been said to suggest, at times,
was bashfulness; because he would sit, in business offices ashore,
sunburnt and smiling faintly, with downcast eyes. When he raised
them, they were perceived to be direct in their glance and of blue
colour. His hair was fair and extremely fine, clasping from temple to
temple the bald dome of his skull in a clamp as of fluffy silk. The hair
of his face, on the contrary, carroty and flaming, resembled a growth
of copper wire clipped short to the line of the lip; while, no matter
how close he shaved, fiery metallic gleams passed, when he moved his
head, over the surface of his cheeks. He was rather below the medium
height, a bit round-shouldered, and so sturdy of limb that his clothes
always looked a shade too tight for his arms and legs. As if unable
to grasp what is due to the difference of latitudes, he wore a brown
bowler hat, a complete suit of a brownish hue, and clumsy black
boots. These harbour togs gave to his thick figure an air of stiff and
uncouth smartness. A thin silver watch-chain looped his waistcoat, and
he never left his ship for the shore without clutching in his powerful,
hairy fist an elegant umbrella of the very best quality, but generally
unrolled. Young Jukes, the chief mate, attending his commander to
the gangway, would sometimes venture to say, with the greatest gentle-

ness, "Allow me, sir"—and possessing himself of the umbrella defer-
entially, would elevate the ferule, shake the folds, twirl a neat furl in
a jiffy, and hand it back; going through the performance with a face
of such portentous gravity, that Mr. Solomon Rout, the chief engineer,
smoking his morning cigar over the skylight, would turn away his head
in order to hide a smile. "Oh! aye! The blessed gamp. . . . Thank'ee,
Jukes, thank'ee," would mutter Captain MacWhirr, heartily, without
looking up.

Having just enough imagination to carry him through each successive day, and no more, he was tranquilly sure of himself; and from the
very same cause he was not in the least conceited. It is your imaginative superior who is touchy, overbearing, and difficult to please; but
every ship Captain MacWhirr commanded was the floating abode of
harmony and peace. It was, in truth, as impossible for him to take a
flight of fancy as it would be for a watchmaker to put together a chro-
nometer with nothing except a two-pound hammer and a whip-saw in
the way of tools. Yet the uninteresting lives of men so entirely given
to the actuality of the bare existence have their mysterious side. It was
impossible in Captain MacWhirr's case, for instance, to understand
what under heaven could have induced that perfectly satisfactory son
of a petty grocer in Belfast to run away to sea. And yet he had done
that very thing at the age of fifteen. It was enough, when you thought
it over, to give you the idea of an immense, potent, and invisible hand
thrust into the ant-heap of the earth, laying hold of shoulders, knocking heads together, and setting the unconscious faces of the multitude
towards inconceivable goals and in undreamt-of directions.

His father never really forgave him for this undutiful stupidity. "We
could have got on without him," he used to say later on, "but there's
the business. And he an only son, too!" His mother wept very much
after his disappearance. As it had never occurred to him to leave word
behind, he was mourned over for dead till, after eight months, his
first letter arrived from Talcahuano. It was short, and contained the
statement: "We had very fine weather on our passage out." But evidently, in the writer's mind, the only important intelligence was to the
effect that his captain had, on the very day of writing, entered him
regularly on the ship's articles as Ordinary Seaman. "Because I can do
the work," he explained. The mother again wept copiously, while the

remark, "Tom's an ass," expressed the emotions of the father. He was a corpulent man, with a gift for sly chaffing, which to the end of his life he exercised in his intercourse with his son, a little pityingly, as if upon a half-witted person.

MacWhirr's visits to his home were necessarily rare, and in the course of years he despatched other letters to his parents, informing them of his successive promotions and of his movements upon the vast earth. In these missives could be found sentences like this: "The heat here is very great." Or: "On Christmas day at 4 P.M. we fell in with some icebergs." The old people ultimately became acquainted with a good many names of ships, and with the names of the skippers who commanded them—with the names of Scots and English ship-owners—with the names of seas, oceans, straits, promontories—with outlandish names of lumber-ports, of rice-ports, of cotton-ports—with the names of islands—with the name of their son's young woman. She was called Lucy. It did not suggest itself to him to mention whether he thought the name pretty. And then they died.

The great day of MacWhirr's marriage came in due course, following shortly upon the great day when he got his first command.

All these events had taken place many years before the morning when, in the chart-room of the steamer *Nan-Shan,* he stood confronted by the fall of a barometer he had no reason to distrust. The fall—taking into account the excellence of the instrument, the time of the year, and the ship's position on the terrestrial globe—was of a nature omi-nously prophetic; but the red face of the man betrayed no sort of inward disturbance. Omens were as nothing to him, and he was unable to discover the message of a prophecy till the fulfilment had brought it home to his very door. "That's a fall, and no mistake," he thought. "There must be some uncommonly dirty weather knocking about."

The *Nan-Shan* was on her way from the southward to the treaty port of Fu-chau, with some cargo in her lower holds, and two hundred Chinese coolies returning to their village homes in the province of Fo-kien, after a few years of work in various tropical colonies. The morn-ing was fine, the oily sea heaved without a sparkle, and there was a queer white misty patch in the sky like a halo of the sun. The fore-deck, packed with Chinamen, was full of sombre clothing, yellow faces, and pigtails, sprinkled over with a good many naked shoulders, for there was no wind, and the heat was close. The coolies lounged, talked, smoked, or stared over the rail; some, drawing water over the side, sluiced each other; a few slept on hatches, while several small parties of six sat on their heels surrounding iron trays with plates of rice and tiny teacups; and every single Celestial of them was carrying with him all he had in the world—a wooden chest with a ringing lock and brass on the corners, containing the savings of his labours: some clothes of ceremony, sticks of incense, a little opium maybe, bits of nameless rubbish of conventional value, and a small hoard of silver dollars, toiled for in coal lighters, won in gambling-houses or in petty trading, grubbed out of earth, sweated out in mines, on railway lines, in deadly jungle, under heavy burdens—amassed patiently, guarded with care, cherished fiercely.

A cross swell had set in from the direction of Formosa Channel about ten o'clock, without disturbing these passengers much, because the *Nan-Shan,* with her flat bottom, rolling chocks on bilges, and great breadth of beam, had the reputation of an exceptionally steady ship in a sea-way. Mr. Jukes, in moments of expansion on shore, would proclaim loudly that the "old girl was as good as she was pretty." It would never have occurred to Captain MacWhirr to express his favourable opinion so loud or in terms so fanciful.

She was a good ship, undoubtedly, and not old either. She had been built in Dumbarton less than three years before, to the order of a firm of merchants in Siam—Messrs. Sigg and Son. When she lay afloat, finished in every detail and ready to take up the work of her life, the builders contemplated her with pride.

"Sigg has asked us for a reliable skipper to take her out," remarked one of the partners; and the other, after reflecting for a while, said: "I think MacWhirr is ashore just at present." "Is he? Then wire him at once. He's the very man," declared the senior, without a moment's hesitation.

Next morning MacWhirr stood before them unperturbed, having travelled from London by the midnight express after a sudden but undemonstrative parting with his wife. She was the daughter of a superior couple who had seen better days.

"We had better be going together over the ship, Captain," said the senior partner; and the three men started to view the perfections of the *Nan-Shan* from stem to stern, and from her keelson to the trucks of her two stumpy pole-masts.

Captain MacWhirr had begun by taking off his coat, which he hung on the end of a steam windlass embodying all the latest improvements.

"My uncle wrote of you favourably by yesterday's mail to our good friends—Messrs. Sigg, you know—and doubtless they'll continue you out there in command," said the junior partner. "You'll be able to boast of being in charge of the handiest boat of her size on the coast of China, Captain," he added.

"Have you? Thank 'ee," mumbled vaguely MacWhirr, to whom the view of a distant eventuality could appeal no more than the beauty of a wide landscape to a purblind tourist; and his eyes happening at the moment to be at rest upon the lock of the cabin door, he walked up to it, full of purpose, and began to rattle the handle vigorously, while he observed, in his low, earnest voice, "You can't trust the workmen nowadays. A brand-new lock, and it won't act at all. Stuck fast. See? See?"

As soon as they found themselves alone in their office across the yard: "You praised that fellow up to Sigg. What is it you see in him?" asked the nephew, with faint contempt.

"I admit he has nothing of your fancy skipper about him, if that's what you mean," said the elder man, curtly. "Is the foreman of the joiners on the *Nan-Shan* outside? . . . Come in, Bates. How is it that you let Tait's people put us off with a defective lock on the cabin door? The Captain could see directly he set eye on it. Have it replaced at once. The little straws, Bates . . . the little straws. . . ."

The lock was replaced accordingly, and a few days afterwards the *Nan-Shan* steamed out to the East, without MacWhirr having offered any further remark as to her fittings, or having been heard to utter a single word hinting at pride in his ship, gratitude for his appointment, or satisfaction at his prospects.

With a temperament neither loquacious nor taciturn he found very little occasion to talk. There were matters of duty, of course—directions, orders, and so on; but the past being to his mind done with, and the future not there yet, the more general actualities of the day required no comment—because facts can speak for themselves with overwhelming precision.

Old Mr. Sigg liked a man of few words, and one that "you could be sure would not try to improve upon his instructions." MacWhirr satisfying these requirements, was continued in command of the *Nan-Shan,* and applied himself to the careful navigation of his ship in the China seas. She had come out on a British register, but after some time Messrs. Sigg judged it expedient to transfer her to the Siamese flag.

At the news of the contemplated transfer Jukes grew restless, as if under a sense of personal affront. He went about grumbling to himself, and uttering short scornful laughs. "Fancy having a ridiculous Noah's Ark elephant in the ensign of one's ship," he said once at the engine-room door. "Dash me if I can stand it: I'll throw up the billet. Don't it make *you* sick, Mr. Rout?" The chief engineer only cleared his throat with the air of a man who knows the value of a good billet.

The first morning the new flag floated over the stern of the *Nan-Shan* Jukes stood looking at it bitterly from the bridge. He struggled with his feelings for a while, and then remarked, "Queer flag for a man to sail under, sir."

"What's the matter with the flag?" inquired Captain MacWhirr. "Seems all right to me." And he walked across to the end of the bridge to have a good look.

"Well, it looks queer to me," burst out Jukes, greatly exasperated, and flung off the bridge.

Captain MacWhirr was amazed at these manners. After a while he stepped quietly into the chart-room, and opened his International Signal Code-book at the plate where the flags of all the nations are correctly figured in gaudy rows. He ran his finger over them, and when he came to Siam he contemplated with great attention the red field and the white elephant. Nothing could be more simple; but to make sure he brought the book out on the bridge for the purpose of comparing the coloured drawing with the real thing at the flag-staff astern. When next Jukes, who was carrying on the duty that day with a sort of suppressed fierceness, happened on the bridge, his commander observed:

"There's nothing amiss with that flag."

"Isn't there?" mumbled Jukes, falling on his knees before a deck-locker and jerking therefrom viciously a spare lead-line.

"No. I looked up the book. Length twice the breadth and the elephant exactly in the middle. I thought the people ashore would know how to make the local flag. Stands to reason. You were wrong, Jukes. . . ."

"Well, sir," began Jukes, getting up excitedly, "all I can say—" He fumbled for the end of the coil of line with trembling hands.

"That's all right." Captain MacWhirr soothed him, sitting heavily on a little canvas folding-stool he greatly affected. "All you have to do is to take care they don't hoist the elephant upside-down before they get quite used to it."

Jukes flung the new lead-line over on the fore-deck with a loud "Here you are, boss'n—don't forget to wet it thoroughly," and turned with immense resolution towards his commander; but Captain Mac-Whirr spread his elbows on the bridge-rail comfortably.

"Because it would be, I suppose, understood as a signal of distress," he went on. "What do you think? That elephant there, I take it, stands for something in the nature of the Union Jack in the flag. . . ."

"Does it!" yelled Jukes, so that every head on the *Nan-Shan's* decks looked towards the bridge. Then he sighed, and with sudden resignation: "It would certainly be a dam' distressful sight," he said, meekly.

Later in the day he accosted the chief engineer with a confidential, "Here, let me tell you the old man's latest."

Mr. Solomon Rout (frequently alluded to as Long Sol, Old Sol, or Father Rout), from finding himself almost invariably the tallest man on board every ship he joined, had acquired the habit of a stooping, leisurely condescension. His hair was scant and sandy, his flat cheeks were pale, his bony wrists and long scholarly hands were pale, too, as though he had lived all his life in the shade.

He smiled from on high at Jukes, and went on smoking and glancing about quietly, in the manner of a kind uncle lending an ear to the tale of an excited schoolboy. Then, greatly amused but impassive, he asked:

"And did you throw up the billet?"

"No," cried Jukes, raising a weary, discouraged voice above the harsh buzz of the *Nan-Shan's* friction winches. All of them were hard at work, snatching slings of cargo, high up, to the end of long derricks, only, as it seemed, to let them rip down recklessly by the run. The cargo chains groaned in the gins, clinked on coamings, rattled over the side; and the whole ship quivered, with her long gray flanks smoking in wreaths of steam. "No," cried Jukes, "I didn't. What's the good? I might just as well fling my resignation at this bulkhead. I don't believe you can make a man like that understand anything. He simply knocks me over."

At that moment Captain MacWhirr, back from the shore, crossed the deck, umbrella in hand, escorted by a mournful, self-possessed Chinaman, walking behind in paper-soled silk shoes, and who also carried an umbrella.

The master of the *Nan-Shan,* speaking just audibly and gazing at his boots as his manner was, remarked that it would be necessary to call at Fu-chau this trip, and desired Mr. Rout to have steam up to-morrow afternoon at one o'clock sharp. He pushed back his hat to wipe his forehead, observing at the same time that he hated going ashore anyhow; while overtopping him Mr. Rout, without deigning a word, smoked austerely, nursing his right elbow in the palm of his left hand. Then Jukes was directed in the same subdued voice to keep the forward 'tween-deck clear of cargo. Two hundred coolies were going to be put down there. The Bun Hin Company were sending that lot home. Twenty-five bags of rice would be coming off in a sampan directly, for stores. All seven-years'-men they were, said Captain MacWhirr, with a camphor-wood chest to every man. The carpenter should be set to work nailing three-inch battens along the deck below, fore and aft, to keep these boxes from shifting in a sea-way. Jukes had better look to it at once. "D'ye hear, Jukes?" This Chinaman here was coming with the ship as far as Fu-chau—a sort of interpreter he would be. Bun Hin's clerk he was, and wanted to have a look at the space. Jukes had better take him forward. "D'ye hear, Jukes?"

Jukes took care to punctuate these instructions in proper places with the obligatory "Yes, sir," ejaculated without enthusiasm. His brusque "Come along, John; make look see" set the Chinaman in motion at his heels.

"Wanchee look see, all same look see can do," said Jukes, who having no talent for foreign languages mangled the very pidgin-English cruelly. He pointed at the open hatch. "Catchee number one piecie place to sleep in. Eh?"

He was gruff, as became his racial superiority, but not unfriendly.

The Chinaman, gazing sad and speechless into the darkness of the hatchway, seemed to stand at the head of a yawning grave.

"No catchee rain down there—savee?" pointed out Jukes. "Suppose all'ee same fine weather, one piecie coolie-man come topside," he pursued, warming up imaginatively. "Make so—Phooooo!" He expanded his chest and blew out his cheeks. "Savee, John? Breathe—fresh air. Good. Eh? Washee him piecie pants, chow-chow top-side—see, John?"

With his mouth and hands he made exuberant motions of eating rice and washing clothes; and the Chinaman, who concealed his distrust of this pantomime under a collected demeanour tinged by a gentle and refined melancholy, glanced out of his almond eyes from Jukes to the hatch and back again. "Velly good," he murmured, in a disconsolate undertone, and hastened smoothly along the decks, dodging obstacles in his course. He disappeared, ducking low under a sling of ten dirty gunny-bags full of some costly merchandise and exhaling a repulsive smell.

Captain MacWhirr meantime had gone on the bridge, and into the chart-room, where a letter, commenced two days before, awaited termination. These long letters began with the words, "My darling wife," and the steward, between the scrubbing of the floors and the dusting of chronometer-boxes, snatched at every opportunity to read them. They interested him much more than they possibly could the woman for whose eye they were intended; and this for the reason that they related in minute detail each successive trip of the *Nan-Shan*.

Her master, faithful to facts, which alone his consciousness reflected, would set them down with painstaking care upon many pages. The house in a northern suburb to which these pages were addressed had a bit of garden before the bow-windows, a deep porch of good appearance, coloured glass with imitation lead frame in the front door. He paid five-and-forty pounds a year for it, and did not think the rent too high, because Mrs. MacWhirr (a pretentious person with a scraggy neck and a disdainful manner) was admittedly ladylike, and in the neighbourhood considered as "quite superior." The only secret of her life was her abject terror of the time when her husband would come home to stay for good. Under the same roof there dwelt also a daughter called Lydia and a son, Tom. These two were but slightly acquainted with their father. Mainly, they knew him as a rare but privileged visitor, who of an evening smoked his pipe in the dining-room and slept in the house. The lanky girl, upon the whole, was rather ashamed of him; the boy was frankly and utterly indifferent in a straightforward, delightful, unaffected way manly boys have.

And Captain MacWhirr wrote home from the coast of China twelve times every year, desiring quaintly to be "remembered to the children," and subscribing himself "your loving husband," as calmly as if the words so long used by so many men were, apart from their shape, worn-out things, and of a faded meaning.

The China seas north and south are narrow seas. They are seas full of every-day, eloquent facts, such as islands, sand-banks, reefs, swift and changeable currents—tangled facts that nevertheless speak to a seaman in clear and definite language. Their speech appealed to Captain MacWhirr's sense of realities so forcibly that he had given up his state-room below and practically lived all his days on the bridge of his ship, often having his meals sent up, and sleeping at night in the chart-room. And he indited there his home letters. Each of them, without exception, contained the phrase, "The weather has been very fine this trip," or some other form of a statement to that effect. And this statement, too, in its wonderful persistence, was of the same perfect accuracy as all the others they contained.

Mr. Rout likewise wrote letters; only no one on board knew how chatty he could be pen in hand, because the chief engineer had enough imagination to keep his desk locked. His wife relished his style greatly. They were a childless couple, and Mrs. Rout, a big, high-bosomed, jolly woman of forty, shared with Mr. Rout's toothless and venerable mother a little cottage near Teddington. She would run over her correspondence, at breakfast, with lively eyes, and scream out interesting passages in a joyous voice at the deaf old lady, prefacing each extract by the warning shout, "Solomon says!" She had the trick of firing off Solomon's utterances also upon strangers, astonishing them easily by the unfamiliar text and the unexpectedly jocular vein of these quotations. On the day the new curate called for the first time at the cottage, she found occasion to remark, "As Solomon says: 'the engineers that go down to the sea in ships behold the wonders of sailor nature,'" when a change in the visitor's countenance made her stop and stare.

"Solomon.... Oh! ... Mrs. Rout," stuttered the young man, very red in the face, "I must say ... I don't. ...."

"He's my husband," she announced in a great shout, throwing herself back in the chair. Perceiving the joke, she laughed immoderately with a handkerchief to her eyes, while he sat wearing a forced smile, and, from his inexperience of jolly women, fully persuaded that she must be deplorably insane. They were excellent friends afterwards; for, absolving her from irreverent intention, he came to think she was a very worthy person indeed; and he learned in time to receive without flinching other scraps of Solomon's wisdom.

"For my part," Solomon was reported by his wife to have said once, "give me the dullest ass for a skipper before a rogue. There is a way to take a fool; but a rogue is smart and slippery." This was an airy generalization drawn from the particular case of Captain MacWhirr's honesty, which, in itself, had the heavy obviousness of a lump of clay. On the other hand, Mr. Jukes, unable to generalize, unmarried, and unengaged, was in the habit of opening his heart after another fashion to an old chum and former shipmate, actually serving as second officer on board an Atlantic liner.

First of all he would insist upon the advantages of the Eastern trade, hinting at its superiority to the Western ocean service. He extolled the sky, the seas, the ships, and the easy life of the Far East. The *Nan-Shan,* he affirmed, was second to none as a sea-boat.

"We have no brass-bound uniforms, but then we are like brothers here," he wrote. "We all mess together and live like fighting-cocks. . . . All the chaps of the black-squad are as decent as they make that kind, and old Sol, the Chief, is a dry stick. We are good friends. As to our old man, you could not find a quieter skipper. Sometimes you would think he hadn't sense enough to see anything wrong. And yet it isn't that. Can't be. He has been in command for a good few years now. He doesn't do anything actually foolish, and gets his ship along all right without worrying anybody. I believe he hasn't brains enough to enjoy kicking up a row. I don't take advantage of him. I would scorn it. Outside the routine of duty he doesn't seem to understand more than half of what you tell him. We get a laugh out of this at times; but it is dull, too, to be with a man like this—in the long-run. Old Sol says he hasn't much conversation. Conversation! O Lord! He never talks. The other day I had been yarning under the bridge with one of the engineers, and he must have heard us. When I came up to take my watch, he steps out of the chart-room and has a good look all round, peeps over at the sidelights, glances at the compass, squints upwards at the stars. That's his regular performance. By-and-by he says: 'Was that you talking just now in the port alleyway?' 'Yes, sir.' 'With the third engineer?' 'Yes, sir.' He walks off to starboard, and sits under the dodger on a little camp-stool of his, and for half an hour perhaps he makes no sound, except that I heard him sneeze once. Then after a while I hear him getting up over there, and he strolls across to port, where I was. 'I can't understand what you can find to talk about,' says he. 'Two solid hours. I am not blaming you. I see people ashore at it all day long, and then in the evening they sit down and keep at it over the drinks. Must be saying the same things over and over again. I can't understand.'

"Did you ever hear anything like that? And he was so patient about it. It made me quite sorry for him. But he is exasperating, too, sometimes. Of course one would not do anything to vex him even if it were worth while. But it isn't. He's so jolly innocent that if you were to put your thumb to your nose and wave your fingers at him he would only wonder gravely to himself what got into you. He told me once quite simply that he found it very difficult to make out what made people always act so queerly. He's too dense to trouble about, and that's the truth."

Thus wrote Mr. Jukes to his chum in the Western ocean trade, out of the fulness of his heart and the liveliness of his fancy.

He had expressed his honest opinion. It was not worth while trying to impress a man of that sort. If the world had been full of such men, life would have probably appeared to Jukes an unentertaining and unprofitable business. He was not alone in his opinion. The sea itself, as if sharing Mr. Jukes' good-natured forbearance, had never put itself out to startle the silent man, who seldom looked up, and wandered innocently over the waters with the only visible purpose of getting food, raiment, and house-room for three people ashore. Dirty weather he had known, of course. He had been made wet, uncomfortable, tired in the usual way, felt at the time and presently forgotten. So that upon the whole he had been justified in reporting fine weather at home. But he had never been given a glimpse of immeasurable strength and of immoderate wrath, the wrath that passes exhausted but never appeased—the wrath and fury of the passionate sea. He knew it existed, as we know that crime and abominations exist; he had heard of it as a peaceable citizen in a town hears of battles, famines, and floods, and yet knows nothing of what these things mean—though, indeed, he may have been mixed up in a street row, have gone without his dinner once, or been soaked to the skin in a shower. Captain MacWhirr had sailed over the surface of the oceans as some men go skimming over the years of existence to sink gently into a placid grave, ignorant of life to the last, without ever having been made to see all it may contain of perfidy, of violence, and of terror. There are on sea and land such men thus fortunate—or thus disdained by destiny or by the sea.

· II ·

Observing the steady fall of the barometer, Captain MacWhirr thought, "There's some dirty weather knocking about." This is precisely what he thought. He had had an experience of moderately dirty weather—the term dirty as applied to the weather implying only moderate discomfort to the seaman. Had he been informed by an indisputable authority that the end of the world was to be finally accomplished by a catastrophic disturbance of the atmosphere, he would have assimilated the information under the simple idea of dirty weather, and no other, because he had no experience of cataclysms, and belief does not necessarily imply comprehension. The wisdom of his country had pronounced by means of an Act of Parliament that before he could be considered as fit to take charge of a ship he should be able to answer certain simple questions on the subject of circular storms such as hurricanes, cyclones, typhoons; and apparently he had answered them, since he was now in command of the *Nan-Shan* in the China seas during the season of typhoons. But if he had answered he remembered nothing of it. He was, however, conscious of being made uncomfortable by the clammy heat. He came out on the bridge and found no relief to this oppression. The air seemed thick. He gasped like a fish, and began to believe himself greatly out of sorts.

The *Nan-Shan* was ploughing a vanishing furrow upon the circle of the sea that had the surface and the shimmer of an undulating piece of gray silk. The sun, pale and without rays, poured down leaden heat in a strangely indecisive light, and the Chinamen were lying prostrate about the decks. Their bloodless, pinched, yellow faces were like the faces of bilious invalids. Captain MacWhirr noticed two of them especially, stretched out on their backs below the bridge. As soon as they had closed their eyes they seemed dead. Three others, however, were quarrelling barbarously away forward; and one big fellow, half naked, with herculean shoulders, was hanging limply over a winch; another, sitting on the deck, his knees up and his head drooping sideways in a girlish attitude, was plaiting his pigtail with infinite languor depicted in his whole person and in the very movement of his fingers. The smoke struggled with difficulty out of the funnel, and instead of streaming away spread itself out like an infernal sort of cloud, smelling of sulphur and raining soot all over the decks.

"What the devil are you doing there, Mr. Jukes?" asked Captain MacWhirr.

This unusual form of address, though mumbled rather than spoken, caused the body of Mr. Jukes to start as though it had been prodded under the fifth rib. He had had a low bench brought on the bridge, and sitting on it, with a length of rope curled about his feet and a piece of canvas stretched over his knees, was pushing a sail-needle vigorously. He looked up, and his surprise gave to his eyes an expression of innocence and candour.

"I am only roping some of that new set of bags we made last trip for whipping up coals," he remonstrated, gently. "We shall want them for the next coaling, sir."

"What became of the others?"

"Why, worn out of course, sir."

Captain MacWhirr, after glaring down irresolutely at his chief mate, disclosed the gloomy and cynical conviction that more than half of them had been lost overboard, "if only the truth was known," and retired to the other end of the bridge. Jukes, exasperated by this unprovoked attack, broke the needle at the second stitch, and dropping his work got up and cursed the heat in a violent undertone.

The propeller thumped, the three Chinamen forward had given up squabbling very suddenly, and the one who had been plaiting his tail clasped his legs and stared dejectedly over his knees. The lurid sun-shine cast faint and sickly shadows. The swell ran higher and swifter every moment, and the ship lurched heavily in the smooth, deep hol-lows of the sea.

"I wonder where that beastly swell comes from," said Jukes aloud, recovering himself after a stagger.

"North-east," grunted the literal MacWhirr, from his side of the bridge. "There's some dirty weather knocking about. Go and look at the glass."

When Jukes came out of the chart-room, the cast of his countenance had changed to thoughtfulness and concern. He caught hold of the bridge-rail and stared ahead.

The temperature in the engine-room had gone up to a hundred and seventeen degrees. Irritated voices were ascending through the skylight and through the fiddle of the stokehold in a harsh and resonant up-roar, mingled with angry clangs and scrapes of metal, as if men with limbs of iron and throats of bronze had been quarrelling down there. The second engineer was falling foul of the stokers for letting the steam go down. He was a man with arms like a blacksmith, and gener-ally feared; but that afternoon the stokers were answering him back recklessly, and slammed the furnace doors with the fury of despair. Then the noise ceased suddenly, and the second engineer appeared, emerging out the stokehold streaked with grime and soaking wet like a chimney-sweep coming out of a well. As soon as his head was clear of the fiddle he began to scold Jukes for not trimming properly the stokehold ventilators; and in answer Jukes made with his hands depre-catory soothing signs meaning: No wind—can't be helped—you can see for yourself. But the other wouldn't hear reason. His teeth flashed angrily in his dirty face. He didn't mind, he said, the trouble of punch-ing their blanked heads down there, blank his soul, but did the con-demned sailors think you could keep steam up in the God-forsaken boilers simply by knocking the blanked stokers about? No, by George! You had to get some draught, too—may he be everlastingly blanked for a swab-headed deck-hand if you didn't! And the chief, too, ram-paging before the steam-gauge and carrying on like a lunatic up and down the engine-room ever since noon. What did Jukes think he was stuck up there for, if he couldn't get one of his decayed, good-for-nothing deck-cripples to turn the ventilators to the wind?

The relations of the "engine-room" and the "deck" of the *Nan-Shan* were, as is known, of a brotherly nature; therefore Jukes leaned over and begged the other in a restrained tone not to make a disgusting ass of himself; the skipper was on the other side of the bridge. But the second declared mutinously that he didn't care a rap who was on the other side of the bridge, and Jukes, passing in a flash from lofty disapproval into a state of exaltation, invited him in unflattering terms to come up and twist the beastly things to please himself, and catch such wind as a donkey of his sort could find. The second rushed up to the fray. He flung himself at the port ventilator as though he meant to tear it out bodily and toss it overboard. All he did was to move the cowl round a few inches, with an enormous expenditure of force, and seemed spent in the effort. He leaned against the back of the wheel-house, and Jukes walked up to him.

"Oh, Heavens!" ejaculated the engineer in a feeble voice. He lifted his eyes to the sky, and then let his glassy stare descend to meet the horizon that, tilting up to an angle of forty degrees, seemed to hang on a slant for a while and settled down slowly. "Heavens! Phew! What's up, anyhow?"

Jukes, straddling his long legs like a pair of compasses, put on an air of superiority. "We're going to catch it this time," he said. "The barometer is tumbling down like anything, Harry. And you trying to kick up that silly row. . . ."

The word "barometer" seemed to revive the second engineer's mad animosity. Collecting afresh all his energies, he directed Jukes in a low and brutal tone to shove the unmentionable instrument down his gory throat. Who cared for his crimson barometer? It was the steam—the steam—that was going down; and what between the firemen going faint and the chief going silly, it was worse than a dog's life for him; he didn't care a tinker's curse how soon the whole show was blown out of the water. He seemed on the point of having a cry, but after regaining his breath he muttered darkly, "I'll faint them," and dashed off. He stopped upon the fiddle long enough to shake his fist at the unnatural daylight, and dropped into the dark hole with a whoop.

When Jukes turned, his eyes fell upon the rounded back and the big red ears of Captain MacWhirr, who had come across. He did not look at his chief officer, but said at once, "That's a very violent man, that second engineer."

"Jolly good second, anyhow," grunted Jukes. "They can't keep up steam," he added, rapidly, and made a grab at the rail against the coming lurch.

Captain MacWhirr, unprepared, took a run and brought himself up with a jerk by an awning stanchion.

"A profane man," he said, obstinately. "If this goes on, I'll have to get rid of him the first chance."

"It's the heat," said Jukes. "The weather's awful. It would make a saint swear. Even up here I feel exactly as if I had my head tied up in a woollen blanket."

Captain MacWhirr looked up. "D'ye mean to say, Mr. Jukes, you ever had your head tied up in a blanket? What was that for?"

"It's a manner of speaking, sir," said Jukes, stolidly.

"Some of you fellows do go on! What's that about saints swearing? I wish you wouldn't talk so wild. What sort of saint would that be that would swear? No more saint than yourself, I expect. And what's a blanket got to do with it—or the weather either. . . . The heat does not make me swear—does it? It's filthy bad temper. That's what it is. And what's the good of your talking like this?"

Thus Captain MacWhirr expostulated against the use of images in speech, and at the end electrified Jukes by a contemptuous snort, followed by words of passion and resentment: "Damme! I'll fire him out of the ship if he don't look out."

And Jukes, incorrigible, thought: "Goodness me! Somebody's put a new inside to my old man. Here's temper, if you like. Of course it's the weather; what else? It would make an angel quarrelsome—let alone a saint."

All the Chinamen on deck appeared at their last gasp.

At its setting the sun had a diminished diameter and an expiring brown, rayless glow, as if millions of centuries elapsing since the morning had brought it near its end. A dense bank of cloud became visible to the northward; it had a sinister dark olive tint, and lay low and motionless upon the sea, resembling a solid obstacle in the path of the ship. She went floundering towards it like an exhausted creature driven to its death. The coppery twilight retired slowly, and the darkness brought out overhead a swarm of unsteady, big stars, that, as if blown upon, flickered exceedingly and seemed to hang very near the earth. At eight o'clock Jukes went into the chart-room to write up the ship's log.

He copied neatly out of the rough-book the number of miles, the course of the ship, and in the column for "wind" scrawled the word "calm" from top to bottom of the eight hours since noon. He was exasperated by the continuous, monotonous rolling of the ship. The heavy inkstand would slide away in a manner that suggested perverse intelligence in dodging the pen. Having written in the large space under the head of "Remarks" "Heat very oppressive," he stuck the end of the pen-holder in his teeth, pipe fashion, and mopped his face carefully.

"Ship rolling heavily in a high cross swell," he began again, and commented to himself, "Heavily is no word for it." Then he wrote: "Sunset threatening, with a low bank of clouds to N. and E. Sky clear overhead."

Sprawling over the table with arrested pen, he glanced out of the door, and in that frame of his vision he saw all the stars flying upwards between the teak-wood jambs on a black sky. The whole lot took flight together and disappeared, leaving only a blackness flecked with white flashes, for the sea was as black as the sky and speckled with foam afar. The stars that had flown to the roll came back on the return swing of the ship, rushing downwards in their glittering multitude, not of fiery points, but enlarged to tiny discs brilliant with a clear wet sheen.

Jukes watched the flying big stars for a moment, and then wrote: "8 P.M. Swell increasing. Ship labouring and taking water on her decks. Battened down the coolies for the night. Barometer still falling." He paused, and thought to himself, "Perhaps nothing whatever'll come of it." And then he closed resolutely his entries: "Every appearance of a typhoon coming on."

On going out he had to stand inside, and Captain MacWhirr strode over the doorstep without saying a word or making a sign.

"Shut the door, Mr. Jukes, will you?" he cried from within.

Jukes turned back to do so, muttering ironically: "Afraid to catch cold, I suppose." It was his watch below, but he yearned for communion with his kind; and he remarked cheerily to the second mate: "Doesn't look so bad, after all—does it?"

The second mate was marching to and fro on the bridge, tripping down with small steps one moment, and the next climbing with difficulty the shifting slope of the deck. At the sound of Jukes' voice he stood still, facing forward, but made no reply.

"Hallo! That's a heavy one," said Jukes, swaying to meet the long roll till his lowered hand touched the planks. This time the second mate made in his throat a noise of an unfriendly nature.

He was an oldish, shabby little fellow, with bad teeth and no hair on his face. He had been shipped in a hurry in Shanghai, that trip when the second officer brought from home had delayed the ship three hours in port by contriving (in some manner Captain MacWhirr could never understand) to fall overboard into an empty coal-lighter lying alongside, and had to be sent ashore to the hospital with concussion of the brain and a broken limb or two.

Jukes was not discouraged by the unsympathetic sound. "The Chinamen must be having a lovely time of it down there," he said. "It's lucky for them the old girl has the easiest roll of any ship I've ever been in. There now! This one wasn't so bad."

"You wait," snarled the second mate.

With his sharp nose, red at the tip, and his thin pinched lips, he always looked as though he were raging inwardly; and he was concise in his speech to the point of rudeness. All his time off duty he spent in his cabin with the door shut, keeping so still in there that he was supposed to fall asleep as soon as he had disappeared; but the man who came in to wake him for his watch on deck would invariably find him with his eyes wide open, flat on his back in the bunk, and glaring irritably from a soiled pillow. He never wrote any letters, did not seem to hope for news from anywhere; and though he had been heard once to mention West Hartlepool, it was with extreme bitterness, and only in connection with the extortionate charges of a boarding-house. He was one of those men who are picked up at need in the ports of the world. They are competent enough, appear hopelessly hard up, show no evidence of any sort of vice, and carry about them all the signs of manifest failure. They come aboard on an emergency, care for no ship afloat, live in their own atmosphere of casual connection amongst their shipmates who know nothing of them, and make up their minds to leave at inconvenient times. They clear out with no words of leave-taking in some God-forsaken port other men would fear to be stranded in, and go ashore in company of a shabby sea-chest, corded like a treasure-box, and with an air of shaking the ship's dust off their feet.

"You wait," he repeated, balanced in great swings with his back to Jukes, motionless and implacable.

"Do you mean to say we are going to catch it hot?" asked Jukes with boyish interest.

"Say? . . . I say nothing. You don't catch me," snapped the little second mate, with a mixture of pride, scorn, and cunning, as if Jukes' question had been a trap cleverly detected. "Oh, no! None of you here shall make a fool of me if I know it," he mumbled to himself.

Jukes reflected rapidly that this second mate was a mean little beast, and in his heart he wished poor Jack Allen had never smashed himself up in the coal-lighter. The far-off blackness ahead of the ship was like another night seen through the starry night of the earth—the starless night of the immensities beyond the created universe, revealed in its appalling stillness through a low fissure in the glittering sphere of which the earth is the kernel.

"Whatever there might be about," said Jukes, "we are steaming straight into it."

"*You've* said it," caught up the second mate, always with his back to Jukes. "You've said it, mind—not I."

"Oh, go to Jericho!" said Jukes, frankly; and the other emitted a triumphant little chuckle.

"You've said it," he repeated.

"And what of that?"

"I've known some real good men get into trouble with their skippers for saying a dam' sight less," answered the second mate feverishly. "Oh, no! You don't catch me."

"You seem deucedly anxious not to give yourself away," said Jukes, completely soured by such absurdity. "I wouldn't be afraid to say what I think."

"Aye, to me! That's no great trick. I am nobody, and well I know it."

The ship, after a pause of comparative steadiness, started upon a series of rolls, one worse than the other, and for a time Jukes, preserving his equilibrium, was too busy to open his mouth. As soon as the violent swinging had quieted down somewhat, he said: "This is a bit too much of a good thing. Whether anything is coming or not I think she ought to be put head on to that swell. The old man is just gone in to lie down. Hang me if I don't speak to him."

But when he opened the door of the chart-room he saw his captain reading a book. Captain MacWhirr was not lying down: he was standing up with one hand grasping the edge of the bookshelf and the other holding open before his face a thick volume. The lamp wriggled in the gimbals, the loosened books toppled from side to side on the shelf, the long barometer swung in jerky circles, the table altered its slant every moment. In the midst of all this stir and movement Captain MacWhirr, holding on, showed his eyes above the upper edge, and asked, "What's the matter?"

"Swell getting worse, sir."

"Noticed that in here," muttered Captain MacWhirr. "Anything wrong?"

Jukes, inwardly disconcerted by the seriousness of the eyes looking at him over the top of the book, produced an embarrassed grin.

"Rolling like old boots," he said, sheepishly.

"Aye! Very heavy—very heavy. What do you want?"

At this Jukes lost his footing and began to flounder.

"I was thinking of our passengers," he said, in the manner of a man clutching at a straw.

"Passengers?" wondered the Captain, gravely. "What passengers?"

"Why, the Chinamen, sir," explained Jukes, very sick of this conversation.

"The Chinamen! Why don't you speak plainly? Couldn't tell what you meant. Never heard a lot of coolies spoken of as passengers before. Passengers, indeed! What's come to you?"

Captain MacWhirr, closing the book on his forefinger, lowered his arm and looked completely mystified. "Why are you thinking of the Chinamen, Mr. Jukes?" he inquired.

Jukes took a plunge, like a man driven to it. "She's rolling her decks full of water, sir. Thought you might put her head on perhaps—for a while. Till this goes down a bit—very soon, I dare say. Head to the eastward. I never knew a ship roll like this."

He held on in the doorway, and Captain MacWhirr, feeling his grip on the shelf inadequate, made up his mind to let go in a hurry, and fell heavily on the couch.

"Head to the eastward?" he said, struggling to sit up. "That's more than four points off her course."

"Yes, sir. Fifty degrees. . . . Would just bring her head far enough round to meet this. . . ."

Captain MacWhirr was now sitting up. He had not dropped the book, and he had not lost his place.

"To the eastward?" he repeated, with dawning astonishment. "To the . . . Where do you think we are bound to? You want me to haul a full-powered steamship four points off her course to make the Chinamen comfortable! Now, I've heard more than enough of mad things done in the world—but this. . . . If I didn't know you, Jukes, I would think you were in liquor. Steer four points off. . . . And what afterwards? Steer four points over the other way, I suppose, to make the course good. What put it into your head that I would start to tack a steamer as if she were a sailing-ship?"

"Jolly good thing she isn't," threw in Jukes, with bitter readiness. "She would have rolled every blessed stick out of her this afternoon."

"Aye! And you just would have had to stand and see them go," said Captain MacWhirr, showing a certain animation. "It's a dead calm, isn't it?"

"It is, sir. But there's something out of the common coming, for sure."

"Maybe. I suppose you have a notion I should be getting out of the way of that dirt," said Captain MacWhirr, speaking with the utmost simplicity of manner and tone, and fixing the oilcloth on the floor with a heavy stare. Thus he noticed neither Jukes' discomfiture nor the mixture of vexation and astonished respect on his face.

"Now, here's this book," he continued with deliberation, slapping his thigh with the closed volume. "I've been reading the chapter on the storms there."

This was true. He had been reading the chapter on the storms. When he had entered the chart-room, it was with no intention of taking the book down. Some influence in the air—the same influence, probably, that caused the steward to bring without orders the Captain's sea-boots and oilskin coat up to the chart-room—had as it were guided his hand to the shelf; and without taking the time to sit down he had waded with a conscious effort into the terminology of the subject. He lost himself amongst advancing semi-circles, left- and right-hand quadrants, the curves of the tracks, the probable bearing of the centre, the shifts of wind and the readings of barometer. He tried to bring all these things into a definite relation to himself, and ended by becoming contemptuously angry with such a lot of words and with so much advice, all head-work and supposition, without a glimmer of certitude.

"It's the damnedest thing, Jukes," he said. "If a fellow was to believe all that's in there, he would be running most of his time all over the sea trying to get behind the weather."

Again he slapped his leg with the book; and Jukes opened his mouth, but said nothing.

"Running to get behind the weather! Do you understand that, Mr. Jukes? It's the maddest thing!" ejaculated Captain MacWhirr, with pauses, gazing at the floor profoundly. "You would think an old woman had been writing this. It passes me. If that thing means anything useful, then it means that I should at once alter the course away, away to the devil somewhere, and come booming down on Fu-chau from the northward at the tail of this dirty weather that's supposed to be knocking about in our way. From the north! Do you understand, Mr. Jukes? Three hundred extra miles to the distance, and a pretty coal bill to show. I couldn't bring myself to do that if every word in there was gospel truth, Mr. Jukes. Don't you expect me. . . ."

And Jukes, silent, marvelled at this display of feeling and loquacity.

"But the truth is that you don't know if the fellow is right, anyhow. How can you tell what a gale is made of till you get it? He isn't aboard here, is he? Very well. Here he says that the centre of them things bears eight points off the wind; but we haven't got any wind, for all the barometer falling. Where's his centre now?"

"We will get the wind presently," mumbled Jukes.

"Let it come, then," said Captain MacWhirr, with dignified indignation. "It's only to let you see, Mr. Jukes, that you don't find everything in books. All these rules for dodging breezes and circumventing the winds of heaven, Mr. Jukes, seem to me the maddest thing, when you come to look at it sensibly."

He raised his eyes, saw Jukes gazing at him dubiously, and tried to illustrate his meaning.

"About as queer as your extraordinary notion of dodging the ship head to sea, for I don't know how long, to make the Chinamen comfortable; whereas all we've got to do is to take them to Fu-chau, being timed to get there before noon on Friday. If the weather delays me—very well. There's your log-book to talk straight about the weather. But suppose I went swinging off my course and came in two days late, and they asked me: 'Where have you been all that time, Captain?' What could I say to that? 'Went around to dodge the bad weather,' I would say. 'It must've been dam' bad,' they would say. 'Don't know,' I would have to say; 'I've dodged clear of it.' See that, Jukes? I have been thinking it all out this afternoon."

He looked up again in his unseeing, unimaginative way. No one had ever heard him say so much at one time. Jukes, with his arms open in the doorway, was like a man invited to behold a miracle. Unbounded wonder was the intellectual meaning of his eye, while incredulity was seated in his whole countenance.

"A gale is a gale, Mr. Jukes," resumed the Captain, "and a full-powered steam-ship has got to face it. There's just so much dirty weather knocking about the world, and the proper thing is to go through it with none of what old Captain Wilson of the *Melita* calls 'storm strategy.' The other day ashore I heard him hold forth about it to a lot of shipmates who came in and sat at a table next to mine. It seemed to me the greatest nonsense. He was telling them how he out-manœuvred, I think he said, a terrific gale so that it never came nearer than fifty miles to him. A neat piece of head-work he called it. How he knew there was a terrific gale fifty miles off beats me altogether. It was like listening to a crazy man. I would have thought Captain Wilson was old enough to know better."

Captain MacWhirr ceased for a moment, then said, "It's your watch below, Mr. Jukes?"

Jukes came to himself with a start. "Yes, sir."

"Leave orders to call me at the slightest change," said the Captain.

He reached up to put the book away, and tucked his legs upon the couch. "Shut the door so that it don't fly open, will you? I can't stand a door banging. They've put a lot of rubbishy locks into this ship, I must say."

Captain MacWhirr closed his eyes.

He did so to rest himself. He was tired, and he experienced that state of mental vacuity which comes at the end of an exhaustive discussion that has liberated some belief matured in the course of meditative years. He had indeed been making his confession of faith, had he only known it; and its effect was to make Jukes, on the other side of the door, stand scratching his head for a good while.

Captain MacWhirr opened his eyes.

He thought he must have been asleep. What was that loud noise? Wind? Why had he not been called? The lamp wriggled in its gimbals, the barometer swung in circles, the table altered its slant every moment; a pair of limp sea-boots with collapsed tops went sliding past the couch. He put out his hand instantly, and captured one.

Jukes' face appeared in a crack of the door: only his face, very red, with staring eyes. The flame of the lamp leaped, a piece of paper flew up, a rush of air enveloped Captain MacWhirr. Beginning to draw on the boot, he directed an expectant gaze at Jukes' swollen, excited features.

"Came on like this," shouted Jukes, "five minutes ago . . . all of a sudden."

The head disappeared with a bang, and a heavy splash and patter of drops swept past the closed door as if a pailful of melted lead had been flung against the house. A whistling could be heard now upon the deep vibrating noise outside. The stuffy chart-room seemed as full of draughts as a shed. Captain MacWhirr collared the other sea-boot on its violent passage along the floor. He was not flustered, but he could not find at once the opening for inserting his foot. The shoes he had flung off were scurrying from end to end of the cabin, gambolling playfully over each other like puppies. As soon as he stood up he kicked at them viciously, but without effect.

He threw himself into the attitude of a lunging fencer, to reach after his oilskin coat; and afterwards he staggered all over the confined space while he jerked himself into it. Very grave, straddling his legs far apart, and stretching his neck, he started to tie deliberately the strings of his sou'-wester under his chin, with thick fingers that trembled slightly. He went through all the movements of a woman putting on her bonnet before a glass, with a strained, listening attention, as though he had expected every moment to hear the shout of his name in the confused clamour that had suddenly beset his ship. Its increase filled his ears while he was getting ready to go out and confront whatever it might mean. It was tumultuous and very loud—made up of the rush of the wind, the crashes of the sea, with that prolonged deep vibration of the air, like the roll of an immense and remote drum beating the charge of the gale.

He stood for a moment in the light of the lamp, thick, clumsy, shapeless in his panoply of combat, vigilant and red-faced.

"There's a lot of weight in this," he muttered.

As soon as he attempted to open the door the wind caught it. Clinging to the handle, he was dragged out over the doorstep, and at once found himself engaged with the wind in a sort of personal scuffle whose object was the shutting of that door. At the last moment a tongue of air scurried in and licked out the flame of the lamp.

Ahead of the ship he perceived a great darkness lying upon a multitude of white flashes; on the starboard beam a few amazing stars drooped, dim and fitful, above an immense waste of broken seas, as if seen through a mad drift of smoke.

On the bridge a knot of men, indistinct, and toiling, were making great efforts in the light of the wheelhouse windows that shone mistily on their heads and backs. Suddenly darkness closed upon one pane, then on another. The voices of the lost group reached him after the manner of men's voices in a gale, in shreds and fragments of forlorn shouting snatched past the ear. All at once Jukes appeared at his side, yelling, with his head down.

"Watch—put in—wheelhouse shutters—glass—afraid—blow in."

Jukes heard his commander upbraiding.

"This—come—anything—warning—call me."

He tried to explain, with the uproar pressing on his lips.

"Light air—remained—bridge—sudden—north-east—could turn—thought—you—sure—hear."

They had gained the shelter of the weather-cloth, and could converse with raised voices, as people quarrel.

"I got the hands along to cover up all the ventilators. Good job I had remained on deck. I didn't think you would be asleep, and so . . . What did you say, sir? What?"

"Nothing," cried Captain MacWhirr. "I said—all right."

"By all the powers! We've got it this time," observed Jukes in a howl.

"You haven't altered her course?" inquired Captain MacWhirr, straining his voice.

"No, sir. Certainly not. Wind came out right ahead. And here comes the head sea."

A plunge of the ship ended in a shock as if she had landed her forefoot upon something solid. After a moment of stillness a lofty flight of sprays drove hard with the wind upon their faces.

"Keep her at it as long as we can," shouted Captain MacWhirr.

Before Jukes had squeezed the salt water out of his eyes all the stars had disappeared.

· III ·

Jukes was as ready a man as any half-dozen young mates that may be caught by casting a net upon the waters; and though he had been somewhat taken aback by the startling viciousness of the first squall, he had pulled himself together on the instant, had called out the hands and had rushed them along to secure such openings about the deck as had not been already battened down earlier in the evening. Shouting in his fresh, stentorian voice, "Jump, boys, and bear a hand!" he led in the work, telling himself the while that he had "just expected this."

But at the same time he was growing aware that this was rather more than he had expected. From the first stir of the air felt on his cheek the gale seemed to take upon itself the accumulated impetus of an avalanche. Heavy sprays enveloped the *Nan-Shan* from stem to stern, and instantly in the midst of her regular rolling she began to jerk and plunge as though she had gone mad with fright.

Jukes thought, "This is no joke." While he was exchanging explanatory yells with his captain, a sudden lowering of the darkness came upon the night, falling before their vision like something palpable. It was as if the masked lights of the world had been turned down. Jukes was uncritically glad to have his captain at hand. It relieved him as though that man had, by simply coming on deck, taken most of the gale's weight upon his shoulders. Such is the prestige, the privilege, and the burden of command.

Captain MacWhirr could expect no relief of that sort from any one on earth. Such is the loneliness of command. He was trying to see, with that watchful manner of a seaman who stares into the wind's eye as if into the eye of an adversary, to penetrate the hidden intention and guess the aim and force of the thrust. The strong wind swept at him out of a vast obscurity; he felt under his feet the uneasiness of his ship, and he could not even discern the shadow of her shape. He wished it were not so; and very still he waited, feeling stricken by a blind man's helplessness.

To be silent was natural to him, dark or shine. Jukes, at his elbow, made himself heard yelling cheerily in the gusts, "We must have got the worst of it at once, sir." A faint burst of lightning quivered all round, as if flashed into a cavern—into a black and secret chamber of the sea, with a floor of foaming crests.

It unveiled for a sinister, fluttering moment a ragged mass of clouds hanging low, the lurch of the long outlines of the ship, the black figures of men caught on the bridge, heads forward, as if petrified in the act of butting. The darkness palpitated down upon all this, and then the real thing came at last.

It was something formidable and swift, like the sudden smashing of a vial of wrath. It seemed to explode all round the ship with an overpowering concussion and a rush of great waters, as if an immense dam had been blown up to windward. In an instant the men lost touch of each other. This is the disintegrating power of a great wind: it isolates one from one's kind. An earthquake, a landslip, an avalanche, overtake a man incidentally, as it were—without passion. A furious gale attacks him like a personal enemy, tries to grasp his limbs, fastens upon his mind, seeks to rout his very spirit out of him.

Jukes was driven away from his commander. He fancied himself whirled a great distance through the air. Everything disappeared—even, for a moment, his power of thinking; but his hand had found one of the rail-stanchions. His distress was by no means alleviated by an inclination to disbelieve the reality of this experience.

Though young, he had seen some bad weather, and had never doubted his ability to imagine the worst; but this was so much beyond his powers of fancy that it appeared incompatible with the existence of any ship whatever. He would have been incredulous about himself in the same way, perhaps, had he not been so harassed by the necessity of exerting a wrestling effort against a force trying to tear him away from his hold. Moreover, the conviction of not being utterly destroyed returned to him through the sensations of being half-drowned, bestially shaken, and partly choked.

It seemed to him he remained there precariously alone with the stanchion for a long, long time. The rain poured on him, flowed, drove in sheets. He breathed in gasps; and sometimes the water he swallowed was fresh and sometimes it was salt. For the most part he kept his eyes shut tight, as if suspecting his sight might be destroyed in the immense flurry of the elements. When he ventured to blink hastily, he derived some moral support from the green gleam of the starboard light shining feebly upon the flight of rain and sprays. He was actually looking at it when its ray fell upon the uprearing sea which put it out. He saw the head of the wave topple over, adding the mite of its crash to the tremendous uproar raging around him, and almost at the same instant the stanchion was wrenched away from his embracing arms. After a crushing thump on his back he found himself suddenly afloat and borne upwards. His first irresistible notion was that the whole China Sea had climbed on the bridge. Then, more sanely, he concluded himself gone overboard. All the time he was being tossed, flung, and rolled in great volumes of water, he kept on repeating mentally, with the utmost precipitation, the words: "My God! My God! My God! My God!"

All at once, in a revolt of misery and despair, he formed the crazy resolution to get out of that. And he began to thresh about with his arms and legs. But as soon as he commenced his wretched struggles he discovered that he had become somehow mixed up with a face, an oilskin coat, somebody's boots. He clawed ferociously all these things in turn, lost them, found them again, lost them once more, and finally was himself caught in the firm clasp of a pair of stout arms. He returned the embrace closely round a thick solid body. He had found his captain.

They tumbled over and over, tightening their hug. Suddenly the water let them down with a brutal bang; and, stranded against the side of the wheelhouse, out of breath and bruised, they were left to stagger up in the wind and hold on where they could.

Jukes came out of it rather horrified, as though he had escaped some unparalleled outrage directed at his feelings. It weakened his faith in himself. He started shouting aimlessly to the man he could feel near him in that fiendish blackness, "Is it you, sir? Is it you, sir?" till his temples seemed ready to burst. And he heard in answer a voice, as if crying far away, as if screaming to him fretfully from a very great distance, the one word "Yes!" Other seas swept again over the bridge. He received them defencelessly right over his bare head, with both his hands engaged in holding.

The motion of the ship was extravagant. Her lurches had an appalling helplessness: she pitched as if taking a header into a void, and seemed to find a wall to hit every time. When she rolled she fell on her side headlong, and she would be righted back by such a demolishing blow that Jukes felt her reeling as a clubbed man reels before he collapses. The gale howled and scuffled about gigantically in the darkness, as though the entire world were one black gully. At certain moments the air streamed against the ship as if sucked through a tunnel with a concentrated solid force of impact that seemed to lift her clean out of the water and keep her up for an instant with only a quiver running through her from end to end. And then she would begin her tumbling again as if dropped back into a boiling cauldron. Jukes tried hard to compose his mind and judge things coolly.

The sea, flattened down in the heavier gusts, would uprise and overwhelm both ends of the *Nan-Shan* in snowy rushes of foam, expanding wide, beyond both rails, into the night. And on this dazzling sheet, spread under the blackness of the clouds and emitting a bluish glow, Captain MacWhirr could catch a desolate glimpse of a few tiny specks black as ebony, the tops of the hatches, the battened companions, the heads of the covered winches, the foot of a mast. This was all he could see of his ship. Her middle structure, covered by the bridge which bore him, his mate, the closed wheelhouse where a man was steering shut up with the fear of being swept overboard together with the whole thing in one great crash—her middle structure was like a half-tide rock awash upon a coast. It was like an outlying rock with the water boiling up, streaming over, pouring off, beating round—like a rock in the surf to which shipwrecked people cling before they let go—only it rose, it sank, it rolled continuously, without respite and rest, like a rock that should have miraculously struck adrift from a coast and gone wallowing upon the sea.

The *Nan-Shan* was being looted by the storm with a senseless, destructive fury: trysails torn out of the extra gaskets, double-lashed awnings blown away, bridge swept clean, weather-cloths burst, rails twisted, light-screens smashed—and two of the boats had gone already. They had gone unheard and unseen, melting, as it were, in the shock and smother of the wave. It was only later, when upon the white flash of another high sea hurling itself amidships, Jukes had a vision of two pairs of davits leaping black and empty out of the solid blackness, with one overhauled fall flying and an iron-bound block capering in the air, that he became aware of what had happened within about three yards of his back.

He poked his head forward, groping for the ear of his commander. His lips touched it—big, fleshy, very wet. He cried in an agitated tone, "Our boats are going now, sir."

And again he heard that voice, forced and ringing feebly, but with a penetrating effect of quietness in the enormous discord of noises, as if sent out from some remote spot of peace beyond the black wastes of the gale; again he heard a man's voice—the frail and indomitable sound that can be made to carry an infinity of thought, resolution and purpose, that shall be pronouncing confident words on the last day, when heavens fall, and justice is done—again he heard it, and it was crying to him, as if from very, very far—"All right."

He thought he had not managed to make himself understood. "Our boats—I say boats—the boats, sir! Two gone!"

The same voice, within a foot of him and yet so remote, yelled sensibly, "Can't be helped."

Captain MacWhirr had never turned his face, but Jukes caught some more words on the wind.

"What can—expect—when hammering through—such— Bound to leave—something behind—stands to reason."

Watchfully Jukes listened for more. No more came. This was all

Captain MacWhirr had to say; and Jukes could picture to himself rather than see the broad squat back before him. An impenetrable obscurity pressed down upon the ghostly glimmers of the sea. A dull conviction seized upon Jukes that there was nothing to be done.

If the steering-gear did not give way, if the immense volumes of water did not burst the deck in or smash one of the hatches, if the engines did not give up, if way could be kept on the ship against this terrific wind, and she did not bury herself in one of these awful seas, of whose white crests alone, topping high above her bows, he could now and then get a sickening glimpse—then there was a chance of her coming out of it. Something within him seemed to turn over, bringing uppermost the feeling that the *Nan-Shan* was lost.

"She's done for," he said to himself, with a surprising mental agitation, as though he had discovered an unexpected meaning in this thought. One of these things was bound to happen. Nothing could be prevented now, and nothing could be remedied. The men on board did not count, and the ship could not last. This weather was too impossible.

Jukes felt an arm thrown heavily over his shoulders; and to this overture he responded with great intelligence by catching hold of his captain round the waist.

They stood clasped thus in the blind night, bracing each other against the wind, cheek to cheek and lip to ear, in the manner of two hulks lashed stem to stern together.

And Jukes heard the voice of his commander hardly any louder than before, but nearer, as though, starting to march athwart the prodigious rush of the hurricane, it had approached him, bearing that strange effect of quietness like the serene glow of a halo.

"D'ye know where the hands got to?" it asked, vigorous and evanescent at the same time, overcoming the strength of the wind, and swept away from Jukes instantly.

Jukes didn't know. They were all on the bridge when the real force of the hurricane struck the ship. He had no idea where they had crawled to. Under the circumstances they were nowhere, for all the use that could be made of them. Somehow the Captain's wish to know distressed Jukes.

"Want the hands, sir?" he cried, apprehensively.

"Ought to know," asserted Captain MacWhirr. "Hold hard."

They held hard. An outburst of unchained fury, a vicious rush of the wind absolutely steadied the ship; she rocked only, quick and light like a child's cradle, for a terrific moment of suspense, while the whole atmosphere, as it seemed, streamed furiously past her, roaring away from the tenebrous earth.

It suffocated them, and with eyes shut they tightened their grasp. What from the magnitude of the shock might have been a column of water running upright in the dark, butted against the ship, broke short, and fell on her bridge, crushingly, from on high, with a dead burying weight.

A flying fragment of that collapse, a mere splash, enveloped them in one swirl from their feet over their heads, filling violently their ears, mouths and nostrils with salt water. It knocked out their legs, wrenched in haste at their arms, seethed away swiftly under their chins; and opening their eyes, they saw the piled-up masses of foam dashing to and fro amongst what looked like the fragments of a ship. She had given way as if driven straight in. Their panting hearts yielded, too, before the tremendous blow; and all at once she sprang up again to her desperate plunging, as if trying to scramble out from under the ruins.

The seas in the dark seemed to rush from all sides to keep her back where she might perish. There was hate in the way she was handled, and a ferocity in the blows that fell. She was like a living creature thrown to the rage of a mob: hustled terribly, struck at, borne up, flung down, leaped upon. Captain MacWhirr and Jukes kept hold of each other, deafened by the noise, gagged by the wind; and the great physical tumult beating about their bodies, brought, like an unbridled display of passion, a profound trouble to their souls. One of those wild and appalling shrieks that are heard at times passing mysteriously overhead in the steady roar of a hurricane, swooped, as if borne on wings, upon the ship, and Jukes tried to outscream it.

"Will she live through this?"

The cry was wrenched out of his breast. It was as unintentional as the birth of a thought in the head, and he heard nothing of it himself. It all became extinct at once—thought, intention, effort—and of his cry the inaudible vibration added to the tempest waves of the air.

He expected nothing from it. Nothing at all. For indeed what answer could be made? But after a while he heard with amazement the frail and resisting voice in his ear, the dwarf sound, unconquered in the giant tumult.

"She may!"

It was a dull yell, more difficult to seize than a whisper. And presently the voice returned again, half submerged in the vast crashes, like a ship battling against the waves of an ocean.

"Let's hope so!" it cried—small, lonely and unmoved, a stranger to the visions of hope or fear; and it flickered into disconnected words: "Ship. . . . This. . . . Never—Anyhow . . . for the best." Jukes gave it up.

Then, as if it had come suddenly upon the one thing fit to withstand the power of a storm, it seemed to gain force and firmness for the last broken shouts:

"Keep on hammering . . . builders . . . good men. . . . And chance it . . . engines. . . . Rout . . . good man."

Captain MacWhirr removed his arm from Jukes' shoulders, and thereby ceased to exist for his mate, so dark it was; Jukes, after a tense stiffening of every muscle, would let himself go limp all over. The gnawing of profound discomfort existed side by side with an incredible disposition to somnolence, as though he had been buffeted and worried into drowsiness. The wind would get hold of his head and try to shake it off his shoulders; his clothes, full of water, were as heavy as lead, cold and dripping like an armour of melting ice: he shivered—it lasted a long time; and with his hands closed hard on his hold, he was letting himself sink slowly into the depths of bodily misery. His mind became concentrated upon himself in an aimless, idle way, and when something pushed lightly at the back of his knees he nearly, as the saying is, jumped out of his skin.

In the start forward he bumped the back of Captain MacWhirr, who didn't move; and then a hand gripped his thigh. A lull had come, a menacing lull of the wind, the holding of a stormy breath—and he felt himself pawed all over. It was the boatswain. Jukes recognized these hands, so thick and enormous that they seemed to belong to some new species of man.

The boatswain had arrived on the bridge, crawling on all fours against the wind, and had found the chief mate's legs with the top of his head. Immediately he crouched and began to explore Jukes' person upwards with prudent, apologetic touches, as became an inferior.

He was an ill-favoured, undersized, gruff sailor of fifty, coarsely hairy, short-legged, long-armed, resembling an elderly ape. His strength was immense; and in his great lumpy paws, bulging like brown boxing-gloves on the end of furry forearms, the heaviest objects were handled like playthings. Apart from the grizzled pelt on his chest, the menacing demeanour and the hoarse voice, he had none of the classical attributes of his rating. His good nature almost amounted to imbecility: the men did what they liked with him, and he had not an ounce of initiative in his character, which was easy-going and talkative. For these reasons Jukes disliked him; but Captain MacWhirr, to Jukes' scornful disgust, seemed to regard him as a first-rate petty officer.

He pulled himself up by Jukes' coat, taking that liberty with the greatest moderation, and only so far as it was forced upon him by the hurricane.

"What is it, boss'n, what is it?" yelled Jukes, impatiently. What could that fraud of a boss'n want on the bridge? The typhoon had got on Jukes' nerves. The husky bellowings of the other, though unintelligible, seemed to suggest a state of lively satisfaction. There could be no mistake. The old fool was pleased with something.

The boatswain's other hand had found some other body, for in a changed tone he began to inquire: "Is it you, sir? Is it you, sir?" The wind strangled his howls.

"Yes!" cried Captain MacWhirr.

· IV ·

All that the boatswain, out of a superabundance of yells, could make clear to Captain MacWhirr was the bizarre intelligence that "All them Chinamen in the fore 'tween deck have fetched away, sir."

Jukes to leeward could hear these two shouting within six inches of his face, as you may hear on a still night half a mile away two men conversing across a field. He heard Captain MacWhirr's exasperated "What? What?" and the strained pitch of the other's hoarseness. "In a lump . . . seen them myself. . . . Awful sight, sir . . . thought . . . tell you."

Jukes remained indifferent, as if rendered irresponsible by the force of the hurricane, which made the very thought of action utterly vain. Besides, being very young, he had found the occupation of keeping his heart completely steeled against the worst so engrossing that he had come to feel an overpowering dislike towards any other form of activity whatever. He was not scared; he knew this because, firmly believing he would never see another sunrise, he remained calm in that belief.

These are the moments of do-nothing heroics to which even good men surrender at times. Many officers of ships can no doubt recall a case in their experience when just such a trance of confounded stoicism would come all at once over a whole ship's company. Jukes, however, had no wide experience of men or storms. He conceived himself to be calm—inexorably calm; but as a matter of fact he was daunted; not abjectly, but only so far as a decent man may, without becoming loathsome to himself.

It was rather like a forced-on numbness of spirit. The long, long stress of a gale does it; the suspense of the interminably culminating catastrophe; and there is a bodily fatigue in the mere holding on to existence within the excessive tumult; a searching and insidious fatigue that penetrates deep into a man's breast to cast down and sadden his heart, which is incorrigible, and of all the gifts of the earth—even before life itself—aspires to peace.

Jukes was benumbed much more than he supposed. He held on—very wet, very cold, stiff in every limb; and in a momentary hallucination of swift visions (it is said that a drowning man thus reviews all his life) he beheld all sorts of memories altogether unconnected with his present situation. He remembered his father, for instance: a worthy business man, who at an unfortunate crisis in his affairs went quietly to bed and died forthwith in a state of resignation. Jukes did not recall these circumstances, of course, but remaining otherwise unconcerned he seemed to see distinctly the poor man's face; a certain game of nap played when quite a boy in Table Bay on board a ship, since lost with all hands; the thick eyebrows of his first skipper; and without any emotion, as he might years ago have walked listlessly into her room and found her sitting there with a book, he remembered his mother—dead, too, now—the resolute woman, left badly off, who had been very firm in his bringing up.

It could not have lasted more than a second, perhaps not so much. A heavy arm had fallen about his shoulders; Captain MacWhirr's voice was speaking his name into his ear.

"Jukes! Jukes!"

He detected the tone of deep concern. The wind had thrown its weight on the ship, trying to pin her down amongst the seas. They made a clean breach over her, as over a deep-swimming log; and the gathered weight of crashes menaced monstrously from afar. The breakers flung out of the night with a ghostly light on their crests—the light of sea-foam that in a ferocious, boiling-up pale flash showed upon the slender body of the ship the toppling rush, the downfall, and the seething mad scurry of each wave. Never for a moment could she shake herself clear of the water; Jukes, rigid, perceived in her motion the ominous sign of haphazard floundering. She was no longer struggling intelligently. It was the beginning of the end; and the note of busy concern in Captain MacWhirr's voice sickened him like an exhibition of blind and pernicious folly.

The spell of the storm had fallen upon Jukes. He was penetrated by it, absorbed by it; he was rooted in it with a rigour of dumb attention. Captain MacWhirr persisted in his cries, but the wind got between them like a solid wedge. He hung around Jukes' neck as heavy as a millstone, and suddenly the sides of their heads knocked together.

"Jukes! Mr. Jukes, I say!"

He had to answer that voice that would not be silenced. He answered in the customary manner: ". . . Yes, sir."

And directly, his heart, corrupted by the storm that breeds a craving for peace, rebelled against the tyranny of training and command.

Captain MacWhirr had his mate's head fixed firm in the crook of his elbow, and pressed it to his yelling lips mysteriously. Sometimes Jukes would break in, admonishing hastily: "Look out, sir!" or Captain MacWhirr would bawl an earnest exhortation to "Hold hard, there!" and the whole black universe seemed to reel together with the ship. They paused. She floated yet. And Captain MacWhirr would resume his shouts. ". . . Says . . . whole lot . . . fetched away. . . . Ought to see . . . what's the matter."

Directly the full force of the hurricane had struck the ship, every part of her deck became untenable; and the sailors, dazed and dismayed, took shelter in the port alleyway under the bridge. It had a door aft, which they shut; it was very black, cold, and dismal. At each heavy fling of the ship they would groan all together in the dark, and tons of water could be heard scuttling about as if trying to get at them from above. The boatswain had been keeping up a gruff talk, but a more unreasonable lot of men, he said afterwards, he had never been with. They were snug enough there, out of harm's way, and not wanted to do anything, either; and yet they did nothing but grumble and complain peevishly like so many sick kids. Finally, one of them said that if there had been at least some light to see each other's noses by, it wouldn't be so bad. It was making him crazy, he declared, to lie there in the dark waiting for the blamed hooker to sink.

"Why don't you step outside, then, and be done with it at once?" the boatswain turned on him.

This called up a shout of execration. The boatswain found himself overwhelmed with reproaches of all sorts. They seemed to take it ill that a lamp was not instantly created for them out of nothing. They would whine after a light to get drowned by—anyhow! And though the unreason of their revilings was patent—since no one could hope to reach the lamp-room, which was forward—he became greatly distressed. He did not think it was decent of them to be nagging at him like this. He told them so, and was met by general contumely. He sought refuge, therefore, in an embittered silence. At the same time their grumbling and sighing and muttering worried him greatly, but by-and-by it occurred to him that there were six globe lamps hung in the 'tween-deck, and that there could be no harm in depriving the coolies of one of them.

The *Nan-Shan* had an athwartship coal-bunker, which, being at times used as cargo space, communicated by an iron door with the fore 'tween-deck. It was empty then, and its manhole was the foremost one in the alleyway. The boatswain could get in, therefore, without coming out on deck at all; but to his great surprise he found he could induce no one to help him in taking off the manhole cover. He groped for it all the same, but one of the crew lying in his way refused to budge.

"Why, I only want to get you that blamed light you are crying for," he expostulated, almost pitifully.

Somebody told him to go and put his head in a bag. He regretted he could not recognize the voice, and that it was too dark to see, otherwise, as he said, he would have put a head on *that* son of a sea-cook, anyway, sink or swim. Nevertheless, he had made up his mind to show them he could get a light, if he were to die for it.

Through the violence of the ship's rolling, every movement was dangerous. To be lying down seemed labour enough. He nearly broke his neck dropping into the bunker. He fell on his back, and was sent shooting helplessly from side to side in the dangerous company of a heavy iron bar—a coal-trimmer's slice probably—left down there by somebody. This thing made him as nervous as though it had been a wild beast. He could not see it, the inside of the bunker coated with coal-dust being perfectly and impenetrably black; but he heard it sliding and clattering, and striking here and there, always in the neighbourhood of his head. It seemed to make an extraordinary noise, too—to give heavy thumps as though it had been as big as a bridge girder. This was remarkable enough for him to notice while he was flung from port to starboard and back again, and clawing desperately the smooth sides of the bunker in the endeavour to stop himself. The door into the 'tween-deck not fitting quite true, he saw a thread of dim light at the bottom.

Being a sailor, and a still active man, he did not want much of a chance to regain his feet; and as luck would have it, in scrambling up he put his hand on the iron slice, picking it up as he rose. Otherwise he would have been afraid of the thing breaking his legs, or at least knocking him down again. At first he stood still. He felt unsafe in this darkness that seemed to make the ship's motion unfamiliar, unforeseen, and difficult to counteract. He felt so much shaken for a moment that he dared not move for fear of "taking charge again." He had no mind to get battered to pieces in that bunker.

He had struck his head twice; he was dazed a little. He seemed to hear yet so plainly the clatter and bangs of the iron slice flying about his ears that he tightened his grip to prove to himself he had it there safely in his hand. He was vaguely amazed at the plainness with which down there he could hear the gale raging. Its howls and shrieks seemed to take on, in the emptiness of the bunker, something of the human character, of human rage and pain—being not vast but infinitely poignant. And there were, with every roll, thumps, too—profound, ponderous thumps, as if a bulky object of five-ton weight or so had got play in the hold. But there was no such thing in the cargo. Something on deck? Impossible. Or alongside? Couldn't be.

He thought all this quickly, clearly, competently, like a seaman, and in the end remained puzzled. This noise, though, came deadened from outside, together with the washing and pouring of water on deck above his head. Was it the wind? Must be. It made down there a row like the shouting of a big lot of crazed men. And he discovered in himself a desire for a light, too—if only to get drowned by—and a nervous anxiety to get out of that bunker as quickly as possible.

He pulled back the bolt: the heavy iron plate turned on its hinges; and it was as though he had opened the door to the sounds of the tempest. A gust of hoarse yelling met him: the air was still; and the rushing of water overhead was covered by a tumult of strangled, throaty shrieks that produced an effect of desperate confusion. He straddled his legs the whole width of the doorway and stretched his neck. And at first he perceived only what he had come to seek: six small yellow flames swinging violently on the great body of the dusk.

It was stayed like the gallery of a mine, with a row of stanchions in the middle, and cross-beams overhead, penetrating into the gloom ahead—indefinitely. And to port there loomed, like the caving in of one of the sides, a bulky mass with a slanting outline. The whole place, with the shadows and the shapes, moved all the time. The boatswain glared: the ship lurched to starboard, and a great howl came from that mass that had the slant of fallen earth.

Pieces of wood whizzed past. Planks, he thought, inexpressibly startled, and flinging back his head. At his feet a man went sliding over, open-eyed, on his back, straining with uplifted arms for nothing: and another came bounding like a detached stone with his head between his legs and his hands clenched. His pigtail whipped in the air; he made a grab at the boatswain's legs, and from his opened hand a bright white disc rolled against the boatswain's foot. He recognized a silver dollar, and yelled at it with astonishment. With a precipitated sound of trampling and shuffling of bare feet, and with guttural cries, the mound of writhing bodies piled up to port detached itself from the ship's side and sliding, inert and struggling, shifted to starboard, with a dull, brutal thump. The cries ceased. The boatswain heard a long moan through the roar and whistling of the wind; he saw an inextricable confusion of heads and shoulders, naked soles kicking upwards, fists raised, tumbling backs, legs, pigtails, faces.

"Good Lord!" he cried, horrified, and banged-to the iron door upon this vision.

This was what he had come on the bridge to tell. He could not keep it to himself; and on board ship there is only one man to whom it is worth while to unburden yourself. On his passage back the hands in the alleyway swore at him for a fool. Why didn't he bring that lamp? What the devil did the coolies matter to anybody? And when he came out, the extremity of the ship made what went on inside of her appear of little moment.

At first he thought he had left the alleyway in the very moment of her sinking. The bridge ladders had been washed away, but an enormous sea filling the after-deck floated him up. After that he had to lie on his stomach for some time, holding to a ring-bolt, getting his breath now and then, and swallowing salt water. He struggled farther on his hands and knees, too frightened and distracted to turn back. In this way he reached the after-part of the wheelhouse. In that comparatively sheltered spot he found the second mate. The boatswain was pleasantly surprised—his impression being that everybody on deck must have been washed away a long time ago. He asked eagerly where the Captain was.

The second mate was lying low, like a malignant little animal under a hedge.

"Captain? Gone overboard, after getting us into this mess." The mate, too, for all he knew or cared. Another fool. Didn't matter. Everybody was going by-and-by.

The boatswain crawled out again into the strength of the wind; not because he much expected to find anybody, he said, but just to get away from "that man." He crawled out as outcasts go to face an inclement world. Hence his great joy at finding Jukes and the Captain. But what was going on in the 'tween-deck was to him a minor matter by that time. Besides, it was difficult to make yourself heard. But he managed to convey the idea that the Chinamen had broken adrift together with their boxes, and that he had come up on purpose to report this. As to the hands, they were all right. Then, appeased, he subsided on the deck in a sitting posture, hugging with his arms and legs, the stand of the engine-room telegraph—an iron casting as thick as a post. When that went, why, he expected he would go, too. He gave no more thought to the coolies.

Captain MacWhirr had made Jukes understand that he wanted him to go down below—to see.

"What am I to do then, sir?" And the trembling of his whole wet body caused Jukes' voice to sound like bleating.

"See first . . . Boss'n . . . says . . . adrift."

"That boss'n is a confounded fool," howled Jukes, shakily.

The absurdity of the demand made upon him revolted Jukes. He was as unwilling to go as if the moment he had left the deck the ship were sure to sink.

"I must know . . . can't leave. . . ."

"They'll settle, sir."

"Fight . . . boss'n says they fight. . . . Why? Can't have . . . fighting . . . board ship. . . . Much rather keep you here . . . case . . . I should . . . washed overboard myself. . . . Stop it . . . some way. You see and tell me . . . through engine-room tube. Don't want you . . . come up here . . . too often. Dangerous . . . moving about . . . deck."

Jukes, held with his head in chancery, had to listen to what seemed horrible suggestions.

"Don't want . . . you get lost . . . so long . . . ship isn't. . . . Rout . . . Good man. . . . Ship . . . may . . . through this . . . all right yet."

All at once Jukes understood he would have to go.

"Do you think she may?" he screamed.

But the wind devoured the reply, out of which Jukes heard only the one word, pronounced with great energy ". . . Always. . . ."

Captain MacWhirr released Jukes, and bending over the boatswain, yelled, "Get back with the mate." Jukes only knew that the arm was gone off his shoulders. He was dismissed with his orders—to do what? He was exasperated into letting go his hold carelessly, and on the instant was blown away. It seemed to him that nothing could stop him from being blown right over the stern. He flung himself down hastily, and the boatswain, who was following, fell on him.

"Don't you get up yet, sir," cried the boatswain. "No hurry!"

A sea swept over. Jukes understood the boatswain to splutter that the bridge ladders were gone. "I'll lower you down, sir, by your hands," he screamed. He shouted also something about the smoke-stack being as likely to go overboard as not. Jukes thought it very possible, and imagined the fires out, the ship helpless. . . . The boat-swain by his side kept on yelling. "What? What is it?" Jukes cried distressfully; and the other repeated, "What would my old woman say if she saw me now?"

In the alleyway, where a lot of water had got in and splashed in the dark, the men were still as death, till Jukes stumbled against one of them and cursed him savagely for being in the way. Two or three voices then asked, eager and weak, "Any chance for us, sir?"

"What's the matter with you fools?" he said brutally. He felt as though he could throw himself down amongst them and never move any more. But they seemed cheered; and in the midst of obsequious warnings, "Look out! Mind that manhole lid, sir," they lowered him into the bunker. The boatswain tumbled down after him, and as soon as he had picked himself up he remarked, "She would say, 'Serve you right, you old fool, for going to sea.'"

The boatswain had some means, and made a point of alluding to them frequently. His wife—a fat woman—and two grown-up daugh-ters kept a greengrocer's shop in the East-end of London.

In the dark, Jukes, unsteady on his legs, listened to a faint thunder-ous patter. A deadened screaming went on steadily at his elbow, as it were; and from above the louder tumult of the storm descended upon these near sounds. His head swam. To him, too, in that bunker, the motion of the ship seemed novel and menacing, sapping his resolution as though he had never been afloat before.

He had half a mind to scramble out again; but the remembrance of Captain MacWhirr's voice made this impossible. His orders were to go and see. What was the good of it, he wanted to know. Enraged, he told himself he would see—of course. But the boatswain, staggering clumsily, warned him to be careful how he opened that door; there was a blamed fight going on. And Jukes, as if in great bodily pain, desired irritably to know what the devil they were fighting for.

"Dollars! Dollars, sir. All their rotten chests got burst open. Blamed money skipping all over the place, and they are tumbling after it head over heels—tearing and biting like anything. A regular little hell in there."

Jukes convulsively opened the door. The short boatswain peered under his arm.

One of the lamps had gone out, broken perhaps. Rancorous, guttural cries burst out loudly on their ears, and a strange panting sound, the working of all these straining breasts. A hard blow hit the side of the ship: water fell above with a stunning shock, and in the forefront of the gloom, where the air was reddish and thick, Jukes saw a head bang the deck violently, two thick calves waving on high, muscular arms twined round a naked body, a yellow-face, open-mouthed and with a set wild stare, look up and slide away. An empty chest clattered turning over; a man fell head first with a jump, as if lifted by a kick; and farther off, indistinct, others streamed like a mass of rolling stones down a bank, thumping the deck with their feet and flourishing their arms wildly. The hatchway ladder was loaded with coolies swarming on it like bees on a branch. They hung on the steps in a crawling, stirring cluster, beating madly with their fists the underside of the battened hatch, and the headlong rush of the water above was heard in the intervals of their yelling. The ship heeled over more, and they began to drop off: first one, then two, then all the rest went away together, falling straight off with a great cry.

Jukes was confounded. The boatswain, with gruff anxiety, begged him, "Don't you go in there, sir."

The whole place seemed to twist upon itself, jumping incessantly the while; and when the ship rose to a sea Jukes fancied that all these men would be shot upon him in a body. He backed out, swung the door to, and with trembling hands pushed at the bolt. . . .

As soon as his mate had gone Captain MacWhirr, left alone on the bridge, sidled and staggered as far as the wheelhouse. Its door being hinged forward, he had to fight the gale for admittance, and when at last he managed to enter it, it was with an instantaneous clatter and a bang, as though he had been fired through the wood. He stood within, holding on to the handle.

The steering-gear leaked steam, and in the confined space the glass of the binnacle made a shiny oval of light in a thin white fog. The wind howled, hummed, whistled, with sudden booming gusts that rattled the doors and shutters in the vicious patter of sprays. Two coils of lead-line and a small canvas bag hung on a long lanyard, swung wide off, and came back clinging to the bulkheads. The gratings underfoot were nearly afloat; with every seeping blow of a sea, water squirted violently through the cracks all round the door, and the man at the helm had flung down his cap, his coat, and stood propped against the gear-casing in a striped cotton shirt open on his breast. The little brass wheel in his hands had the appearance of a bright and fragile toy. The cords of his neck stood hard and lean, a dark patch lay in the hollow of his throat, and his face was still and sunken as in death.

Captain MacWhirr wiped his eyes. The sea that had nearly taken him overboard had, to his great annoyance, washed his sou'-wester hat off his bald head. The fluffy, fair hair, soaked and darkened, resembled a mean skein of cotton threads festooned round his bare skull. His face, glistening with sea-water, had been made crimson with the wind, with the sting of sprays. He looked as though he had come off sweating from before a furnace.

"You here?" he muttered, heavily.

The second mate had found his way into the wheelhouse some time before. He had fixed himself in a corner with his knees up, a fist pressed against each temple; and this attitude suggested rage, sorrow, resignation, surrender, with a sort of concentrated unforgiveness. He said mournfully and defiantly, "Well, it's my watch below now: ain't it?"

The steam gear clattered, stopped, clattered again; and the helmsman's eyeballs seemed to project out of a hungry face as if the compass card behind the binnacle glass had been meat. God knows how long he had been left there to steer, as if forgotten by all his shipmates. The bells had not been struck; there had been no reliefs; the ship's routine had gone down wind; but he was trying to keep her head north-north-east. The rudder might have been gone for all he knew, the fires out, the engines broken down, the ship ready to roll over like a corpse. He was anxious not to get muddled and lose control of her head, because the compass-card swung far both ways, wriggling on the pivot, and sometimes seemed to whirl right round. He suffered from mental stress. He was horribly afraid, also, of the wheelhouse going. Mountains of water kept on tumbling against it. When the ship took one of her desperate dives the corners of his lips twitched.

Captain MacWhirr looked up at the wheelhouse clock. Screwed to the bulk-head, it had a white face on which the black hands appeared to stand quite still. It was half-past one in the morning.

"Another day," he muttered to himself.

The second mate heard him, and lifting his head, as one grieving amongst ruins, "You won't see it break," he exclaimed. His wrists and his knees could be seen to shake violently. "No, by God! You won't. . . ."

He took his face again between his fists.

The body of the helmsman had moved slightly, but his head didn't budge on his neck,—like a stone head fixed to look one way from a column. During a roll that all but took his booted legs from under him, and in the very stagger to save himself, Captain MacWhirr said austerely, "Don't you pay any attention to what that man says." And then, with an indefinable change of tone, very grave, he added, "He isn't on duty."

The sailor said nothing.

The hurricane boomed, shaking the little place, which seemed air-tight; and the light of the binnacle flickered all the time.

"You haven't been relieved," Captain MacWhirr went on, looking down. "I want you to stick to the helm, though, as long as you can. You've got the hang of her. Another man coming here might make a mess of it. Wouldn't do. No child's play. And the hands are probably busy with a job down below. . . . Think you can?"

The steering-gear leaped into an abrupt short clatter, stopped smouldering like an ember; and the still man, with a motionless gaze, burst out, as if all the passion in him had gone into his lips: "By Heavens, sir! I can steer for ever if nobody talks to me."

"Oh! aye! All right. . . ." The Captain lifted his eyes for the first time to the man, ". . . Hackett."

And he seemed to dismiss this matter from his mind. He stooped to the engine-room speaking-tube, blew in, and bent his head. Mr. Rout below answered, and at once Captain MacWhirr put his lips to the mouthpiece.

With the uproar of the gale around him he applied alternately his lips and his ear, and the engineer's voice mounted to him, harsh and as if out of the heat of an engagement. One of the stokers was disabled, the others had given in, the second engineer and the donkeyman were firing-up. The third engineer was standing by the steam-valve. The engines were being tended by hand. How was it above?

"Bad enough. It mostly rests with you," said Captain MacWhirr. Was the mate down there yet? No? Well, he would be presently. Would Mr. Rout let him talk through the speaking-tube?—through the deck speaking-tube, because he—the Captain—was going out again on the bridge directly. There was some trouble amongst the Chinamen. They were fighting, it seemed. Couldn't allow fighting anyhow. . . .

Mr. Rout had gone away, and Captain MacWhirr could feel against his ear the pulsation of the engines, like the beat of the ship's heart. Mr. Rout's voice down there shouted something distantly. The ship pitched headlong, the pulsation leaped with a hissing tumult, and stopped dead. Captain MacWhirr's face was impassive, and his eyes were fixed aimlessly on the crouching shape of the second mate. Again Mr. Rout's voice cried out in the depths, and the pulsating beats recommenced, with slow strokes—growing swifter.

Mr. Rout had returned to the tube. "It don't matter much what they do," he said, hastily; and then, with irritation, "She takes these dives as if she never meant to come up again."

"Awful sea," said the Captain's voice from above.

"Don't let me drive her under," barked Solomon Rout up the pipe.

"Dark and rain. Can't see what's coming," uttered the voice. "Must—keep—her—moving—enough to steer—and chance it," it went on to state distinctly.

"I am doing as much as I dare."

"We are—getting—smashed up—a good deal up here," proceeded the voice mildly. "Doing—fairly well—though. Of course, if the wheelhouse should go. . . ."

Mr. Rout, bending an attentive ear, muttered peevishly something under his breath.

But the deliberate voice up there became animated to ask: "Jukes turned up yet?" Then, after a short wait, "I wish he would bear a hand. I want him to be done and come up here in case of anything. To look after the ship. I am all alone. The second mate's lost. . . ."

"What?" shouted Mr. Rout into the engine-room, taking his head away. Then up the tube he cried, "Gone overboard?" and clapped his ear to.

"Lost his nerve," the voice from above continued in a matter-of-fact tone. "Damned awkward circumstance."

Mr. Rout, listening with bowed neck, opened his eyes wide at this. However, he heard something like the sounds of a scuffle and broken exclamations coming down to him. He strained his hearing; and all the time Beale, the third engineer, with his arms uplifted, held between the palms of his hands the rim of a little black wheel projecting at the side of a big copper pipe. He seemed to be poising it above his head, as though it were a correct attitude in some sort of game.

To steady himself, he pressed his shoulder against the white bulkhead, one knee bent, and a sweat-rag tucked in his belt hanging on his hip. His smooth cheek was begrimed and flushed, and the coal dust on his eyelids, like the black pencilling of a make-up, enhanced the liquid brilliance of the whites, giving to his youthful face something of a feminine, exotic and fascinating aspect. When the ship pitched he would with hasty movements of his hands screw hard at the little wheel.

"Gone crazy," began the Captain's voice suddenly in the tube. "Rushed at me. . . . Just now. Had to knock him down. . . . This minute. You heard, Mr. Rout?"

"The devil!" muttered Mr. Rout. "Look out, Beale!"

His shout rang out like the blast of a warning trumpet, between the iron walls of the engine-room. Painted white, they rose high into the dusk of the skylight, sloping like a roof; and the whole lofty space resembled the interior of a monument, divided by floors of iron grating, with lights flickering at different levels, and a mass of gloom lingering in the middle, within the columnar stir of machinery under the motionless swelling of the cylinders. A loud and wild resonance, made up of all the noises of the hurricane, dwelt in the still warmth of the air. There was in it the smell of hot metal, of oil, and a slight mist of steam. The blows of the sea seemed to traverse it in an unringing, stunning shock, from side to side.

Gleams, like pale long flames, trembled upon the polish of metal; from the flooring below the enormous crank-heads in their turns with a flash of brass and steel—going over; while the connecting-rods, big-jointed, like skeleton limbs, seemed to thrust them down and pull them up again with an irresistible precision. And deep in the half-light other rods dodged deliberately to and fro, crossheads nodded, discs of metal rubbed smoothly against each other, slow and gentle, in a commingling of shadows and gleams.

Sometimes all those powerful and unerring movements would slow down simultaneously, as if they had been the functions of a living organism, stricken suddenly by the blight of languor; and Mr. Rout's eyes would blaze darker in his long sallow face. He was fighting this fight in a pair of carpet slippers. A short shiny jacket barely covered his loins, and his white wrists protruded far out of the tight sleeves, as though the emergency had added to his stature, had lengthened his limbs, augmented his pallor, hollowed his eyes.

He moved, climbing high up, disappearing low down, with a rest-less, purposeful industry, and when he stood still, holding the guard-rail in front of the starting-gear, he would keep glancing to the right at the steam-gauge, at the water-gauge, fixed upon the white wall in the light of a swaying lamp. The mouths of two speaking-tubes gaped stupidly at his elbow, and the dial of the engine-room telegraph resembled a clock of large diameter, bearing on its face curt words instead of figures. The grouped letters stood out heavily black, around the pivot-head of the indicator, emphatically symbolic of loud exclamations: AHEAD, ASTERN, SLOW, HALF, STAND BY; and the fat black hand pointed downwards to the word FULL, which, thus singled out, captured the eye as a sharp cry secures attention.

The wood-encased bulk of the low-pressure cylinder, frowning portly from above, emitted a faint wheeze at every thrust, and except for that low hiss the engines worked their steel limbs headlong or slow with a silent, determined smoothness. And all this, the white walls, the moving steel, the floor plates under Solomon Rout's feet, the floors of iron grating above his head, the dusk and the gleams, uprose and sank continuously, with one accord, upon the harsh wash of the waves against the ship's side. The whole loftiness of the place, booming hol-low to the great voice of the wind, swayed at the top like a tree, would go over bodily, as if borne down this way and that by the tremendous blasts.

"You've got to hurry up," shouted Mr. Rout, as soon as he saw Jukes appear in the stokehold doorway.

Jukes' glance was wandering and tipsy; his red face was puffy, as though he had overslept himself. He had had an arduous road, and had travelled over it with immense vivacity, the agitation of his mind corresponding to the exertions of his body. He had rushed up out of the bunker, stumbling in the dark alleyway amongst a lot of bewildered men who, trod upon, asked "What's up, sir?" in awed mutters all round him;—down the stokehold ladder, missing many iron rungs in his hurry, down into a place deep as a well, black as Tophet, tipping over back and forth like a see-saw. The water in the bilges thundered at each roll, and lumps of coal skipped to and fro, from end to end, rattling like an avalanche of pebbles on a slope of iron.

Somebody in there moaned with pain, and somebody else could be seen crouching over what seemed the prone body of a dead man; a lusty voice blasphemed; and the glow under each fire-door was like a pool of flaming blood radiating quietly in a velvety blackness.

A gust of wind struck upon the nape of Jukes' neck and next moment he felt it streaming about his wet ankles. The stokehold ventilators hummed: in front of the six fire-doors two wild figures, stripped to the waist, staggered and stooped, wrestling with two shovels.

"Hallo! Plenty of draught now," yelled the second engineer at once, as though he had been all the time looking out for Jukes. The donkeyman, a dapper little chap with a dazzling fair skin and a tiny, gingery moustache, worked in a sort of mute transport. They were keeping a full head of steam, and a profound rumbling, as of an empty furniture van trotting over a bridge, made a sustained bass to all the other noises of the place.

"Blowing off all the time," went on yelling the second. With a sound as of a hundred scoured saucepans, the orifice of a ventilator spat upon his shoulder a sudden gush of salt water, and he volleyed a stream of curses upon all things on earth including his own soul, ripping and raving, and all the time attending to his business. With a sharp clash of metal the ardent pale glare of the fire opened upon his bullet head, showing his spluttering lips, his insolent face, and with another clang closed like the white-hot wink of an iron eye.

"Where's the blooming ship? Can you tell me? blast my eyes! Under water—or what? It's coming down here in tons. Are the condemned cowls gone to Hades? Hey? Don't you know anything—you jolly sailor-man you. . . ?"

Jukes, after a bewildered moment, had been helped by a roll to dart through; and as soon as his eyes took in the comparative vastness, peace and brilliance of the engine-room, the ship, setting her stern heavily in the water, sent him charging head down upon Mr. Rout.

The chief's arm, long like a tentacle, and straightening as if worked by a spring, went out to meet him, and deflected his rush into a spin towards the speaking-tubes. At the same time Mr. Rout repeated earnestly:

"You've got to hurry up, whatever it is."

Jukes yelled "Are you there, sir?" and listened. Nothing. Suddenly the roar of the wind fell straight into his ear, but presently a small voice shoved aside the shouting hurricane quietly.

"You, Jukes?—Well?"

Jukes was ready to talk: it was only time that seemed to be wanting. It was easy enough to account for everything. He could perfectly imagine the coolies battened down in the reeking 'tween-deck, lying sick and scared between the rows of chests. Then one of these chests—or perhaps several at once—breaking loose in a roll, knocking out others, sides splitting, lids flying open, and all these clumsy Chinamen rising up in a body to save their property. Afterwards every fling of the ship would hurl that tramping, yelling mob here and there, from side to side, in a whirl of smashed wood, torn clothing, rolling dollars. A struggle once started, they would be unable to stop themselves. Nothing could stop them now except main force. It was a disaster. He had seen it, and that was all he could say. Some of them must be dead, he believed. The rest would go on fighting. . . .

He sent up his words, tripping over each other, crowding the narrow tube. They mounted as if into a silence of an enlightened comprehension dwelling alone up there with a storm. And Jukes wanted to be dismissed from the face of that odious trouble intruding on the great need of the ship.

· V ·

He waited. Before his eyes the engines turned with slow labour, that in the moment of going off into a mad fling would stop dead at Mr. Rout's shout, "Look out, Beale!" They paused in an intelligent immobility, stilled in mid-stroke, a heavy crank arrested on the cant, as if conscious of danger and the passage of time. Then, with a "Now, then!" from the chief, and the sound of a breath expelled through clenched teeth, they would accomplish the interrupted revolution and begin another.

There was the prudent sagacity of wisdom and the deliberation of enormous strength in their movements. This was their work—this patient coaxing of a distracted ship over the fury of the waves and into the very eye of the wind. At times Mr. Rout's chin would sink on his breast, and he watched them with knitted eyebrows as if lost in thought.

The voice that kept the hurricane out of Jukes' ear began: "Take the hands with you, . . ." and left off unexpectedly.

"What could I do with them, sir?"

A harsh, abrupt, imperious clang exploded suddenly. The three pairs of eyes flew up to the telegraph dial to see the hand jump from FULL to STOP, as if snatched by a devil. And then these three men in the engine-room had the intimate sensation of a check upon the ship, of a strange shrinking, as if she had gathered herself for a desperate leap.

"Stop her!" bellowed Mr. Rout.

Nobody—not even Captain MacWhirr, who alone on deck had caught sight of a white line of foam coming on at such a height that he couldn't believe his eyes—nobody was to know the steepness of that sea and the awful depth of the hollow the hurricane had scooped out behind the running wall of water.

It raced to meet the ship, and, with a pause, as of girding the loins, the *Nan-Shan* lifted her bows and leaped. The flames in all the lamps sank, darkening the engine-room. One went out. With a tearing crash and a swirling, raving tumult, tons of water fell upon the deck, as though the ship had darted under the foot of a cataract.

Down there they looked at each other, stunned.

"Swept from end to end, by God!" bawled Jukes.

She dipped into the hollow straight down, as if going over the edge of the world. The engine-room toppled forward menacingly, like the inside of a tower nodding in an earthquake. An awful racket, of iron things falling, came from the stokehold. She hung on this appalling slant long enough for Beale to drop on his hands and knees and begin to crawl as if he meant to fly on all fours out of the engine-room, and for Mr. Rout to turn his head slowly, rigid, cavernous, with the lower jaw dropping. Jukes had shut his eyes, and his face in a moment became hopelessly blank and gentle, like the face of a blind man.

At last she rose slowly, staggering, as if she had to lift a mountain with her bows.

Mr. Rout shut his mouth; Jukes blinked; and little Beale stood up hastily.

"Another one like this, and that's the last of her," cried the chief.

He and Jukes looked at each other, and the same thought came into their heads. The Captain! Everything must have been swept away. Steering-gear gone—ship like a log. All over directly.

"Rush!" ejaculated Mr. Rout thickly, glaring with enlarged, doubtful eyes at Jukes, who answered him by an irresolute glance.

The clang of the telegraph gong soothed them instantly. The black hand dropped in a flash from Stop to Full.

"Now then, Beale!" cried Mr. Rout.

The steam hissed low. The piston-rods slid in and out. Jukes put his ear to the tube. The voice was ready for him. It said: "Pick up all the money. Bear a hand now. I'll want you up here." And that was all.

"Sir?" called up Jukes. There was no answer.

He staggered away like a defeated man from the field of battle. He had got, in some way or other, a cut above his left eyebrow—a cut to the bone. He was not aware of it in the least: quantities of the China Sea, large enough to break his neck for him, had gone over his head, had cleaned, washed, and salted that wound. It did not bleed, but only gaped red; and this gash over the eye, his dishevelled hair, the disorder of his clothes, gave him the aspect of a man worsted in a fight with fists.

"Got to pick up the dollars." He appealed to Mr. Rout, smiling pitifully at random.

"What's that?" asked Mr. Rout, wildly. "Pick up . . . ? I don't care. . . ." Then, quivering in every muscle, but with an exaggeration of paternal tone, "Go away now, for God's sake. You deck people'll drive me silly. There's that second mate been going for the old man. Don't you know? You fellows are going wrong for want of something to do. . . ."

At these words Jukes discovered in himself the beginnings of anger. Want of something to do—indeed. . . . Full of hot scorn against the chief, he turned to go the way he had come. In the stokehold the plump donkeyman toiled with his shovel mutely, as if his tongue had been cut out; but the second was carrying on like a noisy, undaunted maniac, who had preserved his skill in the art of stoking under a marine boiler.

"Hallo, you wandering officer! Hey! Can't you get some of your slush-slingers to wind up a few of them ashes? I am getting choked with them here. Curse it! Hallo! Hey! Remember the articles: *Sailors and firemen to assist each other.* Hey! D'ye hear?"

Jukes was climbing out frantically, and the other, lifting up his face after him, howled, "Can't you speak? What are you poking about here for? What's your game, anyhow?"

A frenzy possessed Jukes. By the time he was back amongst the men in the darkness of the alleyway, he felt ready to wring all their necks at the slightest sign of hanging back. The very thought of it exasperated him. *He* couldn't hang back. They shouldn't.

The impetuosity with which he came amongst them carried them along. They had already been excited and startled at all his comings and goings—by the fierceness and rapidity of his movements; and more felt than seen in his rushes, he appeared formidable—busied with matters of life and death that brooked no delay. At his first word he heard them drop into the bunker one after another obediently, with heavy thumps.

They were not clear as to what would have to be done. "What is it? What is it?" they were asking each other. The boatswain tried to explain; the sounds of a great scuffle surprised them: and the mighty shocks, reverberating awfully in the black bunker, kept them in mind of their danger. When the boatswain threw open the door it seemed that an eddy of the hurricane, stealing through the iron sides of the ship, had set all these bodies whirling like dust: there came to them a confused uproar, a tempestuous tumult, a fierce mutter, gusts of screams dying away, and the tramping of feet mingling with the blows of the sea.

For a moment they glared amazed, blocking the doorway. Jukes pushed through them brutally. He said nothing, and simply darted in. Another lot of coolies on the ladder, struggling suicidally to break through the battened hatch to a swamped deck, fell off as before, and he disappeared under them like a man overtaken by a landslide.

The boatswain yelled excitedly: "Come along. Get the mate out. He'll be trampled to death. Come on."

They charged in, stamping on breasts, on fingers, on faces, catching their feet in heaps of clothing, kicking broken wood; but before they could get hold of him Jukes emerged waist deep in a multitude of clawing hands. In the instant he had been lost to view, all the buttons of his jacket had gone, its back had got split up to the collar, his waistcoat had been torn open. The central struggling mass of Chinamen went over to the roll, dark, indistinct, helpless, with a wild glean of many eyes in the dim light of the lamps.

"Leave me alone—damn you. I am all right," screeched Jukes. "Drive them forward. Watch your chance when she pitches. Forward with 'em. Drive them against the bulkhead. Jam 'em up."

The rush of the sailors into the seething 'tween-deck was like a splash of cold water into a boiling cauldron. The commotion sank for a moment.

The bulk of Chinamen were locked in such a compact scrimmage that, linking their arms and aided by an appalling dive of the ship, the seamen sent it forward in one great shove, like a solid block. Behind their backs small clusters and loose bodies tumbled from side to side.

The boatswain performed prodigious feats of strength. With his long arms open, and each great paw clutching at a stanchion, he stopped the rush of seven entwined Chinamen rolling like a boulder. His joints cracked; he said, "Ha!" and they flew apart. But the carpenter showed the greater intelligence. Without saying a word to anybody he went back into the alleyway, to fetch several coils of cargo gear he had seen there—chain and rope. With these life-lines were rigged.

There was really no resistance. The struggle, however it began, had turned into a scramble of blind panic. If the coolies had started up after their scattered dollars they were by that time fighting only for their footing. They took each other by the throat merely to save themselves from being hurled about. Whoever got a hold anywhere would kick at the others who caught at his legs and hung on, till a roll sent them flying together across the deck.

The coming of the white devils was a terror. Had they come to kill? The individuals torn out of the ruck became very limp in the seamen's hands: some, dragged aside by the heels, were passive, like dead bodies, with open, fixed eyes. Here and there a coolie would fall on his knees as if begging for mercy; several, whom the excess of fear made unruly, were hit with hard fists between the eyes, and cowered; while those who were hurt submitted to rough handling, blinking rapidly without a plaint. Faces streamed with blood; there were raw places on the shaven heads, scratches, bruises, torn wounds, gashes. The broken porcelain out of the chests was mostly responsible for the latter. Here and there a Chinaman, wild-eyed, with his tail unplaited, nursed a bleeding sole.

They had been ranged closely, after having been shaken into submission, cuffed a little to allay excitement, addressed in gruff words of encouragement that sounded like promises of evil. They sat on the deck in ghastly, drooping rows, and at the end the carpenter, with two hands to help him, moved busily from place to place, setting taut and hitching the life-lines. The boatswain, with one leg and one arm embracing a stanchion, struggled with a lamp pressed to his breast, trying to get a light, and growling all the time like an industrious gorilla. The figures of seamen stooped repeatedly, with the movements of gleaners, and everything was being flung into the bunker: clothing, smashed wood, broken china, and the dollars, too, gathered up in men's jackets. Now and then a sailor would stagger towards the doorway with his arms full of rubbish; and dolorous, slanting eyes followed his movements.

With every roll of the ship the long rows of sitting Celestials would sway forward brokenly, and her head-long dives knocked together the line of shaven polls from end to end. When the wash of water rolling on the deck died away for a moment, it seemed to Jukes, yet quivering from his exertions, that in his mad struggle down there he had overcome the wind somehow: that a silence had fallen upon the ship, a silence in which the sea struck thunderously at her sides.

Everything had been cleared out of the 'tween-deck—all the wreckage, as the men said. They stood erect and tottering above the level of heads and drooping shoulders. Here and there a coolie sobbed for his breath. Where the high light fell, Jukes could see the salient ribs of one, the yellow, wistful face of another; bowed necks; or would meet a dull stare directed at his face. He was amazed that there had been no corpses; but the lot of them seemed at their last gasp, and they appeared to him more pitiful than if they had been all dead.

Suddenly one of the coolies began to speak. The light came and went on his lean, straining face; he threw his head up like a baying hound. From the bunker came the sounds of knocking and the tinkle of some dollars rolling loose; he stretched out his arm, his mouth yawned black, and the incomprehensible guttural hooting sounds, that did not seem to belong to a human language, penetrated Jukes with a strange emotion as if a brute had tried to be eloquent.

Two more started mouthing what seemed to Jukes fierce denunciations; the others stirred with grunts and growls. Jukes ordered the hands out of the 'tween-decks hurriedly. He left last himself, backing through the door, while the grunts rose to a loud murmur and hands were extended after him as after a malefactor. The boatswain shot the bolt, and remarked uneasily, "Seems as if the wind had dropped, sir."

The seamen were glad to get back into the alleyway. Secretly each of them thought that at the last moment he could rush out on deck—and that was a comfort. There is something horribly repugnant in the idea of being drowned under a deck. Now they had done with the Chinamen, they again became conscious of the ship's position.

Jukes on coming out of the alleyway found himself up to the neck in the noisy water. He gained the bridge, and discovered he could detect obscure shapes as if his sight had become preternaturally acute. He saw faint outlines. They recalled not the familiar aspect of the *Nan-Shan*, but something remembered—an old dismantled steamer he had seen years ago rotting on a mudbank. She recalled that wreck.

There was no wind, not a breath, except the faint currents created by the lurches of the ship. The smoke tossed out of the funnel was settling down upon her deck. He breathed it as he passed forward. He felt the deliberate throb of the engines, and heard small sounds that seemed to have survived the great uproar: the knocking of broken fittings, the rapid tumbling of some piece of wreckage on the bridge. He perceived dimly the squat shape of his captain holding on to a twisted bridge-rail, motionless and swaying as if rooted to the planks. The unexpected stillness of the air oppressed Jukes.

"We have done it, sir," he gasped.

"Thought you would," said Captain MacWhirr.

"Did you?" murmured Jukes to himself.

"Wind fell all at once," went on the Captain.

Jukes burst out: "If you think it was an easy job—"

But his captain, clinging to the rail, paid no attention. "According to the books the worst is not over yet."

"If most of them hadn't been half dead with seasickness and fright, not one of us would have come out of that 'tween-deck alive," said Jukes.

"Had to do what's fair by them," mumbled MacWhirr, stolidly. "You don't find everything in books."

"Why, I believe they would have risen on us if I hadn't ordered the hands out of that pretty quick," continued Jukes with warmth.

After the whisper of their shouts, their ordinary tones, so distinct, rang out very loud to their ears in the amazing stillness of the air. It seemed to them they were talking in a dark and echoing vault.

Through a jagged aperture in the dome of clouds the light of a few stars fell upon the black sea, rising and falling confusedly. Sometimes the head of a watery cone would topple on board and mingle with the rolling flurry of foam on the swamped deck; and the *Nan-Shan* wallowed heavily at the bottom of a circular cistern of clouds. This ring of dense vapours, gyrating madly round the calm of the centre, encompassed the ship like a motionless and unbroken wall of an aspect inconceivably sinister. Within, the sea, as if agitated by an internal commotion, leaped in peaked mounds that jostled each other, slapping heavily against her sides; and a low moaning sound, the infinite plaint of the storm's fury, came from beyond the limits of the menacing calm. Captain MacWhirr remained silent, and Jukes' ready ear caught suddenly the faint, long-drawn roar of some immense wave rushing unseen under that thick blackness, which made the appalling boundary of his vision.

"Of course," he started resentfully, "they thought we had caught at the chance to plunder them. Of course! You said—pick up the money. Easier said than done. They couldn't tell what was in our heads. We came in, smash—right into the middle of them. Had to do it by a rush."

"As long as it's done, . . ." mumbled the Captain, without attempting to look at Jukes. "Had to do what's fair."

"We shall find yet there's the devil to pay when this is over," said Jukes, feeling very sore. "Let them only recover a bit, and you'll see. They will fly at our throats, sir. Don't forget, sir, she isn't a British ship now. These brutes know it well, too. The damned Siamese flag."

"We are on board, all the same," remarked Captain MacWhirr.

"The trouble's not over yet," insisted Jukes, prophetically, reeling and catching on. "She's a wreck," he added, faintly.

"The trouble's not over yet," assented Captain MacWhirr, half aloud. . . . "Look out for her a minute."

"Are you going off the deck, sir?" asked Jukes, hurriedly, as if the storm were sure to pounce upon him as soon as he had been left alone with the ship.

He watched her, battered and solitary, labouring heavily in a wild scene of mountainous black waters lit by the gleams of distant worlds. She moved slowly, breathing into the still core of the hurricane the excess of her strength in a white cloud of steam—and the deep-toned vibration of the escape was like the defiant trumpeting of a living creature of the sea impatient for the renewal of the contest. It ceased suddenly. The still air moaned. Above Jukes' head a few stars shone into a pit of black vapours. The inky edge of the cloud-disc frowned upon the ship under the patch of glittering sky. The stars, too, seemed to look at her intently, as if for the last time, and the cluster of their splendour sat like a diadem on a lowering brow.

Captain MacWhirr had gone into the chart-room. There was no light there; but he could feel the disorder of that place where he used to live tidily. His armchair was upset. The books had tumbled out on the floor: he scrunched a piece of glass under his boot. He groped for the matches, and found a box on a shelf with a deep ledge. He struck one, and puckering the corners of his eyes, held out the little flame towards the barometer whose glittering top of glass and metals nodded at him continuously.

It stood very low—incredibly low, so low that Captain MacWhirr grunted. The match went out, and hurriedly he extracted another, with thick, stiff fingers.

Again a little flame flared up before the nodding glass and metal of the top. His eyes looked at it, narrowed with attention, as if expecting an imperceptible sign. With his grave face he resembled a booted and misshapen pagan burning incense before the oracle of a Joss. There was no mistake. It was the lowest reading he had ever seen in his life.

Captain MacWhirr emitted a low whistle. He forgot himself till the flame diminished to a blue spark, burnt his fingers and vanished. Perhaps something had gone wrong with the thing!

There was an aneroid glass screwed above the couch. He turned that way, struck another match, and discovered the white face of the other instrument looking at him from the bulkhead, meaningly, not to be gainsaid, as though the wisdom of men were made unerring by the indifference of matter. There was no room for doubt now. Captain MacWhirr pshawed at it, and threw the match down.

The worst was to come, then—and if the books were right this worst would be very bad. The experience of the last six hours had enlarged his conception of what heavy weather could be like. "It'll be terrific," he pronounced, mentally. He had not consciously looked at anything by the light of the matches except at the barometer; and yet somehow he had seen that his water-bottle and the two tumblers had been flung out of their stand. It seemed to give him a more intimate knowledge of the tossing the ship had gone through. "I wouldn't have believed it," he thought. And his table had been cleared, too; his rulers, his pencils, the inkstand—all the things that had their safe appointed places—they were gone, as if a mischievous hand had plucked them out one by one and flung them on the wet floor. The hurricane had broken in upon the orderly arrangements of his privacy. This had never happened before, and the feeling of dismay reached the very seat of his composure. And the worst was to come yet! He was glad the trouble in the 'tween-deck had been discovered in time. If the ship had to go after all, then, at least, she wouldn't be going to the bottom with a lot of people in her fighting teeth and claw. That would have been odious. And in that feeling there was a humane intention and a vague sense of the fitness of things.

These instantaneous thoughts were yet in their essence heavy and slow, partaking of the nature of the man. He extended his hand to put back the matchbox in its corner of the shelf. There were always matches there—by his order. The steward had his instructions impressed upon him long before. "A box . . . just there, see? Not so very full . . . where I can put my hand on it, steward. Might want a light in a hurry. Can't tell on board ship *what* you might want in a hurry. Mind, now."

And of course on his side he would be careful to put it back in its place scrupulously. He did so now, but before he removed his hand it occurred to him that perhaps he would never have occasion to use that box any more. The vividness of the thought checked him and for an infinitesimal fraction of a second his fingers closed again on the small object as though it had been the symbol of all these little habits that chain us to the weary round of life. He released it at last, and letting himself fall on the settee, listened for the first rounds of returning wind.

Not yet. He heard only the wash of water, the heavy splashes, the dull shocks of the confused seas boarding his ship from all sides. She would never have a chance to clear her decks.

But the quietude of the air was startlingly tense and unsafe, like a slender hair holding a sword suspended over his head. By this awful pause the storm penetrated the defences of the man and unsealed his lips. He spoke out in the solitude and the pitch darkness of the cabin, as if addressing another being awakened within his breast.

"I shouldn't like to lose her," he said half aloud.

He sat unseen, apart from the sea, from his ship, isolated, as if withdrawn from the very current of his own existence, where such freaks as talking to himself surely had no place. His palms reposed on his knees, he bowed his short neck and puffed heavily, surrendering to a strange sensation of weariness he was not enlightened enough to recognize for the fatigue of mental stress.

From where he sat he could reach the door of a washstand locker. There should have been a towel there. There was. Good. . . . He took it out, wiped his face, and afterwards went on rubbing his wet head. He towelled himself with energy in the dark, and then remained motionless with the towel on his knees. A moment passed, of a stillness so profound that no one could have guessed there was a man sitting in that cabin. Then a murmur rose.

"She may come out of it yet."

When Captain MacWhirr came out on deck, which he did brusquely, as though he had suddenly become conscious of having stayed away too long, the calm had lasted already more than fifteen minutes—long enough to make itself intolerable even to his imagination. Jukes, motionless on the forepart of the bridge, began to speak at once. His voice, blank and forced as though he were talking through hard-set teeth, seemed to flow away on all sides into the darkness, deepening again upon the sea.

"I had the wheel relieved. Hackett began to sing out that he was done. He's lying in there alongside the steering-gear with a face like death. At first I couldn't get anybody to crawl out and relieve the poor devil. That boss'n's worse than no good, I always said. Thought I would have had to go myself and haul out one of them by the neck."

"Ah, well," muttered the Captain. He stood watchful by Jukes' side.

"The second mate's in there, too, holding his head. Is he hurt, sir?"

"No—crazy," said Captain MacWhirr, curtly.

"Looks as if he had a tumble, though."

"I had to give him a push," explained the Captain.

Jukes gave an impatient sigh.

"It will come very sudden," said Captain MacWhirr, "and from over there, I fancy. God only knows though. These books are only good to muddle your head and make you jumpy. It will be bad, and there's an end. If we only can steam her round in time to meet it. . . ."

A minute passed. Some of the stars winked rapidly and vanished.

"You left them pretty safe?" began the Captain abruptly, as though the silence were unbearable.

"Are you thinking of the coolies, sir? I rigged life-lines all ways across that 'tween-deck."

"Did you? Good idea, Mr. Jukes."

"I didn't . . . think you cared to . . . know," said Jukes—the lurching of the ship cut his speech as though somebody had been jerking him around while he talked—"how I got on with . . . that infernal job. We did it. And it may not matter in the end."

"Had to do what's fair, for all—they are only Chinamen. Give them the same chance with ourselves—hang it all. She isn't lost yet. Bad enough to be shut up below in a gale—"

"That's what I thought when you gave me the job, sir," interjected Jukes, moodily.

"—without being battered to pieces," pursued Captain MacWhirr with rising vehemence. "Couldn't let that go on in my ship, if I knew she hadn't five minutes to live. Couldn't bear it, Mr. Jukes."

A hollow echoing noise, like that of a shout rolling in a rocky chasm, approached the ship and went away again. The last star, blurred, enlarged, as if returning to the fiery mist of its beginning, struggled with the colossal depth of blackness hanging over the ship—and went out.

"Now for it!" muttered Captain MacWhirr. "Mr. Jukes."

"Here, sir."

The two men were growing indistinct to each other.

"We must trust her to go through it and come out on the other side. That's plain and straight. There's no room for Captain Wilson's storm-strategy here."

"No, sir."

"She will be smothered and swept again for hours," mumbled the Captain. "There's not much left by this time above deck for the sea to take away—unless you or me."

"Both, sir," whispered Jukes, breathlessly.

"You are always meeting trouble half way, Jukes," Captain MacWhirr remonstrated quaintly. "Though it's a fact that the second mate is no good. D'ye hear, Mr. Jukes? You would be left alone if. . . ."

Captain MacWhirr interrupted himself, and Jukes, glancing on all sides, remained silent.

"Don't you be put out by anything," the Captain continued, mumbling rather fast. "Keep her facing it. They may say what they like, but the heaviest seas run with the wind. Facing it—always facing it—that's the way to get through. You are a young sailor. Face it. That's enough for any man. Keep a cool head."

"Yes, sir," said Jukes, with a flutter of the heart.

In the next few seconds the Captain spoke to the engine-room and got an answer.

For some reason Jukes experienced an access of confidence, a sensation that came from outside like a warm breath, and made him feel equal to every demand. The distant muttering of the darkness stole into his ears. He noted it unmoved, out of that sudden belief in himself, as a man safe in a shirt of mail would watch a point.

The ship laboured without intermission amongst the black hills of water, paying with this hard tumbling the price of her life. She rumbled in her depths, shaking a white plummet of steam into the night, and Jukes' thought skimmed like a bird through the engine-room, where Mr. Rout—good man—was ready. When the rumbling ceased it seemed to him that there was a pause of every sound, a dead pause in which Captain MacWhirr's voice rang out startlingly.

"What's that? A puff of wind?"—it spoke much louder than Jukes had ever heard it before—"On the bow. That's right. She may come out of it yet."

The mutter of the winds drew near apace. In the forefront could be distinguished a drowsy waking plaint passing on, and far off the growth of a multiple clamour, marching and expanding. There was the throb as of many drums in it, a vicious rushing note, and like the chant of a tramping multitude.

Jukes could no longer see his captain distinctly. The darkness was absolutely piling itself upon the ship. At most he made out movements, a hint of elbows spread out, of a head thrown up.

Captain MacWhirr was trying to do up the top button of his oilskin coat with unwonted haste. The hurricane, with its power to madden the seas, to sink ships, to uproot trees, to overturn strong walls and dash the very birds of the air to the ground, had found this taciturn man in its path, and, doing its utmost, had managed to wring out a few words. Before the renewed wrath of winds swooped on his ship, Captain MacWhirr was moved to declare, in a tone of vexation, as it were: "I wouldn't like to lose her."

He was spared that annoyance.

· VI ·

On a bright sunshiny day, with the breeze chasing her smoke far ahead, the *Nan-Shan* came into Fu-chau. Her arrival was at once noticed on shore, and the seamen in harbour said: "Look! Look at that steamer. What's that? Siamese—isn't she? Just look at her!"

She seemed, indeed, to have been used as a running target for the secondary batteries of a cruiser. A hail of minor shells could not have given her upper works a more broken, torn, and devastated aspect: and she had about her the worn, weary air of ships coming from the far ends of the world—and indeed with truth, for in her short passage she had been very far; sighting, verily, even the coast of the Great Beyond, whence no ship ever returns to give up her crew to the dust of the earth. She was incrusted and gray with salt to the trucks of her masts and to the top of her funnel; as though (as some facetious seaman said) "the crowd on board had fished her out somewhere from the bottom of the sea and brought her in here for salvage." And further, excited by the felicity of his own wit, he offered to give five pounds for her—"as she stands."

Before she had been quite an hour at rest, a meagre little man, with a red-tipped nose and a face cast in an angry mould, landed from a sampan on the quay of the Foreign Concession, and incontinently turned to shake his fist at her.

A tall individual, with legs much too thin for a rotund stomach, and with watery eyes, strolled up and remarked, "Just left her—eh? Quick work."

He wore a soiled suit of blue flannel with a pair of dirty cricketing shoes; a dingy gray moustache drooped from his lip, and daylight could be seen in two places between the rim and the crown of his hat.

"Hallo! what are you doing here?" asked the ex-second-mate of the *Nan-Shan,* shaking hands hurriedly.

"Standing by for a job—chance worth taking—got a quiet hint," explained the man with the broken hat, in jerky, apathetic wheezes.

The second shook his fist again at the *Nan-Shan.* "There's a fellow there that ain't fit to have the command of a scow," he declared, quivering with passion, while the other looked about listlessly.

"Is there?"

But he caught sight on the quay of a heavy seaman's chest, painted brown under a fringed sailcloth cover, and lashed with new manila line. He eyed it with awakened interest.

"I would talk and raise trouble if it wasn't for that damned Siamese flag. Nobody to go to—or I would make it hot for him. The fraud! Told his chief engineer—that's another fraud for you—I had lost my nerve. The greatest lot of ignorant fools that ever sailed the seas. No! You can't think . . ."

"Got your money all right?" inquired his seedy acquaintance suddenly.

"Yes. Paid me off on board," raged the second mate. "'Get your breakfast on shore,' says he."

"Mean skunk!" commented the tall man, vaguely, and passed his tongue on his lips. "What about having a drink of some sort?"

"He struck me," hissed the second mate.

"No! Struck! You don't say?" The man in blue began to bustle about sympathetically. "Can't possibly talk here. I want to know all about it. Struck—eh? Let's get a fellow to carry your chest. I know a quiet place where they have some bottled beer. . . ."

Mr. Jukes, who had been scanning the shore through a pair of glasses, informed the chief engineer afterwards that "our late second mate hasn't been long in finding a friend. A chap looking uncommonly like a bummer. I saw them walk away together from the quay."

The hammering and banging of the needful repairs did not disturb Captain MacWhirr. The steward found in the letter he wrote, in a tidy chart-room, passages of such absorbing interest that twice he was nearly caught in the act. But Mrs. MacWhirr, in the drawing-room of the forty-pound house, stifled a yawn—perhaps out of self-respect—for she was alone.

She reclined in a plush-bottomed and gilt hammock-chair near a tiled fireplace, with Japanese fans on the mantel and a glow of coals in the grate. Lifting her hands, she glanced wearily here and there into the many pages. It was not her fault they were so prosy, so completely uninteresting—from "My darling wife" at the beginning, to "Your loving husband" at the end. She couldn't be really expected to understand all these ship affairs. She was glad, of course, to hear from him, but she had never asked herself why, precisely.

". . . They are called typhoons . . . The mate did not seem to like it . . . Not in books . . . Couldn't think of letting it go on. . . ."

The paper rustled sharply. ". . . A calm that lasted more than twenty minutes," she read perfunctorily; and the next words her thoughtless eyes caught, on the top of another page, were: "see you and the children again. . . ." She had a movement of impatience. He was always thinking of coming home. He had never had such a good salary before. What was the matter now?

It did not occur to her to turn back overleaf to look. She would have found it recorded there that between 4 and 6 A.M. on December 25th, Captain MacWhirr did actually think that his ship could not possibly live another hour in such a sea, and that he would never see his wife and children again. Nobody was to know this (his letters got mislaid so quickly)—nobody whatever but the steward, who had been greatly impressed by that disclosure. So much so, that he tried to give the cook some idea of the "narrow squeak we all had" by saying solemnly, "The old man himself had a dam' poor opinion of our chance."

"How do you know?" asked, contemptuously, the cook, an old soldier. "He hasn't told you, maybe?"

"Well, he did give me a hint to that effect," the steward brazened it out.

"Get along with you! He will be coming to tell *me* next," jeered the old cook, over his shoulder.

Mrs. MacWhirr glanced farther, on the alert. ". . . Do what's fair. . . . Miserable objects. . . . Only three, with a broken leg each, and one . . . Thought had better keep the matter quiet . . . hope to have done the fair thing. . . ."

She let fall her hands. No: there was nothing more about coming home. Must have been merely expressing a pious wish. Mrs. MacWhirr's mind was set at ease, and a black marble clock, priced by the local jeweller at £3 18s. 6d., had a discreet stealthy tick.

The door flew open, and a girl in the long-legged, short-frocked period of existence, flung into the room. A lot of colourless, rather lanky hair was scattered over her shoulders. Seeing her mother, she stood still, and directed her pale prying eyes upon the letter.

"From father," murmured Mrs. MacWhirr. "What have you done with your ribbon?"

The girl put her hands up to her head and pouted.

"He's well," continued Mrs. MacWhirr, languidly. "At least I think so. He never says." She had a little laugh. The girl's face expressed a wandering indifference, and Mrs. MacWhirr surveyed her with fond pride.

"Go and get your hat," she said after a while. "I am going out to do some shopping. There is a sale at Linom's."

"Oh, how jolly!" uttered the child, impressively, in unexpectedly grave vibrating tones, and bounded out of the room.

It was a fine afternoon, with a gray sky and dry sidewalks. Outside the draper's Mrs. MacWhirr smiled upon a woman in a black mantle of generous proportions armoured in jet and crowned with flowers blooming falsely above a bilious matronly countenance. They broke into a swift little babble of greetings and exclamations both together, very hurried, as if the street were ready to yawn open and swallow all that pleasure before it could be expressed.

Behind them the high glass doors were kept on the swing. People couldn't pass, men stood aside waiting patiently, and Lydia was absorbed in poking the end of her parasol between the stone flags. Mrs. MacWhirr talked rapidly.

"Thank you very much. He's not coming home yet. Of course it's very sad to have him away, but it's such a comfort to know he keeps so well." Mrs. MacWhirr drew breath. "The climate there agrees with him," she added, beamingly, as if poor MacWhirr had been away touring in China for the sake of his health.

Neither was the chief engineer coming home yet. Mr. Rout knew too well the value of a good billet.

"Solomon says wonders will never cease," cried Mrs. Rout joyously at the old lady in her armchair by the fire. Mr. Rout's mother moved slightly, her withered hands lying in black half-mittens on her lap.

The eyes of the engineer's wife fairly danced on the paper. "That captain of the ship he is in—a rather simple man, you remember, mother?—has done something rather clever, Solomon says."

"Yes, my dear," said the old woman meekly, sitting with bowed silvery head, and that air of inward stillness characteristic of very old people who seem lost in watching the last flickers of life. "I think I remember."

Solomon Rout, Old Sol, Father Sol, the Chief, "Rout, good man"—Mr. Rout, the condescending and paternal friend of youth, had been the baby of her many children—all dead by this time. And she remembered him best as a boy of ten—long before he went away to serve his apprenticeship in some great engineering works in the North. She had seen so little of him since, she had gone through so many years, that she had now to retrace her steps very far back to recognize him plainly in the mist of time. Sometimes it seemed that her daughter-in-law was talking of some strange man.

Mrs. Rout junior was disappointed. "H'm. H'm." She turned the page. "How provoking! He doesn't say what it is. Says I couldn't understand how much there was in it. Fancy! What could it be so very clever? What a wretched man not to tell us!"

She read on without further remark soberly, and at last sat looking into the fire. The chief wrote just a word or two of the typhoon; but something had moved him to express an increased longing for the companionship of the jolly woman. "If it hadn't been that mother must be looked after, I would send you your passage-money to-day. You could set up a small house out here. I would have a chance to see you sometimes then. We are not growing younger. . . ."

"He's well, mother," sighed Mrs. Rout, rousing herself.

"He always was a strong healthy boy," said the old woman, placidly.

But Mr. Jukes' account was really animated and very full. His friend in the Western Ocean trade imparted it freely to the other officers of his liner. "A chap I know writes to me about an extraordinary affair that happened on board his ship in that typhoon—you know—that we read of in the papers two months ago. It's the funniest thing! Just see for yourself what he says. I'll show you his letter."

There were phrases in it calculated to give the impression of light-hearted, indomitable resolution. Jukes had written them in good faith, for he felt thus when he wrote. He described with lurid effect the scenes in the 'tween-deck. ". . . It struck me in a flash that those confounded Chinamen couldn't tell we weren't a desperate kind of robbers. 'Tisn't good to part the Chinaman from his money if he is the stronger party. We need have been desperate indeed to go thieving in such weather, but what could these beggars know of us? So, without thinking of it twice, I got the hands away in a jiffy. Our work was done—that the old man had set his heart on. We cleared out without staying to inquire how they felt. I am convinced that if they had not been so unmercifully shaken, and afraid—each individual one of them—to stand up, we would have been torn to pieces. Oh! It was pretty complete, I can tell you; and you may run to and fro across the Pond to the end of time before you find yourself with such a job on your hands."

After this he alluded professionally to the damage done to the ship, and went on thus:

"It was when the weather quieted down that the situation became confoundedly delicate. It wasn't made any better by us having been lately transferred to the Siamese flag; though the skipper can't see that it makes any difference—'as long as *we* are on board'—he says. There are feelings that this man simply hasn't got—and there's an end of it. You might just as well try to make a bedpost understand. But apart from this it is an infernally lonely state for a ship to be going about the China seas with no proper consuls, not even a gunboat of her own anywhere, nor a body to go to in case of some trouble.

"My notion was to keep these Johnnies under hatches for another fifteen hours or so; as we weren't much farther than that from Fu-chau. We would find there, most likely, some sort of a man-of-war, and once under her guns we were safe enough; for surely any skipper of a man-of-war—English, French or Dutch—would see white men through as far as row on board goes. We could get rid of them and their money afterwards by delivering them to their Mandarin or Tao-tai, or whatever they call these chaps in goggles you see being carried about in sedan-chairs through their stinking streets.

"The old man wouldn't see it somehow. He wanted to keep the matter quiet. He got that notion into his head, and a steam windlass couldn't drag it out of him. He wanted as little fuss made as possible, for the sake of the ship's name and for the sake of the owners—'for the sake of all concerned,' says he, looking at me very hard. It made me angry hot. Of course you couldn't keep a think like that quiet; but the chests had been secured in the usual manner and were safe enough for any earthly gale, while this had been an altogether fiendish business I couldn't give you even an idea of.

"Meantime, I could hardly keep on my feet. None of us had a spell of any sort for nearly thirty hours, and there the old man sat rubbing his chin, rubbing the top of his head, and so bothered he didn't even think of pulling his boots off.

"'I hope, sir,' says I, 'you won't be letting them out on deck before we make ready for them in some shape or other.' Not, mind you, that I felt very sanguine about controlling these beggars if they meant to take charge. A trouble with a cargo of Chinamen is no child's play. I was dam' tired, too. 'I wish,' said I, 'you would let us throw the whole lot of these dollars down to them and leave them to fight it out amongst themselves, while we get a rest.'

"'Now you talk wild, Jukes,' says he, looking up in his slow way that makes you ache all over, somehow. 'We must plan out something that would be fair to all parties.'

"I had no end of work on hand, as you may imagine, so I set the hands going, and then I thought I would turn in a bit. I hadn't been asleep in my bunk ten minutes when in rushes the steward and begins to pull at my leg.

"'For God's sake, Mr. Jukes, come out! Come on deck quick, sir. Oh, do come out!'

"The fellow scared all the sense out of me. I didn't know what had happened: another hurricane—or what. Could hear no wind.

"'The Captain's letting them out. Oh, he is letting them out! Jump on deck, sir, and save us. The chief engineer has just run below for his revolver.'

"That's what I understood the fool to say. However, Father Rout swears he went in there only to get a clean pocket-handkerchief. Anyhow, I made one jump into my trousers and flew on deck aft. There was certainly a good deal of noise going on forward of the bridge. Four of the hands with the boss'n were at work abaft. I passed up to them some of the rifles all the ships on the China coast carry in the cabin, and led them on the bridge. On the way I ran against Old Sol, looking startled and sucking at an unlighted cigar.

"'Come along,' I shouted to him.

"We charged, the seven of us, up to the chart-room. All was over. There stood the old man with his sea-boots still drawn up to his hips and in shirt-sleeves—got warm thinking it out, I suppose. Bun Hin's dandy clerk at his elbow, as dirty as a sweep, was still green in the face. I could see directly I was in for something.

"'What the devil are these monkey tricks, Mr. Jukes?' asks the old man, as angry as ever he could be. I tell you frankly it made me lose my tongue. 'For God's sake, Mr. Jukes,' says he, 'do take away these rifles from the men. Somebody's sure to get hurt before long if you don't. Damme, if this ship isn't worse than Bedlam! Look sharp now. I want you up here to help me and Bun Hin's Chinaman to count that money. You wouldn't mind lending a hand, too, Mr. Rout, now you are here. The more of us the better.'

"He had settled it all in his mind while I was having a snooze. Had we been an English ship, or only going to land our cargo of coolies in an English port, like Hong-Kong, for instance, there would have been no end of inquiries and bother, claims for damages and so on. But these Chinamen know their officials better than we do.

"The hatches had been taken off already, and they were all on deck after a night and a day down below. It made you feel queer to see so many gaunt, wild faces together. The beggars stared about at the sky, at the sea, at the ship, as though they had expected the whole thing to have been blown to pieces. And no wonder! They had had a doing that would have shaken the soul out of a white man. But then they say a Chinaman has no soul. He has, though, something about him that is deuced tough. There was a fellow (amongst others of the badly hurt) who had had his eye all but knocked out. It stood out of his head the size of half a hen's egg. This would have laid out a white man on his back for a month: and yet there was that chap elbowing here and there in the crowd and talking to the others as if nothing had been the matter. They made a great hubbub amongst themselves, and whenever the old man showed his bald head on the foreside of the bridge, they would all leave off jawing and look at him from below.

"It seems that after he had done his thinking he made that Bun Hin's fellow go down and explain to them the only way they could get their money back. He told me afterwards that, all the coolies having worked in the same place and for the same length of time, he reckoned he would be doing the fair thing by them as near as possible if he shared all the cash we had picked up equally among the lot. You couldn't tell one man's dollars from another's, he said, and if you asked each man how much money he brought on board he was afraid they would lie, and he would find himself a long way short. I think he was right there. As to giving up the money to any Chinese official he could scare up in Fu-chau, he said he might just as well put the lot in his own pocket at once for all the good it would be to them. I suppose they thought so, too.

"We finished the distribution before dark. It was rather a sight: the sea running high, the ship a wreck to look at, these Chinamen staggering up on the bridge one by one for their share, and the old man still booted, and in his shirt-sleeves, busy paying out at the chart-room door, perspiring like anything, and now and then coming down sharp on myself or Father Rout about one thing or another not quite to his mind. He took the share of those who were disabled himself to them on the No. 2 hatch. There were three dollars left over, and these went to the three most damaged coolies, one to each. We turned-to afterwards, and shovelled out on deck heaps of wet rags, all sorts of fragments of things without shape, and that you couldn't give a name to, and let them settle the ownership themselves.

"This certainly is coming as near as can be to keeping the thing quiet for the benefit of all concerned. What's your opinion, you pampered mail-boat swell? The old chief says that this was plainly the only thing that could be done. The skipper remarked to me the other day, 'There are things you find nothing about in books.' I think that he got out of it very well for such a stupid man."

THE END OF THE TETHER

· I ·

FOR a long time after the course of the steamer *Sofala* had been altered for the land, the low swampy coast had retained its appearance of a mere smudge of darkness beyond a belt of glitter. The sunrays fell violently upon the calm sea—seemed to shatter themselves upon an adamantine surface into sparkling dust, into a dazzling vapour of light that blinded the eye and wearied the brain with its unsteady brightness.

Captain Whalley did not look at it. When his Serang, approaching the roomy cane arm-chair which he filled capably, had informed him in a low voice that the course was to be altered, he had risen at once and had remained on his feet, face forward, while the head of his ship swung through a quarter of a circle. He had not uttered a single word, not even the word to steady the helm. It was the Serang, an elderly, alert, little Malay, with a very dark skin, who murmured the order to the helmsman. And then slowly Captain Whalley sat down again in the arm-chair on the bridge and fixed his eyes on the deck between his feet.

He could not hope to see anything new upon this lane of the sea. He had been on these coasts for the last three years. From Low Cape to Malantan the distance was fifty miles, six hours' steaming for the old ship with the tide, or seven against. Then you steered straight for the land, and by and by three palms would appear on the sky, tall and slim, and with their dishevelled heads in a bunch, as if in confidential criticism of the dark mangroves. The *Sofala* would be headed towards the sombre strip of the coast, which at a given moment, as the ship closed with it obliquely, would show several clean shining fractures—the brimful estuary of a river. Then on through a brown liquid, three parts water and one part black earth, on and on between the low shores, three parts black earth and one part brackish water, the *Sofala* would plough her way upstream, as she had done once every month for these seven years or more, long before he was aware of her existence, long before he had ever thought of having anything to do with her and her invariable voyages. The old ship ought to have known the road better than her men, who had not been kept so long at it without a change; better than the faithful Serang, whom he had brought over from his last ship to keep the captain's watch; better than he himself, who had been her captain for the last three years only. She could always be depended upon to make her courses. Her compasses were never out. She was no trouble at all to take about, as if her great age had given her knowledge, wisdom, and steadiness. She made her landfalls to a degree of the bearing, and almost to a minute of her allowed time. At any moment, as he sat on the bridge without looking up, or lay sleepless in his bed, simply by reckoning the days and the hours he could tell where he was—the precise spot of the beat. He knew it well, too, this monotonous huckster's round, up and down the Straits; he knew its order and its sights and its people. Malacca to begin with, in at daylight and out at dusk, to cross over with a rigid phosphorescent wake this highway of the Far East. Darkness and gleams on the water, clear stars on a black sky, perhaps the lights of a home steamer keeping her unswerving course in the middle, or maybe the elusive shadow of a native craft with her mat sails flitting by silently—and low land on the other side in sight at daylight. At noon the three palms of the next place of call, up a sluggish river. The only white man residing there was a retired young sailor, with whom he had become friendly in the course of many voyages. Sixty miles farther on there was another place of call, a deep bay with only a couple of houses on the beach. And so on, in and out, picking up coastwise cargo here and there, and finishing with a hundred miles' steady steaming through the maze of an archipelago of small islands up to a large native town at the end of the beat. There was a three days' rest for the old ship before he started her again in inverse order, seeing the same shores from another bearing, hearing the same voices in the same places, back again to the *Sofala's* port of registry on the great highway to the East, where he would take up a berth nearly opposite the big stone pile of the harbour office till it was time to start again on the old round of 1,600 miles and thirty days. Not a very enterprising life, this, for Captain Whalley, Henry Whalley, otherwise Daredevil Harry Whalley, of the *Condor,* a famous clipper in her day. No. Not a very enterprising life for a man who had served famous firms, who had sailed famous ships (more than one or two of them his own); who had made famous passages, had been the pioneer of new routes and new trades; who had steered across the unsurveyed tracts of the South Seas, and had seen the sun rise on uncharted islands. Fifty years at sea, and forty out in the East ("a pretty thorough apprenticeship," he used to remark smilingly), had made him honourably known to a generation of shipowners and merchants in all the ports from Bombay clear over to where the East merges into the West upon the coast of the two Americas. His fame remained writ, not very large but plain enough, on the Admiralty charts. Was there not somewhere between Australia and China a Whalley Island and a Condor Reef? On that dangerous coral formation the celebrated clipper had hung stranded for three days, her captain and crew throwing her cargo overboard with one hand and with the other, as it were, keeping off her a flotilla of savage war-canoes. At that time neither the island nor the reef had any official existence. Later the officers of her Majesty's steam-vessel *Fusilier,* despatched to make a survey of the route, recognized in the adoption of these two names the enterprise of the man and the solidity of the ship. Besides, as any one who cares may see, the *General Directory* vol. ii. p. 410, begins the description of the "Malotu or Whalley Passage" with the words: "This advantageous route, first discovered in 1850 by Captain Whalley in the ship *Condor,*" etc., and ends by recommending it warmly to sailing vessels leaving the China ports for the south in the months from December to April inclusive.

This was the clearest gain he had out of life. Nothing could rob him of this kind of fame. The piercing of the Isthmus of Suez, like the breaking of a dam, had let in upon the East a flood of new ships, new men, new methods of trade. It had changed the face of the Eastern seas and the very spirit of their life; so that his early experiences meant nothing whatever to the new generation of seamen.

In those bygone days he had handled many thousands of pounds of his employers' money and of his own; he had attended faithfully, as by law a shipmaster is expected to do, to the conflicting interests of owners, charterers, and underwriters. He had never lost a ship or consented to a shady transaction; and he had lasted well, outlasting in the end the conditions that had gone to the making of his name. He had buried his wife (in the Gulf of Petchili), had married off his daughter to the man of her unlucky choice, and had lost more than an ample competence in the crash of the notorious Travancore and Deccan Banking Corporation, whose downfall had shaken the East like an earthquake. And he was sixty-seven years old.

· II ·

His age sat lightly enough on him; and of his ruin he was not ashamed. He had not been alone in believing in the stability of the Banking Corporation. Men whose judgment in matters of finance was as expert as his seamanship had commended the prudence of his investments, and had themselves lost much money in the great failure. The only difference between him and them was that he had lost his all. And yet not his all. There had remained to him from his lost fortune a very pretty little barque, *Fair Maid,* which he had bought to occupy his leisure of a retired sailor—"to play with," as he expressed it himself.

He had formally declared himself tired of the sea the year preceding his daughter's marriage. But after the young couple had gone to settle in Melbourne he found out that he could not make himself happy on shore. He was too much of a merchant sea-captain for mere yachting to satisfy him. He wanted the illusion of affairs; and his acquisition of the *Fair Maid* preserved the continuity of his life. He introduced her to his acquaintances in various ports as "my last command." When he grew too old to be trusted with a ship, he would lay her up and go ashore to be buried, leaving directions in his will to have the barque towed out and scuttled decently in deep water on the day of the funeral. His daughter would not grudge him the satisfaction of knowing that no stranger would handle his last command after him. With the fortune he was able to leave her, the value of a 500-ton barque was neither here nor there. All this would be said with a jocular twinkle in his eye: the vigorous old man had too much vitality for the sentimentalism of regret; and a little wistfully withal, because he was at home in life, taking a genuine pleasure in its feelings and its possessions; in the dignity of his reputation and his wealth, in his love for his daughter, and in his satisfaction with the ship—the plaything of his lonely leisure.

He had the cabin arranged in accordance with his simple ideal of comfort at sea. A big bookcase (he was a great reader) occupied one side of his stateroom; the portrait of his late wife, a flat bituminous oil-painting representing the profile and one long black ringlet of a young woman, faced his bedplace. Three chronometers ticked him to sleep and greeted him on waking with the tiny competition of their beats. He rose at five every day. The officer of the morning watch, drinking his early cup of coffee aft by the wheel, would hear through the wide orifice of the copper ventilators all the splashings, blowings, and sputterings of his captain's toilet. These noises would be followed by a sustained deep murmur of the Lord's Prayer recited in a loud earnest voice. Five minutes afterwards the head and shoulders of Captain Whalley emerged out of the companion-hatchway. Invariably he paused for a while on the stairs, looking all round at the horizon; upwards at the trim of the sails; inhaling deep draughts of the fresh air. Only then he would step out on the poop, acknowledging the hand raised to the peak of the cap with a majestic and benign "Good morning to you." He walked the deck till eight scrupulously. Sometimes, not above twice a year, he had to use a thick cudgel-like stick on account of a stiffness in the hip—a slight touch of rheumatism, he supposed. Otherwise he knew nothing of the ills of the flesh. At the ringing of the breakfast bell he went below to feed his canaries, wind up the chronometers, and take the head of the table. From there he had before his eyes the big carbon photographs of his daughter, her husband, and two fat-legged babies—his grandchildren—set in black frames into the maple-wood bulkheads of the cuddy. After breakfast he dusted the glass over these portraits himself with a cloth, and brushed the oil painting of his wife with a plummet kept suspended from a small brass hook by the side of the heavy gold frame. Then with the door of his state-room shut, he would sit down on the couch under the portrait to read a chapter out of a thick pocket Bible—her

Bible. But on some days he only sat there for half an hour with his finger between the leaves and the closed book resting on his knees. Perhaps he had remembered suddenly how fond of boat-sailing she used to be.

She had been a real shipmate and a true woman, too. It was like an article of faith with him that there never had been, and never could be, a brighter, cheerier home anywhere afloat or ashore than his home under the poop-deck of the *Condor,* with the big main cabin all white and gold, garlanded as if for a perpetual festival with an unfading wreath. She had decorated the centre of every panel with a cluster of home flowers. It took her a twelvemonth to go round the cuddy with this labour of love. To him it had remained a marvel of painting, the highest achievement of taste and skill; and as to old Swinburne, his mate, every time he came down to his meals he stood transfixed with admiration before the progress of the work. You could almost smell these roses, he declared, sniffing the faint flavour of turpentine which at that time pervaded the saloon, and (as he confessed afterwards) made him somewhat less hearty than usual in tackling his food. But there was nothing of the sort to interfere with his enjoyment of her singing. "Mrs. Whalley is a regular out-and-out nightingale, sir," he would pronounce with a judicial air after listening profoundly over the skylight to the very end of the piece. In fine weather, in the second dog-watch, the two men could hear her trills and roulades going on to the accompaniment of the piano in the cabin. On the very day they got engaged he had written to London for the instrument; but they had been married for over a year before it reached them, coming out round the Cape. The big case made part of the first direct general cargo landed in Hongkong harbour—an event that to the men who walked the busy quays of to-day seemed as hazily remote as the dark ages of history. But Captain Whalley could in a half-hour of solitude live again all his life, with its romance, its idyl, and its sorrow. He had to close her eyes himself. She went away from under the ensign like a sailor's wife, a sailor herself at heart. He had read the service over her, out of her own prayer-book, without a break in his voice. When he raised his eyes he could see old Swinburne facing him with his cap pressed to his breast, and his rugged, weather-beaten, impassive face streaming with drops of water like a lump of chipped red granite in a shower. It was all very well for that old sea-dog to cry. He had to read on to the end; but after the splash he did not remember much of what happened for the next few days. An elderly sailor of the crew, deft at needlework, put together a mourning frock for the child out of one of her black skirts.

He was not likely to forget; but you cannot dam up life like a sluggish stream. It will break out and flow over a man's troubles, it will close upon a sorrow like the sea upon a dead body, no matter how much love has gone to the bottom. And the world is not bad. People had been very kind to him; especially Mrs. Gardner, the wife of the senior partner in Gardner, Patteson & Co., the owners of the *Condor*. It was she who volunteered to look after the little one, and in due course took her to England (something of a journey in those days, even by the overland mail route) with her own girls to finish her education. It was ten years before he saw her again.

As a little child she had never been frightened of bad weather; she would beg to be taken up on deck in the bosom of his oilskin coat to watch the big seas hurling themselves upon the *Condor*. The swirl and crash of the waves seemed to fill her small soul with a breathless delight. "A good boy spoiled," he used to say of her in joke. He had named her Ivy because of the sound of the word, and obscurely fascinated by a vague association of ideas. She had twined herself tightly round his heart, and he intended her to cling close to her father as to a tower of strength; forgetting while she was little, that in the nature of things she would probably elect to cling to someone else. But he loved life well enough for even that event to give him a certain satisfaction, apart from his more intimate feeling of loss.

After he had purchased the *Fair Maid* to occupy his loneliness, he hastened to accept a rather unprofitable freight to Australia simply for the opportunity of seeing his daughter in her own home. What made him dissatisfied there was not to see that she clung now to somebody else, but that the prop she had selected seemed on closer examination "a rather poor stick"—even in the matter of health. He disliked his son-in-law's studied civility perhaps more than his method of handling the sum of money he had given Ivy at her marriage. But of his apprehensions he said nothing. Only on the day of his departure, with the hall-door open all ready, holding her hands and looking steadily into her eyes, he had said, "You know, my dear, all I have is for you and the chicks. Mind you write to me openly." She had answered him by an almost imperceptible movement of her head. She resembled her mother in the colour of her eyes, and in character—and also in this, that she understood him without many words.

Sure enough she had to write; and some of these letters made Captain Whalley lift his white eyebrows. For the rest he considered he was reaping the true reward of his life by being thus able to produce on demand whatever was needed. He had not enjoyed himself so much in a way since his wife had died. Characteristically enough his son-in-law's punctuality in failure caused him at a distance to feel a sort of kindness towards the man. The fellow was so perpetually being jammed on a lee shore that to charge it all to his reckless navigation would be manifestly unfair. No, no! He knew well what that meant. It was bad luck. His own had been simply marvellous, but he had seen in his life too many good men—seamen and others—go under with the sheer weight of bad luck not to recognize the fatal signs. For all that, he was cogitating on the best way of tying up very strictly every penny he had to leave, when with a preliminary rumble of rumours (whose first sound reached him in Shanghai as it happened), the shock of the big failure came; and, after passing through the phases of stupor, of incredulity, of indignation, he had to accept the fact that he had nothing to speak of to leave.

Upon that, as if he had only waited for this catastrophe, the unlucky man, away there in Melbourne, gave up his unprofitable game, and sat down—in an invalid's bath-chair at that, too. "He will never walk again," wrote the wife. For the first time in his life Captain Whalley was a bit staggered.

The *Fair Maid* had to go to work in bitter earnest now. It was no longer a matter of preserving alive the memory of Dare-devil Harry Whalley in the Eastern Seas, or of keeping an old man in pocket-money and clothes, with, perhaps, a bill for a few hundred first-class cigars thrown in at the end of the year. He would have to buckle-to, and keep her going hard on a scant allowance of gilt for the ginger-bread scrolls at her stem and stern.

This necessity opened his eyes to the fundamental changes of the world. Of his past only the familiar names remained, here and there, but the things and the men, as he had known them, were gone. The name of Gardner, Patteson & Co. was still displayed on the walls of warehouses by the waterside, on the brass plates and window-panes in the business quarters of more than one Eastern port, but there was no longer a Gardner or a Patteson in the firm. There was no longer for Captain Whalley an arm-chair and a welcome in the private office, with a bit of business ready to be put in the way of an old friend, for the sake of bygone services. The husbands of the Gardner girls sat behind the desks in that room where, long after he had left the employ, he had kept his right of entrance in the old man's time. Their ships now had yellow funnels with black tops, and a time-table of appointed routes like a confounded service of tramways. The winds of December and June were all one to them; their captains (excellent young men he doubted not) were, to be sure, familiar with Whalley Island, because of late years the Government had established a white fixed light on the north end (with a red danger sector over the Condor Reef), but most of them would have been extremely surprised to hear that a flesh-and-blood Whalley still existed—an old man going about the world trying to pick up a cargo here and there for his little barque.

And everywhere it was the same. Departed the men who would have nodded appreciatively at the mention of his name, and would have thought themselves bound in honour to do something for Daredevil Harry Whalley. Departed the opportunities which he would have known how to seize; and gone with them the white-winged flock of clippers that lived in the boisterous uncertain life of the winds, skimming big fortunes out of the foam of the sea. In a world that pared down the profits to an irreducible minimum, in a world that was able to count its disengaged tonnage twice over every day and in which lean charters were snapped up by cable three months in advance, there were no chances of fortune for an individual wandering haphazard with a little barque—hardly indeed any room to exist.

He found it more difficult from year to year. He suffered greatly from the smallness of remittances he was able to send his daughter. Meantime he had given up good cigars, and even in the matter of inferior cheroots limited himself to six a day. He never told her of his difficulties, and she never enlarged upon her struggle to live. Their confidence in each other needed no explanations, and their perfect understanding endured without protestations of gratitude or regret. He would have been shocked if she had taken it into her head to thank him in so many words, but he found it perfectly natural that she should tell him she needed two hundred pounds.

He had come in with the *Fair Maid* in ballast to look for a freight in the *Sofala's* port of registry, and her letter met him there. Its tenor was that it was no use mincing matters. Her only resource was in opening a boarding-house, for which the prospects, she judged, were good. Good enough, at any rate, to make her tell him frankly that with two hundred pounds she could make a start. He had torn the envelope open, hastily, on deck, where it was handed to him by the ship-chandler's runner, who had brought his mail at the moment of anchoring. For the second time in his life he was appalled, and remained stock-still at the cabin door with the paper trembling between his fingers. Open a boarding-house! Two hundred pounds for a start! The only resource! And he did not know where to lay his hands on two hundred pence.

All that night Captain Whalley walked the poop of his anchored ship, as though he had been about to close with the land in thick weather, and uncertain of his position after a run of many gray days without a sight of sun, moon, or stars. The black night twinkled with the guiding lights of seamen and the steady straight lines of lights on shore; and all around the *Fair Maid* the riding lights of ships cast trembling trails upon the water of the roadstead. Captain Whalley saw not a gleam anywhere till the dawn broke and he found out that his clothing was soaked through with the heavy dew.

His ship was awake. He stopped short, stroked his wet beard, and descended the poop ladder backwards, with tired feet. At the sight of him the chief officer, lounging about sleepily on the quarterdeck, remained open-mouthed in the middle of a great early-morning yawn.

"Good morning to you," pronounced Captain Whalley, solemnly, passing into the cabin. But he checked himself in the doorway, and without looking back. "By the bye," he said, "there should be an empty wooden case put away in the lazarette. It has not been broken up—has it?"

The mate shut his mouth, and then asked as if dazed, "What empty case, sir?"

"A big flat packing-case belonging to that painting in my room. Let it be taken up on deck and tell the carpenter to look it over. I may want to use it before long."

The chief officer did not stir a limb till he had heard the door of the captain's stateroom slam within the cuddy. Then he beckoned aft the second mate with his forefinger to tell him that there was something "in the wind."

When the bell rang Captain Whalley's authoritative voice boomed out through a closed door, "Sit down and don't wait for me." And his impressed officers took their places, exchanging looks and whispers across the table. What! No breakfast? And after apparently knocking about all night on deck, too! Clearly, there was something in the wind. In the skylight above their heads, bowed earnestly over the plates, three wire cages rocked and rattled to the restless jumping of the hungry canaries; and they could detect the sounds of their "old man's" deliberate movements within his stateroom. Captain Whalley was methodically winding up the chronometers, dusting the portrait of his late wife, getting a clean white shirt out of the drawers, making himself ready in his punctilious, unhurried manner to go ashore. He could not have swallowed a single mouthful of food that morning. He had made up his mind to sell the *Fair Maid.*

· III ·

Just at that time the Japanese were casting far and wide for ships of European build, and he had no difficulty in finding a purchaser, a speculator who drove a hard bargain, but paid cash down for the *Fair Maid,* with a view to a profitable resale. Thus it came about that Captain Whalley found himself on a certain afternoon descending the steps of one of the most important post offices of the East with a slip of bluish paper in his hand. This was the receipt of a registered letter enclosing a draft for two hundred pounds, and addressed to Melbourne. Captain Whalley pushed the paper into his waistcoat-pocket, took his stick from under his arm, and walked down the street.

It was a recently opened and untidy thoroughfare with rudimentary side-walks and a soft layer of dust cushioning the whole width of the road. One end touched the slummy street of Chinese shops near the harbour, the other drove straight on, without houses, for a couple of miles, through patches of jungle-like vegetation, to the yard gates of the new Consolidated Docks Company. The crude frontages of the new Government buildings alternated with the blank fencing of vacant plots, and the view of the sky seemed to give an added spaciousness to the broad vista. It was empty and shunned by natives after business hours, as though they had expected to see one of the tigers from the neighbourhood of the New Waterworks on the hill coming at a loping canter down the middle to get a Chinese shopkeeper for supper. Captain Whalley was not dwarfed by the solitude of the grandly planned street. He had too fine a presence for that. He was only a lonely figure walking purposefully, with a great white beard like a pilgrim, and with a thick stick that resembled a weapon. On one side the new Courts of Justice had a low and unadorned portico of squat columns half concealed by a few old trees left in the approach. On the other the pavilion wings of the new Colonial Treasury came out to the line of the street. But Captain Whalley, who had now no ship and no home, remembered in passing that on that very site when he first came out from England there had stood a fishing village, a few mat huts erected on piles between a muddy tidal creek and a miry pathway that went writhing into a tangled wilderness without any docks or waterworks.

No ship—no home. And his poor Ivy away there had no home either. A boarding-house is no sort of home though it may get you a living. His feelings were horribly rasped by the idea of the boarding-house. In his rank of life he had that truly aristocratic temperament characterized by a scorn of vulgar gentility and by prejudiced views as to the derogatory nature of certain occupations. For his own part he had always preferred sailing merchant ships (which is a straightforward occupation) to buying and selling merchandise of which the essence is to get the better of somebody in a bargain—an undignified trial of wits at best. His father had been Colonel Whalley (retired) of the H.E.I. Company's service, with very slender means besides his pension, but with distinguished connections. He could remember as a boy how frequently waiters at the inns, country tradesmen and small people of that sort, used to "My lord" the old warrior on the strength of his appearance.

Captain Whalley himself (he would have entered the Navy if his father had not died before he was fourteen) had something of a grand air which would have suited an old and glorious admiral; but he became lost like a straw in the eddy of a brook amongst the swarm of brown and yellow humanity filling a thoroughfare, that by contrast with the vast and empty avenue he had left seemed as narrow as a lane and absolutely riotous with life. The walls of the houses were blue; the shops of the Chinamen yawned like cavernous lairs; heaps of nondescript merchandise overflowed the gloom of the long range of arcades, and the fiery serenity of sunset took the middle of the street from end to end with a glow like the reflection of a fire. It fell on the bright colours and the dark faces of the bare-footed crowd, on the pallid yellow backs of the half-naked jostling coolies, on the accoutrements of a tall Sikh trooper with a parted beard and fierce moustaches on sentry before the gate of the police compound. Looming very big above the heads in a red haze of dust, the tightly packed car of the cable tramway navigated cautiously up the human stream, with the incessant blare of its horn, in the manner of a steamer groping in a fog.

Captain Whalley emerged like a diver on the other side, and in the desert shade between the walls of closed warehouses removed his hat to cool his brow. A certain disrepute attached to the calling of a land-lady of a boarding-house. These women were said to be rapacious, unscrupulous, untruthful; and though he condemned no class of his fellow-creatures—God forbid!—these were suspicions to which it was unseemly that a Whalley should lay herself open. He had not expostulated with her, however. He was confident she shared his feelings; he was sorry for her; he trusted her judgment; he considered it a merciful dispensation that he could help her once more—but in his aristocratic heart of hearts he would have found it more easy to reconcile himself to the idea of her turning seamstress. Vaguely he remembered reading years ago a touching piece called the "Song of the Shirt." It was all very well making songs about poor women. The granddaughter of Colonel Whalley, the landlady of a boarding-house! Pooh! He replaced his hat, dived into two pockets, and stopping a moment to apply a flaring match to the end of a cheap cheroot, blew an embittered cloud of smoke at a world that could hold such surprises.

Of one thing he was certain—that she was the own child of a clever mother. Now he had got over the wrench of parting with his ship, he perceived clearly that such a step had been unavoidable. Perhaps he had been growing aware of it all along with an unconfessed knowledge. But she, far away there, must have had an intuitive perception of it, with the pluck to face that truth and the courage to speak out—all the qualities which had made her mother a woman of such excellent counsel.

It would have had to come to that in the end! It was fortunate she had forced his hand. In another year or two it would have been an utterly barren sale. To keep the ship going he had been involving himself deeper every year. He was defenceless before the insidious work of adversity, to whose more open assaults he could present a firm front; like a cliff that stands unmoved the open battering of the sea, with a lofty ignorance of the treacherous backwash undermining its base. As it was, every liability satisfied, her request answered, and owing no man a penny, there remained to him from the proceeds a sum of five hundred pounds put away safely. In addition he had upon his person some forty odd dollars—enough to pay his hotel bill, providing he did not linger too long in the modest bedroom where he had taken refuge.

Scantily furnished, and with a waxed floor, it opened into one of the side-verandahs. The straggling building of bricks, as airy as a bird-cage, resounded with the incessant flapping of rattan screens worried by the wind between the whitewashed square pillars of the sea-front. The rooms were lofty, a ripple of sunshine flowed over the ceilings; and the periodical invasions of tourists from some passenger steamer in the harbour flitted through the wind-swept dusk of the apartments with the tumult of their unfamiliar voices and impermanent presences, like relays of migratory shades condemned to speed headlong round the earth without leaving a trace. The babble of their irruptions ebbed out as suddenly as it had arisen; the draughty corridors and the long chairs of the verandahs knew their sightseeing hurry or their prostrate repose no more; and Captain Whalley, substantial and dignified, left well nigh alone in the vast hotel by each light-hearted skurry, felt more and more like a stranded tourist with no aim in view, like a forlorn traveller without a home. In the solitude of his room he smoked thoughtfully, gazing at the two sea-chests which held all that he could call his own in this world. A thick roll of charts in a sheath of sailcloth leaned in a corner; the flat packing-case containing the portrait in oils and the three carbon photographs had been pushed under the bed. He was tired of discussing terms, of assisting at surveys, of all the routine of the business. What to the other parties was merely the sale of a ship was to him a momentous event involving a radically new view of existence. He knew that after this ship there would be no other; and the hopes of his youth, the exercise of his abilities, every feeling and achievement of his manhood, had been indissolubly con- nected with ships. He had served ships; he had owned ships; and even the years of his actual retirement from the sea had been made bearable by the idea that he had only to stretch out his hand full of money to get a ship. He had been at liberty to feel as though he were the owner of all the ships in the world. The selling of this one was weary work; but when she passed from him at last, when he signed the last receipt, it was as though all the ships had gone out of the world together, leaving him on the shore of inaccessible oceans with seven hundred pounds in his hands.

Striding firmly, without haste, along the quay, Captain Whalley averted his glances from the familiar roadstead. Two generations of seamen born since his first day at sea stood between him and all these ships at the anchorage. His own was sold, and he had been asking himself, What next?

From the feeling of loneliness, of inward emptiness—and of loss, too, as if his very soul had been taken out of him forcibly—there had sprung at first a desire to start right off and join his daughter. "Here are the last pence," he would say to her; "take them, my dear. And here's your old father: you must take him, too."

His soul recoiled, as if afraid of what lay hidden at the bottom of this impulse. Give up! Never! When one is thoroughly weary all sorts of nonsense come into one's head. A pretty gift it would have been for a poor woman—this seven hundred pounds with the incumbrance of a hale old fellow more than likely to last for years and years to come. Was he not as fit to die in harness as any of the youngsters in charge of these anchored ships out yonder? He was as solid now as ever he had been. But as to who would give him work to do, that was another matter. Were he, with his appearance and antecedents, to go about looking for a junior's berth, people, he was afraid, would not take him seriously; or else if he succeeded in impressing them, he would maybe obtain their pity, which would be like stripping yourself naked to be kicked. He was not anxious to give himself away for less than nothing. He had no use for anybody's pity. On the other hand, a command—the only thing he could try for with due regard for common decency—was not likely to be lying in wait for him at the corner of the next street. Commands don't go a-begging nowadays. Ever since he had come ashore to carry out the business of the sale he had kept his ears open, but had heard no hint of one being vacant in the port. And even if there had been one, his successful past itself stood in his way. He had been his own employer too long. The only credential he could produce was the testimony of his whole life. What better recommendation could any one require? But vaguely he felt that the unique document would be looked upon as an archaic curiosity of the Eastern waters, a screed traced in obsolete words—in a half-forgotten language.

· IV ·

Revolving these thoughts, he strolled on near the railings of the quay, broad-chested, without a stoop, as though his big shoulders had never felt the burden of the loads that must be carried between the cradle and the grave. No single betraying fold or line of care disfigured the reposeful modelling of his face. It was full and untanned; and the upper part emerged, massively quiet, out of the downward flow of silvery hair, with the striking delicacy of its clear complexion and the powerful width of the forehead. The first cast of his glance fell on you candid and swift, like a boy's; but because of the ragged snowy thatch of the eyebrows the affability of his attention acquired the character of a keen and searching scrutiny. With age he had put on flesh a little, had increased his girth like an old tree presenting no symptoms of decay; and even the opulent, lustrous ripple of white hairs upon his chest seemed an attribute of unquenchable vitality and vigour.

Once rather proud of his great bodily strength, and even of his personal appearance, conscious of his worth, and firm in his rectitude, there had remained to him, like the heritage of departed prosperity, the tranquil bearing of a man who had proved himself fit in every sort of way for the life of his choice. He strode on squarely under the projecting brim of an ancient Panama hat. It had a low crown, a crease through its whole diameter, a narrow black ribbon. Imperishable and a little discoloured, this headgear made it easy to pick him out from afar on thronged wharves and in the busy streets. He had never adopted the comparatively modern fashion of pipeclayed cork helmets. He disliked the form; and he hoped he could manage to keep a cool head to the end of his life without all these contrivances for hygienic ventilation. His hair was cropped close, his linen always of immaculate whiteness; a suit of thin gray flannel, worn threadbare but scrupulously brushed, floated about his burly limbs, adding to his bulk by the looseness of its cut. The years had mellowed the good-humoured, imperturbable audacity of his prime into a temper carelessly serene; and the leisurely tapping of his iron-shod stick accompanied his footfalls with a self-confident sound on the flagstones. It was impossible to connect such a fine presence and this unruffled aspect with the belittling troubles of poverty; the man's whole existence appeared to pass before you, facile and large, in the freedom of means as ample as the clothing of his body.

The irrational dread of having to break into his five hundred pounds for personal expenses in the hotel disturbed the steady poise of his mind. There was no time to lose. The bill was running up. He nourished the hope that this five hundred would perhaps be the means, if everything else failed, of obtaining some work which, keeping his body and soul together (not a matter of great outlay), would enable him to be of use to his daughter. To his mind it was her own money which he employed, as it were, in backing her father and solely for her benefit. Once at work, he would help her with the greater part of his earnings; he was good for many years yet, and this boarding-house business, he argued to himself, whatever the prospects, could not be much of a gold-mine from the first start. But what work? He was ready to lay hold of anything in an honest way so that it came quickly to his hand; because the five hundred pounds must be preserved intact for eventual use. That was the great point. With the entire five hundred one felt a substance at one's back; but it seemed to him that should he let it dwindle to four-fifty or even four-eighty, all the efficiency would be gone out of the money, as though there were some magic power in the round figure. But what sort of work?

Confronted by that haunting question as by an uneasy ghost, for whom he had no exorcising formula, Captain Whalley stopped short on the apex of a small bridge spanning steeply the bed of a canalized creek with granite shores. Moored between the square blocks a sea-going Malay prau floated half hidden under the arch of masonry, with her spars lowered down, without a sound of life on board, and covered from stem to stern with a ridge of palm-leaf mats. He had left behind him the overheated pavements bordered by the stone frontages that, like the sheer face of cliffs, followed the sweep of the quays; and an unconfined spaciousness of orderly and sylvan aspect opened before him its wide plots of rolled grass, like pieces of green carpet smoothly pegged out, its long ranges of trees lined up in colossal porticos of dark shafts roofed with a vault of branches.

Some of these avenues ended at the sea. It was a terraced shore; and beyond, upon the level expanse, profound and glistening like the gaze of a dark-blue eye, an oblique band of stippled purple lengthened itself indefinitely through the gap between a couple of verdant twin islets. The masts and spars of a few ships far away, hull down in the outer roads, sprang straight from the water in a fine maze of rosy lines pencilled on the clear shadow of the eastern board. Captain Whalley gave them a long glance. The ship, once his own, was anchored out there. It was staggering to think that it was open to him no longer to take a boat at the jetty and get himself pulled off to her when the evening came. To no ship. Perhaps never more. Before the sale was concluded, and till the purchase-money had been paid, he had spent daily some time on board the *Fair Maid*. The money had been paid this very morning, and now, all at once, there was positively no ship that he could go on board of when he liked; no ship that would need his presence in order to do her work—to live. It seemed an incredible state of affairs, something too bizarre to last. And the sea was full of craft of all sorts. There was that prau lying so still swathed in her shroud of sewn palm-leaves—she, too, had her indispensable man. They lived through each other, this Malay he had never seen, and this high-sterned thing of no size that seemed to be resting after a long journey. And of all the ships in sight, near and far, each was provided with a man, the man without whom the finest ship is a dead thing, a floating and purposeless log.

After his one glance at the roadstead he went on since there was nothing to turn back for, and the time must be got through somehow. The avenues of big trees ran straight over the Esplanade, cutting each other at diverse angles, columnar below and luxuriant above. The interlaced boughs high up there seemed to slumber; not a leaf stirred overhead: and the reedy cast-iron lamp-posts in the middle of the road, gilt like sceptres diminished in a long perspective, with their globes of white porcelain atop, resembling a barbarous decoration of ostriches' eggs displayed in a row. The flaming sky kindled a tiny crimson spark upon the glistening surface of each glassy shell.

With his chin sunk a little, his hands behind his back, and the end of his stick marking the gravel with a faint wavering line at his heels, Captain Whalley reflected that if a ship without a man was like a body without a soul, a sailor without a ship was of not much more account in this world than an aimless log adrift upon the sea. The log might be sound enough by itself, tough of fibre, and hard to destroy—but what of that! And a sudden sense of irremediable idleness weighted his feet like a great fatigue.

A succession of open carriages came bowling along the newly opened sea-road. You could see across the wide grass-plots the discs of vibration made by the spokes. The bright domes of the parasols swayed lightly outwards like full-blown blossoms on the rim of a vase; and the quiet sheet of dark-blue water, crossed by a bar of purple, made a background for the spinning wheels and the high action of the horses, whilst the turbaned heads of the Indian servants elevated above the line of the sea horizon glided rapidly on the paler blue of the sky. In an open space near the little bridge each turn-out trotted smartly in a wide curve away from the sunset; then pulling up sharp, entered the main alley in a long slow-moving file with the great red stillness of the sky at the back. The trunks of mighty trees stood all touched with red on the same side, the air seemed aflame under the high foliage, the very ground under the hoofs of the horses was red. The wheels turned solemnly; one after another the sunshades drooped, folding their colours like gorgeous flowers shutting their petals at the end of the day. In the whole half-mile of human beings no voice uttered a distinct word, only a faint thudding noise went on mingled with slight jingling sounds, and the motionless heads and shoulders of men and women sitting in couples emerged stolidly above the lowered hoods—as if wooden. But one carriage and pair coming late did not join the line.

It fled along in a noiseless roll; but on entering the avenue one of the dark bays snorted, arching his neck and shying against the steel-tipped pole; a flake of foam fell from the bit upon the point of a satiny shoulder, and the dusky face of the coachman leaned forward at once over the hands taking a fresh grip of the reins. It was a long dark-green landau, having a dignified and buoyant motion between the sharply curved C-springs, and a sort of strictly official majesty in its supreme elegance. It seemed more roomy than is usual, its horses seemed slightly bigger, the appointments a shade more perfect, the servants perched somewhat higher on the box. The dresses of three women—two young and pretty, and one, handsome, large, of mature age—seemed to fill completely the shallow body of the carriage. The fourth face was that of a man, heavy lidded, distinguished and sallow, with a sombre, thick, iron-gray imperial and moustaches, which somehow had the air of solid appendages. His Excellency—

The rapid motion of that one equipage made all the others appear utterly inferior, blighted, and reduced to crawl painfully at a snail's pace. The landau distanced the whole file in a sort of sustained rush; the features of the occupants whirling out of sight left behind an impression of fixed stares and impassive vacancy; and after it had vanished in full flight as it were, notwithstanding the long line of vehicles hugging the curb at a walk, the whole lofty vista of the avenue seemed to lie open and emptied of life in the enlarged impression of an august solitude.

Captain Whalley had lifted his head to look, and his mind, disturbed in its meditation, turned with wonder (as men's minds will do) to matters of no importance. It struck him that it was to this port, where he had just sold his last ship, that he had come with the very first he had ever owned, and with his head full of a plan for opening a new trade with a distant part of the Archipelago. The then governor had given him no end of encouragement. No Excellency he—this Mr. Denham—this governor with his jacket off; a man who tended night and day, so to speak, the growing prosperity of the settlement with the self-forgetful devotion of a nurse for a child she loves; a lone bachelor who lived as in a camp with the few servants and his three dogs in what was called then the Government Bungalow: a low-roofed structure on the half-cleared slope of a hill, with a new flagstaff in front and a police orderly on the verandah. He remembered toiling up that hill under a heavy sun for his audience; the unfurnished aspect of the cool shaded room; the long table covered at one end with piles of papers, and with two guns, a brass telescope, a small bottle of oil with a feather stuck in the neck at the other—and the flattering attention given to him by the man in power. It was an undertaking full of risk he had come to expound, but a twenty minutes' talk in the Government Bungalow on the hill had made it go smoothly from the start. And as he was retiring Mr. Denham, already seated before the papers, called out after him, "Next month the *Dido* starts for a cruise that way, and I shall request her captain officially to give you a look-in and see how you get on." The *Dido* was one of the smart frigates on the China station—and five-and-thirty years make a big slice of time. Five-and-thirty years ago an enterprise like his had for the colony enough importance to be looked after by a Queen's ship. A big slice of time. Individuals were of some account then. Men like himself; men, too, like poor Evans, for instance, with his red face, his coal-black whiskers, and his restless eyes, who had set up the first patent slip for repairing small ships, on the edge of the forest, in a lonely bay three miles up the coast. Mr. Denham had encouraged that enterprise, too, and yet somehow poor Evans had ended by dying at home deucedly hard up. His son, they said, was squeezing oil out of cocoanuts for a living on some God-forsaken islet of the Indian Ocean; but it was from that patent slip in a lonely wooded bay that had sprung the workshops of the Consolidated Docks Company, with its three graving basins carved out of solid rock, its wharves, its jetties, its electric-light plant, its steam-power houses—with its gigantic sheer-legs, fit to lift the heaviest weight ever carried afloat, and whose head could be seen like the top of a queer white monument peeping over bushy points of land and sandy promontories, as you approached the New Harbour from the west.

There had been a time when men counted: there were not so many carriages in the colony then, though Mr. Denham, he fancied, had a buggy. And Captain Whalley seemed to be swept out of the great avenue by the swirl of a mental backwash. He remembered muddy shores, a harbour without quays, the one solitary wooden pier (but that was a public work) jutting out crookedly, the first coal-sheds erected on Monkey Point, that caught fire mysteriously and smouldered for days, so that amazed ships came into a roadstead full of sulphurous fog, and the sun hung blood-red at midday. He remembered the things, the faces, and something more besides—like the faint flavour of a cup quaffed to the bottom, like a subtle sparkle of the air that was not to be found in the atmosphere of to-day.

In this evocation, swift and full of detail like a flash of magnesium light into the niches of a dark memorial hall, Captain Whalley contemplated things once important, the efforts of small men, the growth of a great place, but now robbed of all consequence by the greatness of accomplished facts, by hopes greater still; and they gave him for a moment such an almost physical grip upon time, such a comprehension of our unchangeable feelings, that he stopped short, struck the ground with his stick, and ejaculated mentally, "What the devil am I doing here!" He seemed lost in a sort of surprise; but he heard his name called out in wheezy tones once, twice—and turned on his heels slowly.

He beheld then, waddling towards him autocratically, a man of an old-fashioned and gouty aspect, with hair as white as his own, but with shaved, florid cheeks, wearing a necktie—almost a neckcloth—whose stiff ends projected far beyond his chin; with round legs, round arms, a round body, a round face—generally producing the effect of his short figure having been distended by means of an air-pump as much as the seams of his clothing would stand. This was the Master-Attendant of the port. A master-attendant is a superior sort of harbour-master; a person, out in the East, of some consequence in his sphere; a Government official, a magistrate for the waters of the port, and possessed of vast but ill-defined disciplinary authority over seamen of all classes. This particular Master-Attendant was reported to consider it miserably inadequate, on the ground that it did not include the power of life and death. This was a jocular exaggeration. Captain Eliott was fairly satisfied with his position, and nursed no inconsiderable sense of such power as he had. His conceited and tyrannical disposition did not allow him to let it dwindle in his hands for want of use. The uproarious, choleric frankness of his comments on people's character and conduct caused him to be feared at bottom. Though in conversation many pretended not to mind him in the least, others would only smile sourly at the mention of his name, and there were even some who dared to pronounce him "a meddlesome old ruffian." But for almost all of them one of Captain Eliott's outbreaks was nearly as distasteful to face as a chance of annihilation.

· V ·

As soon as he had come up quite close he said, mouthing in a growl—

"What's this I hear, Whalley? Is it true you're selling the *Fair Maid?*"

Captain Whalley, looking away, said the thing was done—money had been paid that morning; and the other expressed at once his approbation of such an extremely sensible proceeding. He had got out of his trap to stretch his legs, he explained, on his way home to dinner. Sir Frederick looked well at the end of his time. Didn't he?

Captain Whalley could not say; had only noticed the carriage going past.

The Master-Attendant, plunging his hands into the pockets of an alpaca jacket inappropriately short and tight for a man of his age and appearance, strutted with a slight limp, and with his head reaching only to the shoulder of Captain Whalley, who walked easily, staring straight before him. They had been good comrades years ago, almost intimates. At the time when Whalley commanded the renowned *Condor,* Eliott had charge of the nearly as famous *Ringdove* for the same owners; and when the appointment of Master-Attendant was created, Whalley would have been the only other serious candidate. But Captain Whalley, then in the prime of life, was resolved to serve no one but his own auspicious Fortune. Far away, tending his hot irons, he was glad to hear the other had been successful. There was a worldly suppleness in bluff Ned Eliott that would serve him well in that sort of official appointment. And they were so dissimilar at bottom that as they came slowly to the end of the avenue before the Cathedral, it had never come into Whalley's head that he might have been in that man's place—provided for to the end of his days.

The sacred edifice, standing in solemn isolation amongst the converging avenues of enormous trees, as if to put grave thoughts of heaven into the hours of ease, presented a closed Gothic portal to the light and glory of the west. The glass of the rosace above the ogive glowed like fiery coal in the deep carvings of a wheel of stone. The two men faced about.

"I'll tell you what they ought to do next, Whalley," growled Captain Eliott suddenly.

"Well?"

"They ought to send a real live lord out here when Sir Frederick's time is up. Eh?"

Captain Whalley perfunctorily did not see why a lord of the right sort should not do as well as any one else. But this was not the other's point of view.

"No, no. Place runs itself. Nothing can stop it now. Good enough for a lord," he growled in short sentences. "Look at the changes in our own time. We need a lord here now. They have got a lord in Bombay."

He dined once or twice every year at the Government House—a many-windowed, arcaded palace upon a hill laid out in roads and gardens. And lately he had been taking about a duke in his Master-Attendant's steam-launch to visit the harbour improvements. Before that he had "most obligingly" gone out in person to pick out a good berth for the ducal yacht. Afterwards he had an invitation to lunch on board. The duchess herself lunched with them. A big woman with a red face. Complexion quite sunburnt. He should think ruined. Very gracious manners. They were going on to Japan. . . .

He ejaculated these details for Captain Whalley's edification, pausing to blow out his cheeks as if with a pent-up sense of importance, and repeatedly protruding his thick lips till the blunt crimson end of his nose seemed to dip into the milk of his moustache. The place ran itself; it was fit for any lord; it gave no trouble except in its Marine department—in its Marine department, he repeated twice, and after a heavy snort began to relate how the other day her Majesty's Consul-General in French Cochin-China had cabled to him—in his official capacity—asking for a qualified man to be sent over to take charge of a Glasgow ship whose master had died in Saigon.

"I sent word of it to the officers' quarters in the Sailors' Home," he continued, while the limp in his gait seemed to grow more accentuated with the increasing irritation of his voice. "Place's full of them. Twice as many men as there are berths going in the local trade. All hungry for an easy job. Twice as many—and—What d'you think, Whalley? . . ."

He stopped short; his hands, clenched and thrust deeply downwards, seemed ready to burst the pockets of his jacket. A slight sigh escaped Captain Whalley.

"Hey? You would think they would be falling over each other. Not a bit of it. Frightened to go home. Nice and warm out here to lie about a verandah waiting for a job. I sit and wait in my office. Nobody. What did they suppose? That I was going to sit there like a dummy with the Consul-General's cable before me? Not likely. So I looked up a list of them I keep by me and sent word for Hamilton—the worst loafer of them all—and just made him go. Threatened to instruct the steward of the Sailors' Home to have him turned out neck and crop. He did not think the berth was good enough—if you—please. 'I've your record by me,' said I. 'You came ashore here eighteen months ago, and you haven't done six months' work since. You are in debt for your board now at the Home, and I suppose you reckon the Marine Office will pay in the end. Eh? So it shall; but if you don't take this chance, away you go to England, assisted passage, by the first homeward steamer that comes along. You are no better than a pauper. We don't want any white paupers here.' I scared him. But look at the trouble all this gave me."

"You would not have had any trouble," Captain Whalley said almost involuntarily, "if you had sent for me."

Captain Eliott was immensely amused; he shook with laughter as he walked. But suddenly he stopped laughing. A vague recollection had crossed his mind. Hadn't he heard it said at the time of the Travancore and Deccan smash that poor Whalley had been cleaned out completely? "Fellow's hard up, by heavens!" he thought; and at once he cast a sidelong upwards glance at his companion. But Captain Whalley was smiling austerely straight before him, with a carriage of the head inconceivable in a penniless man—and he became reassured. Impossible. Could not have lost everything. That ship had been only a hobby of his. And the reflection that a man who had confessed to receiving that very morning a presumably large sum of money was not likely to spring upon him a demand for a small loan put him entirely at his ease again. There had come a long pause in their talk, however, and not knowing how to begin again, he growled out soberly, "We old fellows ought to take a rest now."

"The best thing for some of us would be to die at the oar," Captain Whalley said, negligently.

"Come, now. Aren't you a bit tired by this time of the whole show?" muttered the other, sullenly.

"Are you?"

Captain Eliott was. Infernally tired. He only hung on to his berth so long in order to get his pension on the highest scale before he went home. It would be no better than poverty, anyhow; still, it was the only thing between him and the workhouse. And he had a family. Three girls, as Whalley knew. He gave "Harry, old boy," to understand that these three girls were a source of the greatest anxiety and worry to him. Enough to drive a man distracted.

"Why? What have they been doing now?" asked Captain Whalley with a sort of amused absent-mindedness.

"Doing! Doing nothing. That's just it. Lawn-tennis and silly novels from morning to night. . . ."

If one of them at least had been a boy! But all three! And, as ill-luck would have it, there did not seem to be any decent young fellows left in the world. When he looked around in the club he saw only a lot of conceited popinjays too selfish to think of making a good woman happy. Extreme indigence stared him in the face with all that crowd to keep at home. He had cherished the idea of building himself a little house in the country—in Surrey—to end his days in, but he was afraid it was out of the question . . . and his staring eyes rolled upwards with such a pathetic anxiety that Captain Whalley charitably nodded down at him, restraining a sort of sickening desire to laugh.

"You must know what it is yourself, Harry. Girls are the very devil for worry and anxiety."

"Ay! But mine is doing well," Captain Whalley pronounced slowly, staring to the end of the avenue.

The Master-Attendant was glad to hear this. Uncommonly glad. He remembered her well. A pretty girl she was.

Captain Whalley, stepping out carelessly, assented as if in a dream: "She was pretty."

The procession of carriages was breaking up.

One after another they left the file to go off at a trot, animating the vast avenue with their scattered life and movement; but soon the aspect of dignified solitude returned and took possession of the straight wide road. A syce in white stood at the head of a Burmah pony harnessed to a varnished two-wheel cart; and the whole thing waiting by the curb seemed no bigger than a child's toy forgotten under the soaring trees. Captain Eliott waddled up to it and made as if to clamber in, but refrained; and keeping one hand resting easily on the shaft, he changed the conversation from his pension, his daughters, and his poverty back again to the only other topic in the world—the Marine Office, the men and the ships of the port.

He proceeded to give instances of what was expected of him; and his thick voice drowsed in the still air like the obstinate droning of an enormous bumble-bee. Captain Whalley did not know what was the force or the weakness that prevented him from saying goodnight and walking away. It was as though he had been too tired to make the effort. How queer. More queer than any of Ned's instances. Or was it that overpowering sense of idleness alone that made him stand there and listen to these stories? Nothing very real had ever troubled Ned Eliott; and gradually he seemed to detect deep in, as if wrapped up in the gross wheezy rumble, something of the clear hearty voice of the young captain of the *Ringdove*. He wondered if he, too, had changed to the same extent; and it seemed to him that the voice of his old chum had not changed so very much—that the man was the same. Not a bad fellow the pleasant, jolly Ned Eliott, friendly, well up to his business—and always a bit of a humbug. He remembered how he used to amuse his poor wife. She could read him like an open book. When the *Condor* and the *Ringdove* happened to be in port together, she would frequently ask him to bring Captain Eliott to dinner. They had not met often since those old days. Not once in five years, perhaps. He regarded from under his white eyebrows this man he could not bring himself to take into his confidence at this juncture; and the other went on with his intimate outpourings, and as remote from his hearer as though he had been talking on a hill-top a mile away.

He was in a bit of a quandary now as to the steamer *Sofala*. Ultimately every hitch in the port came into his hands to undo. They would miss him when he was gone in another eighteen months, and most likely some retired naval officer had been pitchforked into the appointment—a man that would understand nothing and care less. That steamer was a coasting craft having a steady trade connection as far north as Tenasserim; but the trouble was she could get no captain to take her on her regular trip. Nobody would go in her. He really had no power, of course, to order a man to take a job. It was all very well to stretch a point on the demand of a consul-general, but. . . .

"What's the matter with the ship?" Captain Whalley interrupted in measured tones.

"Nothing's the matter. Sound old steamer. Her owner has been in my office this afternoon tearing his hair."

"Is he a white man?" asked Whalley in an interested voice.

"He calls himself a white man," answered the Master-Attendant scornfully; "but if so, it's just skin-deep and no more. I told him that to his face, too."

"But who is he, then?"

"He's the chief engineer of her. See *that*, Harry?"

"I see," Captain Whalley said, thoughtfully. "The engineer. I see."

How the fellow came to be a shipowner at the same time was quite a tale. He came out third in a home ship nearly fifteen years ago, Captain Eliott remembered, and got paid off after a bad sort of row both with his skipper and his chief. Anyway, they seemed jolly glad to get rid of him at all costs. Clearly a mutinous sort of chap. Well, he remained out here, a perfect nuisance, everlastingly shipped and unshipped, unable to keep a berth very long; pretty nigh went through every engine-room afloat belonging to the colony. Then suddenly, "What do you think happened, Harry?"

Captain Whalley, who seemed lost in a mental effort as of doing a sum in his head, gave a slight start. He really couldn't imagine. The Master-Attendant's voice vibrated dully with hoarse emphasis. The man actually had the luck to win the second great prize in the Manila lottery. All these engineers and officers of ships took tickets in that gamble. It seemed to be a perfect mania with them all.

Everybody expected now that he would take himself off home with his money, and go to the devil in his own way. Not at all. The *Sofala,* judged too small and not quite modern enough for the sort of trade she was in, could be got for a moderate price from her owners, who had ordered a new steamer from Europe. He rushed in and bought her. This man had never given any signs of that sort of mental intoxication the mere fact of getting hold of a large sum of money may produce—not till he got a ship of his own; but then he went off his balance all at once: came bouncing into the Marine Office on some transfer business, with his hat hanging over his left eye and switching a little cane in his hand, and told each one of the clerks separately that "Nobody could put him out now. It was his turn. There was no one over him on earth, and there never would be either." He swaggered and strutted between the desks, talking at the top of his voice, and trembling like a leaf all the while, so that the current business of the office was suspended for the time he was in there, and everybody in the big room stood open-mouthed looking at his antics. Afterwards he could be seen during the hottest hours of the day with his face as red as fire rushing along up and down the quays to look at his ship from different points of view: he seemed inclined to stop every stranger he came across just to let them know "that there would be no longer any one over him; he had bought a ship; nobody on earth could put him out of his engine-room now."

Good bargain as she was, the price of the *Sofala* took up pretty near all the lottery-money. He had left himself no capital to work that. That did not matter so much, for these were the halcyon days of steam coasting trade, before some of the home shipping firms had thought of establishing local fleets to feed their main lines. These, when once organized, took the biggest slices out of that cake, of course; and by and by a squad of confounded German tramps turned up east of Suez Canal and swept up all the crumbs. They prowled on the cheap to and fro along the coast and between the islands, like a lot of sharks in the water ready to snap up anything you let drop. And then the high old times were over for good; for years the *Sofala* had made no more, he judged, than a fair living. Captain Eliott looked upon it as his duty in every way to assist an English ship to hold her own; and it stood to reason that if for want of a captain the *Sofala* began to miss her trips she would very soon lose her trade. There was the quandary. The man was too impracticable. "Too much of a beggar on horseback from the first," he explained. "Seemed to grow worse as the time went on. In the last three years he's run through eleven skippers; he had tried every single man here, outside of the regular lines. I had warned him before that this would not do. And now, of course, no one will look at the *Sofala*. I had one or two men up at my office and talked to them; but, as they said to me, what was the good of taking the berth to lead a regular dog's life for a month and then get the sack at the end of the first trip? The fellow, of course, told me it was all nonsense; there has been a plot hatching for years against him. And now it had come. All the horrid sailors in the port had conspired to bring him to his knees, because he was an engineer." Captain Eliott emitted a throaty chuckle.

"And the fact is, that if he misses a couple more trips he need never trouble himself to start again. He won't find any cargo in his old trade. There's too much competition nowadays for people to keep their stuff lying about for a ship that does not turn up when she's expected. It's a bad lookout for him. He swears he will shut himself on board and starve to death in his cabin rather than sell her—even if he could find a buyer. And that's not likely in the least. Not even the Japs would give her insured value for her. It isn't like selling sailing-ships. Steamers *do* get out of date, besides getting old."

"He must have laid by a good bit of money though," observed Captain Whalley, quietly.

The Harbour-master puffed out his purple cheeks to an amazing size.

"Not a stiver, Harry. Not—a—single sti-ver."

He waited; but as Captain Whalley, stroking his beard slowly, looked down on the ground without a word, he tapped him on the forearm, tiptoed, and said in a hoarse whisper—

"The Manila lottery has been eating him up."

He frowned a little, nodding in tiny affirmative jerks. They all were going in for it; a third of the wages paid to ships' officers ("in my port," he snorted) went to Manila. It was a mania. That fellow Massy had been bitten by it like the rest of them from the first; but after winning once he seemed to have persuaded himself he had only to try again to get another big prize. He had taken dozens and scores of tickets for every drawing since. What with this vice and his ignorance of affairs, ever since he had improvidently bought that steamer he had been more or less short of money.

This, in Captain Eliott's opinion, gave an opening for a sensible sailor-man with a few pounds to step in and save that fool from the consequences of his folly. It was his craze to quarrel with his captains. He had had some really good men, too, who would have been too glad to stay if he would only let them. But no. He seemed to think he was no owner unless he was kicking somebody out in the morning and having a row with the new man in the evening. What was wanted for him was a master with a couple of hundred or so to take an interest in the ship on proper conditions. You don't discharge a man for no fault, only because of the fun of telling him to pack up his traps and go ashore, when you know that in that case you are bound to buy back his share. On the other hand, a fellow with an interest in the ship is not likely to throw up his job in a huff about a trifle. He had told Massy that. He had said: "'This won't do, Mr. Massy. We are getting very sick of you here in the Marine Office. What you must do now is to try whether you could get a sailor to join you as partner. That seems to be the only way.' And that was sound advice, Harry."

Captain Whalley, leaning on his stick, was perfectly still all over, and his hand, arrested in the act of stroking, grasped his whole beard. And what did the fellow say to that?

The fellow had the audacity to fly out at the Master-Attendant. He had received the advice in a most impudent manner. "I didn't come here to be laughed at," he had shrieked. "I appeal to you as an Englishman and a shipowner brought to the verge of ruin by an illegal conspiracy of your beggarly sailors, and all you condescend to do for me is to tell me to go and get a partner!" . . . The fellow had presumed to stamp with rage on the floor of the private office. Where was he going to get a partner? Was he being taken for a fool? Not a single one of that contemptible lot ashore at the "Home" had twopence in his pocket to bless himself with. The very native curs in the bazaar knew that much. . . . "And it's true enough, Harry," rumbled Captain Eliott, judicially. "They are much more likely one and all to owe money to the Chinamen in Denham Road for the clothes on their backs. 'Well,' said I, 'you make too much noise over it for my taste, Mr. Massy. Good morning.' He banged the door after him; he dared to bang my door, confound his cheek!''

The head of the Marine department was out of breath with indignation; then recollecting himself as it were, "I'll end by being late to dinner—yarning with you here . . . wife doesn't like it."

He clambered ponderously into the trap; leaned out side-ways, and only then wondered wheezily what on earth Captain Whalley could have been doing with himself of late. They had had no sight of each other for years and years till the other day when he had seen him unexpectedly in the office.

What on earth. . . .

Captain Whalley seemed to be smiling to himself in his white beard. "The earth is big," he said, vaguely.

The other, as if to test the statement, stared all round from his driving-seat. The Esplanade was very quiet; only from afar, from very far, a long way from the sea-shore, across the stretches of grass, through the long ranges of trees, came faintly the toot—toot—toot of the cable car beginning to roll before the empty peristyle of the Public Library on its three-mile journey to the New Harbour Docks.

"Doesn't seem to be so much room on it," growled the Master-Attendant, "since these Germans came along shouldering us at every turn. It was not so in our time."

He fell into deep thought, breathing stertorously, as though he had been taking a nap open-eyed. Perhaps he, too, on his side, had detected in the silent pilgrim-like figure, standing there by the wheel, like an arrested wayfarer, the buried lineaments of the features belonging to the young captain of the *Condor*. Good fellow—Harry Whalley—never very talkative. You never knew what he was up to—a bit too off-hand with people of consequence, and apt to take a wrong view of a fellow's actions. Fact was he had a too good opinion of himself. He would have liked to tell him to get in and drive him home to dinner. But one never knew. Wife would not like it.

"And it's funny to think, Harry," he went on in a big subdued drone, "that of all the people on it there seems only you and I left to remember this part of the world as it used to be. . . ."

He was ready to indulge in the sweetness of a sentimental mood had it not struck him suddenly that Captain Whalley, unstirring and without a word, seemed to be awaiting something—perhaps expecting. . . . He gathered the reins at once and burst out in bluff hearty growls—

"Ha! My dear boy. The men we have known—the ships we've sailed—ay! and the things we've done. . . ."

The pony plunged—the syce skipped out of the way. Captain Whalley raised his arm.

"Good-bye."

· VI ·

The sun had set. And when, after drilling a deep hole with his stick, he moved from that spot the night had massed its army of shadows under the trees. They filled the eastern ends of the avenue as if only waiting the signal for a general advance upon the open spaces of the world; they were gathering low between the deep stone-faced banks of the canal. The Malay prau, half concealed under the arch of the bridge, had not altered its position a quarter of an inch. For a long time Captain Whalley stared down over the parapet, till at last the floating immobility of that beshrouded thing seemed to grow upon him into something inexplicable and alarming. The twilight abandoned the zenith; its reflected gleams left the world below, and the water of the canal seemed to turn into pitch. Captain Whalley crossed it.

The turning to the right, which was his way to his hotel, was only a very few steps farther. He stopped again (all the houses of the seafront were shut up, the quayside was deserted, but for one or two figures of natives walking in the distance) and began to reckon the amount of his bill. So many days in the hotel at so many dollars a day. To count the days he used his fingers: plunging one hand into his pocket, he jingled a few silver coins. All right for three days more; and then, unless something turned up, he must break into the five hundred—Ivy's money—invested in her father. It seemed to him that the first meal coming out of that reserve would choke him—for certain. Reason was of no use. It was a matter of feeling. His feelings had never played him false.

He did not turn to the right. He walked on, as if there still had been a ship in the roadstead to which he could get himself pulled off in the evening. Far away, beyond the houses, on the slope of an indigo promontory closing the view of the quays, the slim column of a factory-chimney smoked quietly straight up into the clear air. A Chinaman, curled down in the stern of one of the half-dozen sampans floating off the end of the jetty, caught sight of a beckoning hand. He jumped up, rolled his pigtail round his head swiftly, tucked in two rapid movements his wide dark trousers high up his yellow thighs, and by a single, noiseless, finlike stir of the oars, sheered the sampan alongside the steps with the ease and precision of a swimming fish.

"*Sofala,*" articulated Captain Whalley from above; and the Chinaman, a new emigrant probably, stared upwards with a tense attention as if waiting to see the queer word fall visibly from the white man's lips. "*Sofala,*" Captain Whalley repeated; and suddenly his heart failed him. He paused. The shores, the islets, the high ground, the low points, were dark: the horizon had grown sombre; and across the eastern sweep of the shore the white obelisk, marking the landing-place of the telegraph-cable, stood like a pale ghost on the beach before the dark spread of uneven roofs, intermingled with palms, of the native town. Captain Whalley began again:

"*Sofala.* Savee *So-fa-la,* John?"

This time the Chinaman made out that bizarre sound, and grunted his assent uncouthly, low down in his bare throat. With the first yellow twinkle of a star that appeared like the head of a pin stabbed deep into the smooth, pale, shimmering fabric of the sky, the edge of a keen chill seemed to cleave through the warm air of the earth. At the moment of stepping into the sampan to go and try for the command of the *Sofala* Captain Whalley shivered a little.

When on his return he landed on the quay again, Venus, like a choice jewel set low on the hem of the sky, cast a faint gold trail behind him upon the roadstead, as level as a floor made of one dark and polished stone. The lofty vaults of the avenues were black—all black overhead—and the porcelain globes on the lamp-posts resembled egg-shaped pearls, gigantic and luminous, displayed in a row whose farther end seemed to sink in the distance, down to the level of his knees. He put his hands behind his back. He would now consider calmly the discretion of it before saying the final word to-morrow. His feet scrunched the gravel loudly—the discretion of it. It would have been easier to appraise had there been a workable alternative. The honesty of it was indubitable: he meant well by the fellow; and periodically his shadow leaped up intense by his side on the trunks of the trees, to lengthen itself, oblique and dim, far over the grass—repeating his stride.

The discretion of it. Was there a choice? He seemed already to have lost something of himself; to have given up to a hungry spectre something of his truth and dignity in order to live. But his life was necessary. Let poverty do its worst in exacting its toll of humiliation. It was certain that Ned Eliott had rendered him, without knowing it, a service for which it would have been impossible to ask. He hoped Ned would not think there had been something underhand in his action. He supposed that now when he heard of it he would understand—or perhaps he would only think Whalley an eccentric old fool. What would have been the good of telling him—any more than of blurting the whole tale to that man Massy? Five hundred pounds ready to invest. Let him make the best of that. Let him wonder. You want a captain—I want a ship. That's enough. B-r-r-r. What a disagreeable impression that empty, dark, echoing steamer had made upon him. . . .

A laid-up steamer was a dead thing and no mistake; a sailing-ship somehow seems always ready to spring into life with the breath of the incorruptible heaven; but a steamer, thought Captain Whalley, with her fires out, without the warm whiffs from below meeting you on her decks, without the hiss of steam, the clangs of iron in her breast—lies there as cold and still and pulseless as a corpse.

In the solitude of the avenue, all black above and lighted below, Captain Whalley, considering the discretion of his course, met, as it were incidentally, the thought of death. He pushed it aside with dislike and contempt. He almost laughed at it; and in the unquenchable vitality of his age only thought with a kind of exultation how little he needed to keep body and soul together. Not a bad investment for the poor woman this solid carcass of her father. And for the rest—in case of anything—the agreement should be clear: the whole five hundred to be paid back to her integrally within three months. Integrally. Every penny. He was not to lose any of her money whatever else had to go—a little dignity—some of his self-respect. He had never before allowed anybody to remain under any sort of false impression as to himself. Well, let that go—for her sake. After all, he had never *said* anything misleading—and Captain Whalley felt himself corrupt to the marrow of his bones. He laughed a little with the intimate scorn of his worldly prudence. Clearly, with a fellow of that sort, and in the peculiar relation they were to stand to each other, it would not have done to blurt out everything. He did not like the fellow. He did not like his spells of fawning loquacity and bursts of resentfulness. In the end—a poor devil. He would not have liked to stand in his shoes. Men were not evil, after all. He did not like his sleek hair, his queer way of standing at right angles, with his nose in the air, and glancing along his shoulder at you. No. On the whole, men were not bad—they were only silly or unhappy.

Captain Whalley had finished considering the discretion of that step—and there was the whole long night before him. In the full light his long beard would glisten like a silver breastplate covering his heart; in the spaces between the lamps his burly figure passed less distinct, loomed very big, wandering, and mysterious. No; there was not much real harm in men: and all the time a shadow marched with him, slanting on his left hand—which in the East is a presage of evil.

"Can you make out the clump of palms yet, Serang?" asked Captain Whalley from his chair on the bridge of the *Sofala* approaching the bar of Batu Beru.

"No, Tuan. By and by see." The old Malay, in a blue dungaree suit, planted on his bony dark feet under the bridge awning, put his hands behind his back and stared ahead out of the innumerable wrinkles at the corners of his eyes.

Captain Whalley sat still, without lifting his head to look for himself. Three years—thirty-six times. He had made these palms thirty-six times from the southward. They would come into view at the proper time. Thank God, the old ship made her courses and distances trip after trip, as correct as clockwork. At last he murmured again—

"In sight yet?"

"The sun makes a very great glare, Tuan."

"Watch well, Serang."

"Ya, Tuan."

A white man had ascended the ladder from the deck noiselessly, and had listened quietly to this short colloquy. Then he stepped out on the bridge and began to walk from end to end, holding up the long cherrywood stem of a pipe. His black hair lay plastered in long lanky wisps across the bald summit of his head; he had a furrowed brow, a yellow complexion, and a thick shapeless nose. A scanty growth of whisker did not conceal the contour of his jaw. His aspect was of brooding care; and sucking at a curved black mouthpiece, he presented such a heavy overhanging profile that even the Serang could not help reflecting sometimes upon the extreme unloveliness of some white men.

Captain Whalley seemed to brace himself up in his chair, but gave no recognition whatever to his presence. The other puffed jets of smoke; then suddenly—

"I could never understand that new mania of yours of having this Malay here for your shadow, partner."

Captain Whalley got up from the chair in all his imposing stature and walked across to the binnacle, holding such an unswerving course that the other had to back away hurriedly, and remained as if intimidated, with the pipe trembling in his hand. "Walk over me now," he muttered in a sort of astounded and discomfited whisper. Then slowly and distinctly he said—

"I—am—not—dirt." And then added defiantly, "As you seem to think."

The Serang jerked out—

"See the palms now, Tuan."

Captain Whalley strode forward to the rail; but his eyes, instead of going straight to the point, with the assured keen glance of a sailor, wandered irresolutely in space, as though he, the discoverer of new routes, had lost his way upon this narrow sea.

Another white man, the mate, came up on the bridge. He was tall, young, lean, with a moustache like a trooper, and something malicious in the eye. He took up a position beside the engineer. Captain Whalley with his back to them, inquired—

"What's on the log?"

"Eighty-five," answered the mate quickly, and nudged the engineer with his elbow.

Captain Whalley's muscular hands squeezed the iron rail with an extraordinary force; his eyes glared with an enormous effort; he knitted his eyebrows, the perspiration fell from under his hat—and in a faint voice he murmured, "Steady her, Serang—when she is on the proper bearing."

The silent Malay stepped back, waited a little, and lifted his arm warningly to the helmsman. The wheel revolved rapidly to meet the swing of the ship. Again the mate nudged the engineer. But Massy turned upon him.

"Mr. Sterne," he said, violently, "let me tell you—as a shipowner—that you are no better than a confounded fool."

· VII ·

Sterne went down smirking and apparently not at all disconcerted, but the engineer Massy remained on the bridge, moving about with uneasy self-assertion. Everybody on board was his inferior—everyone without exception. He paid their wages and found them in their food. They ate more of his bread and pocketed more of his money than they were worth; and they had no care in the world, while he alone had to meet all the difficulties of shipowning. When he contemplated his position in all its menacing entirety, it seemed to him that he had been for years the prey of a band of parasites; and for years he had scowled at everybody connected with the *Sofala* except, perhaps, at the Chinese firemen who served to get her along. Their use was manifest: they were an indispensable part of the machinery of which he was the master.

When he passed along his decks he shouldered those he came across brutally; but the Malay deck hands had learned to dodge out of his way. He had to bring himself to tolerate them because of the necessary manual labour of the ship which must be done. He had to struggle and plan and scheme to keep the *Sofala* afloat—and what did he get for it? Not even enough respect. They could not have given him enough of that if all their thoughts and all their actions had been directed to that end. The vanity of possession, the vainglory of power, had passed away by this time, and there remained only the material embarrassments, the fear of losing that position which had turned out not worth having, and an anxiety of thought which no abject subservience of men could repay.

He walked up and down. The bridge was his own after all. He had paid for it; and with the stem of the pipe in his hand he would stop short at times as if to listen with a profound and concentrated attention to the deadened beat of the engines (his own engines) and the slight grinding of the steering chains upon the continuous low wash of water alongside. But for these sounds, the ship might have been lying as still as if moored to a bank, and as silent as if abandoned by every living soul; only the coast, the low coast of mud and mangroves with the three palms in a bunch at the back, grew slowly more distinct in its long straight line; without a single feature to arrest attention. The native passengers of the *Sofala* lay about on mats under the awnings; the smoke of her funnel seemed the only sign of her life and connected with her gliding motion in a mysterious manner.

Captain Whalley on his feet, with a pair of binoculars in his hand and the little Malay Serang at his elbow, like an old giant attended by a wizened pigmy, was taking her over the shallow water of the bar.

This submarine ridge of mud, scoured by the stream out of the soft bottom of the river and heaped up far out on the hard bottom of the sea, was difficult to get over. The alluvial coast having no distinguishing marks, the bearings of the crossing-place had to be taken from the shape of the mountains inland. The guidance of a form flattened and uneven at the top like a grinder tooth, and of another smooth, saddle-backed summit, had to be searched for within the great unclouded glare that seemed to shift and float like a dry fiery mist, filling the air, ascending from the water, shrouding the distances, scorching to the eye. In this veil of light the near edge of the shore alone stood out almost coal-black with an opaque and motionless solidity. Thirty miles away the serrated range of the interior stretched across the horizon, its outlines and shades of blue, faint and tremulous like a background painted on airy gossamer on the quivering fabric of an impalpable curtain let down to the plain of alluvial soil; and the openings of the estuary appeared, shining white, like bits of silver let into the square pieces snipped clean and sharp out of the body of the land bordered with mangroves.

On the forepart of the bridge the giant and the pigmy muttered to each other frequently in quiet tones. Behind them Massy stood sideways with an expression of disdain and suspense on his face. His globular eyes were perfectly motionless, and he seemed to have forgotten the long pipe he held in his hand.

On the fore-deck below the bridge, steeply roofed with the white slopes of the awnings, a young lascar seaman had clambered outside the rail. He adjusted quickly a broad band of sail canvas under his armpits, and throwing his chest against it, leaned out far over the water. The sleeve of his thin cotton shirt, cut off close to the shoulder, bared his brown arm of full rounded form and with a satiny skin like a woman's. He swung it rigidly with the rotary and menacing action of a slinger: the 14-lb. weight hurtled circling in the air, then suddenly flew ahead as far as the curve of the bow. The wet thin line swished like scratched silk running through the dark fingers of the man, and the plunge of the lead close to the ship's side made a vanishing silvery scar upon the golden glitter; then after an interval the voice of the young Malay uplifted and long-drawn declared the depth of the water in his own language.

"Tiga stengah," he cried after each splash and pause, gathering the line busily for another cast. "Tiga stengah," which means three fathom and a half. For a mile or so from seaward there was a uniform depth of water right up to the bar. "Half-three. Half-three. Half-three,"—and his modulated cry, returned leisurely and monotonous, like the repeated call of a bird, seemed to float away in sunshine and disappear in the spacious silence of the empty sea and of a lifeless shore lying open, north and south, east and west, without the stir of a single cloud-shadow or the whisper of any other voice.

The owner-engineer of the *Sofala* remained very still behind the two seamen of different race, creed, and colour; the European with the time-defying vigour of his old frame, the little Malay, old, too, but slight and shrunken like a withered brown leaf blown by a chance wind under the mighty shadow of the other. Very busy looking forward at the land, they had not a glance to spare; and Massy, glaring at them from behind, seemed to resent their attention to their duty like a personal slight upon himself.

This was unreasonable; but he had lived in his own world of unreasonable resentments for many years. At last, passing his moist palm over the rare lanky wisps of coarse hair on the top of his yellow head, he began to talk slowly.

"A leadsman, you want! I suppose that's your correct mail-boat style. Haven't you enough judgment to tell where you are by looking at the land? Why, before I had been a twelvemonth in the trade I was up to that trick—and I am only an engineer. I can point to you from here where the bar is, and I could tell you besides that you are likely as not to stick her in the mud in about five minutes from now; only you would call it interfering, I suppose. And there's that written agreement of ours, that says I mustn't interfere."

His voice stopped. Captain Whalley, without relaxing the set severity of his features, moved his lips to ask in a quick mumble—

"How near, Serang?"

"Very near now, Tuan," the Malay muttered, rapidly.

"Dead slow," said the Captain aloud in a firm tone.

The Serang snatched at the handle of the telegraph. A gong clanged down below. Massy with a scornful snigger walked off and put his head down the engine-room skylight.

"You may expect some rare fooling with the engines, Jack," he bellowed. The space into which he stared was deep and full of gloom; and the gray gleams of steel down there seemed cool after the intense glare of the sea around the ship. The air, however, came up clammy and hot on his face. A short hoot on which it would have been impossible to put any sort of interpretation came from the bottom cavernously. This was the way in which the second engineer answered his chief.

He was a middle-aged man with an inattentive manner, and apparently wrapped up in such a taciturn concern for his engines that he seemed to have lost the use of speech. When addressed directly his only answer would be a grunt or a hoot, according to the distance. For all the years he had been in the *Sofala* he had never been known to exchange as much as a frank Good-morning with any of his shipmates. He did not seem aware that men came and went in the world; he did not seem to see them at all. Indeed he never recognized his shipmates on shore. At table (the four white men of the *Sofala* messed together) he sat looking into his plate dispassionately, but at the end of the meal would jump up and bolt down below as if a sudden thought had impelled him to rush and see whether somebody had not stolen the engines while he dined. In port at the end of the trip he went ashore regularly, but no one knew where he spent his evenings or in what manner. The local coasting fleet had preserved a wild and incoherent tale of his infatuation for the wife of a sergeant in an Irish infantry regiment. The regiment, however, had done its turn of garrison duty there ages before, and was gone somewhere to the other side of the earth, out of men's knowledge. Twice or perhaps three times in the course of the year he would take too much to drink. On these occasions he would return on board at an earlier hour than usual; run across the deck balancing himself with his spread arms like a tightrope walker; and locking the door of his cabin, he would converse and argue with himself the livelong night in an amazing variety of tones; storm, sneer, and whine with an inexhaustible persistence. Massy in his berth next door, raising himself on his elbow, would discover that his second remembered the name of every white man that had passed through the *Sofala* for years and years back. He remembered the names of men that had died, that had gone home, that had gone to America; he remembered in his cups the names of men whose connection with the ship had been so short that Massy had almost forgotten its circumstances and could barely recall their faces. The inebriated voice on the other side of the bulkhead commented upon them all with an extraordinary and ingenious venom of scandalous inventions. It seems they had all offended him in some way, and in return he had found them all out. He muttered darkly; he laughed sardonically; he crushed them one after another; but of his chief, Massy, he babbled with an envious and naïve admiration. Clever scoundrel! Don't meet the likes of him every day. Just look at him. Ha! Great! Ship of his own. Wouldn't catch *him* going wrong. No fear—the beast! And Massy, after listening with a gratified smile to these artless tributes to his greatness, would begin to shout, thumping at the bulkhead with both fists—

"Shut up, you lunatic! Won't you let me go to sleep, you fool!"

But a half smile of pride lingered on his lips; outside the solitary lascar told off for night duty in harbour, perhaps a youth fresh from a forest village, would stand motionless in the shadows of the deck listening to the endless drunken gabble. His heart would be thumping with breathless awe of white men: the arbitrary and obstinate men who pursue inflexibly their incomprehensible purposes—beings with weird intonations in the voice, moved by unaccountable feelings, actuated by inscrutable motives.

· VIII ·

For a while after his second's answering hoot Massy hung over the engine-room gloomily. Captain Whalley who, by the power of five hundred pounds, had kept his command for three years, might have been suspected of never having seen that coast before. He seemed unable to put down his glasses, as though they had been glued under his contracted eyebrows. This settled frown gave to his face an air of invincible and just severity; but his raised elbow trembled slightly, and the perspiration poured from under his hat as if a second sun had suddenly blazed up at the zenith by the side of the ardent still globe already there, in whose blinding white heat the earth whirled and shone like a mote of dust.

From time to time, still holding up his glasses, he raised his other hand to wipe his streaming face. The drops rolled down his cheeks, fell like rain upon the white hairs of his beard, and brusquely, as if guided by an uncontrollable and anxious impulse, his arm reached out to the stand of the engine-room telegraph.

The gong clanged down below. The balanced vibration of the dead-slow speed ceased together with every sound and tremor in the ship, as if the great stillness that reigned upon the coast had stolen in through her sides of iron and taken possession of her innermost recesses. The illusion of perfect immobility seemed to fall upon her from the luminous blue dome without a stain arching over a flat sea without a stir. The faint breeze she had made for herself expired, as if all at once the air had become too thick to budge; even the slight hiss of the water on her stem died out. The narrow, long hull, carrying its way without a ripple, seemed to approach the shoal water of the bar by stealth. The plunge of the lead with the mournful, mechanical cry of the lascar came at longer and longer intervals; and the men on her bridge seemed to hold their breath. The Malay at the helm looked fixedly at the compass card, the Captain and the Serang stared at the coast.

Massy had left the skylight, and, walking flat-footed, had returned softly to the very spot on the bridge he had occupied before. A slow, lingering grin exposed his set of big white teeth: they gleamed evenly in the shade of the awning like the keyboard of a piano in a dusky room.

At last, pretending to talk to himself in excessive astonishment, he said not very loud—

"Stop the engines now. What next, I wonder?"

He waited, stooping from the shoulders, his head bowed, his glance oblique. Then raising his voice a shade—

"If I dared make an absurd remark I would say that you haven't the stomach to. . . ."

But a yelling spirit of excitement, like some frantic soul wandering unsuspected in the vast stillness of the coast, had seized upon the body of the lascar at the lead. The languid monotony of his sing-song changed to a swift, sharp clamour. The weight flew after a single whirr, the line whistled, splash followed splash in haste. The water had shoaled, and the man, instead of the drowsy tale of fathoms, was calling out the soundings in feet.

"Fifteen feet. Fifteen, fifteen! Fourteen, fourteen. . . ."

Captain Whalley lowered the arm holding the glasses. It descended slowly as if by its own weight; no other part of his towering body stirred; and the swift cries with their eager warning note passed him by as though he had been deaf.

Massy, very still, and turning an attentive ear, had fastened his eyes upon the silvery, close-cropped back of the steady old head. The ship herself seemed to be arrested but for the gradual decrease of depth under her keel.

"Thirteen feet . . . Thirteen! Twelve!" cried the leadsman anxiously below the bridge. And suddenly the barefooted Serang stepped away noiselessly to steal a glance over the side.

Narrow of shoulder, in a suit of faded blue cotton, an old gray felt hat rammed down on his head, with a hollow in the nape of his dark neck, and with his slender limbs, he appeared from the back no bigger than a boy of fourteen. There was a childlike impulsiveness in the curiosity with which he watched the spread of the voluminous, yellowish convolutions rolling up from below to the surface of the blue water like massive clouds driving slowly upwards on the unfathomable sky. He was not startled at the sight in the least. It was not doubt, but the certitude that the keel of the *Sofala* must be stirring the mud now, which made him peep over the side.

His peering eyes, set aslant in a face of the Chinese type, a little old face, immovable, as if carved in old brown oak, had informed him long before that the ship was not headed at the bar properly. Paid off from the *Fair Maid,* together with the rest of the crew, after the completion of the sale, he had hung, in his faded blue suit and floppy gray hat, about the doors of the Harbour Office, till one day, seeing Captain Whalley coming along to get a crew for the *Sofala,* he had put himself quietly in the way, with his bare feet in the dust and an upward mute glance. The eyes of his old commander had fallen on him favourably—it must have been an auspicious day—and in less than half an hour the white men in the "Ofiss" had written his name on a document as Serang of the fire-ship *Sofala*. Since that time he had repeatedly looked at that estuary, upon that coast, from this bridge and from this side of the bar. The record of the visual world fell through his eyes upon his unspeculating mind as on a sensitized plate through the lens of a camera. His knowledge was absolute and precise; nevertheless, had he been asked his opinion, and especially if questioned in the downright, alarming manner of white men, he would have displayed the hesitation of ignorance. He was certain of his facts—but such a certitude counted for little against the doubt what answer would be pleasing. Fifty years ago, in a jungle village, and before he was a day old, his father (who died without ever seeing a white face) had had his nativity cast by a man of skill and wisdom in astrology, because in the arrangement of the stars may be read the last word of human destiny. His destiny had been to thrive by the favour of various white men on the sea. He had swept the decks of ships, had tended their helms, had minded their stores, had risen at last to be a Serang; and his placid mind had remained as incapable of penetrating the simplest motives of those he served as they themselves were incapable of detecting through the crust of the earth the secret nature of its heart, which may be fire or may be stone. But he had no doubt whatever that the *Sofala* was out of the proper track for crossing the bar at Batu Beru.

It was a slight error. The ship could not have been more than twice her own length too far to the northward; and a white man at a loss for a cause (since it was impossible to suspect Captain Whalley of blundering ignorance, of want of skill, or of neglect) would have been inclined to doubt the testimony of his senses. It was some such feeling that kept Massy motionless, with his teeth laid bare by an anxious grin. Not so the Serang. He was not troubled by any intellectual mistrust of his senses. If his captain chose to stir the mud it was well. He had known in his life white men indulge in outbreaks equally strange. He was only genuinely interested to see what would come of it. At last, apparently satisfied, he stepped back from the rail.

He had made no sound: Captain Whalley, however, seemed to have observed the movements of his Serang. Holding his head rigidly, he asked with a mere stir of his lips—

"Going ahead still, Serang?"

"Still going a little, Tuan," answered the Malay. Then added casually, "She is over."

The lead confirmed his words; the depth of water increased at every cast, and the soul of excitement departed suddenly from the lascar swung in the canvas belt over the *Sofala's* side. Captain Whalley ordered the lead in, set the engines ahead without haste, and averting his eyes from the coast directed the Serang to keep a course for the middle of the entrance.

Massy brought the palm of his hand with a loud smack against his thigh.

"You grazed on the bar. Just look astern and see if you didn't. Look at the track she left. You can see it plainly. Upon my soul, I thought you would! What made you do that? What on earth made you do that? I believe you are trying to scare me."

He talked slowly, as it were circumspectly, keeping his prominent black eyes on his captain. There was also a slight plaintive note in his rising choler, for, primarily, it was the clear sense of a wrong suffered undeservedly that made him hate the man who, for a beggarly five hundred pounds, claimed a sixth part of the profits under the three years' agreement. Whenever his resentment got the better of the awe the person of Captain Whalley inspired he would positively whimper with fury.

"You don't know what to invent to plague my life out of me. I would not have thought that a man of your sort would condescend. . . ."

He paused, half hopefully, half timidly, whenever Captain Whalley made the slightest movement in the deck-chair, as though expecting to be conciliated by a soft speech or else rushed upon and hunted off the bridge.

"I am puzzled," he went on again, with the watchful, unsmiling baring of his big teeth. "I don't know what to think. I do believe you are trying to frighten me. You very nearly planted her on the bar for at least twelve hours, besides getting the engines choked with mud. Ships can't afford to lose twelve hours on a trip nowadays—as you ought to know very well, and do know very well to be sure, only. . . ."

His slow volubility, the sideways cranings of his neck, the black glances out of the very corners of his eyes, left Captain Whalley unmoved. He looked at the deck with a severe frown. Massy waited for some little time, then began to threaten plaintively.

"You think you've got me bound hand and foot in that agreement. You think you can torment me in any way you please. Ah! But remember it has another six weeks to run yet. There's time for me to dismiss you before the three years are out. You will do yet something that will give me the chance to dismiss you, and make you wait a twelvemonth for your money before you can take yourself off and pull out your five hundred, and leave me without a penny to get the new boilers for her. You gloat over that idea—don't you? I do believe you sit here gloating. It's as if I had sold my soul for five hundred pounds to be everlastingly damned in the end. . . ."

He paused, without apparent exasperation, then continued evenly—

". . . With the boilers worn out and the survey hanging over my head. Captain Whalley— Captain Whalley, I say, what do you do with your money? You must have stacks of money somewhere—a man like you must. It stands to reason. I am not a fool, you know, Captain Whalley—partner."

Again he paused, as though he had done for good. He passed his tongue over his lips, gave a backward glance at the Serang conning the ship with quiet whispers and slight signs of the hand. The wash of the propeller sent a swift ripple, crested with dark froth, upon a long flat spit of black slime. The *Sofala* had entered the river; the trail she had stirred up over the bar was a mile astern of her now, out of sight, had disappeared utterly; and the smooth, empty sea along the coast was left behind in the glittering desolation of sunshine. On each side of her, low down, the growth of sombre twisted mangroves covered the semi-liquid banks; and Massy continued in his old tone, with an abrupt start, as if his speech had been ground out of him, like the tune of a music-box, by turning a handle.

"Though if anybody ever got the best of me, it is you. I don't mind saying this. I've said it—there! What more can you want? Isn't that enough for your pride, Captain Whalley? You got over me from the first. It's all of a piece, when I look back at it. You allowed me to insert that clause about intemperance without saying anything, only looking very sick when I made a point of it going in black on white. How could I tell what was wrong about you? There's generally something wrong somewhere. And, lo and behold! when you come on board it turns out that you've been in the habit of drinking nothing but water for years and years."

His dogmatic, reproachful whine stopped. He brooded profoundly, after the manner of craft and unintelligent men. It seemed inconceivable that Captain Whalley should not laugh at the expression of disgust that overspread the heavy, yellow countenance. But Captain Whalley never raised his eyes—sitting in his arm-chair, outraged, dignified, and motionless.

"Much good it was to me," Massy remonstrated, monotonously, "to insert a clause of dismissal for intemperance against a man who drinks nothing but water. And you looked so upset, too, when I read my draft in the lawyer's office that morning. Captain Whalley—you looked so crestfallen, that I made sure I had gone home on your weak spot. A shipowner can't be too careful as to the sort of skipper he gets. You must have been laughing at me in your sleeve all the blessed time. . . . Eh? What were you going to say?"

Captain Whalley had only shuffled his feet slightly. A dull animosity became apparent in Massy's sideways stare.

"But recollect that there are other grounds of dismissal. There's habitual carelessness, amounting to incompetence—there's gross and persistent neglect of duty. I am not quite as big a fool as you try to make me out to be. You have been careless of late—leaving everything to that Serang. Why! I've seen you letting that old fool of a Malay take bearings for you, as if you were too big to attend to your work yourself. And what do you call that silly touch-and-go manner in which you took the ship over the bar just now? You expect me to put up with that."

Leaning on his elbow against the ladder abaft the bridge, Sterne, the mate, tried to hear, blinking the while from the distance at the second engineer, who had come up for a moment, and stood in the engine-room companion. Wiping his hands on a bunch of cotton waste, he looked about with indifference to the right and left at the river banks slipping astern of the *Sofala* steadily.

Massy turned full at the chair. The character of his whine became again threatening.

"Take care. I may yet dismiss you and freeze to your money for a year. I may. . . ."

But before the silent, rigid immobility of the man whose money had come in the nick of time to save him from utter ruin, his voice died out in his throat.

"Not that I want you to go," he resumed after a silence, and in an absurdly insinuating tone. "I want nothing better than to be friends and renew the agreement, if you will consent to find another couple of hundred to help with the new boilers, Captain Whalley. I've told you before. She must have new boilers; you know it as well as I do. Have you thought this over?"

He waited. The slender stem of the pipe with its bulky lump of a bowl at the end hung down from his thick lips. It had gone out. Suddenly he took it from between his teeth and wrung his hands slightly.

"Don't you believe me?" He thrust the pipe bowl into the pocket of his shiny black jacket.

"It's like dealing with the devil," he said. "Why don't you speak? At first you were so high and mighty with me I hardly dared to creep about my own deck. Now I can't get a word from you. You don't seem to see me at all. What does it mean? Upon my soul, you terrify me with this deaf and dumb trick. What's going on in that head of yours? What are you plotting against me there so hard that you can't say a word? You will never make me believe that you—you—don't know where to lay your hands on a couple of hundred. You have made me curse the day I was born. . . ."

"Mr. Massy," said Captain Whalley, suddenly, without stirring.

The engineer started violently.

"If that is so I can only beg you to forgive me."

"Starboard," muttered the Serang to the helmsman; and the *Sofala* began to swing round the bend into the second reach.

"Ough!" Massy shuddered. "You make my blood run cold. What made you come here? What made you come aboard that evening all of a sudden, with your high talk and your money—tempting me? I always wondered what was your motive. You fastened yourself on me to have easy times and grow fat on my life blood, I tell you. Was that it? I believe you are the greatest miser in the world, or else why. . . ."

"No. I am only poor," interrupted Captain Whalley, stonily.

"Steady," murmured the Serang. Massy turned away with his chin on his shoulder.

"I don't believe it," he said in his dogmatic tone. Captain Whalley made no movement. "There you sit like a gorged vulture—exactly like a vulture."

He embraced the middle of the reach and both the banks in one blank, unseeing, circular glance, and left the bridge slowly.

· IX ·

On turning to descend Massy perceived the head of Sterne the mate loitering, with his sly, confident smile, his red moustaches and blinking eyes, at the foot of the ladder.

Sterne had been a junior in one of the larger shipping concerns before joining the *Sofala*. He had thrown up his berth, he said, "on general principles." The promotion in the employ was very slow, he complained, and he thought it was time for him to try and get on a bit in the world. It seemed as though nobody would ever die or leave the firm; they all stuck fast in their berths till they got mildewed; he was tired of waiting; and he feared that when a vacancy did occur the best servants were by no means sure of being treated fairly. Besides, the captain he had to serve under—Captain Provost—was an unaccountable sort of man and had taken a dislike to him for some reason or other. For doing rather more than his bare duty as likely as not. When he had done anything wrong he could take a talking-to, like a man; but he expected to be treated like a man, too, and not to be addressed invariably as though he were a dog. He had asked Captain Provost plump and plain to tell him where he was at fault, and Captain Provost, in a most scornful way, had told him that he was a perfect officer, and that if he disliked the way he was being spoken to there was the gangway—he could take himself off ashore at once. But everybody knew what sort of man Captain Provost was. It was no use appealing to the office. Captain Provost had too much influence in the employ. All the same, they had to give him a good character. He made bold to say there was nothing in the world against him, and, as he had happened to hear that the mate of the *Sofala* had been taken to the hospital that morning with a sunstroke, he thought there would be no harm in seeing whether he would not do. . . .

He had come to Captain Whalley freshly shaved, red-faced, thin-flanked, throwing out his lean chest; and had recited his little tale with an open and manly assurance. Now and then his eyelids quivered slightly, his hand would steal up to the end of the flaming moustache; his eyebrows were straight, furry, of a chestnut colour, and the directness of his gaze seemed to tremble on the verge of impudence. Captain Whalley had engaged him temporarily; then, the other man having been ordered home by the doctors, Sterne had remained for the next trip, and then the next. He had now attained permanency, and the performance of his duties was marked by an air of serious, single-minded application. Directly he was spoken to, he began to smile attentively, with a great deference expressed in his whole attitude; but there was in the rapid winking which went on all the time something quizzical, as though he had possessed the secret of some universal joke cheating all creation and impenetrable to other mortals.

Grave and smiling he watched Massy come down step by step; when the chief engineer had reached the deck he swung about, and they found themselves face to face. Matched as to height and utterly dissimilar, they confronted each other as if there had been something between them—something else than the bright strip of sunlight that, falling through the wide lacing of two awnings, cut crosswise the narrow planking of the deck and separated their feet as it were a stream;

something profound and subtle and incalculable, like an unexpressed understanding, a secret mistrust, or some sort of fear.

At last Sterne, blinking his deep-set eyes and sticking forward his scraped, clean-cut chin, as crimson as the rest of his face, murmured—

"You've seen? He grazed! You've seen?"

Massy, contemptuous, and without raising his yellow, fleshy countenance, replied in the same pitch—

"Maybe. But if it had been you we would have been stuck fast in the mud."

"Pardon me, Mr. Massy. I beg to deny it. Of course a shipowner may say what he jolly well pleases on his own deck. That's all right; but I beg to. . . ."

"Get out of my way!"

The other had a slight start, the impulse of suppressed indignation perhaps, but held his ground. Massy's downward glance wandered right and left, as though the deck all round Sterne had been bestrewn with eggs that must not be broken, and he had looked irritably for places where he could set his feet in flight. In the end he, too, did not move, though there was plenty of room to pass on.

"I heard you say up there," went on the mate—"and a very just remark it was, too—that there's always something wrong. . . ."

"Eavesdropping is what's wrong with *you*, Mr. Sterne."

"Now, if you would only listen to me for a moment, Mr. Massy, sir, I could. . . ."

"You are a sneak," interrupted Massy in a great hurry, and even managed to get so far as to repeat, "a common sneak," before the mate had broken in argumentatively—

"Now, sir, what is it you want? You want. . . ."

"I want—I want," stammered Massy, infuriated and astonished—"I want? How do you know that I want anything? How dare you? . . . What do you mean? . . . What are you after—you. . . ."

"Promotion." Sterne silenced him with candid bravado. The engineer's round soft cheeks quivered still, but he said quietly enough—

"You are only worrying my head off," and Sterne met him with a confident little smile.

"A chap in business I know (well up in the world he is now) used to tell me that this was the proper way. 'Always push on to the front,' he would say. 'Keep yourself well before your boss. Interfere whenever you get a chance. Show him what you know. Worry him into seeing you.' That was his advice. Now I know no other boss than you here. You are the owner, and no one else counts for *that* much in my eyes. See, Mr. Massy? I want to get on. I make no secret of it that I am one of the sort that means to get on. These are the men to make use of, sir. You haven't arrived at the top of the tree, sir, without finding that out—I daresay."

"Worry your boss in order to get on," repeated Massy, as if awestruck by the irreverent originality of the idea. "I shouldn't wonder if this was just what the Blue Anchor people kicked you out of their employ for. Is that what you call getting on? You shall get on in the same way here if you aren't careful—I can promise you."

At this Sterne hung his head, thoughtful, perplexed, winking hard at the deck. All his attempts to enter into confidential relations with his owner had led of late to nothing better than these dark threats of dismissal; and a threat of dismissal would check him at once into a hesitating silence as though he were not sure that the proper time for defying it had come. On this occasion he seemed to have lost his tongue for a moment, and Massy, getting in motion, heavily passed him by with an abortive attempt at shouldering. Sterne defeated it by stepping aside. He turned then swiftly, opening his mouth very wide as if to shout something after the engineer, but seemed to think better of it.

Always—as he was ready to confess—on the lookout for an opening to get on, it had become an instinct with him to watch the conduct of his immediate superiors for something "that one could lay hold of." It was his belief that no skipper in the world would keep his command for a day if only the owners could be "made to know." This romantic and naïve theory had led him into trouble more than once, but he remained incorrigible; and his character was so instinctively disloyal that whenever he joined a ship the intention of ousting his commander out of the berth and taking his place was always present at the back of his head, as a matter of course. It filled the leisure of his waking hours with the reveries of careful plans and compromising discoveries—the dreams of his sleep with images of lucky turns and favourable accidents. Skippers had been known to sicken and die at sea, than

which nothing could be better to give a smart mate a chance of showing what he's made of. They also would tumble overboard sometimes:
he had heard of one or two such cases. Others again. . . . But, as it
were constitutionally, he was faithful to the belief that the conduct of
no single one of them would stand the test of careful watching by a
man who "knew what's what" and who kept his eyes "skinned pretty
well" all the time.

After he had gained a permanent footing on board the *Sofala* he
allowed his perennial hope to rise high. To begin with, it was a great
advantage to have an old man for captain: the sort of man besides
who in the nature of things was likely to give up the job before long
from one cause or another. Sterne was greatly chagrined, however, to
notice that he did not seem anyway near being past his work yet. Still,
these old men go to pieces all at once sometimes. Then there was the
owner-engineer close at hand to be impressed by his zeal and steadiness. Sterne never for a moment doubted the obvious nature of his
own merits (he was really an excellent officer); only, nowadays, professional merit alone does not take a man along fast enough. A chap must
have some push in him, and must keep his wits at work, too, to help
him forward. He made up his mind to inherit the charge of this
steamer if it was to be done at all; not indeed estimating the command
of the *Sofala* as a very great catch, but for the reason that, out East
especially, to make a start is everything, and one command leads to
another.

He began by promising himself to behave with great circumspection; Massy's sombre and fantastic humours intimidated him as being
outside one's usual sea experience; but he was quite intelligent enough
to realize almost from the first that he was there in the presence of
an exceptional situation. His peculiar prying imagination penetrated it
quickly; the feeling that there was in it an element which eluded his
grasp exasperated his impatience to get on. And so one trip came to
an end, then another, and he had begun his third before he saw an
opening by which he could step in with any sort of effect. It had all
been very queer and very obscure; something had been going on near
him, as if separated by a chasm from the common life and the working
routine of the ship, which was exactly like the life and the routine of
any other coasting steamer of that class.

Then one day he made his discovery.

It came to him after all these weeks of watchful observation and puzzled surmises, suddenly, like the long-sought solution of a riddle that suggests itself to the mind in a flash. Not with the same authority, however. Great heavens! Could it be that? And after remaining thunderstruck for a few seconds he tried to shake it off with self-contumely, as though it had been the product of an unhealthy bias toward the Incredible, the Inexplicable, the Unheard-of—the Mad!

This—the illuminating moment—had occurred the trip before, on the return passage. They had just left a place of call on the mainland called Pangu; they were steaming straight out of a bay. To the east a massive headland closed the view, with the tilted edges of the rocky strata showing through its ragged clothing of rank bushes and thorny creepers. The wind had begun to sing in the rigging; the sea along the coast, green and as if swollen a little above the line of the horizon, seemed to pour itself over, time after time, with a slow and thundering fall, into the shadow of the leeward cape; and across the wide opening the nearest of a group of small islands stood enveloped in the hazy yellow light of a breezy sunrise; still farther out the hummocky tops of other islets peeped out motionless above the water of the channels between, scoured tumultuously by the breeze.

The usual track of the *Sofala* both going and returning on every trip led her for a few miles along this reef-infested region. She followed a broad lane of water, dropping astern, one after another, these crumbs of the earth's crust resembling a squadron of dismasted hulks run in disorder upon a foul ground of rocks and shoals. Some of these fragments of land appeared, indeed, no bigger than a stranded ship; others, quite flat, lay awash like anchored rafts, like ponderous, black rafts of stone; several, heavily timbered and round at the base, emerged in squat domes of deep green foliage that shuddered darkly all over to the flying touch of cloud shadows driven by the sudden gusts of the squally season. The thunderstorms of the coast broke frequently over that cluster; it turned then shadowy in its whole extent; it turned more dark, and as if more still in the play of fire; as if more impenetrably silent in the peals of thunder; its blurred shapes vanished—dissolving utterly at times in the thick rain—to reappear clear-cut and black in the stormy light against the gray sheet of the cloud—scattered on the

slaty round table of the sea. Unscathed by storms, resisting the work
of years, unfretted by the strife of the world, there it lay unchanged
as on that day, four hundred years ago, when first beheld by Western
eyes from the deck of a high-pooped caravel.

It was one of those secluded spots that may be found on the busy
sea, as on land you come sometimes upon the clustered houses of a
hamlet untouched by men's restlessness, untouched by their need, by
their thought, and as if forgotten by time itself. The lives of uncounted
generations had passed it by, and the multitudes of seafowl, urging
their way from all the points of the horizon to sleep on the outer rocks
of the group, unrolled the converging evolutions of their flight in long,
sombre streamers upon the glow of the sky. The palpitating cloud of
their wings soared and stooped over the pinnacles of the rocks, over
the rocks slender like spires, squat like martello towers; over the pyra-
midal heaps like fallen ruins, over the lines of bald boulders showing
like a wall of stones battered to pieces and scorched by lightning—with the sleepy, clear glimmer of water in every breach. The
noise of their continuous and violent screaming filled the air.

This great noise would meet the *Sofala* coming up from Batu Beru;
it would meet her on quiet evenings, a pitiless and savage clamour
enfeebled by distance, the clamour of seabirds settling to rest, and
struggling for a footing at the end of the day. No one noticed it especially on board; it was the voice of their ship's unerring landfall, ending the steady stretch of a hundred miles. She had made good her
course, she had run her distance till the punctual islets began to
emerge one by one, the points of rocks, the hummocks of earth . . .
and the cloud of birds hovered—the restless cloud emitting a strident
and cruel uproar, the sound of the familiar scene, the living part of
the broken land beneath, of the outspread sea, and of the high sky
without a flaw.

But when the *Sofala* happened to close with the land after sunset she
would find everything very still there under the mantle of the night. All
would be still, dumb, almost invisible—but for the blotting out of the
low constellations occulted in turns behind the vague masses of the
islets whose true outlines eluded the eye amongst the dark spaces of
the heaven: and the ship's three lights, resembling three stars—the
red and the green with the white above—her three lights, like three

companion stars wandering on the earth, held their unswerving course for the passage at the southern end of the group. Sometimes there were human eyes open to watch them come nearer, travelling smoothly in the sombre void; the eyes of a naked fisherman in his canoe floating over a reef. He thought drowsily: "Ha! The fire-ship that once in every moon goes in and comes out of Pangu Bay." More he did not know of her. And just as he had detected the faint rhythm of the propeller beating the calm water a mile and half away, the time would come for the *Sofala* to alter her course, the lights would swing off him their triple beam—and disappear.

A few miserable, half-naked families, a sort of outcast tribe of long-haired, lean, and wild-eyed people, strove for their living in this lonely wilderness of islets, lying like an abandoned outwork of the land at the gates of the bay. Within the knots and loops of the rocks the water rested more transparent than crystal under their crooked and leaky canoes, scooped out of the trunk of a tree: the forms of the bottom undulated slightly to the dip of a paddle; and the men seemed to hang in the air, they seemed to hang enclosed within the fibres of a dark, sodden log, fishing patiently in a strange, unsteady, pellucid, green air above the shoals.

Their bodies stalked brown and emaciated as if dried up in the sunshine; their lives ran out silently; the homes where they were born, went to rest, and died—flimsy sheds of rushes and coarse grass eked out with a few ragged mats—were hidden out of sight from the open sea. No glow of their household fires ever kindled for a seaman a red spark upon the blind night of the group: and the calms of the coast, the flaming long calms of the equator, the unbreathing, concentrated calms like the deep introspection of a passionate nature, brooded aw-fully for days and weeks together over the unchangeable inheritance of their children; till at last the stones, hot like live embers, scorched the naked sole, till the water clung warm, and sickly, and as if thick-ened about the legs of lean men with girded loins, wading thigh-deep in the pale blaze of the shallows. And it would happen now and then that the *Sofala,* through some delay in one of the ports of call, would heave in sight making for Pangu Bay as late as noonday.

Only a blurring cloud at first, the thin mist of her smoke would arise mysteriously from an empty point on the clear line of sea and sky. The taciturn fishermen within the reefs would extend their lean arms toward the offing; and the brown figures stooping on the tiny beaches, the brown figures of men, women, and children grubbing in the sand in search of turtles' eggs, would rise up, crooked elbow aloft and hand over the eyes, to watch this monthly apparition glide straight on, swerve off—and go by. Their ears caught the panting of that ship; their eyes followed her till she passed between the two capes of the mainland going at full speed as though she hoped to make her way unchecked into the very bosom of the earth.

On such days the luminous sea would give no sign of the dangers lurking on both sides of her path. Everything remained still, crushed by the overwhelming power of the light; and the whole group, opaque in the sunshine,—the rocks resembling pinnacles, the rocks resembling spires, the rocks resembling ruins; the forms of islets resembling bee-hives, resembling mole-hills; the islets recalling the shapes of hay-stacks, the contours of ivy-clad towers—would stand reflected together upside down in the unwrinkled water, like carved toys of ebony disposed on the silvered plate-glass of a mirror.

The first touch of blowing weather would envelop the whole at once in the spume of the windward breakers, as if in a sudden cloudlike burst of steam; and the clear water seemed fairly to boil in all the passages. The provoked sea outlined exactly in a design of angry foam the wide base of the group; the submerged level of broken waste and refuse left over from the building of the coast near by, projecting its dangerous spurs, all awash, far into the channel, and bristling with wicked long spits often a mile long: with deadly spits made of froth and stones.

And even nothing more than a brisk breeze—as on that morning, the voyage before, when the *Sofala* left Pangu Bay early, and Mr. Sterne's discovery was to blossom out like a flower of incredible and evil aspect from the tiny seed of instinctive suspicion—even such a breeze had enough strength to tear the placid mask from the face of the sea. To Sterne, gazing with indifference, it had been like a revelation to behold for the first time the dangers marked by the hissing livid patches on the water as distinctly as on the engraved paper of a chart. It came into his mind that this was the sort of day most favourable for a stranger attempting the passage: a clear day, just windy enough for the sea to break on every ledge, buoying, as it were, the channel plainly to the sight; whereas during a calm you had nothing to depend on but the compass and the practised judgment of your eye. And yet the successive captains of the *Sofala* had had to take her through at night more than once. Nowadays you could not afford to throw away six or seven hours of a steamer's time. That you couldn't. But then use is everything, and with proper care. . . . The channel was broad and safe enough; the main point was to hit upon the entrance correctly in the dark—for if a man got himself involved in that stretch of broken water over yonder he would never get out with a whole ship—if he ever got out at all.

This was Sterne's last train of thought independent of the great discovery. He had just seen to the securing of the anchor, and had remained forward idling away a moment or two. The captain was in charge on the bridge. With a slight yawn he had turned away from his survey of the sea and had leaned his shoulders against the fish davit.

These, properly speaking, were the very last moments of ease he was to know on board the *Sofala.* All the instants that came after were to be pregnant with purpose and intolerable with perplexity. No more idle, random thoughts; the discovery would put them on the rack, till sometimes he wished to goodness he had been fool enough not to make it at all. And yet, if his chance to get on rested on the discovery of "something wrong," he could not have hoped for a greater stroke of luck.

· X ·

The knowledge was too disturbing, really. There was "something wrong" with a vengeance, and the moral certitude of it was at first simply frightful to contemplate. Sterne had been looking aft in a mood so idle, that for once he was thinking no harm of any one. His captain on the bridge presented himself naturally to his sight. How insignificant, how casual was the thought that had started the train of discovery—like an accidental spark that suffices to ignite the charge of a tremendous mine!

Caught under by the breeze, the awnings of the foredeck bellied upwards and collapsed slowly, and above their heavy flapping the gray stuff of Captain Whalley's roomy coat fluttered incessantly around his arms and trunk. He faced the wind in full light, with his great silvery beard blown forcibly against his chest; the eyebrows overhung heavily the shadows whence his glance appeared to be staring ahead piercingly. Sterne could just detect the twin gleam of the whites shifting under the shaggy arches of the brow. At short range these eyes, for all the man's affable manner, seemed to look you through and through. Sterne never could defend himself from that feeling when he had occasion to speak with his captain. He did not like it. What a big heavy man he appeared up there, with that little shrimp of a Serang in close attendance—as was usual in this extraordinary steamer! Confounded absurd custom that. He resented it. Surely the old fellow could have looked after his ship without that loafing native at his elbow. Sterne wriggled his shoulders with disgust. What was it? Indolence or what?

That old skipper must have been growing lazy for years. They all grew lazy out East here (Sterne was very conscious of his own unimpaired activity); they got slack all over. But he towered very erect on the bridge; and quite low by his side, as you see a small child looking over the edge of a table, the battered soft hat and the brown face of the Serang peeped over the white canvas screen of the rail.

No doubt the Malay was standing back, nearer to the wheel; but the great disparity of size in close association amused Sterne like the observation of a bizarre fact in nature. There were as queer fish out of the sea as any in it.

He saw Captain Whalley turn his head quickly to speak to his Serang; the wind whipped the whole white mass of the beard sideways. He would be directing the chap to look at the compass for him, or what not. Of course. Too much trouble to step over and see for himself. Sterne's scorn for that bodily indolence which overtakes white men in the East increased on reflection. Some of them would be utterly lost if they hadn't all these natives at their beck and call; they grew perfectly shameless about it, too. He was not of that sort, thank God! It wasn't in him to make himself dependent for his work on any shrivelled-up little Malay like that. As if one could ever trust a silly native for anything in the world! But that fine old man thought differently, it seems. There they were together, never far apart; a pair of them, recalling to the mind an old whale attended by a little pilot-fish.

The fancifulness of the comparison made him smile. A whale with an inseparable pilot-fish! That's what the old man looked like; for it could not be said he looked like a shark, though Mr. Massy had called him that very name. But Mr. Massy did not mind what he said in his savage fits. Sterne smiled to himself—and gradually the ideas evoked by the sound, by the imagined shape of the word pilot-fish, the ideas of aid, of guidance needed and received, came uppermost in his mind: the word pilot awakened the idea of trust, of dependence, the idea of the welcome, clear-eyed help brought to the seaman groping for the land in the dark: groping blindly in fogs: feeling his way in the thick weather of the gales that, filling the air with a salt mist blown up from the sea, contract the range of sight on all sides to a shrunken horizon that seems within reach of the hand.

A pilot sees better than a stranger, because his local knowledge, like a sharper vision, completes the shapes of things hurriedly glimpsed; penetrates the veils of mist spread over the land by the storms of the sea; defines with certitude the outlines of a coast lying under the pall of fog, the forms of landmarks half buried in a starless night as in a shallow grave. He recognizes because he already knows. It is not to his far-reaching eye but to his more extensive knowledge that the pilot looks for certitude; for this certitude of the ship's position on which may depend a man's good fame and the peace of his conscience, the justification of the trust deposited in his hands, with his own life, too, which is seldom wholly his to throw away, and the humble lives of others rooted in distant affections, perhaps, and made as weighty as the lives of kings by the burden of the awaiting mystery. The pilot's knowledge brings relief and certitude to the commander of a ship; the Serang, however, in his fanciful suggestion of a pilot-fish attending a whale, could not in any way be credited with a superior knowledge. Why should he have it? These two men had come on that run together—the white and the brown—on the same day: and of course a white man would learn more in a week than the best native would in a month. He was made to stick to the skipper as though he were of some use—as the pilot-fish, they say, is to the whale. But how—it was very marked—how? A pilot-fish—a pilot—a . . . But if not superior knowledge then. . . .

Sterne's discovery was made. It was repugnant to his imagination, shocking to his ideas of honesty, shocking to his conception of mankind. This enormity affected one's outlook on what was possible in this world: it was as if for instance the sun had turned blue, throwing a new and sinister light on men and nature. Really in the first moment he had felt sickish, as though he had got a blow below the belt: for a second the very colour of the sea seemed changed—appeared queer to his wandering eye; and he had a passing, unsteady sensation in all his limbs as though the earth had started turning the other way.

A very natural incredulity succeeding this sense of upheaval brought a measure of relief. He had gasped; it was over. But afterwards, during all that day, sudden paroxysms of wonder would come over him in the midst of his occupations. He would stop and shake his head. The revolt of his incredulity had passed away almost as quick as the first emotion of discovery, and for the next twenty-four hours he had no sleep. That would never do. At meal-times (he took the foot of the table set up for the white men on the bridge) he could not help losing himself in a fascinated contemplation of Captain Whalley opposite. He watched the deliberate upward movements of the arm; the old man put his food to his lips as though he never expected to find any taste in his daily bread, as though he did not know anything about it. He fed himself like a somnambulist. "It's an awful sight," thought Sterne; and he watched the long period of mournful, silent immobility, with a big brown hand lying closed by the side of the plate, till he noticed the two engineers to the right and left looking at him in astonishment. He would close his mouth in a hurry then, and lowering his eyes, wink rapidly at his plate. It was awful to see the old chap sitting there: it was even awful to think that with three words he could blow him up sky-high. All he had to do was to raise his voice and pronounce a single short sentence, and yet that simple act seemed as impossible to attempt as moving the sun out of its place in the sky. The old chap could eat in his terrific mechanical way; but Sterne, from mental excitement, could not—not that evening, at any rate.

He had had ample time since to get accustomed to the strain of the meal-hours. He would never have believed it. But then use is everything; only the very potency of his success prevented anything resembling elation. He felt like a man who, in his legitimate search for a loaded gun to help him on his way through the world, chances to come upon a torpedo—upon a live torpedo with a shattering charge in its head and a pressure of many atmospheres in its tail. It is the sort of weapon to make its possessor careworn and nervous. He had no mind to be blown up himself; and he could not get rid of the notion that the explosion was bound to damage him, too, in some way.

This vague apprehension had restrained him at first. He was able now to eat and sleep with that fearful weapon by his side, with the conviction of its power always in his mind. It had not been arrived at by any reflective process; but once the idea had entered his head, the conviction had followed overwhelmingly in a multitude of observed little facts to which before he had given only a languid attention. The abrupt and faltering intonations of the deep voice; the taciturnity put on like an armour; the deliberate, as if guarded, movements; the long immobilities, as if the man he watched had been afraid to disturb the very air: every familiar gesture, every word uttered in his hearing, every sigh overheard, had acquired a special significance, a confirmatory import.

Every day that passed over the *Sofala* appeared to Sterne simply crammed full with proofs—with incontrovertible proofs. At night, when off duty, he would steal out of his cabin in pyjamas (for more proofs) and stand a full hour, perhaps, on his bare feet below the bridge, as absolutely motionless as the awning stanchion in its deck socket near by. On the stretches of easy navigation it is not usual for a coasting captain to remain on deck all the time of his watch. The Serang keeps it for him as a matter of custom; in open water, on a straight course, he is usually trusted to look after the ship by himself. But this old man seemed incapable of remaining quietly down below. No doubt he could not sleep. And no wonder. This was also a proof. Suddenly in the silence of the ship panting upon the still, dark sea, Sterne would hear a low voice above him exclaiming nervously—

"Serang!"

"Tuan!"

"You are watching the compass well?"

"Yes, I am watching, Tuan."

"The ship is making her course?"

"She is, Tuan. Very straight."

"It is well; and remember, Serang, that the order is, that you are to mind the helmsmen and keep a lookout with care, the same as if I were not on deck."

Then, when the Serang had made his answer, the low tones on the bridge would cease, and everything round Sterne seemed to become more still and more profoundly silent. Slightly chilled and with his back aching a little from long immobility, he would steal away to his room on the port side of the deck. He had long since parted with the last vestige of incredulity; of the original emotions, set into a tumult by the discovery, some trace of the first awe alone remained. Not the awe of the man himself—he could blow him up sky-high with six words—rather it was an awestruck indignation at the reckless perversity of avarice (what else could it be?), at the mad and sombre resolution that for the sake of a few dollars more seemed to set at nought the common rule of conscience and pretended to struggle against the very decree of Providence.

You could not find another man like this one in the whole round world—thank God. There was something devilishly dauntless in the character of such a deception which made you pause.

Other considerations occurring to his prudence had kept him tongue-tied from day to day. It seemed to him now that it would yet have been easier to speak out in the first hour of discovery. He almost regretted not having made a row at once. But then the very monstrosity of the disclosure . . . Why! he could hardly face it himself, let alone pointing it out to somebody else. Moreover, with a desperado of that sort one never knew. The object was not to get him out (that was as well as done already), but to step into his place. Bizarre as the thought seemed, he might have shown fight. A fellow up to working such a fraud would have enough cheek for anything; a fellow that, as it were, stood up against God Almighty Himself. He was a horrid marvel—that's what he was: he was perfectly capable of brazening out the affair scandalously till he got him (Sterne) kicked out of the ship and everlastingly damaged his prospects in this part of the East. Yet if you want to get on something must be risked. At times Sterne thought he had been unduly timid of taking action in the past; and what was worse, it had come to this, that in the present he did not seem to know what action to take.

Massy's savage moroseness was too disconcerting. It was an incalculable factor of the situation. You could not tell what there was behind that insulting ferocity. How could one trust such a temper? It did not put Sterne in bodily fear for himself, but it frightened him exceedingly as to his prospects.

Though of course inclined to credit himself with exceptional powers of observation, he had by now lived too long with his discovery. He had gone on looking at nothing else, till at last one day it occurred to him that the thing was so obvious that no one could miss seeing it. There were four white men in all on board the *Sofala*. Jack, the second engineer, was too dull to notice anything that took place out of his engine-room. Remained Massy—the owner—the interested person—nearly going mad with worry. Sterne had heard and seen more than enough on board to know what ailed him; but his exasperation seemed to make him deaf to cautious overtures. If he had only known it, there was the very thing he wanted. But how could you bargain with a man of that sort? It was like going into a tiger's den with a piece of raw meat in your hand. He was as likely as not to rend you for your pains. In fact, he was always threatening to do that very thing; and the urgency of the case, combined with the impossibility of handling it with safety, made Sterne in his watches below toss and mutter open-eyed in his bunk, for hours, as though he had been burning with fever.

Occurrences like the crossing of the bar just now were extremely alarming to his prospects. He did not want to be left behind by some swift catastrophe. Massy being on the bridge, the old man had to brace himself up, and make a show, he supposed. But it was getting very bad with him, very bad indeed, now. Even Massy had been emboldened to find fault this time; Sterne, listening at the foot of the ladder, had heard the other's whimpering and artless denunciations. Luckily the beast was very stupid and could not see the why of all this. However, small blame to him; it took a clever man to hit upon the cause. Nevertheless, it was high time to do something. The old man's game could not be kept up for many days more.

"I may yet lose my life at this fooling—let alone my chance," Sterne mumbled angrily to himself, after the stooping back of the chief engineer had disappeared round the corner of the skylight. Yes, no doubt—he thought; but to blurt out his knowledge would not advance his prospects. On the contrary, it would blast them utterly as likely as not. He dreaded another failure. He had a vague consciousness of not being much liked by his fellows in this part of the world; inexplicably enough, for he had done nothing to them. Envy, he supposed. People were always down on a clever chap who made no bones about his determination to get on. To do your duty and count on the gratitude of that brute Massy would be sheer folly. He was a bad lot. Unmanly! A vicious man! Bad! Bad! A brute! A brute without a spark of anything human about him; without so much as simple curiosity even, or else surely he would have responded in some way to all these hints he had been given. . . . Such insensibility was almost mysterious. Massy's state of exasperation seemed to Sterne to have made him stupid beyond the ordinary silliness of shipowners.

Sterne, meditating on the embarrassments of that stupidity, forgot himself completely. His stony, unwinking stare was fixed on the planks of the deck.

The slight quiver agitating the whole fabric of the ship was more perceptible in the silent river, shaded and still like a forest path. The *Sofala,* gliding with an even motion, had passed beyond the coast-belt of mud and mangroves. The shores rose higher, in firm sloping banks, and the forest of big trees came down to the brink. Where the earth had been crumbled by the floods it showed a steep brown cut, denuding a mass of roots intertwined as if wrestling underground; and in the air, the interlaced boughs, bound and loaded with creepers, carried on the struggle for life, mingled their foliage in one solid wall of leaves, with here and there the shape of an enormous dark pillar soaring, or a ragged opening, as if torn by the flight of a cannon-ball, disclosing the impenetrable gloom within, the secular inviolable shade of the virgin forest. The thump of the engines reverberated regularly like the strokes of a metronome beating the measure of the vast silence, the shadow of the western wall had fallen across the river, and the smoke pouring backwards from the funnel eddied down behind the ship, spread a thin dusky veil over the sombre water, which, checked by the flood-tide, seemed to lie stagnant in the whole straight length of the reaches.

Sterne's body, as if rooted on the spot, trembled slightly from top to toe with the internal vibration of the ship; from under his feet came sometimes a sudden clang of iron, the noisy burst of a shout below; to the right the leaves of the tree-tops caught the rays of the low sun, and seemed to shine with a golden green light of their own shimmering around the highest boughs which stood out black against a smooth blue sky that seemed to droop over the bed of the river like the roof of a tent. The passengers for Batu Beru, kneeling on the planks, were engaged in rolling their bedding of mats busily; they tied up bundles, they snapped the locks of wooden chests. A pockmarked pedlar of small wares threw his head back to drain into his throat the last drops out of an earthenware bottle before putting it away in a roll of blankets. Knots of travelling traders standing about the deck conversed in low tones; the followers of a small Rajah from down the coast, broad-faced simple young fellows in white drawers and round white cotton caps with their coloured sarongs twisted across their bronze shoulders, squatted on their hams on the hatch, chewing betel with bright red mouths as if they had been tasting blood. Their spears, lying piled up together within the circle of their bare toes, resembled a casual bundle of dry bamboos; a thin, livid Chinaman, with a bulky package wrapped up in leaves already thrust under his arm, gazed ahead eagerly; a wandering Kling rubbed his teeth with a bit of wood, pouring over the side a bright stream of water out of his lips; the fat Rajah dozed in a shabby deck-chair—and at the turn of every bend the two walls of leaves reappeared running parallel along the banks, with their impenetrable solidity fading at the top to a vaporous mistiness of countless slender twigs growing free, of young delicate branches shooting from the topmost limbs of hoary trunks, of feathery heads of climbers like delicate silver sprays standing up without a quiver. There was not a sign of a clearing anywhere; not a trace of human habitation, except when in one place, on the bare end of a low point under an isolated group of slender tree-ferns, the jagged, tangled remnants of an old hut on piles appeared with that peculiar aspect of ruined bamboo walls that look as if smashed with a club. Farther on, half hidden under the drooping bushes, a canoe containing a man and a woman together with a dozen green cocoanuts in a heap, rocked helplessly after the *Sofala* had passed, like a navigating contrivance of venturesome insects, of travelling ants; while two glassy folds of water streaming away from each bow of the steamer across the whole width of the river ran with her upstream smoothly, fretting their outer ends into a brown whispering tumble of froth against the miry foot of each bank.

"I must," thought Sterne, "bring that brute Massy to his bearings. It's getting too absurd in the end. Here's the old man up there buried in his chair—he may just as well be in his grave for all the use he'll ever be in the world—and the Serang's in charge. Because that's what he is. In charge. In the place that's mine by rights. I must bring that savage brute to his bearings. I'll do it at once, too. . . ."

When the mate made an abrupt start, a little brown, half-naked boy, with large black eyes, and the string of a written charm round his neck, became panic-struck at once. He dropped the banana he had been munching, and ran to the knee of a grave dark Arab in flowing robes, sitting like a Biblical figure, incongruously, on a yellow tin trunk corded with a rope of twisted rattan. The father, unmoved, put out his hand to pat the little shaven poll protectingly.

· XI ·

Sterne crossed the deck upon the track of the chief engineer. Jack, the second, retreating backwards down the engine-room ladder, and still wiping his hands, treated him to an incomprehensible grin of white teeth out of his grimy hard face; Massy was nowhere to be seen. Sterne scratched at the door softly, then, putting his lips to the rose of the ventilator, said—

"I must speak to you, Mr. Massy. Just give me a minute or two."

"I am busy. Go away from my door."

"But pray, Mr. Massy. . . ."

"You go away. D'you hear? Take yourself off altogether—to the other end of the ship—quite away. . . ." The voice inside dropped low. "To the devil."

Sterne paused: then very quietly—

"It's rather pressing. When do you think you will be at liberty, sir?"

The answer to this was an exasperated "Never"; and at once Sterne, with a very firm expression of face, turned the handle.

Mr. Massy's stateroom—a narrow, one-berth cabin—smelt strongly of soap, and presented to view a swept, dusted, unadorned neatness, not so much bare as barren, not so much severe as starved and lacking in humanity, like the ward of a public hospital, or rather (owing to the small size) like the clean retreat of a desperately poor but exemplary person. Not a single photograph frame ornamented the bulkheads; not a single article of clothing, not as much as a spare cap, hung from the brass hooks. All the inside was painted in one plain tint of pale blue; two big sea-chests in sailcloth covers and with iron padlocks fitted exactly in the space under the bunk. One glance was enough to embrace all the strip of scrubbed planks within the four unconcealed corners. The absence of the usual settee was striking; the teak-wood top of the washing-stand seemed hermetically closed, and so was the lid of the writing-desk, which protruded from the partition at the foot of the bed-place, containing a mattress as thin as a pancake under a threadbare blanket with a faded red stripe, and a folded mosquito-net against the nights spent in harbour. There was not a scrap of paper anywhere in sight, no boots on the floor, no litter of any sort, not a speck of dust anywhere; no traces of pipe-ash even, which, in a heavy smoker, was morally revolting, like a manifestation of extreme hypocrisy; and the bottom of the old wooden arm-chair (the only seat there), polished with much use, shone as if its shabbiness had been waxed. The screen of leaves on the bank, passing as if unrolled endlessly in the round opening of the port, sent a wavering network of light and shade into the place.

Sterne, holding the door open with one hand, had thrust in his head and shoulders. At this amazing intrusion Massy, who was doing absolutely nothing, jumped up speechless.

"Don't call names," murmured Sterne, hurriedly. "I won't be called names. I think of nothing but your good, Mr. Massy."

A pause as of extreme astonishment followed. They both seemed to have lost their tongues. Then the mate went on with discreet glibness:

"You simply couldn't conceive what's going on on board your ship. It wouldn't enter your head for a moment. You are too good—too—too upright, Mr. Massy, to suspect anybody of such a . . . It's enough to make your hair stand on end."

He watched for the effect: Massy seemed dazed, uncomprehending. He only passed the palm of his hand on the coal-black wisps plastered across the top of his head. In a tone suddenly changed to confidential audacity Sterne hastened on:

"Remember that there's only six weeks left to run. . . ." The other was looking at him stonily . . . "So anyhow you will require a captain for the ship before long."

Then only, as if that suggestion had scarified his flesh in the manner of red-hot iron, Massy gave a start and seemed ready to shriek. He contained himself by a great effort.

"Require—a—captain," he repeated with scathing slowness. "Who requires a captain? You dare tell me that I need any of you humbugging sailors to run my ship. You and your likes have been fattening on me for years. It would have hurt me less to throw my money overboard. Pam—pe—red us—e—less f-f-f-frauds. The old ship knows as much as the best of you." He snapped his teeth audibly and growled through them. "The silly law requires a captain."

Sterne had taken heart of grace meantime.

"And the silly insurance people, too, as well," he said, lightly. "But never mind that. What I want to ask is: Why shouldn't *I* do, sir? I don't say but you could take a steamer about the world as well as any of us sailors. I don't pretend to tell *you* that it is a very great trick. . . ." He emitted a short, hollow guffaw, familiarly. . . . "I didn't make the law—but there it is; and I am an active young fellow; I quite hold with your ideas; I know your ways by this time, Mr. Massy. I wouldn't try to give myself airs like that—that—er—lazy specimen of an old man up there."

He put a marked emphasis on the last sentence, to lead Massy away from the track in case . . . but he did not doubt of now holding his success. The chief engineer seemed nonplussed, like a slow man invited to catch hold of a whirligig of some sort.

"What you want, sir, is a chap with no nonsense about him, who would be content to be your sailing-master. Quite right, too. Well, I am fit for the work as much as that Serang. Because that's what it amounts to. Do you know, sir, that a dam' Malay like a monkey is in charge of your ship—and no one else? Just listen to his feet pit-patting above us on the bridge—real officer in charge. He's taking her up the river while the great man is wallowing in the chair—perhaps asleep; and if he is, that would not make it much worse either—take my word for it."

He tried to thrust himself farther in. Massy, with lowered forehead, one hand grasping the back of the arm-chair, did not budge.

"You think, sir, that the man has got you tight in his agreement. . . ." Massy raised a heavy snarling face at this. . . . "Well, sir, one can't help hearing of it on board. It's no secret. And it has been the talk on shore for years; fellows have been making bets about it. No, sir! It's *you* who have got him at your mercy. You will say that you can't dismiss him for indolence. Difficult to prove in court, and so on. Why, yes. But if you say the word, sir, I can tell you something about his indolence that will give you the clear right to fire him out on the spot and put me in charge for the rest of this very trip—yes, sir, before we leave Batu Beru—and make him pay a dollar a day for his keep till we get back, if you like. Now, what do you think of that? Come, sir. Say the word. It's really well worth your while, and I am quite ready to take your bare word. A definite statement from you would be as good as a bond."

His eyes began to shine. He insisted. A simple statement—and he thought to himself that he would manage somehow to stick in his berth as long as it suited him. He would make himself indispensable; the ship had a bad name in her port; it would be easy to scare the fellows off. Massy would have to keep him.

"A definite statement from me would be enough," Massy repeated, slowly.

"Yes, sir. It would." Sterne stuck out his chin cheerily and blinked at close quarters with that unconscious impudence which had the power to enrage Massy beyond anything.

The engineer spoke very distinctly:

"Listen well to me, then, Mr. Sterne: I wouldn't—d'ye hear?—I wouldn't promise you the value of two pence for anything *you* can tell me."

He struck Sterne's arm away with a smart blow, and catching hold of the handle pulled the door to. The terrific slam darkened the cabin instantaneously to his eyes as if after the flash of an explosion. At once he dropped into the chair. "Oh, no! You don't!" he whispered faintly.

The ship had in that place to shave the bank so close that the gigantic wall of leaves came gliding like a shutter against the port; the darkness of the primeval forest seemed to flow into that bare cabin with the odour of rotting leaves, of sodden soil—the strong muddy smell of the living earth steaming uncovered after the passing of a deluge. The bushes swished loudly alongside; above there was a series of crackling sounds, with a sharp rain of small broken branches falling on the bridge; a creeper with a great rustle snapped on the head of a boat davit, and a long, luxuriant green twig actually whipped in and out of the open port, leaving behind a few torn leaves that remained suddenly at rest on Mr. Massy's blanket. Then, the ship sheering out in the stream, the light began to return, but did not augment beyond a subdued clearness: for the sun was very low already, and the river, wending its sinuous course through a multitude of secular trees as if at the bottom of a precipitous gorge, had been already invaded by a deepening gloom—the swift precursor of the night.

"Oh, no, you don't!" murmured the engineer again. His lips trembled almost imperceptibly; his hands, too, a little: and to calm himself he opened the writing-desk, spread out a sheet of thin grayish paper covered with a mass of printed figures and began to scan them attentively for the twentieth time this trip at least.

With his elbows propped, his head between his hands, he seemed to lose himself in the study of an abstruse problem in mathematics. It was the list of the winning numbers from the last drawing of the great lottery which had been the one inspiring fact of so many years of his existence. The conception of a life deprived of that periodical sheet of paper had slipped away from him entirely, as another man, according to his nature, would not have been able to conceive a world without fresh air, without activity, or without affection. A great pile of flimsy sheets had been growing for years in his desk, while the *Sofala*, driven by the faithful Jack, wore out her boilers in tramping up and down the Straits, from cape to cape, from river to river, from bay to bay; accumulating by that hard labour of an overworked, starved ship the blackened mass of these documents. Massy kept them under lock and key like a treasure. There was in them, as in the experience of life, the fascination of hope, the excitement of a half-penetrated mystery, the longing of a half-satisfied desire.

For days together, on a trip, he would shut himself up in his berth with them: the thump of the toiling engines pulsated in his ear; and he would weary his brain poring over the rows of disconnected figures, bewildering by their senseless sequence, resembling the hazards of destiny itself. He nourished a conviction that there must be some logic lurking somewhere in the results of chance. He thought he had seen its very form. His head swam; his limbs ached; he puffed at his pipe mechanically; a contemplative stupor would soothe the fretfulness of his temper, like the passive bodily quietude procured by a drug, while the intellect remains tensely on the stretch. Nine, nine, nought, four, two. He made a note. The next winning number of the great prize was forty-seven thousand and five. These numbers of course would have to be avoided in the future when writing to Manila for the tickets. He mumbled, pencil in hand ... "and five. Hm ... hm." He wetted his finger: the papers rustled. Ha! But what's this? Three years ago, in the September drawing, it was number nine, nought, four, two that took the first prize. Most remarkable. There was a hint there of a definite rule! He was afraid of missing some recondite principle in the overwhelming wealth of his material. What could it be? And for half an hour he would remain dead still, bent low over the desk, without twitching a muscle. At his back the whole berth would be thick with a heavy body of smoke, as if a bomb had burst in there, unnoticed, unheard.

At last he would lock up the desk with the decision of unshaken confidence, jump up and go out. He would walk swiftly back and forth on that part of the foredeck which was kept clear of the lumber and of the bodies of the native passengers. They were a great nuisance, but they were also a source of profit that could not be disdained. He needed every penny of profit the *Sofala* could make. Little enough it was, in all conscience! The incertitude of chance gave him no concern, since he had somehow arrived at the conviction that, in the course of years, every number was bound to have its winning turn. It was simply a matter of time and of taking as many tickets as he could afford for every drawing. He generally took rather more; all the earnings of the ship went that way, and also the wages he allowed himself as chief engineer. It was the wages he paid to others that he begrudged with a reasoned and at the same time a passionate regret. He scowled at the lascars with their deck brooms, at the quartermasters rubbing the brass rails with greasy rags; he was eager to shake his fist and roar abuse in bad Malay at the poor carpenter—a timid, sickly, opium-fuddled Chinaman, in loose blue drawers for all costume, who invariably dropped his tools and fled below, with streaming tail and shaking all over, before the fury of that "devil." But it was when he raised up his eyes to the bridge where one of these sailor frauds was always planted by law in charge of his ship that he felt almost dizzy with rage. He abominated them all; it was an old feud, from the time he first went to sea, an unlicked cub with a great opinion of himself, in the engine-room. The slights that had been put upon him. The persecutions he had suffered at the hands of skippers—of absolute nobodies in a steamship after all. And now that he had risen to be a shipowner they were still a plague to him: he had absolutely to pay away precious money to the conceited useless loafers:—As if a fully qualified engineer—who was the owner as well—were not fit to be trusted with the whole charge of a ship. Well! he made it pretty warm for them; but it was a poor consolation. He had come in time to hate the ship, too, for the repairs she required, for the coal-bills he had to pay, for the poor beggarly freights she earned. He would clench his hand as he walked and hit the rail a sudden blow, viciously, as though she could be made to feel pain. And yet he could not do without her; he needed her; he must hang on to her tooth and nail to keep his head above water till the expected flood of fortune came sweeping up and landed him safely on the high shore of his ambition.

It was now to do nothing, nothing whatever, and have plenty of money to do it on. He had tasted of power, the highest form of it his limited experience was aware of—the power of shipowning. What a deception! Vanity of vanities! He wondered at his folly. He had thrown away the substance for the shadow. Of the gratification of wealth he did not know enough to excite his imagination with any visions of luxury. How would he—the child of a drunken boiler-maker—going straight from the workshop into the engine-room of a north-country collier! But the notion of the absolute idleness of wealth he could very well conceive. He revelled in it, to forget his present troubles; he imagined himself walking about the streets of Hull (he knew their gutters well as a boy) with his pockets full of sovereigns. He would buy himself a house; his married sisters, their husbands, his old workshop chums, would render him infinite homage. There would be nothing to think of. His word would be law. He had been out of work for a long time before he won his prize, and he remembered how Carlo Mariani (commonly known as Paunchy Charley), the Maltese hotel-keeper at the slummy end of Denham Street, had cringed joyfully before him in the evening, when the news had come. Poor Charley, though he made his living by ministering to various abject vices, gave credit for the food to many a piece of white wreckage. He was naïvely overjoyed at the idea of his old bills being paid, and he reckoned confidently on a spell of festivities in the cavernous grog-shop downstairs. Massy remembered the curious, respectful looks of the "trashy" white men in the place. His heart had swelled within him. Massy had left Charley's infamous den directly he had realized the possibilities open to him, with his nose in the air. Afterwards the memory of these adulations was a great sadness.

This was the true power of money—and no trouble with it, nor any thinking required either. He thought with difficulty and felt vividly; to his blunt brain the problems offered by any ordered scheme of life seemed in their cruel toughness to have been put in his way by the obvious malevolence of men. As a shipowner everyone had conspired to make him a nobody. How could he have been such a fool as to purchase that accursed ship? He had been abominably swindled; there was no end to this swindling, and as the difficulties of his improvident ambition gathered thicker round him, he really came to hate everybody he had ever come in contact with. A temper naturally irritable and an amazing sensitiveness to the claims of his own personality had ended by making life for him a sort of inferno—a place where his lost soul had been given up to the torment of savage brooding.

But he had never hated any one so much as that old man who turned up one evening to save him from an utter disaster,—from the conspiracy of the wretched sailors. He seemed to have fallen on board from the sky. His footsteps echoed on the empty steamer, and the strange deep-toned voice on deck repeating interrogatively the words, "Mr. Massy, Mr. Massy there?" had been startling like a wonder. And coming up from the depths of the cold engine-room, where he had been pottering dismally with a candle amongst the enormous shadows, thrown on all sides by the skeleton limbs of machinery, Massy had been struck dumb by astonishment in the presence of that imposing old man with a beard like a silver plate, towering in the dusk rendered lurid by the expiring flames of sunset.

"Want to see me on business? What business? I am doing no business. Can't you see that this ship is laid up?" Massy had turned at bay before the pursuing irony of his disaster. Afterwards he could not believe his ears. What was that old fellow getting at? Things don't happen that way. It was a dream. He would presently wake up and find the man vanished like a shape of mist. The gravity, the dignity, the firm and courteous tone of that athletic old stranger impressed Massy. He was almost afraid. But it was no dream. Five hundreds pounds are no dream. At once he became suspicious. What did it mean? Of course it was an offer to catch hold of for dear life. But what could there be behind?

Before they had parted, after appointing a meeting in a solicitor's office early on the morrow, Massy was asking himself, What is his motive? He spent the night in hammering out the clauses of the agreement—a unique instrument of its sort whose tenor got bruited abroad somehow and became the talk and wonder of the port.

Massy's object had been to secure for himself as many ways as possible of getting rid of his partner without being called upon at once to pay back his share. Captain Whalley's efforts were directed to making the money secure. Was it not Ivy's money—a part of her fortune whose only other asset was the time-defying body of her old father? Sure of his forbearance in the strength of his love for her, he accepted, with stately serenity, Massy's stupidly cunning paragraphs against his incompetence, his dishonesty, his drunkenness, for the sake of other stringent stipulations. At the end of three years he was at liberty to withdraw from the partnership, taking his money with him. Provision was made for forming a fund to pay him off. But if he left the *Sofala* before the term, from whatever cause (barring death), Massy was to have a whole year for paying. "Illness?" the lawyer had suggested: a young man fresh from Europe and not overburdened with business, who was rather amused. Massy began to whine unctuously, "How could he be expected? . . ."

"Let that go," Captain Whalley had said with a superb confidence in his body. "Acts of God," he added. In the midst of life we are in death, but he trusted his Maker with a still greater fearlessness—his Maker who knew his thoughts, his human affections, and his motives. His Creator knew what use he was making of his health—how much he wanted it. . . . "I trust my first illness will be my last. I've never been ill that I can remember," he had remarked. "Let it go."

But at this early stage he had already awakened Massy's hostility by refusing to make it six hundred instead of five. "I cannot do that," was all he had said, simply, but with so much decision that Massy desisted at once from pressing the point, but had thought to himself, "Can't! Old curmudgeon. *Won't!* He must have lots of money, but he would like to get hold of a soft berth and the sixth part of my profits for nothing if he only could."

And during these years Massy's dislike grew under the restraint of something resembling fear. The simplicity of that man appeared dangerous. Of late he had changed, however, had appeared less formidable and with a lessened vigour of life, as though he had received a secret wound. But still he remained incomprehensible in his simplicity, fearlessness, and rectitude. And when Massy learned that he meant to leave him at the end of the time, to leave him confronted with the problem of the boilers, his dislike blazed up secretly into hate.

It had made him so clear-eyed that for a long time now Mr. Sterne could have told him nothing he did not know. He had much ado in trying to terrorize that mean sneak into silence; he wanted to deal alone with the situation; and—incredible as it might have appeared to Mr. Sterne—he had not yet given up the desire and the hope of inducing that hated old man to stay. Why! there was nothing else to do, unless he were to abandon his chances of fortune. But now, suddenly, since the crossing of the bar at Batu Beru things seemed to be coming rapidly to a point. It disquieted him so much that the study of the winning numbers failed to soothe his agitation: and the twilight in the cabin deepened, very sombre.

He put the list away, muttering once more, "Oh, no, my boy, you don't. Not if I know it." He did not mean the blinking, eavesdropping humbug to force his action. He took his head again into his hands; his immobility confined in the darkness of this shut-up little place seemed to make him a thing apart infinitely removed from the stir and the sounds of the deck.

He heard them: the passengers were beginning to jabber excitedly; somebody dragged a heavy box past his door. He heard Captain Whalley's voice above—

"Stations, Mr. Sterne." And the answer from somewhere on deck forward—

"Ay, ay, sir."

"We shall moor head upstream this time; the ebb has made."

"Head upstream, sir."

"You will see to it, Mr. Sterne."

The answer was covered by the autocratic clang of the engine-room gong. The propeller went on beating slowly: one, two, three; one, two, three—with pauses as if hesitating on the turn. The gong clanged time after time, and the water churned this way and that by the blades was making a great noisy commotion alongside. Mr. Massy did not move. A shore-light on the other bank, a quarter of a mile across the river, drifted, no bigger than a tiny star, passing slowly athwart the circle of the port. Voices from Mr. Van Wyk's jetty answered the hails from the ship; ropes were thrown and missed and thrown again; the swaying flame of a torch carried in a large sampan coming to fetch away in state the Rajah from down the coast cast a sudden ruddy glare into his cabin, over his very person. Mr. Massy did not move. After a few last ponderous turns the engines stopped, and the prolonged clanging of the gong signified that the captain had done with them. A great number of boats and canoes of all sizes boarded the off-side of the *Sofala*. Then after a time the tumult of splashing, of cries, of shuffling feet, of packages dropped with a thump, the noise of the native passengers going away, subsided slowly. On the shore, a voice, cultivated, slightly authoritative, spoke very close alongside—

"Brought any mail for me this time?"

"Yes, Mr. Van Wyk." This was from Sterne, answering over the rail in a tone of respectful cordiality. "Shall I bring it up to you?"

But the voice asked again—

"Where's the captain?"

"Still on the bridge, I believe. He hasn't left his chair. Shall I. . . ."

The voice interrupted negligently—

"I will come on board."

"Mr. Van Wyk," Sterne suddenly broke out with an eager effort, "will you do me the favour. . . ."

The mate walked away quickly towards the gangway. A silence fell. Mr. Massy in the dark did not move.

He did not move even when he heard slow shuffling footsteps pass his cabin lazily. He contented himself to bellow out through the closed door—

"You—Jack!"

The footsteps came back without haste; the door-handle rattled, and the second engineer appeared in the opening, shadowy in the sheen of the skylight at his back, with his face apparently as black as the rest of his figure.

"We have been very long coming up this time," Mr. Massy growled, without changing his attitude.

"What do you expect with half the boiler tubes plugged up for leaks?" the second defended himself loquaciously.

"None of your lip," said Massy.

"None of your rotten boilers—I say," retorted his faithful subordinate without animation, huskily.

"Go down there and carry a head of steam on them yourself—if you dare. I don't."

"You aren't worth your salt then," Massy said. The other made a faint noise which resembled a laugh but might have been a snarl.

"Better go slow than stop the ship altogether," he admonished his admired superior. Mr. Massy moved at last. He turned in his chair, and grinding his teeth—

"Dam' you and the ship! I wish she were at the bottom of the sea. Then you would have to starve."

The trusty second engineer closed the door gently.

Massy listened. Instead of passing on to the bathroom where he should have gone to clean himself, the second entered his cabin, which was next door. Mr. Massy jumped up and waited. Suddenly he heard the lock snap in there. He rushed out and gave a violent kick to the door.

"I believe you are locking yourself up to get drunk," he shouted.

A muffled answer came after a while.

"My own time."

"If you take to boozing on the trip I'll fire you out," Massy cried.

An obstinate silence followed that threat. Massy moved away, perplexed. On the bank two figures appeared, approaching the gangway. He heard a voice tinged with contempt—

"I would rather doubt your word. But I shall certainly speak to him of this."

The other voice, Sterne's, said with a sort of regretful formality—

"Thanks. That's all I want. I must do my duty."

Mr. Massy was surprised. A short, dapper figure leaped lightly on the deck and nearly bounded into him where he stood beyond the circle of light from the gangway lamp. When it had passed towards the bridge, after exchanging a hurried "Good evening," Massy said surlily to Sterne, who followed with slow steps—

"What is it you're making up to Mr. Van Wyk for, now?"

"Far from it, Mr. Massy. I am not good enough for Mr. Van Wyk. Neither are you, sir, in his opinion, I am afraid. Captain Whalley is, it seems. He's gone to ask him to dine up at the house this evening."

Then he murmured to himself darkly—

"I hope he will like it."

· XII ·

Mr. Van Wyk, the white man of Batu Beru, an ex-naval officer who, for reasons best known to himself, had thrown away the promise of a brilliant career to become the pioneer of tobacco-planting on that remote part of the coast, had learned to like Captain Whalley. The appearance of the new skipper had attracted his attention. Nothing more unlike all the diverse types he had seen succeeding each other on the bridge of the *Sofala* could be imagined.

At that time Batu Beru was not what it has become since: the centre of a prosperous tobacco-growing district, a tropically suburban-looking little settlement of bungalows in one long street shaded with two rows of trees, embowered by the flowering and trim luxuriance of the gardens, with a three-mile-long carriage-road for the afternoon drives and a first-class Resident with a fat, cheery wife to lead the society of married estate-managers and unmarried young fellows in the service of the big companies.

All this prosperity was not yet; and Mr. Van Wyk prospered alone on the left bank on his deep clearing carved out of the forest, which came down above and below to the water's edge. His lonely bungalow faced across the river the houses of the Sultan: a restless and melancholy old ruler who had done with love and war, for whom life no longer held any savour (except of evil forebodings) and time never had any value. He was afraid of death, and hoped he would die before the white men were ready to take his country from him. He crossed the river frequently (with never less than ten boats crammed full of people), in the wistful hope of extracting some information on the subject from his own white man. There was a certain chair on the verandah he always took: the dignitaries of the court squatted on the rugs and skins between the furniture: the inferior people remained below on the grass-plot between the house and the river in rows three or four deep all along the front. Not seldom the visit began at day-break. Mr. Van Wyk tolerated these inroads. He would nod out of his bedroom window, toothbrush or razor in hand, or pass through the throng of courtiers in his bathing robe. He appeared and disappeared humming a tune, polished his nails with attention, rubbed his shaved face with eau-de-Cologne, drank his early tea, went out to see his coolies at work; returned, looked through some papers on his desk, read a page or two in a book or sat before his cottage piano leaning back on the stool, his arms extended, fingers on the keys, his body swaying slightly from side to side. When absolutely forced to speak he gave evasive, vaguely soothing answers out of pure compassion: the same feeling perhaps made him so lavishly hospitable with the aerated drinks that more than once he left himself without soda-water for a whole week. That old man had granted him as much land as he cared to have cleared: it was neither more nor less than a fortune.

Whether it was fortune or seclusion from his kind that Mr. Van Wyk sought, he could not have pitched upon a better place. Even the mail-boats of the subsidized company calling on the veriest clusters of palm-thatched hovels along the coast steamed past the mouth of Batu Beru river far away in the offing. The contract was old: perhaps in a few years' time, when it had expired, Batu Beru would be included in the service; meantime all Mr. Van Dyk's mail was addressed to Malacca, whence his agent sent it across once a month by the *Sofala*. It followed that whenever Massy had run short of money (through taking too many lottery tickets), or got into a difficulty about a skipper, Mr. Van Wyk was deprived of his letters and newspapers. In so far he had a personal interest in the fortunes of the *Sofala*. Though he considered himself a hermit (and for no passing whim evidently, since he had stood eight years of it already), he liked to know what went on in the world.

Handy on the verandah upon a walnut étagère (it had come last year by the *Sofala*—everything came by the *Sofala*) there lay, piled up under bronze weights, a pile of *The Times* weekly edition, the large sheets of the *Rotterdam Courant,* the *Graphic* in its world-wide green wrappers, an illustrated Dutch publication without a cover, the numbers of a German magazine with covers of the "Bismarck malade" colour. There were also parcels of new music—though the piano (it had come years ago by the *Sofala*) in the damp atmosphere of the forests was generally out of tune. It was vexing to be cut off from everything for sixty days at a stretch sometimes, without any means of knowing what was the matter. And when the *Sofala* reappeared Mr. Van Wyk would descend the steps of the verandah and stroll over the grass-plot in front of his house, down to the water-side, with a frown on his white brow.

"You've been laid up after an accident, I presume."

He addressed the bridge, but before anybody could answer Massy was sure to have already scrambled ashore over the rail and pushed in, squeezing the palms of his hands together, bowing his sleek head as if gummed all over the top with black threads and tapes. And he would be so enraged at the necessity of having to offer such an explanation that his moaning would be positively pitiful, while all the time he tried to compose his big lips into a smile.

"No, Mr. Van Wyk. You would not believe it. I couldn't get one of those wretches to take the ship out. Not a single one of the lazy beasts could be induced, and the law, you know, Mr. Van Wyk. . . ."

He moaned at great length apologetically; the words conspiracy, plot, envy, came out prominently, whined with greater energy. Mr. Van Wyk, examining with a faint grimace his polished fingernails, would say, "H'm. Very unfortunate," and turn his back on him.

Fastidious, clever, slightly sceptical, accustomed to the best society (he had held a much-envied shore appointment at the Ministry of Marine for a year preceding his retreat from his profession and from Europe), he possessed a latent warmth of feeling and a capacity for sympathy which were concealed by a sort of haughty, arbitrary indifference of manner arising from his early training; and by a something an enemy might have called foppish, in his aspect—like a distorted echo of past elegancies. He managed to keep an almost military discipline amongst the coolies of the estate he had dragged into the light of day out of the tangle and shadows of the jungle; and the white shirt he put on every evening with its stiff glossy front and high collar looked as if he had meant to preserve the decent ceremony of evening-dress, but had wound a thick crimson sash above his hips as a concession to the wilderness, once his adversary, now his vanquished companion. Moreover, it was a hygienic precaution. Worn wide open in front, a short jacket of some airy silken stuff floated from his shoulders. His fluffy, fair hair, thin at the top, curled slightly at the sides; a carefully arranged moustache, an ungarnished forehead, the gleam of low patent shoes peeping under the wide bottom of trousers cut straight from the same stuff as the gossamer coat, completed a figure recalling, with its sash, a pirate chief of romance, and at the same time the elegance of a slightly bald dandy indulging, in seclusion, a taste for unorthodox costume.

It was his evening get-up. The proper time for the *Sofala* to arrive at Batu Beru was an hour before sunset, and he looked picturesque, and somehow quite correct, too, walking at the water's edge on the background of grass slope crowned with a low, long bungalow with an immensely steep roof of palm thatch, and clad to the eaves in flowering creepers. While the *Sofala* was being made fast he strolled in the shade of the few trees left near the landing-place, waiting till he could go on board. Her white men were not of his kind. The old Sultan (though his wistful invasions were a nuisance) was really much more acceptable to his fastidious taste. But still they were white; the periodical visits of the ship made a break in the well-filled sameness of the days without disturbing his privacy. Moreover, they were necessary from a business point of view; and through a strain of preciseness in his nature he was irritated when she failed to appear at the appointed time.

The cause of the irregularity was too absurd, and Massy, in his opinion, was a contemptible idiot. The first time the *Sofala* reappeared under the new agreement swinging out of the bend below, after he had almost given up all hope of ever seeing her again, he felt so angry that he did not go down at once to the landing-place. His servants had come running to him with the news, and he had dragged a chair close against the front rail of the verandah, spread his elbows out, rested his chin on his hands, and went on glaring at her fixedly while she was being made fast opposite his house. He could make out easily all the white faces on board. Who on earth was that kind of patriarch they had got there on the bridge now?

At last he sprang up and walked down the gravel path. It was a fact that the very gravel for his paths had been imported by the *Sofala*. Exasperated out of his quiet superciliousness, without looking at any one right or left, he accosted Massy straightway in so determined a manner that the engineer, taken aback, began to stammer unintelligibly. Nothing could be heard but the words: "Mr. Van Wyk . . . Indeed, Mr. Van Wyk. . . . For the future, Mr. Van Wyk"—and by the suffusion of blood Massy's vast bilious face acquired an unnatural orange tint, out of which the disconcerted coal-black eyes shone in an extraordinary manner.

"Nonsense. I am tired of this. I wonder you have the impudence to come alongside my jetty as if I had it made for your convenience alone."

Massy tried to protest earnestly. Mr. Van Wyk was very angry. He had a good mind to ask that German firm—those people in Malacca—what was their name?—boats with green funnels. They would be only too glad of the opening to put one of their small steamers on the run. Yes; Schnitzler, Jacob Schnitzler, would in a moment. Yes. He had decided to write without delay.

In his agitation Massy caught up his falling pipe.

"You don't mean it, sir!" he shrieked.

"You shouldn't mismanage your business in this ridiculous manner."

Mr. Van Wyk turned on his heel. The other three whites on the bridge had not stirred during the scene. Massy walked hastily from side to side, puffed out his cheeks, suffocated.

"Stuck-up Dutchman!"

And he moaned out feverishly a long tale of griefs. The efforts he had made for all these years to please that man. This was the return you got for it, eh? Pretty. Write to Schnitzler—let in the green-funnel boats—get an old Hamburg Jew to ruin him. No, really he could laugh. . . . He laughed sobbingly. . . . Ha! ha! ha! And make him carry the letter in his own ship presumably.

He stumbled across a grating and swore. He would not hesitate to fling the Dutchman's correspondence overboard—the whole confounded bundle. He had never, never made any charge for that accommodation. But Captain Whalley, his new partner, would not let him probably; besides, it would be only putting off the evil day. For his own part he would make a hole in the water rather than look on tamely at the green funnels overrunning his trade.

He raved aloud. The China boys hung back with the dishes at the foot of the ladder. He yelled from the bridge down at the deck, "Aren't we going to have any chow this evening at all?" then turned violently to Captain Whalley, who waited, grave and patient, at the head of the table, smoothing his beard in silence now and then with a forbearing gesture.

"You don't seem to care what happens to me. Don't you see that this affects your interests as much as mine? It's no joking matter."

He took the foot of the table growling between his teeth.

"Unless you have a few thousands put away somewhere. I haven't."

Mr. Van Wyk dined in his thoroughly lit-up bungalow, putting a point of splendour in the night of his clearing above the dark bank of the river. Afterwards he sat down to his piano, and in a pause he became aware of slow footsteps passing on the path along the front. A plank or two creaked under a heavy tread; he swung half round on the music-stool, listening with his finger-tips at rest on the keyboard. His little terrier barked violently, backing in from the verandah. A deep voice apologized gravely for "this intrusion." He walked out quickly.

At the head of the steps the patriarchal figure, who was the new captain of the *Sofala* apparently (he had seen a round dozen of them, but not one of that sort), towered without advancing. The little dog barked unceasingly, till a flick of Mr. Van Wyk's handkerchief made him spring aside into silence. Captain Whalley, opening the matter, was met by a punctiliously polite but determined opposition.

They carried on their discussion standing where they had come face to face. Mr. Van Wyk observed his visitor with attention. Then at last, as if forced out of his reserve—

"I am surprised that you should intercede for such a confounded fool."

This outbreak was almost complimentary, as if its meaning had been, "That such a man as you should intercede!" Captain Whalley let it pass by without flinching. One would have thought he had heard nothing. He simply went on to state that he was personally interested in putting things straight between them. Personally. . . .

But Mr. Van Wyk, really carried away by his disgust with Massy, became very incisive—

"Indeed—if I am to be frank with you—his whole character does not seem to me particularly estimable or trustworthy. . . ."

Captain Whalley, always straight, seemed to grow an inch taller and broader, as if the girth of his chest had suddenly expanded under his beard.

"My dear sir, you don't think I came here to discuss a man with whom I am—I am—h'm—closely associated."

A sort of solemn silence lasted for a moment. He was not used to asking favours, but the importance he attached to this affair had made him willing to try. . . . Mr. Van Wyk, favourably impressed, and suddenly mollified by a desire to laugh, interrupted—

"That's all right if you make it a personal matter; but you can do no less than sit down and smoke a cigar with me."

A slight pause, then Captain Whalley stepped forward heavily. As to the regularity of the service, for the future he made himself responsible for it; and his name was Whalley—perhaps to a sailor (he was speaking to a sailor, was he not?) not altogether unfamiliar. There was a lighthouse now, on an island. Maybe Mr. Van Wyk himself. . . .

"Oh, yes. Oh, indeed." Mr. Van Wyk caught on at once. He indicated a chair. How very interesting. For his own part he had seen some service in the last Acheen War, but had never been so far East. Whalley Island? Of course. Now that was very interesting. What changes his guest must have seen since.

"I can look further back even—on a whole half-century."

Captain Whalley expanded a bit. The flavour of a good cigar (it was a weakness) had gone straight to his heart, also the civility of that young man. There was something in that accidental contact of which he had been starved in his years of struggle.

The front wall retreating made a square recess furnished like a room. A lamp with a milky glass shade, suspended below the slope of the high roof at the end of a slender brass chain, threw a bright round of light upon a little table bearing an open book and an ivory paper-knife. And, in the translucent shadows beyond, other tables could be seen, a number of easy-chairs of various shapes, with a great profusion of skin rugs strewn on the teakwood planking all over the verandah. The flowering creepers scented the air. Their foliage clipped out between the uprights made as if several frames of thick, unstirring leaves reflecting the lamplight in a green glow. Through the opening at his elbow Captain Whalley could see the gangway lantern of the *Sofala* burning dim by the shore, the shadowy masses of the town beyond the open lustrous darkness of the river, and, as if hung along the straight edge of the projecting eaves, a narrow black strip of the night sky full of stars—resplendent. The famous cigar in hand he had a moment of complacency.

"A trifle. Somebody must lead the way. I just showed that the thing could be done; but you men brought up to the use of steam cannot conceive the vast importance of my bit of venturesomeness to the Eastern trade of the time. Why, that new route reduced the average time of a southern passage by eleven days for more than half the year. Eleven days! It's on record. But the remarkable thing—speaking to a sailor—I should say was. . . ."

He talked well, without egotism, professionally. The powerful voice, produced without effort, filled the bungalow even into the empty rooms with a deep and limpid resonance, seemed to make a stillness outside; and Mr. Van Wyk was surprised by the serene quality of its tone, like the perfection of manly gentleness. Nursing one small foot, in a silk sock and a patent leather shoe, on his knee, he was immensely entertained. It was as if nobody could talk like this now, and the overshadowed eyes, the flowing white beard, the big frame, the serenity, the whole temper of the man, were an amazing survival from the prehistoric times of the world coming up to him out of the sea.

Captain Whalley had been also the pioneer of the early trade in the Gulf of Petchili. He even found occasion to mention that he had buried his "dear wife" there six-and-twenty years ago. Mr. Van Wyk, impassive, could not help speculating in his mind swiftly as to the sort of woman that would mate with such a man. Did they make an adventurous and well-matched pair? No. Very possibly she had been small, frail, no doubt very feminine—or most likely commonplace with domestic instincts, utterly insignificant. But Captain Whalley was no garrulous bore, and shaking his head as if to dissipate the momentary gloom that had settled on his handsome old face, he alluded conversationally to Mr. Van Wyk's solitude.

Mr. Van Wyk affirmed that sometimes he had more company than he wanted. He mentioned smilingly some of the peculiarities of his intercourse with "My Sultan." He made his visits in force. Those people damaged his grass-plot in front (it was not easy to obtain some approach to a lawn in the tropics), and the other day had broken down some rare bushes he had planted over there. And Captain Whalley remembered immediately that, in 'forty-seven, the then Sultan, "this man's grandfather," had been notorious as a great protector of the piratical fleets of praus from farther East. They had a safe refuge in the river at Batu Beru. He financed more especially a Balinini chief called Haji Daman. Captain Whalley, nodding significantly his bushy white eyebrows, had a very good reason to know something of that. The world had progressed since that time.

Mr. Van Wyk demurred with unexpected acrimony. Progressed in what? he wanted to know.

Why, in knowledge of truth, in decency, in justice, in order—in honesty, too, since men harmed each other mostly from ignorance. It was, Captain Whalley concluded quaintly, more pleasant to live in.

Mr. Van Wyk whimsically would not admit that Mr. Massy, for instance, was more pleasant naturally than the Balinini pirates.

The river had not gained much by the change. They were in their way every bit as honest. Massy was less ferocious than Haji Daman no doubt, but. . . .

"And what about you, my good sir?" Captain Whalley laughed a deep soft laugh. "*You!* are an improvement, surely."

He continued in a vein of pleasantry. A good cigar was better than a knock on the head—the sort of welcome he would have found on this river forty or fifty years ago. Then leaning forward slightly, he became earnestly serious. It seems as if, outside their own sea-gipsy tribes, these rovers had hated all mankind with an incomprehensible, bloodthirsty hatred. Meantime their depredations had been stopped, and what was the consequence? The new generation was orderly, peaceable, settled in prosperous villages. He could speak from personal knowledge. And even the few survivors of that time—old men now—had changed so much, that it would have been unkind to remember against them that they had ever slit a throat in their lives. He had one especially in his mind's eye: a dignified, venerable headman of a certain large coast village about sixty miles sou'west of Tampasuk. It did one's heart good to see him—to hear that man speak. He might have been a ferocious savage once. What men wanted was to be checked by superior intelligence, by superior knowledge, by superior force, too—yes, by force held in trust from God and sanctified by its use in accordance with His declared will. Captain Whalley believed a disposition for good existed in every man, even if the world were not a very happy place as a whole. In the wisdom of men he had not so much confidence.

The disposition had to be helped up pretty sharply sometimes, he admitted. They might be silly, wrongheaded, unhappy; but naturally evil—no. There was at bottom a complete harmlessness at least. . . .

"Is there?" Mr. Van Wyk snapped acrimoniously.

Captain Whalley laughed at the interjection, in the good humour of large, tolerating certitude. He could look back at half a century, he pointed out. The smoke oozed placidly through the white hairs hiding his kindly lips.

"At all events," he resumed after a pause, "I am glad that they've had no time to do you much harm as yet."

This allusion to his comparative youthfulness did not offend Mr. Van Wyk, who got up and wriggled his shoulders with an enigmatic half-smile. They walked out together amicably into the starry night towards the river-side. Their footsteps resounded unequally on the dark path. At the shore end of the gangway the lantern, hung low to the handrail, threw a vivid light on the white legs and the big black feet of Mr. Massy waiting about anxiously. From the waist upwards he remained shadowy, with a row of buttons gleaming up to the vague outline of his chin.

"You may thank Captain Whalley for this," Mr. Van Wyk said, curtly, to him before turning away.

The lamps on the verandah flung three long squares of light between the uprights far over the grass. A bat flitted before his face like a circling flake of velvety blackness. Along the jasmine hedge the night air seemed heavy with the fall of perfumed dew; flower-beds bordered the path; the clipped bushes uprose in dark, rounded clumps here and there before the house; the dense foliage of creepers filtered the sheen of the lamplight within in a soft glow all along the front; and everything near and far stood still in a great immobility, in a great sweetness.

Mr. Van Wyk (a few years before he had had occasion to imagine himself treated more badly than anybody alive had ever been by a woman) felt for Captain Whalley's optimistic views the disdain of a man who had once been credulous himself. His disgust with the world (the woman for a time had filled it for him completely) had taken the form of activity in retirement, because, though capable of great depth of feeling, he was energetic and essentially practical. But there was in that uncommon old sailor, drifting on the outskirts of his busy solitude, something that fascinated his scepticism. His very simplicity (amusing enough) was like a delicate refinement of an upright character. The striking dignity of manner could be nothing else, in a man reduced to such a humble position, but the expression of something essentially noble in the character. With all his trust in mankind he was no fool; the serenity of his temper at the end of so many years, since it could not obviously have been appeased by success, wore an air of profound wisdom. Mr. Van Wyk was amused at it sometimes. Even the very physical traits of the old captain of the *Sofala,* his powerful frame, his reposeful mien, his intelligent, handsome face, the big limbs, the benign courtesy, the touch of rugged severity in the shaggy eyebrows, made up a seductive personality. Mr. Van Wyk disliked littleness of every kind, but there was nothing small about that man, and in the exemplary regularity of many trips an intimacy had grown up between them, a warm feeling at bottom under a kindly stateliness of forms agreeable to his fastidiousness.

They kept their respective opinions on all worldly matters. His other convictions Captain Whalley never intruded. The difference of their ages was like another bond between them. Once, when twitted with the uncharitableness of his youth, Mr. Van Wyk, running his eye over the vast proportions of his interlocutor, retorted in friendly banter—

"Oh. You'll come to my way of thinking yet. You'll have plenty of time. Don't call yourself old: you look good for a round hundred."

But he could not help his stinging incisiveness, and though moderating it by an almost affectionate smile, he added—

"And by then you will probably consent to die from sheer disgust."

Captain Whalley, smiling, too, shook his head. "God forbid!"

He thought that perhaps on the whole he deserved something better than to die in such sentiments. The time of course would have to come, and he trusted to his Maker to provide a manner of going out of which he need not be ashamed. For the rest he hoped he would live to a hundred if need be; other men had been known; it would be no miracle. He expected no miracles.

The pronounced, argumentative tone caused Mr. Van Wyk to raise his head and look at him steadily. Captain Whalley was gazing fixedly with a rapt expression, as though he had seen his Creator's favourable decree written in mysterious characters on the wall. He kept perfectly motionless for a few seconds, then got his vast bulk on to his feet so impetuously that Mr. Van Wyk was startled.

He struck first a heavy blow on his inflated chest: and, throwing out horizontally a big arm that remained steady, extended in the air like the limb of a tree on a windless day—

"Not a pain or an ache there. Can you see this shake in the least?"

His voice was low, in an awing, confident contrast with the headlong emphasis of his movements. He sat down abruptly.

"This isn't to boast of it, you know. I am nothing," he said in his effortless strong voice, that seemed to come out as naturally as a river flows. He picked up the stump of the cigar he had laid aside, and added peacefully, with a slight nod, "As it happens, my life is necessary; it isn't my own, it isn't—God knows."

He did not say much for the rest of the evening, but several times Mr. Van Wyk detected a faint smile of assurance flitting under the heavy moustache.

Later on Captain Whalley would now and then consent to dine "at the house." He could even be induced to drink a glass of wine. "Don't think I'm afraid of it, my good sir," he explained. "There was a very good reason why I should give it up."

On another occasion, leaning back at ease, he remarked, "You have treated me most—most humanely, my dear Mr. Van Wyk, from the very first."

"You'll admit there was some merit," Mr. Van Wyk hinted, slily. "An associate of that excellent Massy. . . . Well, well, my dear captain, I won't say a word against him."

"It would be no use your saying anything against him," Captain Whalley affirmed a little moodily. "As I've told you before, my life—my work, is necessary, not for myself alone. I can't choose. . . ." He paused, turned the glass before him right round. . . . "I have an only child—a daughter."

The ample downward sweep of his arm over the table seemed to suggest a small girl at a vast distance. "I hope to see her once more before I die. Meantime it's enough to know that she has me sound and solid, thank God. You can't understand how one feels. Bone of my bone, flesh of my flesh; the very image of my poor wife. Well, she. . . ."

Again, he paused, then pronounced stoically the words, "She has a hard struggle."

And his head fell on his breast, his eyebrows remained knitted, as by an effort of meditation. But generally his mind seemed steeped in the serenity of boundless trust in a higher power. Mr. Van Wyk wondered sometimes how much of it was due to the splendid vitality of the man, to the bodily vigour which seems to impart something of its force to the soul. But he had learned to like him very much.

· XIII ·

This was the reason why Mr. Sterne's confidential communication, delivered hurriedly on the shore alongside the dark silent ship, had disturbed his equanimity. It was the most incomprehensible and unexpected thing that could happen; and the perturbation of his spirit was so great that, forgetting all about his letters, he ran rapidly up the bridge ladder.

The portable table was being put together for dinner to the left of the wheel by two pig-tailed "boys," who as usual snarled at each other over the job, while another, a doleful, burly, very yellow Chinaman, resembling Mr. Massy, waited apathetically with the cloth over his arm and a pile of thick dinner-plates against his chest. A common cabin lamp with its globe missing, brought up from below, had been hooked to the wooden framework of the awning; the side-screens had been lowered all round; Captain Whalley, filling the depths of the wicker-chair, seemed to sit benumbed in a canvas tent crudely lighted, and used for the storing of nautical objects; a shabby steering-wheel, a battered brass binnacle on a stout mahogany stand, two dingy life-buoys, an old cork fender lying in a corner, dilapidated deck-lockers with loops of tin rope instead of door-handles.

He shook off the appearance of numbness to return Mr. Van Wyk's unusually brisk greeting, but relapsed directly afterwards. To accept a pressing invitation to dinner "up at the house" cost him another very visible physical effort. Mr. Van Wyk, perplexed, folded his arms, and leaning back against the rail, with his little, black, shiny feet well out, examined him covertly.

"I've noticed of late that you are not quite yourself, old friend."

He put an affectionate gentleness into the last two words. The real intimacy of their intercourse had never been so vividly expressed before.

"Tut, tut, tut!"

The wicker-chair creaked heavily.

"Irritable," commented Mr. Van Wyk to himself; and aloud, "I'll expect to see you in half an hour, then," he said, negligently, moving off.

"In half an hour," Captain Whalley's rigid silvery head repeated behind him as if out of a trance.

Amidships, below, two voices, close against the engine-room, could be heard answering each other—one angry and slow, the other alert.

"I tell you the beast has locked himself in to get drunk."

"Can't help it now, Mr. Massy. After all, a man has a right to shut himself up in his cabin in his own time."

"Not to get drunk."

"I heard him swear that the worry with the boilers was enough to drive any man to drink," Sterne said, maliciously.

Massy hissed out something about bursting the door in. Mr. Van Wyk, to avoid them, crossed in the dark to the other side of the deserted deck. The planking of the little wharf rattled faintly under his hasty feet.

"Mr. Van Wyk! Mr. Van Wyk!"

He walked on: somebody was running on the path. "You've forgotten to get your mail."

Sterne, holding a bundle of papers in his hand, caught up with him. "Oh, thanks."

But, as the other continued at his elbow, Mr. Van Wyk stopped short. The overhanging eaves, descending low upon the lighted front of the bungalow, threw their black straight-edged shadow into the great body of the night on that side. Everything was very still. A tinkle of cutlery and a slight jingle of glasses were heard. Mr. Van Wyk's servants were laying the table for two on the verandah.

"I am afraid you give me no credit whatever for my good intentions in the matter I've spoken to you about," said Sterne.

"I simply don't understand you."

"Captain Whalley is a very audacious man, but he will understand that his game is up. That's all that anybody need ever know of it from me. Believe me, I am very considerate in this, but duty is duty. I don't want to make a fuss. All I ask you, as his friend, is to tell him from me that the game's up. That will be sufficient."

Mr. Van Wyk felt a loathsome dismay at this queer privilege of friendship. He would not demean himself by asking for the slightest explanation; to drive the other away with contumely he did not think prudent—as yet, at any rate. So much assurance staggered him. Who could tell what there could be in it? he thought. His regard for Captain Whalley had the tenacity of a disinterested sentiment, and his practical instinct coming to his aid, he concealed his scorn.

"I gather, then, that this is something grave."

"Very grave," Sterne assented, solemnly, delighted at having produced an effect at last. He was ready to add some effusive protestations of regret at the "unavoidable necessity," but Mr. Van Wyk cut him short—very civilly, however.

Once on the verandah Mr. Van Wyk put his hands in his pockets, and, straddling his legs, stared down at a black panther skin lying on the floor before a rocking-chair. "It looks as if the fellow had not the pluck to play his own precious game openly," he thought.

This was true enough. In the face of Massy's last rebuff Sterne dared not declare his knowledge. His object was simply to get charge of the steamer and keep it for some time. Massy would never forgive him for forcing himself on; but if Captain Whalley left the ship of his own accord, the command would devolve upon him for the rest of the trip; so he hit upon the brilliant idea of scaring the old man away. A vague menace, a mere hint, would be enough in such a brazen case; and, with a strange admixture of compassion, he thought that Batu Beru was a very good place for throwing up the sponge. The skipper could go ashore quietly, and stay with that Dutchman of his. Weren't these two as thick as thieves together? And on reflection he seemed to see that there was a way to work the whole thing through that great friend of the old man's. This was another brilliant idea. He had an inborn preference for circuitous methods. In this particular case he desired to remain in the background as much as possible, to avoid exasperating Massy needlessly. No fuss! Let it all happen naturally.

Mr. Van Wyk all through the dinner was conscious of a sense of isolation that invades sometimes the closeness of human intercourse. Captain Whalley failed lamentably and obviously in his attempts to eat something. He seemed overcome by a strange absentmindedness. His hand would hover irresolutely, as if left without guidance by a preoccupied mind. Mr. Van Wyk had heard him coming up from a long way off in the profound stillness of the river-side, and had noticed the irresolute character of the footfalls. The toe of his boot had struck the bottom stair as though he had come along mooning with his head in the air right up to the steps of the verandah. Had the captain of the *Sofala* been another sort of man he would have suspected the work of age there. But one glance at him was enough. Time—after, indeed, marking him for its own—had given him up to his usefulness, in which his simple faith would see a proof of Divine mercy. "How could I contrive to warn him?" Mr. Van Wyk wondered, as if Captain Whalley had been miles and miles away, out of sight and earshot of all evil. He was sickened by an immense disgust of Sterne. Even to mention his threat to a man like Whalley would be positively indecent. There was something more vile and insulting in its hint than in a definite charge of crime—the debasing taint of blackmailing. "What could any one bring against him?" he asked himself. This was a limpid personality. "And for what object?" The Power that man trusted had thought fit to leave him nothing on earth that envy could lay hold of, except a bare crust of bread.

"Won't you try some of this?" he asked, pushing a dish slightly. Suddenly it occurred to Mr. Van Wyk that Sterne might possibly be coveting the command of the *Sofala*. His cynicism was quite startled by what looked like a proof that no man may count himself safe from his kind unless in the very abyss of misery. An intrigue of that sort was hardly worth troubling about, he judged; but still, with such a fool as Massy to deal with, Whalley ought to and must be warned.

At this moment Captain Whalley, bolt upright, the deep cavities of the eyes overhung by a bushy frown, and one large brown hand resting on each side of his empty plate, spoke across the table-cloth abruptly—

"Mr. Van Wyk, you've always treated me with the most humane consideration."

"My dear captain, you make too much of the simple fact that I am not a savage." Mr. Van Wyk, utterly revolted by the thought of Sterne's obscure attempt, raised his voice incisively, as if the mate had been hiding somewhere within earshot. "Any consideration I have been able to show was no more than the rightful due of a character I've learned to regard by this time with an esteem that nothing can shake."

A slight ring of glass made him lift his eyes from the slice of pineapple he was cutting into small pieces on his plate. In changing his position Captain Whalley had contrived to upset an empty tumbler.

Without looking that way, leaning sideways on his elbow, his other hand shading his brow, he groped shadily for it, then desisted. Van Wyk stared blankly, as if something momentous had happened all at once. He did not know why he should feel so startled; but he forgot Sterne utterly for the moment,

"Why, what's the matter?"

And Captain Whalley, half-averted, in a deadened, agitated voice, muttered—

"Esteem!"

"And I may add something more," Mr. Van Wyk, very steady-eyed, pronounced slowly.

"Hold! Enough!" Captain Whalley did not change his attitude or raise his voice. "Say no more! I can make you no return. I am too poor even for that now. Your esteem is worth having. You are not a man that would stoop to deceive the poorest sort of devil on earth, or make a ship unseaworthy every time he takes her to sea."

Mr. Van Wyk, leaning forward, his face gone pink all over, with the starched table-napkin over his knees, was inclined to mistrust his senses, his power of comprehension, the sanity of his guest.

"Where? Why? In the name of God!—what's this? What ship? I don't understand who. . . ."

"Then, in the name of God, it is I! A ship's unseaworthy when her captain can't see. I am going blind."

Mr. Van Wyk made a slight movement, and sat very still afterwards for a few seconds; then, with the thought of Sterne's "The game's up," he ducked under the table to pick up the napkin which had slipped off his knees. This was the game that was up. And at the same time the muffled voice of Captain Whalley passed over him—

"I've deceived them all. Nobody knows."

He emerged flushed to the eyes. Captain Whalley, motionless under the full blaze of the lamp, shaded his face with his hand.

"And you had that courage?"

"Call it by what name you like. But you are a humane man—a—a—gentleman, Mr. Van Wyk. You may have asked me what I had done with my conscience."

He seemed to muse, profoundly silent, very still in his mournful pose.

"I began to tamper with it in my pride. You begin to see a lot of things when you are going blind. I could not be frank with an old chum even. I was not frank with Massy—no, not altogether. I knew he took me for a wealthy sailor fool, and I let him. I wanted to keep up my importance—because there was poor Ivy away there—my daughter. What did I want to trade on his misery for? I did trade on it—for her. And now, what mercy could I expect from him? He would trade on mine if he knew it. He would hunt the old fraud out, and stick to the money for a year. Ivy's money. And I haven't kept a penny for myself. How am I going to live for a year. A year! In a year there will be no sun in the sky for her father."

His deep voice came out, awfully veiled, as though he had been overwhelmed by the earth of a landslide and talking of the thoughts that haunt the dead in their graves. A cold shudder ran down Mr. Van Wyk's back.

"And how long is it since you have. . . ?" he began.

"It was a long time before I could bring myself to believe in this—this—visitation." Captain Whalley spoke with gloomy patience from under his hand.

He had not thought he had deserved it. He had begun by deceiving himself from day to day, from week to week. He had the Serang at hand there—an old servant. It came on gradually, and when he could no longer deceive himself. . . .

His voice died out almost.

"Rather than give her up I set myself to deceive you all."

"It's incredible," whispered Mr. Van Wyk. Captain Whalley's appalling murmur flowed on.

"Not even the sign of God's anger could make me forget her. How could I forsake my child, feeling my vigour all the time—the blood warm within me? Warm as yours. It seems to me that, like the blinded Samson, I would find the strength to shake down a temple upon my head. She's a struggling woman—my own child that we used to pray over together, my poor wife and I. Do you remember that day I as well as told you that I believed God would let me live to a hundred for her sake? What sin is there in loving your child? Do you see it? I was ready for her sake to live for ever. I half believed I would. I've been praying for death since. Ha! Presumptuous man—you wanted to live. . . ."

A tremendous, shuddering upheaval of that big frame, shaken by a gasping sob, set the glasses jingling all over the table, seemed to make the whole house tremble to the roof-tree. And Mr. Van Wyk, whose feeling of outraged love had been translated into a form of struggle with nature, understood very well that, for that man whose whole life had been conditioned by action, there could exist no other expression for all the emotions; that, voluntarily to cease venturing, doing, enduring, for his child's sake, would have been exactly like plucking his warm love for her out of his living heart. Something too monstrous, too impossible, even to conceive.

Captain Whalley had not changed his attitude, that seemed to express something of shame, sorrow, and defiance.

"I have even deceived you. If it had not been for that word 'esteem.' These are not the words for me. I would have lied to you. Haven't I lied to you? Weren't you going to trust your property on board this very trip?"

"I have a floating yearly policy," Mr. Van Wyk said almost unwittingly, and was amazed at the sudden cropping up of a commercial detail.

"The ship is unseaworthy, I tell you. The policy would be invalid if it were known. . . ."

"We shall share the guilt, then."

"Nothing could make mine less," said Captain Whalley.

He had not dared to consult a doctor; the man would have perhaps asked who he was, what he was doing; Massy might have heard something. He had lived on without any help, human or divine. The very prayers stuck in his throat. What was there to pray for? and death seemed as far as ever. Once he got into his cabin he dared not come out again; when he sat down he dared not get up; he dared not raise his eyes to anybody's face, he felt reluctant to look upon the sea or up to the sky. The world was fading before his great fear of giving himself away. The old ship was his last friend; he was not afraid of her; he knew every inch of her deck; but at her, too, he hardly dared to look, for fear of finding he could see less than the day before. A great incertitude enveloped him. The horizon was gone; the sky mingled darkly with the sea. Who was this figure standing over yonder? what was this thing lying down there? And a frightful doubt of the reality of what he could see made even the remnant of sight that remained to him an added torment, a pitfall always open for his miserable pretence. He was afraid to stumble inexcusably over something—to say a fatal Yes or No to a question. The hand of God was upon him, but it could not tear him away from his child. And, as if in a nightmare of humiliation, every featureless man seemed an enemy.

He let his hand fall heavily on the table. Mr. Van Wyk, arms down, chin on breast, with a gleam of white teeth pressing on the lower lip, meditated on Sterne's "The game's up."

"The Serang of course does not know."

"Nobody," said Captain Whalley, with assurance.

"Ah, yes. Nobody. Very well. Can you keep it up to the end of the trip? That is the last under the agreement with Massy."

Captain Whalley got up and stood erect, very stately, with the great white beard lying like a silver breastplate over the awful secret of his heart. Yes; that was the only hope there was for him of ever seeing her again, of securing the money, the last he could do for her, before he crept away somewhere—useless, a burden, a reproach to himself. His voice faltered.

"Think of it! Never see her any more: the only human being besides myself now on earth that can remember my wife. She's just like her mother. Lucky the poor woman is where there are no tears shed over those they loved on earth and that remain to pray not to be led into temptation—because, I suppose, the blessed know the secret of grace in God's dealings with His created children."

He swayed a little, said with austere dignity—

"I don't. I know only the child He has given me."

And he began to walk. Mr. Van Wyk, jumping up, saw the full meaning of the rigid head, the hesitating feet, the vaguely extended hand. His heart was beating fast; he moved a chair aside, and instinctively advanced as if to offer his arm. But Captain Whalley passed him by, making for the stairs quite straight.

"He could not see me at all out of his line," Van Wyk thought, with a sort of awe. Then going to the head of the stairs, he asked a little tremulously—

"What is it like—like a mist—like. . . ." Captain Whalley, half-way down, stopped, and turned round undismayed to answer:

"It is as if the light were ebbing out of the world. Have you ever watched the ebbing sea on an open stretch of sands withdrawing farther and farther away from you? It is like this—only there will be no flood to follow. Never. It is as if the sun were growing smaller, the stars going out one by one. There can't be many left that I can see by this. But I haven't had the courage to look of late. . . ." He must have been able to make out Mr. Van Wyk, because he checked him by an authoritative gesture and a stoical—

"I can get about alone yet."

It was as if he had taken his line, and would accept no help from men, after having been cast out, like a presumptuous Titan, from his heaven. Mr. Van Wyk, arrested, seemed to count the footsteps right out of earshot. He walked between the tables, tapping smartly with his heels, took up a paper-knife, dropped it after a vague glance along the blade; then happening upon the piano, struck a few chords, standing up before the keyboard with an attentive poise of the head like a piano-tuner; closing it, he pivoted on his heels brusquely, avoided the little terrier sleeping trustfully on crossed forepaws, came upon the stairs next, and, as though he had lost his balance on the top step, ran down headlong out of the house. His servants, beginning to clear the table, heard him mutter to himself (evil words no doubt) down there, and then after a pause go away with a strolling gait in the direction of the wharf.

The bulwarks of the *Sofala* lying alongside the bank made a low, black wall on the undulating contour of the shore. Two masts and a funnel uprose from behind it with a great rake, as if about to fall: a solid, square elevation in the middle bore the ghostly shapes of white boats, the curves of davits, lines of rail and stanchions, all confused and mingling darkly everywhere; but low down, amidships, a single lighted port stared out on the night, perfectly round, like a small, full moon, whose yellow beam caught a patch of wet mud, the edge of trodden grass, two turns of heavy cable wound round the foot of a thick wooden post in the ground.

Mr. Van Wyk, peering alongside, heard a muzzy boastful voice apparently jeering at a person called Prendergast. It mouthed abuse thickly, choked; then pronounced very distinctly the word "Murphy," and chuckled. Glass tinkled tremulously. All these sounds came from the lighted port. Mr. Van Wyk hesitated, stooped; it was impossible to look through unless he went down into the mud.

"Sterne," he said half aloud.

The drunken voice within said gladly:

"Sterne—of course. Look at him blink. Look at him! Sterne, Whalley, Massy. Massy, Whalley, Sterne. But Massy's the best. You can't come over him. He would just love to see you starve."

Mr. Van Wyk moved away, made out farther forward a shadowy head stuck out from under the awnings as if on the watch, and spoke quietly in Malay, "Is the mate asleep?"

"No. Here, at your service."

In a moment Sterne appeared, walking as noiselessly as a cat on the wharf.

"It's so jolly dark, and I had no idea you would be down to-night."

"What's this horrible raving?" asked Mr. Van Wyk, as if to explain the cause of a shudder that ran over him audibly.

"Jack's broken out on a drunk. That's our second. It's his way. He will be right enough by to-morrow afternoon, only Mr. Massy will keep on worrying up and down the deck. We had better get away."

He muttered suggestively of a talk "up at the house." He had long desired to effect an entrance there, but Mr. Van Wyk nonchalantly demurred: it would not, he feared, be quite prudent, perhaps; and the opaque black shadow under one of the two big trees left at the landing-place swallowed them up, impenetrably dense by the side of the wide river that seemed to spin into threads of glitter the light of a few big stars dropped here and there upon its outspread and flowing stillness.

"The situation is grave beyond doubt," Mr. Van Wyk said. Ghostlike in their white clothes they could not distinguish each other's features, and their feet made no sound on the soft earth. A sort of purring was heard. Mr. Sterne felt gratified by such a beginning.

"I thought, Mr. Van Wyk, a gentleman of your sort would see at once how awkwardly I was situated."

"Yes, very. Obviously his health is bad. Perhaps he's breaking up. I see, and he himself is well aware—I assume I am speaking to a man of sense—he is well aware that his legs are giving out."

"His legs—ah!" Mr. Sterne was disconcerted, and then turned sulky. "You may call it his legs if you like; what I want to know is whether he intends to clear out quietly. That's a good one, too! His legs! Pooh!"

"Why, yes. Only look at the way he walks," Van Wyk took him up in a perfectly cool and undoubting tone. "The question, however, is whether your sense of duty does not carry you too far from your true interest. After all, I, too, could do something to serve you. You know who I am."

"Everybody along the Straits has heard of you, sir."

Mr. Van Wyk presumed that this meant something favourable.

Sterne had a soft laugh at this pleasantry. He should think so! To the opening statement, that the partnership agreement was to expire at the end of this very trip, he gave an attentive assent. He was aware. One heard of nothing else on board all the blessed day long. As to Massy, it was no secret that he was in a jolly deep hole with these worn-out boilers. He would have to borrow somewhere a couple of hundred first of all to pay off the captain; and then he would have to raise money on mortgage upon the ship for the new boilers—that is, if he could find a lender at all. At best it meant loss of time, a break in the trade, short earnings for the year—and there was always the danger of having his connection filched away from him by the Germans. It was whispered about that he had already tried two firms. Neither would have anything to do with him. Ship too old, and the man too well known in the place. . . . Mr. Sterne's final rapid winking remained buried in the deep darkness sibilating with his whispers.

"Supposing, then, he got the loan," Mr. Van Wyk resumed in a deliberate undertone, "on your own showing he's more than likely to get a mortgagee's man thrust upon him as captain. For my part, I know that I would make that very stipulation myself if I had to find the money. And as a matter of fact I am thinking of doing so. It would be worth my while in many ways. Do you see how this would bear on the case under discussion?"

"Thank you, sir. I am sure you couldn't get anybody that would care more for your interests."

"Well, it suits my interest that Captain Whalley should finish his time. I shall probably take a passage with you down the Straits. If that can be done, I'll be on the spot when all these changes take place, and in a position to look after *your* interests."

"Mr. Van Wyk, I want nothing better. I am sure I am infinitely. . . ."

"I take it, then, that this may be done without any trouble."

"Well, sir, what risk there is can't be helped; but (speaking to you as my employer now) the thing is more safe than it looks. If anybody had told me of it I wouldn't have believed it, but I have been looking on myself. That old Serang has been trained up to the game. There's nothing the matter with his—his—limbs, sir. He's got used to do things on his own in a remarkable way. And let me tell you, sir, that Captain Whalley, poor man, is by no means useless. Fact. Let me explain to you, sir. He stiffens up that old monkey of a Malay, who knows well enough what to do. Why, he must have kept captain's watches in all sorts of country ships off and on for the last five-and-twenty years. These natives, sir, as long as they have a white man close at the back, will go on doing the right thing most surprisingly well—even if left quite to themselves. Only the white man must be of the sort to put starch into them, and the captain is just the one for that. Why, sir, he has drilled him so well that now he needs hardly speak at all. I have seen that little wrinkled ape made to take the ship out of Pangu Bay on a blowy morning and on all through the islands; take her out first-rate, sir, dodging under the old man's elbow, and in such quiet style that you could not have told for the life of you which of the two was doing the work up there. That's where our poor friend would be still of use to the ship even if—if—he could no longer lift a foot, sir. Providing the Serang does not know that there's anything wrong."

"He doesn't."

"Naturally not. Quite beyond his apprehension. They aren't capable of finding out anything about us, sir."

"You seem to be a shrewd man," said Mr. Van Wyk in a choked mutter, as though he were feeling sick.

"You'll find me a good enough servant, sir."

Mr. Sterne hoped now for a handshake at least, but unexpectedly with a "What's this? Better not to be seen together," Mr. Van Wyk's white shape wavered, and instantly seemed to melt away in the black air under the roof of boughs. The mate was startled. Yes. There was that faint thumping clatter.

He stole out silently from under the shade. The lighted port-hole shone from afar. His head swam with the intoxication of sudden success. What a thing it was to have a gentleman to deal with! He crept aboard, and there was something weird in the shadowy stretch of empty decks, echoing with shouts and blows proceeding from a darker part amidships. Mr. Massy was raging before the door of the berth: the drunken voice within flowed on undisturbed in the violent racket of kicks.

"Shut up! Put your light out and turn in, you confounded swilling pig—you! D'you hear me, you beast?"

The kicking stopped, and in the pause the muzzy oracular voice announced from within—

"Ah! Massy, now—that's another thing. Massy's deep."

"Who's that aft there? You, Sterne? He'll drink himself into a fit of horrors." The chief engineer appeared vague and big at the corner of the engine-room skylight.

"He will be good enough for duty to-morrow. I would let him be, Mr. Massy."

Sterne slipped away into his berth, and at once had to sit down. His head swam with exultation. He got into his bunk as if in a dream. A feeling of profound peace, of pacific joy, came over him. On deck all was quiet.

Mr. Massy, with his ear against the door of Jack's cabin, listened critically to a deep, stertorous breathing within. This was a dead-drunk sleep. The bout was over: tranquillized on that score, he, too, went in, and with slow wriggles got out of his old tweed jacket. It was a garment with many pockets, which he used to put on at odd times of the day, being subject to sudden chilly fits, and when he felt warmed he would take it off and hang it about anywhere all over the ship. It would be seen swinging on belaying-pins, thrown over the heads of winches, suspended on people's very door-handles for that matter. Was he not the owner? But his favourite place was a hook on a wooden awning stanchion on the bridge, almost against the binnacle. He had even in the early days more than one tussle on that point with Captain Whalley, who desired the bridge to be kept tidy. He had been overawed then. Of late, though, he had been able to defy his partner with impunity. Captain Whalley never seemed to notice anything now. As to the Malays, in their awe of that scowling man not one of the crew would dream of laying a hand on the thing, no matter where or what it swung from.

With an unexpectedness which made Mr. Massy jump and drop the coat at his feet, there came from the next berth the crash and thud of a headlong, jingling, clattering fall. The faithful Jack must have dropped to sleep suddenly as he sat at his revels, and now had gone over chair and all, breaking, as it seemed by the sound, every single glass and bottle in the place. After the terrific smash all was still for a time in there, as though he had killed himself on the spot. Mr. Massy held his breath. At last a sleepy, uneasy groaning sigh was exhaled slowly on the other side of the bulkhead.

"I hope to goodness he's too drunk to wake up now," muttered Mr. Massy.

The sound of a softly knowing laugh nearly drove him to despair. He swore violently under his breath. The fool would keep him awake all night now for certain. He cursed his luck. He wanted to forget his maddening troubles in sleep sometimes. He could detect no movements. Without apparently making the slightest attempt to get up, Jack went on sniggering to himself where he lay; then began to speak, where he had left off as it were—

"Massy! I love the dirty rascal. He would like to see his poor old Jack starve—but just you look where he has climbed to. . . ." He hiccoughed in a superior, leisurely manner. . . . "Shipowning it with the best. A lottery ticket you want. Ha! ha! I will give you lottery tickets, my boy. Let the old ship sink and the old chum starve—that's right. He don't go wrong—Massy don't. Not he. He's a genius—that man is. That's the way to win your money. Ship and chum must go."

"The silly fool has taken it to heart," muttered Massy to himself. And, listening with a softened expression of face for any slight sign of returning drowsiness, he was discouraged profoundly by a burst of laughter full of joyful irony.

"Would like to see her at the bottom of the sea! Oh, you clever, clever devil! Wish her sunk, eh? I should think you would, my boy; the damned old thing and all your troubles with her. Rake in the insurance money—turn your back on your old chum—all's well—gentleman again."

A grim stillness had come over Massy's face. Only his big black eyes rolled uneasily. The raving fool. And yet it was all true. Yes. Lottery tickets, too. All true. What? Beginning again? He wished he wouldn't. . . .

But it was even so. The imaginative drunkard on the other side of the bulkhead shook off the deathlike stillness that after his last words had fallen on the dark ship moored to a silent shore.

"Don't you dare to say anything against George Massy, Esquire. When he's tired of waiting he will do away with her. Look out! Down she goes—chum and all. He'll know how to. . . ."

The voice hesitated, weary, dreamy, lost, as if dying away in a vast open space.

". . . Find a trick that will work. He's up to it—never fear. . . ."

He must have been very drunk, for at last the heavy sleep gripped him with the suddenness of a magic spell, and the last word lengthened itself into an interminable, noisy, indrawn snore. And then even the snoring stopped, and all was still.

But it seemed as though Mr. Massy had suddenly come to doubt the efficacy of sleep as against a man's troubles; or perhaps he had found the relief he needed in the stillness of a calm contemplation that may contain the vivid thoughts of wealth, of a stroke of luck, of long idleness, and may bring before you the imagined form of every desire; for, turning about and throwing his arms over the edge of his bunk, he stood there with his feet on his favourite old coat, looking out through the round port into the night over the river. Sometimes a breath of wind would enter and touch his face, a cool breath charged with the damp, fresh feel from a vast body of water. A glimmer here and there was all he could see of it; and once he might after all suppose he had dozed off, since there appeared before his vision, unexpectedly and connected with no dream, a row of flaming and gigantic figures—three nought seven one two—making up a number such as you may see on a lottery ticket. And then all at once the port was no longer black: it was pearly gray, framing a shore crowded with houses, thatched roof beyond thatched roof, walls of mats and bamboo, gables of carved teak timber. Rows of dwellings raised on a forest of piles lined the steely bank of the river, brimful and still, with the tide on the turn. This was Batu Beru—and the day had come.

Mr. Massy shook himself, put on the tweed coat, and, shivering nervously as if from some great shock, made a note of the number. A fortunate, rare hint that. Yes; but to pursue fortune one wanted money—ready cash.

Then he went out and prepared to descend into the engine-room. Several small jobs had to be seen to, and Jack was lying dead drunk on the floor of his cabin, with the door locked at that. His gorge rose at the thought of work. Ay! But if you wanted to do nothing you had to get first a good bit of money. A ship won't save you. True, all true. He was tired of waiting for some chance that would rid him at last of that ship that had turned out a curse on his life.

· XIV ·

The deep, interminable hoot of the steam-whistle had, in its grave, vibrating note, something intolerable, which sent a slight shudder down Mr. Van Wyk's back. It was the early afternoon; the *Sofala* was leaving Batu Beru for Pangu, the next place of call. She swung in the stream, scantily attended by a few canoes, and, gliding on the broad river, became lost to view from the Van Wyk bungalow.

Its owner had not gone this time to see her off. Generally he came down to the wharf, exchanged a few words with the bridge while she cast off, and waved his hand to Captain Whalley at the last moment. This day he did not even go as far as the balustrade of the verandah. "He couldn't see me if I did," he said to himself. "I wonder whether he can make out the house at all." And this thought somehow made him feel more alone than he had ever felt for all these years. What was it? six or seven? Seven. A long time.

He sat on the verandah with a closed book on his knee, and, as it were, looked out upon his solitude, as if the fact of Captain Whalley's blindness had opened his eyes to his own. There were many sorts of heartaches and troubles, and there was no place where they could not find a man out. And he felt ashamed, as though he had for six years behaved like a peevish boy.

His thought followed the *Sofala* on her way. On the spur of the moment he had acted impulsively, turning to the thing most pressing. And what else could he have done? Later on he should see. It seemed necessary that he should come out into the world, for a time at least. He had money—something could be arranged; he would grudge no time, no trouble, no loss of his solitude. It weighed on him now—and Captain Whalley appeared to him as he had sat shading his eyes, as if, being deceived in the trust of his faith, he were beyond all the good and evil that can be wrought by the hands of men.

Mr. Van Wyk's thoughts followed the *Sofala* down the river, winding about through the belt of the coast forest, between the buttressed shafts of the big trees, through the mangrove strip, and over the bar. The ship crossed it easily in broad daylight, piloted, as it happened, by Mr. Sterne, who took the watch from four to six, and then went below to hug himself with delight at the prospect of being virtually employed by a rich man—like Mr. Van Wyk. He could not see how any hitch could occur now. He did not seem able to get over the feeling of being "fixed up at last." From six to eight, in the course of duty, the Serang looked alone after the ship. She had a clear road before her now till about three in the morning, when she would close with the Pangu group. At eight Mr. Sterne came out cheerily to take charge again till midnight. At ten he was still chirruping and humming to himself on the bridge, and about that time Mr. Van Wyk's thought abandoned the *Sofala.* Mr. Van Wyk had fallen asleep at last.

Massy, blocking the engine-room companion, jerked himself into his tweed jacket surlily, while the second waited with a scowl.

"Oh. You came out! You sot! Well, what have you got to say for yourself?"

He had been in charge of the engines till then. A sombre fury darkened his mind: a hot anger against the ship, against the facts of life, against the men for their cheating, against himself, too—because of an inward tremor in his heart.

An incomprehensible growl answered him.

"What? Can't you open your mouth now? You yelp out your infernal rot loud enough when you are drunk. What do you mean by abusing people in that way?—you old useless boozer, you!"

"Can't help it. Don't remember anything about it. You shouldn't listen."

"You dare to tell me! What do you mean by going on a drunk like this?"

"Don't ask me. Sick of the dam' boilers—you would be. Sick of Life."

"I wish you were dead, then. You've made me sick of you. Don't you remember the uproar you made last night? You miserable old soaker!"

"No; I don't. Don't want to. Drink is drink."

"I wonder what prevents me from kicking you out. What do you want here?"

"Relieve you. You've been long enough down there, George."

"Don't you George me—you tippling old rascal, you! If I were to die to-morrow you would starve. Remember that. Say Mr. Massy."

"Mr. Massy," repeated the other, stolidly.

Dishevelled, with dull blood-shot eyes, a snuffy, grimy shirt, greasy trousers, naked feet thrust into ragged slippers, he bolted in head down directly Massy had made way for him.

The chief engineer looked around. The deck was empty as far as the taffrail. All the native passengers had left in Batu Beru this time, and no others had joined. The dial of the patent log tinkled periodically in the dark at the end of the ship. It was a dead calm, and, under the clouded sky, through the still air that seemed to cling warm, with a seaweed smell, to her slim hull, on a sea of sombre gray and unwrinkled, the ship moved on an even keel, as if floating detached in empty space. But Mr. Massy slapped his forehead, tottered a little, and caught hold of a belaying-pin at the foot of the mast.

"I shall go mad," he muttered, walking across the deck unsteadily. A shovel was scraping loose coal down below—a fire-door clanged. Sterne on the bridge began whistling a new tune.

Captain Whalley, sitting on the couch, awake and fully dressed, heard the door of his cabin open. He did not move in the least, waiting to recognize the voice, with an appalling strain of prudence.

A bulkhead lamp blazed on the white paint, the crimson plush, the brown varnish of mahogany tops. The white wood packing-case under the bed-place had remained unopened for three years now, as though Captain Whalley had felt that, after the *Fair Maid* was gone, there could be no abiding-place on earth for his affections. His hands rested on his knees; his handsome head with big eyebrows presented a rigid profile to the doorway. The expected voice spoke out at last.

"Once more, then. What am I to call you?"

Ha! Massy. Again. The weariness of it crushed his heart—and the pain of shame was almost more than he could bear without crying out.

"Well. Is it to be 'partner' still?"

"You don't know what you ask."

"I know what I want. . . ."

Massy stepped in and closed the door.

". . . And I am going to have a try for it with you once more."

His whine was half persuasive, half menacing.

"For it's no manner of use to tell me that you are poor. You don't spend anything on yourself, that's true enough; but there's another name for that. You think you are going to have what you want out of me for three years, and then cast me off without hearing what I think of you. You think I would have submitted to your airs if I had known you had only a beggarly five hundred pounds in the world. You ought to have told me."

"Perhaps," said Captain Whalley, bowing his head. "And yet it has saved you. . . ." Massy laughed scornfully. . . . "I have told you often enough since."

"And I don't believe you now. When I think how I let you lord it over my ship! Do you remember how you used to bullyrag me about my coat and *your* bridge? It was in his way. *His* bridge! 'And I won't be a party to this—and I couldn't think of doing that.' Honest man! And now it all comes out. 'I am poor, and I can't. I have only this five hundred in the world.'"

He contemplated the immobility of Captain Whalley, that seemed to present an inconquerable obstacle in his path. His face took a mournful cast.

"You are a hard man."

"Enough," said Captain Whalley, turning upon him. "You shall get nothing from me, because I have nothing of mine to give away now."

"Tell that to the marines!"

Mr. Massy, going out, looked back once; then the door closed, and Captain Whalley, alone, sat as still as before. He had nothing of his own—even his own past of honour, of truth, of just pride, was gone. All his spotless life had fallen into the abyss. He had said his last good-bye to it. But what belonged to *her,* that he meant to save. Only a little money. He would take it to her in his own hands—this last gift of a man that had lasted too long. And an immense and fierce impulse, the very passion of paternity, flamed up with all the unquenched vigour of his worthless life in a desire to see her face.

Just across the deck Massy had gone straight to his cabin, struck a light, and hunted up the note of the dreamed number whose figures had flamed up also with the fierceness of another passion. He must contrive somehow not to miss a drawing. That number meant something. But what expedient could he contrive to keep himself going?

"Wretched miser!" he mumbled.

If Mr. Sterne could at no time have told him anything new about his partner, he could have told Mr. Sterne that another use could be made of a man's affliction than just to kick him out, and thus defer the term of a difficult payment for a year. To keep the secret of the affliction and induce him to stay was a better move. If without means, he would be anxious to remain; and that settled the question of refunding him his share. He did not know exactly how much Captain Whalley was disabled; but if it so happened that he put the ship ashore somewhere for good and all, it was not the owner's fault—was it? He was not obliged to know that there was anything wrong. But probably nobody would raise such a point, and the ship was fully insured. He had had enough self-restraint to pay up the premiums. But this was not all. He could not believe Captain Whalley to be so confoundedly destitute as not to have some more money put away somewhere. If he, Massy, could get hold of it, that would pay for the boilers, and everything would go on as before. And if she got lost in the end, so much the better. He hated her: he loathed the troubles that took his mind off the chances of fortune. He wished her at the bottom of the sea, and the insurance money in his pocket. And as, baffled, he left Captain Whalley's cabin, he enveloped in the same hatred the ship with the worn-out boilers and the man with the dimmed eyes.

And our conduct after all is so much a matter of outside suggestion, that had it not been for his Jack's drunken gabble he would have there and then had it out with this miserable man, who would neither help, nor stay, nor yet lose the ship. The old fraud! He longed to kick him out. But he restrained himself. Time enough for that—when he liked. There was a fearful new thought put into his head. Wasn't he up to it after all? How that beast Jack had raved! "Find a safe trick to get rid of her." Well, Jack was not so far wrong. A very clever trick had occurred to him. Ay! But what of the risk?

A feeling of pride—the pride of superiority to common prejudices—crept into his breast, made his heart beat fast, his mouth turn dry. Not everybody would dare; but he was Massy, and he was up to it!

Six bells were struck on deck. Eleven! He drank a glass of water, and sat down for ten minutes or so to calm himself. Then he got out of his chest a small bull's-eye lantern of his own and lit it.

Almost opposite his berth, across the narrow passage under the bridge, there was, in the iron deck-structure covering the stokehold fiddle and the boiler-space, a storeroom with iron sides, iron roof, iron-plated floor, too, on account of the heat below. All sorts of rubbish was shot there: it had a mound of scrap-iron in a corner; rows of empty oil-cans; sacks of cotton-waste, with a heap of charcoal, a deck-forge, fragments of an old hen-coop, winch-covers all in rags, remnants of lamps, and a brown felt hat, discarded by a man dead now (of a fever on the Brazil coast), who had been once mate of the *Sofala,* had remained for years jammed forcibly behind a length of burst copper pipe, flung at some time or other out of the engine-room. A complete and impervious blackness pervaded that Capharnaum of forgotten things. A small shaft of light from Mr. Massy's bull's-eye fell slanting right through it.

His coat was unbuttoned; he shot the bolt of the door (there was no other opening), and, squatting before the scrap-heap, began to pack his pockets with pieces of iron. He packed them carefully, as if the rusty nuts, the broken bolts, the links of cargo chain, had been so much gold he had that one chance to carry away. He packed his side-pockets till they bulged, the breast-pocket, the pockets inside. He turned over the pieces. Some he rejected. A small mist of powdered rust began to rise about his busy hands. Mr. Massy knew something of the scientific basis of his clever trick. If you want to deflect the magnetic needle of a ship's compass, soft iron is the best; likewise many small pieces in the pockets of a jacket would have more effect than a few large ones, because in that way you obtain a greater amount of surface for weight in your iron, and it's surface that tells.

He slipped out swiftly—two strides sufficed—and in his cabin he perceived that his hands were all red—red with rust. It disconcerted him, as though he had found them covered with blood: he looked himself over hastily. Why, his trousers, too! He had been rubbing his rusty palms on his legs.

He tore off the waistband button in his haste, brushed his coat, washed his hands. Then the air of guilt left him, and he sat down to wait.

He sat bolt upright and weighted with iron in his chair. He had a hard, lumpy bulk against each hip, felt the scrappy iron in his pockets touch his ribs at every breath, the downward drag of all these pounds hanging upon his shoulders. He looked very dull, too, sitting idle there, and his yellow face, with motionless black eyes, had something passive and sad in its quietness.

When he heard eight bells struck above his head, he rose and made ready to go out. His movements seemed aimless, his lower lip had dropped a little, his eyes roamed about the cabin, and the tremendous tension of his will had robbed them of every vestige of intelligence.

With the last stroke of the bell the Serang appeared noiselessly on the bridge to relieve the mate. Sterne overflowed with good nature, since he had nothing more to desire.

"Got your eyes well open yet, Serang? It's middling dark; I'll wait till you get your sight properly."

The old Malay murmured, looked up with his worn eyes, sidled away into the light of the binnacle, and, clasping his hands behind his back, fixed his eyes on the compass-card.

"You'll have to keep a good lookout ahead for land, about half-past three. It's fairly clear, though. You have looked in on the captain as you came along—eh? He knows the time? Well, then, I am off."

At the foot of the ladder he stood aside for the captain. He watched him go up with an even, certain tread, and remained thoughtful for a moment. "It's funny," he said to himself, "but you can never tell whether that man has seen you or not. He might have heard me breathe this time."

He was a wonderful man when all was said and done. They said he had had a name in his day. Mr. Sterne could well believe it; and he concluded serenely that Captain Whalley must be able to see people more or less—as himself just now, for instance—but not being certain of anybody, had to keep up that unnoticing silence of manner for fear of giving himself away. Mr. Sterne was a shrewd guesser.

This necessity of every moment brought home to Captain Whalley's heart the humiliation of his falsehood. He had drifted into it from paternal love, from incredulity, from boundless trust in divine justice meted out to men's feelings on this earth. He would give his poor Ivy the benefit of another month's work; perhaps the affliction was only temporary. Surely God would not rob his child of his power to help, and cast him naked into a night without end. He had caught at every hope; and when the evidence of his misfortune was stronger than hope, he tried not to believe the manifest thing.

In vain. In the steadily darkening universe a sinister clearness fell upon his ideas. In the illuminating moments of suffering he saw life, men, all things, the whole earth with all her burden of created nature, as he had never seen them before.

Sometimes he was seized with a sudden vertigo and an overwhelming terror; and then the image of his daughter appeared. Her, too, he had never seen so clearly before. Was it possible that he should ever be unable to do anything whatever for her? Nothing. And not see her any more? Never.

Why? The punishment was too great for a little presumption, for a little pride. And at last he came to cling to his deception with a fierce determination to carry it out to the end, to save her money intact, and behold her once more with his own eyes. Afterwards—what? The idea of suicide was revolting to the vigour of his manhood. He had prayed for death till the prayers had stuck in his throat. All the days of his life he had prayed, for daily bread, and not to be led into temptation, in a childlike humility of spirit. Did words mean anything? Whence did the gift of speech come? The violent beating of his heart reverberated in his head—seemed to shake his brain to pieces.

He sat down heavily in the deck-chair to keep the pretence of his watch. The night was dark. All the nights were dark now.

"Serang," he said, half aloud.

"Ada, Tuan. I am here."

"There are clouds on the sky?"

"There are, Tuan."

"Let her be steered straight. North."

"She is going north, Tuan."

The Serang stepped back. Captain Whalley recognized Massy's footfalls on the bridge.

The engineer walked over to port and returned, passing behind the chair several times. Captain Whalley detected an unusual character as of prudent care in this prowling. The near presence of that man brought with it always a recrudescence of moral suffering for Captain Whalley. It was not remorse. After all, he had done nothing but good to the poor devil. There was also a sense of danger—the necessity of greater caution.

Massy stopped and said—

"So you still say you must go?"

"I must indeed."

"And you couldn't at least leave the money for a term of years?"

"Impossible."

"Can't trust it with me without your care, eh?"

Captain Whalley remained silent. Massy sighed deeply over the back of the chair.

"It would just do to save me," he said in a tremulous voice.

"I've saved you once."

The chief engineer took off his coat with careful movements, and proceeded to feel for the brass hook screwed into the wooden stanchion. For this purpose he placed himself right in front of the binnacle, thus hiding completely the compass-card from the quartermaster at the wheel. "Tuan!" the lascar at last murmured softly, meaning to let the white man know that he could not see to steer.

Mr. Massy had accomplished his purpose. The coat was hanging from the nail, within six inches of the binnacle. And directly he had stepped aside the quartermaster, a middle-aged, pock-marked, Sumatra Malay, almost as dark as a negro, perceived with amazement that in that short time, in this smooth water, with no wind at all, the ship had gone swinging far out of her course. He had never known her get away like this before. With a slight grunt of astonishment he turned the wheel hastily to bring her head back north, which was the course. The grinding of the steering-chains, the chiding murmurs of the Serang, who had come over to the wheel, made a slight stir, which attracted Captain Whalley's anxious attention. He said, "Take better care." Then everything settled to the usual quiet on the bridge. Mr. Massy had disappeared.

But the iron in the pockets of the coat had done its work; and the *Sofala,* heading north by the compass made untrue by this simple device, was no longer making a safe course for Pangu Bay.

The hiss of water parted by her stem, the throb of her engines, all the sounds of her faithful and laborious life, went on uninterrupted in the great calm of the sea joining on all sides the motionless layer of cloud over the sky. A gentle stillness as vast as the world seemed to wait upon her path, enveloping her lovingly in a supreme caress. Mr. Massy thought there could be no better night for an arranged shipwreck.

Run up high and dry on one of the reefs east of Pangu—wait for daylight—hole in the bottom—out boats—Pangu Bay same evening. That's about it. As soon as she touched he would hasten on the bridge, get hold of the coat (nobody would notice in the dark), and shake it upside down over the side, or even fling it into the sea. A detail. Who could guess? Coat been seen hanging there from that hook hundreds of times. Nevertheless, when he sat down on the lower step of the bridge-ladder his knees knocked together a little. The waiting part was the worst of it. At times he would begin to pant quickly, as though he had been running, and then breathe largely, swelling with the intimate sense of a mastered fate. Now and then he would hear the shuffle of the Serang's bare feet up there: quiet, low voices would exchange a few words, and lapse almost at once into silence. . . .

"Tell me directly you see any land, Serang."

"Yes, Tuan. Not yet."

"No, not yet," Captain Whalley would agree.

The ship had been the best friend of his decline. He had sent all the money he had made by and in the *Sofala* to his daughter. His thought lingered on the name. How often he and his wife had talked over the cot of the child in the big stern-cabin of the *Condor;* she would grow up, she would marry, she would love them, they would live near her and look at her happiness—it would go on without end. Well, his wife was dead, to the child he had given all he had to give; he wished he could come near her, see her, see her face once, live in the sound of her voice, that could make the darkness of the living grave ready for him supportable. He had been starved of love too long. He imagined her tenderness.

The Serang had been peering forward, and now and then glancing at the chair. He fidgeted restlessly, and suddenly burst out close to Captain Whalley—

"Tuan, do you see anything of the land?"

The alarmed voice brought Captain Whalley to his feet at once. He! See! And at the question, the curse of his blindness seemed to fall on him with a hundredfold force.

"What's the time?" he cried.

"Half-past three, Tuan."

"We are close. You *must* see. Look, I say. Look."

Mr. Massy, awakened by the sudden sound of talking from a short doze on the lowest step, wondered why he was there. Ah! A faintness came over him. It is one thing to sow the seed of an accident and another to see the monstrous fruit hanging over your head ready to fall in the sound of agitated voices. "There's no danger," he muttered thickly to himself.

The horror of incertitude had seized upon Captain Whalley, the miserable mistrust of men, of things—of the very earth. He had steered that very course thirty-six times by the same compass—if anything was certain in this world it was its absolute, unerring correctness. Then what had happened? Did the Serang lie? Why lie? Why? Was he going blind, too?

"Is there a mist? Look low on the water. Low down, I say."

"Tuan, there's no mist. See for yourself."

Captain Whalley steadied the trembling of his limbs by an effort. Should he stop the engines at once and give himself away? A gust of irresolution swayed all sorts of bizarre notions in his mind. The unusual had come, and he was not fit to deal with it. In this passage of inexpressible anguish he saw her face—the face of a young girl—with an amazing strength of illusion. No, he must not give himself away after having gone so far for her sake. "You steered the course? You made it? Speak the truth."

"Ya, Tuan. On the course now. Look."

Captain Whalley strode to the binnacle, which to him made such a dim spot of light in an infinity of shapeless shadow. By bending his face right down to the glass he had been able before. . . .

Having to stoop so low, he put out, instinctively, his arm to where he knew there was a stanchion to steady himself against. His hand closed on something that was not wood but cloth. The slight pull adding to the weight, the loop broke, and Mr. Massy's coat, falling, struck the deck heavily with a dull thump, accompanied by a lot of clicks.

"What's this?"

Captain Whalley fell on his knees, with groping hands extended in a frank gesture of blindness. They trembled, these hands feeling for the truth. He saw it. Iron near the compass. Wrong course. Wreck her! His ship. Oh, no. Not that.

"Jump and stop her!" he roared out in a voice not his own.

He ran himself—hands forward, a blind man, and while the clanging of the gong echoed still all over the ship, she seemed to butt full tilt into the side of a mountain.

It was low water along the north side of the strait. Mr. Massy had not reckoned on that. Instead of running aground for half her length, the *Sofala* butted the sheer ridge of a stone reef which would have been awash at high water. This made the shock absolutely terrific. Everybody in the ship that was standing was thrown down headlong: the shaken rigging made a great rattling to the very trucks. All the lights went out; several chain-guys, snapping, clattered against the funnel; there were crashes, pings of parted wire-rope, splintering sounds, loud cracks; the masthead lamp flew over the bows, and all the doors about the deck began to bang heavily. Then, after having hit, she rebounded, hit the second time the very same spot like a battering-ram. This completed the havoc: the funnel, with all the guys gone, fell over with a hollow sound of thunder, smashing the wheel to bits, crushing the frame of the awnings, breaking the lockers, filling the bridge with a mass of broken wood. Captain Whalley picked himself up and stood knee-deep in wreckage, torn, bleeding, knowing the nature of the danger he had escaped mostly by the sound, and holding Mr. Massy's coat in his arms.

By this time Sterne (he had been flung out of his bunk) had set the engines astern. They worked for a few turns, then a voice bawled out, "Get out of the damned engine-room, Jack!"—and they stopped; but the ship had gone clear of the reef and lay still, with a heavy cloud of steam issuing from the broken deck-pipes, and vanishing in wispy shapes into the night. Notwithstanding the suddenness of the disaster there was no shouting, as if the very violence of the shock had half-stunned the shadowy lot of people swaying here and there about her decks. The voice of the Serang pronounced distinctly above the confused murmurs—

"No bottom." He had heaved the lead.

Mr. Sterne cried out next in a strained pitch—

"Where the devil has she got to? Where are we?"

Captain Whalley replied in a calm bass—

"Amongst the reefs to the eastward."

"You know it, sir? Then she will never get out again."

"She will be gone in five minutes. Boats, Sterne. Even one will save you all in this calm."

The Chinaman stokers went in a disorderly rush for the port boats. Nobody tried to check them. The Malays, after a moment of confusion, became quiet, and Mr. Sterne showed a good countenance. Captain Whalley had not moved. His thoughts were darker than this night in which he had lost his first ship.

"He made me lose a ship."

Another tall figure standing before him amongst the litter of the smash on the bridge whispered insanely—

"Say nothing of it."

Massy stumbled closer. Captain Whalley heard the chattering of his teeth.

"I have the coat."

"Throw it down and come along," urged the chattering voice. "B-b-b-b-boat!"

"You will get five years for this."

Mr. Massy had lost his voice. His speech was a mere dry rustling in his throat.

"Have mercy!"

"Had you any when you made me lose my ship? Mr. Massy, you shall get five years for this!"

"I wanted money! Money! My own money! I will give you some money. Take half of it. You love money yourself."

"There's a justice. . . ."

Massy made an awful effort, and in a strange, half-choked utterance—

"You blind devil! It's you that drove me to it."

Captain Whalley, hugging the coat to his breast, made no sound. The light had ebbed for ever from the world—let everything go. But this man should not escape scot-free.

Sterne's voice commanded—

"Lower away!"

The blocks rattled.

"Now then," he cried, "over with you. This way. You, Jack, here. Mr. Massy! Mr. Massy! Captain! Quick, sir! Let's get—"

"I shall go to prison for trying to cheat the insurance, but you'll get exposed; you, honest man, who has been cheating me. You are poor. Aren't you? You've nothing but the five hundred pounds. Well, you have nothing at all now. The ship's lost, and the insurance won't be paid."

Captain Whalley did not move. True! Ivy's money! Gone in this wreck. Again he had a flash of insight. He was indeed at the end of his tether.

Urgent voices cried out together alongside. Massy did not seem able to tear himself away from the bridge. He chattered and hissed despairingly—

"Give it up to me! Give it up!"

"No," said Captain Whalley; "I could not give it up. You had better go. Don't wait, man, if you want to live. She's settling down by the head fast. No; I shall keep it, but I shall stay on board."

Massy did not seem to understand; but the love of life, awakened suddenly, drove him away from the bridge.

Captain Whalley laid the coat down, and stumbled amongst the heaps of wreckage to the side.

"Is Mr. Massy with you?" he called out into the night.

Sterne from the boat shouted—

"Yes; we've got him. Come along, sir. It's madness to stay longer."

Captain Whalley felt along the rail carefully, and without a word, cast off the painter. They were expecting him still down there. They were waiting, till a voice suddenly exclaimed—

"We are adrift! Shove off!"

"Captain Whalley! Leap! . . . pull up a little . . . leap! You can swim."

In that old heart, in that vigorous body, there was, that nothing should be wanting, a horror of death that apparently could not be overcome by the horror of blindness. But after all, for Ivy he had carried his point, walking in his darkness to the very verge of a crime. God had not listened to his prayers. The light had finished ebbing out of the world; not a glimmer. It was a dark waste; but it was unseemly that a Whalley who had gone so far to carry a point should continue to live. He must pay the price.

"Leap as far as you can, sir; we will pick you up."

They did not hear him answer. But their shouting seemed to remind him of something. He groped his way back, and sought for Mr. Massy's coat. He could swim indeed; people sucked down by the whirlpool of a sinking ship do come up sometimes to the surface, and it was unseemly that a Whalley, who had made up his mind to die, should be beguiled by chance into a struggle. He would put all these pieces of iron into his own pockets.

They, looking from the boat, saw the *Sofala,* a black mass upon a black sea, lying still at an appalling cant. No sound came from her. Then, with a great bizarre shuffling noise, as if the boilers had broken through the bulkheads, and with a faint muffled detonation, where the ship had been there appeared for a moment something standing upright and narrow, like a rock out of the sea. Then that, too, disappeared.

When the *Sofala* failed to come back to Batu Beru at the proper time, Mr. Van Wyk understood at once that he would never see her any more. But he did not know what had happened till some weeks afterwards, when, in a native craft lent him by his Sultan, he had made his way to the *Sofala's* port of registry, where already her existence and the official inquiry into her loss were beginning to be forgotten.

It had not been a very remarkable or interesting case, except for the fact that the captain had gone down with his sinking ship. It was the only life lost; and Mr. Van Wyk would not have been able to learn any details had it not been for Sterne, whom he met one day on the quay near the bridge over the creek, almost on the very spot where Captain Whalley, to preserve his daughter's five hundred pounds intact, had turned to get a sampan which would take him on board the *Sofala.*

From afar Mr. Van Wyk saw Sterne blink straight at him and raise his hand to his hat. They drew into the shade of a building (it was a bank), and the mate related how the boats with the crew got into Pangu Bay about six hours after the accident, and how they had lived for a fortnight in a state of destitution before they found an opportunity to get away from that beastly place. The inquiry had exonerated everybody from all blame. The loss of the ship was put down to an unusual set of the current. Indeed, it could not have been anything else: there was no other way to account for the ship being set seven miles to the eastward of her position during the middle watch.

"A piece of bad luck for me, sir."

Sterne passed his tongue on his lips and glanced aside. "I lost the advantage of being employed by you, sir. I can never be sorry enough. But here it is: one man's poison, another man's meat. This could not have been handier for Mr. Massy if he had arranged that shipwreck himself. The most timely total loss I've ever heard of."

"What became of that Massy?" asked Mr. Van Wyk.

"He, sir? Ha! ha! He would keep on telling me that he meant to buy another ship; but as soon as he had the money in his pocket he cleared out for Manila by mail-boat early in the morning. I gave him chase right aboard, and he told me then he was going to make his fortune dead sure in Manila. I could go to the devil for all he cared. And yet he as good as promised to give me the command if I didn't talk too much."

"You never said anything. . . ." Mr. Van Wyk began.

"Not I, sir. Why should I? I mean to get on, but the dead aren't in my way," said Sterne. His eyelids were beating rapidly, then drooped for an instant. "Besides, sir, it would have been an awkward business. You made me hold my tongue just a bit too long."

"Do you know how it was that Captain Whalley remained on board? Did he really refuse to leave? Come now! Or was it perhaps an accidental . . . ?"

"Nothing!" Sterne interrupted with energy. "I tell you I yelled for him to leap overboard. He simply *must* have cast off the painter of the boat himself. We all yelled to him—that is, Jack and I. He wouldn't even answer us. The ship was as silent as a grave to the last. Then the boilers fetched away, and down she went. Accident! Not it! The game was up, sir, I tell you."

This was all that Sterne had to say.

Mr. Van Wyk had been of course made the guest of the club for a fortnight, and it was there that he met the lawyer in whose office had been signed the agreement between Massy and Captain Whalley.

"Extraordinary old man," he said. "He came into my office from nowhere in particular as you may say, with his five hundred pounds to invest, and that engineer fellow following him anxiously. And now he is gone out a little inexplicably, just as he came. I could never understand him quite. There was no mystery at all about that Massy, eh? I wonder whether Whalley refused to leave the ship. It would have been foolish. He was blameless, as the court found."

Mr. Van Wyk had known him well, he said, and he could not believe in suicide. Such an act would not have been in character with what he knew of the man.

"It is my opinion, too," the lawyer agreed. The general theory was that the captain had remained too long on board trying to save something of importance. Perhaps the chart which would clear him, or else something of value in his cabin. The painter of the boat had come adrift of itself, it was supposed. However, strange to say, some little time before that voyage poor Whalley had called in his office and had left with him a sealed envelope addressed to his daughter, to be forwarded to her in case of his death. Still it was nothing very unusual, especially in a man of his age. Mr. Van Wyk shook his head. Captain Whalley looked good for a hundred years.

"Perfectly true," assented the lawyer. "The old fellow looked as though he had come into the world full grown and with that long beard. I could never, somehow, imagine him either younger or older—don't you know. There was a sense of physical power about that man, too. And perhaps that was the secret of that something peculiar in his person which struck everybody who came in contact with him. He looked indestructible by any ordinary means that put an end to the rest of us. His deliberate, stately courtesy of manner was full of significance. It was as though he were certain of having plenty of time for everything. Yes, there was something indestructible about him; and the way he talked sometimes you might have thought he believed it himself. When he called on me last with that letter he wanted me to take charge of, he was not depressed at all. Perhaps a shade more deliberate in his talk and manner. Not depressed in the least. Had he a presentiment, I wonder? Perhaps! Still it seems a miserable end for such a striking figure."

"Oh, yes! It was a miserable end," Mr. Van Wyk said, with so much fervour that the lawyer looked up at him curiously; and afterwards, after parting with him, he remarked to an acquaintance—

"Queer person that Dutch tobacco-planter from Batu Beru. Know anything of him?"

"Heaps of money," answered the bank manager. "I hear he's going home by the next mail to form a company to take over his estates. Another tobacco district thrown open. He's wise, I think. These good times won't last for ever."

In the southern hemisphere Captain Whalley's daughter had no pre-sentiment of evil when she opened the envelope addressed to her in the lawyer's handwriting. She had received it in the afternoon; all the boarders had gone out, her boys were at school, her husband sat up-stairs in his big arm-chair with a book, thin-faced, wrapped up in rugs to the waist. The house was still, and the grayness of a cloudy day lay against the panes of the windows.

In a shabby dining-room, where a faint cold smell of dishes lingered all the year round, sitting at the end of a long table surrounded by many chairs pushed in with their backs close against the edge of the perpetually laid table-cloth, she read the opening sentences: "Most profound regret—painful duty—your father is no more—in accor-dance with his instructions—fatal casualty—consolation—no blame attached to his memory. . . ."

Her face was thin, her temples a little sunk under the smooth bands of black hair, her lips remained resolutely compressed, while her dark eyes grew larger, till at last, with a low cry, she stood up, and instantly stooped to pick up another envelope which had slipped off her knees on to the floor.

She tore it open, snatched out the enclosure. . . .

"My dearest child," it said, "I am writing this while I am able yet to write legibly. I am trying hard to save for you all the money that is left; I have only kept it to serve you better. It is yours. It shall not be lost; it shall not be touched. There's five hundred pounds. Of what I have earned I have kept nothing back till now. For the future, if I live, I must keep back some—a little—to bring me to you. I must come to you. I must see you once more.

"It is hard to believe that you will ever look on these lines. God seems to have forgotten me. I want to see you—and yet death would be a greater favour. If you ever read these words, I charge you to begin by thanking a God merciful at last, for I shall be dead then, and it will be well. My dear, I am at the end of my tether."

The next paragraph began with the words: "My sight is going. . . ."

She read no more that day. The hand holding up the paper to her eyes fell slowly, and her slender figure in a plain black dress walked rigidly to the window. Her eyes were dry: no cry of sorrow or whisper of thanks went up to heaven from her lips. Life had been too hard, for all the efforts of his love. It had silenced her emotions. But for the first time in all these years its sting had departed, the carking care of poverty, the meanness of a hard struggle for bread. Even the image of her husband and of her children seemed to glide away from her into the gray twilight; it was her father's face alone that she saw, as though he had come to see her, always quiet and big, as she had seen him last, but with something more august and tender in his aspect.

She slipped his folded letter between the two buttons of her plain black bodice, and leaning her forehead against a window-pane remained there till dusk, perfectly motionless, giving him all the time she could spare. Gone! Was it possible? My God, was it possible? The blow had come softened by the spaces of the earth, by the years of absence. There had been whole days when she had not thought of him at all—had no time. But she had loved him, she felt she had loved him after all.

FALK:

A Reminiscence

SEVERAL of us, all more or less connected with the sea, were dining in a small river-hostelry not more than thirty miles from London, and less than twenty from that shallow and dangerous puddle to which our coasting men give the grandiose name of "German Ocean." And through the wide windows we had a view of the Thames; an enfilading view down the Lower Hope Reach. But the dinner was execrable, and all the feast was for the eyes.

That flavour of salt-water which for so many of us had been the very water of life permeated our talk. He who hath known the bitterness of the Ocean shall have its taste for ever in his mouth. But one or two of us, pampered by the life of the land, complained of hunger. It was impossible to swallow any of that stuff. And indeed there was a strange mustiness in everything. The wooden dining-room stuck out over the mud of the shore like a lacustrine dwelling; the planks of the floor seemed rotten; a decrepid old waiter tottered pathetically to and fro before an antediluvian and worm-eaten sideboard; the chipped plates might have been disinterred from some kitchen midden near an inhabited lake; and the chops recalled times more ancient still. They brought forcibly to one's mind the night of ages when the primeval man, evolving the first rudiments of cookery from his dim consciousness, scorched lumps of flesh at a fire of sticks in the company of other good fellows; then, gorged and happy, sat him back among the gnawed bones to tell his artless tales of experience—the tales of hunger and hunt—and of women, perhaps!

But luckily the wine happened to be as old as the waiter. So, comparatively empty, but upon the whole fairly happy, we sat back and told our artless tales. We talked of the sea and all its works. The sea never changes, and its works for all the talk of men are wrapped in mystery. But we agreed that the times were changed. And we talked of old ships, of sea-accidents, of break-downs, dismastings; and of a man who brought his ship safe to Liverpool all the way from the River Platte under a jury rudder. We talked of wrecks, of short rations and of heroism—or at least of what the newspapers would have called heroism at sea—a manifestation of virtues quite different from the heroism of primitive times. And now and then falling silent all together we gazed at the sights of the river.

A P. & O. boat passed bound down. "One gets jolly good dinners on board these ships," remarked one of our band. A man with sharp eyes read out the name on her bows: *Arcadia.* "What a beautiful model of a ship!" murmured some of us. She was followed by a small cargo-steamer, and the flag they hauled down aboard while we were looking showed her to be a Norwegian. She made an awful lot of smoke, and before it had quite blown away, a high-sided, short, wooden barque, in ballast and towed by a paddle-tug, appeared in front of the windows. All her hands were forward busy setting up the headgear; and aft a woman in a red hood, quite alone with the man at the wheel, paced the length of the poop back and forth, with the gray wool of some knitting work in her hands. "German I should think," muttered one. "The skipper has his wife on board," remarked another; and the light of the crimson sunset all ablaze behind the London smoke, throwing a glow of Bengal light upon the barque's spars, faded away from the Hope Reach.

Then one of us, who had not spoken before, a man of more than fifty, that had commanded ships for a quarter of a century, looking after the barque now gliding far away, all black on the lustre of the river, said:

This reminds me of an absurd episode in my life, now many years ago, when I got first the command of an iron barque, loading then in a certain Eastern seaport. It was also the capital of an Eastern kingdom, lying up a river as might be London lies up this old Thames of ours. No more need be said of the place; for this sort of thing might have happened anywhere where there are ships, skippers, tugboats, and orphan nieces of indescribable splendour. And the absurdity of the episode concerns only me, my enemy Falk, and my friend Hermann.

There seemed to be something like peculiar emphasis on the words

"My friend Hermann," which caused one of us (for we had just been speaking of heroism at sea) to say idly and nonchalantly:

"And was this Hermann a hero?"

Not at all, said our grizzled friend. No hero at all. He was a Schiff-führer: Ship-conductor. That's how they call a Master Mariner in Germany. I prefer our way. The alliteration is good, and there is something in the nomenclature that gives to us as a body the sense of corporate existence: Apprentice, Mate, Master, in the ancient and honourable craft of the sea. As to my friend Hermann, he might have been a consummate master of the honourable craft, but he was called officially Schiff-führer, and had the simple, heavy appearance of a well-to-do farmer, combined with the good-natured shrewdness of a small shop-keeper. With his shaven chin, round limbs, and heavy eyelids he did not look like a toiler, and even less like an adventurer of the sea. Still, he toiled upon the seas, in his own way, much as a shopkeeper works behind his counter. And his ship was the means by which he maintained his growing family.

She was a heavy, strong, blunt-bowed affair, awakening the ideas of primitive solidity, like the wooden plough of our forefathers. And there were, about her, other suggestions of a rustic and homely nature. The extraordinary timber projections which I have seen in no other vessel made her square stern resemble the tail end of a miller's waggon. But the four stern ports of her cabin, glazed with six little greenish panes each, and framed in wooden sashes painted brown, might have been the windows of a cottage in the country. The tiny white curtains and the greenery of flower-pots behind the glass completed the resemblance. On one or two occasions when passing under her stern I had detected from my boat a round arm in the act of tilting a watering-pot, and the bowed sleek head of a maiden whom I shall always call Hermann's niece, because as a matter of fact I've never heard her name, for all my intimacy with the family.

This, however, sprang up later on. Meantime in common with the rest of the shipping in that Eastern port, I was left in no doubt as to Hermann's notions of hygienic clothing. Evidently he believed in wearing good stout flannel next his skin. On most days little frocks and pinafores could be seen drying in the mizzen rigging of his ship, or a tiny row of socks fluttering on the signal halyards; but once a fortnight the family washing was exhibited in force. It covered the poop entirely.

The afternoon breeze would incite to a weird and flabby activity all that crowded mass of clothing, with its vague suggestions of drowned, mutilated and flattened humanity. Trunks without heads waved at you arms without hands; legs without feet kicked fantastically with collapsible flourishes; and there were long white garments, that taking the wind fairly through their neck openings edged with lace, became for a moment violently distended as by the passage of obese and invisible bodies. On these days you could make out that ship at a great distance by the multicoloured grotesque riot going on abaft her mizzen-mast.

She had her berth just ahead of me, and her name was *Diana,*—Diana not of Ephesus but of Bremen. This was proclaimed in white letters a foot long spaced widely across the stern (somewhat like the lettering of a shop-sign) under the cottage windows. This ridiculously unsuitable name struck one as an impertinence towards the memory of the most charming of goddesses; for, apart from the fact that the old craft was physically incapable of engaging in any sort of chase, there was a gang of four children belonging to her. They peeped over the rail at passing boats and occasionally dropped various objects into them. Thus, sometime before I knew Hermann to speak to, I received on my hat a horrid rag-doll belonging to Hermann's eldest daughter. However, these youngsters were upon the whole well behaved. They had fair heads, round eyes, round little knobby noses, and they resembled their father a good deal.

This *Diana* of Bremen was a most innocent old ship, and seemed to know nothing of the wicked sea, as there are on shore households that know nothing of the corrupt world. And the sentiments she suggested were unexceptionable and mainly of a domestic order. She was a home. All these dear children had learned to walk on her roomy quarter-deck. In such thoughts there is something pretty, even touching. Their teeth, I should judge, they cut on the ends of her running gear. I have many times observed the baby Hermann (Nicholas) engaged in gnawing the whipping of the fore-royal brace. Nicholas' favourite place of residence was under the main fife-rail. Directly he was let loose he would crawl off there, and the first seaman who came along would bring him, carefully held aloft in tarry hands, back to the cabin door. I fancy there must have been a standing order to that effect. In the course of these transportations the baby, who was the only peppery person in the ship, tried to smite these stalwart young German sailors on the face.

Mrs. Hermann, an engaging, stout housewife, wore on board baggy blue dresses with white dots. When, as happened once or twice, I caught her at an elegant little wash-tub rubbing hard on white collars, baby's socks, and Hermann's summer neckties, she would blush in girlish confusion, and raising her wet hands greet me from afar with many friendly nods. Her sleeves would be rolled up to the elbows, and the gold hoop of her wedding ring glittered among the soapsuds. Her voice was pleasant, she had a serene brow, smooth bands of very fair hair, and a good-humoured expression of the eyes. She was motherly and moderately talkative. When this simple matron smiled, youthful dimples broke out on her fresh broad cheeks. Hermann's niece, on the other hand, an orphan and very silent, I never saw attempt a smile. This, however, was not gloom on her part but the restraint of youthful gravity.

They had carried her about with them for the last three years, to help with the children and be company for Mrs. Hermann, as Hermann mentioned once to me. It had been very necessary while they were all little, he had added in a vexed manner. It was her arm and her sleek head that I had glimpsed one morning, through the stern-windows of the cabin, hovering over the pots of fuchsias and mignonette; but the first time I beheld her full length I surrendered to her proportions. They fix her in my mind, as great beauty, great intelligence, quickness of wit or kindness of heart might have made some other woman memorable.

With her it was form and size. It was her physical personality that had this imposing charm. She might have been witty, intelligent, and kind to an exceptional degree. I don't know, and this is not to the point. All I know is that she was built on a magnificent scale. Built is the only word. She was constructed, she was erected, as it were, with regal lavishness. It staggered you to see this reckless expenditure of material upon a chit of a girl. She was youthful and also perfectly mature, as though she had been some fortunate immortal. She was heavy, too, perhaps, but that's nothing. It only added to that notion of permanence. She was barely nineteen. But such shoulders! Such round arms! Such a shadowing forth of mighty limbs when with three long strides she pounced across the deck upon the overturned Nicholas—it's perfectly indescribable! She seemed a good, quiet girl, vigilant as to Lena's needs, Gustav's tumbles, the state of Karl's dear little nose—conscientious, hardworking, and all that. But what magnificent hair she had! Abundant, long, thick, of a tawny colour. It had the sheen of precious metals. She wore it plaited tightly into one single tress hanging girlishly down her back; and its end reached down to her waist. The massiveness of it surprised you. On my word it reminded one of a club. Her face was big, comely, of an unruffled expression. She had a good complexion, and her blue eyes were so pale that she appeared to look at the world with the empty white candour of a statue. You could not call her good-looking. It was something much more impressive. The simplicity of her apparel, the opulence of her form, her imposing stature, and the extraordinary sense of vigorous life that seemed to emanate from her like a perfume exhaled by a flower, made her beautiful with a beauty of a rustic and olympian order. To watch her reaching up to the clothes-line with both arms raised high above her head, caused you to fall a musing in a strain of pagan piety. Excellent Mrs. Hermann's baggy cotton gowns had some sort of rudimentary frills at neck and bottom, but this girl's print frocks hadn't even a wrinkle; nothing but a few straight folds in the skirt falling to her feet, and these, when she stood still, had a severe and statuesque quality. She was inclined naturally to be still whether sitting or standing. However, I don't mean to say she was statuesque. She was too generously alive; but she could have stood for an allegoric statue of the Earth. I don't mean the worn-out earth of our possession, but a young Earth, a virginal planet undisturbed by the vision of a future teeming with the monstrous forms of life, clamorous with the cruel battles of hunger and thought.

The worthy Hermann himself was not very entertaining, though his English was fairly comprehensible. Mrs. Hermann, who always let off one speech at least at me in an hospitable, cordial tone (and in Platt-Deutsch, I suppose), I could not understand. As to their niece, however satisfactory to look upon (and she inspired you somehow with a hopeful view as to the prospects of mankind) she was a modest and silent presence, mostly engaged in sewing, only now and then, as I observed, falling over that work into a state of maidenly meditation. Her aunt sat opposite her, sewing also, with her feet propped on a wooden foot-stool. On the other side of the deck Hermann and I would get a couple of chairs out of the cabin and settle down to a smoking match, accompanied at long intervals by the pacific exchange of a few words. I came nearly every evening. Hermann I would find in his shirt-sleeves. As soon as he returned from the shore on board his ship he commenced operations by taking off his coat; then he put on his head an embroidered round cap with a tassel, and changed his boots for a pair of cloth slippers. Afterwards he smoked at the cabin-door, looking at his children with an air of civic virtue, till they got caught one after another and put to bed in various staterooms. Lastly, we would drink some beer in the cabin, which was furnished with a wooden table on cross legs, and with black straight-backed chairs—more like a farm kitchen than a ship's cuddy. The sea and all nautical affairs seemed very far removed from the hospitality of this exemplary family.

And I liked this because I had a rather worrying time on board my own ship. I had been appointed ex-officio by the British Consul to take charge of her after a man who had died suddenly, leaving for the guidance of his successor some suspiciously unreceipted bills, a few dry-dock estimates hinting at bribery, and a quantity of vouchers for three years' extravagant expenditure; all these mixed up together in a dusty old violin-case lined with ruby velvet. I found besides a large account-book, which, when opened hopefully, turned out to my infinite conster-nation to be filled with verses—page after page of rhymed doggerel of a jovial and improper character, written in the neatest minute hand I ever did see. In the same fiddle-case a photograph of my predecessor, taken lately in Saigon, represented in front of a garden view, and in company of a female in strange draperies, an elderly, squat, rugged man of stern aspect in a clumsy suit of black broad-cloth, and with the hair brushed forward above the temples in a manner reminding one of a boar's tusks. Of a fiddle, however, the only trace on board was the case, its empty husk as it were; but of the two last freights the ship had indubitably earned of late, there were not even the husks left. It was impossible to say where all that money had gone to. It wasn't on board. It had not been remitted home; for a letter from the owners, preserved in a desk evidently by the merest accident, complained mildly enough that they had not been favoured by a scratch of the pen for the last eighteen months. There were next to no stores on board, not an inch of spare rope or a yard of canvas. The ship had been run bare, and I foresaw no end of difficulties before I could get her ready for sea.

As I was young then—not thirty yet—I took myself and my troubles very seriously. The old mate, who had acted as chief mourner at the captain's funeral, was not particularly pleased at my coming. But the fact is the fellow was not legally qualified for command, and the Consul was bound, if at all possible, to put a properly certificated man on board.

As to the second mate, all I can say his name was Tottersen, or something like that. His practice was to wear on his head, in that tropical climate, a mangy fur cap. He was, without exception, the stupidest man I had ever seen on board ship. And he looked it, too. He looked so confoundedly stupid that it was a matter of surprise for me when he answered to his name.

I drew no great comfort from their company, to say the least of it; while the prospect of making a long sea passage with those two fellows was depressing. And my other thoughts in solitude could not be of a gay complexion. The crew was sickly, the cargo was coming very slow; I foresaw I would have lots of trouble with the characters, and doubted whether they would advance me enough money for the ship's expenses. Their attitude towards me was unfriendly. Altogether I was not getting on. I would discover at odd times (generally about midnight) that I was totally inexperienced, greatly ignorant of business, and hopelessly unfit for any sort of command; and when the steward had to be taken to the hospital ill with choleraic symptoms I felt bereaved of the only decent person at the after end of the ship. He was fully expected to recover, but in the meantime had to be replaced by some sort of servant. And on the recommendation of a certain Schomberg, the proprietor of the smaller of the two hotels in the place, I engaged a Chinaman. Schomberg, a brawny, hairy Alsatian, and an awful gossip, assured me that it was all right. "First-class boy that. Came in the *suite* of his Excellency Tseng the Commissioner—you know. His Excellency Tseng lodged with me here for three weeks."

He mouthed the Chinese Excellency at me with great unction, though the specimen of the "*suite*" did not seem very promising. At the time, however, I did not know what an untrustworthy humbug Schomberg was. The "boy" might have been forty or a hundred and forty for all you could tell—one of those Chinamen of the death's-head type of face and completely inscrutable. Before the end of the third day he had revealed himself as a confirmed opium-smoker, a gambler, a most audacious thief, and a first-class sprinter. When he departed at the top of his speed with thirty-two golden sovereigns of my own hard-earned savings it was the last straw. I had reserved that money in case my difficulties came to the worst. Now it was gone I felt as poor and naked as a fakir. I clung to my ship, for all the bother she caused me, but what I could not bear were the long lonely evenings in her cuddy, where the atmosphere, made smelly by a leaky lamp, was agitated by the snoring of the mate. That fellow shut himself up in his stuffy cabin punctually at eight, and made gross and revolting noises like a water-logged trombone. It was odious not to be able to worry oneself in comfort on board one's own ship. Everything in this world, I reflected, even the command of a nice little barque, may be made a delusion and a snare for the unwary spirit of pride in man.

From such reflections I was glad to make my escape on board that Bremen *Diana.* There apparently no whisper of the world's iniquities had ever penetrated. And yet she lived upon the wide sea: and the sea tragic and comic, the sea with its horrors and its peculiar scandals, the sea peopled by men and ruled by iron necessity is indubitably a part of the world. But that patriarchal old tub, like some saintly retreat, echoed nothing of it. She was world proof. Her venerable innocence apparently put a restraint on the roaring lusts of the sea. And yet I have known the sea too long to believe in its respect for decency. An elemental force is ruthlessly frank. It may, of course, have been Hermann's skilful seamanship, but to me it looked as if the allied oceans had refrained from smashing these high bulwarks, unshipping the lumpy rudder, frightening the children, and generally opening this family's eyes out of sheer reticence. It looked like reticence. The ruthless disclosure was, in the end, left for a man to make; a man strong and elemental enough and driven to unveil some secrets of the sea by the power of a simple and elemental desire.

This, however, occurred much later, and meantime I took sanctuary in that serene old ship early every evening. The only person on board that seemed to be in trouble was little Lena, and in due course I perceived that the health of the rag-doll was more than delicate. This object led a sort of "in extremis" existence in a wooden box placed against the starboard mooring-bitts tended and nursed with the greatest sympathy and care by all the children, who greatly enjoyed pulling long faces and moving with hushed footsteps. Only the baby—Nicholas—looked on with a cold, ruffianly leer, as if he had belonged to another tribe altogether. Lena perpetually sorrowed over the box, and all of them were in deadly earnest. It was wonderful the way these children would work up their compassion for that bedraggled thing I wouldn't have touched with a pair of tongs. I suppose they were exercising and developing their racial sentimentalism by the means of that dummy. I was only surprised that Mrs. Hermann let Lena cherish and hug that bundle of rags to that extent, it was so disreputably and completely unclean. But Mrs. Hermann would raise her fine womanly eyes from her needlework to look on with amused sympathy, and did not seem to see it, somehow, that this object of affection was a disgrace to the ship's purity. Purity, not cleanliness, is the word. It was pushed so far that I seemed to detect in this, too, a sentimental excess, as if dirt had been removed in very love. It is impossible to give you an idea of such a meticulous neatness. It was as if every morning that ship had been arduously explored with—with toothbrushes. Her very bowsprit three times a week had its toilette made with a cake of soap and a piece of soft flannel. Arrayed—I *must* say arrayed—arrayed artlessly in dazzling white paint as to wood and dark green as to ironwork the simple-minded distribution of these colours evoked the images of guileless peace, of arcadian felicity; and the childish comedy of disease and sorrow struck me sometimes as an abominably real blot upon that ideal state.

I enjoyed it greatly, and on my part I brought a little mild excitement into it. Our intimacy arose from the pursuit of that thief. It was in the evening, and Hermann, who, contrary to his habits, had stayed on shore late that day, was extricating himself backwards out of a little gharry on the river bank, opposite his ship, when the hunt passed. Realizing the situation as though he had eyes in his shoulder-blades, he joined us with a leap and took the lead. The Chinaman fled silent like a rapid shadow on the dust of an extremely oriental road. I followed. A long way in the rear my mate whooped like a savage. A young moon threw a bashful light on a plain like a monstrous waste ground: the architectural mass of a Buddhist temple far away projected itself in dead black on the sky. We lost the thief of course; but in my disappointment I had to admire Hermann's presence of mind. The velocity that stodgy man developed in the interests of a complete stranger earned my warm gratitude—there was something truly cordial in his exertions.

He seemed as vexed as myself at our failure, and would hardly listen to my thanks. He said it was "nothings," and invited me on the spot to come on board his ship and drink a glass of beer with him. We poked sceptically for a while amongst the bushes, peered without conviction into a ditch or two. There was not a sound: patches of slime glimmered feebly amongst the reeds. Slowly we trudged back, drooping under the thin sickle of the moon, and I heard him mutter to himself, "Himmel!

Zwei und dreissig Pfund!" He was impressed by the figure of my loss. For a long time we had ceased to hear the mate's whoops and yells.

Then he said to me, "Everybody has his troubles," and as we went on remarked that he would never have known anything of mine hadn't he by an extraordinary chance been detained on shore by Captain Falk. He didn't like to stay late ashore—he added with a sigh. The something doleful in his tone I put to his sympathy with my misfortune, of course.

On board the *Diana* Mrs. Hermann's fine eyes expressed much interest and commiseration. We had found the two women sewing face to face under the open skylight in the strong glare of the lamp. Hermann walked in first, starting in the very doorway to pull off his coat, and encouraging me with loud, hospitable ejaculations: "Come in! This way! Come in, captain!" At once, coat in hand, he began to tell his wife all about it. Mrs. Hermann put the palms of her plump hands together; I smiled and bowed with a heavy heart: the niece got up from her sewing to bring Hermann's slippers and his embroidered calotte, which he assumed pontifically, talking (about me) all the time. Billows of white stuff lay between the chairs on the cabin floor; I caught the words "Zwei und dreissig Pfund" repeated several times, and presently came the beer, which seemed delicious to my throat, parched with running and the emotions of the chase.

I didn't get away till well past midnight, long after the women had retired. Hermann had been trading in the East for three years or more, carrying freights of rice and timber mostly. His ship was well known in all the ports from Vladivostok to Singapore. She was his own property. The profits had been moderate, but the trade answered well enough while the children were small yet. In another year or so he hoped he would be able to sell the old *Diana* to a firm in Japan for a fair price. He intended to return home, to Bremen, by mail boat, second class, with Mrs. Hermann and the children. He told me all this stolidly, with slow puffs at his pipe. I was sorry when knocking the ashes out he began to rub his eyes. I would have sat with him till morning. What had I to hurry on board my own ship for? To face the broken rifled drawer in my stateroom. Ugh! The very thought made me feel unwell.

I became their daily guest, as you know. I think that Mrs. Hermann from the first looked upon me as a romantic person. I did not, of course, tear my hair *coram populo* over my loss, and she took it for lordly indifference. Afterwards, I daresay, I did tell them some of my adventures—such as they were—and they marvelled greatly at the extent of my experience. Hermann would translate what he thought the most striking passages. Getting upon his legs, and as if delivering a lecture on a phenomenon, he addressed himself, with gestures, to the two women, who would let their sewing sink slowly on their laps. Meantime I sat before a glass of Hermann's beer, trying to look modest. Mrs. Hermann would glance at me quickly, emit slight "Ach's!" The girl never made a sound. Never. But she, too, would sometimes raise her pale eyes to look at me in her unseeing, gentle way. Her glance was by no means stupid; it beamed out soft and diffuse as the moon beams upon a landscape—quite differently from the scrutinizing inspection of the stars. You were drowned in it, and imagined yourself to appear blurred. And yet this same glance when turned upon Christian Falk must have been as efficient as the searchlight of a battle-ship.

Falk was the other assiduous visitor on board, but from his behaviour he might have been coming to see the quarter-deck capstan. He certainly used to stare at it a good deal when keeping us company outside the cabin door, with one muscular arm thrown over the back of the chair, and his big shapely legs, in very tight white trousers, extended far out and ending in a pair of black shoes as roomy as punts. On arrival he would shake Hermann's hand with a mutter, bow to the women, and take up his careless and misanthropic attitude by our side. He departed abruptly, with a jump, going through the performance of grunts, hand-shakes, bow, as if in a panic. Sometimes, with a sort of discreet and convulsive effort, he approached the women and exchanged a few low words with them, half a dozen at most. On these occasions Hermann's usual stare became positively glassy and Mrs. Hermann's kind counte-nance would colour up. The girl herself never turned a hair.

Falk was a Dane or perhaps a Norwegian, I can't tell now. At all events he was a Scandinavian of some sort, and a bloated monopolist to boot. It is possible he was unacquainted with the word, but he had a clear perception of the thing itself. His tariff of charges for towing ships in and out was the most brutally inconsiderate document of the sort I had ever seen. He was the commander and owner of the only tug-boat on the river, a very trim white craft of 150 tons or more, as elegantly neat as a yacht, with a round wheelhouse rising like a glazed turret high above her sharp bows, and with one slender varnished pole mast for-ward. I daresay there are yet a few shipmasters afloat who remember

Falk and his tug very well. He extracted his pound and a half of flesh
from each of us merchant-skippers with an inflexible sort of indifference
which made him detested and even feared. Schomberg used to remark:
"I won't talk about the fellow. I don't think he has six drinks from
year's end to year's end in my place. But my advice is, gentlemen, don't
you have anything to do with him, if you can help it."

This advice, apart from unavoidable business relations, was easy to
follow because Falk intruded upon no one. It seems absurd to compare
a tug-boat skipper to a centaur: but he reminded me somehow of an
engraving in a little book I had as a boy, which represented centaurs at
a stream, and there was one especially, in the foreground, prancing bow
and arrows in hand, with regular severe features and an immense curled
wavy beard, flowing down his breast. Falk's face reminded me of that
centaur. Besides, he was a composite creature. Not a man-horse, it is
true, but a man-boat. He lived on board his tug, which was always
dashing up and down the river from early morn till dewy eve. In the
last rays of the setting sun, you could pick out far away down the reach
his beard borne high up on the white structure, foaming up stream to
anchor for the night. There was the white-clad man's body, and the rich
brown patch of the hair, and nothing below the waist but the 'thwart-
ship white lines of the bridge-screens, that led the eye to the sharp white
lines of the bows cleaving the muddy water of the river.

Separated from his boat, to me at least he seemed incomplete. The
tug herself without his head and torso on the bridge looked mutilated
as it were. But he left her very seldom. All the time I remained in harbour
I saw him only twice on shore. On the first occasion it was at my
charterers, where he came in misanthropically to get paid for towing
out a French barque the day before. The second time I could hardly
believe my eyes, for I beheld him reclining under his beard in a cane-
bottomed chair in the billiard-room of Schomberg's hotel.

It was very funny to see Schomberg ignoring him pointedly. The
artificiality of it contrasted strongly with Falk's natural unconcern. The
big Alsatian talked loudly with his other customers, going from one little
table to the other, and passing Falk's place of repose with his eyes fixed
straight ahead. Falk sat there with an untouched glass at his elbow. He
must have known by sight and name every white man in the room, but
he never addressed a word to anybody. He acknowledged my presence
by a drop of his eyelids, and that was all. Sprawling there in the chair,

he would, now and again, draw the palms of both his hands down his face, giving at the same time a slight, almost imperceptible, shudder.

It was a habit he had, and of course I was perfectly familiar with it, since you could not remain an hour in his company without being made to wonder at such a passionate and inexplicable gesture breaking some long period of stillness. He used to make it at all sorts of times; as likely as not after he had been listening to little Lena's chatter about the suffering doll, for instance. The Hermann children always besieged him about his legs closely, though, in a gentle way, he shrank from them a little. He seemed, however, to feel a great affection for the whole family. For Hermann himself especially. He sought his company. In this case, for instance, he must have been waiting for him, because as soon as he appeared Falk rose hastily, and they went out together. Then Schomberg expounded in my hearing to three or four people his theory that Falk was after Captain Hermann's niece, and asserted confidently that nothing would come of it. It was the same last year when Captain Hermann was loading here, he said.

Naturally, I did not believe Schomberg, but I own that for a time I observed closely what went on. All I discovered was some impatience on Hermann's part. At the sight of Falk, stepping over the gangway, the excellent man would begin to mumble and chew between his teeth something that sounded like German swear-words. However, as I've said, I'm not familiar with the language, and Hermann's soft, round-eyed countenance remained unchanged. Staring stolidly ahead he greeted him with, "Wie geht's," or in English, "How are you?" with a throaty enunciation. The girl would look up for an instant and move her lips slightly: Mrs. Hermann let her hands rest on her lap to talk volubly to him for a minute or so in her pleasant voice before she went on with her sewing again. Falk would throw himself into a chair, stretch his big legs, as like as not draw his hands down his face passionately. As to myself, he was not pointedly impertinent: it was rather as though he could not be bothered with such trifles as my existence; and the truth is that being a monopolist he was under no necessity to be amiable. He was sure to get his own extortionate terms out of me for towage whether he frowned or smiled. As a matter of fact, he did neither: but before many days went by he managed to astonish me not a little and to set Schomberg's tongue clacking more than ever.

It came about in this way. There was a shallow bar at the mouth of the river which ought to have been kept down, but the authorities of the State were piously busy gliding afresh the great Buddhist Pagoda just then, and had no money to spare for dredging operations. I don't know how it may be now, but at the time I speak of that sandbank was a great nuisance to the shipping. One of its consequences was that vessels of a certain draught of water, like Hermann's or mine, could not complete their loading in the river. After taking in as much as possible of their cargo, they had to go outside to fill up. The whole procedure was an unmitigated bore. When you thought you had as much on board as your ship could carry safely over the bar, you went and gave notice to your agents. They, in their turn, notified Falk that so-and-so was ready to go out. Then Falk (ostensibly when it fitted in with his other work, but, if the truth were known, simply when his arbitrary spirit moved him), after ascertaining carefully in the office that there was enough money to meet his bill, would come along unsympathetically, glaring at you with his yellow eyes from the bridge, and would drag you out dishevelled as to rigging, lumbered as to the decks, with unfeeling haste, as if to execution. And he would force you, too, to take the end of his own wire hawser, for the use of which there was of course an extra charge. To your shouted remonstrances against this extortion this towering trunk with one hand on the engine-room telegraph only shook its bearded head above the splash, the racket and the clouds of smoke, in which the tug, backing and filling in the smother of churning paddle-wheels behaved like a ferocious and impatient creature. He had her manned by the cheekiest gang of lascars I ever did see, whom he allowed to bawl at you insolently, and, once fast, he plucked you out of your berth as if he did not care what he smashed. Eighteen miles down the river you had to go behind him, and then three more along the coast to where a group of uninhabited rocky islets enclosed a sheltered anchorage. There you would have to lie at single anchor with your naked spars showing to seaward over these barren fragments of land scattered upon a very intensely blue sea. There was nothing to look at besides but a bare coast, the muddy edge of the brown plain with the sinuosities of the river you had left, traced in dull green, and the Great Pagoda uprising lonely and massive with shining curves and pinnacles like the gorgeous and stony efflorescence of tropical rocks. You had nothing to do but to wait fretfully for the balance of your cargo, which was sent out of the river with the greatest irregularity. And it was open to you to console yourself with the thought that, after all, this stage of bother meant that your departure from these shores was indeed approaching at last.

We both had to go through that stage, Hermann and I, and there was a sort of tacit emulation between the ships as to which should be ready first. We kept on neck and neck almost to the finish, when I won the race by going personally to give notice in the forenoon; whereas Hermann, who was very slow in making up his mind to go ashore, did not get to the agents' office till late in the day. They told him there that my ship was first on turn for next morning, and I believe he told them he was in no hurry. It suited him better to go the day after.

That evening, on board the *Diana*, he sat staring with his plump knees well apart and puffing at the curved mouthpiece of his pipe. Presently he spoke with some impatience to his niece about putting the children to bed. Mrs. Hermann, who was talking to Falk, stopped short and looked at her husband uneasily, but the girl got up at once and drove the children before her into the cabin. In a little while Mrs. Hermann had to leave us to quell what, from the sounds inside, must have been a dangerous mutiny. At this Hermann grumbled to himself. For half an hour longer Falk left alone with us fidgeted on his chair, sighed lightly, then at last, after drawing his hands down his face, got up, and as if renouncing the hope of making himself understood (he hadn't opened his mouth once) he said in English: "Well . . . Good-night, Captain Hermann." He stopped for a moment before my chair and looked down fixedly, I may even say he glared, and he went so far as to make a deep noise in his throat. All this was so marked that for the first time in our limited intercourse of nods and grunts he excited in me something like interest. But next moment he disappointed me—for he strode away hastily without a nod even.

His manner was usually odd it is true, and I certainly did not pay much attention to it; but that sort of obscure intention, which seemed to lurk in his nonchalance like a wary old carp in a pond, had never before come so near the surface. He had distinctly aroused my expectations. I would have been unable to say what it was I expected, but at all events I did not expect the absurd developments he sprung upon me no later than the break of the very next day.

I remember only that there was, on that evening, enough point in his behaviour to make me, after he had fled, wonder audibly what he might mean. To this Hermann, crossing his legs with a swing and settling himself viciously away from me in his chair, said: "That fellow don't know himself what he means."

There might have been some insight in such a remark. I said nothing, and, still averted, Hermann added: "When I was here last year he was just the same." An eruption of tobacco smoke enveloped his head as if his temper had exploded like gunpowder.

I had half a mind to ask him point blank whether he, at least, didn't know why Falk, a notoriously unsociable man, had taken to visiting his ship with such assiduity. After all, I reflected suddenly, it was a most remarkable thing. I wonder now what Hermann would have said. As it turned out he didn't let me ask. Forgetting all about Falk apparently, he started a monologue on his plans for the future: the selling of the ship, the going home; and falling into a reflective and calculating mood he mumbled between regular jets of smoke about the expense. The necessity of disbursing passage-money for all his tribe seemed to disturb him in a manner that was the more striking because otherwise he gave no signs of a miserly disposition. And yet he fussed over the prospect of that voyage home in a mail-boat like a sedentary grocer who has made up his mind to see the world. He was racially thrifty I suppose, and for him there must have been a great novelty in finding himself obliged to pay for travelling—for sea travelling which was the normal state of life for the family—from the very cradle for most of them. I could see he grudged prospectively every single shilling which must be spent so absurdly. It was rather funny. He would become doleful over it, and then again, with a fretful sigh, he would suppose there was nothing for it now but to take three second-class tickets—and there were the four children to pay for besides. A lot of money that to spend at once. A big lot of money.

I sat with him listening (not for the first time) to these heart-searchings till I grew thoroughly sleepy, and then I left him and turned in on board my ship. At daylight I was awakened by a yelping of shrill voices, accompanied by a great commotion in the water, and the short, bullying blasts of a steam-whistle. Falk with his tug had come for me.

I began to dress. It was remarkable that the answering noise on board my ship together with the patter of feet above my head ceased suddenly. But I heard more remote guttural cries which seemed to express surprise and annoyance. Then the voice of my mate reached me howling expostulations to somebody at a distance. Other voices joined, apparently indignant; a chorus of something that sounded like abuse replied. Now and then the steam-whistle screeched.

Altogether that unnecessary uproar was distracting, but down there in my cabin I took it calmly. In another moment, I thought, I should be going down that wretched river, and in another week at the most I should be totally quit of the odious place and all the odious people in it.

Greatly cheered by the idea, I seized the hair-brushes and looking at myself in the glass began to use them. Suddenly a hush fell upon the noise outside, and I heard (the ports of my cabin were thrown open)— I heard a deep calm voice, not on board my ship, however, hailing resolutely in English, but with a strong foreign twang, "Go ahead!"

There may be tides in the affairs of men which taken at the flood . . . and so on. Personally I am still on the look-out for that important turn. I am, however, afraid that most of us are fated to flounder for ever in the dead water of a pool the shores of which are arid indeed. But I know that there are often in men's affairs unexpectedly—even irrationally— illuminating moments when an otherwise insignificant sound, perhaps only some perfectly commonplace gesture, suffices to reveal to us all the unreason, all the fatuous unreason, of our complacency. "Go ahead" are not particularly striking words even when pronounced with a foreign accent; yet they petrified me in the very act of smiling at myself in the glass. And then, refusing to believe my ears, but already boiling with indignation, I ran out of the cabin and up on deck.

It was incredibly true. It was perfectly true. I had no eyes for anything but the *Diana*. It was she that was being taken away. She was already out of her berth and shooting athwart the river. "The way this loonatic plucked that ship out is a caution," said the awed voice of my mate close to my ear. "Hey! Hallo! Falk! Hermann! What's this infernal trick?" I yelled in a fury.

Nobody heard me. Falk certainly could not hear me. His tug was turning at full speed away under the other bank. The wire hawser between her and the *Diana*, stretched as taut as a harpstring, vibrated alarmingly.

The high black craft careened over to the awful strain. A loud crack came out of her, followed by the tearing and splintering of wood. "There!" said the awed voice in my ear. "He's carried away their towing chock." And then, with enthusiasm, "Oh! Look! Look, sir! Look at them Dutchmen skipping out of the way on the forecastle. I hope to goodness he'll break a few of their shins before he's done with 'em."

I yelled my vain protests. The rays of the rising sun coursing level along the plain warmed my back, but I was hot enough with rage. I could not have believed that a simple towing operation could suggest so plainly the idea of abduction, of rape. Falk was simply running off with the *Diana*.

The white tug careered out into the middle of the river. The red floats of her paddle-wheels revolving with mad rapidity tore up the whole reach into foam. The *Diana* in mid-stream waltzed round with as much grace as an old barn, and flew after her ravisher. Through the ragged fog of smoke driving headlong upon the water I had a glimpse of Falk's square motionless shoulders under a white hat as big as a cart-wheel, of his red face, his yellow staring eyes, his great beard. Instead of keeping a look-out ahead, he was deliberately turning his back on the river to glare at his tow. The tall heavy craft, never so used before in her life, seemed to have lost her senses; she took a wild sheer against her helm, and for a moment came straight at us, menacing and clumsy, like a runaway mountain. She piled up a streaming, hissing, boiling wave halfway up her blunt stem, my crew let out one great howl,—and then we held our breaths. It was a near thing. But Falk had her! He had her in his clutch. I fancied I could hear the steel hawser ping as it surged across the *Diana's* forecastle, with the hands on board of her bolting away from it in all directions. It was a near thing. Hermann, with his hair rumpled, in a snuffy flannel shirt and a pair of mustard-coloured trousers, had rushed to help with the wheel. I saw his terrified round face; I saw his very teeth uncovered by a sort of ghastly fixed grin; and in a great leaping tumult of water between the two ships the *Diana* whisked past so close that I could have flung a hair-brush at his head, for it seems, I had kept them in my hands all the time. Meanwhile Mrs. Hermann sat placidly on the skylight, with a woollen shawl on her shoulders. The excellent woman in response to my indignant gesticulations fluttered a handkerchief, nodding and smiling in the kindest way imaginable. The boys, only half-dressed, were jumping about the poop in great glee, displaying their gaudy braces; and Lena in a short scarlet petticoat, with peaked elbows and thin bare arms, nursed the rag-doll with devotion. The whole family passed before my sight as if dragged across a scene of unparalleled violence. The last I saw was Hermann's niece with the baby Hermann in her arms standing apart from the others. Magnificent in her close-fitting print frock, she displayed something so commanding in the manifest perfection of her figure that the sun seemed to be rising for her alone. The flood of light brought out the opulence of her form and the vigour of her youth in a glorifying way. She went by perfectly motionless and as if lost in meditation; only the hem of her skirt stirred in the draught; the sun rays broke on her sleek tawny hair; that bald-headed ruffian, Nicholas, was whacking her on the shoulder. I saw his tiny fat arm rise and fall in a workmanlike manner. And then the four cottage windows of the *Diana* came into view retreating swiftly down the river. The sashes were up, and one of the white calico curtains fluttered straight out like a streamer above the agitated water of the wake.

To be thus tricked out of one's turn was an unheard of occurrence. In my agent's office, where I went to complain at once, they protested with apologies they couldn't understand how the mistake arose: but Schomberg, when I dropped in later to get some tiffin, though surprised to see me, was perfectly ready with an explanation. I found him seated at the end of a long narrow table, facing his wife—a scraggy little woman, with long ringlets and a blue tooth, who smiled abroad stupidly and looked frightened when you spoke to her. Between them a waggling punkah fanned twenty vacant cane-bottomed chairs and two rows of shiny plates. Three Chinamen in white jackets loafed with napkins in their hands around that desolation. Schomberg's pet *table d'hôte* was not much of a success that day. He was feeding himself furiously and seemed to overflow with bitterness.

He began by ordering in a brutal voice the chops to be brought back for me, and turning in his chair: "Mistake, they told you? Not a bit of it! Don't you believe it for a moment, captain! Falk isn't a man to make mistakes unless on purpose." His firm conviction was that Falk had been trying all along to curry favour on the cheap with Hermann. "On the cheap—mind you! It doesn't cost him a cent to put that insult upon you, and Captain Hermann gets in a day ahead of your ship. Time's money! Eh? You are very friendly with Captain Hermann I believe, but a man is bound to be pleased at any little advantage he may get. Captain Hermann is a good business man, and there's no such thing as a friend in business. Is there?" He leaned forward and began to cast stealthy glances as usual. "But Falk is, and always was, a miserable fellow. I would despise him."

I muttered, grumpily, that I had no particular respect for Falk.

"I would despise him," he insisted, with an appearance of anxiety which would have amused me if I had not been fathoms deep in discontent. To a young man fairly conscientious and as well-meaning as only the young man can be, the current ill-usage of life comes with a peculiar cruelty. Youth that is fresh enough to believe in guilt, in innocence, and in itself, will always doubt whether it have not perchance deserved its fate. Sombre of mind and without appetite, I struggled with the chop while Mrs. Schomberg sat with her everlasting stupid grin and Schomberg's talk gathered way like a slide of rubbish.

"Let me tell you. It's all about that girl. I don't know what Captain Hermann expects, but if he asked me I could tell him something about Falk. He's a miserable fellow. That man is a perfect slave. That's what I call him. A slave. Last year I started this *table d'hôte*, and sent cards out—you know. You think he had one meal in the house? Give the thing a trial? Not once. He has got hold now of a Madras cook—a blamed fraud that I hunted out of my cook-house with a rattan. He was not fit to cook for white men. No, not for the white men's dogs either; but see, any damned native that can boil a pot of rice is good enough for Mr. Falk. Rice and a little fish he buys for a few cents from the fishing-boats outside is what he lives on. You would hardly credit it— eh? A white man, too. . . ."

He wiped his lips, using the napkin with indignation, and looking at me. It flashed through my mind in the midst of my depression that if all the meat in the town was like these *table d'hôte* chops, Falk wasn't so much to blame. I was on the point of saying this, but Schomberg's stare was intimidating. "He's a vegetarian, perhaps," I murmured instead.

"He's a miser. A miserable miser," affirmed the hotel-keeper with great force. "The meat here is not so good as at home—of course. And dear, too. But look at me. I only charge a dollar for the tiffin, and one dollar and fifty cents for the dinner. Show me anything cheaper. Why am I doing it? There's little profit in this game. Falk wouldn't look at it. I do it for the sake of a lot of young white fellows here that hadn't a place where they could get a decent meal and eat it decently in good company. There's first-rate company always at my table."

The convinced way he surveyed the empty chairs made me feel as if I had intruded upon a tiffin of ghostly Presences.

"A white man should eat like a white man, dash it all," he burst out impetuously. "Ought to eat meat, must eat meat. I manage to get meat for my patrons all the year round. Don't I? I am not catering for a dam' lot of coolies: Have another chop, captain. . . . No? You, boy—take away!"

He threw himself back and waited grimly for the curry. The half-closed jalousies darkened the room pervaded by the smell of fresh whitewash; a swarm of flies buzzed and settled in turns, and poor Mrs. Schomberg's smile seemed to express the quintessence of all the imbecility that had ever spoken, had ever breathed, had ever been fed on infamous buffalo meat within these bare walls. Schomberg did not open his lips till he was ready to thrust therein a spoonful of greasy rice. He rolled his eyes ridiculously before he swallowed the hot stuff, and only then broke out afresh.

"It is the most degrading thing. They take the dish up to the wheel-house for him with a cover on it, and he shuts both the doors before he begins to eat. Fact! Must be ashamed of himself. Ask the engineer. He can't do without an engineer—don't you see—and as no respectable man can be expected to put up with such a table, he allows them fifteen dollars a month extra mess money. I assure you it is so! You just ask Mr. Ferdinand da Costa. That's the engineer he has now. You may have seen him about my place, a delicate dark young man, with very fine eyes and a little moustache. He arrived here a year ago from Calcutta. Between you and me, I guess the money-lenders there must have been after him. He rushes here for a meal every chance he can get, for just please tell me what satisfaction is that for a well-educated young fellow to feed all alone in his cabin—like a wild beast? That's what Falk expects his engineers to put up with for fifteen dollars extra. And the rows on board every time a little smell of cooking gets about the deck! You wouldn't believe! The other day da Costa got the cook to fry a steak for him—a turtle steak it was, too, not beef at all—and the fat caught or something. Young da Costa himself was telling me of it here in this room. 'Mr. Schomberg'—says he—'if I had let a cylinder cover blow off through my negligence Captain Falk couldn't have been more savage. He frightened the cook so that he won't put anything on the fire for me now.' Poor da Costa had tears in his eyes. Only try to put yourself in his place, captain: a sensitive, gentlemanly young fellow. Is he expected to eat his food raw? But that's your Falk all over. Ask any one you like. I suppose the fifteen dollars extra he has to give keep on rankling—in there."

And Schomberg tapped his manly breast. I sat half stunned by his irrelevant babble. Suddenly he gripped my forearm in an impressive and cautious manner, as if to lead me into a very cavern of confidence.

"It's nothing but enviousness," he said in a lowered tone, which had a stimulating effect upon my wearied hearing. "I don't suppose there is one person in this town that he isn't envious of. I tell you he's dangerous. Even I myself am not safe from him. I know for certain he tried to poison. . . ."

"Oh, come now," I cried, disgusted.

"But I know for certain. The people themselves came and told me of it. He went about saying everywhere I was a worse pest to this town than the cholera. He had been talking against me ever since I opened this hotel. And he poisoned Captain Hermann's mind, too. Last time the *Diana* was loading here Captain Hermann used to come in every day for a drink or a cigar. This time he hasn't been here twice in a week. How do you account for that?"

He squeezed my arm till he extorted from me some sort of mumble.

"Falk makes ten times the money I do. I've another hotel to fight against, and there is no other tug on the river. I am not in his way, am I? He wouldn't be fit to run an hotel if he tried. But that's just his nature. He can't bear to think I am making a living. I only hope it makes him properly wretched. He's like that in everything. He would like to keep a decent table well enough. But no—for the sake of a few cents. Can't do it. It's too much for him. That's what I call being a slave to it. But he's mean enough to kick up a row when his nose gets tickled a bit. See that? That just paints him. Miserly and envious. You can't account for it any other way. Can you? I have been studying him these three years."

He was anxious I should assent to his theory. And indeed on thinking it over it would have been plausible enough if there hadn't been always the essential falseness of irresponsibility in Schomberg's chatter. However, I was not disposed to investigate the psychology of Falk. I was engaged just then in eating despondently a piece of stale Dutch cheese, being too much crushed to care what I swallowed myself, let alone bothering my head about Falk's ideas of gastronomy. I could expect from their study no clue to his conduct in matters of business, which seemed to me totally unrestrained by morality or even by the commonest sort of decency. How insignificant and contemptible I must appear, for the fellow to dare treat me like this—I reflected suddenly, writhing in silent agony. And I consigned Falk and all his peculiarities to the devil with so much mental fervour as to forget Schomberg's existence, till he grabbed my arm urgently. "Well, you may think and think till every hair of your head falls off, captain; but you can't explain it in any other way."

For the sake of peace and quietness I admitted hurriedly that I couldn't; persuaded that now he would leave off. But the only result was to make his moist face shine with the pride of cunning. He removed his hand for a moment to scare a black mass of flies off the sugar-basin, and caught hold of my arm again.

"To be sure. And in the same way everybody is aware he would like to get married. Only he can't. Let me quote you an instance. Well, two years ago a Miss Vanlo, a very ladylike girl, came from home to keep house for her brother, Fred, who had an engineering shop for small repairs by the waterside. Suddenly Falk takes to going up to their bungalow after dinner and sitting for hours in the verandah saying nothing. The poor girl couldn't tell for the life of her what to do with such a man, so she would keep on playing the piano and singing to him evening after evening till she was ready to drop. And it wasn't as if she had been a strong young woman either. She was thirty, and the climate had been playing the deuce with her. Then—don't you see—Fred had to sit up with them for propriety, and during whole weeks on end never got a chance to get to bed before midnight. That was not pleasant for a tired man—was it? And besides Fred had worries then because his shop didn't pay and he was dropping money fast. He just longed to get away from here and try his luck somewhere else, but for the sake of his sister he hung on and on till he ran himself into debt over his ears—I can tell you. I, myself, could show a handful of his chits for meals and drinks in my drawer. I could never find out tho' where Fred found all the money at last. Can't be but he must have got something out of that brother of his, a coal merchant in Port Said. Anyhow he paid everybody before he left, but the girl nearly broke her heart. Disappointment, of course, and at her age, don't you know. . . . Mrs. Schomberg here was very friendly with her, and she could tell you. Awful despair. Fainting fits. It was a scandal. A notorious scandal. To that extent that old Mr. Siegers—not your present charterer, but Mr. Siegers, the father, the old gentleman who retired from business on a fortune and got buried at sea going home, *he* had to interview Falk in his private office. He was a man who could speak like a Dutch Uncle, and, besides, Messrs. Siegers had been helping Falk with a good bit of money from the start. In fact, you may say they made him as far as that goes. It so happened that just at the time he turned up here, their firm was chartering a lot of sailing-ships every year, and it suited their business that there should be good towing facilities on the river. See? . . . Well—there's always an ear at the keyhole—isn't there? In fact," he lowered his tone confidentially, "in this case it was a good friend of mine; a man you can see here any evening; only they conversed rather low. Anyhow my friend's certain that Falk was trying to make all sorts of excuses, and old Mr. Siegers was coughing a lot. And yet Falk wanted all the time to be married, too. Why! It's notorious the man has been longing for years to make a home for himself. Only he can't face the expense. When it comes to putting his hand in his pocket—it chokes him off. That's the truth and no other. I've always said so, and everybody agrees with me by this time. What do you think of that—eh?"

He appealed confidently to my indignation, but having a mind to annoy him I remarked, "that it seemed to me very pitiful—if true."

He bounced in his chair as if I had run a pin into him. I don't know what he might have said, only at that moment we heard through the half-open door of the billiard-room the footsteps of two men entering from the verandah, a murmur of two voices; at the sharp tapping of a coin on a table Mrs. Schomberg half rose irresolutely. "Sit still," he hissed at her, and then, in an hospitable, jovial tone, contrasting amazingly with the angry glance that had made his wife sink in her chair, he cried very loud: "Tiffin still going on in here, gentlemen."

There was no answer, but the voices dropped suddenly. The head Chinaman went out. We heard the clink of ice in the glasses, pouring sounds, the shuffling of feet, the scraping of chairs. Schomberg, after wondering in a low mutter who the devil could be there at this time of the day, got up napkin in hand to peep through the doorway cautiously. He retreated rapidly on tip-toe, and whispering behind his hand informed me that it was Falk, Falk himself who was in there, and what's more, he had Captain Hermann with him.

The return of the tug from the outer Roads was unexpected but possible, for Falk had taken away the *Diana* at half-past five, and it was now two o'clock. Schomberg wished me to observe that neither of these men would spend a dollar on a tiffin, which they must have wanted. But by the time I was ready to leave the dining-room Falk had gone. I heard the last of his big boots on the planks of the verandah. Hermann was sitting quite alone in the large, wooden room with the two lifeless billiard tables shrouded in striped covers, mopping his face diligently. He wore his best go-ashore clothes, a stiff collar, black coat, large white waistcoat, gray trousers. A white cotton sunshade with a cane handle reposed between his legs, his side whiskers were neatly brushed, his chin had been freshly shaved; and he only distantly resembled the dishevelled and terrified man in a snuffy night shirt and ignoble old trousers I had seen in the morning hanging on to the wheel of the *Diana*.

He gave a start at my entrance, and addressed me at once in some confusion, but with genuine eagerness. He was anxious to make it clear he had nothing to do with what he called the "tam pizness" of the morning. It was most inconvenient. He had reckoned upon another day up in town to settle his bills and sign certain papers. There were also some few stores to come, and sundry pieces of "my ironwork," as he called it quaintly, landed for repairs, had been left behind. Now he would have to hire a native boat to take all this out to the ship. It would cost five to six dollars perhaps. He had had no warning from Falk. Nothing. . . . He hit the table with his dumpy fist. . . . Der verfluchte Kerl came in the morning like a "tam' ropper," making a great noise, and took him away. His mate was not prepared, his ship was moored fast—he protested it was shameful to come upon a man in that way. Shameful! Yet such was the power Falk had on the river that when I suggested in a chilling tone that he might have simply refused to have his ship moved, Hermann was quite startled at the idea. I never realized so well before that this is an age of steam. The exclusive possession of a marine boiler had given Falk the whip hand of us all. Hermann, recovering, put it to me appealingly that I knew very well how unsafe it was to contradict that fellow. At this I only smiled distantly.

"Der Kerl!" he cried. He was sorry he had not refused. He was indeed. The damage! The damage! What for all that damage! There was no occasion for damage. Did I know how much damage he had done? It gave me a certain satisfaction to tell him that I had heard his old waggon of a ship crack fore and aft as she went by. "You passed close enough to me," I added, significantly.

He threw both his hands up to heaven at the recollection. One of them grasped by the middle the white parasol, and he resembled curiously a caricature of a shopkeeping citizen in one of his own German comic papers. "Ach! That was dangerous," he cried. I was amused. But directly he added with an appearance of simplicity, "The side of your iron ship would have been crushed in like—like this matchbox."

"Would it?" I growled, much less amused now; but by the time I had decided that this remark was not meant for a dig at me he had worked himself into a high state of resentfulness against Falk. The inconvenience, the damage, the expense! Gottferdam! Devil take the fellow. Behind the bar Schomberg, with a cigar in his teeth, pretended to be writing with a pencil on a large sheet of paper; and as Hermann's excitement increased it made me comfortingly aware of my own calmness and superiority. But it occurred to me while I listened to his revilings, that after all the good man had come up in the tug. There perhaps—since he must come to town—he had no option. But evidently he had had a drink with Falk, either accepted or offered. How was that? So I checked him by saying loftily that I hoped he would make Falk pay for every penny of the damage.

"That's it! That's it! Go for him," called out Schomberg from the bar, flinging his pencil down and rubbing his hands.

We ignored his noise. But Hermann's excitement suddenly went off the boil as when you remove a sauce-pan from the fire. I urged on his consideration that he had done now with Falk and Falk's confounded tug. He, Hermann, would not, perhaps, turn up again in this part of the world for years to come, since he was going to sell the *Diana* at the end of this very trip ("Go home passenger in a mail-boat," he murmured mechanically). He was therefore safe from Falk's malice. All he had to do was to race off to his consignees and stop payment of the towage bill before Falk had the time to get in and lift the money.

Nothing could have been less in the spirit of my advice than the thoughtful way in which he set about to make his parasol stay propped against the edge of the table.

While I watched his concentrated efforts with astonishment he threw at me one or two perplexed, half-shy glances. Then he sat down. "That's all very well," he said, reflectively.

It cannot be doubted that the man had been thrown off his balance by being hauled out of the harbour against his wish. His stolidity had been profoundly stirred, else he would never have made up his mind to ask me unexpectedly whether I had not remarked that Falk had been casting eyes upon his niece. "No more than myself," I answered with literal truth. The girl was of the sort one necessarily casts eyes at in a sense. She made no noise, but she filled most satisfactorily a good bit of space.

"But you, captain, are not the same kind of man," observed Hermann.

I was not, I am happy to say, in a position to deny this. "What about the lady?" I could not help asking. At this he gazed for a time into my face, earnestly, and made as if to change the subject. I heard him beginning to mutter something unexpected, about his children growing old enough to require schooling. He would have to leave them ashore with their grandmother when he took up that new command he expected to get in Germany.

This constant harping on his domestic arrangements was funny. I suppose it must have been like the prospect of a complete alteration in his life. An epoch. He was going, too, to part with the *Diana!* He had served in her for years. He had inherited her. From an uncle, if I remember rightly. And the future loomed big before him, occupying his thought exclusively with all its aspects as on the eve of a venturesome enterprise. He sat there frowning and biting his lip, and suddenly he began to fume and fret.

I discovered to my momentary amusement that he seemed to imagine I could, should or ought, have caused Falk in some way to declare himself. Such a hope was incomprehensible, but funny. Then the contact with all this foolishness irritated me. I said crossly that I had seen no symptoms, but if there were any—since he, Hermann, was so sure— then it was still worse. What pleasure Falk found in humbugging people in just that way I couldn't say. It was, however, my solemn duty to warn him. It had lately, I said, come to my knowledge that there was a man (not a very long time ago either) who had been taken in just like this.

All this passed in undertones, and at this point Schomberg, exasperated at our secrecy, went out of the room, slamming the door with a crash that positively lifted us in our chairs. This, or else what I had said, huffed my Hermann. He supposed, with a contemptuous toss of his head towards the door which trembled yet, that I had got hold of some of that man's silly tales. It looked, indeed, as though his mind had been thoroughly poisoned against Schomberg. "His tales were—they were," he repeated, seeking for the word—"trash." They were trash, he reiterated and moreover I was young yet . . .

This horrid aspersion (I regret I am no longer exposed to that sort of insult) made me huffy, too. I felt ready in my own mind to back up every assertion of Schomberg's and on any subject. In a moment, devil only knows why, Hermann and I were looking at each other most inimically. He caught up his hat without more ado and I gave myself the pleasure of calling after him:

"Take my advice and make Falk pay for breaking up your ship. You aren't likely to get anything else out of him."

When I got on board my ship, the old mate, who was very full of the events of the morning, remarked:

"I saw the tug coming back from the outer Roads just before two P.M." (He never by any chance used the words morning or afternoon. Always P.M. or A.M., log-book style.) "Smart work that. Man's always in a state of hurry. He's a regular chucker-out, ain't he, sir? There's a few pubs I know of in the East-end of London that would be all the better for one of his sort around the bar." He chuckled at his joke. "A regular chucker-out. Now he has fired out that Dutchman head over heels, I suppose our turn's coming to-morrow morning."

We were all on deck at break of day (even the sick—poor devils— had crawled out) ready to cast off in the twinkling of an eye. Nothing came. Falk did not come. At last, when I began to think that probably something had gone wrong in his engine-room, we perceived the tug going by, full pelt, down the river, as if we hadn't existed. For a moment I entertained the wild notion that he was going to turn round in the next reach. Afterwards, I watched his smoke appear above the plain, now here, now there, according to the windings of the river. It disappeared. Then without a word I went down to breakfast. I just simply went down to breakfast.

Not one of us uttered a sound till the mate, after imbibing—by means of suction out of a saucer—his second cup of tea, exclaimed: "Where the devil is the man gone to?"

"Courting!" I shouted, with such a fiendish laugh that the old chap didn't venture to open his lips any more.

I started to the office perfectly calm. Calm with excessive rage. Evidently they knew all about it already, and they treated me to a show of consternation. The manager, a soft-footed, obese man, breathing short, got up to meet me, while all round the room the young clerks, bending over their desks, cast glances in my direction. The fat man, without waiting for my complaint, wheezing heavily and in a tone as if he himself were incredulous, conveyed to me the news that Falk—Captain Falk— had declined—had absolutely declined—to tow my ship—to have anything to to with my ship—this day or any other day. Never!

I did my best to preserve a cool appearance, but, all the same, I must have shown how much taken aback I was. We were talking in the middle of the room. Suddenly, behind my back some ass blew his nose with a great noise and at the same time another quill-driver got up and went out on the landing hastily. It occurred to me I was cutting a foolish figure there. I demanded angrily to see the principal in his private room.

The skin of Mr. Siegers' head showed dead white between the iron gray streaks of hair lying plastered cross-wise from ear to ear over the top of his skull in the manner of a bandage. His narrow sunken face was of an uniform and permanent terra-cotta colour, like a piece of pottery. He was sickly, thin, and short, with wrists like a boy of ten. But from that debile body there issued a bullying voice, tremendously loud, harsh and resonant, as if produced by some powerful mechanical contrivance in the nature of a fog-horn. I do not know what he did with it in the private life of his home, but in the larger sphere of business it presented the advantage of overcoming arguments without the slightest mental effort, by the mere volume of sound. We had had several passages of arms. It took me all I knew to guard the interest of my owners— whom, *nota bene*, I had never seen—while Siegers (who had made their acquaintance some years before, during a business tour in Australia) pretended to the knowledge of their innermost minds, and, in the character of "our very good friends," threw them perpetually at my head.

He looked at me with a jaundiced eye (there was no love lost between us), and declared at once that it was strange, very strange. His pronunciation of English was so extravagant that I can't even attempt to reproduce it. For instance, he said "Fferie strantch." Combined with the bellowing intonation it made the language of one's childhood sound weirdly startling, and even if considered purely as a kind of unmeaning noise it filled you with astonishment at first. "They had," he continued, "been acquainted with Captain Falk for very many years, and never had any reason. . . ."

"That's why I come to you, of course," I interrupted. "I've the right to know the meaning of this infernal nonsense." In the half-light of the room, which was greenish, because of the tree-tops screening the window, I saw him writhe his meagre shoulders. It came into my head, as disconnected ideas will come at all sorts of times into one's head, that this, most likely, was the very room where, if the tale were true, Falk had been lectured by Mr. Siegers, the father. Mr. Siegers' (the son's) overwhelming voice, in brassy blasts, as though he had been trying to articulate words through a trumpet, was expressing his great regret at conduct characterized by a very marked want of discretion . . . As I lived I was being lectured, too! His deafening gibberish was difficult to follow, but it was *my* conduct—mine!—that . . . Damn! I wasn't going to stand this.

"What on earth are you driving at?" I asked in a passion. I put my hat on my head (he never offered a seat to anybody), and as he seemed for the moment struck dumb by my irreverence, I turned my back on him and marched out. His vocal arrangements blared after me a few threats of coming down on the ship for the demurrage of the lighters, and all the other expenses consequent upon the delays arising from my frivolity.

Once outside in the sunshine my head swam. It was no longer a question of mere delay. I perceived myself involved in hopeless and humiliating absurdities that were leading me to something very like a disaster. "Let us be calm," I muttered to myself, and ran into the shade of a leprous wall. From that short side-street I could see the broad main thoroughfare ruinous and gay, running away, away between stretches of decaying masonry, bamboo fences, ranges of arcades of brick and plaster, hovels of lath and mud, lofty temple gates of carved timber, huts of rotten mats—an immensely wide thoroughfare, loosely packed as far as the eye could reach with a barefooted and brown multitude paddling ankle deep in the dust. For a moment I felt myself about to go out of my mind with worry and desperation.

Some allowance must be made for the feelings of a young man new to responsibility. I thought of my crew. Half of them were ill, and I really began to think that some of them would end by dying on board if I couldn't get them out to sea soon. Obviously I should have to take my ship down the river, either working under canvas or dredging with the anchor down; operations which, in common with many modern sailors, I only knew theoretically. And I almost shrank from undertaking them shorthanded and without local knowledge of the river bed, which is so necessary for the confident handling of a ship. There were no pilots, no beacons, no buoys of any sort; but there was a very devil of a current for anybody to see, no end of shoal places, and at least two obviously awkward turns of the channel between me and the sea. But how dangerous these turns were I could not tell. I didn't even know what my ship was capable of! I had never handled her in my life. A misunderstanding between a man and his ship, in a difficult river with no room to make it up, is bound to end in trouble for the man. On the other hand, it must be owned I had not much reason to count upon a general run of good luck. And suppose I had the misfortune to pile her up high and dry on some beastly shoal? That would have been the final undoing of that voyage. It was plain that if Falk refused to tow me out he would also refuse to pull me off. This meant—what? A day lost at the very best; but more likely a whole fortnight of frizzling on some pestilential mudflat, of desperate work, of discharging cargo; more than likely it meant borrowing money at an exorbitant rate of interest—from the Siegers' gang, too, at that. They were a power in the port. And that elderly seaman of mine, Gambril, had looked pretty ghastly when I went forward to dose him with quinine that morning. *He* would certainly die—not to speak of two or three others that seemed nearly as bad, and of the rest of them just ready to catch any tropical disease going. Horror, ruin and everlasting remorse. And no help. None. I had fallen amongst a lot of unfriendly lunatics!

At any rate, if I must take my ship down myself it was my duty to procure if possible some local knowledge. But that was not easy. The only person I could think of for that service was a certain Johnson, formerly captain of a country ship, but now spliced to a country wife and gone utterly to the bad. I had only heard of him in the vaguest way, as living concealed in the thick of two hundred thousand natives, and only emerging into the light of day for the purpose of hunting up some brandy. I had a notion that if I could lay my hands on him I would sober him on board my ship and use him for a pilot. Better than nothing.

Once a sailor always a sailor—and he had known the river for years. But in our Consulate (where I arrived dripping after a sharp walk) they could tell me nothing. The excellent young men on the staff, though willing to help me, belonged to a sphere of the white colony for which that sort of Johnson does not exist. Their suggestion was that I should hunt the man up myself with the help of the Consulate's constable—an ex-sergeant-major of a regiment of Hussars.

This man, whose usual duty apparently consisted in sitting behind a little table in an outer room of Consular offices, when ordered to assist me in my search for Johnson displayed lots of energy and a marvellous amount of local knowledge of a sort. But he did not conceal an immense and sceptical contempt for the whole business. We explored together on that afternoon an infinity of infamous grog shops, gambling dens, opium dens. We walked up narrow lanes where our gharry—a tiny box of a thing on wheels, attached to a jibbing Burmah pony—could by no means have passed. The constable seemed to be on terms of scornful intimacy with Maltese, with Eurasians, with Chinamen, with Klings, and with the sweepers belonging to a temple, with whom he talked at the gate. We interviewed also through a grating in a mud wall closing a blind alley an immensely corpulent Italian, who, the ex-sergeant-major remarked to me perfunctorily, had "killed another man last year." There-upon he addressed him as "Antonio" and "Old Buck," though that bloated carcase, apparently more than half filling the sort of cell wherein it sat, recalled rather a fat pig in a stye. Familiar and never unbending, the sergeant chucked—absolutely chucked—under the chin a horribly wrinkled and shrivelled old hag propped on a stick, who had volunteered some sort of information: and with the same stolid face he kept up an animated conversation with the groups of swathed brown women, who sat smoking cheroots on the doorsteps of a long range of clay hovels. We got out of the gharry and clambered into dwellings airy like packing crates, or descended into places sinister like cellars. We got in, we drove on, we got out again for the sole purpose, as it seemed, of looking behind a heap of rubble. The sun declined; my companion was curt and sardonic in his answers, but it appears we were just missing Johnson all along. At last our conveyance stopped once more with a jerk, and the driver jumping down opened the door.

A black mudhole blocked the lane. A mound of garbage crowned with the dead body of a dog arrested us not. An empty Australian beef tin bounded cheerily before the toe of my boot. Suddenly we clambered through a gap in a prickly fence. . . .

It was a very clean native compound: and the big native woman, with bare brown legs as thick as bed-posts, pursuing on all fours a silver dollar that came rolling out from somewhere, was Mrs. Johnson herself. "Your man's at home," said the ex-sergeant, and stepped aside in complete and marked indifference to anything that might follow. Johnson—at home—stood with his back to a native house built on posts and with its walls made of mats. In his left hand he held a banana. Out of the right he dealt another dollar into space. The woman captured this one on the wing, and there and then plumped down on the ground to look at us with greater comfort.

"My man" was sallow of face, grizzled, unshaven, muddy on elbows and back; where the seams of his serge coat yawned you could see his white nakedness. The vestiges of a paper collar encircled his neck. He looked at us with a grave, swaying surprise. "Where do you come from?" he asked. My heart sank. How could I have been stupid enough to waste energy and time for this?

But having already gone so far I approached a little nearer and declared the purpose of my visit. He would have to come at once with me, sleep on board my ship, and to-morrow, with the first of the ebb, he would give me his assistance in getting my ship down to the sea, without steam. A six-hundred-ton barque, drawing nine feet aft. I proposed to give him eighteen dollars for his local knowledge; and all the time I was speaking he kept on considering attentively the various aspects of the banana, holding first one side up to his eye, then the other.

"You've forgotten to apologize," he said at last with extreme precision. "Not being a gentleman yourself, you don't know apparently when you intrude upon a gentleman. I am one. I wish you to understand that when I am in funds I don't work, and now . . ."

I would have pronounced him perfectly sober had he not paused in great concern to try and brush a hole off the knee of his trousers.

"I have money—and friends. Every gentleman has. Perhaps you would like to know my friend? His name is Falk. You could borrow some money. Try to remember. F-A-L-K. Falk." Abruptly his tone changed. "A noble heart," he said, muzzily.

"Has Falk been giving you some money?" I asked, appalled by the detailed finish of the dark plot.

"Lent me, my good man, not given me," he corrected, suavely. "Met me taking the air last evening, and being as usual anxious to oblige—— Hadn't you better go to the devil out of my compound?"

And upon this, without other warning, he let fly with the banana, which missed my head and took the constable just under the left eye. He rushed at the miserable Johnson, stammering with fury. They fell. . . . But why dwell on the wretchedness, the breathlessness, the degradation, the senselessness, the weariness, the ridicule and humiliation and—and—the perspiration, of these moments? I dragged the ex-hussar off. He was like a wild beast. It seems he had been greatly annoyed at losing his free afternoon on my account. The garden of his bungalow required his personal attention, and at the slight blow of the banana the brute in him had broken loose. We left Johnson on his back still black in the face, but beginning to kick feebly. Meantime, the big woman had remained sitting on the ground, apparently paralyzed with extreme terror.

For half an hour we jolted inside our rolling box, side by side, in profound silence. The ex-sergeant was busy staunching the blood of a long scratch on his cheek. "I hope you're satisfied," he said, suddenly. "That's what comes of all that tomfool business. If you hadn't quarrelled with that tugboat skipper over some girl or other, all this wouldn't have happened."

"You heard *that* story?" I said.

"Of course I heard. And I shouldn't wonder if the Consul-General himself doesn't come to hear of it. How am I to go before him to-morrow with that thing on my cheek—I want to know. It's *you* who ought to have got this!"

After that, till the gharry stopped and he jumped out without leave-taking, he swore to himself steadily, horribly; muttering great, purposeful, trooper oaths, to which the worst a sailor can do is like the prattle of a child. For my part I had just the strength to crawl into Schomberg's coffee-room, where I wrote at a little table a note to the mate instructing him to get everything ready for dropping down the river next day. I couldn't face my ship. Well! she had a clever sort of skipper and no mistake—poor thing! What a horrid mess! I took my head between my hands. At times the obviousness of my innocence would reduce me to despair. What had I done? If I had done something to bring about the situation I should at least have learned not to do it again. But I felt guiltless to the point of imbecility. The room was empty yet; only Schomberg prowled round me goggle-eyed and with a sort of awed respectful curiosity. No doubt he had set the story going himself; but he was a good-hearted chap, and I am really persuaded he participated in all my troubles. He did what he could for me. He ranged aside the heavy matchstand, set a chair straight, pushed a spittoon slightly with his foot—as you show small attentions to a friend under a great sorrow—sighed, and at last, unable to hold his tongue:

"Well! I warned you, captain. That's what comes of running your head against Mr. Falk. Man'll stick at nothing."

I sat without stirring, and after surveying me with a sort of commiseration in his eyes, he burst out in a hoarse whisper: "But for a fine lump of a girl, she's a fine lump of a girl." He made a loud smacking noise with his thick lips. "The finest lump of a girl that I ever . . ." he was going on with great unction, but for some reason or other broke off. I fancied myself throwing something at his head. "I don't blame you, captain. Hang me if I do," he said with a patronizing air.

"Thank you," I said, resignedly. It was no use fighting against this false fate. I don't know even if I was sure myself where the truth of the matter began. The conviction that it would end disastrously had been driven into me by all the successive shocks my sense of security had received. I began to ascribe an extraordinary potency to agents in themselves powerless. It was as if Schomberg's baseless gossip had the power to bring about the thing itself or the abstract enmity of Falk could put my ship ashore.

I have already explained how fatal this last would have been. For my further action, my youth, my inexperience, my very real concern for the health of my crew must be my excuse. The action itself, when it came, was purely impulsive. It was set in movement quite undiplomatically and simply by Falk's appearance in the doorway of the coffee-room.

The room was full by then and buzzing with voices. I had been looked at with curiosity by every one, but how am I to describe the sensation produced by the appearance of Falk himself blocking the doorway? The tension of expectation could be measured by the profundity of the silence that fell upon the very click of the billiard balls. As to Schomberg, he looked extremely frightened; he hated mortally any sort of row (*fracas* he called it) in his establishment. *Fracas* was bad for business, he affirmed; but in truth, this specimen of portly, middle-aged manhood was of a timid disposition. I don't know what, considering my presence in the place, they all hoped would come of it. A sort of stag fight, perhaps. Or they may have supposed Falk had come in only to annihilate me completely. As a matter of fact, Falk had come in because Hermann had asked him to inquire after the precious white cotton parasol which, in the worry and excitement of the previous day, he had forgotten at the table where we had held our little discussion.

It was this that gave me my opportunity. I don't think I would have gone to seek Falk out. No. I don't think so. There are limits. But there was an opportunity and I seized it—I have already tried to explain why. Now I will merely state that, in my opinion, to get his sickly crew into the sea air and secure a quick despatch for his ship a skipper would be justified in going to any length, short of absolute crime. He should put his pride in his pocket; he may accept confidences; he must explain his innocence as if it were a sin; he may take advantage of misconceptions, of desires and of weaknesses; he ought to conceal his horror and other emotions, and, if the fate of a human being, and that human being a magnificent young girl, is strangely involved—why, he should contemplate that fate (whatever it might seem to be) without turning a hair. And all these things I have done; the explaining, the listening, the pretending—even to the discretion—and nobody, not even Hermann's niece, I believe, need throw stones at me now. Schomberg at all events needn't, since from first to last, I am happy to say there was not the slightest "*fracas.*"

Overcoming a nervous contraction of the windpipe, I had managed to exclaim "Captain Falk!" His start of surprise was perfectly genuine, but afterwards he neither smiled nor scowled. He simply waited. Then, when I had said, "I must have a talk with you," and had pointed to a chair at my table, he moved up to me, though he didn't sit down. Schomberg, however, with a long tumbler in his hand, was making towards us prudently, and I discovered then the only sign of weakness in Falk. He had for Schomberg a repulsion resembling that sort of physical fear some people experience at the sight of a toad. Perhaps to a man so essentially and silently concentrated upon himself (though he could talk well enough, as I was to find out presently) the other's irrepressible loquacity, embracing every human being within range of the tongue, might have appeared unnatural, disgusting, and monstrous. He suddenly gave signs of restiveness—positively like a horse about to rear, and, muttering hurriedly as if in great pain, "No. I can't stand that fellow," seemed ready to bolt. This weakness of his gave me the advantage at the very start. "Verandah," I suggested, as if rendering him a service, and walked him out by the arm. We stumbled over a few chairs; we had the feeling of open space before us, and felt the fresh breath of the river—fresh, but tainted. The Chinese theatres across the water made, in the sparsely twinkling masses of gloom an Eastern town presents at night, blazing centres of light, and of a distant and howling uproar. I felt him become suddenly tractable again like an animal, like a good-tempered horse when the object that scares him is removed. Yes. I felt in the darkness there how tractable he was, without my conviction of his inflexibility—tenacity, rather, perhaps—being in the least weakened. His very arm abandoning itself to my grasp was as hard as marble—like a limb of iron. But I heard a tumultuous scuffling of boot-soles within. The unspeakable idiots inside were crowding to the windows, climbing over each other's backs behind the blinds, billiard cues and all. Somebody broke a window-pane, and with the sound of falling glass, so suggestive of riot and devastation, Schomberg reeled out after us in a state of funk which had prevented him from parting with his brandy and soda. He must have trembled like an aspen leaf. The piece of ice in the long tumbler he held in his hand tinkled with an effect of chattering teeth. "I beg you, gentlemen," he expostulated, thickly. "Come! Really, now, I must insist . . ."

How proud I am of my presence of mind! "Hallo," I said instantly in a loud and naïve tone, "somebody's breaking your windows, Schomberg. Would you please tell one of your boys to bring out here a pack of cards and a couple of lights? And two long drinks. Will you?"

To receive an order soothed him at once. It was business. "Certainly," he said in an immensely relieved tone. The night was rainy, with wandering gusts of wind, and while we waited for the candles Falk said, as if to justify his panic, "I don't interfere in anybody's business. I don't give any occasion for talk. I am a respectable man. But this fellow is always making out something wrong and can never rest till he gets somebody to believe him."

This was the first of my knowledge of Falk. This desire of respectability, of being like everybody else, was the only recognition he vouchsafed to the organization of mankind. For the rest he might have been the member of a herd, not of a society. Self-preservation was his only concern. Not selfishness, but mere self-preservation. Selfishness presupposes consciousness, choice, the presence of other men; but his instinct acted as though he were the last of mankind nursing that law like the only spark of a sacred fire. I don't mean to say that living naked in a cavern would have satisfied him. Obviously he was the creature of the conditions to which he was born. No doubt self-preservation meant also the preservation of these conditions. But essentially it meant something much more simple, natural, and powerful. How shall I express it? It meant the preservation of the five senses of his body—let us say—taking it in its narrowest as well as in its widest meaning. I think you will admit before long the justice of this judgment. However, as we stood there together in the dark verandah I had judged nothing as yet—and I had no desire to judge—which is an idle practice anyhow. The light was long in coming.

"Of course," I said in a tone of mutual understanding, "it isn't exactly a game of cards I want with you."

I saw him draw his hands down his face—the vague stir of the passionate and meaningless gesture; but he waited in silent patience. It was only when the lights had been brought out that he opened his lips. I understood his mumble to mean that "he didn't know any card-games."

"Like this, Schomberg and all the other fools will have to keep off," I said, tearing open the pack. "Have you heard that we are universally supposed to be quarrelling about a girl? You know who—of course. I am really ashamed to ask, but is it possible that you do me the honour to think me dangerous?"

As I said these words I felt how absurd it was and also I felt flattered—for, really, what else could it be? His answer, spoken in his usual dispassionate undertone, made it clear that it was so, but not precisely as flattering as I supposed. He thought me dangerous with Hermann, more than with the girl herself; but, as to quarrelling, I saw at once how inappropriate the word was. We had no quarrel. Natural forces are not quarrelsome. You can't quarrel with the wind that inconveniences and humiliates you by blowing off your hat in a street full of people. He had no quarrel with me. Neither would a boulder, falling on my head, have had. He fell upon me in accordance with the law by which he was moved—not of gravitation, like a detached stone, but of self-preservation. Of course this is giving it a rather wide interpretation. Strictly speaking, he had existed and could have existed without being married. Yet he told me that he had found it more and more difficult to live alone. Yes. He told me this in his low, careless voice, to such a pitch of confidence had we arrived at the end of half an hour.

It took me just about that time to convince him that I had never dreamed of marrying Hermann's niece. Could any necessity have been more extravagant? And the difficulty was the greater because he was so hard hit himself that he couldn't imagine anybody else being able to remain in a state of indifference. Any man with eyes in his head, he seemed to think, could not help coveting so much bodily magnificence. This profound belief was conveyed by the manner he listened sitting sideways to the table and playing absently with a few cards I had dealt to him at random. And the more I saw into him the more I saw of him. The wind swayed the lights so that his sunburnt face, whiskered to the eyes, seemed to successively flicker crimson at me and to go out. I saw the extraordinary breadth of the high cheek-bones, the perpendicular style of the features, the massive forehead, steep like a cliff, denuded at the top, largely uncovered at the temples. The fact is I had never before seen him without his hat; but now, as if my fervour had made him hot, he had taken it off and laid it gently on the floor. Something peculiar in the shape and setting of his yellow eyes gave them the provoking silent intensity which characterized his glance. But the face was thin, furrowed, worn; I discovered this through the bush of his hair, as you may detect the gnarled shape of a tree trunk in a dense undergrowth. These over-grown cheeks were sunken. It was an anchorite's bony head fitted with a Capuchin's beard and adjusted to a herculean body. I don't mean athletic. Hercules, I take it, was not an athlete. He was a strong man, susceptible to female charms, and not afraid of dirt. And thus with Falk, who was a strong man. He was extremely strong, just as the girl (since I must think of them together) was magnificently attractive by the masterful power of flesh and blood, expressed in shape, in size, in attitude—that is by a straight appeal to the senses. His mind meantime, preoccupied with respectability, quailed before Schomberg's tongue and seemed absolutely impervious to my protestations; and I went so far as to protest that I would just as soon think of marrying my mother's (dear old lady!)

faithful female cook as Hermann's niece. Sooner, I protested, in my desperation, much sooner; but it did not appear that he saw anything outrageous in the proposition, and in his sceptical immobility he seemed to nurse the argument that at all events the cook was very, very far away. It must be said that, just before, I had gone wrong by appealing to the evidence of my manner whenever I called on board the *Diana.* I had never attempted to approach the girl, or to speak to her, or even to look at her in any marked way. Nothing could be clearer. But, as his own idea of—let us say—courting, seemed to consist precisely in sitting silently for hours in the vicinity of the beloved object, that line of argument inspired him with distrust. Staring down his extended legs he let out a grunt—as much as to say, "That's all very fine, but you can't throw dust in *my* eyes."

As last I was exasperated into saying, "Why don't you put the matter at rest by talking to Hermann?" and I added, sneeringly: "You don't expect me perhaps to speak for you?"

To this he said, very loud for him, "Would you?"

And for the first time he lifted his head to look at me with wonder and incredulity. He lifted his head so sharply that there could be no mistake. I had touched a spring. I saw the whole extent of my opportunity, and could hardly believe in it.

"Why! Speak to . . . Well, of course," I proceeded very slowly, watching him with great attention, for, on my word, I feared a joke. "Not, perhaps, to the young lady herself. I can't speak German, you know. But . . ."

He interrupted me with the earnest assurance that Hermann had the highest opinion of me; and at once I felt the need for the greatest possible diplomacy at this juncture. So I demurred just enough to draw him on. Falk sat up, but except for a very noticeable enlargement of the pupils, till the irises of his eyes were reduced to two narrow yellow rings, his face, I should judge, was incapable of expressing excitement. "Oh, yes! Hermann did have the greatest . . ."

"Take up your cards. Here's Schomberg peeping at us through the blind!" I said.

We went through the motions of what might have been a game of écarté. Presently the intolerable scandalmonger withdrew, probably to inform the people in the billiard-room that we two were gambling on the verandah like mad.

We were not gambling, but it was a game; a game in which I felt I held the winning cards. The stake, roughly speaking, was the success of the voyage—for me; and he, I apprehended, had nothing to lose. Our intimacy matured rapidly, and before many words had been exchanged I perceived that the excellent Hermann had been making use of me. That simple and astute Teuton had been, it seems, holding me up to Falk in the light of a rival. I was young enough to be shocked at so much duplicity. "Did he tell you that in so many words?" I asked with indignation.

Hermann had not. He had given hints only; and of course it had not taken very much to alarm Falk; but, instead of declaring himself, he had taken steps to remove the family from under my influence. He was perfectly straightforward about it—as straightforward as a tile falling on your head. There was no duplicity in that man; and when I congratulated him on the perfection of his arrangements—even to the bribing of the wretched Johnson against me—he had a genuine movement of protest. Never bribed. He knew the man wouldn't work as long as he had a few cents in his pocket to get drunk on, and, naturally (he said—"*naturally*") he let him have a dollar or two. He was himself a sailor, he said, and anticipated the view another sailor, like myself, was bound to take. On the other hand, he was sure that I should have to come to grief. He hadn't been knocking about for the last seven years up and down that river for nothing. It would have been no disgrace to me—but he asserted confidently I would have had my ship very awkwardly ashore at a spot two miles below the Great Pagoda. . . .

And with all that he had no ill-will. That was evident. This was a crisis in which his only object had been to gain time—I fancy. And presently he mentioned that he had written for some jewellery, real good jewellery—had written to Hong-Kong for it. It would arrive in a day or two.

"Well, then," I said, cheerily, "everything is all right. All you've got to do is to present it to the lady together with your heart, and live happy ever after."

Upon the whole he seemed to accept that view as far as the girl was concerned, but his eyelids drooped. There was still something in the way. For one thing Hermann disliked him so much. As to me, on the contrary, it seemed as though he could not praise me enough. Mrs. Hermann, too. He didn't know why they disliked him so. It made everything most difficult.

I listened impassive, feeling more and more diplomatic. His speech was not transparently clear. He was one of those men who seem to live, feel, suffer in a sort of mental twilight. But as to being fascinated by the girl and possessed by the desire of home life with her—it was as clear as daylight. So much being at stake, he was afraid of putting it to the hazard of the declaration. Besides, there was something else. And with Hermann being so set against him . . .

"I see," I said, thoughtfully, while my heart beat fast with the excitement of my diplomacy. "I don't mind sounding Hermann. In fact, to show you how mistaken you were, I am ready to do all I can for you in that way."

A light sigh escaped him. He drew his hands down his face, and it emerged, bony, unchanged of expression, as if all the tissues had been ossified. All the passion was in those big brown hands. He was satisfied. Then there was that other matter. If there were anybody on earth it was I who could persuade Hermann to take a reasonable view! I had a knowledge of the world and lots of experience. Hermann admitted this himself. And then I was a sailor, too. Falk thought that a sailor would be able to understand certain things best. . . .

He talked as if the Hermanns had been living all their life in a rural hamlet, and I alone had been capable, with my practice in life, of a large and indulgent view of certain occurrences. That was what my diplomacy was leading me to. I began suddenly to dislike it.

"I say, Falk," I asked quite brusquely, "you haven't already a wife put away somewhere?"

The pain and disgust of his denial were very striking. Couldn't I understand that he was as respectable as any white man hereabouts; earning his living honestly? He was suffering from my suspicion, and the low undertone of his voice made his protestations sound very pathetic. For a moment he shamed me, but, my diplomacy notwithstanding, I seemed to develop a conscience, as if in very truth it were in my power to decide the success of this matrimonial enterprise. By pretending hard enough we come to believe anything—anything to our advantage. And I had been pretending very hard, because I meant yet to be towed safely down the river. But, through conscience or stupidity, I couldn't help alluding to the Vanlo affair. "You acted rather badly there. Didn't you?" was what I ventured actually to say—for the logic of our conduct is always at the mercy of obscure and unforeseen impulses.

His dilated pupils swerved from my face, glancing at the window with a sort of scared fury. We heard behind the blinds the continuous and sudden clicking of ivory, a jovial murmur of many voices, and Schomberg's deep manly laugh.

"That confounded old woman of a hotel-keeper then would never, never let it rest!" Falk exclaimed. Well, yes! It had happened two years ago. When it came to the point he owned he couldn't make up his mind to trust Fred Vanlo—no sailor, a bit of a fool, too. He could not trust him, but, to stop his row, he had lent him enough money to pay all his debts before he left. I was greatly surprised to hear this. Then Falk could not be such a miser after all. So much the better for the girl. For a time he sat silent; then he picked up a card and while looking at it he said:

"You need not think of anything bad. It was an accident. I've been unfortunate once."

"Then in heaven's name say nothing about it."

As soon as these words were out of my mouth I fancied I had said something immoral. He shook his head negatively. It had to be told. He considered it proper that the relations of the lady should know. No doubt—I thought to myself—had Miss Vanlo not been thirty and damaged by the climate he would have found it possible to entrust Fred Vanlo with this confidence. And then the figure of Hermann's niece appeared before my mind's eye, with the wealth of her opulent form, her rich youth, her lavish strength. With that powerful and immaculate vitality, her girlish form must have shouted aloud of life to that man, whereas poor Miss Vanlo could only sing sentimental songs to the strumming of a piano.

"And that Hermann hates me, I know it!" he cried in his undertone, with a sudden recrudescence of anxiety. "I must tell them. It is proper that they should know. You would say so yourself."

He then murmured an utterly mysterious allusion to the necessity for peculiar domestic arrangements. Though my curiosity was excited I did not want to hear any of his confidences. I feared he might give me a piece of information that would make my assumed *rôle* of match-maker odious—however unreal it was. I was aware that he could have the girl for the asking; and keeping down a desire to laugh in his face, I expressed a confident belief in my ability to argue away Hermann's dislike for him. "I am sure I can make it all right," I said. He looked very pleased.

And when we rose not a word had been said about towage! Not a word! The game was won and the honour was safe. Oh! blessed white cotton umbrella! We shook hands, and I was holding myself with difficulty from breaking into a dance of joy when he came back, striding all the length of the verandah, and said doubtfully:

"I say, captain, I have your word? You—you—won't turn round?"

Heavens! The fright he gave me. Behind his tone of doubt there was something desperate and menacing. The infatuated ass. But I was equal to the situation.

"My dear Falk," I said, beginning to lie with a glibness and effrontery that amazed me even at the time—"confidence for confidence." (He had made no confidences.) "I will tell you that I am already engaged to an extremely charming girl at home, and so you understand . . ."

He caught my hand and wrung it in a crushing grip.

"Pardon me. I feel it every day more difficult to live alone . . ."

"On rice and fish," I interrupted smartly, giggling with the sheer nervousness of escaped danger.

He dropped my hand as if it had become suddenly red hot. A moment of profound silence ensued, as though something extraordinary had happened.

"I promise you to obtain Hermann's consent," I faltered out at last, and it seemed to me that he could not help seeing through that humbugging promise. "If there's anything else to get over I shall endeavour to stand by you," I conceded further, feeling somehow defeated and overborne; "but you must do your best yourself."

"I have been unfortunate once," he muttered, unemotionally, and turning his back on me he went away, thumping slowly the plank floor as if his feet had been shod with iron.

Next morning, however, he was lively enough as man-boat, a combination of splashing and shouting; of the insolent commotion below with the steady overbearing glare of the silent head-piece above. He turned us out most unnecessarily at an ungodly hour, but it was nearly eleven in the morning before he brought me up a cable's length from Hermann's ship. And he did it very badly, too, in a hurry, and nearly contriving to miss altogether the patch of good holding ground, because, forsooth, he had caught sight of Hermann's niece on the poop. And so did I; and probably as soon as he had seen her himself. I saw the modest, sleek glory of the tawny head, and the full, gray shape of the girlish print frock she filled so perfectly, so satisfactorily, with the seduction of unfaltering curves—a very nymph of Diana the Huntress. And *Diana* the ship sat, high-walled and as solid as an institution, on the smooth level of the water, the most uninspiring and respectable craft upon the seas, useful and ugly, devoted to the support of domestic virtues like any grocer's shop on shore. At once Falk steamed away; for there was some work for him to do. He would return in the evening.

He ranged close by us, passing out dead slow, without a hail. The beat of the paddle-wheels reverberating amongst the stony islets, as if from the ruined walls of a vast arena, filled the anchorage confusedly with the clapping sounds as of a mighty and leisurely applause. Abreast of Hermann's ship Falk stopped the engines; and a profound silence reigned over the rocks, the shore and the sea, for the time it took him to raise his hat aloft before the nymph of the gray print frock. I had snatched up my binoculars, and I can answer for it she didn't stir a limb, standing by the rail shapely and erect, with one of her hands grasping a rope at the height of her head, while the way of the tug carried slowly past her the lingering and profound homage of the man. There was for me an enormous significance in the scene, the sense of having witnessed a solemn declaration. The die was cast. After such a manifestation he couldn't back out. And I reflected that it was nothing whatever to me now. With a rush of black smoke belching suddenly out of the funnel, and a mad swirl of paddle-wheels provoking a burst of weird and precipitated clapping, the tug shot out of the desolate arena. The rocky islets lay on the sea like the heaps of a cyclopean ruin on a plain; the centipedes and scorpions lurked under the stones; there was not a single blade of grass in sight anywhere, not a single lizard sunning himself on a boulder by the shore. When I looked again at Hermann's ship the girl had disappeared. I could not detect the smallest dot of a bird on the immense sky, and the flatness of the land continued the flatness of the sea to the naked line of the horizon.

This is the setting now inseparably connected with my knowledge of Falk's misfortune. My diplomacy had brought me there, and now I had only to wait the time for taking up the *rôle* of an ambassador. My diplomacy was a success; my ship was safe; old Gambril would probably live; a feeble sound of a tapping hammer came intermittently from the *Diana*. During the afternoon I looked at times at the old homely ship, the faithful nurse of Hermann's progeny, or yawned towards the distant temple of Buddha, like a lonely hillock on the plain, where shaven priests cherish the thoughts of that Annihilation which is the worthy reward of us all. Unfortunate! He had been unfortunate once. Well, that was not so bad as life goes. And what the devil could be the nature of that misfortune? I remembered that I had known a man before who had declared himself to have fallen, years ago, a victim to misfortune; but this misfortune, whose effects appeared permanent (he looked desperately hard up) when considered dispassionately, seemed indistinguishable from a breach of trust. Could it be something of that nature? Apart, however, from the utter improbability that he would offer to talk of it even to his future uncle-in-law I had a strange feeling that Falk's physique unfitted him for that sort of delinquency. As the person of Hermann's niece exhaled the profound physical charm of feminine form, so her adorer's big frame embodied to my senses the hard, straight masculinity that would conceivably kill but would not condescend to cheat. The thing was obvious. I might just as well have suspected the girl of a curvature of the spine. And I perceived that the sun was about to set.

The smoke of Falk's tug hove in sight, far away at the mouth of the river. It was time for me to assume the character of an ambassador, and the negotiation would not be difficult except in the matter of keeping my countenance. It was all too extravagantly nonsensical, and I conceived that it would be best to compose for myself a grave demeanour. I practised this in my boat as I went along, but the bashfulness that came secretly upon me the moment I stepped on the deck of the *Diana* is inexplicable. As soon as we had exchanged greetings Hermann asked me eagerly if I knew whether Falk had found his white parasol.

"He's going to bring it to you himself directly," I said with great solemnity. "Meantime, I am charged with an important message for which he begs your favourable consideration. He is in love with your niece. . . ."

"*Ach So!*" he hissed with an animosity that made my assumed gravity change into the most genuine concern. What meant this tone? And I hurried on.

"He wishes, with your consent of course, to ask her to marry him at once—before you leave here, that is. He would speak to his Consul."

Hermann sat down and smoked violently. Five minutes passed in that furious meditation, and then, taking the long pipe out of his mouth, he burst into a hot diatribe against Falk—against his cupidity, his stupidity (a fellow that can hardly be got to say "yes" or "no" to the simplest question)—against his outrageous treatment of the shipping in port (because he saw they were at his mercy)—and against his manner of walking, which to his (Hermann's) mind showed a conceit positively unbearable. The damage to the old *Diana* was not forgotten, of course, and there was nothing of any nature said or done by Falk (even to the last offer of refreshment in the hotel) that did not seem to have been a cause of offence. "Had the cheek" to drag him (Hermann) into that coffee-room; as though a drink from him could make up for forty-seven dollars and fifty cents of damage in the cost of wood alone—not counting two days' work for the carpenter. Of course he would not stand in the girl's way. He was going home to Germany. There were plenty of poor girls walking about in Germany.

"He's very much in love," was all I found to say.

"Yes," he cried. "And it is time, too, after making himself and me talked about ashore the last voyage I was here, and then now again; coming on board every evening unsettling the girl's mind, and saying nothing. What sort of conduct is that?"

The seven thousand dollars the fellow was always talking about did not, in his opinion, justify such behaviour. Moreover, nobody had seen them. He (Hermann) seriously doubted if Falk possessed seven thousand cents, and the tug, no doubt, was mortgaged up to the top of the funnel to the firm of Siegers. But let that pass. He wouldn't stand in the girl's way. Her head was so turned that she had become no good to them of late. Quite unable even to put the children to bed without her aunt. It was bad for the children; they got unruly; and yesterday he actually had to give Gustav a thrashing.

For that, too, Falk was made responsible apparently. And looking at my Hermann's heavy, puffy, good-natured face, I knew he would not exert himself till greatly exasperated, and, therefore, would thrash very hard, and being fat would resent the necessity. How Falk had managed to turn the girl's head was more difficult to understand. I supposed Hermann would know. And then hadn't there been Miss Vanlo? It could not be his silvery tongue, or the subtle seduction of his manner; he had no more of what is called "manner" than an animal—which, however, on the other hand, is never, and can never be called vulgar. Therefore it must have been his bodily appearance, exhibiting a virility of nature as exaggerated as his beard, and resembling a sort of constant ruthlessness. It was seen in the very manner he lolled in the chair. He meant no offence, but his intercourse was characterized by that sort of frank disregard of susceptibilities a tall man, living in a world of dwarfs, would naturally assume, without in the least wishing to be unkind. But amongst men of his own stature, or nearly, this frank use of his advantages, in such matters as the awful towage bills for instance, caused much impotent gnashing of teeth. When attentively considered it seemed appalling at times. He was a strange beast. But maybe women liked it. Seen in that light he was well worth taming, and I suppose every woman at the bottom of her heart considers herself as a tamer of strange beasts. But Hermann arose with precipitation to carry the news to his wife. I had barely the time, as he made for the cabin door, to grab him by the seat of his inexpressibles. I begged him to wait till Falk in person had spoken with him. There remained some small matter to talk over as I understood.

He sat down again at once, full of suspicion.

"What matter?" he said, surlily. "I have had enough of his nonsense. There's no matter at all, as he knows very well; the girl has nothing in the world. She came to us in one thin dress when my brother died, and I have a growing family."

"It can't be anything of that kind," I opined. "He's desperately enamoured of your niece. I don't know why he did not say so before. Upon my word, I believe it is because he was afraid to lose, perhaps, the felicity of sitting near her on your quarter-deck."

I intimated my conviction that Falk's love was so great as to be in a sense cowardly. The effects of a great passion are unaccountable. It has been known to make a man timid. But Hermann looked at me as if I had raved; and the twilight was dying out rapidly.

"You don't believe in passion, do you, Hermann?" I continued, cheerily. "The passion of fear will make a cornered rat courageous. Falk's in a corner. He will take her off your hands in one thin frock just as she came to you. And after ten years' service it isn't a bad bargain," I added.

Far from taking offence, he resumed his air of civic virtue. The sudden night came upon him while he stared placidly along the deck, bringing in contact with his thick lips, and taking away again after a jet of smoke, the curved mouthpiece fitted to the stem of his pipe. The night came upon him and buried in haste his whiskers, his globular eyes, his puffy pale face, his fat knees and the vast flat slippers on his fatherly feet.

Only his short arms in respectable white shirt-sleeves remained very visible, propped up like the flippers of a seal reposing on the strand.

"Falk wouldn't settle anything about repairs. Told me to find out first how much wood I should require and he would see," he remarked; and after he had spat peacefully in the dusk we heard over the water the beat of the tug's floats. There is, on a calm night, nothing more suggestive of fierce and headlong haste than the rapid sound made by the paddle-wheels of a boat threshing her way through a quiet sea; and the approach of Falk towards his fate seemed to be urged by an impatient and passionate desire. The engines must have been driven to the very utmost of their revolutions. We heard them slow down at last, and, vaguely, the white hull of the tug appeared moving against the black islets, whilst a slow and rhythmical clapping as of thousands of hands rose on all sides. It ceased all at once, just before Falk brought her up. A single brusque splash was followed by the long-drawn rumbling of iron links running through the hawse pipe. Then a solemn silence fell upon the roadstead.

"He will soon be here," I murmured, and after that we waited for him without a word. Meantime, raising my eyes, I beheld the glitter of a lofty sky above the *Diana's* mastheads. The multitude of stars gathered into clusters, in rows, in lines, in masses, in groups, shone all together, unanimously—and the few isolated ones, blazing by themselves in the midst of dark patches, seemed to be of a superior kind and of an inextinguishable nature. But long striding footsteps were heard hastening along the deck; the high bulwarks of the *Diana* made a deeper darkness. We rose from our chairs quickly, and Falk, appearing before us, all in white, stood still.

Nobody spoke at first, as though we had been covered with confusion. His arrival was fiery, but his white bulk, of indefinite shape and without features, made him loom up like a man of snow.

"The captain here has been telling me . . ." Hermann began in a homely and amicable voice; and Falk gave a low, nervous laugh. His cool, negligent undertone had no inflexions, but the strength of a powerful emotion made him ramble in his speech. He had always desired a home. It was difficult to live alone, though he was not answerable. He was domestic; there had been difficulties; but since he had seen Hermann's niece he found that it had become at last impossible to live by himself. "I mean—impossible," he repeated with no sort of emphasis and only with the slightest of pauses, but the word fell into my mind with the force of a new idea.

"I have not said anything to her yet," Hermann observed, quietly. And Falk dismissed this by a "That's all right. Certainly. Very proper." There was a necessity for perfect frankness—in marrying, especially. Hermann seemed attentive, but he seized the first opportunity to ask us into the cabin. "And by-the-by, Falk," he said, innocently, as we passed in, "the timber came to no less than forty-seven dollars and fifty cents."

Falk, uncovering his head, lingered in the passage. "Some other time," he said; and Hermann nudged me angrily—I don't know why. The girl alone in the cabin sat sewing at some distance from the table. Falk stopped short in the doorway. Without a word, without a sign, without the slightest inclination of his bony head, by the silent intensity of his look alone, he seemed to lay his herculean frame at her feet. Her hands sank slowly on her lap, and raising her clear eyes, she let her soft, beaming glance enfold him from head to foot like a slow and pale caress. He was very hot when he sat down; she, with bowed head, went on with her sewing; her neck was very white under the light of the lamp; but Falk, hiding his face in the palms of his hands shuddered faintly. He drew them down, even to his beard, and his uncovered eyes aston- ished me by their tense and irrational expression—as though he had just swallowed a heavy gulp of alcohol. It passed away while he was binding us to secrecy. Not that he cared, but he did not like to be spoken about; and I looked at the girl's marvellous, at her wonderful, at her regal hair, plaited tight into that one astonishing and maidenly tress. Whenever she moved her well-shaped head it would stir stiffly to and fro on her back. The thin cotton sleeve fitted the irreproachable roundness of her arm like a skin; and her very dress, stretched on her bust, seemed to palpitate like a living tissue with the strength of vitality animating her body. How good her complexion was, the outline of her soft cheek and the small convoluted conch of her rosy ear! To pull her needle she kept the little finger apart from the others; it seemed a waste of power to see her sewing—eternally sewing—with that industrious and precise movement of her arm, going on eternally upon all the oceans, under all the skies, in innumerable harbours. And suddenly I heard Falk's voice declare that he could not marry a woman unless she knew of something in his life that had happened ten years ago. It was an accident. An unfortunate accident. It would affect the domestic arrangements of their home, but, once told, it need not be alluded to again for the rest of their lives. "I should want my wife to feel for me," he said. "It has made me unhappy." And how could he keep the knowledge of it to himself—he asked us—perhaps through years and years of companionship? What sort of companionship would that be? He had thought it over. A wife must know. Then why not at once? He counted on Hermann's kindness for presenting the affair in the best possible light. And Hermann's countenance, mystified before, became very sour. He stole an inquisitive glance at me. I shook my head blankly. Some people thought, Falk went on, that such an experience changed a man for the rest of his life. He couldn't say. It was hard, awful, and not to be forgotten, but he did not think himself a worse man than before. Only he talked in his sleep now, he believed. . . . At last I began to think he had accidentally killed someone; perhaps a friend—his own father maybe; when he went on to say that probably we were aware he never touched meat. Throughout he spoke English, of course on my account.

He swayed forward heavily.

The girl, with her hands raised before her pale eyes, was threading her needle. He glanced at her and his mighty trunk overshadowed the table, bringing nearer to us the breadth of his shoulders, the thickness of his neck, and that incongruous, anchorite head, burnt in the desert, hollowed and lean as if by excesses of vigils and fasting. His beard flowed imposingly downwards, out of sight, between the two brown hands gripping the edge of the table, and his persistent glance made sombre by the wide dilations of the pupils, fascinated.

"Imagine to yourselves," he said in his ordinary voice, "that I have eaten man."

I could only ejaculate a faint "Ah!" of complete enlightenment. But Hermann, dazed by the excessive shock, actually murmured, "Himmel! What for?"

"It was my terrible misfortune to do so," said Falk in a measured undertone. The girl, unconscious, sewed on. Mrs. Hermann was absent in one of the state-rooms, sitting up with Lena, who was feverish; but Hermann suddenly put both his hands up with a jerk. The embroidered calotte fell, and, in the twinkling of an eye, he had rumpled his hair all ends up in a most extravagant manner. In this state he strove to speak; with every effort his eyes seemed to start further out of their sockets; his head looked like a mop. He choked, gasped, swallowed, and managed to shriek out the one word, "Beast!"

From that moment till Falk went out of the cabin the girl, with her hands folded on the work lying in her lap, never took her eyes off him. His own, in the blindness of his heart, darted all over the cabin, only seeking to avoid the sight of Hermann's raving. It was ridiculous, and was made almost terrible by the stillness of every other person present. It was contemptible, and was made appalling by the man's overmastering horror of this awful sincerity, coming to him suddenly, with the confession of such a fact. He walked with great strides; he gasped. He wanted to know from Falk how dared he to come and tell him this? Did he think himself a proper person to be sitting in this cabin where his wife and children lived? Tell his niece! Expected him to tell his niece! His own brother's daughter! Shameless! Did I ever hear tell of such impudence?—he appealed to me. "This man here ought to have gone and hidden himself out of sight instead of . . ."

"But it's a great misfortune for me. But it's a great misfortune for me," Falk would ejaculate from time to time.

However, Hermann kept on running frequently against the corners of the table. At last he lost a slipper, and crossing his arms on his breast, walked up with one stocking foot very close to Falk, in order to ask him whether he did think there was anywhere on earth a woman abandoned enough to mate with such a monster. "Did he? Did he? Did he?" I tried to restrain him. He tore himself out of my hands; he found his slipper, and, endeavouring to put it on, stormed standing on one leg—and Falk, with a face unmoved and averted eyes, grasped all his mighty beard in one vast palm.

"Was it right then for me to die myself?" he asked thoughtfully. I laid my hand on his shoulder.

"Go away," I whispered imperiously, without any clear reason for this advice, except that I wished to put an end to Hermann's odious noise. "Go away."

He looked searchingly for a moment at Hermann before he made a move. I left the cabin, too, to see him out of the ship. But he hung about the quarter-deck.

"It is my misfortune," he said in a steady voice.

"You were stupid to blurt it out in such a manner. After all, we don't hear such confidences every day."

"What does the man mean?" he mused in deep undertones. "Somebody had to die—but why me?"

He remained still for a time in the dark—silent; almost invisible. All at once he pinned my elbows to my sides. I felt utterly powerless in his grip, and his voice, whispering in my ear, vibrated.

"It's worse than hunger. Captain, do you know what that means? And I could kill then—or be killed. I wish the crowbar had smashed my skull ten years ago. And I've got to live now. Without her. Do you understand? Perhaps many years. But how? What can be done? If I had allowed myself to look at her once I would have carried her off before that man in my hands—like this."

I felt myself snatched off the deck, then suddenly dropped—and I staggered backwards, feeling bewildered and bruised. What a man! All was still; he was gone. I heard Hermann's voice declaiming in the cabin, and went in.

I could not at first make out a single word, but Mrs. Hermann, who, attracted by the noise, had come in some time before, with an expression of surprise and mild disapproval depicted broadly on her face, was giving now all the signs of profound, helpless agitation. Her husband shot a string of guttural words at her, and instantly putting out one hand to the bulkhead as if to save herself from falling, she clutched the loose bosom of her dress with the other. He harangued the two women extraordinarily, with much of his shirt hanging out of his waistbelt, stamping his foot, turning from one to the other, sometimes flinging both his arms straight up above his rumpled hair and keeping them in that position while he uttered a passage of loud denunciation; at others folding them tight across his breast—and then he hissed with indignation, elevating his shoulders and protruding his head. The girl was crying.

She had not changed her attitude. From her steady eyes that, following Falk in his retreat, had remained fixed wistfully on the cabin door, the tears fell rapid, thick, on her hands, on the work in her lap, warm and gentle like a shower in spring. She wept without grimacing, without noise—very touching, very quiet, with something more of pity than of pain in her face, as one weeps in compassion rather than grief—and Hermann, before her, declaimed. I caught several times the word "Mensch," man; and also "Fressen," which last I looked up afterwards in my dictionary. It means "Devour." Hermann seemed to be requesting an answer of some sort from her; his whole body swayed. She remained mute and perfectly still; at last his agitation gained her; she put the palms of her hands together, her full lips parted, no sound came. His voice scolded shrilly, his arms went like a windmill—suddenly he shook his thick fist at her. She burst out into loud sobs. He seemed stupefied.

Mrs. Hermann rushed forward babbling rapidly.

The two women fell on each other's necks, and, with an arm round her niece's waist, she led her away. Her own eyes were simply streaming, her face was flooded. She shook her head back at me negatively, I wonder why to this day. The girl's head dropped heavily on her shoulder. They disappeared together.

Then Hermann sat down and stared at the cabin floor.

"We don't know all the circumstances," I ventured to break the silence. He retorted tartly that he didn't want to know of any. According to his ideas no circumstances could excuse a crime—and certainly not such a crime. This was the opinion generally received. The duty of a human being was to starve. Falk therefore was a beast, an animal; base, low, vile, despicable, shameless, and deceitful. He had been deceiving him since last year. He was, however, inclined to think that Falk must have gone mad quite recently; for no sane person, without necessity, uselessly, for no earthly reason, and regardless of another's self-respect and peace of mind, would own to having devoured human flesh. "Why tell?" he cried. "Who was asking him?" It showed Falk's brutality because after all he had selfishly caused him (Hermann) much pain. He would have preferred not to know that such an unclean creature had been in the habit of caressing his children. He hoped I would say nothing of all this ashore, though. He wouldn't like it to get about that he had been intimate with an eater of men—a common cannibal. As to the scene he had made (which I judged quite unnecessary) he was not going to inconvenience and restrain himself for a fellow that went about courting and upsetting girls' heads, while he knew all the time that no decent housewifely girl would think of marrying him. At least he (Hermann) could not conceive how any girl could. "Fancy Lena! . . . No, it was impossible. The thoughts that would come into their heads every time they sat down to a meal. Horrible! Horrible!"

"You are too squeamish, Hermann," I said.

He seemed to think it was eminently proper to be squeamish if the word meant disgust at Falk's conduct; and turning up his eyes

sentimentally he drew my attention to the horrible fate of the victims—
the victims of that Falk. I said that I knew nothing about them. He
seemed surprised. Could not anybody imagine without knowing? He—
for instance—felt he would like to avenge them. But what if—said I—
there had not been any? They might have died as it were, naturally—
of starvation. He shuddered. But to be eaten—after death! To be devoured! He gave another deep shudder, and asked suddenly, "Do you
think it is true?"

His indignation and his personality together would have been enough
to spoil the reality of the most authentic thing. When I looked at him I
doubted the story—but the remembrance of Falk's words, looks, gestures, invested it not only with an air of reality but with the absolute
truth of primitive passion.

"It is true just as much as you are able to make it; and exactly in the
way you like to make it. For my part, when I hear you clamouring about
it, I don't believe it is true at all."

And I left him pondering. The men in my gig lying at the foot of
Diana's side-ladder, told me that the captain of the tug had gone away
in his boat sometime ago.

I let my fellows pull an easy stroke; because of the heavy dew the
clear sparkle of the stars seemed to fall on me cold and wetting. There
was a sense of lurking gruesome horror somewhere in my mind, and it
was mingled with clear and grotesque images. Schomberg's gastronomic
tittle-tattle was responsible for these; and I half hoped I should never
see Falk again. But the first thing my anchor-watchman told me was that
the captain of the tug was on board. He had sent his boat away and was
now waiting for me in the cuddy.

He was lying full length on the stern settee, his face buried in the
cushions. I had expected to see it discomposed, contorted, despairing.
It was nothing of the kind; it was just as I had seen it twenty times,
steady and glaring from the bridge of the tug. It was immovably set and
hungry, dominated like the whole man by the singleness of one instinct.

He wanted to live. He had always wanted to live. So we all do—but
in us the instinct serves a complex conception, and in him this instinct
existed alone. There is in such simple development a gigantic force, and
like the pathos of a child's naïve and uncontrolled desire. He wanted
that girl, and the utmost that can be said for him was that he wanted
that particular girl alone. I think I saw then the obscure beginning, the

seed germinating in the soil of an unconscious need, the first shoot of that tree bearing now for a mature mankind the flower and the fruit, the infinite gradation in shades and in flavour of our discriminating love. He was a child. He was as frank as a child, too. He was hungry for the girl, terribly hungry, as he had been terribly hungry for food.

Don't be shocked if I declare that in my belief it was the same need, the same pain, the same torture. We are in his case allowed to contemplate the foundation of all the emotions—that one joy which is to live, and the one sadness at the root of the innumerable torments. It was made plain by the way he talked. He had never suffered so. It was gnawing, it was fire; it was there, like this! And after pointing below his breastbone, he made a hard wringing motion with his hands. And I assure you that, seen as I saw it with my bodily eyes, it was anything but laughable. And again, as he was presently to tell me (alluding to an early incident of the disastrous voyage when some damaged meat had been flung overboard), he said that a time soon came when his heart ached (that was the expression he used), and he was ready to tear his hair out at the thought of all that rotten beef thrown away.

I heard all this; I witnessed his physical struggles, seeing the working of the rack and hearing the true voice of pain. I witnessed it all patiently, because the moment I came into the cuddy he had called upon me to stand by him—and this, it seems, I had diplomatically promised.

His agitation was impressive and alarming in the little cabin, like the floundering of a great whale driven into a shallow cove in a coast. He stood up; he flung himself down headlong; he tried to tear the cushion with his teeth; and again hugging it fiercely to his face he let himself fall on the couch. The whole ship seemed to feel the shock of his despair; and I contemplated with wonder the lofty forehead, the noble touch of time on the uncovered temples, the unchanged hungry character of the face—so strangely ascetic and so incapable of portraying emotion.

What should he do? He had lived by being near her.

He had sat—in the evening—I knew?—all his life! She sewed. Her head was bent—so. Her head—like this—and her arms. Ah! Had I seen? Like this.

He dropped on a stool, bowed his powerful neck whose nape was red, and with his hands stitched the air, ludicrous, sublimely imbecile and comprehensible.

And now he couldn't have her? No! That was too much. After thinking, too, that . . . What had he done? What was my advice? Take her by force? No? Mustn't he? Who was there to stop him? For the first time I saw one of his features move; a fighting teeth-baring curl of the lip? . . . "Not Hermann, perhaps." He lost himself in thought as though he had fallen out of the world.

I may note that the idea of suicide apparently did not enter his head for a single moment. It occurred to me to ask:

"Where was it that this shipwreck of yours took place?"

"Down south," he said, vaguely, with a start.

"You are not down south now," I said. "Violence won't do. They would take her away from you in no time. And what was the name of the ship?"

"*Borgmester Dahl,*" he said. "It was no shipwreck."

He seemed to be waking up by degrees from that trance, and waking up calmed.

"Not a shipwreck? What was it?"

"Break down," he answered, looking more like himself every moment. By this only I learned that it was a steamer. I had till then supposed they had been starving in boats or on a raft—or perhaps on a barren rock.

"She did not sink then?" I asked in surprise. He nodded. "We sighted the southern ice," he pronounced, dreamily.

"And you alone survived?"

He sat down. "Yes. It was a terrible misfortune for me. Everything went wrong. All the men went wrong. I survived."

Remembering the things one reads of it was difficult to realize the true meaning of his answers. I ought to have seen at once—but I did not; so difficult is it for our minds, remembering so much, instructed so much, informed of so much, to get in touch with the real actuality at our elbow. And with my head full of preconceived notions as to how a case of "Cannibalism and suffering at sea" should be managed I said—"You were then so lucky in the drawing of lots?"

"Drawing of lots?" he said. "What lots? Do you think I would have allowed my life to go for the drawing of lots?"

Not if he could help it, I perceived, no matter what other life went.

"It was a great misfortune. Terrible. Awful," he said. "Many heads went wrong, but the best men would live."

"The toughest, you mean," I said. He considered the word. Perhaps it was strange to him, though his English was so good.

"Yes," he asserted at last. "The best. It was everybody for himself at last and the ship open to all."

Thus from question to question I got the whole story. I fancy it was the only way I could that night have stood by him. Outwardly at least he was himself again; the first sign of it was the return of that incongruous trick he had of drawing both his hands down his face—and it had its meaning now, with that slight shudder of the frame and the passionate anguish of these hands uncovering a hungry immovable face, the wide pupils of the intent, silent, fascinating eyes.

It was an iron steamer of a most respectable origin. The burgomaster of Falk's native town had built her. She was the first steamer ever launched there. The burgomaster's daughter had christened her. Country people drove in carts from miles around to see her. He told me all this. He got the berth as, what we would call, chief mate. He seemed to think it had been a feather in his cap; and, in his own corner of the world, this lover of life was of good parentage.

The burgomaster had advanced ideas in the ship-owning line. At that time not everyone would have known enough to think of despatching a cargo steamer to the Pacific. But he loaded her with pitch-pine deals and sent her off to hunt for her luck. Wellington was to be the first port, I fancy. It doesn't matter, because in latitude 44° south and somewhere halfway between Good Hope and New Zealand the tail-shaft broke and the propeller dropped off.

They were steaming then with a fresh gale on the quarter and all their canvas set, to help the engines. But by itself the sail power was not enough to keep way on her. When the propeller went the ship broached-to at once, and the masts got whipped overboard.

The disadvantage of being dismasted consisted in this, that they had nothing to hoist flags on to make themselves visible at a distance. In the course of the first few days several ships failed to sight them; and the gale was drifting them out of the usual track. The voyage had been, from the first, neither very successful nor very harmonious. There had been quarrels on board. The captain was a clever, melancholic man, who had no unusual grip on his crew. The ship had been amply provisioned for the passage, but, somehow or other, several barrels of meat were found spoiled on opening, and had been thrown overboard soon after leaving home, as a sanitary measure. Afterwards the crew of the *Borgmester Dahl* thought of that rotten carrion with tears of regret, covetousness and despair.

She drove south. To begin with, there had been an appearance of organization, but soon the bonds of discipline became relaxed. A sombre idleness succeeded. They looked with sullen eyes at the horizon. The gales increased, she lay in the trough and the seas made a clean breach over her. One frightful night, when they expected their hulk to turn over with them every moment, a heavy sea broke on board, deluged the store-rooms and spoiled the best part of the remaining provisions. It seems the hatch had not been properly secured. This instance of neglect is characteristic of utter discouragement. Falk tried to inspire some energy into his captain, but failed. From that time he retired more into himself, always trying to do his utmost in the situation. It grew worse. Gale succeeded gale, with black mountains of water hurling themselves on the *Borgmester Dahl*. Some of the men never left their bunks; many became quarrelsome. The chief-engineer, an old man, refused to speak at all to anybody. Others shut themselves up in their berths to cry. On calm days the inert steamer rolled on a leaden sea under a murky sky, or showed, in sunshine, the squalor of sea waifs, the dried white salt, the rust, the jagged broken places. Then the gales came again. They kept body and soul together on short rations. Once, an English ship, scudding in a storm, tried to stand by them, heaving-to pluckily under their lee. The seas swept her decks; the men in oilskins clinging to her rigging looked at them, and they made desperate signs over their shattered bulwarks. Suddenly her main-topsail went, yard and all, in a terrific squall; she had to bear up under bare poles and disappeared.

Other ships had spoken them before, but at first they had refused to be taken off, expecting the assistance of some steamer. There were very few steamers in those latitudes then; and when they desired to leave this dead and drifting carcase, no ship came in sight. They had drifted south out of men's knowledge. They failed to attract the attention of a lonely whaler: and very soon the edge of the polar ice-cap rose from the sea and closed the southern horizon like a wall. One morning they were alarmed by finding themselves floating amongst detached pieces of ice. But the fear of sinking passed away like their vigour, like their hopes;

the shocks of the floes knocking against the ship's side could not rouse them from their apathy: and the *Borgmester Dahl* drifted out again, unharmed, into open water. They hardly noticed the change.

The funnel had gone overboard in one of the heavy rolls; two of their three boats had disappeared, washed away in bad weather, and the davits swung to and fro, unsecured, with chafed rope's ends waggling to the roll. Nothing was done on board, and Falk told me how he had often listened to the water washing about the dark engine-room where the engines, stilled for ever, were decaying slowly into a mass of rust, as the stilled heart decays within the lifeless body. At first, after the loss of the motive power, the tiller had been thoroughly secured by lashings. But in course of time these had rotted, chafed, rusted, parting one by one; and the rudder, freed, banged heavily to and fro night and day, sending dull shocks through the whole frame of the vessel. This was dangerous. Nobody cared enough to lift a little finger. He told me that even now sometimes waking up at night, he fancied he could hear the dull vibrating thuds. The pintles carried away, and it dropped off at last.

The final catastrophe came with the sending off of their one remaining boat. It was Falk who had managed to preserve her intact, and now it was agreed that some of the hands should sail away into the track of the shipping to procure assistance. She was provisioned with all the food they could spare for the six who were to go. They waited for a fine day. It was long in coming. At last one morning they lowered her into the water.

Directly, in that demoralized crowd, trouble broke out. Two men who had no business there had jumped into the boat under the pretence of unhooking the tackles, while some sort of squabble arose on the deck amongst these weak, tottering spectres of a ship's company. The captain, who had been for days living secluded and unapproachable in the chart-room, came to the rail. He ordered the two men to come up on board and threatened them with his revolver. They pretended to obey, but suddenly cutting the boat's painter, gave a shove against the ship's side and made ready to hoist the sail.

"Shoot, sir! Shoot them down!" cried Falk—"and I will jump overboard to regain the boat." But the captain, after taking aim with an irresolute arm, turned suddenly away.

A howl of rage arose. Falk dashed into his cabin for his own pistol.

When he returned it was too late. Two more men had leaped into the water, but the fellows in the boat beat them off with the oars, hoisted the boat's lug and sailed away. They were never heard of again.

Consternation and despair possessed the remaining ship's company, till the apathy of utter hopelessness re-asserted its sway. That day a fireman committed suicide, running up on deck with his throat cut from ear to ear, to the horror of all hands. He was thrown overboard. The captain had locked himself in the chart-room, and Falk, knocking vainly for admittance, heard him reciting over and over again the names of his wife and children, not as if calling upon them or commending them to God, but in a mechanical voice like an exercise of memory. Next day the doors of the chart-room were swinging open to the roll of the ship, and the captain had disappeared. He must during the night have jumped into the sea. Falk locked both the doors and kept the keys.

The organized life of the ship had come to an end. The solidarity of the men had gone. They became indifferent to each other. It was Falk who took in hand the distribution of such food as remained. Sometimes whispers of hate were heard passing between the languid skeletons that drifted endlessly to and fro, north and south, east and west, upon that carcase of a ship.

And in this lies the grotesque horror of this sombre story. The last extremity of sailors, overtaking a small boat or a frail craft, seems easier to bear, because of the direct danger of the seas. The confined space, the close contact, the imminent menace of the waves, seem to draw men together, in spite of madness, suffering and despair. But there was a ship—safe, convenient, roomy: a ship with beds, bedding, knives, forks, comfortable cabins, glass and china, and a complete cook's galley, pervaded, ruled and possessed by the pitiless spectre of starvation. The lamp oil had been drunk, the wicks cut up for food, the candles eaten. At night she floated dark in all her recesses and full of fears. One day Falk came upon a man gnawing a splinter of pine wood. Suddenly he threw the piece of wood away, tottered to the rail, and fell over. Falk, too late to prevent the act, saw him claw the ship's side desperately before he went down. Next day another man did the same thing, after uttering horrible imprecations. But this one somehow managed to get hold of the broken rudder chains and hung on there, silently. Falk set about trying to save him, and all the time the man, holding with both hands, looked at him anxiously with his sunken eyes. Then, just as Falk was ready to put his hand on him, the man let go his hold and sank like a stone. Falk reflected on these sights. His heart revolted against the horror of death, and he said to himself that he would struggle for every precious minute of his life.

One afternoon—as the survivors lay about on the after-deck—the carpenter, a tall man with a black beard, spoke of the last sacrifice. There was nothing eatable left on board. Nobody said a word to this; but that company separated quickly, these listless feeble spectres slunk off one by one to hide in fear of each other. Falk and the carpenter remained on deck together. Falk liked the big carpenter. He had been the best man of the lot, helpful and ready as long as there was anything to do, the longest hopeful, and had preserved to the last some vigour and decision of mind.

They did not speak to each other. Henceforth no voices were to be heard conversing sadly on board that ship. After a time the carpenter tottered away forward; but later in the day Falk going to drink at the fresh-water pump, had the inspiration to turn his head. The carpenter had stolen upon him from behind, and, summoning all his strength, was aiming with a crowbar a blow at the back of his skull.

Dodging just in time, Falk made his escape and ran into his cabin. While he was loading his revolver there, he heard the sound of heavy blows struck upon the bridge. The locks of the chart-room doors were slight, they flew open, and the carpenter, possessing himself of the captain's revolver, fired a shot of defiance.

Falk was about to go on deck and have it out at once, when he remarked that one of the ports of his cabin commanded the approaches to the fresh-water pump. Instead of going out he stayed within and secured the door. "The best man shall survive," he said to himself— and the other, he reasoned, must at some time or other come there to drink. These starving men would drink often to cheat the pangs of their hunger. But the carpenter, too, must have noticed the position of the port. They were the two best men in the ship, and the game was with them. All the rest of the day Falk saw no one and heard no sound. At night he strained his eyes. It was dark—he heard a rustling noise once, but he was certain that no one could have come near the pump. It was to the left of his deck port, and he could not have failed to see a man, for the night was clear and starry. He saw nothing; towards morning another faint noise made him suspicious. Deliberately and quietly he unlocked his door. He had not slept, and had not given way to the horror of the situation. He wanted to live.

But during the night the carpenter, without even trying to approach the pump, had managed to creep quietly along the starboard bulwark, and, unseen, had crouched down right under Falk's deck port. When daylight came he rose up suddenly, looked in, and putting his arm through the round, brass-framed opening, fired at Falk within a foot. He missed—and Falk, instead of attempting to seize the arm holding the weapon, opened his door unexpectedly, and with the muzzle of his revolver nearly touching the other's side, shot him dead.

The best man had survived. Both of them had at the beginning just strength enough to stand on their feet, and both had displayed pitiless resolution, endurance, cunning and courage—all the qualities of classic heroism. At once Falk threw overboard the captain's revolver. He was a born monopolist. Then after the report of the two shots, followed by a profound silence, there crept out into the cold, cruel dawn of Antarctic regions, from various hiding-places, over the deck of that dismantled corpse of a ship floating on a gray sea ruled by iron necessity and with a heart of ice—there crept into view one by one, cautious, slow, eager, glaring, and unclean, a band of hungry and livid skeletons. Falk faced them, the possessor of the only fire-arm on board; and the second best man—the carpenter—was lying dead between him and them.

"He was eaten, of course," I said.

Falk bent his head slowly, shuddered a little, drawing his hands over his face, and said, "I had never any quarrel with that man. But there were our lives between him and me."

Why continue the story of that ship, that story before which—with its fresh-water pump like a spring of death, its man with the weapon, the sea ruled by iron necessity, its spectral band swayed by terror and hope, its mute and unhearing heaven—the fable of the *Flying Dutchman* with its convention of crime and its sentimental retribution fades like a graceful wreath, like a wisp of white mist. What is there to say that everyone of us cannot guess for himself? I believe Falk began by going through the ship, revolver in hand, to annex all the matches. Those starving wretches had plenty of matches! He had no mind to have the ship set on fire under his feet, either from hate or from despair. He lived in the open, camping on the bridge, commanding all the after-deck and the only approach to the pump. He lived! Some of the others lived, too—concealed, anxious, coming out one by one from their hiding-places at the seductive sound of a shot. And he was not selfish. They shared all alike. But only three of them all remained alive when a whaler, returning from her cruising-ground, nearly ran over the water-logged hull of the *Borgmester Dahl*, which, it seems, in the end had in some way sprung a leak in both her holds, but being loaded with deals could not sink.

"They all died," Falk said. "These three, too, afterwards. But I would not die. All died, all! under this terrible misfortune. But was I, too, to throw away my life? Could I? Tell me, captain? I was alone there, quite alone, just like the others. Each man was alone. Was I to give up my revolver? Who to? Or was I to throw it into the sea? What would have been the good? Only the best man would survive. It was a great, terrible, and cruel misfortune."

He had survived! I saw him before me as though preserved for a witness to the mighty truth of an unerring and eternal principle. Great beads of perspiration stood on his forehead. And suddenly it struck the table with a heavy blow, as he fell forward throwing his hands out.

"And this is worse," he cried. "This is a worse pain! This is more terrible."

He made my heart thump with the profound conviction of his cry. And after he had left me to go on board his ship I called up before my mental eye the image of the girl weeping silently, abundantly, patiently, and as if irresistibly. I thought of her tawny hair. I thought how, if unplaited, it would have covered her all round as low as the hips, like the hair of a siren. And she had bewitched him. Fancy a man who would guard his own life with the inflexibility of a pitiless and immovable fate, being brought to lament that once a crowbar had missed his skull! The sirens sing and lure to death, but this one had been weeping silently as if for the pity of his life. She was the tender and voiceless siren of this appalling navigator. He evidently wanted to live his whole conception of life. Nothing else would do. And she, too, was a servant of that life that, in the midst of death, cries aloud to our senses. She was eminently fitted to interpret for him its feminine side. And in her own way, and with her own profusion of sensuous charms she also seemed to illustrate the eternal truth of an unerring principle. I don't know though what sort of principle Hermann illustrated when he turned up early on board my ship with a most perplexed air. It struck me, however, that he, too, would do his best to survive. He seemed greatly calmed on the subject of Falk, but still very full of it.

"What is it you said I was last night? You know—" he asked after some preliminary talk. "Too—too—I don't know. A very funny word."

"Squeamish?" I suggested.

"Yes. What does it mean?"

"That you exaggerate things—to yourself. Without inquiry, and so on."

He seemed to turn it over in his mind. We went on talking. This Falk was the plague of his life. Upsetting everybody like this! Mrs. Hermann was unwell this morning. His niece was crying still. There was nobody to look after the children. He struck his umbrella on the deck. The girl would be like that for months. Fancy carrying all the way home, second class, a perfectly useless girl who is crying all the time. It was bad for Lena, too, he observed; but on what grounds I could not guess. Perhaps of the bad example. That child was already sorrowing and crying enough over the rag doll. Nicholas was really the least sentimental person of the family.

"Why does your niece weep?" I asked.

"From pity," cried Hermann.

It was impossible to make out women. Mrs. Hermann was the only one he pretended to understand. She was very, very upset and doubtful.

"Doubtful about what?" I asked.

He averted his eyes and did not answer this. It was impossible to make women out. For instance, his niece was weeping for Falk. Now he (Hermann) would like to wring his neck—but then . . . He supposed he had too tender a heart. "Frankly," he asked at last, "what do you think of what we heard last night, captain?"

"In all these tales," I observed, "there is always a good deal of exaggeration."

And not letting him recover from his surprise I assured him that I knew all the details. He begged me not to repeat them. His heart was too tender. They would make him feel unwell. Then, looking at his feet and speaking very slowly, he supposed that he need not see much of them after they were married. For, indeed, he could not bear the sight of Falk. On the other hand, it was ridiculous to take home a girl with her head turned. A girl that weeps all the time and is of no help to her aunt.

"Now you will be able to do with one cabin only on your passage home," I said.

"Yes, I had thought of that," he said brightly, almost. Yes! Himself, his wife, four children—one cabin might do. Whereas if his niece went . . .

"And what does Mrs. Hermann say to it?" I inquired.

Mrs. Hermann did not know whether a man of that sort could make a girl happy—she had been greatly deceived in Captain Falk. She had passed a very bad night.

Those good people did not seem to be able to retain an impression for a whole twelve hours. I assured him on my own personal knowledge that Falk possessed in himself all the qualities to make his niece's future prosperous. He said he was glad to hear this, and that he would tell his wife. Then the object of the visit came out. He wished me to help him to resume relations with Falk. His niece, he said, had expressed the hope I would do so in my kindness. He was evidently anxious that I should, for though he seemed to have forgotten nine-tenths of his last night's opinions and the whole of his indignation, yet he evidently feared to be sent to the right-about. "You told me he was very much in love," he concluded, slyly, and leered in a sort of bucolic way.

As soon as he had left my ship I called Falk on board by signal—the tug still lying at the anchorage. He took the news with calm gravity, as though he had all along trusted the stars to fight for him in their courses.

I saw them once more together, and only once—on the quarter-deck of the *Diana*. Hermann sat smoking with a shirt-sleeved elbow hooked over the back of his chair. Mrs. Hermann was sewing alone. As Falk stepped over the gangway, Hermann's niece, with a slight swish of the skirt and a friendly nod to me, glided past my chair.

Those two met in sunshine abreast of the mainmast. He held her hands and looked down at them, and she looked up at him with her candid and unseeing glance. It seemed to me they had come together as if attracted, drawn and guided to each other by a mysterious influence. They were a complete couple. In her gray frock, palpitating with life, generous of form, olympian and simple, she was indeed the siren to fascinate that dark navigator, this ruthless lover of the five senses. From afar I seemed to feel the masculine strength with which he grasped those hands she had extended to him with a womanly swiftness. Lena, a little pale, nursing her beloved lump of dirty rags, ran towards her big friend;

and then in the drowsy silence of the good old ship Mrs. Hermann's voice rang out so changed that it made me spin round in my chair to see what was the matter.

"Lena, come here!" she screamed. And this good-natured matron gave me a wavering glance, dark and full of fearsome distrust. The child ran back, surprised, to her knee. But the two, standing before each other in sunlight with clasped hands, had heard nothing, had seen nothing and no one. Three feet away from them, in the shade, a seaman sat on a spar, very busy splicing a strop and dipping his fingers into a tar-pot, as if utterly unaware of their existence.

When I returned in command of another vessel some five years afterwards, Mr. and Mrs. Falk had left the place. I shouldn't wonder if Schomberg's tongue had succeeded at last in scaring Falk away for good; and, indubitably, there was some vague tale still going about the town of a certain Falk, owner of a tug, who had won his wife at cards from the captain of an English ship.

THE DUEL

· I ·

NAPOLEON I., whose career had the quality of a duel against the whole of Europe, disliked duelling between the officers of his army. The great military emperor was not a swashbuckler, and had little respect for tradition.

Nevertheless, a story of duelling, which became a legend in the army, runs through the epic of imperial wars. To the surprise and admiration of their fellows, two officers, like insane artists trying to gild refined gold or paint the lily, pursued a private contest through the years of universal carnage. They were officers of cavalry, and their connection with the high-spirited but fanciful animal which carries men into battle seems particularly appropriate. It would be difficult to imagine for heroes of this legend two officers of infantry of the line, for example, whose fantasy is tamed by much walking exercise, and whose valour necessarily must be of a more plodding kind. As to gunners or engineers, whose heads are kept cool on a diet of mathematics, it is simply unthinkable.

The names of the two officers were Feraud and D'Hubert, and they were both lieutenants in a regiment of hussars, but not in the same regiment.

Feraud was doing regimental work, but Lieut. D'Hubert had the good fortune to be attached to the person of the general commanding the division, as *officier d'ordonnance*. It was in Strasbourg, and in this agreeable and important garrison they were enjoying greatly a short interval of peace. They were enjoying it, though both intensely warlike, because it was a sword-sharpening, firelock-cleaning peace, dear to a military

heart and undamaging to military prestige, inasmuch that no one believed in its sincerity or duration.

Under those historical circumstances, so favourable to the proper
appreciation of military leisure, Lieut. D'Hubert, one fine afternoon,
made his way along a quiet street of a cheerful suburb towards Lieut.
Feraud's quarters, which were in a private house with a garden at the
back, belonging to an old maiden lady.

His knock at the door was answered instantly by a young maid in
Alsatian costume. Her fresh complexion and her long eyelashes, lowered
demurely at the sight of the tall officer, caused Lieut. D'Hubert, who
was accessible to esthetic impressions, to relax the cold, severe gravity
of his face. At the same time he observed that the girl had over her arm
a pair of hussar's breeches, blue with a red stripe.

"Lieut. Feraud in?" he inquired, benevolently.

"Oh, no, sir! He went out at six this morning."

The pretty maid tried to close the door. Lieut. D'Hubert, opposing
this move with gentle firmness, stepped into the ante-room, jingling his
spurs.

"Come, my dear! You don't mean to say he has not been home since
six o'clock this morning?"

Saying these words, Lieut. D'Hubert opened without ceremony the
door of a room so comfortably and neatly ordered that only from internal
evidence in the shape of boots, uniforms, and military accoutrements
did he acquire the conviction that it was Lieut. Feraud's room. And he
saw also that Lieut. Feraud was not at home. The truthful maid had
followed him, and raised her candid eyes to his face.

"H'm!" said Lieut. D'Hubert, greatly disappointed, for he had already visited all the haunts where a lieutenant of hussars could be found
of a fine afternoon. "So he's out? And do you happen to know, my dear,
why he went out at six this morning?"

"No," she answered, readily. "He came home late last night, and
snored. I heard him when I got up at five. Then he dressed himself in
his oldest uniform and went out. Service, I suppose."

"Service? Not a bit of it!" cried Lieut. D'Hubert. "Learn, my angel,
that he went out thus early to fight a duel with a civilian."

She heard this news without a quiver of her dark eyelashes. It was
very obvious that the actions of Lieut. Feraud were generally above
criticism. She only looked up for a moment in mute surprise, and Lieut.

D'Hubert concluded from this absence of emotion that she must have seen Lieut. Feraud since the morning. He looked around the room.

"Come!" he insisted, with confidential familiarity. "He's perhaps somewhere in the house now?"

She shook her head.

"So much the worse for him!" continued Lieut. D'Hubert, in a tone of anxious conviction. "But he has been home this morning."

This time the pretty maid nodded slightly.

"He has!" cried Lieut. D'Hubert. "And went out again? What for? Couldn't he keep quietly indoors! What a lunatic! My dear girl——"

Lieut. D'Hubert's natural kindness of disposition and strong sense of comradeship helped his powers of observation. He changed his tone to a most insinuating softness, and, gazing at the hussar's breeches hanging over the arm of the girl, he appealed to the interest she took in Lieut. Feraud's comfort and happiness. He was pressing and persuasive. He used his eyes, which were kind and fine, with excellent effect. His anxiety to get hold at once of Lieut. Feraud, for Lieut. Feraud's own good, seemed so genuine that at last it overcame the girl's unwillingness to speak. Unluckily she had not much to tell. Lieut. Feraud had returned home shortly before ten, had walked straight into his room, and had thrown himself on his bed to resume his slumbers. She had heard him snore rather louder than before far into the afternoon. Then he got up, put on his best uniform, and went out. That was all she knew.

She raised her eyes, and Lieut. D'Hubert stared into them incredulously.

"It's incredible. Gone parading the town in his best uniform! My dear child, don't you know he ran that civilian through this morning? Clean through, as you spit a hare."

The pretty maid heard the gruesome intelligence without any signs of distress. But she pressed her lips together thoughtfully.

"He isn't parading the town," she remarked in a low tone. "Far from it."

"The civilian's family is making an awful row," continued Lieut. D'Hubert, pursuing his train of thought. "And the general is very angry. It's one of the best families in the town. Feraud ought to have kept close at least——"

"What will the general do to him?" inquired the girl, anxiously.

"He won't have his head cut off, to be sure," grumbled Lieut. D'Hubert. "His conduct is positively indecent. He's making no end of trouble for himself by this sort of bravado."

"But he isn't parading the town," the maid insisted in a shy murmur.

"Why, yes! Now I think of it, I haven't seen him anywhere about. What on earth has he done with himself?"

"He's gone to pay a call," suggested the maid, after a moment of silence.

Lieut. D'Hubert started.

"A call! Do you mean a call on a lady? The cheek of the man! And how do you know this, my dear?"

Without concealing her woman's scorn for the denseness of the masculine mind, the pretty maid reminded him that Lieut. Feraud had arrayed himself in his best uniform before going out. He had also put on his newest dolman, she added, in a tone as if this conversation were getting on her nerves, and turned away brusquely.

Lieut. D'Hubert, without questioning the accuracy of the deduction, did not see that it advanced him much on his official quest. For his quest after Lieut. Feraud had an official character. He did not know any of the women this fellow, who had run a man through in the morning, was likely to visit in the afternoon. The two young men knew each other but slightly. He bit his gloved finger in perplexity.

"Call!" he exclaimed. "Call on the devil!"

The girl, with her back to him, and folding the hussar's breeches on a chair, protested with a vexed little laugh:

"Oh, dear, no! On Madame de Lionne."

Lieut. D'Hubert whistled softly. Madame de Lionne was the wife of a high official who had a well-known *salon* and some pretensions to sensibility and elegance. The husband was a civilian, and old; but the society of the *salon* was young and military. Lieut. D'Hubert had whistled, not because the idea of pursuing Lieut. Feraud into that very *salon* was disagreeable to him, but because, having arrived in Strasbourg only lately, he had not had the time as yet to get an introduction to Madame de Lionne. And what was that swashbuckler Feraud doing there, he wondered. He did not seem the sort of man who——

"Are you certain of what you say?" asked Lieut. D'Hubert.

The girl was perfectly certain. Without turning round to look at him, she explained that the coachman of their next door neighbors knew the *maître-d'hôtel* of Madame de Lionne. In this way she had her information. And she was perfectly certain. In giving this assurance she sighed. Lieut. Feraud called there nearly every afternoon, she added.

"Ah, bah!" exclaimed D'Hubert, ironically. His opinion of Madame de Lionne went down several degrees. Lieut. Feraud did not seem to him specially worthy of attention on the part of a woman with a reputation for sensibility and elegance. But there was no saying. At bottom they were all alike—very practical rather than idealistic. Lieut. D'Hubert, however, did not allow his mind to dwell on these considerations.

"By thunder!" he reflected aloud. "The general goes there sometimes. If he happens to find the fellow making eyes at the lady there will be the devil to pay! Our general is not a very accommodating person, I can tell you."

"Go quickly, then! Don't stand here now I've told you where he is!" cried the girl, colouring to the eyes.

"Thanks, my dear! I don't know what I would have done without you."

After manifesting his gratitude in an aggressive way, which at first was repulsed violently, and then submitted to with a sudden and still more repellent indifference, Lieut. D'Hubert took his departure.

He clanked and jingled along the streets with a martial swagger. To run a comrade to earth in a drawing-room where he was not known did not trouble him in the least. A uniform is a passport. His position as *officier d'ordonnance* of the general added to his assurance. Moreover, now that he knew where to find Lieut. Feraud, he had no option. It was a service matter.

Madame de Lionne's house had an excellent appearance. A man in livery, opening the door of a large drawing-room with a waxed floor, shouted his name and stood aside to let him pass. It was a reception day. The ladies wore big hats surcharged with a profusion of feathers; their bodies sheathed in clinging white gowns, from the armpits to the tips of the low satin shoes, looked sylph-like and cool in a great display of bare necks and arms. The men who talked with them, on the contrary, were arrayed heavily in multi-coloured garments with collars up to their ears and thick sashes round their waists. Lieut. D'Hubert made his unabashed way across the room and, bowing low before a sylph-like form reclining on a couch, offered his apologies for this intrusion, which nothing could excuse but the extreme urgency of the service order he had to communicate to his comrade Feraud. He proposed to himself to return presently in a more regular manner and beg forgiveness for interrupting the interesting conversation . . .

A bare arm was extended towards him with gracious nonchalance even before he had finished speaking. He pressed the hand respectfully to his lips, and made the mental remark that it was bony. Madame de Lionne was a blonde, with too fine a skin and a long face.

"*C'est ça!*" she said, with an ethereal smile, disclosing a set of large teeth. "Come this evening to plead for your forgiveness."

"I will not fail, madame."

Meantime, Lieut. Feraud, splendid in his new dolman and the extremely polished boots of his calling, sat on a chair within a foot of the couch, one hand resting on his thigh, the other twirling his moustache to a point. At a significant glance from D'Hubert he rose without alacrity, and followed him into the recess of a window.

"What is it you want with me?" he asked, with astonishing indifference. Lieut. D'Hubert could not imagine that in the innocence of his heart and simplicity of his conscience Lieut. Feraud took a view of his duel in which neither remorse nor yet a rational apprehension of consequences had any place. Though he had no clear recollection how the quarrel had originated (it was begun in an establishment where beer and wine are drunk late at night), he had not the slightest doubt of being himself the outraged party. He had had two experienced friends for his seconds. Everything had been done according to the rules governing that sort of adventures. And a duel is obviously fought for the purpose of someone being at least hurt, if not killed outright. The civilian got hurt. That also was in order. Lieut. Feraud was perfectly tranquil; but Lieut. D'Hubert took it for affectation, and spoke with a certain vivacity.

"I am directed by the general to give you the order to go at once to your quarters, and remain there under close arrest."

It was now the turn of Lieut. Feraud to be astonished. "What the devil are you telling me there?" he murmured, faintly, and fell into such profound wonder that he could only follow mechanically the motions of Lieut. D'Hubert. The two officers, one tall, with an interesting face and a moustache the colour of ripe corn, the other, short and sturdy, with a hooked nose and a thick crop of black curly hair, approached the mistress of the house to take their leave. Madame de Lionne, a woman of eclectic taste, smiled upon these armed young men with impartial sensibility and an equal share of interest. Madame de Lionne took her delight in the infinite variety of the human species. All the other eyes in the drawing-room followed the departing officers; and when they had gone out one or two men, who had already heard of the duel, imparted the information to the sylph-like ladies, who received it with faint shrieks of humane concern.

Meantime, the two hussars walked side by side, Lieut. Feraud trying to master the hidden reason of things which in this instance eluded the grasp of his intellect; Lieut. D'Hubert feeling annoyed at the part he had to play, because the general's instructions were that he should see personally that Lieut. Feraud carried out his orders to the letter, and at once.

"The chief seems to know this animal," he thought, eyeing his companion, whose round face, the round eyes, and even the twisted-up jet black little moustache seemed animated by a mental exasperation against the incomprehensible. And aloud he observed rather reproachfully, "The general is in a devilish fury with you!"

Lieut. Feraud stopped short on the edge of the pavement, and cried in accents of unmistakable sincerity, "What on earth for?" The innocence of the fiery Gascon soul was depicted in the manner in which he seized his head in both hands as if to prevent it bursting with perplexity.

"For the duel," said Lieut. D'Hubert, curtly. He was annoyed greatly by this sort of perverse fooling.

"The duel! The . . ."

Lieut. Feraud passed from one paroxysm of astonishment into another. He dropped his hands and walked on slowly, trying to reconcile this information with the state of his own feelings. It was impossible. He burst out indignantly, "Was I to let that sauerkraut-eating civilian wipe his boots on the uniform of the 7th Hussars?"

Lieut. D'Hubert could not remain altogether unmoved by that simple sentiment. This little fellow was a lunatic, he thought to himself, but there was something in what he said.

"Of course, I don't know how far you were justified," he began, soothingly. "And the general himself may not be exactly informed. Those people have been deafening him with their lamentations."

"Ah! the general is not exactly informed," mumbled Lieut. Feraud, walking faster and faster as his choler at the injustice of his fate began to rise. "He is not exactly . . . And he orders me under close arrest, with God knows what afterwards!"

"Don't excite yourself like this," remonstrated the other. "Your adversary's people are very influential, you know, and it looks bad enough on the face of it. The general had to take notice of their complaint at once. I don't think he means to be over-severe with you. It's the best thing for you to be kept out of sight for a while."

"I am very much obliged to the general," muttered Lieut. Feraud through his teeth. "And perhaps you would say I ought to be grateful to you, too, for the trouble you have taken to hunt me up in the drawing-room of a lady who——"

"Frankly," interrupted Lieut. D'Hubert, with an innocent laugh, "I think you ought to be. I had no end of trouble to find out where you were. It wasn't exactly the place for you to disport yourself in under the circumstances. If the general had caught you there making eyes at the goddess of the temple . . . oh, my word! . . . He hates to be bothered with complaints against his officers, you know. And it looked uncommonly like sheer bravado."

The two officers had arrived now at the street door of Lieut. Feraud's lodgings. The latter turned towards his companion. "Lieut. D'Hubert," he said, "I have something to say to you, which can't be said very well in the street. You can't refuse to come up."

The pretty maid had opened the door. Lieut. Feraud brushed past her brusquely, and she raised her scared and questioning eyes to Lieut. D'Hubert, who could do nothing but shrug his shoulders slightly as he followed with marked reluctance.

In his room Lieut. Feraud unhooked the clasp, flung his new dolman on the bed, and, folding his arms across his chest, turned to the other hussar.

"Do you imagine I am a man to submit tamely to injustice?" he inquired, in a boisterous voice.

"Oh, do be reasonable!" remonstrated Lieut. D'Hubert.

"I am reasonable! I am perfectly reasonable!" retorted the other with ominous restraint. "I can't call the general to account for his behaviour, but you are going to answer me for yours."

"I can't listen to this nonsense," murmured Lieut. D'Hubert, making a slightly contemptuous grimace.

"You call this nonsense? It seems to me a perfectly plain statement. Unless you don't understand French."

"What on earth do you mean?"

"I mean," screamed suddenly Lieut. Feraud, "to cut off your ears to teach you to disturb me with the general's orders when I am talking to a lady!"

A profound silence followed this mad declaration; and through the open window Lieut. D'Hubert heard the little birds singing sanely in the garden. He said, preserving his calm, "Why! If you take that tone, of course I shall hold myself at your disposition whenever you are at liberty to attend to this affair; but I don't think you will cut my ears off."

"I am going to attend to it at once," declared Lieut. Feraud, with extreme truculence. "If you are thinking of displaying your airs and graces to-night in Madame de Lionne's *salon* you are very much mistaken."

"Really!" said Lieut. D'Hubert, who was beginning to feel irritated, "you are an impracticable sort of fellow. The general's orders to me were to put you under arrest, not to carve you into small pieces. Goodmorning!" And turning his back on the little Gascon, who, always sober in his potations, was as though born intoxicated with the sunshine of his vine-ripening country, the Northman, who could drink hard on occasion, but was born sober under the watery skies of Picardy, made for the door. Hearing, however, the unmistakable sound behind his back of a sword drawn from the scabbard, he had no option but to stop.

"Devil take this mad Southerner!" he thought, spinning round and surveying with composure the warlike posture of Lieut. Feraud, with a bare sword in his hand.

"At once!—at once!" stuttered Feraud, beside himself.

"You had my answer," said the other, keeping his temper very well.

At first he had been only vexed, and somewhat amused; but now his face got clouded. He was asking himself seriously how he could manage to get away. It was impossible to run from a man with a sword, and as to fighting him, it seemed completely out of the question. He waited awhile, then said exactly what was in his heart.

"Drop this! I won't fight with you. I won't be made ridiculous."

"Ah, you won't?" hissed the Gascon. "I suppose you prefer to be made infamous. Do you hear what I say? . . . Infamous! Infamous!

Infamous!'' he shrieked, rising and falling on his toes and getting very red in the face.

Lieut. D'Hubert, on the contrary, became very pale at the sound of the unsavoury word for a moment, then flushed pink to the roots of his fair hair. "But you can't go out to fight; you are under arrest, you lunatic!" he objected, with angry scorn.

"There's the garden: it's big enough to lay out your long carcass in," spluttered the other with such ardour that somehow the anger of the cooler man subsided.

"This is perfectly absurd," he said, glad enough to think he had found a way out of it for the moment. "We shall never get any of our comrades to serve as seconds. It's preposterous."

"Seconds! Damn the seconds! We don't want any seconds. Don't you worry about any seconds. I shall send word to your friends to come and bury you when I am done. And if you want any witnesses, I'll send word to the old girl to put her head out of a window at the back. Stay! There's the gardener. He'll do. He's as deaf as a post, but he has two eyes in his head. Come along! I will teach you, my staff officer, that the carrying about of a general's orders is not always child's play."

While thus discoursing he had unbuckled his empty scabbard. He sent it flying under the bed, and, lowering the point of the sword, brushed past the perplexed Lieut. D'Hubert, exclaiming, "Follow me!" Directly he had flung open the door a faint shriek was heard and the pretty maid, who had been listening at the keyhole, staggered away, putting the backs of her hands over her eyes. Feraud did not seem to see her, but she ran after him and seized his left arm. He shook her off, and then she rushed towards Lieut. D'Hubert and clawed at the sleeve of his uniform.

"Wretched man!" she sobbed. "Is this what you wanted to find him for?"

"Let me go," entreated Lieut. D'Hubert, trying to disengage himself gently. "It's like being in a madhouse," he protested, with exasperation. "Do let me go! I won't do him any harm."

A fiendish laugh from Lieut. Feraud commented that assurance. "Come along!" he shouted, with a stamp of his foot.

And Lieut. D'Hubert did follow. He could do nothing else. Yet in vindication of his sanity it must be recorded that as he passed through the ante-room the notion of opening the street door and bolting out presented itself to this brave youth, only of course to be instantly dismissed, for he felt sure that the other would pursue him without shame or compunction. And the prospect of an officer of hussars being chased along the street by another officer of hussars with a naked sword could not be for a moment entertained. Therefore he followed into the garden. Behind them the girl tottered out, too. With ashy lips and wild, scared eyes, she surrendered herself to a dreadful curiosity. She had also the notion of rushing if need be between Lieut. Feraud and death.

The deaf gardener, utterly unconscious of approaching footsteps, went on watering his flowers till Lieut. Feraud thumped him on the back. Beholding suddenly an enraged man flourishing a big sabre, the old chap trembling in all his limbs dropped the watering-pot. At once Lieut. Feraud kicked it away with great animosity, and, seizing the gardener by the throat, backed him against a tree. He held him there, shouting in his ear, "Stay here, and look on! You understand? You've got to look on! Don't dare budge from the spot!"

Lieut. D'Hubert came slowly down the walk, unclasping his dolman with unconcealed disgust. Even then, with his hand already on the hilt of his sword, he hesitated to draw'till a roar "*En garde, fichtre!* What do you think you came here for?" and the rush of his adversary forced him to put himself as quickly as possible in a posture of defence.

The clash of arms filled that prim garden, which hitherto had known no more warlike sound than the click of clipping shears; and presently the upper part of an old lady's body was projected out of a window upstairs. She tossed her arms above her white cap, scolding in a cracked voice. The gardener remained glued to the tree, his toothless mouth open in idiotic astonishment, and a little farther up the path the pretty girl, as if spellbound to a small grass plot, ran a few steps this way and that, wringing her hands and muttering crazily. She did not rush between the combatants: the onslaughts of Lieut. Feraud were so fierce that her heart failed her. Lieut. D'Hubert, his faculties concentrated upon defence, needed all his skill and science of the sword to stop the rushes of his adversary. Twice already he had to break ground. It bothered him to feel his foothold made insecure by the round, dry gravel of the path rolling under the hard soles of his boots. This was most unsuitable ground, he thought, keeping a watchful, narrowed gaze, shaded by long eyelashes, upon the fiery stare of his thick-set adversary. This absurd affair would ruin his reputation of a sensible, well-behaved, promising young officer. It would damage, at any rate, his immediate prospects, and lose him the good-will of his general. These worldly preoccupations were no doubt misplaced in view of the solemnity of the moment. A duel, whether regarded as a ceremony in the cult of honour, or even when reduced in its moral essence to a form of manly sport, demands a perfect singleness of intention, a homicidal austerity of mood. On the other hand, this vivid concern for his future had not a bad effect inasmuch as it began to rouse the anger of Lieut. D'Hubert. Some seventy seconds had elapsed since they had crossed blades, and Lieut. D'Hubert had to break ground again in order to avoid impaling his reckless adversary like a beetle for a cabinet of specimens. The result was that misapprehending the motive, Lieut. Feraud with a triumphant sort of snarl pressed his attack.

"This enraged animal will have me against the wall directly," thought Lieut. D'Hubert. He imagined himself much closer to the house than he was, and he dared not turn his head; it seemed to him that he was keeping his adversary off with his eyes rather more than with his point. Lieut. Feraud crouched and bounded with a fierce tigerish agility fit to trouble the stoutest heart. But what was more appalling than the fury of a wild beast, accomplishing in all innocence of heart a natural function, was the fixity of savage purpose man alone is capable of displaying. Lieut. D'Hubert in the midst of his worldly preoccupations perceived it at last. It was an absurd and damaging affair to be drawn into, but whatever silly intention the fellow had started with, it was clear enough that by this time he meant to kill—nothing less. He meant it with an intensity of will utterly beyond the inferior faculties of a tiger.

As is the case with constitutionally brave men, the full view of the danger interested Lieut. D'Hubert. And directly he got properly interested, the length of his arm and the coolness of his head told in his favour. It was the turn of Lieut. Feraud to recoil, with a blood-curdling grunt of baffled rage. He made a swift feint, and then rushed straight forward.

"Ah! you would, would you?" Lieut. D'Hubert exclaimed, mentally. The combat had lasted nearly two minutes, time enough for any man to get embittered, apart from the merits of the quarrel. And all at once it was over. Trying to close breast to breast under his adversary's guard Lieut. Feraud received a slash on his shortened arm. He did not feel it in the least, but it checked his rush, and his feet slipping on the gravel he fell backwards with great violence. The shock jarred his boiling brain into the perfect quietude of insensibility. Simultaneously with his fall the pretty servant-girl shrieked; but the old maiden lady at the window ceased her scolding, and began to cross herself piously.

Beholding his adversary stretched out perfectly still, his face to the sky, Lieut. D'Hubert thought he had killed him outright. The impression of having slashed hard enough to cut his man clean in two abode with him for a while in an exaggerated memory of the right good-will he had put into the blow. He dropped on his knees hastily by the side of the prostrate body. Discovering that not even the arm was severed, a slight sense of disappointment mingled with the feeling of relief. The fellow deserved the worst. But truly he did not want the death of that sinner. The affair was ugly enough as it stood, and Lieut. D'Hubert addressed himself at once to the task of stopping the bleeding. In this task it was his fate to be ridiculously impeded by the pretty maid. Rending the air with screams of horror, she attacked him from behind and, twining her fingers in his hair, tugged back at his head. Why she should choose to hinder him at this precise moment he could not in the least understand. He did not try. It was all like a very wicked and harassing dream. Twice to save himself from being pulled over he had to rise and fling her off. He did this stoically, without a word, kneeling down again at once to go on with his work. But the third time, his work being done, he seized her and held her arms pinned to her body. Her cap was half off, her face was red, her eyes blazed with crazy boldness. He looked mildly into them while she called him a wretch, a traitor, and a murderer many times in succession. This did not annoy him so much as the conviction that she had managed to scratch his face abundantly. Ridicule would be added to the scandal of the story. He imagined the adorned tale making its way through the garrison of the town, through the whole army on the frontier, with every possible distortion of motive and sentiment and circumstance, spreading a doubt upon the sanity of his conduct and the distinction of his taste even to the very ears of his honourable family. It was all very well for that fellow Feraud, who had no connections, no family to speak of, and no quality but courage, which, anyhow, was a matter of course, and possessed by every single trooper in the whole mass of French cavalry. Still holding down the arms of the girl in a strong grip, Lieut. D'Hubert glanced over his shoulder. Lieut. Feraud had opened his eyes. He did not move. Like a man just waking from a deep sleep he stared without any expression at the evening sky.

Lieut. D'Hubert's urgent shouts to the old gardener produced no effect—not so much as to make him shut his toothless mouth. Then he remembered that the man was stone deaf. All that time the girl struggled, not with maidenly coyness, but like a pretty, dumb fury, kicking his shins now and then. He continued to hold her as if in a vice, his instinct telling him that were he to let her go she would fly at his eyes. But he was greatly humiliated by his position. At last she gave up. She was more exhausted than appeased, he feared. Nevertheless, he attempted to get out of this wicked dream by way of negotiation.

"Listen to me," he said, as calmly as he could. "Will you promise to run for a surgeon if I let you go?"

With real affliction he heard her declare that she would do nothing of the kind. On the contrary, her sobbed out intention was to remain in the garden, and fight tooth and nail for the protection of the vanquished man. This was shocking.

"My dear child!" he cried in despair, "is it possible that you think me capable of murdering a wounded adversary? Is it. . . . Be quiet, you little wild cat, you!"

They struggled. A thick, drowsy voice said behind him, "What are you after with that girl?"

Lieut. Feraud had raised himself on his good arm. He was looking sleepily at his other arm, at the mess of blood on his uniform, at a small red pool on the ground, at his sabre lying a foot away on the path. Then he laid himself down gently again to think it all out, as far as a thundering headache would permit of mental operations.

Lieut. D'Hubert released the girl who crouched at once by the side of the other lieutenant. The shades of night were falling on the little trim garden with this touching group, whence proceeded low murmurs of sorrow and compassion, with other feeble sounds of a different character, as if an imperfectly awake invalid were trying to swear. Lieut. D'Hubert went away.

He passed through the silent house, and congratulated himself upon the dusk concealing his gory hands and scratched face from the passers-by. But this story could by no means be concealed. He dreaded the discredit and ridicule above everything, and was painfully aware of sneaking through the back streets in the manner of a murderer. Presently the sounds of a flute coming out of the open window of a lighted upstairs room in a modest house interrupted his dismal reflections. It was being played with a persevering virtuosity, and through the *fioritures* of the tune one could hear the regular thumping of the foot beating time on the floor.

Lieut. D'Hubert shouted a name, which was that of an army surgeon whom he knew fairly well. The sounds of the flute ceased, and the musician appeared at the window, his instrument still in his hand, peering into the street.

"Who calls? You, D'Hubert? What brings you this way?"

He did not like to be disturbed at the hour when he was playing the flute. He was a man whose hair had turned grey already in the thankless task of tying up wounds on battlefields where others reaped advancement and glory.

"I want you to go at once and see Feraud. You know Lieut. Feraud? He lives down the second street. It's but a step from here."

"What's the matter with him?"

"Wounded."

"Are you sure?"

"Sure!" cried D'Hubert. "I come from there."

"That's amusing," said the elderly surgeon. Amusing was his favourite word; but the expression of his face when he pronounced it never corresponded. He was a stolid man. "Come in," he added. "I'll get ready in a moment."

"Thanks! I will. I want to wash my hands in your room."

Lieut. D'Hubert found the surgeon occupied in unscrewing his flute, and packing the pieces methodically in a case. He turned his head.

"Water there—in the corner. Your hands do want washing."

"I've stopped the bleeding," said Lieut. D'Hubert. "But you had better make haste. It's rather more than ten minutes ago, you know."

The surgeon did not hurry his movements.

"What's the matter? Dressing came off? That's amusing. I've been at work in the hospital all day but I've been told this morning by somebody that he had come off without a scratch."

"Not the same duel probably," growled moodily Lieut. D'Hubert, wiping his hands on a coarse towel.

"Not the same. . . . What? Another. It would take the very devil to make me go out twice in one day." The surgeon looked narrowly at Lieut. D'Hubert. "How did you come by that scratched face? Both sides, too—and symmetrical. It's amusing."

"Very!" snarled Lieut. D'Hubert. "And you will find his slashed arm amusing, too. It will keep both of you amused for quite a long time."

The doctor was mystified and impressed by the brusque bitterness of Lieut. D'Hubert's tone. They left the house together, and in the street he was still more mystified by his conduct.

"Aren't you coming with me?" he asked.

"No," said Lieut. D'Hubert. "You can find the house by yourself. The front door will be standing open very likely."

"All right. Where's his room?"

"Ground floor. But you had better go right through and look in the garden first."

This astonishing piece of information made the surgeon go off without further parley. Lieut. D'Hubert regained his quarters nursing a hot and uneasy indignation. He dreaded the chaff of his comrades almost as much as the anger of his superiors. The truth was confoundedly grotesque and embarrassing, even putting aside the irregularity of the combat itself, which made it come abominably near a criminal offence. Like all men without much imagination, a faculty which helps the process of reflective thought, Lieut. D'Hubert became frightfully harassed by the obvious aspects of his predicament. He was certainly glad that he had not killed Lieut. Feraud outside all rules, and without the regular witnesses proper to such a transaction. Uncommonly glad. At the same time he felt as though he would have liked to wring his neck for him without ceremony.

He was still under the sway of these contradictory sentiments when the surgeon amateur of the flute came to see him. More than three days had elapsed. Lieut. D'Hubert was no longer *officer d'ordonnance* to the general commanding the division. He had been sent back to his regiment. And he was resuming his connection with the soldiers' military family by being shut up in close confinement, not at his own quarters in town, but in a room in the barracks. Owing to the gravity of the incident, he was forbidden to see any one. He did not know what had happened, what was being said, or what was being thought. The arrival of the surgeon was a most unexpected thing to the worried captive. The amateur of the flute began by explaining that he was there only by a special favour of the colonel.

"I represented to him that it would be only fair to let you have some authentic news of your adversary," he continued. "You'll be glad to hear he's getting better fast."

Lieut. D'Hubert's face exhibited no conventional signs of gladness. He continued to walk the floor of the dusty bare room.

"Take this chair, doctor," he mumbled.

The doctor sat down.

"This affair is variously appreciated—in town and in the army. In fact, the diversity of opinions is amusing."

"Is it!" mumbled Lieut. D'Hubert, tramping steadily from wall to wall. But within himself he marvelled that there could be two opinions on the matter. The surgeon continued.

"Of course, as the real facts are not known——"

"I should have thought," interrupted D'Hubert, "that the fellow would have put you in possession of facts."

"He said something," admitted the other, "the first time I saw him. And, by the by, I did find him in the garden. The thump on the back of his head had made him a little incoherent then. Afterwards he was rather reticent than otherwise."

"Didn't think he would have the grace to be ashamed!" mumbled D'Hubert, resuming his pacing while the doctor murmured, "It's very amusing. Ashamed! Shame was not exactly his frame of mind. However, you may look at the matter otherwise."

"What are you talking about? What matter?" asked D'Hubert, with a sidelong look at the heavy-faced, grey-haired figure seated on a wooden chair.

"Whatever it is," said the surgeon a little impatiently, "I don't want to pronounce any opinion on your conduct——"

"By heavens, you had better not!" burst out D'Hubert.

"There!—there! Don't be so quick in flourishing the sword. It doesn't pay in the long run. Understand once for all that I would not carve any of you youngsters except with the tools of my trade. But my advice is good. If you go on like this you will make for yourself an ugly reputation."

"Go on like what?" demanded Lieut. D'Hubert, stopping short, quite startled. "I!—I!—make for myself a reputation. . . . What do you imagine?"

"I told you I don't wish to judge of the rights and wrongs of this incident. It's not my business. Nevertheless——"

"What on earth has he been telling you?" interrupted Lieut. D'Hubert, in a sort of awed scare.

"I told you already, that at first, when I picked him up in the garden, he was incoherent. Afterwards he was naturally reticent. But I gather at least that he could not help himself."

"He couldn't?" shouted Lieut. D'Hubert in a great voice. Then, lowering his tone impressively, "And what about me? Could I help myself?"

The surgeon stood up. His thoughts were running upon the flute, his constant companion with a consoling voice. In the vicinity of field ambulances, after twenty-four hours' hard work, he had been known to trouble with its sweet sounds the horrible stillness of battlefields, given over to silence and the dead. The solacing hour of his daily life was approaching, and in peace time he held on to the minutes as a miser to his hoard.

"Of course!—of course!" he said, perfunctorily. "You would think so. It's amusing. However, being perfectly neutral and friendly to you both, I have consented to deliver his message to you. Say that I am humouring an invalid if you like. He wants you to know that this affair is by no means at an end. He intends to send you his seconds directly he has regained his strength—providing, of course, the army is not in the field at that time."

"He intends, does he? Why, certainly," spluttered Lieut. D'Hubert in a passion.

The secret of his exasperation was not apparent to the visitor; but this passion confirmed the surgeon in the belief which was gaining ground outside that some very serious difference had arisen between these two young men, something serious enough to wear an air of mystery, some fact of the utmost gravity. To settle their urgent difference about that fact, those two young men had risked being broken and disgraced at the outset almost of their career. The surgeon feared that the forthcoming inquiry would fail to satisfy the public curiosity. They would not take the public into their confidence as to that something which had passed between them of a nature so outrageous as to make them face a charge of murder—neither more nor less. But what could it be?

The surgeon was not very curious by temperament; but that question haunting his mind caused him twice that evening to hold the instrument off his lips and sit silent for a whole minute—right in the middle of a tune—trying to form a plausible conjecture.

· II ·

He succeeded in this object no better than the rest of the garrison and the whole of society. The two young officers, of no especial consequence till then, became distinguished by the universal curiosity, as to the origin of their quarrel. Madame de Lionne's *salon* was the centre of ingenious surmises; that lady herself was for a time assailed by inquiries as being the last person known to have spoken to these unhappy and reckless young men before they went out together from her house to a savage encounter with swords, at dusk, in a private garden. She protested she had not observed anything unusual in their demeanour. Lieut. Feraud had been visibly annoyed at being called away. That was natural enough; no man likes to be disturbed in a conversation with a lady famed for her elegance and sensibility. But in truth the subject bored Madame de Lionne, since her personality could by no stretch of reckless gossip be connected with this affair. And it irritated her to hear it advanced that there might have been some woman in the case. This irritation arose, not from her elegance or sensibility, but from a more instinctive side of her nature. It became so great at last that she peremptorily forbade the subject to be mentioned under her roof. Near her couch the prohibition was obeyed, but father off in the *salon* the pall of the imposed silence continued to be lifted more or less. A personage with a long, pale face, resembling the countenance of a sheep, opined, shaking his head, that it was a quarrel of long standing envenomed by time. It was objected to him that the men themselves were too young for such a theory. They belonged also to different and distant parts of France. There were other physical impossibilities, too. A sub-commissary of the Intendence, an agreeable and cultivated bachelor in kerseymere breeches, Hessian boots, and a blue coat embroidered with silver lace, who affected to believe in the transmigration of souls, suggested that the two had met perhaps in some previous existence. The feud was in the forgotten past.

It might have been something quite inconceivable in the present state of their being; but their souls remembered the animosity, and manifested an instinctive antagonism. He developed this theme jocularly. Yet the affair was so absurd from the worldly, the military, the honourable, or the prudential point of view, that his weird explanation seemed rather more reasonable than any other.

The two officers had confided nothing definite to any one. Humiliation at having been worsted arms in hand, and an uneasy feeling of having been involved in a scrape by the injustice of fate, kept Lieut. Feraud savagely dumb. He mistrusted the sympathy of mankind. That would, of course, go to that dandified staff officer. Lying in bed, he raved aloud to the pretty maid who administered to his needs with devotion, and listened to his horrible imprecations with alarm. That Lieut. D'Hubert should be made to "pay for it," seemed to her just and natural. Her principal care was that Lieut. Feraud should not excite himself. He appeared so wholly admirable and fascinating to the humility of her heart that her only concern was to see him get well quickly, even if it were only to resume his visits to Madame de Lionne's *salon*.

Lieut. D'Hubert kept silent for the immediate reason that there was no one, except a stupid young soldier servant, to speak to. Further, he was aware that the episode, so grave professionally, had its comic side. When reflecting upon it, he still felt that he would like to wring Lieut. Feraud's neck for him. But this formula was figurative rather than precise, and expressed more a state of mind than an actual physical impulse. At the same time, there was in that young man a feeling of comradeship and kindness which made him unwilling to make the position of Lieut. Feraud worse than it was. He did not want to talk at large about this wretched affair. At the inquiry he would have, of course, to speak the truth in self-defence. This prospect vexed him.

But no inquiry took place. The army took the field instead. Lieut. D'Hubert, liberated without remark, took up his regimental duties; and Lieut. Feraud, his arm just out of the sling, rode unquestioned with his squadron to complete his convalescence in the smoke of battlefields and the fresh air of night bivouacs. This bracing treatment suited him so well, that at the first rumour of an armistice being signed he could turn without misgivings to the thoughts of his private warfare.

This time it was to be regular warfare. He sent two friends to Lieut.

D'Hubert, whose regiment was stationed only a few miles away. Those friends had asked no questions of their principal. "I owe him one, that pretty staff officer," he had said, grimly, and they went away quite contentedly on their mission. Lieut. D'Hubert had no difficulty in finding two friends equally discreet and devoted to their principal. "There's a crazy fellow to whom I must give a lesson," he had declared curtly; and they asked for no better reasons.

On these grounds an encounter with duelling-swords was arranged one early morning in a convenient field. At the third set-to Lieut. D'Hubert found himself lying on his back on the dewy grass with a hole in his side. A serene sun rising over a landscape of meadows and woods hung on his left. A surgeon—not the flute player, but another—was bending over him, feeling around the wound.

"Narrow squeak. But it will be nothing," he pronounced.

Lieut. D'Hubert heard these words with pleasure. One of his seconds, sitting on the wet grass, and sustaining his head on his lap, said, "The fortune of war, *mon pauvre vieux*. What will you have? You had better make it up like two good fellows. Do!"

"You don't know what you ask," murmured Lieut, D'Hubert, in a feeble voice. "However, if he . . ."

In another part of the meadow the seconds of Lieut. Feraud were urging him to go over and shake hands with his adversary.

"You have paid him off now—*que diable*. It's the proper thing to do. This D'Hubert is a decent fellow."

"I know the decency of these generals' pets," muttered Lieut. Feraud through his teeth, and the sombre expression of his face discouraged further efforts at reconciliation. The seconds, bowing from a distance, took their men off the field. In the afternoon Lieut. D'Hubert, very popular as a good comrade uniting great bravery with a frank and equable temper, had many visitors. It was remarked that Lieut. Feraud did not, as is customary, show himself much abroad to receive the felicitations of his friends. They would not have failed him, because he, too, was liked for the exuberance of his southern nature and the simplicity of his character. In all the places where officers were in the habit of assembling at the end of the day the duel of the morning was talked over from every point of view. Though Lieut. D'Hubert had got worsted this time, his sword play was commended. No one could deny that it was very close, very scientific. It was even whispered that if he got touched it was because he wished to spare his adversary. But by many the vigour and dash of Lieut. Feraud's attack were pronounced irresistible.

The merits of the two officers as combatants were frankly discussed; but their attitude to each other after the duel was criticised lightly and with caution. It was irreconcilable, and that was to be regretted. But after all they knew best what the care of their honour dictated. It was not a matter for their comrades to pry into over-much. As to the origin of the quarrel, the general impression was that it dated from the time they were holding garrison in Strasbourg. The musical surgeon shook his head at that. It went much farther back, he thought.

"Why, of course! You must know the whole story," cried several voices, eager with curiosity. "What was it?"

He raised his eyes from his glass deliberately. "Even if I knew ever so well, you can't expect me to tell you, since both the principals choose to say nothing."

He got up and went out, leaving the sense of mystery behind him. He could not stay any longer, because the witching hour of flute-playing was drawing near.

After he had gone a very young officer observed solemnly, "Obviously, his lips are sealed!"

Nobody questioned the high correctness of that remark. Somehow it added to the impressiveness of the affair. Several older officers of both regiments, prompted by nothing but sheer kindness and love of harmony, proposed to form a Court of Honour, to which the two young men would leave the task of their reconciliation. Unfortunately they began by approaching Lieut. Feraud, on the assumption that, having just scored heavily, he would be found placable and disposed to moderation.

The reasoning was sound enough. Nevertheless, the move turned out unfortunate. In that relaxation of moral fibre, which is brought about by the ease of soothed vanity, Lieut. Feraud had condescended in the secret of his heart to review the case, and even had come to doubt not the justice of his cause, but the absolute sagacity of his conduct. This being so, he was disinclined to talk about it. The suggestion of the regimental wise men put him in a difficult position. He was disgusted at it, and this disgust, by a paradoxical logic, reawakened his animosity against Lieut. D'Hubert. Was he to be pestered with this fellow for ever—the fellow who had an infernal knack of getting round people somehow? And yet it was difficult to refuse point blank that mediation sanctioned by the code of honour.

He met the difficulty by an attitude of grim reserve. He twisted his moustache and used vague words. His case was perfectly clear. He was not ashamed to state it before a proper Court of Honour, neither was he afraid to defend it on the ground. He did not see any reason to jump at the suggestion before ascertaining how his adversary was likely to take it.

Later in the day, his exasperation growing upon him, he was heard in a public place saying sardonically, "that it would be the very luckiest thing for Lieut. D'Hubert, because the next time of meeting he need not hope to get off with the mere trifle of three weeks in bed."

This boastful phrase might have been prompted by the most profound Machiavellism. Southern natures often hide, under the outward impulsiveness of action and speech, a certain amount of astuteness.

Lieut. Feraud, mistrusting the justice of men, by no means desired a Court of Honour; and the above words, according so well with his temperament, had also the merit of serving his turn. Whether meant so or not, they found their way in less than four-and-twenty hours into Lieut. D'Hubert's bedroom. In consequence Lieut. D'Hubert, sitting propped up with pillows, received the overtures made to him next day by the statement that the affair was of a nature which could not bear discussion.

The pale face of the wounded officer, his weak voice which he had yet to use cautiously, and the courteous dignity of his tone had a great effect on his hearers. Reported outside all this did more for deepening the mystery than the vapourings of Lieut. Feraud. This last was greatly relieved at the issue. He began to enjoy the state of general wonder, and was pleased to add to it by assuming an attitude of fierce discretion.

The colonel of Lieut. D'Hubert's regiment was a grey-haired, weather-beaten warrior, who took a simple view of his responsibilities. "I can't," he said to himself, "let the best of my subalterns get damaged like this for nothing. I must get to the bottom of this affair privately. He must speak out if the devil were in it. The colonel should be more than a father to these youngsters." And indeed he loved all his men with as much affection as a father of a large family can feel for every individual member of it. If human beings by an oversight of Providence came into the world as mere civilians, they were born again into a regiment as infants are born into a family, and it was that military birth alone which counted.

At the sight of Lieut. D'Hubert standing before him very bleached and hollow-eyed the heart of the old warrior felt a pang of genuine compassion. All his affection for the regiment—that body of men which he held in his hand to launch forward and draw back, who ministered to his pride and commanded all his thoughts—seemed centred for a moment on the person of the most promising subaltern. He cleared his throat in a threatening manner, and frowned terribly. "You must understand," he began, "that I don't care a rap for the life of a single man in the regiment. I would send the eight hundred and forty-three of you men and horses galloping into the pit of perdition with no more compunction than I would kill a fly!"

"Yes, Colonel. You would be riding at our head," said Lieut. D'Hubert with a wan smile.

The colonel, who felt the need of being very diplomatic, fairly roared at this. "I want you to know, Lieut. D'Hubert, that I could stand aside and see you all riding to Hades if need be. I am a man to do even that if the good of the service and my duty to my country required it from me. But that's unthinkable, so don't you even hint at such a thing." He glared awfully, but his tone softened. "There's some milk yet about that moustache of yours, my boy. You don't know what a man like me is capable of. I would hide behind a haystack if . . . Don't grin at me, sir! How dare you? If this were not a private conversation I would . . . Look here! I am responsible for the proper expenditure of lives under my command for the glory of our country and the honour of the regiment. Do you understand that? Well, then, what the devil do you mean by letting yourself be spitted like this by that fellow of the 7th Hussars? It's simply disgraceful!"

Lieut. D'Hubert felt vexed beyond measure. His shoulders moved slightly. He made no other answer. He could not ignore his responsibility.

The colonel veiled his glance and lowered his voice still more. "It's deplorable!" he murmured. And again he changed his tone. "Come!" he went on, persuasively, but with that note of authority which dwells in the throat of a good leader of men, "this affair must be settled. I desire to be told plainly what it is all about. I demand, as your best friend, to know."

The compelling power of authority, the persuasive influence of kindness, affected powerfully a man just risen from a bed of sickness. Lieut. D'Hubert's hand, which grasped the knob of a stick, trembled slightly. But his northern temperament, sentimental yet cautious and clearsighted, too, in its idealistic way, checked his impulse to make a clean breast of the whole deadly absurdity. According to the precept of transcendental wisdom, he turned his tongue seven times in his mouth before he spoke. He made then only a speech of thanks.

The colonel listened, interested at first, then looked mystified. At last he frowned. "You hesitate?—*mille tonnerres!* Haven't I told you that I will condescend to argue with you—as a friend?"

"Yes, Colonel!" answered Lieut. D'Hubert, gently. "But I am afraid that after you have heard me out as a friend you will take action as my superior officer."

The attentive colonel snapped his jaws. "Well, what of that?" he said, frankly. "Is it so damnably disgraceful?"

"It is not," negatived Lieut. D'Hubert, in a faint but firm voice.

"Of course, I shall act for the good of the service. Nothing can prevent me doing that. What do you think I want to be told for?"

"I know it is not from idle curiosity," protested Lieut. D'Hubert. "I know you will act wisely. But what about the good fame of the regiment?"

"It cannot be affected by any youthful folly of a lieutenant," said the colonel, severely.

"No. It cannot be. But it can be by evil tongues. It will be said that a lieutenant of the 4th Hussars, afraid of meeting his adversary, is hiding behind his colonel. And that would be worse than hiding behind a haystack—for the good of the service. I cannot afford to do that, Colonel."

"Nobody would dare to say anything of the kind," began the colonel very fiercely, but ended the phrase on an uncertain note. The bravery of Lieut. D'Hubert was well known. But the colonel was well aware that the duelling courage, the single combat courage, is rightly or wrongly supposed to be courage of a special sort. And it was eminently necessary that an officer of his regiment should possess every kind of courage— and prove it, too. The colonel stuck out his lower lip, and looked far away with a peculiar glazed stare. This was the expression of his perplexity—an expression practically unknown to his regiment; for perplexity is a sentiment which is incompatible with the rank of colonel of cavalry. The colonel himself was overcome by the unpleasant novelty of the sensation. As he was not accustomed to think except on professional matters connected with the welfare of men and horses, and the proper use thereof on the field of glory, his intellectual efforts degenerated into mere mental repetitions of profane language. "*Mille tonnerres! . . . Sacré nom de nom . . .*" he thought.

Lieut. D'Hubert coughed painfully, and added in a weary voice: "There will be plenty of evil tongues to say that I've been cowed. And I am sure you will not expect me to pass that over. I may find myself suddenly with a dozen duels on my hands instead of this one affair."

The direct simplicity of this argument came home to the colonel's understanding. He looked at his subordinate fixedly. "Sit down, Lieutenant!" he said, gruffly. "This is the very devil of a . . . Sit down!"

"*Mon Colonel,*" D'Hubert began again, "I am not afraid of evil tongues. There's a way of silencing them. But there's my peace of mind, too. I wouldn't be able to shake off the notion that I've ruined a brother officer.

Whatever action you take, it is bound to go farther. The inquiry has been dropped—let it rest now. It would have been absolutely fatal to Feraud."

"Hey! What! Did he behave so badly?"

"Yes. It was pretty bad," muttered Lieut. D'Hubert. Being still very weak, he felt a disposition to cry.

As the other man did not belong to his own regiment the colonel had no difficulty in believing this. He began to pace up and down the room. He was a good chief, a man capable of discreet sympathy. But he was human in other ways, too, and this became apparent because he was not capable of artifice.

"The very devil, Lieutenant," he blurted out, in the innocence of his heart, "is that I have declared my intention to get to the bottom of this affair. And when a colonel says something . . . you see . . ."

Lieut. D'Hubert broke in earnestly: "Let me entreat you, Colonel, to be satisfied with taking my word of honour that I was put into a damnable position where I had no option; I had no choice whatever, consistent with my dignity as a man and an officer. . . . After all, Colonel, this fact is the very bottom of this affair. Here you've got it. The rest is mere detail. . . ."

The colonel stopped short. The reputation of Lieut. D'Hubert for good sense and good temper weighed in the balance. A cool head, a warm heart, open as the day. Always correct in his behaviour. One had to trust him. The colonel repressed manfully an immense curiosity. "H'm! You affirm that as a man and an officer. . . . No option? Eh?"

"As an officer—an officer of the 4th Hussars, too," insisted Lieut. D'Hubert, "I had not. And that is the bottom of the affair, Colonel."

"Yes. But still I don't see why, to one's colonel. . . . A colonel is a father—*que diable!*"

Lieut. D'Hubert ought not to have been allowed out as yet. He was becoming aware of his physical insufficiency with humiliation and despair. But the morbid obstinacy of an invalid possessed him, and at the same time he felt with dismay his eyes filling with water. This trouble seemed too big to handle. A tear fell down the thin, pale cheek of Lieut. D'Hubert.

The colonel turned his back on him hastily. You could have heard a pin drop. "This is some silly woman story—is it not?"

Saying these words the chief spun round to seize the truth, which is not a beautiful shape living in a well, but a shy bird best caught by stratagem. This was the last move of the colonel's diplomacy. He saw the truth shining unmistakably in the gesture of Lieut. D'Hubert raising his weak arms and his eyes to heaven in supreme protest.

"Not a woman affair—eh?" growled the colonel, staring hard. "I don't ask you who or where. All I want to know is whether there is a woman in it?"

Lieut. D'Hubert's arms dropped, and his weak voice was pathetically broken.

"Nothing of the kind, *mon Colonel.*"

"On your honour?" insisted the old warrior.

"On my honour."

"Very well," said the colonel, thoughtfully, and bit his lip. The arguments of Lieut. D'Hubert, helped by his liking for the man, had convinced him. On the other hand, it was highly improper that his intervention, of which he had made no secret, should produce no visible effect. He kept Lieut. D'Hubert a few minutes longer, and dismissed him kindly.

"Take a few days more in bed, Lieutenant. What the devil does the surgeon mean by reporting you fit for duty?"

On coming out of the colonel's quarters, Lieut. D'Hubert said nothing to the friend who was waiting outside to take him home. He said nothing to anybody. Lieut. D'Hubert made no confidences. But on the evening of that day the colonel, strolling under the elms growing near his quarters, in the company of his second in command, opened his lips.

"I've got to the bottom of this affair," he remarked.

The lieut.-colonel, a dry, brown chip of a man with short side-whiskers, pricked up his ears at that without letting a sign of curiosity escape him.

"It's no trifle," added the colonel, oracularly. The other waited for a long while before he murmured:

"Indeed, sir!"

"No trifle," repeated the colonel, looking straight before him. "I've, however, forbidden D'Hubert either to send to or receive a challenge from Feraud for the next twelve months."

He had imagined this prohibition to save the prestige a colonel should have. The result of it was to give an official seal to the mystery surrounding this deadly quarrel. Lieut. D'Hubert repelled by an impassive silence all attempts to worm the truth out of him. Lieut. Feraud, secretly uneasy at first, regained his assurance as time went on. He disguised his ignorance of the meaning of the imposed truce by slight sardonic laughs, as though he were amused by what he intended to keep to himself. "But what will you do?" his chums used to ask him. He contented himself by replying "*Qui vivra verra*" with a little truculent air. And everybody admired his discretion.

Before the end of the truce Lieut. D'Hubert got his troop. The promotion was well earned, but somehow no one seemed to expect the event. When Lieut. Feraud heard of it at a gathering of officers, he muttered through his teeth, "Is that so?" At once he unhooked his sabre from a peg near the door, buckled it on carefully, and left the company without another word. He walked home with measured steps, struck a light with his flint and steel, and lit his tallow candle. Then snatching an unlucky glass tumbler off the mantelpiece he dashed it violently on the floor.

Now that D'Hubert was an officer of superior rank there could be no question of a duel. Neither of them could send or receive a challenge without rendering himself amenable to a court-martial. It was not to be thought of. Lieut. Feraud, who for many days now had experienced no real desire to meet Lieut. D'Hubert arms in hand, chafed again at the systematic injustice of fate. "Does he think he will escape me in that way?" he thought, indignantly. He saw in this promotion an intrigue, a conspiracy, a cowardly manœuvre. That colonel knew what he was doing. He had hastened to recommend his favourite for a step. It was outrageous that a man should be able to avoid the consequences of his acts in such a dark and tortuous manner.

Of a happy-go-lucky disposition, of a temperament more pugnacious than military, Lieut. Feraud had been content to give and receive blows for sheer love of armed strife, and without much thought of advancement; but now an urgent desire to get on sprang up in his breast. This fighter by vocation resolved in his mind to seize showy occasions and to court the favourable opinion of his chiefs like a mere worldling. He knew he was as brave as any one, and never doubted his personal charm. Nevertheless, neither the bravery nor the charm seemed to work very swiftly. Lieut. Feraud's engaging, careless truculence of a *beau sabreur* underwent a change. He began to make bitter allusions to "clever fellows who stick at nothing to get on." The army was full of them, he would say; you had only to look round. But all the time he had in view one person only, his adversary, D'Hubert. Once he confided to an appreciative friend: "You see, I don't know how to fawn on the right sort of people. It isn't in my character."

He did not get his step till a week after Austerlitz. The Light Cavalry of the Grand Army had its hands very full of interesting work for a little while. Directly the pressure of professional occupation had been eased Captain Feraud took measures to arrange a meeting without loss of time. "I know my bird," he observed, grimly. "If I don't look sharp he will take care to get himself promoted over the heads of a dozen better men than himself. He's got the knack for that sort of thing."

This duel was fought in Silesia. If not fought to a finish, it was, at any rate, fought to a standstill. The weapon was the cavalry sabre, and the skill, the science, the vigour, and the determination displayed by the adversaries compelled the admiration of the beholders. It became the subject of talk on both shores of the Danube, and as far as the garrisons of Gratz and Laybach. They crossed blades seven times. Both had many cuts which bled profusely. Both refused to have the combat stopped, time after time, with what appeared the most deadly animosity. This appearance was caused on the part of Captain D'Hubert by a rational desire to be done once for all with this worry; on the part of Captain Feraud by a tremendous exaltation of his pugnacious instincts and the incitement of wounded vanity. At last, dishevelled, their shirts in rags, covered with gore and hardly able to stand, they were led away forcibly by their marvelling and horrified seconds. Later on, besieged by comrades avid of details, these gentlemen declared that they could not have allowed that sort of hacking to go on indefinitely. Asked whether the quarrel was settled this time, they gave it out as their conviction that it was a difference which could only be settled by one of the parties remaining lifeless on the ground. The sensation spread from army corps to army corps, and penetrated at last to the smallest detachments of the troops cantoned between the Rhine and the Save. In the cafés in Vienna it was generally estimated, from details to hand, that the adversaries would be able to meet again in three weeks' time on the outside. Something really transcendent in the way of duelling was expected.

These expectations were brought to naught by the necessities of the service which separated the two officers. No official notice had been taken of their quarrel. It was now the property of the army, and not to be meddled with lightly. But the story of the duel, or rather their duelling propensities, must have stood somewhat in the way of their advancement, because they were still captains when they came together again during the war with Prussia. Detached north after Jena, with the army commanded by Marshal Bernadotte, Prince of Ponte Corvo, they entered Lübeck together.

It was only after the occupation of that town that Captain Feraud found leisure to consider his future conduct in view of the fact that Captain D'Hubert had been given the position of third aide-de-camp to the marshal. He considered it a great part of a night, and in the morning summoned two sympathetic friends.

"I've been thinking it over calmly," he said, gazing at them with blood-shot, tired eyes. "I see that I must get rid of that intriguing personage. Here he's managed to sneak on to the personal staff of the marshal. It's a direct provocation to me. I can't tolerate a situation in which I am exposed any day to receive an order through him. And God knows what order, too! That sort of thing has happened once before— and that's once too often. He understands this perfectly, never fear. I can't tell you any more. Now you know what it is you have to do."

This encounter took place outside the town of Lübeck, on very open ground, selected with special care in deference to the general sentiment of the cavalry division belonging to the army corps, that this time the two officers should meet on horseback. After all, this duel was a cavalry affair, and to persist in fighting on foot would look like a slight on one's own arm of the service. The seconds, startled by the unusual nature of the suggestion, hastened to refer to their principals. Captain Feraud jumped at it with alacrity. For some obscure reason, depending, no doubt, on his psychology, he imagined himself invincible on horseback. All alone within the four walls of his room he rubbed his hands and muttered triumphantly, "Aha! my pretty staff officer, I've got you now."

Captain D'Hubert on his side, after staring hard for a considerable time at his friends, shrugged his shoulders slightly. This affair had hopelessly and unreasonably complicated his existence for him. One absurdity more or less in the development did not matter—all absurdity was distasteful to him; but, urbane as ever, he produced a faintly ironical smile, and said in his calm voice, "It certainly will do away to some extent with the monotony of the thing."

When left alone, he sat down at a table and took his head into his hands. He had not spared himself of late and the marshal had been working all his aides-de-camp particularly hard. The last three weeks of campaigning in horrible weather had affected his health. When overtired he suffered from a stitch in his wounded side, and that uncomfortable sensation always depressed him. "It's that brute's doing, too," he thought bitterly.

The day before he had received a letter from home, announcing that his only sister was going to be married. He reflected that from the time she was nineteen and he twenty-six, when he went away to garrison life in Strasbourg, he had had but two short glimpses of her. They had been great friends and confidants; and now she was going to be given away to a man whom he did not know—a very worthy fellow no doubt, but not half good enough for her. He would never see his old Léonie again. She had a capable little head, and plenty of tact; she would know how to manage the fellow, to be sure. He was easy in his mind about her happiness but he felt ousted from the first place in her thoughts which had been his ever since the girl could speak. A melancholy regret of the days of his childhood settled upon Captain D'Hubert, third aide-de-camp to the Prince of Ponte Corvo.

He threw aside the letter of congratulation he had begun to write as in duty bound, but without enthusiasm. He took a fresh piece of paper, and traced on it the words: "This is my last will and testament." Looking at these words he gave himself up to unpleasant reflection; a presentiment that he would never see the scenes of his childhood weighed down the equable spirits of Captain D'Hubert. He jumped up, pushing his chair back, yawned elaborately in sign that he didn't care anything for presentiments, and throwing himself on the bed went to sleep. During the night he shivered from time to time without waking up. In the morning he rode out of town between his two seconds, talking of indifferent things, and looking right and left with apparent detachment into the heavy morning mists shrouding the flat green fields bordered by hedges. He leaped a ditch, and saw the forms of many mounted men moving in the fog. "We are to fight before a gallery, it seems," he muttered to himself, bitterly.

His seconds were rather concerned at the state of the atmosphere, but presently a pale, sickly sun struggled out of the low vapours, and Captain D'Hubert made out, in the distance, three horsemen riding a little apart from the others. It was Captain Feraud and his seconds. He drew his sabre, and assured himself that it was properly fastened to his wrist. And now the seconds, who had been standing in close group with the heads of their horses together, separated at an easy canter, leaving a large, clear field between him and his adversary. Captain D'Hubert looked at the pale sun, at the dismal fields, and the imbecility of the impending fight filled him with desolation. From a distant part of the field a stentorian voice shouted commands at proper intervals: *Au pas— Au trot—Charrrgez!* . . . Presentiments of death don't come to a man for nothing, he thought at the very moment he put spurs to his horse.

And therefore he was more than surprised when, at the very first set-to, Captain Feraud laid himself open to a cut over the forehead, which blinding him with blood, ended the combat almost before it had fairly begun. It was impossible to go on. Captain D'Hubert, leaving his enemy swearing horribly and reeling in the saddle between his two appalled friends, leaped the ditch again into the road and trotted home with his two seconds, who seemed rather awestruck at the speedy issue of that encounter. In the evening Captain D'Hubert finished the congratulatory letter on his sister's marriage.

He finished it late. It was a long letter. Captain D'Hubert gave reins to his fancy. He told his sister that he would feel rather lonely after this great change in her life; but then the day would come for him, too, to get married. In fact, he was thinking already of the time when there would be no one left to fight with in Europe and the epoch of wars would be over. "I expect then," he wrote, "to be within measurable distance of a marshal's baton, and you will be an experienced married woman. You shall look out a wife for me. I will be, probably, bald by then, and a little *blasé*. I shall require a young girl, pretty of course, and with a large fortune, which should help me to close my glorious career in the splendour befitting my exalted rank." He ended with the information that he had just given a lesson to a worrying, quarrelsome fellow who imagined he had a grievance against him. "But if you, in the depths of your province," he continued, "ever hear it said that your brother is of a quarrelsome disposition, don't you believe it on any account. There is no saying what gossip from the army may reach your innocent ears. Whatever you hear you may rest assured that your ever-loving brother is not a duellist." Then Captain D'Hubert crumpled up the blank sheet of paper headed with the words "This is my last will and testament," and threw it in the fire with a great laugh at himself. He didn't care a snap for what that lunatic could do. He had suddenly acquired the conviction that his adversary was utterly powerless to affect his life in any sort of way; except, perhaps, in the way of putting a special excitement into the delightful, gay intervals between the campaigns.

From this on there were, however, to be no peaceful intervals in the career of Captain D'Hubert. He saw the fields of Eylau and Friedland, marched and counter-marched in the snow, in the mud, in the dust of Polish plains, picking up distinction and advancement on all the roads of North-eastern Europe. Meantime, Captain Feraud, despatched southwards with his regiment, made unsatisfactory war in Spain. It was only when the preparations for the Russian campaign began that he was ordered north again. He left the country of mantillas and oranges without regret.

The first signs of a not unbecoming baldness added to the lofty aspect of Colonel D'Hubert's forehead. This feature was no longer white and smooth as in the days of his youth; the kindly open glance of his blue eyes had grown a little hard as if from much peering through the smoke of battles. The ebony crop on Colonel Feraud's head, coarse and crinkly like a cap of horsehair, showed many silver threads about the temples. A detestable warfare of ambushes and inglorious surprises had not improved his temper. The beak-like curve of his nose was unpleasantly set off by a deep fold on each side of his mouth. The round orbits of his eyes radiated wrinkles. More than ever he recalled an irritable and staring bird—something like a cross between a parrot and an owl. He was still extremely outspoken in his dislike of "intriguing fellows." He seized every opportunity to state that he did not pick up his rank in the ante-rooms of marshals. The unlucky persons, civil or military, who, with an intention of being pleasant, begged Colonel Feraud to tell them how he came by that very apparent scar on the forehead, were astonished to find themselves snubbed in various ways, some of which were simply rude and others mysteriously sardonic. Young officers were warned kindly by their more experienced comrades not to stare openly at the colonel's scar. But indeed an officer need have been very young in his profession not to have heard the legendary tale of that duel originating in a mysterious, unforgivable offence.

· III ·

The retreat from Moscow submerged all private feelings in a sea of disaster and misery. Colonels without regiments, D'Hubert and Feraud carried the musket in the ranks of the so-called sacred battalion—a battalion recruited from officers of all arms who had no longer any troops to lead.

In that battalion promoted colonels did duty as sergeants; the generals captained the companies; a marshal of France, Prince of the Empire, commanded the whole. All had provided themselves with muskets picked up on the road, and with cartridges taken from the dead. In the general destruction of the bonds of discipline and duty holding together the companies, the battalions, the regiments, the brigades, and divisions of an armed host, this body of men put its pride in preserving some semblance of order and formation. The only stragglers were those who fell out to give up to the frost their exhausted souls. They plodded on, and their passage did not disturb the mortal silence of the plains, shining with the livid light of snows under a sky the colour of ashes. Whirlwinds ran along the fields, broke against the dark column, enveloped it in a turmoil of flying icicles, and subsided, disclosing it creeping on its tragic way without the swing and rhythm of the military pace. It struggled onwards, the men exchanging neither words nor looks; whole ranks marched touching elbow, day after day and never raising their eyes from the ground, as if lost in despairing reflections. In the dumb, black forests of pines the cracking of overloaded branches was the only sound they heard. Often from daybreak to dusk no one spoke in the whole column. It was like a *macabre* march of struggling corpses towards a distant grave. Only an alarm of Cossacks could restore to their eyes a semblance of martial resolution. The battalion faced about and deployed, or formed square under the endless fluttering of snowflakes. A cloud of horsemen with fur caps on their heads, levelled long lances, and yelled "Hurrah! Hurrah!" around their menacing immobility whence, with muffled detonations, hundreds of dark red flames darted through the air thick with falling snow. In a very few moments the horsemen would disappear, as if carried off yelling in the gale, and the sacred battalion standing still, alone in the blizzard, heard only the howling of the wind, whose blasts searched their very hearts. Then, with a cry or two of "*Vive l'Empereur!*" it would resume its march, leaving behind a few lifeless bodies lying huddled up, tiny black specks on the white immensity of the snows.

Though often marching in the ranks, or skirmishing in the woods side by side, the two officers ignored each other; this not so much from inimical intention as from a very real indifference. All their store of moral energy was expended in resisting the terrific enmity of nature and the crushing sense of irretrievable disaster. To the last they counted among the most active, the least demoralized of the battalion; their vigorous vitality invested them both with the appearance of an heroic pair in the eyes of their comrades. And they never exchanged more than a casual word or two, except one day, when skirmishing in front of the battalion against a worrying attack of cavalry, they found themselves cut off in the woods by a small party of Cossacks. A score of fur-capped, hairy horsemen rode to and fro, brandishing their lances in ominous silence; but the two officers had no mind to lay down their arms, and Colonel Feraud suddenly spoke up in a hoarse, growling voice, bringing his firelock to the shoulder. "You take the nearest brute, Colonel D'Hubert; I'll settle the next one. I am a better shot than you are."

Colonel D'Hubert nodded over his levelled musket. Their shoulders were pressed against the trunk of a large tree; on their front enormous snowdrifts protected them from a direct charge. Two carefully aimed shots rang out in the frosty air, two Cossacks reeled in their saddles. The rest, not thinking the game good enough, closed round their wounded comrades and galloped away out of range. The two officers managed to rejoin their battalion halted for the night. During that afternoon they had leaned upon each other more than once, and towards the end, Colonel D'Hubert, whose long legs gave him an advantage in walking through soft snow, peremptorily took the musket of Colonel Feraud from him and carried it on his shoulder, using his own as a staff.

On the outskirts of a village half buried in the snow an old wooden barn burned with a clear and an immense flame. The sacred battalion of skeletons, muffled in rags, crowded greedily the windward side, stretching hundreds of numbed, bony hands to the blaze. Nobody had noted their approach. Before entering the circle of light playing on the sunken, glassy-eyed, starved faces, Colonel D'Hubert spoke in his turn:

"Here's your musket, Colonel Feraud. I can walk better than you."

Colonel Feraud nodded, and pushed on towards the warmth of the fierce flames. Colonel D'Hubert was more deliberate, but not the less bent on getting a place in the front rank. Those they shouldered aside tried to greet with a faint cheer the reappearance of the two indomitable companions in activity and endurance. Those manly qualities had never perhaps received a higher tribute than this feeble acclamation.

This is the faithful record of speeches exchanged during the retreat from Moscow by Colonels Feraud and D'Hubert. Colonel Feraud's taciturnity was the outcome of concentrated rage. Short, hairy, black faced, with layers of grime and the thick sprouting of a wiry beard, a frost-bitten hand wrapped up in filthy rags carried in a sling, he accused fate of unparalleled perfidy towards the sublime Man of Destiny. Colonel D'Hubert, his long moustaches pendent in icicles on each side of his cracked blue lips, his eyelids inflamed with the glare of snows, the principal part of his costume consisting of a sheepskin coat looted with difficulty from the frozen corpse of a camp follower found in an abandoned cart, took a more thoughtful view of events. His regularly handsome features, now reduced to mere bony lines and fleshless hollows, looked out of a woman's black velvet hood, over which was rammed forcibly a cocked hat picked up under the wheels of an empty army fourgon, which must have contained at one time some general officer's luggage. The sheepskin coat being short for a man of his inches ended very high up, and the skin of his legs, blue with the cold, showed through the tatters of his nether garments. This under the circumstances provoked neither jeers nor pity. No one cared how the next man felt or looked. Colonel D'Hubert himself, hardened to exposure, suffered mainly in his self-respect from the lamentable indecency of his costume. A thoughtless person may think that with a whole host of inanimate bodies bestrewing the path of retreat there could not have been much difficulty in supplying the deficiency. But to loot a pair of breeches from a frozen corpse is not so easy as it may appear to a mere theorist. It requires time and labour. You must remain behind while your companions march on. Colonel D'Hubert had his scruples as to falling out. Once he had stepped aside he could not be sure of ever rejoining his battalion; and the ghastly intimacy of a wrestling match with the frozen dead opposing the unyielding rigidity of iron to your violence was repugnant to the delicacy of his feelings. Luckily, one day, grubbing in a mound of snow between the huts of a village in the hope of finding there a frozen potato or some vegetable garbage he could put between his long and shaky teeth, Colonel D'Hubert uncovered a couple of mats of the sort Russian peasants use to line the sides of their carts with. These, beaten free of frozen snow, bent about his elegant person and fastened solidly round his waist, made a bell-shaped nether garment, a sort of stiff petticoat, which rendered Colonel D'Hubert a perfectly decent, but a much more noticeable figure than before.

Thus accoutred, he continued to retreat, never doubting of his personal escape, but full of other misgivings. The early buoyancy of his belief in the future was destroyed. If the road of glory led through such unforeseen passages, he asked himself—for he was reflective—whether the guide was altogether trustworthy. It was a patriotic sadness, not unmingled with some personal concern, and quite unlike the unreasoning indignation against men and things nursed by Colonel Feraud. Recruiting his strength in a little German town for three weeks, Colonel D'Hubert was surprised to discover within himself a love of repose. His returning vigour was strangely pacific in its aspirations. He meditated silently upon this bizarre change of mood. No doubt many of his brother officers of field rank went through the same moral experience. But these were not the times to talk of it. In one of his letters home Colonel D'Hubert wrote, "All your plans, my dear Léonie, for marrying me to the charming girl you have discovered in your neighbourhood, seem farther off than ever. Peace is not yet. Europe wants another lesson. It will be a hard task for us, but it shall be done, because the Emperor is invincible."

Thus wrote Colonel D'Hubert from Pomerania to his married sister Léonie, settled in the south of France. And so far the sentiments expressed would not have been disowned by Colonel Feraud, who wrote no letters to anybody, whose father had been in life an illiterate blacksmith, who had no sister or brother, and whom no one desired ardently to pair off for a life of peace with a charming young girl. But Colonel D'Hubert's letter contained also some philosophical generalities upon the uncertainty of all personal hopes, when bound up entirely with the prestigious fortune of one incomparably great it is true, yet still remaining but a man in his greatness. This view would have appeared rank heresy to Colonel Feraud. Some melancholy forebodings of a military kind, expressed cautiously, would have been pronounced as nothing short of high treason by Colonel Feraud. But Léonie, the sister of Colonel D'Hubert, read them with profound satisfaction, and, folding the letter thoughtfully, remarked to herself that "Armand was likely to prove eventually a sensible fellow." Since her marriage into a Southern family she had become a convinced believer in the return of the legitimate king. Hopeful and anxious she offered prayers night and morning, and burnt candles in churches for the safety and prosperity of her brother.

She had every reason to suppose that her prayers were heard. Colonel D'Hubert passed through Lutzen, Bautzen, and Leipsic losing no limb, and acquiring additional reputation. Adapting his conduct to the needs of that desperate time, he had never voiced his misgivings. He concealed them under a cheerful courtesy of such pleasant character that people were inclined to ask themselves with wonder whether Colonel D'Hubert was aware of any disasters. Not only his manners, but even his glances remained untroubled. The steady amenity of his blue eyes disconcerted all grumblers, and made despair itself pause.

This bearing was remarked favourably by the Emperor himself; for Colonel D'Hubert, attached now to the Major-General's staff, came on several occasions under the imperial eye. But it exasperated the higher strung nature of Colonel Feraud. Passing through Magdeburg on service, this last allowed himself, while seated gloomily at dinner with the *Commandant de Place,* to say of his life-long adversary: "This man does not love the Emperor," and his words were received by the other guests in profound silence. Colonel Feraud, troubled in his conscience at the atrocity of the aspersion felt the need to back it up by a good argument. "I ought to know him," he cried, adding some oaths. "One studies one's adversary. I have met him on the ground half a dozen times, as all the army knows. What more do you want? If that isn't opportunity enough for any fool to size up his man, may the devil take me if I can tell what is." And he looked around the table, obstinate and sombre.

Later on in Paris, while extremely busy reorganizing his regiment, Colonel Feraud learned that Colonel D'Hubert had been made a general. He glared at his informant incredulously, then folded his arms and turned away muttering, "Nothing surprises me on the part of that man."

And aloud he added, speaking over his shoulder, "You would oblige me greatly by telling General D'Hubert at the first opportunity that his advancement saves him for a time from a pretty hot encounter. I was only waiting for him to turn up here."

The other officer remonstrated.

"Could you think of it, Colonel Feraud, at this time, when every life should be consecrated to the glory and safety of France?"

But the strain of unhappiness caused by military reverses had spoiled Colonel Feraud's character. Like many other men, he was rendered wicked by misfortune.

"I cannot consider General D'Hubert's existence of any account either for the glory or safety of France," he snapped viciously. "You don't pretend, perhaps, to know him better than I do—I who have met him half a dozen times on the ground—do you?"

His interlocutor, a young man, was silenced. Colonel Feraud walked up and down the room.

"This is not the time to mince matters," he said. "I can't believe that that man ever loved the Emperor. He picked up his general's stars under the boots of Marshal Berthier. Very well. I'll get mine in another fashion, and then we shall settle this business which has been dragging on too long."

General D'Hubert, informed indirectly of Colonel Feraud's attitude, made a gesture as if to put aside an importunate person. His thoughts were solicited by graver cares. He had had no time to go and see his family. His sister, whose royalist hopes were rising higher every day, though proud of her brother, regretted his recent advancement in a measure, because it put on him a prominent mark of the usurper's favour, which later on could have an adverse influence upon his career. He wrote to her that no one but an inveterate enemy could say he had got his promotion by favour. As to his career, he assured her that he looked no farther forward into the future than the next battlefield.

Beginning the campaign of France in this dogged spirit, General D'Hubert was wounded on the second day of the battle under Laon. While being carried off the field he heard that Colonel Feraud, promoted this moment to general, had been sent to replace him at the head of his brigade. He cursed his luck impulsively, not being able at the first glance to discern all the advantages of a nasty wound. And yet it was by this heroic method that Providence was shaping his future. Travelling slowly south to his sister's country home under the care of a trusty old servant, General D'Hubert was spared the humiliating contacts and the perplexities of conduct which assailed the men of Napoleonic empire at the moment of its downfall. Lying in his bed, with the windows of his room open wide to the sunshine of Provence, he perceived the undisguised aspect of the blessing conveyed by that jagged fragment of a Prussian shell, which, killing his horse and ripping open his thigh, saved him from an active conflict with his conscience. After the last fourteen years spent sword in hand in the saddle, and with the sense of his duty done to the very end, General D'Hubert found resignation an easy virtue. His sister was delighted with his reasonableness. "I leave myself altogether in your hands, my dear Léonie," he had said to her.

He was still laid up when, the credit of his brother-in-law's family being exerted on his behalf, he received from the royal government not only the confirmation of his rank, but the assurance of being retained on the active list. To this was added an unlimited convalescent leave. The unfavourable opinion entertained of him in Bonapartist circles, though it rested on nothing more solid than the unsupported pronouncement of General Feraud, was directly responsible for General D'Hubert's retention on the active list. As to General Feraud, his rank was confirmed, too. It was more than he dared to expect; but Marshal Soult, then Minister of War to the restored king, was partial to officers who had served in Spain. Only not even the marshal's protection could secure for him active employment. He remained irreconcilable, idle, and sinister. He sought in obscure restaurants the company of other half-pay officers who cherished dingy but glorious old tricolour cockades in their breast-pockets, and buttoned with the forbidden eagle buttons their shabby uniforms, declaring themselves too poor to afford the expense of the prescribed change.

The triumphant return from Elba, a historical fact as marvelous and incredible as the exploits of some mythological demi-god, found General D'Hubert still quite unable to sit a horse. Neither could he walk very well. These disabilities, which Madame Léonie accounted most lucky, helped to keep her brother out of all possible mischief. His frame of mind at that time, she noted with dismay, became very far from reasonable. This general officer, still menaced by the loss of a limb, was discovered one night in the stables of the Château by a groom, who, seeing a light, raised an alarm of thieves. His crutch was lying half-buried in the straw of the litter, and the general was hopping on one leg in a loose box around a snorting horse he was trying to saddle. Such were the effects of imperial magic upon a calm temperament and a pondered mind. Beset in the light of stable lanterns, by the tears, entreaties, indignation, remonstrances and reproaches of his family, he got out of the difficult situation by fainting away there and then in the arms of his nearest relatives, and was carried off to bed. Before he got out of it again, the second time reign of Napoleon, the Hundred Days of feverish agitation and supreme effort, passed away like a terrifying dream. The tragic year 1815, begun in the trouble and unrest of consciences, was ending in vengeful proscriptions.

How General Feraud escaped the clutches of the Special Commission and the last offices of a firing squad he never knew himself. It was partly due to the subordinate position he was assigned during the Hundred Days. The Emperor had never given him active command, but had kept him busy at the cavalry depôt in Paris, mounting and despatching hastily drilled troopers into the field. Considering this task as unworthy of his abilities, he had discharged it with no offensively noticeable zeal; but for the greater part he was saved from the excesses of Royalist reaction by the interference of General D'Hubert.

This last, still on convalescent leave, but able now to travel, had been dispatched by his sister to Paris to present himself to this legitimate sovereign. As no one in the capital could possibly know anything of the episode in the stable he was received there with distinction. Military to the very bottom of his soul, the prospect of rising in his profession consoled him from finding himself the butt of Bonapartist malevolence, which pursued him with a persistence he could not account for. All the rancour of that embittered and persecuted party pointed to him as the man who had *never* loved the Emperor—a sort of monster essentially worse than a mere betrayer.

General D'Hubert shrugged his shoulders without anger at this ferocious prejudice. Rejected by his old friends, and mistrusting profoundly the advances of Royalist society, the young and handsome general (he was barely forty) adopted a manner of cold, punctilious courtesy, which at the merest shadow of an intended slight passed easily into harsh haughtiness. Thus prepared, General D'Hubert went about his affairs in Paris feeling inwardly very happy with the peculiar uplifting happiness of a man very much in love. The charming girl looked out by his sister had come upon the scene, and had conquered him in the thorough manner in which a young girl by merely existing in his sight can make a man of forty her own. They were going to be married as soon as General D'Hubert had obtained his official nomination to a promised command.

One afternoon, sitting on the *terrasse* of the *Café Tortoni*, General D'Hubert learned from the conversation of two strangers occupying a table near his own, that General Feraud, included in the batch of superior officers arrested after the second return of the king, was in danger of passing before the Special Commission. Living all his spare moments, as is frequently the case with expectant lovers, a day in advance of reality, and in a state of bestarred hallucination, it required nothing less than the name of his perpetual antagonist pronounced in a loud voice to call the youngest of Napoleon's generals away from the mental contemplation of his betrothed. He looked round. The strangers wore civilian clothes. Lean and weather-beaten, lolling back in their chairs, they scowled at people with moody and defiant abstraction from under their hats pulled low over their eyes. It was not difficult to recognize them for two of the compulsorily retired officers of the Old Guard. As from bravado or carelessness they chose to speak in loud tones, General D'Hubert, who saw no reason why he should change his seat, heard every word. They did not seem to be the personal friends of General Feraud. His name came up amongst others. Hearing it repeated, General D'Hubert's tender anticipations of a domestic future adorned with a woman's grace were traversed by the harsh regret of his warlike past, of that one long, intoxicating clash of arms, unique in the magnitude of its glory and disaster—the marvellous work and the special possession of his own generation. He felt an irrational tenderness towards his old adversary and appreciated emotionally the murderous absurdity their encounter had introduced into his life. It was like an additional pinch of spice in a hot dish. He remembered the flavour with sudden melancholy. He would never taste it again. It was all over. "I fancy it was being left lying in the garden that had exasperated him so against me from the first," he thought, indulgently.

The two strangers at the next table had fallen silent after the third mention of General Feraud's name. Presently the elder of the two, speaking again in a bitter tone, affirmed that General Feraud's account was settled. And why? Simply because he was not like some bigwigs who loved only themselves. The Royalists knew they could never make anything of him. He loved *The Other* too well.

The Other was the Man of St. Helena. The two officers nodded and touched glasses before they drank to an impossible return. Then the same who had spoken before, remarked with a sardonic laugh, "His adversary showed more cleverness."

"What adversary?" asked the younger, as if puzzled.

"Don't you know? They were two hussars. At each promotion they fought a duel. Haven't you heard of the duel going on ever since 1801?"

The other had heard of the duel, of course. Now he understood the allusion. General Baron D'Hubert would be able now to enjoy his fat king's favour in peace.

"Much good may it do to him," mumbled the elder.

"They were both brave men. I never saw this D'Hubert—a sort of intriguing dandy, I am told. But I can well believe what I've heard Feraud say of him—that he *never* loved the Emperor."

They rose and went away.

General D'Hubert experienced the horror of a somnambulist who wakes up from a complacent dream of activity to find himself walking on a quagmire. A profound disgust of the ground on which he was making his way overcame him. Even the image of the charming girl was swept from his view in the flood of moral distress. Everything he had ever been or hoped to be would taste of bitter ignominy unless he could manage to save General Feraud from the fate which threatened so many braves. Under the impulse of this almost morbid need to attend to the safety of his adversary, General D'Hubert worked so well with hands and feet (as the French saying is), that in less than twenty-four hours he found means of obtaining an extraordinary private audience from the Minister of Police.

General Baron D'Hubert was shown in suddenly without preliminaries. In the dusk of the Minister's cabinet, behind the forms of writing-desk, chairs, and tables, between two bunches of wax candles blazing in sconces, he beheld a figure in a gorgeous coat posturing before a tall mirror. The old *conventionnel* Fouché, Senator of the Empire, traitor to every man, to every principle and motive of human conduct, Duke of Otranto, and the wily artizan of the second Restoration, was trying the fit of a court suit in which his young and accomplished *fiancée* had declared her intention to have his portrait painted on porcelain. It was a caprice, a charming fancy which the first Minister of Police of the second Restoration was anxious to gratify. For that man, often compared in wiliness of conduct to a fox, but whose ethical side could be worthily symbolized by nothing less emphatic than a skunk, was as much possessed by his love as General D'Hubert himself.

Startled to be discovered thus by the blunder of a servant, he met this little vexation with the characteristic impudence which had served his turn so well in the endless intrigues of his self-seeking career. Without altering his attitude a hair's-breadth, one leg in a silk stocking advanced, his head twisted over his left shoulder, he called out calmly, "This way, General. Pray approach. Well? I am all attention."

While General D'Hubert, ill at ease as if one of his own little weaknesses had been exposed, presented his request as shortly as possible, the Duke of Otranto went on feeling the fit of his collar, settling the lapels before the glass, and buckling his back in an effort to behold the set of the gold embroidered coat-skirts behind. His still face, his attentive eyes, could not have expressed a more complete interest in those matters if he had been alone.

"Exclude from the operations of the Special Court a certain Feraud, Gabriel Florian, General of brigade of the promotion of 1814?" he repeated, in a slightly wondering tone, and then turned away from the glass. "Why exclude *him* precisely?"

"I am surprised that your Excellency, so competent in the evaluation of men of his time, should have thought worth while to have that name put down on the list."

"A rabid Bonapartist!"

"So is every grenadier and every trooper of the army, as your Excellency well knows. And the individuality of General Feraud can have no more weight than that of any casual grenadier. He is a man of no mental grasp, of no capacity whatever. It is inconceivable that he should ever have any influence."

"He has a well-hung tongue, though," interjected Fouché.

"Noisy, I admit, but not dangerous."

"I will not dispute with you. I know next to nothing of him. Hardly his name, in fact."

"And yet your Excellency has the presidency of the Commission charged by the king to point out those who were to be tried," said General D'Hubert, with an emphasis which did not miss the minister's ear.

"Yes, General," he said, walking away into the dark part of the vast room, and throwing himself into a deep armchair that swallowed him up, all but the soft gleam of gold embroideries and the pallid patch of the face—"yes, General. Take this chair there."

General D'Hubert sat down.

"Yes, General," continued the arch-master in the arts of intrigue and betrayals, whose duplicity, as if at times intolerable to his self-knowledge, found relief in bursts of cynical openness. "I did hurry on the formation of the proscribing Commission, and I took its presidency. And do you know why? Simply from fear that if I did not take it quickly into my hands my own name would head the list of the proscribed. Such are the times in which we live. But I am minister of the king yet, and I ask you plainly why I should take the name of this obscure Feraud off the list? You wonder how his name got there! Is it possible that you should know men so little? My dear General, at the very first sitting of the Commission names poured on us like rain off the roof of the Tuileries. Names! We had our choice of thousands. How do you know that the name of this Feraud, whose life or death don't matter to France, does not keep out some other name?"

The voice out of the armchair stopped. Opposite General D'Hubert sat still, shadowy and silent. Only his sabre clinked slightly. The voice in the armchair began again. "And we must try to satisfy the exigencies of the Allied Sovereigns, too. The Prince de Talleyrand told me only yesterday that Nesselrode had informed him officially of His Majesty the Emperor Alexander's dissatisfaction at the small number of examples the Government of the king intends to make—especially amongst military men. I tell you this confidentially."

"Upon my word!" broke out General D'Hubert, speaking through his teeth, "if your Excellency deigns to favour me with any more confidential information I don't know what I will do. It's enough to break one's sword over one's knee, and fling the pieces. . . ."

"What government you imagined yourself to be serving?" interrupted the minister, sharply.

After a short pause the crestfallen voice of General D'Hubert answered, "The Government of France."

"That's paying your conscience off with mere words, General. The truth is that you are serving a government of returned exiles, of men who have been without country for twenty years. Of men also who have just got over a very bad and humiliating fright. . . . Have no illusions on that score."

The Duke of Otranto ceased. He had relieved himself, and had attained his object of stripping some self-respect off that man who had inconveniently discovered him posturing in a gold-embroidered court costume before a mirror. But they were a hot-headed lot in the army; it occurred to him that it would be inconvenient if a well-disposed general officer, received in audience on the recommendation of one of the Princes, were to do something rashly scandalous directly after a private interview with the minister. In a changed tone he put a question to the point: "Your relation—this Feraud?"

"No. No relation at all."

"Intimate friend?"

"Intimate . . . yes. There is between us an intimate connection of a nature which makes it a point of honour with me to try . . ."

The minister rang a bell without waiting for the end of the phrase. When the servant had gone out, after bringing in a pair of heavy silver candelabra for the writing-desk, the Duke of Otranto rose, his breast glistening all over with gold in the strong light, and taking a piece of paper out of a drawer, held it in his hand ostentatiously while he said with persuasive gentleness: "You must not speak of breaking your sword across your knee, General. Perhaps you would never get another. The Emperor will not return this time. . . . *Diable d'homme!* There was just a moment, here in Paris, soon after Waterloo, when he frightened me.

It looked as though he were ready to begin all over again. Luckily one never does begin all over again, really. You must not think of breaking your sword, General."

General D'Hubert, looking on the ground, moved slightly his hand in a hopeless gesture of renunciation. The Minister of Police turned his eyes away from him, and scanned deliberately the paper he had been holding up all the time.

"There are only twenty general officers selected to be made an example of. Twenty. A round number. And let's see, Feraud. . . . Ah, he's there. Gabriel Florian. *Parfaitement.* That's your man. Well, there will be only nineteen examples made now."

General D'Hubert stood up feeling as though he had gone through an infectious illness. "I must beg your Excellency to keep my interference a profound secret. I attach the greatest importance to his never learning . . ."

"Who is going to inform him, I should like to know?" said Fouché, raising his eyes curiously to General D'Hubert's tense, set face. "Take one of these pens, and run it through the name yourself. This is the only list in existence. If you are careful to take up enough ink no one will be able to tell what was the name struck out. But, *par exemple,* I am not responsible for what Clarke will do with him afterwards. If he persists in being rabid he will be ordered by the Minister of War to reside in some provincial town under the supervision of the police."

A few days later General D'Hubert was saying to his sister, after the first greetings had been got over: "Ah, my dear Léonie! it seemed to me I couldn't get away from Paris quick enough."

"Effect of love," she suggested, with a malicious smile.

"And horror," added General D'Hubert, with profound seriousness. "I have nearly died there of . . . of nausea."

His face was contracted with disgust. And as his sister looked at him attentively he continued, "I have had to see Fouché. I have had an audience. I have been in his cabinet. There remains with one, who had the misfortune to breathe the air of the same room with that man, a sense of diminished dignity, an uneasy feeling of being not so clean, after all, as one hoped one was. . . . But you can't understand."

She nodded quickly several times. She understood very well, on the contrary. She knew her brother thoroughly, and liked him as he was. Moreover, the scorn and loathing of mankind were the lot of the *Jacobin*

Fouché, who, exploiting for his own advantage every weakness, every virtue, every generous illusion of mankind, made dupes of his whole generation, and died obscurely as Duke of Otranto.

"My dear Armand," she said, compassionately, "what could you want from that man?"

"Nothing less than a life," answered General D'Hubert. "And I've got it. It had to be done. But I feel yet as if I could never forgive the necessity to the man I had to save."

General Feraud, totally unable (as is the case with most of us) to comprehend what was happening to him, received the Minister of War's order to proceed at once to a small town of Central France with feelings whose natural expression consisted in a fierce rolling of the eye and savage grinding of the teeth. The passing away of the state of war, the only condition of society he had ever known, the horrible view of a world at peace, frightened him. He went away to his little town firmly convinced that this could not last. There he was informed of his retirement from the army, and that his pension (calculated on the scale of a colonel's rank) was made dependent on the correctness of his conduct, and on the good reports of the police. No longer in the army! He felt suddenly strange to the earth, like a disembodied spirit. It was impossible to exist. But at first he reacted from sheer incredulity. This could not be. He waited for thunder, earthquakes, natural cataclysms; but nothing happened. The leaden weight of an irremediable idleness descended upon General Feraud, who having no resources within himself sank into a state of awe-inspiring hebetude. He haunted the streets of the little town, gazing before him with lacklustre eyes, disregarding the hats raised on his passage; and people, nudging each other as he went by, whispered, "That's poor General Feraud. His heart is broken. Behold how he loved the Emperor."

The other living wreckage of Napoleonic tempest clustered round General Feraud with infinite respect. He, himself, imagined his soul to be crushed by grief. He suffered from quickly succeeding impulses to weep, to howl, to bite his fists till blood came, to spend days on his bed with his head thrust under the pillow; but these arose from sheer ennui, from the anguish of an immense, indescribable, inconceivable boredom. His mental inability to grasp the hopeless nature of his case as a whole saved him from suicide. He never even thought of it once. He thought of nothing. But his appetite abandoned him, and the difficulty he experienced to express the overwhelming nature of his feelings (the most furious swearing could do no justice to it) induced gradually a habit of silence—a sort of death to a southern temperament.

Great, therefore, was the sensation amongst the *anciens militaires* frequenting a certain little café full of flies when one stuffy afternoon "that poor General Feraud" let out suddenly a volley of formidable curses.

He had been sitting quietly in his own privileged corner looking through the Paris gazettes with just as much interest as a condemned man on the eve of execution could be expected to show in the news of the day. A cluster of martial, bronzed faces, amongst which there was one lacking an eye, and another the tip of a nose, frost-bitten in Russia, surrounded him anxiously.

"What's the matter, General?"

General Feraud sat erect, holding the folded newspaper at arm's length in order to make out the small print better. He read to himself, over again, fragments of the intelligence which had caused, what may be called his resurrection.

"*We are informed that General d'Hubert, till now on sick leave in the south, is to be called to the command of the 5th Cavalry brigade in . . .*"

He dropped the paper stonily. . . . "Called to the command" . . . and suddenly gave his forehead a mighty slap. "I had almost forgotten him," he muttered, in a conscience-stricken tone.

A deep-chested veteran shouted across the café: "Some new villainy of the Government, General?"

"The villainies of these scoundrels," thundered General Feraud, "are innumerable. One more, one less!" . . . He lowered his tone. "But I will set good order to one of them at least."

He looked all round the faces. "There's a pomaded, curled staff officer, the darling of some of the marshals who sold their father for a handful of English gold. He will find out presently that I am alive yet," he declared, in a dogmatic tone. "However, this is a private affair. An old affair of honour. Bah! Our honour does not matter. Here we are driven off with a split ear like a lot of cast troop horses—good only for a knacker's yard. But it would be like striking a blow for the Emperor. . . . Messieurs, I shall require the assistance of two of you."

Every man moved forward. General Feraud, deeply touched by this demonstration, called with visible emotion upon the one-eyed veteran cuirassier and the officer of the Chasseurs à Cheval who had left the tip of his nose in Russia. He excused his choice to the others.

"A cavalry affair this—you know."

He was answered with a varied chorus of *"Parfaitement, mon Général. . . . C'est juste. . . . Parbleu, c'est connu. . . ."* Everybody was satisfied. The three left the café together, followed by cries of *"Bonne chance."*

Outside they linked arms, the general in the middle. The three rusty cocked hats worn *en bataille* with a sinister forward slant barred the narrow street nearly right across. The overheated little town of grey stones and red tiles was drowsing away its provincial afternoon under a blue sky. The loud blows of a cooper hooping a cask reverberated regularly between the houses. The general dragged his left foot a little in the shade of the walls.

"This damned winter of 1813 has got into my bones for good. Never mind. We must take pistols, that's all. A little lumbago. We must have pistols. He's game for my bag. My eyes are as keen as ever. You should have seen me in Russia picking off the dodging Cossacks with a beastly old infantry musket. I have a natural gift for firearms."

In this strain General Feraud ran on, holding up his head, with owlish eyes and rapacious beak. A mere fighter all his life, a cavalry man, a *sabreur*, he conceived war with the utmost simplicity, as, in the main, a massed lot of personal contests, a sort of gregarious duelling. And here he had in hand a war of his own. He revived. The shadow of peace passed away from him like the shadow of death. It was the marvellous resurrection of the named Feraud, Gabriel Florian, *engagé volontaire* of 1793, General of 1814, buried without ceremony by means of a service order signed by the War Minister of the Second Restoration.

· IV ·

No man succeeds in everything he undertakes. In that sense we are all failures. The great point is not to fail in ordering and sustaining the effort of our life. In this matter vanity is what leads us astray. It hurries us into situations from which we must come out damaged; whereas pride is our safeguard, by the reserve it imposes on the choice of our endeavour as much as by the virtue of its sustaining power.

General D'Hubert was proud and reserved. He had not been damaged by his casual love affairs, successful or otherwise. In his war-scarred body his heart at forty remained unscratched. Entering with reserve into his sister's matrimonial plans, he had felt himself falling irremediably in love as one falls off a roof. He was too proud to be frightened. Indeed, the sensation was too delightful to be alarming.

The inexperience of a man of forty is a much more serious thing than the inexperience of a youth of twenty, for it is not helped out by the rashness of hot blood. The girl was mysterious, as young girls are by the mere effect of their guarded ingenuity; and to him the mysteriousness of that young girl appeared exceptional and fascinating. But there was nothing mysterious about the arrangements of the match which Madame Léonie had promoted. There was nothing peculiar, either. It was a very appropriate match, commending itself extremely to the young lady's mother (the father was dead) and tolerable to the young lady's uncle—an old *émigré* lately returned from Germany, and pervading, cane in hand, a lean ghost of the *ancien régime,* the garden walks of the young lady's ancestral home.

General D'Hubert was not the man to be satisfied merely with the woman and the fortune—when it came to the point. His pride (and pride aims always at true success) would be satisfied with nothing short of love. But as true pride excludes vanity, he could not imagine any reason why this mysterious creature with deep and brilliant eyes of a violet colour should have any feeling for him warmer than indifference. The young lady (her name was Adèle) baffled every attempt at a clear understanding on that point. It is true that the attempts were clumsy and made timidly, because by then General D'Hubert had become acutely aware of the number of his years, of his wounds, of his many moral imperfections, of his secret unworthiness—and had incidentally learned by experience the meaning of the word funk. As far as he could make out she seemed to imply that, with an unbounded confidence in her mother's affection and sagacity, she felt no unsurmountable dislike for the person of General D'Hubert; and that this was quite sufficient for a well-brought-up young lady to begin married life upon. This view hurt and tormented the pride of General D'Hubert. And yet he asked himself, with a sort of sweet despair, what more could he expect? She had a quiet and luminous forehead. Her violet eyes laughed while the lines of her lips and chin remained composed in admirable gravity. All this was set off by such a glorious mass of fair hair, by a complexion so marvellous, by such a grace of expression, that General D'Hubert really never found the opportunity to examine with sufficient detachment the lofty exigencies of his pride. In fact, he became shy of that line of inquiry since it had led once or twice to a crisis of solitary passion in which it was borne upon him that he loved her enough to kill her rather than lose her. From such passages, not unknown to men of forty, he would come out broken, exhausted, remorseful, a little dismayed. He derived, however, considerable comfort from the quietist practice of sitting now and then half the night by an open window and meditating upon the wonder of her existence, like a believer lost in the mystic contemplation of his faith.

It must not be supposed that all these variations of his inward state were made manifest to the world. General D'Hubert found no difficulty in appearing wreathed in smiles. Because, in fact, he was very happy. He followed the established rules of his condition, sending over flowers (from his sister's garden and hot-houses) early every morning, and a little later following himself to lunch with his intended, her mother, and her *émigré* uncle. The middle of the day was spent in strolling or sitting in the shade. A watchful deference, trembling on the verge of tenderness was the note of their intercourse on his side—with a playful turn of the phrase concealing the profound trouble of his whole being caused by her inaccessible nearness. Late in the afternoon General D'Hubert walked home between the fields of vines, sometimes intensely miserable, sometimes supremely happy, sometimes pensively sad; but always feeling a special intensity of existence, that elation common to artists, poets, and lovers—to men haunted by a great passion, a noble thought, or a new vision of plastic beauty.

The outward world at that time did not exist with any special distinctness for General D'Hubert. One evening, however, crossing a ridge from which he could see both houses, General D'Hubert became aware of two figures far down the road. The day had been divine. The festal decoration of the inflamed sky lent a gentle glow to the sober tints of the southern land. The grey rocks, the brown fields, the purple, undulating distances harmonized in luminous accord, exhaled already the scents of the evening. The two figures down the road presented themselves like two rigid and wooden silhouettes all black on the ribbon of white dust. General D'Hubert made out the long, straight, military *capotes* buttoned closely right up to the black stocks, the cocked hats, the lean, carven, brown countenances—old soldiers—*vieilles moustaches!* The taller of the two had a black patch over one eye; the other's hard, dry countenance presented some bizarre, disquieting peculiarity, which on nearer approach proved to be the absence of the tip of the nose. Lifting their hands with one movement to salute the slightly lame civilian walking with a thick stick, they inquired for the house where the General Baron D'Hubert lived, and what was the best way to get speech with him quietly.

"If you think this quiet enough," said General D'Hubert, looking round at the vine-fields, framed in purple lines, and dominated by the nest of grey and drab walls of a village clustering around the top of a conical hill, so that the blunt church tower seemed but the shape of a crowning rock—"if you think this spot quiet enough, you can speak to him at once. And I beg you, comrades, to speak openly, with perfect confidence."

They stepped back at this, and raised again their hands to their hats with marked ceremoniousness. Then the one with the chipped nose, speaking for both, remarked that the matter was confidential enough, and to be arranged discreetly. Their general quarters were established in that village over there, where the infernal clodhoppers—damn their false, Royalist hearts!—looked remarkably cross-eyed at three unassuming military men. For the present he should only ask for the name of General D'Hubert's friends.

"What friends?" said the astonished General D'Hubert, completely off the track. "I am staying with my brother-in-law over there."

"Well, he will do for one," said the chipped veteran.

"We're the friends of General Feraud," interjected the other, who had kept silent till then, only glowering with his one eye at the man who had *never* loved the Emperor. That was something to look at. For even the gold-laced Judases who had sold him to the English, the marshals and princes, had loved him at some time or other. But this man had *never* loved the Emperor. General Feraud had said so distinctly.

General D'Hubert felt an inward blow in his chest. For an infinitesimal fraction of a second it was as if the spinning of the earth had become perceptible with an awful, slight rustle in the eternal stillness of space. But this noise of blood in his ears passed off at once. Involuntarily he murmured, "Feraud! I had forgotten his existence."

"He's existing at present, very uncomfortably, it is true, in the infamous inn of that nest of savages up there," said the one-eyed cuirassier, drily. "We arrived in your parts an hour ago on post horses. He's awaiting our return with impatience. There is hurry, you know. The General has broken the ministerial order to obtain from you the satisfaction he's entitled to by the laws of honour, and naturally he's anxious to have it all over before the *gendarmerie* gets on his scent."

The other elucidated the idea a little further. "Get back on the quiet— you understand? Phitt! No one the wiser. We have broken out, too. Your friend the king would be glad to cut off our scurvy pittances at the first chance. It's a risk. But honour before everything."

General D'Hubert had recovered his powers of speech. "So you come here like this along the road to invite me to a throat-cutting match with that—that . . ." A laughing sort of rage took possession of him. "Ha! ha! ha! ha!"

His fists on his hips, he roared without restraint, while they stood before him lank and straight, as though they had been shot up with a snap through a trap door in the ground. Only four-and-twenty months ago the masters of Europe, they had already the air of antique ghosts, they seemed less substantial in their faded coats than their own narrow shadows falling so black across the white road: the military and grotesque shadows of twenty years of war and conquests. They had an outlandish appearance of two imperturbable bonzes of the religion of the sword. And General D'Hubert, also one of the ex-masters of Europe, laughed at these serious phantoms standing in his way.

Said one, indicating the laughing General with a jerk of the head: "A merry companion, that."

"There are some of us that haven't smiled from the day The Other went away," remarked his comrade.

A violent impulse to set upon and beat those unsubstantial wraiths to the ground frightened General D'Hubert. He ceased laughing suddenly. His desire now was to get rid of them, to get them away from his sight quickly before he lost control of himself. He wondered at the fury he felt rising in his breast. But he had no time to look into that peculiarity just then.

"I understand your wish to be done with me as quickly as possible. Don't let us waste time in empty ceremonies. Do you see that wood there at the foot of that slope? Yes, the wood of pines. Let us meet there to-morrow at sunrise. I will bring with me my sword or my pistols, or both if you like."

The seconds of General Feraud looked at each other.

"Pistols, General," said the cuirassier.

"So be it. Au revoir—to-morrow morning. Till then let me advise you to keep close if you don't want the *gendarmerie* making inquiries about you before it gets dark. Strangers are rare in this part of the country."

They saluted in silence. General D'Hubert, turning his back on their retreating forms, stood still in the middle of the road for a long time, biting his lower lip and looking on the ground. Then he began to walk straight before him, thus retracing his steps till he found himself before the park gate of his intended's house. Dusk had fallen. Motionless he stared through the bars at the front of the house, gleaming clear beyond the thickets and trees. Footsteps scrunched on the gravel, and presently a tall stooping shape emerged from the lateral alley following the inner side of the park wall.

Le Chevalier de Valmassigue, uncle of the adorable Adèle, ex-brigadier in the army of the Princes, bookbinder in Altona, afterwards shoemaker (with a great reputation for elegance in the fit of ladies' shoes) in another small German town, wore silk stockings on his lean shanks, low shoes with silver buckles, a brocaded waistcoat. A long-skirted coat, *à la française,* covered loosely his thin, bowed back. A small three-cornered hat rested on a lot of powdered hair, tied in a queue.

"*Monsieur le Chevalier,*" called General D'Hubert, softly.

"What? You here again, *mon ami*? Have you forgotten something?"

"By heavens! that's just it. I have forgotten something. I am come to tell you of it. No—outside. Behind this wall. It's too ghastly a thing to be let in at all where she lives."

The Chevalier came out at once with that benevolent resignation some old people display towards the fugue of youth. Older by a quarter of a century than General D'Hubert, he looked upon him in the secret of his heart as a rather troublesome youngster in love. He had heard his enigmatical words very well, but attached no undue importance to what a mere man of forty so hard hit was likely to do or say. The turn of mind of the generation of Frenchmen grown up during the years of his exile was almost unintelligible to him. Their sentiments appeared to him unduly violent, lacking fineness and measure, their language needlessly exaggerated. He joined calmly the General on the road, and they made a few steps in silence, the General trying to master his agitation, and get proper control of his voice.

"It is perfectly true; I forgot something. I forgot till half an hour ago that I had an urgent affair of honour on my hands. It's incredible, but it is so!"

All was still for a moment. Then in the profound evening silence of the countryside the clear, aged voice of the Chevalier was heard trembling slightly: "Monsieur! That's an indignity."

It was his first thought. The girl born during his exile, the posthumous daughter of his poor brother murdered by a band of Jacobins, had grown since his return very dear to his old heart, which had been starving on mere memories of affection for so many years. "It is an inconceivable thing, I say! A man settles such affairs before he thinks of asking for a young girl's hand. Why! If you had forgotten for ten days longer, you would have been married before your memory returned to you. In my time men did not forget such things—nor yet what is due to the feelings of an innocent young woman. If I did not respect them myself, I would qualify your conduct in a way which you would not like."

General D'Hubert relieved himself frankly by a groan. "Don't let that consideration prevent you. You run no risk of offending her mortally."

But the old man paid no attention to this lover's nonsense. It's doubtful whether he even heard. "What is it?" he asked. "What's the nature of . . . ?"

"Call it a youthful folly, *Monsieur le Chevalier.* An inconceivable, incredible result of . . ." He stopped short. "He will never believe the story," he thought. "He will only think I am taking him for a fool, and get offended." General D'Hubert spoke up again: "Yes, originating in youthful folly, it has become . . ."

The Chevalier interrupted: "Well, then it must be arranged."

"Arranged?"

"Yes, no matter at what cost to your *amour propre.* You should have remembered you were engaged. You forgot that, too, I suppose. And then you go and forget your quarrel. It's the most hopeless exhibition of levity I ever heard of."

"Good heavens, Monsieur! You don't imagine I have been picking up this quarrel last time I was in Paris, or anything of the sort, do you?"

"Eh! What matters the precise date of your insane conduct," exclaimed the Chevalier, testily. "The principal thing is to arrange it."

Noticing General D'Hubert getting restive and trying to place a word, the old *émigré* raised his hand, and added with dignity, "I've been a soldier, too. I would never dare suggest a doubtful step to the man whose name my niece is to bear. I tell you that *entre galants hommes* an affair can always be arranged."

"But *saperlotte, Monsieur le Chevalier*, it's fifteen or sixteen years ago. I was a lieutenant of hussars then."

The old Chevalier seemed confounded by the vehemently despairing tone of this information. "You were a lieutenant of hussars sixteen years ago," he mumbled in a dazed manner.

"Why, yes! You did not suppose I was made a general in my cradle like a royal prince."

In the deepening purple twilight of the fields spread with vine leaves, backed by a low band of sombre crimson in the west, the voice of the old ex-officer in the army of the Princes sounded collected, punctiliously civil.

"Do I dream? Is this a pleasantry? Or am I to understand that you have been hatching an affair of honour for sixteen years?"

"It has clung to me for that length of time. That is my precise meaning. The quarrel itself is not to be explained easily. We met on the ground several times during that time, of course."

"What manners! What horrible perversion of manliness! Nothing can account for such inhumanity but the sanguinary madness of the Revolution which has tainted a whole generation," mused the returned *émigré* in a low tone. "Who's your adversary?" he asked a little louder.

"My adversary? His name is Feraud."

Shadowy in his *tricorne* and old-fashioned clothes, like a bowed, thin ghost of the *ancien régime*, the Chevalier voiced a ghostly memory. "I can remember the feud about little Sophie Derval, between Monsieur de Brissac, Captain in the Bodyguards, and d'Anjorrant (not the pockmarked one, the other—the Beau d'Anjorrant, as they called him). They met three times in eighteen months in a most gallant manner. It was the fault of that little Sophie, too, who *would* keep on playing . . ."

"This is nothing of the kind," interrupted General D'Hubert. He laughed a little sardonically. "Not at all so simple," he added. "Nor yet half so reasonable," he finished, inaudibly, between his teeth, and ground them with rage.

After this sound nothing troubled the silence for a long time, till the Chevalier asked, without animation: "What is he—this Feraud?"

"Lieutenant of hussars, too—I mean, he's a general. A Gascon. Son of a blacksmith, I believe."

"There! I thought so. That Bonaparte had a special predilection for the *canaille*. I don't mean this for you, D'Hubert. You are one of us, though you have served this usurper, who . . ."

"Let's leave him out of this," broke in General D'Hubert.

The Chevalier shrugged his peaked shoulders. "Feraud of sorts. Offspring of a blacksmith and some village troll. See what comes of mixing yourself up with that sort of people."

"You have made shoes yourself, Chevalier."

"Yes. But I am not the son of a shoemaker. Neither are you, Monsieur D'Hubert. You and I have something that your Bonaparte's princes, dukes, and marshals have not, because there's no power on earth that could give it to them," retorted the *émigré*, with the rising animation of a man who has got hold of a hopeful argument. "Those people don't exist—all these Ferauds. Feraud! What is Feraud? A *va-nu-pieds* disguised into a general by a Corsican adventurer masquerading as an emperor. There is no earthly reason for a D'Hubert to *s'encanailler* by a duel with a person of that sort. You can make your excuses to him perfectly well. And if the *manant* takes into his head to decline them, you may simply refuse to meet him."

"You say I may do that?"

"I do. With the clearest conscience."

"*Monsieur le Chevalier*! To what do you think you have returned from your emigration?"

This was said in such a startling tone that the old man raised sharply his bowed head, glimmering silvery white under the points of the little *tricorne*. For a time he made no sound.

"God knows!" he said at last, pointing with a slow and grave gesture at a tall roadside cross mounted on a block of stone, and stretching its arms of forged iron all black against the darkening red band in the sky—"God knows! If it were not for this emblem, which I remember seeing on this spot as a child, I would wonder to what we who remained faithful to God and our king have returned. The very voices of the people have changed."

"Yes, it is a changed France," said General D'Hubert. He seemed to have regained his calm. His tone was slightly ironic. "Therefore I cannot take your advice. Besides, how is one to refuse to be bitten by a dog that means to bite? It's impracticable. Take my word for it—Feraud isn't a man to be stayed by apologies or refusals. But there are other ways. I could, for instance, send a messenger with a word to the brigadier of the *gendarmerie* in Senlac. He and his two friends are liable to arrest on my simple order. It would make some talk in the army, both the organized and the disbanded—especially the disbanded. All *canaille!* All once upon a time the companions in arms of Armand D'Hubert. But what need a D'Hubert care what people that don't exist may think? Or, better still, I might get my brother-in-law to send for the mayor of the village and give him a hint. No more would be needed to get the three 'brigands' set upon with flails and pitchforks and hunted into some nice, deep, wet ditch—and nobody the wiser! It has been done only ten miles from here to three poor devils of the disbanded Red Lancers of the Guard going to their homes. What says your conscience, *Chevalier?* Can a D'Hubert do that thing to three men who do not exist?"

A few stars had come out on the blue obscurity, clear as crystal, of the sky. The dry, thin voice of the Chevalier spoke harshly: "Why are you telling me all this?"

The General seized the withered old hand with a strong grip. "Because I owe you my fullest confidence. Who could tell Adèle but you? You understand why I dare not trust my brother-in-law nor yet my own sister. *Chevalier!* I have been so near doing these things that I tremble yet. You don't know how terrible this duel appears to me. And there's no escape from it."

He murmured after a pause, "It's a fatality," dropped the Chevalier's passive hand, and said in his ordinary conversational voice, "I shall have to go without seconds. If it is my lot to remain on the ground, you at least will know all that can be made known of this affair."

The shadowy ghost of the *ancien régime* seemed to have become more bowed during the conversation. "How am I to keep an indifferent face this evening before these two women?" he groaned. "General! I find it very difficult to forgive you."

General D'Hubert made no answer.

"Is your cause good, at least?"

"I am innocent."

This time he seized the Chevalier's ghostly arm above the elbow, and gave it a mighty squeeze. "I must kill him!" he hissed, and opening his hand strode away down the road.

The delicate attentions of his adoring sister had secured for the General perfect liberty of movement in the house where he was a guest. He had even his own entrance through a small door in one corner of the orangery. Thus he was not exposed that evening to the necessity of dissembling his agitation before the calm ignorance of the other inmates. He was glad of it. It seemed to him that if he had to open his lips he would break out into horrible and aimless imprecations, start breaking furniture, smashing china and glass. From the moment he opened the private door and while ascending the twenty-eight steps of a winding staircase, giving access to the corridor on which his room opened, he went through a horrible and humiliating scene in which an infuriated madman with blood-shot eyes and a foaming mouth played inconceivable havoc with everything inanimate that may be found in a well-appointed dining-room. When he opened the door of his apartment the fit was over, and his bodily fatigue was so great that he had to catch at the backs of the chairs while crossing the room to reach a low and broad divan on which he let himself fall heavily. His moral prostration was still greater. That brutality of feeling which he had known only when charging the enemy, sabre in hand, amazed this man of forty, who did not recognize in it the instinctive fury of his menaced passion. But in his mental and bodily exhaustion this passion got cleared, distilled, refined into a sentiment of melancholy despair at having, perhaps, to die before he had taught this beautiful girl to love him.

That night, General D'Hubert stretched out on his back with his hands over his eyes, or lying on his breast with his face buried in a cushion, made the full pilgrimage of emotions. Nauseating disgust at the absurdity of the situation, doubt of his own fitness to conduct his existence, and mistrust of his best sentiments (for what the devil did he want to go to Fouché for?)—he knew them all in turn. "I am an idiot, neither more nor less," he thought—"A sensitive idiot. Because I overheard two men talking in a café. . . . I am an idiot afraid of lies— whereas in life it is only truth that matters."

Several times he got up and, walking in his socks in order not to be heard by anybody downstairs, drank all the water he could find in the dark. And he tasted the torments of jealousy, too. She would marry somebody else. His very soul writhed. The tenacity of that Feraud, the awful persistence of that imbecile brute, came to him with the tremendous force of a relentless destiny. General D'Hubert trembled as he put down the empty water ewer. "He will have me," he thought. General D'Hubert was tasting every emotion that life has to give. He had in his dry mouth the faint sickly flavour of fear, not the excusable fear before a young girl's candid and amused glance, but the fear of death and the honourable man's fear of cowardice.

But if true courage consists in going out to meet an odious danger from which our body, soul, and heart recoil together, General D'Hubert had the opportunity to practise it for the first time in his life. He had charged exultingly at batteries and at infantry squares, and ridden with messages through a hail of bullets without thinking anything about it. His business now was to sneak out unheard, at break of day, to an obscure and revolting death. General D'Hubert never hesitated. He carried two pistols in a leather bag which he slung over his shoulder. Before he had crossed the garden his mouth was dry again. He picked two oranges. It was only after shutting the gate after him that he felt a slight faintness.

He staggered on, disregarding it, and after going a few yards regained the command of his legs. In the colourless and pellucid dawn the wood of pines detached its columns of trunks and its dark green canopy very clearly against the rocks of the grey hillside. He kept his eyes fixed on it steadily, and sucked at an orange as he walked. That temperamental good-humoured coolness in the face of danger which had made him an officer liked by his men and appreciated by his superiors was gradually asserting itself. It was like going into battle. Arriving at the edge of the wood he sat down on a boulder, holding the other orange in his hand, and reproached himself for coming so ridiculously early on the ground. Before very long, however, he heard the swishing of bushes, footsteps on the hard ground, and the sounds of a disjointed, loud conversation. A voice somewhere behind him said boastfully, "He's game for my bag."

He thought to himself, "Here they are. What's this about game? Are they talking of me?" And becoming aware of the other orange in his hand, he thought further, "These are very good oranges. Léonie's own tree. I may just as well eat this orange now instead of flinging it away."

Emerging from a wilderness of rocks and bushes, General Feraud and his seconds discovered General D'Hubert engaged in peeling the orange. They stood still, waiting till he looked up. Then the seconds raised their hats, while General Feraud, putting his hands behind his back, walked aside a little way.

"I am compelled to ask one of you, messieurs, to act for me. I have brought no friends. Will you?"

The one-eyed cuirassier said judicially, "That cannot be refused."

The other veteran remarked, "It's awkward all the same."

"Owing to the state of the people's minds in this part of the country there was no one I could trust safely with the object of your presence here," explained General D'Hubert, urbanely.

They saluted, looked round, and remarked both together:

"Poor ground."

"It's unfit."

"Why bother about ground, measurements, and so on? Let us simplify matters. Load the two pairs of pistols. I will take those of General Feraud, and let him take mine. Or, better still, let us take a mixed pair. One of each pair. Then let us go into the wood and shoot at sight, while you remain outside. We did not come here for ceremonies, but for war—war to the death. Any ground is good enough for that. If I fall, you must leave me where I lie and clear out. It wouldn't be healthy for you to be found hanging about here after that."

It appeared after a short parley that General Feraud was willing to accept these conditions. While the seconds were loading the pistols, he could be heard whistling, and was seen to rub his hands with perfect contentment. He flung off his coat briskly, and General D'Hubert took off his own and folded it carefully on a stone.

"Suppose you take your principal to the other side of the wood and let him enter exactly in ten minutes from now," suggested General D'Hubert, calmly, but feeling as if he were giving directions for his own execution. This, however, was his last moment of weakness. "Wait. Let us compare watches first."

He pulled out his own. The officer with the chipped nose went over to borrow the watch of General Feraud. They bent their heads over them for a time.

"That's it. At four minutes to six by yours. Seven to by mine."

It was the cuirassier who remained by the side of General D'Hubert, keeping his one eye fixed immovably on the white face of the watch he held in the palm of his hand. He opened his mouth, waiting for the beat of the last second long before he snapped out the word, *"Avancez."*

General D'Hubert moved on, passing from the glaring sunshine of the Provençal morning into the cool and aromatic shade of the pines. The ground was clear between the reddish trunks, whose multitude, leaning at slightly different angles, confused his eye at first. It was like going into battle. The commanding quality of confidence in himself woke up in his breast. He was all to his affair. The problem was how to kill the adversary. Nothing short of that would free him from this imbecile nightmare. "It's no use wounding that brute," thought General D'Hubert. He was known as a resourceful officer. His comrades years ago used also to call him The Strategist. And it was a fact that he could think in the presence of the enemy. Whereas Feraud had been always a mere fighter—but a dead shot, unluckily.

"I must draw his fire at the greatest possible range," said General D'Hubert to himself.

At that moment he saw something white moving far off between the trees—the shirt of his adversary. He stepped out at once between the trunks, exposing himself freely; then, quick as lightning, leaped back. It had been a risky move but it succeeded in its object. Almost simultaneously with the pop of a shot a small piece of bark chipped off by the bullet stung his ear painfully.

General Feraud, with one shot expended, was getting cautious. Peeping round the tree, General D'Hubert could not see him at all. This ignorance of the foe's whereabouts carried with it a sense of insecurity. General D'Hubert felt himself abominably exposed on his flank and rear. Again something white fluttered in his sight. Ha! The enemy was still on his front, then. He had feared a turning movement. But apparently General Feraud was not thinking of it. General D'Hubert saw him pass without special haste from one tree to another in the straight line of approach. With great firmness of mind General D'Hubert stayed his hand. Too far yet. He knew he was no marksman. His must be a waiting game—to kill.

Wishing to take advantage of the greater thickness of the trunk, he sank down to the ground. Extended at full length, head on to his enemy, he had his person completely protected. Exposing himself would not do now, because the other was too near by this time. A conviction that Feraud would presently do something rash was like balm to General D'Hubert's soul. But to keep his chin raised off the ground was irksome, and not much use either. He peeped round, exposing a fraction of his head with dread, but really with little risk. His enemy, as a matter of fact, did not expect to see anything of him so far down as that. General D'Hubert caught a fleeting view of General Feraud shifting trees again with deliberate caution. "He despises my shooting," he thought, displaying that insight into the mind of his antagonist which is of such great help in winning battles. He was confirmed in his tactics of immobility. "If I could only watch my rear as well as my front!" he thought anxiously, longing for the impossible.

It required some force of character to lay his pistols down; but, on a sudden impulse, General D'Hubert did this very gently—one on each side of him. In the army he had been looked upon as a bit of a dandy because he used to shave and put on a clean shirt on the days of battle. As a matter of fact, he had always been very careful of his personal appearance. In a man of nearly forty, in love with a young and charming girl, this praiseworthy self-respect may run to such little weaknesses as, for instance, being provided with an elegant little leather folding-case containing a small ivory comb, and fitted with a piece of looking-glass on the outside. General D'Hubert, his hands being free, felt in his breeches' pockets for that implement of innocent vanity excusable in the possessor of long, silky moustaches. He drew it out, and then with the utmost coolness and promptitude turned himself over on his back. In this new attitude, his head a little raised, holding the little looking-glass just clear of his tree, he squinted into it with his left eye, while the right kept a direct watch on the rear of his position. Thus was proved Napoleon's saying, that "for a French soldier, the word impossible does not exist." He had the right tree nearly filling the field of his little mirror.

"If he moves from behind it," he reflected with satisfaction, "I am bound to see his legs. But in any case he can't come upon me unawares."

And sure enough he saw the boots of General Feraud flash in and out, eclipsing for an instant everything else reflected in the little mirror. He shifted its position accordingly. But having to form his judgment of the change from that indirect view he did not realize that now his feet and a portion of his legs were in plain sight of General Feraud.

General Feraud had been getting gradually impressed by the amazing cleverness with which his enemy was keeping cover. He had spotted the right tree with bloodthirsty precision. He was absolutely certain of it. And yet he had not been able to glimpse as much as the tip of an ear. As he had been looking for it at the height of about five feet ten inches from the ground it was no great wonder—but it seemed very wonderful to General Feraud.

The first view of these feet and legs determined a rush of blood to his head. He literally staggered behind his tree, and had to steady himself against it with his hand. The other was lying on the ground, then! On the ground! Perfectly still, too! Exposed! What could it mean. . . . The notion that he had knocked over his adversary at the first shot entered then General Feraud's head. Once there it grew with every second of attentive gazing, overshadowing every other supposition—irresistible, triumphant, ferocious.

"What an ass I was to think I could have missed him," he muttered to himself. "He was exposed *en plein*—the fool!—for quite a couple of seconds."

General Feraud gazed at the motionless limbs, the last vestiges of surprise fading before an unbounded admiration of his own deadly skill with the pistol.

"Turned up his toes! By the god of war, that was a shot!" he exulted mentally. "Got it through the head, no doubt, just where I aimed, staggered behind that tree, rolled over on his back, and died."

And he stared! He stared, forgetting to move, almost awed, almost sorry. But for nothing in the world would he have had it undone. Such a shot!—such a shot! Rolled over on his back and died!

For it was this helpless position, lying on the back, that shouted its direct evidence at General Feraud! It never occurred to him that it might have been deliberately assumed by a living man. It was inconceivable. It was beyond the range of sane supposition. There was no possibility to guess the reason for it. And it must be said, too, that General D'Hubert's turned-up feet looked thoroughly dead. General Feraud expanded his lungs for a stentorian shout to his seconds, but, from what he felt to be an excessive scrupulousness, refrained for a while.

"I will just go and see first whether he breathes yet," he mumbled to himself, leaving carelessly the shelter of his tree. This move was immediately perceived by the resourceful General D'Hubert. He concluded it to be another shift, but when he lost the boots out of the field of the mirror he became uneasy. General Feraud had only stepped a little out of the line, but his adversary could not possibly have supposed him walking up with perfect unconcern. General D'Hubert, beginning to wonder at what had become of the other, was taken unawares so completely that the first warning of danger consisted in the long, early-morning shadow of his enemy falling aslant on his outstretched legs. He had not even heard a footfall on the soft ground between the trees!

It was too much even for his coolness. He jumped up thoughtlessly, leaving the pistols on the ground. The irresistible instinct of an average man (unless totally paralyzed by discomfiture) would have been to stoop for his weapons, exposing himself to the risk of being shot down in that position. Instinct, of course, is irreflective. It is its very definition. But it may be an inquiry worth pursuing whether in reflective mankind the mechanical promptings of instinct are not affected by the customary mode of thought. In his young days, Armand D'Hubert, the reflective, promising officer, had emitted the opinion that in warfare one should "never cast back on the lines of a mistake." This idea, defended and developed in many discussions, had settled into one of the stock notions of his brain, had become a part of his mental individuality. Whether it had gone so inconceivably deep as to affect the dictates of his instinct, or simply because, as he himself declared afterwards, he was "too scared to remember the confounded pistols," the fact is that General D'Hubert never attempted to stoop for them. Instead of going back on his mistake, he seized the rough trunk with both hands, and swung himself behind it with such impetuosity that, going right round in the very flash and report of the pistol-shot, he reappeared on the other side of the tree face to face with General Feraud. This last, completely unstrung by such a show of agility on the part of a dead man, was trembling yet. A very faint mist of smoke hung before his face which had an extraordinary aspect, as if the lower jaw had come unhinged.

"Not missed!" he croaked, hoarsely, from the depths of a dry throat.

This sinister sound loosened the spell that had fallen on General D'Hubert's senses. "Yes, missed—*à bout portant*," he heard himself saying, almost before he had recovered the full command of his faculties. The revulsion of feeling was accompanied by a gust of homicidal fury, resuming in its violence the accumulated resentment of a lifetime. For years General D'Hubert had been exasperated and humiliated by an atrocious absurdity imposed upon him by this man's savage caprice. Besides, General D'Hubert had been in this last instance too unwilling to confront death for the reaction of his anguish not to take the shape of a desire to kill. "And I have my two shots to fire yet," he added, pitilessly.

General Feraud snapped-to his teeth, and his face assumed an irate, undaunted expression. "Go on!" he said, grimly.

These would have been his last words if General D'Hubert had been holding the pistols in his hands. But the pistols were lying on the ground at the foot of a pine. General D'Hubert had the second of leisure necessary to remember that he had dreaded death not as a man, but as a lover; not as a danger, but as a rival; not as a foe to life, but as an obstacle to marriage. And behold! there was the rival defeated!—utterly defeated, crushed, done for!

He picked up the weapons mechanically, and, instead of firing them into General Feraud's breast, he gave expression to the thoughts uppermost in his mind, "You will fight no more duels now."

His tone of leisurely, ineffable satisfaction was too much for General Feraud's stoicism. "Don't dawdle, then, damn you for a cold-blooded staff-coxcomb!" he roared out, suddenly, out of an impassive face held erect on a rigidly still body.

General D'Hubert uncocked the pistols carefully. This proceeding was observed with mixed feelings by the other general. "You missed me twice," the victor said, coolly, shifting both pistols to one hand; "the last time within a foot or so. By every rule of single combat your life belongs to me. That does not mean that I want to take it now."

"I have no use for your forbearance," muttered General Feraud, gloomily.

"Allow me to point out that this is no concern of mine," said General D'Hubert, whose every word was dictated by a consummate delicacy of feeling. In anger he could have killed that man, but in cold blood he recoiled from humiliating by a show of generosity this unreasonable being—a fellow-soldier of the *Grande Armée,* a companion in the wonders and terrors of the great military epic. "You don't set up the pretension of dictating to me what I am to do with what's my own."

General Feraud looked startled, and the other continued, "You've forced me on a point of honour to keep my life at your disposal, as it were, for fifteen years. Very well. Now that the matter is decided to my advantage, I am going to do what I like with your life on the same principle. You shall keep it at my disposal as long as I choose. Neither more nor less. You are on your honour till I say the word."

"I am! But, *sacrebleu*! This is an absurd position for a General of the Empire to be placed in!" cried General Feraud, in accents of profound and dismayed conviction. "It amounts to sitting all the rest of my life with a loaded pistol in a drawer waiting for your word. It's—it's idiotic; I shall be an object of—of—derision."

"Absurd?—idiotic? Do you think so?" queried General D'Hubert with sly gravity. "Perhaps. But I don't see how that can be helped. However, I am not likely to talk at large of this adventure. Nobody need ever know anything about it. Just as no one to this day, I believe, knows the origin of our quarrel. . . . Not a word more," he added, hastily. "I can't really discuss this question with a man who, as far as I am concerned, does not exist."

When the two duellists came out into the open, General Feraud walking a little behind, and rather with the air of walking in a trance, the two seconds hurried towards them, each from his station at the edge of the wood. General D'Hubert addressed them, speaking loud and distinctly, "Messieurs, I make it a point of declaring to you solemnly, in the presence of General Feraud, that our difference is at last settled for good. You may inform all the world of that fact."

"A reconciliation, after all!" they exclaimed together.

"Reconciliation? Not that exactly. It is something much more binding. Is it not so, General?"

General Feraud only lowered his head in sign of assent. The two veterans looked at each other. Later in the day, when they found themselves alone out of their moody friend's earshot, the cuirassier remarked suddenly, "Generally speaking, I can see with my one eye as far as most people; but this beats me. He won't say anything."

"In this affair of honour I understand there has been from first to last always something that no one in the army could quite make out," declared the chasseur with the imperfect nose. "In mystery it began, in mystery it went on, in mystery it is to end, apparently."

General D'Hubert walked home with long, hasty strides, by no means uplifted by a sense of triumph. He had conquered, yet it did not seem to him that he had gained very much by his conquest. The night before he had grudged the risk of his life which appeared to him magnificent, worthy of preservation as an opportunity to win a girl's love. He had known moments when, by a marvellous illusion, this love seemed to be already his, and his threatened life a still more magnificent opportunity of devotion. Now that his life was safe it had suddenly lost its special magnificence. It had acquired instead a specially alarming aspect as a snare for the exposure of unworthiness. As to the marvellous illusion of conquered love that had visited him for a moment in the agitated watches of the night, which might have been his last on earth, he comprehended now its true nature. It had been merely a paroxysm of delirious conceit. Thus to this man, sobered by the victorious issue of a duel, life appeared robbed of its charm, simply because it was no longer menaced.

Approaching the house from the back, through the orchard and the kitchen garden, he could not notice the agitation which reigned in front. He never met a single soul. Only while walking softly along the corridor, he became aware that the house was awake and more noisy than usual. Names of servants were being called out down below in a confused noise of coming and going. With some concern he noticed that the door of his own room stood ajar, though the shutters had not been opened yet. He had hoped that his early excursion would have passed unperceived. He expected to find some servant just gone in; but the sunshine filtering through the usual cracks enabled him to see lying on the low divan something bulky, which had the appearance of two women clasped in each other's arms. Tearful and desolate murmurs issued mysteriously from that appearance. General D'Hubert pulled open the nearest pair of shutters violently. One of the women then jumped up. It was his sister. She stood for a moment with her hair hanging down and her arms raised straight up above her head, and then flung herself with a stifled cry into his arms. He returned her embrace, trying at the same time to disengage himself from it. The other woman had not risen. She seemed, on the contrary, to cling closer to the divan, hiding her face in the cushions. Her hair was also loose; it was admirably fair. General D'Hubert recognized it with staggering emotion. Mademoiselle de Valmassigue! Adèle! In distress!

He became greatly alarmed, and got rid of his sister's hug definitely. Madame Léonie then extended her shapely bare arm out of her *peignoir*, pointing dramatically at the divan. "This poor, terrified child has rushed here from home, on foot, two miles—running all the way."

"What on earth has happened?" asked General D'Hubert in a low, agitated voice.

But Madame Léonie was speaking loudly. "She rang the great bell at the gate and roused all the household—we were all asleep yet. You may imagine what a terrible shock. . . . Adèle, my dear child, sit up."

General D'Hubert's expression was not that of a man who "imagines" with facility. He did, however, fish out of the chaos of surmises the notion that his prospective mother-in-law had died suddenly, but only to dismiss it at once. He could not conceive the nature of the event or the catastrophe which would induce Mademoiselle de Valmassigue, living in a house full of servants, to bring the news over the fields herself, two miles, running all the way.

"But why are you in this room?" he whispered, full of awe.

"Of course, I ran up to see, and this child . . . I did not notice it . . . she followed me. It's that absurd Chevalier," went on Madame Léonie, looking towards the divan. . . . "Her hair is all come down. You may imagine she did not stop to call her maid to dress it before she started. . . . Adèle, my dear, sit up. . . . He blurted it all out to her at half-past five in the morning. She woke up early and opened her shutters to breathe the fresh air, and saw him sitting collapsed on a garden bench at the end of the great alley. At that hour—you may imagine! And the evening before he had declared himself indisposed. She hurried on some clothes and flew down to him. One would be anxious for less. He loves her, but not very intelligently. He had been up all night, fully dressed, the poor old man, perfectly exhausted. He wasn't in a state to invent a plausible story. . . . What a confidant you chose there! My husband was furious. He said, 'We can't interfere now.' So we sat down to wait. It was awful. And this poor child running with her hair loose over here publicly! She has been seen by some people in the fields. She has roused the whole household, too. It's awkward for her. Luckily you are to be married next week. . . . Adèle, sit up. He has come home on his own legs. . . . We expected to see you coming on a stretcher, perhaps—what do I know? Go and see if the carriage is ready. I must take this child home at once. It isn't proper for her to stay here a minute longer."

General D'Hubert did not move. It was as though he had heard nothing. Madame Léonie changed her mind. "I will go and see myself," she cried. "I want also my cloak.—Adèle——" she began, but did not add "sit up." She went out saying, in a very loud and cheerful tone: "I leave the door open."

General D'Hubert made a movement towards the divan, but then Adèle sat up, and that checked him dead. He thought, "I haven't washed this morning. I must look like an old tramp. There's earth on the back of my coat and pine-needles in my hair." It occurred to him that the situation required a good deal of circumspection on his part.

"I am greatly concerned, mademoiselle," he began, vaguely, and abandoned that line. She was sitting up on the divan with her cheeks unusually pink and her hair, brilliantly fair, falling all over her shoulders— which was a very novel sight to the general. He walked away up the room, and looking out of the window for safety said, "I fear you must think I behaved like a madman," in accents of sincere despair. Then he spun round, and noticed that she had followed him with her eyes. They were not cast down on meeting his glance. And the expression of her face was novel to him also. It was, one might have said, reversed. Those eyes looked at him with grave thoughtfulness, while the exquisite lines of her mouth seemed to suggest a restrained smile. This change made her transcendental beauty much less mysterious, much more accessible to a man's comprehension. An amazing ease of mind came to the general—and even some ease of manner. He walked down the room with as much pleasurable excitement as he would have found in walking up to a battery vomiting death, fire, and smoke; then stood looking down with smiling eyes at the girl whose marriage with him (next week) had been so carefully arranged by the wise, the good, the admirable Léonie.

"Ah! mademoiselle," he said, in a tone of courtly regret, "if only I could be certain that you did not come here this morning, two miles, running all the way, merely from affection for your mother!"

He waited for an answer imperturbable but inwardly elated. It came in a demure murmur, eyelashes lowered with fascinating effect. "You must not be *méchant* as well as mad."

And then General D'Hubert made an aggressive movement towards the divan which nothing could check. That piece of furniture was not exactly in the line of the open door. But Madame Léonie, coming back wrapped up in a light cloak and carrying a lace shawl on her arm for

Adèle to hide her incriminating hair under, had a swift impression of her brother getting up from his knees.

"Come along, my dear child," she cried from the doorway.

The general, now himself again in the fullest sense, showed the readiness of a resourceful cavalry officer and the peremptoriness of a leader of men. "You don't expect her to walk to the carriage," he said, indignantly. "She isn't fit. I shall carry her downstairs."

This he did slowly, followed by his awed and respectful sister; but he rushed back like a whirlwind to wash off all the signs of the night of anguish and the morning of war, and to put on the festive garments of a conqueror before hurrying over to the other house. Had it not been for that, General D'Hubert felt capable of mounting a horse and pursuing his late adversary in order simply to embrace him from excess of happiness. "I owe it all to this stupid brute," he thought. "He has made plain in a morning what might have taken me years to find out—for I am a timid fool. No self-confidence whatever. Perfect coward. And the Chevalier! Delightful old man!" General D'Hubert longed to embrace him also.

The Chevalier was in bed. For several days he was very unwell. The men of the Empire and the post-revolution young ladies were too much for him. He got up the day before the wedding, and, being curious by nature, took his niece aside for a quiet talk. He advised her to find out from her husband the true story of the affair of honour, whose claim, so imperative and so persistent, had led her to within an ace of tragedy. "It is right that his wife should be told. And next month or so will be your time to learn from him anything you want to know, my dear child."

Later on, when the married couple came on a visit to the mother of the bride, Madame la Générale D'Hubert communicated to her beloved old uncle the true story she had obtained without any difficulty from her husband.

The Chevalier listened with deep attention to the end, took a pinch of snuff, flicked the grains of tobacco from the frilled front of his shirt, and asked, calmly, "And that's all it was?"

"Yes, uncle," replied Madame la Générale, opening her pretty eyes very wide. "Isn't it funny? C'est insensé—to think what men are capable of!"

"H'm!" commented the old *émigré*. "It depends what sort of men. That Bonaparte's soldiers were savages. It is *insenseé*. As a wife, my dear, you must believe implicitly what your husband says."

But to Léonie's husband the Chevalier confided his true opinion. "If that's the tale the fellow made up for his wife, and during the honeymoon, too, you may depend on it that no one will ever know now the secret of this affair."

Considerably later still, General D'Hubert judged the time come, and the opportunity propitious to write a letter to General Feraud. This letter began by disclaiming all animosity. "I've never," wrote the General Baron D'Hubert, "wished for your death during all the time of our deplorable quarrel. Allow me," he continued, "to give you back in all form your forfeited life. It is proper that we two, who have been partners in so much military glory, should be friendly to each other publicly."

The same letter contained also an item of domestic information. It was in reference to this last that General Feraud answered from a little village on the banks of the Garonne, in the following words:

"If one of your boy's names had been Napoleon—or Joseph—or even Joachim, I could congratulate you on the event with a better heart. As you have thought proper to give him the names of Charles Henri Armand, I am confirmed in my conviction that you *never* loved the Emperor. The thought of that sublime hero chained to a rock in the middle of a savage ocean makes life of so little value that I would receive with positive joy your instructions to blow my brains out. From suicide I consider myself in honour debarred. But I keep a loaded pistol in my drawer."

Madame la Générale D'Hubert lifted up her hands in despair after perusing that answer.

"You see? He *won't* be reconciled," said her husband. "He must never, by any chance, be allowed to guess where the money comes from. It wouldn't do. He couldn't bear it."

"You are a *brave homme*, Armand," said Madame la Générale, appreciatively.

"My dear, I had the right to blow his brains out; but as I didn't, we can't let him starve. He has lost his pension and he is utterly incapable of doing anything in the world for himself. We must take care of him, secretly, to the end of his days. Don't I owe him the most ecstatic moment of my life? . . . Ha! ha! ha! Over the fields, two miles, running all the way! I couldn't believe my ears! . . . But for his stupid ferocity, it would have taken me years to find you out. It's extraordinary how in one way or another this man has managed to fasten himself on my deeper feelings."

A SMILE OF FORTUNE

EVER since the sun rose I had been looking ahead. The ship glided gently in smooth water. After a sixty days' passage I was anxious to make my landfall, a fertile and beautiful island of the tropics. The more enthusiastic of its inhabitants delight in describing it as the "Pearl of the Ocean." Well, let us call it the "Pearl." It's a good name. A pearl distilling much sweetness upon the world.

This is only a way of telling you that first-rate sugar-cane is grown there. All the population of the Pearl lives for it and by it. Sugar is their daily bread, as it were. And I was coming to them for a cargo of sugar in the hope of the crop having been good and of the freights being high.

Mr. Burns, my chief mate, made out the land first; and very soon I became entranced by this blue, pinnacled apparition, almost transparent against the light of the sky, a mere emanation, the astral body of an island risen to greet me from afar. It is a rare phenomenon, such a sight of the Pearl at sixty miles off. And I wondered half seriously whether it was a good omen, whether what would meet me in that island would be as luckily exceptional as this beautiful, dreamlike vision so very few seamen have been privileged to behold.

But horrid thoughts of business interfered with my enjoyment of an accomplished passage. I was anxious for success and I wished, too, to do justice to the flattering latitude of my owners' instructions contained in one noble phrase: "We leave it to you to do the best you can with the ship." . . . All the world being thus given me for a stage, my abilities appeared to me no bigger than a pinhead.

Meantime the wind dropped, and Mr. Burns began to make disagreeable remarks about my usual bad luck. I believe it was his devotion for me which made him critically outspoken on every occasion. All the same, I would not have put up with his humours if it had not been my lot at one time to nurse him through a desperate illness at sea. After snatching him out of the jaws of death, so to speak, it would have been absurd to throw away such an efficient officer. But sometimes I wished he would dismiss himself.

We were late in closing in with the land, and had to anchor outside the harbour till next day. An unpleasant and unrestful night followed. In this road-stead, strange to us both, Burns and I remained on deck almost all the time. Clouds swirled down the porphyry crags under which we lay. The rising wind made a great bullying noise amongst the naked spars, with interludes of sad moaning. I remarked that we had been in luck to fetch the anchorage before dark. It would have been a nasty, anxious night to hang off a harbour under canvas. But my chief mate was uncompromising in his attitude.

"Luck, you call it, sir! Ay—our usual luck. The sort of luck to thank God it's no worse!"

And so he fretted through the dark hours, while I drew on my fund of philosophy. Ah, but it was an exasperating, weary, endless night, to be lying at anchor close under that black coast! The agitated water made snarling sounds all round the ship. At times a wild gust of wind out of a gully high up on the cliffs struck on our rigging a harsh and plaintive note like the wail of a forsaken soul.

· I ·

By half-past seven in the morning, the ship being then inside the harbour at last and moored within a long stone's-throw from the quay, my stock of philosophy was nearly exhausted. I was dressing hurriedly in my cabin when the steward came tripping in with a morning suit over his arm.

Hungry, tired, and depressed, with my head engaged inside a white shirt irritatingly stuck together by too much starch, I desired him peevishly to "heave round with that breakfast." I wanted to get ashore as soon as possible.

"Yes, sir. Ready at eight, sir. There's a gentleman from the shore waiting to speak to you, sir."

This statement was curiously slurred over. I dragged the shirt violently over my head and emerged staring.

"So early!" I cried. "Who's he? What does he want?"

On coming in from sea one has to pick up the conditions of an utterly unrelated existence. Every little event at first has the peculiar emphasis of novelty. I was greatly surprised by that early caller; but there was no reason for my steward to look so particularly foolish.

"Didn't you ask for the name?" I inquired in a stern tone.

"His name's Jacobus, I believe," he mumbled shamefacedly.

"Mr. Jacobus!" I exclaimed loudly, more surprised than ever, but with a total change of feeling. "Why couldn't you say so at once?"

But the fellow had scuttled out of my room. Through the momentarily opened door I had a glimpse of a tall, stout man standing in the cuddy by the table on which the cloth was already laid; a "harbour" table cloth, stainless and dazzlingly white. So far good.

I shouted courteously through the closed door, that I was dressing and would be with him in a moment. In return the assurance that there was no hurry reached me in the visitor's deep, quiet undertone. His time was my own. He dared say I would give him a cup of coffee presently.

"I am afraid you will have a poor breakfast," I cried apologetically. "We have been sixty-one days at sea, you know."

A quiet little laugh, with a "That'll be all right, Captain," was his answer. All this, words, intonation, the glimpsed attitude of the man in the cuddy, had an unexpected character, a something friendly in it— propitiatory. And my surprise was not diminished thereby. What did this call mean? Was it the sign of some dark design against my commercial innocence?

Ah! These commercial interests—spoiling the finest life under the sun. Why must the sea be used for trade—and for war as well? Why kill and traffic on it, pursuing selfish aims of no great importance after all? It would have been so much nicer just to sail about with here and there a port and a bit of land to stretch one's legs on, buy a few books and get a change of cooking for a while. But, living in a world more or less homicidal and desperately mercantile, it was plainly my duty to make the best of its opportunities.

My owners' letter had left it to me, as I have said before, to do my best for the ship, according to my own judgment. But it contained also a postscript worded somewhat as follows:

"Without meaning to interfere with your liberty of action we are writing by the outgoing mail to some of our business friends there who may be of assistance to you. We desire you particularly to call on Mr. Jacobus, a prominent merchant and charterer. Should you hit it off with him he may be able to put you in the way of profitable employment for the ship."

Hit it off! Here was the prominent creature absolutely on board asking for the favour of a cup of coffee! And life not being a fairy-tale the improbability of the event almost shocked me. Had I discovered an enchanted nook of the earth where wealthy merchants rush fasting on board ships before they are fairly moored? Was this white magic or merely some black trick of trade? I came in the end (while making the bow of my tie) to suspect that perhaps I did not get the name right. I had been thinking of the prominent Mr. Jacobus pretty frequently during the passage and my hearing might have been deceived by some remote similarity of sound. . . . The steward might have said Antrobus—or maybe Jackson.

But coming out of my stateroom with an interrogative "Mr. Jacobus?" I was met by a quiet. "Yes," uttered with a gentle smile. The "yes" was rather perfunctory. He did not seem to make much of the fact that he was Mr. Jacobus. I took stock of a big, pale face, hair thin on the top, whiskers also thin, of a faded nondescript color, heavy eyelids. The thick, smooth lips in repose looked as if glued together. The smile was faint. A heavy, tranquil man. I named my two officers, who just then came down to breakfast; but why Mr. Burns's silent demeanour should suggest suppressed indignation I could not understand.

While we were taking our seats round the table some disconnected words of an altercation going on in the companionway reached my ear. A stranger apparently wanted to come down to interview me, and the steward was opposing him.

"You can't see him."

"Why can't I?"

"The Captain is at breakfast, I tell you. He'll be going on shore presently, and you can speak to him on deck."

"That's not fair. You let——"

"I've had nothing to do with that."

"Oh, yes, you have. Everybody ought to have the same chance. You let that fellow——"

The rest I lost. The person having been repulsed successfully, the steward came down. I can't say he looked flushed—he was a mulatto— but he looked flustered. After putting the dishes on the table he remained by the sideboard with that lackadaisical air of indifference he used to assume when he had done something too clever by half and was afraid of getting into a scrape over it. The contemptuous expression of Mr. Burns's face as he looked from him to me was really extraordinary. I couldn't imagine what new bee had stung the mate now.

The Captain being silent, nobody else cared to speak, as is the way in ships. And I was saying nothing simply because I had been made dumb by the splendour of the entertainment. I had expected the usual sea-breakfast, whereas I beheld spread before us a veritable feast of shore provisions: eggs, sausages, butter which plainly did not come from a Danish tin, cutlets, and even a dish of potatoes. It was three weeks since I had seen a real, live potato. I contemplated them with interest, and Mr. Jacobus disclosed himself as a man of human, homely sympathies, and something of a thought-reader.

"Try them, Captain," he encouraged me in a friendly undertone. "They are excellent."

"They look that," I admitted. "Grown on the island, I suppose."

"Oh, no, imported. Those grown here would be more expensive."

I was grieved at the ineptitude of the conversation. Were these the topics for a prominent and wealthy merchant to discuss? I thought the simplicity with which he made himself at home rather attractive; but what is one to talk about to a man who comes on one suddenly, after sixty-one days at sea, out of a totally unknown little town in an island one has never seen before? What were (besides sugar) the interests of that crumb of the earth, its gossip, its topics of conversation? To draw him on business at once would have been almost indecent—or even worse: impolitic. All I could do at the moment was to keep on in the old groove.

"Are the provisions generally dear here?" I asked, fretting inwardly at my inanity.

"I wouldn't say that," he answered placidly, with that appearance of saving his breath his restrained manner of speaking suggested.

He would not be more explicit, yet he did not evade the subject. Eyeing the table in a spirit of complete abstemiousness (he wouldn't let me help him to any eatables) he went into details of supply. The beef was for the most part imported from Madagascar; mutton of course was rare and somewhat expensive, but good goat's flesh——

"Are these goat's cutlets?" I exclaimed hastily, pointing at one of the dishes.

Posed sentimentally by the sideboard, the steward gave a start.

"Lor', no, sir! It's real mutton!"

Mr. Burns got through his breakfast impatiently, as if exasperated by being made a party to some monstrous foolishness, muttered a curt excuse, and went on deck. Shortly afterwards the second mate took his smooth red countenance out of the cabin. With the appetite of a school-boy, and after two months of sea-fare, he appreciated the generous spread. But I did not. It smacked of extravagance. All the same, it was a remarkable feat to have produced it so quickly, and I congratulated the steward on his smartness in a somewhat ominous tone. He gave me a deprecatory smile and, in a way I didn't know what to make of, blinked his fine dark eyes in the direction of the guest.

The latter asked under his breath for another cup of coffee, and nibbled ascetically at a piece of very hard ship's biscuit. I don't think he consumed a square inch in the end; but meantime he gave me, casually as it were, a complete account of the sugar crop, of the local business houses, of the state of the freight market. All that talk was interspersed with hints as to personalities, amounting to veiled warnings, but his pale, fleshy face remained equable, without a gleam, as if ignorant of his voice. As you may imagine I opened my ears very wide. Every word was precious. My ideas as to the value of business friendship were being favourably modified. He gave me the names of all the disponible ships together with their tonnage and the names of their commanders. From that, which was still commercial information, he condescended to mere harbour gossip. The *Hilda* had unaccountably lost her figure-head in the Bay of Bengal, and her captain was greatly affected by this. He and the ship had been getting on in years together and the old gentleman imagined this strange event to be the fore-runner of his own early dissolution. The *Stella* had experienced awful weather off the Cape—had her decks swept, and the chief officer washed overboard. And only a few hours before reaching port the baby died. Poor Captain H—— and his wife were terribly cut up. If they had only been able to bring it into port alive it could have been probably saved; but the wind failed them for the last week or so, light breezes, and . . . the baby was going to be buried this afternoon. He supposed I would attend——

"Do you think I ought to?" I asked, shrinkingly.

He thought so, decidedly. It would be greatly appreciated. All the captains in the harbour were going to attend. Poor Mrs. H——was quite prostrated. Pretty hard on H——altogether.

"And you, Captain—you are not married I suppose?"

"No, I am not married," I said. "Neither married nor even engaged."

Mentally I thanked my stars; and while he smiled in a musing, dreamy fashion, I expressed my acknowledgments for his visit and for the interesting business information he had been good enough to impart to me. But I said nothing of my wonder thereat.

"Of course, I would have made a point of calling on you in a day or two," I concluded.

He raised his eyelids distinctly at me, and somehow managed to look rather more sleepy than before.

"In accordance with my owners' instructions," I explained. "You have had their letter, of course?"

By that time he had raised his eyebrows too but without any particular emotion. On the contrary he struck me then as absolutely imperturbable.

"Oh! You must be thinking of my brother."

It was for me, then, to say "Oh!" But I hope that no more than civil surprise appeared in my voice when I asked him to what, then, I owed the pleasure? . . . He was reaching for an inside pocket leisurely.

"My brother's a very different person. But I am well known in this part of the world. You've probably heard——"

I took a card he extended to me. A thick business card, as I lived! Alfred Jacobus—the other was Ernest—dealer in every description of ship's stores! Provisions salt and fresh, oils, paints, rope, canvas, etc., etc. Ships in harbour victualled by contract on moderate terms——

"I've never heard of you," I said brusquely.

His low-pitched assurance did not abandon him.

"You will be very well satisfied," he breathed out quietly.

I was not placated. I had the sense of having been circumvented somehow. Yet I had deceived myself—if there was any deception. But the confounded cheek of inviting himself to breakfast was enough to deceive any one. And the thought struck me: Why! The fellow had provided all these eatables himself in the way of business. I said:

"You must have got up mighty early this morning."

He admitted with simplicity that he was on the quay before six o'clock waiting for my ship to come in. He gave me the impression that it would be impossible to get rid of him now.

"If you think we are going to live on that scale," I said, looking at the table with an irritated eye, "you are jolly well mistaken."

"You'll find it all right, Captain. I quite understand."

Nothing could disturb his equanimity. I felt dissatisfied, but I could not very well fly out at him. He had told me many useful things—and besides he was the brother of that wealthy merchant. That seemed queer enough.

I rose and told him curtly that I must now go ashore. At once he offered the use of his boat for all the time of my stay in port.

"I only make a nominal charge," he continued equably. "My man remains all day at the landing-steps. You have only to blow a whistle when you want the boat."

And, standing aside at every doorway to let me go through first, he carried me off in his custody after all. As we crossed the quarter-deck two shabby individuals stepped forward and in mournful silence offered me business cards which I took from them without a word under his heavy eye. It was a useless and gloomy ceremony. They were the touts of the other ship-chandlers, and he, placid at my back, ignored their existence.

We parted on the quay, after he had expressed quietly the hope of seeing me often "at the store." He had a smoking-room for captains there, with newspapers and a box of "rather decent cigars." I left him very unceremoniously.

My consignees received me with the usual business heartiness, but their account of the state of the freight-market was by no means so favourable as the talk of the wrong Jacobus had led me to expect. Naturally I became inclined now to put my trust in his version, rather. As I closed the door of the private office behind me I thought to myself: "H'm. A lot of lies. Commercial diplomacy. That's the sort of thing a man coming from sea has got to expect. They would try to charter the ship under the market rate."

In the big, outer room, full of desks, the chief clerk, a tall, lean, shaved person in immaculate white clothes and with a shiny, closely cropped black head on which silvery gleams came and went, rose from his place and detained me affably. Anything they could do for me, they would be most happy. Was I likely to call again in the afternoon? What? Going to a funeral? Oh, yes, poor Captain H——.

He pulled a long, sympathetic face for a moment, then, dismissing from this workaday world the baby, which had got ill in a tempest and had died from too much calm at sea, he asked me with a dental, shark-like smile—if sharks had false teeth—whether I had yet made my little arrangements for the ship's stay in port.

"Yes, with Jacobus," I answered carelessly. "I understand he's the brother of Mr. Ernest Jacobus to whom I have an introduction from my owners."

I was not sorry to let him know I was not altogether helpless in the hands of his firm. He screwed his thin lips dubiously.

"Why," I cried, "isn't he the brother?"

"Oh, yes. . . . They haven't spoken to each other for eighteen years," he added impressively after a pause.

"Indeed! What's the quarrel about?"

"Oh, nothing! Nothing that one would care to mention," he protested primly. "He's got quite a large business. The best ship-chandler here, without a doubt. Business is all very well, but there is such a thing as personal character, too, isn't there? Good-morning, Captain."

He went away mincingly to his desk. He amused me. He resembled an old maid, a commercial old maid, shocked by some impropriety. Was it a commercial impropriety? Commercial impropriety is a serious matter, for it aims at one's pocket. Or was he only a purist in conduct who disapproved of Jacobus doing his own touting? It was certainly undignified. I wondered how the merchant brother liked it. But then different countries, different customs. In a community so isolated and so exclusively "trading" social standards have their own scale.

· II ·

I would have gladly dispensed with the mournful opportunity of becoming acquainted by sight with all my fellow-captains at once. However I found my way to the cemetery. We made a considerable group of bareheaded men in sombre garments. I noticed that those of our company most approaching to the now obsolete sea-dog type were the most moved—perhaps because they had less "manner" than the new generation. The old sea-dog, away from his natural element, was a simple and sentimental animal. I noticed one—he was facing me across the grave—who was dropping tears. They trickled down his weather-beaten face like drops of rain on an old rugged wall. I learned afterwards that he was looked upon as the terror of sailors, a hard man; that he had never had wife or chick of his own, and that, engaged from his tenderest years in deep-sea voyages, he knew women and children merely by sight.

Perhaps he was dropping those tears over his lost opportunities, from sheer envy of paternity and in strange jealousy of a sorrow which he could never know. Man, and even the sea-man, is a capricious animal, the creature and the victim of lost opportunities. But he made me feel ashamed of my callousness. I had no tears.

I listened with horribly critical detachment to that service I had had to read myself, once or twice, over childlike men who had died at sea. The words of hope and defiance, the winged words so inspiring in the free immensity of water and sky, seemed to fall wearily into the little grave. What was the use of asking Death where her sting was, before that small, dark hole in the ground? And then my thoughts escaped me altogether—away into matters of life—and no very high matters at that—ships, freights, business. In the instability of his emotions man resembles deplorably a monkey. I was disgusted with my thoughts—and I thought: Shall I be able to get a charter soon? Time's money . . . Will that Jacobus really put good business in my way? . . . I must go and see him in a day or two.

Don't imagine that I pursued these thoughts with any precision. They pursued me rather: vague, shadowy, restless, shamefaced. Theirs was a callous, abominable, almost revolting, pertinacity. And it was the presence of that pertinacious ship-chandler which had started them. He stood mournfully amongst our little band of men from the sea, and I was angry at his presence, which, suggesting his brother the merchant, had caused me to become outrageous to myself. For indeed I had preserved some decency of feeling. It was only the mind which——

It was over at last. The poor father—a man of forty with black, bushy side-whiskers and a pathetic gash on his freshly shaved chin—thanked us all, swallowing his tears. But for some reason, either because I lingered at the gate of the cemetery, being somewhat hazy as to my way back, or because I was the youngest, or ascribing my moodiness caused by remorse to some more worthy and appropriate sentiment, or simply because I was even more of a stranger to him than the others—he singled me out. Keeping at my side, he renewed his thanks, which I listened to in a gloomy, conscience-stricken silence. Suddenly he slipped one hand under my arm and waved the other after a tall, stout figure walking away by itself down a street in a flutter of thin, grey garments:

"That's a good fellow—a real good fellow"—he swallowed down a belated sob—"this Jacobus."

And he told me in a low voice that Jacobus was the first man to board his ship on arrival, and, learning of their misfortune, had taken charge of everything, volunteered to attend to all routine business, carried off the ship's papers on shore, arranged for the funeral——

"A good fellow. I was knocked over. I had been looking at my wife for ten days. And helpless. Just you think of that! The dear little chap died the very day we made the land. How I managed to take the ship in God alone knows! I couldn't see anything; I couldn't speak; I couldn't. . . . You've heard, perhaps, that we lost our mate overboard on the passage? There was no one to do it for me. And the poor woman nearly crazy down below there all alone with the . . . By the Lord! It isn't fair."

We walked in silence together. I did not know how to part from him. On the quay he let go my arm and struck fiercely his fist into the palm of his other hand.

"By God, it isn't fair!" he cried again. "Don't you ever marry unless you can chuck the sea first. . . . It isn't fair."

I had no intention to "chuck the sea," and when he left me to go aboard his ship I felt convinced that I would never marry. While I was waiting at the steps for Jacobus's boatman, who had gone off somewhere, the captain of the *Hilda* joined me, a slender silk umbrella in his hand and the sharp points of his archaic, Gladstonian shirt-collar framing a small, clean-shaved ruddy face. It was wonderfully fresh for his age, beautifully modelled and lit up by remarkably clear blue eyes. A lot of white hair, glossy like spun glass, curled upwards slightly under the brim of his valuable, ancient, panama hat with a broad black ribbon. In the aspect of that vivacious, neat, little old man there was something quaintly angelic and also boyish.

He accosted me, as though he had been in the habit of seeing me every day of his life from my earliest childhood, with a whimsical remark on the appearance of a stout negro woman who was sitting upon a stool near the edge of the quay. Presently he observed amiably that I had a very pretty little barque.

I returned this civil speech by saying readily:

"Not so pretty as the *Hilda*."

At once the corners of his clear-cut, sensitive mouth dropped dismally. "Oh, dear! I can hardly bear to look at her now."

Did I know, he asked anxiously, that he had lost the figurehead of his ship; a woman in a blue tunic edged with gold, the face perhaps not so very, very pretty, but her bare white arms beautifully shaped and extended as if she were swimming? Did I? Who would have expected such a thing! . . . After twenty years too!

Nobody could have guessed from his tone that the woman was made of wood; his trembling voice, his agitated manner gave to his lamentations a ludicrously scandalous flavour. . . . Disappeared at night—a clear fine night with just a slight swell—in the gulf of Bengal. Went off without a splash; no one in the ship could tell why, how, at what hour— after twenty years last October. . . . Did I ever hear! . . .

I assured him sympathetically that I had never heard—and he became very doleful. This meant no good he was sure. There was something in it which looked like a warning. But when I remarked that surely another figure of a woman could be procured I found myself being soundly rated for my levity. The old boy flushed pink under his clear tan as if I had proposed something improper. One could replace masts, I was told, or a lost rudder—any working part of a ship; but where was the use of sticking up a new figurehead? What satisfaction? How could one care for it? It was easy to see that I had never been shipmates with a figure-head for over twenty years.

"A new figurehead!" he scolded in unquenchable indignation. "Why! I've been a widower now for eight-and-twenty years come next May and I would just as soon think of getting a new wife. You're as bad as that fellow Jacobus."

I was highly amused.

"What has Jacobus done? Did he want you to marry again, Captain?" I inquired in a deferential tone. But he was launched now and only grinned fiercely.

"Procure—indeed! He's the sort of chap to procure you anything you like for a price. I hadn't been moored here for an hour when he got on board and at once offered to sell me a figurehead he happens to have in his yard somewhere. He got Smith, my mate, to talk to me about it. 'Mr. Smith,' says I, 'don't you know me better than that? Am I the sort that would pick up with another man's cast-off figurehead?' And after all these years too! The way some of you young fellows talk——''

I affected great compunction, and as I stepped into the boat I said soberly:

"Then I see nothing for it but to fit in a neat fiddlehead—perhaps. You know, carved scrollwork, nicely gilt."

He became very dejected after his outburst.

"Yes. Scrollwork. Maybe. Jacobus hinted at that too. He's never at a loss when there's any money to be extracted from a sailorman. He would make me pay through the nose for that carving. A gilt fiddlehead did you say—eh? I dare say it would do for you. You young fellows don't seem to have any feeling for what's proper."

He made a convulsive gesture with his right arm.

"Never mind. Nothing can make much difference. I would just as soon let the old thing go about the world with a bare cutwater," he cried sadly. Then as the boat got away from the steps he raised his voice on the edge of the quay with comical animosity:

"I would! If only to spite that figurehead-procuring bloodsucker. I am an old bird here and don't you forget it. Come and see me on board some day!"

I spent my first evening in port quietly in my ship's cuddy; and glad enough was I to think that the shore life which strikes one as so pettily complex, discordant, and so full of new faces on first coming from sea, could be kept off for a few hours longer. I was however fated to hear the Jacobus note once more before I slept.

Mr. Burns had gone ashore after the evening meal to have, as he said, "a look round." As it was quite dark when he announced his intention I didn't ask him what it was he expected to see. Some time about midnight, while sitting with a book in the saloon, I heard cautious movements in the lobby and hailed him by name.

Burns came in, stick and hat in hand, incredibly vulgarised by his smart shore togs, with a jaunty air and an odious twinkle in his eye. Being asked to sit down he laid his hat and stick on the table and after we had talked of ship affairs for a little while:

"I've been hearing pretty tales on shore about that ship-chandler fellow who snatched the job from you so neatly, sir."

I remonstrated with my late patient for his manner of expressing himself. But he only tossed his head disdainfully. A pretty dodge indeed: boarding a strange ship with breakfast in two baskets for all hands and calmly inviting himself to the captain's table! Never heard of anything so crafty and so impudent in his life.

I found myself defending Jacobus's unusual methods.

"He's the brother of one of the wealthiest merchants in the port." The mate's eyes fairly snapped green sparks.

"His grand brother hasn't spoken to him for eighteen or twenty years," he declared triumphantly. "So there!"

"I know all about that," I interrupted loftily.

"Do you, sir? H'm!" His mind was still running on the ethics of commercial competition. "I don't like to see your good nature taken advantage of. He's bribed that steward of ours with a five-rupee note to let him come down—or ten for that matter. He don't care. He will shove that and more into the bill presently."

"Is that one of the tales you have heard ashore?" I asked.

He assured me that his own sense could tell him that much. No; what he had heard on shore was that no respectable person in the whole town would come near Jacobus. He lived in a large old-fashioned house in one of the quiet streets with a big garden. After telling me this Burns put on a mysterious air. "He keeps a girl shut up there who, they say——"

"I suppose you've heard all this gossip in some eminently respectable place?" I snapped at him in a most sarcastic tone.

The shaft told, because Mr. Burns, like many other disagreeable people, was very sensitive himself. He remained as if thunderstruck, with his mouth open for some further communication, but I did not give him the chance. "And, anyhow, what the deuce do I care?" I added, retiring into my room.

And this was a natural thing to say. Yet somehow I was not indifferent. I admit it is absurd to be concerned with the morals of one's ship-chandler, if ever so well connected; but his personality had stamped itself upon my first day in harbour, in the way you know.

After this initial exploit Jacobus showed himself anything but intrusive. He was out in a boat early every morning going round the ships he served, and occasionally remaining on board one of them for breakfast with the captain.

As I discovered that this practice was generally accepted, I just nodded to him familiarly when one morning, on coming out of my room, I found him in the cabin. Glancing over the table I saw that his place was already laid. He stood awaiting my appearance, very bulky and placid, holding a beautiful bunch of flowers in his thick hand. He offered them to my notice with a faint, sleepy smile. From his own garden; had a very fine old garden; picked them himself that morning before going out to business; thought I would like. . . . He turned away. "Steward, can you oblige me with some water in a large jar, please?"

I assured him jocularly, as I took my place at the table, that he made me feel as if I were a pretty girl, and that he mustn't be surprised if I blushed. But he was busy arranging his floral tribute at the sideboard. "Stand it before the Captain's plate, steward, please." He made his request in his usual undertone.

The offering was so pointed that I could do no less than to raise it to my nose, and as he sat down noiselessly he breathed out the opinion that a few flowers improved notably the appearance of a ship's saloon. He wondered why I did not have a shelf fitted all round the skylight for flowers in pots to take with me to sea. He had a skilled workman able to fit up shelves in a day, and he could procure me two or three dozen good plants——

The tips of his thick, round fingers rested composedly on the edge of the table on each side of his cup of coffee. His face remained immovable. Mr. Burns was smiling maliciously to himself. I declared that I hadn't the slightest intention of turning my skylight into a conservatory only to keep the cabin-table in a perpetual mess of mould and dead vegetable matter.

"Rear most beautiful flowers," he insisted with an upward glance. "It's no trouble really."

"Oh, yes, it is. Lots of trouble," I contradicted. "And in the end some fool leaves the skylight open in a fresh breeze, a flick of salt water gets at them and the whole lot is dead in a week."

Mr. Burns snorted a contemptuous approval. Jacobus gave up the subject passively. After a time he unglued his thick lips to ask me if I had seen his brother yet. I was very curt in my answer.

"No, not yet."

"A very different person," he remarked dreamily and got up. His movements were particularly noiseless. "Well—thank you, Captain. If anything is not to your liking please mention it to your steward. I suppose you will be giving a dinner to the office-clerks presently."

"What for?" I cried with some warmth. "If I were a steady trader to the port I could understand it. But a complete stranger! . . . I may not turn up again here for years. I don't see why I . . . Do you mean to say it is customary?"

"It will be expected from a man like you," he breathed out placidly. "Eight of the principal clerks, the manager, that's nine, you three gentlemen, that's twelve. It needn't be very expensive. If you tell your steward to give me a day's notice——"

"It will be expected of me! Why should it be expected of me? Is it because I look particularly soft—or what?"

His immobility struck me as dignified suddenly, his imperturbable quality as dangerous. "There's plenty of time to think about that," I concluded weakly with a gesture that tried to wave him away. But before he departed he took time to mention regretfully that he had not yet had the pleasure of seeing me at his "store" to sample those cigars. He had a parcel of six thousand to dispose of, very cheap.

"I think it would be worth your while to secure some," he added with a fat, melancholy smile and left the cabin.

Mr. Burns struck his fist on the table excitedly.

"Did you ever see such impudence! He's made up his mind to get something out of you one way or another, sir."

At once feeling inclined to defend Jacobus, I observed philosophically that all this was business, I supposed. But my absurd mate, muttering broken disjointed sentences, such as: "I cannot bear! . . . Mark my words! . . ." and so on, flung out of the cabin. If I hadn't nursed him through that deadly fever I wouldn't have suffered such manners for a single day.

· III ·

Jacobus having put me in mind of his wealthy brother I concluded I would pay that business call at once. I had by that time heard a little more of him. He was a member of the Council, where he made himself objectionable to the authorities. He exercised a considerable influence on public opinion. Lots of people owed him money. He was an importer on a great scale of all sorts of goods. For instance, the whole supply of bags for sugar was practically in his hands. This last fact I did not learn till afterwards. The general impression conveyed to me was that of a local personage. He was a bachelor and gave weekly card-parties in his house out of town, which were attended by the best people in the colony.

The greater, then, was my surprise to discover his office in shabby surroundings, quite away from the business quarter, amongst a lot of hovels. Guided by a black board with white lettering, I climbed a narrow wooden staircase and entered a room with a bare floor of planks littered with bits of brown paper and wisps of packing straw. A great number of what looked like wine-cases were piled up against one of the walls. A lanky, inky, light-yellow, mulatto youth, miserably long-necked and generally recalling a sick chicken, got off a three-legged stool behind a cheap deal desk and faced me as if gone dumb with fright. I had some difficulty in persuading him to take in my name, though I could not get from him the nature of his objection. He did it at last with an almost agonised reluctance which ceased to be mysterious to me when I heard him being sworn at menacingly with savage, suppressed growls, then audibly cuffed and finally kicked out without any concealment whatever; because he came back flying head foremost through the door with a stifled shriek.

To say I was startled would not express it. I remained still, like a man lost in a dream. Clapping both his hands to that part of his frail anatomy which had received the shock, the poor wretch said to me simply:

"Will you go in, please."

His lamentable self-possession was wonderful; but it did not do away with the incredibility of the experience. A preposterous notion that I had seen this boy somewhere before, a thing obviously impossible, was like a delicate finishing touch of weirdness added to a scene fit to raise doubts as to one's sanity. I stared anxiously about me like an awakened somnambulist.

"I say," I cried loudly, "there isn't a mistake, is there? This is Mr. Jacobus's office?"

The boy gazed at me with a pained expression—and somehow so familiar! A voice within growled offensively:

"Come in, come in, since you are there. . . . I didn't know."

I crossed the outer room as one approaches the den of some unknown wild beast; with intrepidity but in some excitement. Only no wild beast that ever lived would rouse one's indignation; the power to do that belongs to the odiousness of the human brute. And I was very indignant, which did not prevent me from being at once struck by the extraordinary resemblance of the two brothers.

This one was dark instead of being fair like the other; but he was as big. He was without his coat and waistcoat; he had been doubtless snoozing in the rocking-chair which stood in a corner furthest from the window. Above the great bulk of his crumpled white shirt, buttoned with three diamond studs, his round face looked swarthy. It was moist; his brown moustache hung limp and ragged. He pushed a common, cane-bottomed chair towards me with his foot.

"Sit down."

I glanced at it casually, then, turning my indignant eyes full upon him, I declared in precise and incisive tones that I had called in obedience to my owners' instructions.

"Oh! Yes. H'm! I didn't understand what that fool was saying? . . . But never mind! It will teach the scoundrel to disturb me at this time of the day," he added, grinning at me with savage cynicism.

I looked at my watch. It was past three o'clock—quite the full swing of afternoon office work in the port. He snarled imperiously: "Sit down, Captain."

I acknowledged the gracious invitation by saying deliberately:

"I can listen to all you may have to say without sitting down."

Emitting a loud and vehement "Pshaw!" he glared for a moment, very round-eyed and fierce. It was like a gigantic tomcat spitting at one suddenly. "Look at him! . . . What do you fancy yourself to be? What did you come here for? If you won't sit down and talk business you had better go to the devil."

"I don't know him personally," I said. "But after this I wouldn't mind calling on him. It would be refreshing to meet a gentleman."

He followed me, growling behind my back:

"The impudence! I've a good mind to write to your owners what I think of you."

I turned on him for a moment:

"As it happens I don't care. For my part I assure you I won't even take the trouble to mention you to them."

He stopped at the door of his office while I traversed the littered anteroom. I think he was somewhat taken aback.

"I will break every bone in your body," he roared suddenly at the miserable mulatto lad, "if you ever dare to disturb me before half-past three for anybody. D'ye hear? For anybody! . . . Let alone any damned skipper," he added, in a lower growl.

The frail youngster, swaying like a reed, made a low moaning sound. I stopped short and addressed this sufferer with advice. It was prompted by the sight of a hammer (used for opening the wine-cases, I suppose) which was lying on the floor.

"If I were you, my boy, I would have that thing up my sleeve when I went in next and at the first occasion I would——"

What was there so familiar in that lad's yellow face? Entrenched and quaking behind the flimsy desk, he never looked up. His heavy, lowered eyelids gave me suddenly the clue of the puzzle. He resembled—yes, those thick glued lips—he resembled the brothers Jacobus. He resembled both, the wealthy merchant and the pushing shopkeeper (who resembled each other); he resembled them as much as a thin, light-yellow mulatto lad may resemble a big, stout, middle-aged white man. It was the exotic complexion and the slightness of his build which had put me off so completely. Now I saw in him unmistakably the Jacobus strain, weakened, attenuated, diluted as it were in a bucket of water—and I refrained from finishing my speech. I had intended to say: "Crack this brute's head for him." I still felt the conclusion to be sound. But it is no trifling responsibility to counsel parricide to any one, however deeply injured.

"Beggarly—cheeky—skippers."

I despised the emphatic growl at my back; only, being much vexed and upset, I regret to say that I slammed the door behind me in a most undignified manner.

It may not appear altogether absurd if I say that I brought out from that interview a kindlier view of the other Jacobus. It was with a feeling resembling partisanship that, a few days later, I called at his "store." That long, cavern-like place of business, very dim at the back and stuffed full of all sorts of goods, was entered from the street by a lofty archway. At the far end I saw my Jacobus exerting himself in his shirt-sleeves among his assistants. The captain's room was a small, vaulted apartment with a stone floor and heavy iron bars in its windows like a dungeon converted to hospitable purposes. A couple of cheerful bottles and several gleaming glasses made a brilliant cluster round a tall, cool red earthenware pitcher on the centre table which was littered with newspapers from all parts of the world. A well-groomed stranger in a smart

grey check suit, sitting with one leg flung over his knee, put down one
of these sheets briskly and nodded to me.

I guessed him to be a steamer-captain. It was impossible to get to
know these men. They came and went too quickly and their ships lay
moored far out, at the very entrance of the harbour. Theirs was another
life altogether. He yawned slightly.

"Dull hole, isn't it?"

I understood this to allude to the town.

"Do you find it so?" I murmured.

"Don't you? But I'm off to-morrow, thank goodness."

He was a very gentlemanly person, good-natured and superior. I
watched him draw the open box of cigars to his side of the table, take
a big cigar-case out of his pocket and begin to fill it very methodically.
Presently, on our eyes meeting, he winked like a common mortal and
invited me to follow his example. "They are really decent smokes." I
shook my head.

"I am not off to-morrow."

"What of that? Think I am abusing old Jacobus's hospitality? Heavens! It goes into the bill, of course. He spreads such little matters all
over his account. He can take care of himself! Why, it's business——"

I noted a shadow fall over his well-satisfied expression, a momentary
hesitation in closing his cigar-case. But he ended by putting it in his
pocket jauntily. A placid voice uttered in the doorway: "That's quite
correct, Captain."

The large noiseless Jacobus advanced into the room. His quietness,
in the circumstances, amounted to cordiality. He had put on his jacket
before joining us, and he sat down in the chair vacated by the steamer-
man, who nodded again to me and went out with a short, jarring laugh.
A profound silence reigned. With his drowsy stare Jacobus seemed to be
slumbering open-eyed. Yet, somehow, I was aware of being profoundly
scrutinised by those heavy eyes. In the enormous cavern of the store
somebody began to nail down a case, expertly: tap-tap . . . tap-tap-tap.
Two other experts, one slow and nasal, the other shrill and snappy,
started checking an invoice.

"A half-coil of three-inch manilla rope."

"Right!"

"Six assorted shackles."

"Right!"

"Six tins assorted soups, three of paté, two asparagus, fourteen pounds tobacco, cabin."

"Right!"

"It's for the captain who was here just now," breathed out the immovable Jacobus. "These steamer orders are very small. They pick up what they want as they go along. That man will be in Samarang in less than a fortnight. Very small orders indeed."

The calling over of the items went on in the shop; an extraordinary jumble of varied articles, paint-brushes, Yorkshire Relish, etc., etc. . . . "Three sacks of best potatoes," read out the nasal voice.

At this Jacobus blinked like a sleeping man roused by a shake, and displayed some animation. At his order, shouted into the shop, a smirking half-caste clerk with his ringlets much oiled and with a pen stuck behind his ear, brought in a sample of six potatoes which he paraded in a row on the table.

Being urged to look at their beauty I gave them a cold and hostile glance. Calmly, Jacobus proposed that I should order ten or fifteen tons—tons! I couldn't believe my ears. My crew could not have eaten such a lot in a year; and potatoes (excuse these practical remarks) are a highly perishable commodity. I thought he was joking—or else trying to find out whether I was an unutterable idiot. But his purpose was not so simple. I discovered that he meant me to buy them on my own account.

"I am proposing you a bit of business, Captain. I wouldn't charge you a great price."

I told him that I did not go in for trade. I even added grimly that I knew only too well how that sort of spec. generally ended.

He sighed and clasped his hands on his stomach with exemplary resignation. I admired the placidity of his impudence. Then waking up somewhat:

"Won't you try a cigar, Captain?"

"No, thanks. I don't smoke cigars."

"For once!" he exclaimed, in a patient whisper. A melancholy silence ensued. You know how sometimes a person discloses a certain unsuspected depth and acuteness of thought; that is, in other words, utters something unexpected. It was unexpected enough to hear Jacobus say:

"The man who just went out was right enough. You might take one, Captain. Here everything is bound to be in the way of business."

I felt a little ashamed of myself. The remembrance of his horrid brother made him appear quite a decent sort of fellow. It was with some compunction that I said a few words to the effect that I could have no possible objection to his hospitality.

Before I was a minute older I saw where this admission was leading me. As if changing the subject Jacobus mentioned that his private house was about ten minutes' walk away. It had a beautiful old walled garden. Something really remarkable. I ought to come round some day and have a look at it.

He seemed to be a lover of gardens. I too take extreme delight in them; but I did not mean my compunction to carry me as far as Jacobus's flower-beds, however beautiful and old. He added, with a certain homeliness of tone:

"There's only my girl there."

It is difficult to set everything down in due order; so I must revert here to what happened a week or two before. The medical officer of the port had come on board my ship to have a look at one of my crew who was ailing, and naturally enough he was asked to step into the cabin. A fellow-shipmaster of mine was there too; and in the conversation, somehow or other, the name of Jacobus came to be mentioned. It was pronounced with no particular reverence by the other man, I believe. I don't remember now what I was going to say. The doctor—a pleasant, cultivated fellow, with an assured manner—prevented me by striking in, in a sour tone:

"Ah! You're talking about my respected papa-in-law."

Of course, that sally silenced us at the time. But I remembered the episode, and at this juncture, pushed for something non-committal to say, I inquired with polite surprise:

"You have your married daughter living with you, Mr. Jacobus?"

He moved his big hand from right to left quietly. No! That was another of his girls, he stated, ponderously and under his breath as usual. She . . . He seemed in a pause to be ransacking his mind for some kind of descriptive phrase. But my hopes were disappointed. He merely produced his stereotyped definition.

"She's a very different sort of person."

"Indeed. . . . And by the by, Jacobus, I called on your brother the other day. It's no great compliment if I say that I found him a very different sort of person from you."

He had an air of profound reflection, then remarked quaintly: "He's a man of regular habits."

He might have been alluding to the habit of late siesta; but I mumbled something about "beastly habits anyhow"—and left the store abruptly.

· IV ·

My little passage with Jacobus the merchant became known generally. One or two of my acquaintances made distant allusions to it. Perhaps the mulatto boy had talked. I must confess that people appeared rather scandalised, but not with Jacobus's brutality. A man I knew remonstrated with me for my hastiness.

I gave him the whole story of my visit, not forgetting the tell-tale resemblance of the wretched mulatto boy to his tormentor. He was not surprised. No doubt, no doubt. What of that? In a jovial tone he assured me that there must be many of that sort. The elder Jacobus had been a bachelor all his life. A highly respectable bachelor. But there had never been open scandal in that connection. His life had been quite regular. It could cause no offence to any one.

I said that I had been offended considerably. My interlocutor opened very wide eyes. Why? Because a mulatto lad got a few knocks? That was not a great affair, surely. I had no idea how insolent and untruthful these half-castes were. In fact he seemed to think Mr. Jacobus rather kind than otherwise to employ that youth at all; a sort of amiable weakness which could be forgiven.

This acquaintance of mine belonged to one of the old French families, descendants of the old colonists; all noble, all impoverished, and living a narrow domestic life in dull, dignified decay. The men, as a rule, occupy inferior posts in Government offices or in business houses. The girls are almost always pretty, ignorant of the world, kind and agreeable and generally bilingual; they prattle innocently both in French and English. The emptiness of their existence passes belief. I obtained my entry into a couple of such households because some years before, in Bombay, I had occasion to be of use to a pleasant, ineffectual young man who was rather stranded there, not knowing what to do with himself or even how to get home to his island again. It was a matter of two hundred rupees or so, but, when I turned up, the family made a point of showing their gratitude by admitting me to their intimacy. My knowledge of the French language made me specially acceptable. They had meantime managed to marry the fellow to a woman nearly twice his age, comparatively well off: the only profession he was really fit for. But it was not all cakes and ale. The first time I called on the couple she spied a little spot of grease on the poor devil's pantaloons and made him a screaming scene of reproaches so full of sincere passion that I sat terrified as at a tragedy of Racine.

Of course there was never question of the money I had advanced him; but his sisters, Miss Angele and Miss Mary, and the aunts of both families, who spoke quaint archaic French of pre-Revolution period, and a host of distant relations adopted me for a friend outright in a manner which was almost embarrassing.

It was with the eldest brother (he was employed at a desk in my consignee's office) that I was having this talk about the merchant Jacobus. He regretted my attitude and nodded his head sagely. An influential man. One never knew when one would need him. I expressed my immense preference for the shopkeeper of the two. At that my friend looked grave.

"What on earth are you pulling that long face about?" I cried impatiently. "He asked me to see his garden and I have a good mind to go some day."

"Don't do that," he said, so earnestly that I burst into a fit of laughter; but he looked at me without a smile.

This was another matter altogether. At one time the public conscience of the island had been mightily troubled by my Jacobus. The two brothers had been partners for years in great harmony, when a wandering circus came to the island and my Jacobus became suddenly infatuated with one of the lady-riders. What made it worse was that he was married. He had not even the grace to conceal his passion. It must have been strong indeed to carry away such a large placid creature. His behaviour was perfectly scandalous.

He followed that woman to the Cape, and apparently travelled at the tail of that beastly circus to other parts of the world, in a most degrading position. The woman soon ceased to care for him, and treated him worse than a dog. Most extraordinary stories of moral degradation were reaching the island at that time. He had not the strength of mind to shake himself free. . . .

The grotesque image of a fat, pushing ship-chandler, enslaved by an unholy love-spell, fascinated me; and I listened rather open-mouthed to the tale as old as the world, a tale which had been the subject of legend, of moral fables, of poems, but which so ludicrously failed to fit the personality. What a strange victim for the gods!

Meantime his deserted wife had died. His daughter was taken care of by his brother, who married her as advantageously as was possible in the circumstances.

"Oh! The Mrs. Doctor!" I exclaimed.

"You know that? Yes. A very able man. He wanted a lift in the world, and there was a good bit of money from her mother, besides the expectations. . . . Of course, they don't know him," he added. "The doctor nods in the street, I believe, but he avoids speaking to him when they meet on board a ship, as must happen sometimes."

I remarked that this surely was an old story by now.

My friend assented. But it was Jacobus's own fault that it was neither forgiven nor forgotten. He came back ultimately. But how? Not in a spirit of contrition, in a way to propitiate his scandalized fellow citizens. He must needs drag along with him a child—a girl. . . .

"He spoke to me of a daughter who lives with him," I observed, very much interested.

"She's certainly the daughter of the circus-woman," said my friend. "She may be his daughter too; I am willing to admit that she is. In fact I have no doubt——"

But he did not see why she should have been brought into a respectable community to perpetuate the memory of the scandal. And that was not the worst. Presently something much more distressing happened. That abandoned woman turned up. Landed from a mail-boat. . . .

"What! Here? To claim the child perhaps," I suggested.

"Not she!" My friendly informant was very scornful. "Imagine a painted, haggard, agitated, desperate hag. Been cast off in Mozambique by somebody who paid her passage here. She had been injured internally by a kick from a horse; she hadn't a cent on her when she got ashore; I don't think she even asked to see the child. At any rate, not till the last day of her life. Jacobus hired for her a bungalow to die in. He got a couple of Sisters from the hospital to nurse her through these few months. If he didn't marry her *in extremis* as the good Sisters tried to bring about, it's because she wouldn't even hear of it. As the nuns said: 'The woman died impenitent.' It was reported that she ordered Jacobus out of the room with her last breath. This may be the real reason why he didn't go into mourning himself; He only put the child into black. While she was little she was to be seen sometimes about the streets attended by a negro woman, but since she became of age to put her hair up I don't think she has set foot outside that garden once. She must be over eighteen now."

Thus my friend, with some added details; such as, that he didn't think the girl had spoken to three people of any position in the island; that an elderly female relative of the brothers Jacobus had been induced by extreme poverty to accept the position of gouvernante to the girl. As to Jacobus's business (which certainly annoyed his brother) it was a wise choice on his part. It brought him in contact only with strangers of passage; whereas any other would have given rise to all sorts of awkwardness with his social equals. The man was not wanting in a certain tact— only he was naturally shameless. For why did he want to keep that girl with him? It was most painful for everybody.

I thought suddenly (and with profound disgust) of the other Jacobus, and I could not refrain from saying slily:

"I suppose if he employed her, say, as a scullion in his household and occasionally pulled her hair or boxed her ears, the position would have been more regular—less shocking to the respectable class to which he belongs."

He was not so stupid as to miss my intention, and shrugged his shoulders impatiently.

"You don't understand. To begin with, she's not a mulatto. And a scandal is a scandal. People should be given a chance to forget. I dare say it would have been better for her if she had been turned into a scullion or something of that kind. Of course he's trying to make money in every sort of petty way, but in such a business there'll never be enough for anybody to come forward."

When my friend left me I had a conception of Jacobus and his daughter existing, a lonely pair of castaways, on a desert island; the girl sheltering in the house as if it were a cavern in a cliff, and Jacobus going out to pick up a living for both on the beach—exactly like two shipwrecked people who always hope for some rescuer to bring them back at last into touch with the rest of mankind.

But Jacobus's bodily reality did not fit in with this romantic view.

When he turned up on board in the usual course, he sipped the cup of coffee placidly, asked me if I was satisfied—and I hardly listened to the harbour gossip he dropped slowly in his low, voice-saving enunciation. I had then troubles of my own. My ship chartered, my thoughts dwelling on the success of a quick-round voyage, I had been suddenly confronted by a shortage of bags. A catastrophe! The stock of one especial kind, called pockets, seemed to be totally exhausted. A consignment was shortly expected—it was afloat, on its way, but, meantime, the loading of my ship dead stopped, I had enough to worry about. My consignees, who had received me with such heartiness on my arrival, now, in the character of my charterers, listened to my complaints with polite help-lessness. Their manager, the old-maidish, thin man, who so prudishly didn't even like to speak about the impure Jacobus, gave me the correct commercial view of the position.

"My dear Captain"—he was retracting his leathery cheeks into a condescending, shark-like smile—"we were not morally obliged to tell you of a possible shortage before you signed the charter-party. It was for you to guard against the contingency of a delay—strictly speaking. But of course we shouldn't have taken any advantage. This is no one's fault really. We ourselves have been taken unawares," he concluded primly, with an obvious lie.

This lecture I confess had made me thirsty. Suppressed rage generally produces that effect; and as I strolled on aimlessly I bethought myself of the tall earthenware pitcher in the captains' room of the Jacobus "store."

With no more than a nod to the men I found assembled there, I poured down a deep, cool draught on my indignation, then another, and then, becoming dejected, I sat plunged in cheerless reflections. The others read, talked, smoked, bandied over my head some unsubtle chaff. But my abstraction was respected. And it was without a word to any one that I rose and went out, only to be quite unexpectedly accosted in the bustle of the store by Jacobus the outcast.

"Glad to see you, Captain. What? Going away? You haven't been looking so well these last few days, I notice. Run down, eh?"

He was in his shirt-sleeves, and his words were in the usual course of business, but they had a human note. It was commercial amenity, but I had been a stranger to amenity in that connection. I do verily believe (from the direction of his heavy glance towards a certain shelf) that he was going to suggest the purchase of Clarkson's Nerve Tonic, which he kept in stock, when I said impulsively:

"I am rather in trouble with my loading."

Wide awake under his sleepy, broad mask with glued lips, he understood at once, had a movement of the head so appreciative that I relieved my exasperation by explaining:

"Surely there must be eleven hundred quarter-bags to be found in the colony. It's only a matter of looking for them."

Again that slight movement of the big head, and in the noise and activity of the store that tranquil murmur:

"To be sure. But then people likely to have a reserve of quarter-bags wouldn't want to sell. They'd need that size themselves."

"That's exactly what my consignees are telling me. Impossible to buy. Bosh! They don't want to. It suits them to have the ship hung up. But if I were to discover the lot they would have to——Look here, Jacobus! *You* are the man to have such a thing up your sleeve."

He protested with a ponderous swing of his big head. I stood before him helplessly, being looked at by those heavy eyes with a veiled expression as of a man after some soul-shaking crisis. Then, suddenly:

"It's impossible to talk quietly here," he whispered. "I am very busy. But if you could go and wait for me in my house. It's less than ten minutes' walk. Oh, yes, you don't know the way."

He called for his coat and offered to take me there himself. He would have to return to the store at once for an hour or so to finish his business, and then he would be at liberty to talk over with me that matter of quarter-bags. This programme was breathed out at me through slightly parted, still lips; his heavy, motionless glance rested upon me, placid as ever, the glance of a tired man—but I felt that it was searching, too. I could not imagine what he was looking for in me and kept silent, wondering.

"I am asking you to wait for me in my house till I am at liberty to talk this matter over. You will?"

"Why, of course!" I cried.

"But I cannot promise——"

"I dare say not," I said. "I don't expect a promise."

"I mean I can't even promise to try the move I've in my mind. One must see first . . . h'm!"

"All right. I'll take the chance. I'll wait for you as long as you like. What else have I to do in this infernal hole of a port!"

Before I had uttered my last words we had set off at a swinging pace. We turned a couple of corners and entered a street completely empty of traffic, of semi-rural aspect, paved with cobblestones nestling in grass tufts. The house came to the line of the roadway; a single story on an elevated basement of rough-stones, so that our heads were below the level of the windows as we went along. All the jalousies were tightly shut, like eyes, and the house seemed fast asleep in the afternoon sunshine. The entrance was at the side, in an alley even more grass-grown than the street: a small door, simply on the latch.

With a word of apology as to showing me the way, Jacobus preceded me up a dark passage and led me across the naked parquet floor of what I supposed to be the dining room. It was lighted by three glass doors which stood wide open on to a verandah or rather loggia running its brick arches along the garden side of the house. It was really a magnificent garden: smooth green lawns and a gorgeous maze of flower-beds in the foreground, displayed around a basin of dark water framed in a marble rim, and in the distance the massed foliage of varied trees concealing the roofs of other houses. The town might have been miles away. It was a brilliantly coloured solitude, drowsing in a warm, voluptuous silence. Where the long, still shadows fell across the beds, and in shady nooks, the massed colors of the flowers had an extraordinary magnificence of effect. I stood entranced. Jacobus grasped me delicately above the elbow, impelling me to a half-turn to the left.

I had not noticed the girl before. She occupied a low, deep, wickerwork arm-chair, and I saw her in exact profile like a figure in a tapestry, and as motionless. Jacobus released my arm.

"This is Alice," he announced tranquilly; and his subdued manner of speaking made it sound so much like a confidential communication that I fancied myself nodding understandingly and whispering: "I see, I see." . . . Of course, I did nothing of the kind. Neither of us did anything; we stood side by side looking down at the girl. For quite a time she did not stir, staring straight before her as if watching the vision of some pageant passing through the garden in the deep, rich glow of light and the splendour of flowers.

Then, coming to the end of her reverie, she looked round and up. If I had not at first noticed her, I am certain that she too had been unaware of my presence till she actually perceived me by her father's side. The quickened upward movement of the heavy eyelids, the widening of the languid glance, passing into a fixed stare, put that beyond doubt.

Under her amazement there was a hint of fear, and then came a flash as of anger. Jacobus, after uttering my name fairly loud, said: "Make yourself at home, Captain—I won't be gone long," and went away rapidly. Before I had time to make a bow I was left alone with the girl—who, I remembered suddenly, had not been seen by any man or woman of that town since she had found it necessary to put up her hair. It looked as though it had not been touched again since that distant time of first putting up; it was a mass of black, lustrous locks, twisted anyhow high on her head, with long, untidy wisps hanging down on each side of the clear sallow face; a mass so thick and strong and abundant that, nothing but to look at, it gave you a sensation of heavy pressure on the top of your head and an impression of magnificently cynical untidiness. She leaned forward, hugging herself with crossed legs; a dingy, amber-coloured flounced wrapper of some thin stuff revealed the young supple body drawn together tensely in the deep low seat as if crouching for a spring. I detected a slight, quivering start or two, which looked uncommonly like bounding away. They were followed by the most absolute immobility.

The absurd impulse to run out after Jacobus (for I had been startled, too) once repressed, I took a chair, placed it not very far from her, sat down deliberately, and began to talk about the garden, caring not what I said, but using a gentle caressing intonation as one talks to soothe a startled wild animal. I could not even be certain that she understood me. She never raised her face nor attempted to look my way. I kept on talking only to prevent her from taking flight. She had another of those quivering, repressed starts which made me catch my breath with apprehension.

Ultimately I formed a notion that what prevented her perhaps from going off in one great, nervous leap, was the scantiness of her attire. The wicker arm-chair was the most substantial thing about her person. What she had on under that dingy, loose, amber wrapper must have been of the most flimsy and airy character. One could not help being aware of it. It was obvious. I felt it actually embarrassing at first; but that sort of embarrassment is got over easily by a mind not enslaved by narrow prejudices. I did not avert my gaze from Alice. I went on talking with ingratiating softness, the recollection that, most likely, she had never before been spoken to by a strange man adding to my assurance. I don't know why an emotional tenseness should have crept into the situation. But it did. And just as I was becoming aware of it a slight scream cut short my flow of urbane speech.

The scream did not proceed from the girl. It was emitted behind me, and caused me to turn my head sharply. I understood at once that the apparition in the doorway was the elderly relation of Jacobus, the companion, the gouvernante. While she remained thunderstruck, I got up and made her a low bow.

The ladies of Jacobus's household evidently spent their days in light attire. This stumpy old woman with a face like a large wrinkled lemon, beady eyes, and shock of iron-grey hair, was dressed in a garment of some ash-coloured, silky, light stuff. It fell from her thick neck down to her toes with the simplicity of an unadorned nightgown. It made her appear truly cylindrical. She exclaimed: "How did you get here?"

Before I could say a word she vanished and presently I heard a confusion of shrill protestations in a distant part of the house. Obviously no one could tell her how I got there. In a moment, with great outcries from two negro women following her, she waddled back to the doorway, infuriated.

"What do you want here?"

I turned to the girl. She was sitting straight up now, her hands posed on the arms of the chair. I appealed to her.

"Surely, Miss Alice, you will not let them drive me out into the street?"

Her magnificent black eyes, narrowed, long in shape, swept over me with an indefinable expression, then in a harsh, contemptuous voice she let fall in French a sort of explanation:

"*C'est papa.*"

I made another low bow to the old woman.

She turned her back on me in order to drive away her black hench-women, then surveying my person in a peculiar manner with one small eye nearly closed and her face all drawn up on that side as if with a twinge of toothache, she stepped out on the verandah, sat down in a rocking-chair some distance away, and took up her knitting from a little table. Before she started at it she plunged one of the needles into the mop of her grey hair and stirred it vigorously.

Her elementary nightgown-sort of frock clung to her ancient, stumpy, and floating form. She wore white cotton stockings and flat brown velvet slippers. Her feet and ankles were obtrusively visible on the footrest. She began to rock herself slightly, while she knitted. I had resumed my seat and kept quiet, for I mistrusted that old woman. What if she ordered me to depart? She seemed capable of any outrage. She had snorted once or twice; she was knitting violently. Suddenly she piped at the young girl in French a question which I translate colloquially:

"What's your father up to, now?"

The young creature shrugged her shoulders so comprehensively that her whole body swayed within the loose wrapper; and in that unexpectedly harsh voice which yet had a seductive quality to the senses, like certain kinds of natural rough wines one drinks with pleasure:

"It's some captain. Leave me alone—will you!"

The chair rocked quicker, the old, thin voice was like a whistle.

"You and your father make a pair. He would stick at nothing—that's well known. But I didn't expect this."

I thought it high time to air some of my own French. I remarked modestly, but firmly, that this was business. I had some matters to talk over with Mr. Jacobus.

At once she piped out a derisive "Poor innocent!" Then, with a change of tone: "The shop's for business. Why don't you go to the shop to talk with him?"

The furious speed of her fingers and knitting-needles made one dizzy; and with squeaky indignation:

"Sitting here staring at that girl—is that what you call business?"

"No," I said suavely. "I call this pleasure—an unexpected pleasure. And unless Miss Alice objects——"

I half turned to her. She flung at me an angry and contemptuous "Don't care!" and leaning her elbow on her knees took her chin in her hand—a Jacobus chin undoubtedly. And those heavy eyelids, this black irritated stare reminded me of Jacobus, too—the wealthy merchant, the respected one. The design of her eyebrows also was the same, rigid and ill-omened. Yes! I traced in her a resemblance to both of them. It came to me as a sort of surprising remote inference that both these Jacobuses were rather handsome men after all. I said:

"Oh! Then I shall stare at you till you smile."

She favoured me again with an even more viciously scornful "Don't care!"

The old woman broke in blunt and shrill:

"Hear his impudence! And you too! Don't care! Go at least and put some more clothes on. Sitting there like this before this sailor riff-raff."

The sun was about to leave the Pearl of the Ocean for other seas, for other lands. The walled garden full of shadows blazed with colour as if the flowers were giving up the light absorbed during the day. The amazing old woman became very explicit. She suggested to the girl a corset and a petticoat with a cynical unreserve which humiliated me. Was I of no more account than a wooden dummy? The girl snapped out: "Shan't!"

It was not the naughty retort of a vulgar child; it had a note of desperation. Clearly my intrusion had somehow upset the balance of their established relations. The old woman knitted with furious accuracy, her eyes fastened down on her work.

"Oh, you are the true child of your father! And *that* talks of entering a convent! Letting herself be stared at by a fellow."

"Leave off."

"Shameless thing!"

"Old sorceress," the girl uttered distinctly, preserving her meditative pose, chin in hand, and a far-away stare over the garden.

It was like the quarrel of the kettle and the pot. The old woman flew out of the chair, banged down her work, and with a great play of thick limb perfectly visible in that weird, clinging garment of hers, strode at the girl—who never stirred. I was experiencing a sort of trepidation when, as if awed by that unconscious attitude, the aged relative of Jacobus turned short upon me.

She was, I perceived, armed with a knitting-needle; and as she raised her hand her intention seemed to be to throw it at me like a dart. But she only used it to scratch her head with, examining me the while at close range, one eye nearly shut and her face distorted by a whimsical, one-sided grimace.

"My dear man," she asked abruptly, "do you expect any good to come of this?"

"I do hope so indeed, Miss Jacobus." I tried to speak in the easy tone of an afternoon caller. "You see, I am here after some bags."

"Bags! Look at that now! Didn't I hear you holding forth to that graceless wretch?"

"You would like to see me in my grave," uttered the motionless girl hoarsely.

"Grave! What about me? Buried alive before I am dead for the sake of a thing blessed with such a pretty father!" she cried; and turning to me: "You're one of those men he does business with. Well—why don't you leave us in peace, my good fellow?"

It was said in a tone—this "leave us in peace." There was a sort of ruffianly familiarity, a superiority, a scorn in it. I was to hear it more than once, for you would show an imperfect knowledge of human nature if you thought that this was my last visit to that house—where no respectable person had put foot for ever so many years. No, you would be very much mistaken if you imagined that this reception had scared me away. First of all I was not going to run before a grotesque and ruffianly old woman.

And then you mustn't forget these necessary bags. That first evening Jacobus made me stay to dinner; after, however, telling me loyally that he didn't know whether he could do anything at all for me. He had been thinking it over. It was too difficult, he feared. . . . But he did not give it up in so many words.

We were only three at table; the girl by means of repeated "Won't!" "Shan't!" and "Don't care!" having conveyed and affirmed her intention not to come to the table, not to have any dinner, not to move from the verandah. The old relative hopped about in her flat slippers and piped indignantly, Jacobus towered over her and murmured placidly in his throat; I joined jocularly from a distance, throwing in a few words, for which under the cover of the night I received secretly a most vicious poke in the ribs from the old woman's elbow or perhaps her fist. I restrained a cry. And all the time the girl didn't even condescend to raise her head to look at any of us. All this may sound childish—and yet that stony, petulant sullenness had an obscurely tragic flavour.

And so we sat down to the food around the light of a good many candles while she remained crouching out there, staring in the dark as if feeding her bad temper on the heavily scented air of the admirable garden.

Before leaving I said to Jacobus that I would come next day to hear if the bag affair had made any progress. He shook his head slightly at that.

"I'll haunt your house daily till you pull it off. You'll be always finding me here."

His faint, melancholy smile did not part his thick lips.

"That will be all right, Captain."

Then seeing me to the door, very tranquil, he murmured earnestly the recommendation: "Make yourself at home," and also the hospitable hint about there being always "a plate of soup." It was only on my way to the quay, down the ill-lighted streets, that I remembered I had been engaged to dine that very evening with the S——family. Though vexed with my forgetfulness (it would be rather awkward to explain) I couldn't help thinking that it had procured me a more amusing evening. And besides—business. The sacred business——.

In a barefooted negro who overtook me at a run and bolted down the landing-steps I recognised Jacobus's boatman, who must have been feeding in the kitchen. His usual "Good-night, sah!" as I went up my ship's ladder had a more cordial sound than on previous occasions.

· V ·

I kept my word to Jacobus. I haunted his home. He was perpetually finding me there of an afternoon when he popped in for a moment from the "store." The sound of my voice talking to his Alice greeted him on his doorstep; and when he returned for good in the evening, ten to one he would hear it still going on in the verandah. I just nodded to him; he would sit down heavily and gently, and watch with a sort of approving anxiety my efforts to make his daughter smile.

I called her often "Alice," right before him; sometimes I would address her as Miss "Don't Care," and I exhausted myself in nonsensical chatter without succeeding once in taking her out of her peevish and tragic self. There were moments when I felt I must break out and start swearing at her till all was blue. And I fancied that had I done so Jacobus would not have moved a muscle. A sort of shady, intimate understanding seemed to have been established between us.

I must say the girl treated her father exactly in the same way she treated me.

And how could it have been otherwise? She treated me as she treated her father. She had never seen a visitor. She did not know how men behaved. I belonged to the low lot with whom her father did business at the port. I was of no account. So was her father. The only decent people in the world were the people of the island, who would have nothing to do with him because of something wicked he had done. This was apparently the explanation Miss Jacobus had given her of the household's isolated position. For she had to be told something! And I feel convinced that this version had been assented to by Jacobus. I must say the old woman was putting it forward with considerable gusto. It was on her lips the universal explanation, the universal allusion, the universal taunt.

One day Jacobus came in early and, beckoning me into the dining-room, wiped his brow with a weary gesture and told me that he had managed to unearth a supply of quarter-bags.

"It's fourteen hundred your ship wanted, did you say, Captain?"

"Yes, yes!" I replied eagerly; but he remained calm. He looked more tired than I had ever seen him before.

"Well, Captain, you may go and tell your people that they can get that lot from my brother."

As I remained open-mouthed at this, he added his usual placid formula of assurance:

"You'll find it correct, Captain."

"You spoke to your brother about it?" I was distinctly awed. "And for me? Because he must have known that my ship's the only one hung up for bags. How on earth——"

He wiped his brow again. I noticed that he was dressed with unusual care, in clothes in which I had never seen him before. He avoided my eye.

"You've heard people talk, of course . . . That's true enough. He . . . I . . . We certainly . . . for several years . . ." His voice declined to a mere sleepy murmur. "You see I had something to tell him of, something which——"

His murmur stopped. He was not going to tell me what this something was. And I didn't care. Anxious to carry the news to my charterers, I ran back on the verandah to get my hat.

At the bustle I made the girl turned her eyes slowly in my direction, and even the old woman was checked in her knitting. I stopped a moment to exclaim excitedly:

"Your father's a brick, Miss Don't Care. That's what he is."

She beheld my elation in scornful surprise. Jacobus with unwonted familiarity seized my arm as I flew through the dining-room, and breathed heavily at me a proposal about "A plate of soup" that evening. I answered distractedly: "Eh? What? Oh, thanks! Certainly. With pleasure," and tore myself away. Dine with him? Of course. The merest gratitude——

But some three hours afterwards, in the dusky, silent street, paved with cobble-stones, I became aware that it was not mere gratitude which was guiding my steps towards the house with the old garden, where for years no guest other than myself had ever dined. Mere gratitude does not gnaw at one's interior economy in that particular way. Hunger might; but I was not feeling particularly hungry for Jacobus's food.

On that occasion, too, the girl refused to come to the table.

My exasperation grew. The old woman cast malicious glances at me. I said suddenly to Jacobus: "Here! Put some chicken and salad on that plate." He obeyed without raising his eyes. I carried it with a knife and fork and a serviette out on the verandah. The garden was one mass of gloom, like a cemetery of flowers buried in the darkness, and she, in the chair, seemed to muse mournfully over the extinction of light and colour. Only whiffs of heavy scent passed like wandering, fragrant souls of that departed multitude of blossoms. I talked volubly, jocularly, persuasively, tenderly; I talked in a subdued tone. To a listener it would have sounded like the murmur of a pleading lover. Whenever I paused expectantly there was only a deep silence. It was like offering food to a seated statue.

"I haven't been able to swallow a single morsel thinking of you out here starving yourself in the dark. It's positively cruel to be so obstinate. Think of my sufferings."

"Don't care."

I felt as if I could have done her some violence—shaken her, beaten her maybe. I said:

"Your absurd behaviour will prevent me coming here any more."

"What's that to me?"

"You like it."

"It's false," she snarled.

My hand fell on her shoulder; and if she had flinched I verily believe I would have shaken her. But there was no movement and this immobility disarmed my anger.

"You do. Or you wouldn't be found on the verandah every day. Why are you here, then? There are plenty of rooms in the house. You have your own room to stay in—if you did not want to see me. But you do. You know you do."

I felt a slight shudder under my hand and released my grip as if frightened by that sign of animation in her body. The scented air of the garden came to us in a warm wave like a voluptuous and perfumed sigh.

"Go back to them," she whispered, almost pitifully.

As I re-entered the dining-room I saw Jacobus cast down his eyes. I banged the plate on the table. At this demonstration of ill-humour he murmured something in an apologetic tone, and I turned on him viciously as if he were accountable to me for these "abominable eccentricities," I believe I called them.

"But I dare say Miss Jacobus here is responsible for most of this offensive manner," I added loftily.

She piped out at once in her brazen, ruffianly manner:

"Eh? Why don't you leave us in peace, my good fellow?"

I was astonished that she should dare before Jacobus. Yet what could he have done to repress her? He needed her too much. He raised a heavy, drowsy glance for an instant, then looked down again. She insisted with shrill finality:

"Haven't you done your business, you two? Well, then—"

She had the true Jacobus impudence, that old woman. Her mop of iron-grey hair was parted on the side like a man's raffishly, and she made as if to plunge her fork into it, as she used to do with the knitting-needle, but refrained. Her little black eyes sparkled venomously. I turned to my host at the head of the table—menacingly as it were.

"Well, and what do you say to that, Jacobus? Am I to take it that we have done with each other?"

I had to wait a little. The answer when it came was rather unexpected, and in quite another spirit than the question.

"I certainly think we might do some business yet with those potatoes of mine, Captain. You will find that——"

I cut him short.

"I've told you before that I don't trade."

His broad chest heaved without a sound in a noiseless sigh.

"Think it over, Captain," he murmured, tenacious and tranquil; and I burst into a jarring laugh, remembering how he had stuck to the circus-rider woman—the depth of passion under that placid surface, which even cuts with a riding-whip (so the legend had it) could never ruffle into the semblance of a storm; something like the passion of a fish would be if one could imagine such a thing as a passionate fish.

That evening I experienced more distinctly than ever the sense of moral discomfort which always attended me in that house lying under the ban of all "decent" people. I refused to stay on and smoke after dinner; and when I put my hand into the thickly cushioned palm of Jacobus, I said to myself that it would be for the last time under his roof. I pressed his bulky paw heartily nevertheless. Hadn't he got me out of a serious difficulty? To the few words of acknowledgement I was bound, and indeed quite willing, to utter, he answered by stretching his closed lips in his melancholy, glued-together smile.

"That will be all right, I hope, Captain," he breathed out weightily.

"What do you mean?" I asked, alarmed. "That your brother might yet——"

"Oh, no," he reassured me. "He . . . he's a man of his word, Captain."

My self-communion as I walked away from his door, trying to believe that this was for the last time, was not satisfactory. I was aware myself that I was not sincere in my reflections as to Jacobus's motives, and, of course, the very next day I went back again.

How weak, irrational, and absurd we are! How easily carried away whenever our awakened imagination brings us the irritating hint of a desire! I cared for the girl in a particular way, seduced by the moody expression of her face, by her obstinate silences, her rare, scornful words; by the perpetual pout of her closed lips, the black depths of her fixed gaze turned slowly upon me as if in contemptuous provocation, only to be averted next moment with an exasperating indifference.

Of course the news of my assiduity had spread all over the little town. I noticed a change in the manner of my acquaintances and even something different in the nods of the other captains, when meeting them at the landing-steps or in the offices where business called me. The old-maidish head clerk treated me with distant punctiliousness and, as it were, gathered his skirts round him for fear of contamination. It seemed to me that the very niggers on the quays turned to look after me as I passed; and as to Jacobus's boatman his "Good-night sah!" when he put me on board was no longer merely cordial—it had a familiar, confidential sound as though we had been partners in some villainy.

My friend S——the elder passed me on the other side of the street with a wave of the hand and an ironic smile. The younger brother, the one they had married to an elderly shrew, he, on the strength of an older friendship and as if paying a debt of gratitude, took the liberty to utter a word of warning.

"You're doing yourself no good by your choice of friends, my dear chap," he said with infantile gravity.

As I knew that the meeting of the brothers Jacobus was the subject of excited comment in the whole of the sugary Pearl of the Ocean I wanted to know why I was blamed.

"I have been the occasion of a move which may end in a reconciliation surely desirable from the point of view of the proprieties—don't you know?"

"Of course, if that girl were disposed of it would certainly facilitate——" he mused sagely, then, inconsequential creature, gave me a light tap on the lower part of my waistcoat. "You old sinner," he cried jovially, "much you care for proprieties. But you had better look out for yourself, you know, with a personage like Jacobus who has no sort of reputation to lose."

He had recovered his gravity of a respectable citizen by that time and added regretfully:

"All the women of our family are perfectly scandalized."

But by that time I had given up visiting the S——family and the D——family. The elder ladies pulled such faces when I showed myself, and the multitude of related young ladies received me with such a variety of looks: wondering, awed, mocking (except Miss Mary, who spoke to me and looked at me with hushed pained compassion as though I had been ill), that I had no difficulty in giving them all up. I would have given up the society of the whole town, for the sake of sitting near that girl, snarling and superb and barely clad in that flimsy, dingy, amber wrapper, open low at the throat. She looked, with the wild wisps of hair hanging down her tense face, as though she had just jumped out of bed in the panic of a fire.

She sat leaning on her elbow, looking at nothing. Why did she stay listening to my absurd chatter? And not only that; but why did she powder her face in preparation for my arrival? It seemed to be her idea of making a toilette, and in her untidy negligence a sign of great effort towards personal adornment.

But I might have been mistaken. The powdering might have been her daily practice and her presence in the verandah a sign of an indifference so complete as to take no account of my existence. Well, it was all one to me.

I loved to watch her slow changes of pose, to look at her long immobilities composed in the graceful lines of her body, to observe the mysterious narrow stare of her splendid black eyes, somewhat long in shape, half closed, contemplating the void. She was like a spell-bound creature with the forehead of a goddess crowned by the dishevelled magnificent hair of a gipsy tramp. Even her indifference was seductive. I felt myself growing attached to her by the bond of an irrealizable desire, for I kept my head—quite. And I put up with the moral discomfort of Jacobus's sleepy watchfulness, tranquil, and yet so expressive; as if there had been a tacit pact between us two. I put up with the insolence of the old woman's: "Aren't you ever going to leave us in peace, my good fellow?" with her taunts; with her brazen and sinister scolding. She was of the true Jacobus stock, and no mistake.

Directly I got away from the girl I called myself many hard names. What folly was this? I would ask myself. It was like being the slave of some depraved habit. And I returned to her with my head clear, my heart certainly free, not even moved by pity for that castaway (she was as much of a castaway as any one ever wrecked on a desert island), but as if beguiled by some extraordinary promise. Nothing more unworthy could be imagined. The recollection of that tremulous whisper when I gripped her shoulder with one hand and held a plate of chicken with the other was enough to make me break all my good resolutions.

Her insulting taciturnity was enough sometimes to make one gnash one's teeth with rage. When she opened her mouth it was only to be abominably rude in harsh tones to the associate of her reprobate father; and the full approval of her aged relative was conveyed to her by offensive chuckles. If not that, then her remarks, always uttered in the tone of scathing contempt, were of the most appalling inanity.

How could it have been otherwise? That plump, ruffianly Jacobus old maid in the tight grey frock had never taught her any manners. Manners I suppose are not necessary for born castaways. No educational establishment could ever be induced to accept her as a pupil—on account of the proprieties, I imagine. And Jacobus had not been able to send her away anywhere. How could he have done it? Who with? Where to? He himself was not enough of an adventurer to think of settling down anywhere else. His passion had tossed him at the tail of a circus up and down strange coasts, but, the storm over, he had drifted back shamelessly where, social outcast as he was, he remained still a Jacobus—one of the oldest families on the island, older than the French even. There must have been a Jacobus in at the death of the last Dodo. . . . The girl had learned nothing, she had never listened to a general conversation, she knew nothing, she had heard of nothing. She could read certainly; but all the reading matter that ever came in her way were the newspapers provided for the captains' room of the "store." Jacobus had the habit of taking these sheets home now and then in a very stained and ragged condition.

As her mind could not grasp the meaning of any matters treated there except police-court reports and accounts of crimes, she had formed for herself a notion of the civilised world as a scene of murders, abductions, burglaries, stabbing affrays, and every sort of desperate violence. England and France, Paris and London (the only two towns of which she seemed to have heard), appeared to her sinks of abomination, reeking with blood, in contrast to her little island where petty larceny was about the standard of current misdeeds, with, now and then, some more pronounced crime—and that only amongst the imported coolie labourers on sugar estates or the negroes of the town. But in Europe these things were being done daily by a wicked population of white men amongst whom, as that ruffianly, aristocratic old Miss Jacobus pointed out, the wandering sailors, the associates of her precious papa, were the lowest of the low.

It was impossible to give her a sense of proportion. I suppose she figured England to herself as about the size of the Pearl of the Ocean; in which case it would certainly have been reeking with gore and a mere wreck of burgled houses from end to end. One could not make her understand that these horrors on which she fed her imagination were lost in the mass of orderly life like a few drops of blood in the ocean. She directed upon me for a moment the uncomprehending glance of her narrowed eyes and then would turn her scornful powdered face away without a word. She would not even take the trouble to shrug her shoulders.

At that time the batches of papers brought by the last mail reported a series of crimes in the East End of London, there was a sensational case of abduction in France and a fine display of armed robbery in Australia. One afternoon crossing the dining-room I heard Miss Jacobus piping in the verandah with venomous animosity: "I don't know what your precious papa is plotting with that fellow. But he's just the sort of man who's capable of carrying you off far away somewhere and then cutting your throat some day for your money."

There was a good half of the length of the verandah between their chairs. I came out and sat down fiercely midway between them.

"Yes, that's what we do with girls in Europe," I began in a grimly matter-of-fact tone. I think Miss Jacobus was disconcerted by my sudden appearance. I turned upon her with cold ferocity:

"As to objectionable old women, they are first strangled quietly, then cut up into small pieces and thrown away, a bit here and a bit there. They vanish——"

I cannot go so far as to say I had terrified her. But she was troubled by my truculence, the more so because I had been always addressing her with a politeness she did not deserve. Her plump, knitting hands fell slowly on her knees. She said not a word while I fixed her with severe determination. Then as I turned away from her at last, she laid down her work gently and, with noiseless movements, retreated from the verandah. In fact, she vanished.

But I was not thinking of her. I was looking at the girl. It was what I was coming for daily; troubled, ashamed, eager; finding in my nearness to her a unique sensation which I indulged with dread, self-contempt, and deep pleasure, as if it were a secret vice bound to end in my undoing, like the habit of some drug or other which ruins and degrades its slave.

I looked her over, from the top of her dishevelled head, down the lovely line of the shoulder, following the curve of the hip, the draped form of the long limb, right down to her fine ankle below a torn, soiled flounce; and as far as the point of the shabby, high-heeled, blue slipper, dangling from her well-shaped foot, which she moved slightly, with quick, nervous jerks, as if impatient of my presence. And in the scent of the massed flowers I seemed to breathe her special and inexplicable charm, the heady perfume of the everlastingly irritated captive of the garden.

I looked at her rounded chin, the Jacobus chin; at the full, red lips pouting in the powdered, sallow face; at the firm modelling of the cheek, the grains of white in the hairs of the straight sombre eyebrows; at the long eyes, a narrowed gleam of liquid white and intense motionless black, with their gaze so empty of thought, and so absorbed in their fixity that she seemed to be staring at her own lonely image, in some far-off mirror hidden from my sight amongst the trees.

And suddenly, without looking at me, with the appearance of a person speaking to herself, she asked, in that voice slightly harsh yet mellow and always irritated:

"Why do you keep on coming here?"

"Why do I keep on coming here?" I repeated, taken by surprise. I could not have told her. I could not even tell myself with sincerity why I was coming there. "What's the good of you asking a question like that?"

"Nothing is any good," she observed scornfully to the empty air, her chin propped on her hand, that hand never extended to any man, that no one had ever grasped—for I had only grasped her shoulder once—that generous, fine, somewhat masculine hand. I knew well the peculiarly efficient shape—broad at the base, tapering at the fingers—of that hand, for which there was nothing in the world to lay hold of. I pretended to be playful.

"No! But do you really care to know?"

She shrugged indolently her magnificent shoulders, from which the dingy thin wrapper was slipping a little.

"Oh—never mind—never mind!"

There was something smouldering under those airs of lassitude. She exasperated me by the provocation of her nonchalance, by something elusive and defiant in her very form which I wanted to seize. I said roughly:

"Why? Don't you think I should tell you the truth?"

Her eyes glided my way for a sidelong look, and she murmured, moving only her full, pouting lips:

"I think you would not dare."

"Do you imagine I am afraid of you? What on earth. . . . Well, it's possible, after all, that I don't know exactly why I am coming here. Let us say, with Miss Jacobus, that it is for no good. You seem to believe the outrageous things she says, if you do have a row with her now and then."

She snapped out viciously:

"Who else am I to believe?"

"I don't know," I had to own, seeing her suddenly very helpless and condemned to moral solitude by the verdict of a respectable community. "You might believe me, if you chose."

She made a slight movement and asked me at once, with an effort as if making an experiment:

"What is the business between you and papa?"

"Don't you know the nature of your father's business? Come! He sells provisions to ships."

She became rigid again in her crouching pose.

"Not that. What brings you here—to this house?"

"And suppose it's you? You would not call that business? Would you? And now let us drop the subject. It's no use. My ship will be ready for sea the day after to-morrow."

She murmured a distinctly scared "So soon," and getting up quickly, went to the little table and poured herself a glass of water. She walked with rapid steps and with an indolent swaying of her whole young figure above the hips; when she passed near me I felt with tenfold force the charm of the peculiar, promising sensation I had formed the habit to seek near her. I thought with sudden dismay that this was the end of it; that after one more day I would be no longer able to come into this verandah, sit on this chair, and taste perversely the flavour of contempt in her indolent poses, drink in the provocation of her scornful looks, and listen to the curt, insolent remarks uttered in that harsh and seductive voice. As if my innermost nature had been altered by the action of some moral poison, I felt an abject dread of going to sea.

I had to exercise a sudden self-control, as one puts on a brake, to prevent myself jumping up to stride about, shout, gesticulate, make her a scene. What for? What about? I had no idea. It was just the relief of violence that I wanted; and I lolled back in my chair, trying to keep my lips formed in a smile; that half-indulgent, half-mocking smile which was my shield against the shafts of her contempt and the insulting sallies flung at me by the old woman.

She drank the water at a draught, with the avidity of raging thirst, and let herself fall on the nearest chair, as if utterly overcome. Her attitude, like certain tones of her voice, had in it something masculine: the knees apart in the ample wrapper, the clasped hands hanging between them, her body leaning forward, with drooping head. I stared at the heavy black coil of twisted hair. It was enormous, crowning the bowed head with a crushing and disdained glory. The escaped wisps hung straight down. And suddenly I perceived that the girl was trembling from head to foot, as though that glass of iced water had chilled her to the bone.

"What's the matter now?" I said, startled, but in no very sympathetic mood.

She shook her bowed, overweighted head and cried in a stifled voice but with a rising inflection:

"Go away! Go away! Go away!"

I got up then and approached her, with a strange sort of anxiety. I looked down at her round, strong neck, then stooped low enough to peep at her face. And I began to tremble a little myself.

"What on earth are you gone wild about, Miss Don't Care?"

She flung herself backwards violently, her head going over the back of the chair. And now it was her smooth, full, palpitating throat that lay exposed to my bewildered stare. Her eyes were nearly closed, with only a horrible white gleam under the lids as if she were dead.

"What has come to you?" I asked in awe. "What are you terrifying yourself with?"

She pulled herself together, her eyes open frightfully wide now. The tropical afternoon was lengthening the shadows on the hot, weary earth, the abode of obscure desires, of extravagant hopes, of unimaginable terrors.

"Never mind! Don't care!" Then, after a gasp, she spoke with such frightful rapidity that I could hardly make out the amazing words: "For if you were to shut me up in an empty place as smooth all round as the palm of my hand, I could always strangle myself with my hair."

For a moment, doubting my ears, I let this inconceivable declaration sink into me. It is ever impossible to guess at the wild thoughts that pass through the heads of our fellow-creatures. What monstrous imaginings of violence could have dwelt under the low forehead of that girl who had been taught to regard her father as "capable of anything" more in the light of a misfortune than that of a disgrace; as, evidently, something to be resented and feared rather than to be ashamed of? She seemed, indeed, as unaware of shame as of anything else in the world; but in her ignorance, her resentment and fear took a childish and violent shape.

Of course she spoke without knowing the value of words. What could she know of death—she who knew nothing of life? It was merely as the proof of her being beside herself with some odious apprehension, that this extraordinary speech had moved me, not to pity, but to a fascinated, horrified wonder. I had no idea what notion she had of her danger. Some sort of abduction. It was quite possible with the talk of that atrocious old woman. Perhaps she thought she could be carried off, bound hand and foot and even gagged. At that surmise I felt as if the door of a furnace had been opened in front of me.

"Upon my honour!" I cried. "You will end by going crazy if you listen to that abominable old aunt of yours——"

I studied her haggard expression, her trembling lips. Her cheeks even seemed sunk a little. But how I, the associate of her disreputable father, the "lowest of the low" from the criminal Europe, could manage to reassure her I had no conception. She was exasperating.

"Heavens and earth! What do you think I can do?"

"I don't know."

Her chin certainly trembled. And she was looking at me with extreme attention. I made a step nearer to her chair.

"I shall do nothing. I promise you that. Will that do? Do you understand? I shall do nothing whatever, of any kind; and the day after tomorrow I shall be gone."

What else could I have said? She seemed to drink in my words with the thirsty avidity with which she had emptied the glass of water. She whispered tremulously, in that touching tone I had heard once before on her lips, and which thrilled me again with the same emotion:

"I would believe you. But what about papa——"

"He be hanged!" My emotion betrayed itself by the brutality of my tone. "I've had enough of your papa. Are you so stupid as to imagine that I am frightened of him? He can't make me do anything."

All that sounded feeble to me in the face of her ignorance. But I must conclude that the "accent of sincerity" has, as some people say, a really irresistible power. The effect was far beyond my hopes—and even beyond my conception. To watch the change in the girl was like watching a miracle—the gradual but swift relaxation of her tense glance, of her stiffened muscles, of every fibre of her body. That black, fixed stare into which I had read a tragic meaning more than once, in which I had found a sombre seduction, was perfectly empty now, void of all consciousness whatever, and not even aware any longer of my presence; it had become a little sleepy, in the Jacobus fashion.

But, man being a perverse animal, instead of rejoicing at my complete success, I beheld it with astounded and indignant eyes. There was something cynical in that unconcealed alteration, the true Jacobus shamelessness. I felt as though I had been cheated in some rather complicated deal into which I had entered against my better judgment. Yes, cheated without any regard for, at least, the forms of decency.

With an easy, indolent, and in its indolence supple, feline movement, she rose from the chair, so provokingly ignoring me now, that for very rage I held my ground within less than a foot of her. Leisurely and tranquil, behaving right before me with the ease of a person alone in a room, she extended her beautiful arms, with her hands clenched, her body swaying, her head thrown back a little, revelling contemptuously in a sense of relief, easing her limbs in freedom after all these days of crouching, motionless poses when she had been so furious and so afraid.

All this with supreme indifference, incredible, offensive, exasperating, like ingratitude doubled with treachery.

I ought to have been flattered, perhaps, but, on the contrary, my anger grew; her movement to pass by me as if I were a wooden post or a piece of furniture, that unconcerned movement brought it to a head.

I won't say I did not know what I was doing, but, certainly, cool reflection had nothing to do with the circumstance that next moment both my arms were round her waist. It was an impulsive action, as one snatches at something falling or escaping; and it had no hypocritical gentleness about it either. She had no time to make a sound, and the first kiss I planted on her closed lips was vicious enough to have been a bite.

She did not resist, and of course I did not stop at one. She let me go on, not as if she were inanimate—I felt her there, close against me, young, full of vigour, of life, a strong desirable creature, but as if she did not care in the least, in the absolute assurance of her safety, what I did or left undone. Our faces brought close together in this storm of haphazard caresses, her big, black, wide-open eyes looked into mine without the girl appearing either angry or pleased or moved in any way. In that steady gaze which seemed impersonally to watch my madness I could detect a slight surprise, perhaps—nothing more. I showered kisses upon her face and there did not seem to be any reason why this should not go on for ever.

That thought flashed through my head, and I was on the point of desisting, when, all at once, she began to struggle with a sudden violence which all but freed her instantly, which revived my exasperation with her, indeed a fierce desire never to let her go any more. I tightened my embrace in time, gasping out: "No—you don't!" as if she were my mortal enemy. On her part not a word was said. Putting her hands against my chest, she pushed with all her might without succeeding to break the circle of my arms. Except that she seemed thoroughly awake now, her eyes gave me no clue whatever. To meet her black stare was like looking into a deep well, and I was totally unprepared for her change of tactics. Instead of trying to tear my hands apart, she flung herself upon my breast and with a downward, undulating, serpentine motion, a quick sliding dive, she got away from me smoothly. It was all very swift; I saw her pick up the tail of her wrapper and run for the door at the end of the verandah not very gracefully. She appeared to be limping a little—and then she vanished; the door swung behind her so noiselessly that I could not believe it was completely closed. I had a distinct suspicion of her black eye being at the crack to watch what I would do. I could not make up my mind whether to shake my fist in that direction or blow a kiss.

· VI ·

Either would have been perfectly consistent with my feelings. I gazed at the door, hesitating, but in the end I did neither. The monition of some sixth sense—the sense of guilt, maybe, that sense which always acts too late, alas!—warned me to look round; and at once I became aware that the conclusion of this tumultuous episode was likely to be a matter of lively anxiety. Jacobus was standing in the doorway of the dining-room. How long he had been there it was impossible to guess; and remembering my struggle with the girl I thought he must have been its mute witness from beginning to end. But this supposition seemed almost incredible. Perhaps that impenetrable girl had heard him come in and had got away in time.

He stepped on to the verandah in his usual manner, heavy-eyed, with glued lips. I marvelled at the girl's resemblance to this man. Those long, Egyptian eyes, that low forehead of a stupid goddess, she had found in the sawdust of the circus; but all the rest of the face, the design and the modelling, the rounded chin, the very lips—all that was Jacobus, fined down, more finished, more expressive.

His thick hand fell on and grasped with force the back of a light chair (there were several standing about) and I perceived the chance of a broken head at the end of all this—most likely. My mortification was extreme. The scandal would be horrible; that was unavoidable. But how to act so as to satisfy myself I did not know. I stood on my guard and at any rate faced him. There was nothing else for it. Of one thing I was certain, that, however brazen my attitude, it could never equal the characteristic Jacobus impudence.

He gave me his melancholy, glued smile and sat down. I own I was relieved. The perspective of passing from kisses to blows had nothing particularly attractive in it. Perhaps—perhaps he had seen nothing? He behaved as usual, but he had never before found me alone on the verandah. If he had alluded to it, if he had asked: "Where's Alice?" or something of the sort, I would have been able to judge from the tone. He would give me no opportunity. The striking peculiarity was that he had never looked up at me yet. "He knows," I said to myself confidently. And my contempt for him relieved my disgust with myself.

"You are early home," I remarked.

"Things are very quiet; nothing doing at the store to-day," he explained with a cast-down air.

"Oh, well, you know, I am off," I said, feeling that this, perhaps, was the best thing to do.

"Yes," he breathed out. "Day after to-morrow."

This was not what I had meant; but as he gazed persistently on the floor, I followed the direction of his glance. In the absolute stillness of the house we stared at the high-heeled slipper the girl had lost in her flight. We stared. It lay overturned.

After what seemed a very long time to me, Jacobus hitched his chair forward, stooped with extended arm and picked it up. It looked a slender thing in his big, thick hands. It was not really a slipper, but a low shoe of blue, glazed kid, rubbed and shabby. It had straps to go over the instep, but the girl only thrust her feet in, after her slovenly manner. Jacobus raised his eyes from the shoe to look at me.

"Sit down, Captain," he said at last, in his subdued tone.

As if the sight of that shoe had renewed the spell, I gave up suddenly the idea of leaving the house there and then. It had become impossible. I sat down, keeping my eyes on the fascinating object. Jacobus turned his daughter's shoe over and over in his cushioned paws as if studying the way the thing was made. He contemplated the thin sole for a time; then glancing inside with an absorbed air:

"I am glad I found you here, Captain."

I answered this by some sort of grunt, watching him covertly. Then I added: "You won't have much more of me now."

He was still deep in the interior of that shoe on which my eyes too were resting.

"Have you thought any more of this deal in potatoes I spoke to you about the other day?"

"No, I haven't," I answered curtly. He checked my movement to rise by an austere, commanding gesture of the hand holding that fatal shoe. I remained seated and glared at him. "You know I don't trade."

"You ought to, Captain. You ought to."

I reflected. If I left that house now I would never see the girl again. And I felt I must see her once more, if only for an instant. It was a need, not to be reasoned with, not to be disregarded. No, I did not want to go away. I wanted to stay for one more experience of that strange provoking sensation and of indefinite desire, the habit of which had made me—me of all people!—dread the prospect of going to sea.

"Mr. Jacobus," I pronounced slowly. "Do you really think that upon the whole and taking various matters into consideration—I mean everything, do you understand?—it would be a good thing for me to trade, let us say, with you?"

I waited for a while. He went on looking at the shoe which he held now crushed in the middle, the worn point of the toe and the high heel protruding on each side of his heavy fist.

"That will be all right," he said, facing me squarely at last.

"Are you sure?"

"You'll find it quite correct, Captain." He had uttered his habitual phrases in his usual placid, breath-saving voice and stood my hard, inquisitive stare sleepily without as much as a wink.

"Then let us trade," I said, turning my shoulder to him. "I see you are bent on it."

I did not want an open scandal, but I thought that outward decency may be bought too dearly at times. I included Jacobus, myself, the whole population of the island, in the same contemptuous disgust as though we had been partners in an ignoble transaction. And the remembered vision at sea, diaphanous and blue, of the Pearl of the Ocean at sixty miles off; the unsubstantial, clear marvel of it as if evoked by the art of a beautiful and pure magic, turned into a thing of horrors too. Was this the fortune this vaporous and rare apparition had held for me in its hard heart, hidden within the shape as of fair dreams and mist? Was this my luck?

"I think"—Jacobus became suddenly audible after what seemed the silence of vile meditation—"that you might conveniently take some thirty tons. That would be about the lot, Captain."

"Would it? The lot! I dare say it would be convenient, but I haven't got enough money for that."

I had never seen him so animated.

"No!" he exclaimed with what I took for the accent of grim menace. "That's a pity." He paused, then, unrelenting: "How much money have you got, Captain?" he inquired with awful directness.

It was my turn to face him squarely. I did so and mentioned the amount I could dispose of. And I perceived that he was disappointed. He thought it over, his calculating gaze lost in mine, for quite a long time before he came out in a thoughtful tone with the rapacious suggestion:

"You could draw some more from your charterers. That would be quite easy, Captain."

"No, I couldn't," I retorted brusquely. "I've drawn my salary up to date, and besides, the ship's accounts are closed."

I was growing furious. I pursued: "And I'll tell you what: if I could do it I wouldn't." Then throwing off all restraint, I added: "You are a bit too much of a Jacobus, Mr. Jacobus."

The tone alone was insulting enough, but he remained tranquil, only a little puzzled, till something seemed to dawn upon him; but the unwonted light in his eyes died out instantly. As a Jacobus on his native heath, what a mere skipper chose to say could not touch him, outcast as he was. As a ship-chandler he could stand anything. All I caught of his mumble was a vague—"quite correct," than which nothing could have been more egregiously false at bottom—to my view, at least. But I remembered—I had never forgotten—that I must see the girl. I did not mean to go. I meant to stay in the house till I had seen her once more.

"Look here!" I said finally. "I'll tell you what I'll do. I'll take as many of your confounded potatoes as my money will buy, on condition that you go off at once down to the wharf to see them loaded in the lighter and sent alongside the ship straight away. Take the invoice and a signed receipt with you. Here's the key of my desk. Give it to Burns. He will pay you."

He got up from his chair before I had finished speaking, but he refused to take the key. Burns would never do it. He wouldn't like to ask him even.

"Well, then," I said, eyeing him slightingly, "there's nothing for it, Mr. Jacobus, but you must wait on board till I come off to settle with you."

"That will be all right, Captain. I will go at once."

He seemed at a loss what to do with the girl's shoe he was still holding in his fist. Finally, looking dully at me, he put it down on the chair from which he had risen.

"And you, Captain? Won't you come along, too, just to see——"

"Don't bother about me. I'll take care of myself."

He remained perplexed for a moment, as if trying to understand; and then his weighty: "Certainly, certainly, Captain," seemed to be the outcome of some sudden thought. His big chest heaved. Was it a sigh? As he went out to hurry off those potatoes he never looked back at me.

I waited till the noise of his footsteps had died out of the dining-room, and I waited a little longer. Then turning towards the distant door I raised my voice along the verandah:

"Alice!"

Nothing answered me, not even a stir behind the door. Jacobus's house might have been made empty for me to make myself at home in. I did not call again. I had become aware of a great discouragement. I was mentally jaded, morally dejected. I turned to the garden again, sitting down with my elbows spread on the low balustrade, and took my head in my hands.

The evening closed upon me. The shadows lengthened, deepened, mingled together into a pool of twilight in which the flower-beds glowed like coloured embers; whiffs of heavy scent came to me as if the dusk of this hemisphere were but the dimness of a temple and the garden an enormous censer swinging before the altar of the stars. The colours of the blossoms deepened, losing their glow one by one.

The girl, when I turned my head at a slight noise, appeared to me very tall and slender, advancing with a swaying limp, a floating and uneven motion which ended in the sinking of her shadowy form into the deep low chair. And I don't know why or whence I received the impression that she had come too late. She ought to have appeared at my call. She ought to have . . . It was as if a supreme opportunity had been missed.

I rose and took a seat close to her, nearly opposite her arm-chair. Her ever discontented voice addressed me at once, contemptuously:

"You are still here."

I pitched mine low.

"You have come out at last."

"I came to look for my shoe—before they bring in the lights."

It was her harsh, enticing whisper, subdued, not very steady, but its low tremulousness gave me no thrill now. I could only make out the oval of her face, her uncovered throat, the long, white gleam of her eyes. She was mysterious enough. Her hands were resting on the arms of the chair. But where was the mysterious and provoking sensation which was like the perfume of her flower-like youth? I said quietly:

"I have got your shoe here." She made no sound and I continued: "You had better give me your foot and I will put it on for you."

She made no movement. I bent low down and groped for her foot under the flounces of the wrapper. She did not withdraw it and I put on the shoe, buttoning the instep-strap. It was an inanimate foot. I lowered it gently to the floor.

"If you buttoned the strap you would not be losing your shoe, Miss Don't Care," I said, trying to be playful without conviction. I felt more like wailing over the lost illusion of vague desire, over the sudden conviction that I would never find again near her the strange, half-evil, half-tender sensation which had given its acrid flavour to so many days, which had made her appear tragic and promising, pitiful and provoking. That was all over.

"Your father picked it up," I said, thinking she might just as well be told of the fact.

"I am not afraid of papa—by himself," she declared scornfully.

"Oh! It's only in conjunction with his disreputable associates, strangers, the 'riff-raff of Europe' as your charming aunt or great-aunt says—men like me, for instance—that you——"

"I am not afraid of you," she snapped out.

"That's because you don't know that I am now doing business with your father. Yes, I am in fact doing exactly what he wants me to do. I've broken my promise to you. That's the sort of man I am. And now— aren't you afraid? If you believe what that dear, kind, truthful old lady says you ought to be."

It was with unexpected modulated softness that she affirmed:

"No. I am not afraid." She hesitated. . . . "Not now."

"Quite right. You needn't be. I shall not see you again before I go to sea." I rose and stood near her chair. "But I shall often think of you in this old garden, passing under the trees over there, walking between these gorgeous flower-beds. You must love this garden——"

"I love nothing."

I heard in her sullen tone the faint echo of that resentfully tragic note which I had found once so provoking. But it left me unmoved except for a sudden and weary conviction of the emptiness of all things under Heaven.

"Good-bye, Alice," I said.

She did not answer, she did not move. To merely take her hand, shake it, and go away seemed impossible, almost improper. I stooped without haste and pressed my lips to her smooth forehead. This was the moment when I realised clearly with a sort of terror my complete detachment from that unfortunate creature. And as I lingered in that cruel self-knowledge I felt the light touch of her arms falling languidly on my neck and received a hasty, awkward, haphazard kiss which missed my lips. No! She was not afraid; but I was no longer moved. Her arms slipped off my neck slowly, she made no sound, the deep wicker arm-chair creaked slightly; only a sense of my dignity prevented me fleeing head-long from that catastrophic revelation.

I traversed the dining-room slowly. I thought: She's listening to my footsteps; she can't help it; she'll hear me open and shut that door. And I closed it as gently behind me as if I had been a thief retreating with his ill-gotten booty. During that stealthy act I experienced the last touch of emotion in that house, at the thought of the girl I had left sitting there in the obscurity, with her heavy hair and empty eyes as black as the night itself, staring into the walled garden, silent, warm, odorous with the perfume of imprisoned flowers, which, like herself, were lost to sight in a world buried in darkness.

The narrow, ill-lighted, rustic streets I knew so well on my way to the harbour were extremely quiet. I felt in my heart that the further one ventures the better one understands how everything in our life is common, short, and empty; that it is in seeking the unknown in our sensations that we discover how mediocre are our attempts and how soon defeated! Jacobus's boatman was waiting at the steps with an unusual air of readiness. He put me alongside the ship, but did not give me his confidential "Good-evening, sah," and, instead of shoving off at once, remained holding by the ladder.

I was a thousand miles from commercial affairs, when on the dark quarter-deck Mr. Burns positively rushed at me, stammering with excitement. He had been pacing the deck distractedly for hours awaiting my arrival. Just before sunset a lighter loaded with potatoes had come alongside with that fat ship-chandler himself sitting on the pile of sacks. He was now stuck immovable in the cabin. What was the meaning of it all? Surely I did not——

"Yes, Mr. Burns, I did," I cut him short. He was beginning to make gestures of despair when I stopped that, too, by giving him the key of my desk and desiring him, in a tone which admitted of no argument, to go below at once, pay Mr. Jacobus's bill, and send him out of the ship.

"I don't want to see him," I confessed frankly, climbing the poop-ladder. I felt extremely tired. Dropping on the seat of the skylight, I gave myself up to idle gazing at the lights about the quay and at the black mass of the mountain on the south side of the harbour. I never heard Jacobus leave the ship with every single sovereign of my ready cash in his pocket. I never heard anything till, a long time afterwards, Mr. Burns, unable to contain himself any longer, intruded upon me with his ridiculously angry lamentations at my weakness and good nature.

"Of course, there's plenty of room in the after-hatch. But they are sure to go rotten down there. Well! I never heard . . . seventeen tons! I suppose I must hoist in that lot first thing to-morrow morning."

"I suppose you must. Unless you drop them overboard. But I'm afraid you can't do that. I wouldn't mind myself, but it's forbidden to throw rubbish into the harbour, you know."

"That is the truest word you have said for many a day, sir—rubbish. That's just what I expect they are. Nearly eighty good gold sovereigns gone; a perfectly clean sweep of your drawer, sir. Bless me if I understand!"

As it was impossible to throw the right light on this commercial transaction I left him to his lamentations and under the impression that I was a hopeless fool. Next day I did not go ashore. For one thing, I had no money to go ashore with—no, not enough to buy a cigarette. Jacobus had made a clean sweep. But that was not the only reason. The Pearl of the Ocean had in a few short hours grown odious to me. And I did not want to meet any one. My reputation had suffered. I knew I was the object of unkind and sarcastic comments.

The following morning at sunrise, just as our stern-fasts had been let go and the tug plucked us out from between the buoys, I saw Jacobus standing up in his boat. The nigger was pulling hard; several baskets of provisions for ships were stowed between the thwarts. The father of Alice was going his morning round. His countenance was tranquil and friendly. He raised his arm and shouted something with great heartiness. But his voice was of the sort that doesn't carry any distance; all I could catch faintly, or rather guess at, were the words "next time" and "quite correct." And it was only of these last that I was certain. Raising my arm perfunctorily for all response, I turned away. I rather resented the familiarity of the thing. Hadn't I settled accounts finally with him by means of that potato bargain?

This being a harbour story it is not my purpose to speak of our passage. I was glad enough to be at sea, but not with the gladness of old days. Formerly I had no memories to take away with me. I shared in the blessed forgetfulness of sailors, that forgetfulness natural and invincible, which resembles innocence in so far that it prevents self-examination. Now however I remembered the girl. During the first few days I was for ever questioning myself as to the nature of facts and sensations connected with her person and with my conduct.

And I must say also that Mr. Burns's intolerable fussing with those potatoes was not calculated to make me forget the part which I had played. He looked upon it as a purely commercial transaction of a particularly foolish kind, and his devotion—if it was devotion and not mere cussedness as I came to regard it before long—inspired him with a zeal to minimise my loss as much as possible. Oh, yes! He took care of those infamous potatoes with a vengeance, as the saying goes.

Everlastingly, there was a tackle over the after-hatch and everlastingly the watch on deck were pulling up, spreading out, picking over, rebagging, and lowering down again, some part of that lot of potatoes. My bargain with all its remotest associations, mental and visual—the garden of flowers and scents, the girl with her provoking contempt and her tragic loneliness of a hopeless castaway—was everlastingly dangled before my eyes, for thousands of miles along the open sea. And as if by a satanic refinement of irony it was accompanied by a most awful smell. Whiffs from decaying potatoes pursued me on the poop, they mingled with my thoughts, with my food, poisoned my very dreams. They made an atmosphere of corruption for the ship.

I remonstrated with Mr. Burns about this excessive care. I would have been well content to batten the hatch down and let them perish under the deck.

That perhaps would have been unsafe. The horrid emanations might have flavoured the cargo of sugar. They seemed strong enough to taint the very ironwork. In addition Mr. Burns made it a personal matter. He assured me he knew how to treat a cargo of potatoes at sea—had been in the trade as a boy, he said. He meant to make my loss as small as possible. What between his devotion—it must have been devotion—and his vanity, I positively dared not give him the order to throw my commercial venture overboard. I believe he would have refused point blank to obey my lawful command. An unprecedented and comical situation would have been created with which I did not feel equal to deal.

I welcomed the coming of bad weather as no sailor had ever done. When at last I hove the ship to, to pick up the pilot outside Port Philip Heads, the after-hatch had not been opened for more than a week and I might have believed that no such thing as a potato had ever been on board.

It was an abominable day, raw, blustering, with great squalls of wind and rain; the pilot, a cheery person, looked after the ship and chatted to me, streaming from head to foot; and the heavier the lash of the downpour the more pleased with himself and everything around him he seemed to be. He rubbed his wet hands with a satisfaction, which to me, who had stood that kind of thing for several days and nights, seemed inconceivable in any non-aquatic creature.

"You seem to enjoy getting wet, Pilot," I remarked.

He had a bit of land round his house in the suburbs and it was of his garden he was thinking. At the sound of the word garden, unheard, unspoken for so many days, I had a vision of gorgeous colour, of sweet scents, of a girlish figure crouching in a chair. Yes. That was a distinct emotion breaking into the peace I had found in the sleepless anxieties of my responsibility during a week of dangerous bad weather. The Colony, the pilot explained, had suffered from unparalleled drought. This was the first decent drop of water they had had for seven months. The root crops were lost. And, trying to be casual, but with visible interest, he asked me if I had perchance any potatoes to spare.

Potatoes! I had managed to forget them. In a moment I felt plunged into corruption up to my neck. Mr. Burns was making eyes at me behind the pilot's back.

Finally, he obtained a ton, and paid ten pounds for it. This was twice the price of my bargain with Jacobus. The spirit of covetousness woke up in me. That night, in harbour, before I slept, the Custom House galley came alongside. While his underlings were putting seals on the store-rooms, the officer in charge took me aside confidentially. "I say, Captain, you don't happen to have any potatoes to sell?"

Clearly there was a potato famine in the land. I let him have a ton for twelve pounds and he went away joyfully. That night I dreamt of a pile of gold in the form of a grave in which a girl was buried, and woke up callous with greed. On calling at my ship-broker's office, that man, after the usual business had been transacted, pushed his spectacles up on his forehead.

"I was thinking, Captain, that coming from the Pearl of the Ocean you may have some potatoes to sell."

I said negligently: "Oh, yes, I could spare you a ton. Fifteen pounds."

He exclaimed: "I say!" But after studying my face for a while accepted my terms with a faint grimace. It seems that these people could not exist without potatoes. I could. I didn't want to see a potato as long as I lived; but the demon of lucre had taken possession of me. How the news got about I don't know, but, returning on board rather late, I found a small group of men of the coster type hanging about the waist, while Mr. Burns walked to and fro the quarter-deck loftily, keeping a triumphant eye on them. They had come to buy potatoes.

"These chaps have been waiting here in the sun for hours," Burns whispered to me excitedly. "They have drunk the water-cask dry. Don't you throw away your chances, sir. You are too good-natured."

I selected a man with thick legs and a man with a cast in his eye to negotiate with; simply because they were easily distinguishable from the rest. "You have the money on you?" I inquired, before taking them down into the cabin.

"Yes, sir," they answered in one voice, slapping their pockets. I liked their air of quiet determination. Long before the end of the day all the potatoes were sold at about three times the price I had paid for them. Mr. Burns, feverish and exulting, congratulated himself on his skilful care of my commercial venture, but hinted plainly that I ought to have made more of it.

That night I did not sleep very well. I thought of Jacobus by fits and starts, between snatches of dreams concerned with castaways starving on a desert island covered with flowers. It was extremely unpleasant. In the morning, tired and unrefreshed, I sat down and wrote a long letter to my owners, giving them a carefully-thought-out scheme for the ship's employment in the East and about the China Seas for the next two years. I spent the day at that task and felt somewhat more at peace when it was done.

Their reply came in due course. They were greatly struck with my project; but considering that, notwithstanding the unfortunate difficulty with the bags (which they trusted I would know how to guard against in the future), the voyage showed a very fair profit, they thought it would be better to keep the ship in the sugar trade—at least for the present.

I turned over the page and read on:

"We have had a letter from our good friend Mr. Jacobus. We are pleased to see how well you have hit it off with him; for, not to speak of his assistance in the unfortunate matter of the bags, he writes us that should you, by using all possible dispatch, manage to bring the ship back early in the season he would be able to give us a good rate of freight. We have no doubt that your best endeavours . . . etc. . . . . etc."

I dropped the letter and sat motionless for a long time. Then I wrote my answer (it was a short one) and went ashore myself to post it. But I passed one letter-box, then another, and in the end found myself going up Collins Street with the letter still in my pocket—against my heart. Collins Street at four o'clock in the afternoon is not exactly a desert solitude; but I had never felt more isolated from the rest of mankind than when I walked that day its crowded pavement, battling desperately with my thoughts and feeling already vanquished.

There came a moment when the awful tenacity of Jacobus, the man of one passion and of one idea, appeared to me almost heroic. He had not given me up. He had gone again to his odious brother. And then he appeared to me odious himself. Was it for his own sake or for the sake of the poor girl? And on that last supposition the memory of the kiss which missed my lips appalled me; for whatever he had seen, or guessed at, or risked, he knew nothing of that. Unless the girl had told him. How could I go back to fan that fatal spark with my cold breath? No, no, that unexpected kiss had to be paid for all its full price.

At the first letter-box I came to I stopped and reaching into my breast-pocket I took out the letter—it was as if I were plucking out my very heart—and dropped it through the slit. Then I went straight on board.

I wondered what dreams I would have that night; but as it turned out I did not sleep at all. At breakfast I informed Mr. Burns that I had resigned my command.

He dropped his knife and fork and looked at me with indignation.

"You have, sir! I thought you loved the ship."

"So I do, Burns," I said. "But the fact is that the Indian Ocean and everything that is in it has lost its charm for me. I am going home as passenger by the Suez Canal."

"Everything that is in it," he repeated angrily. "I've never heard anybody talk like this. And to tell you the truth, sir, all the time we have been together I've never quite made you out. What's one ocean more than another? Charm, indeed!"

He was really devoted to me, I believe. But he cheered up when I told him that I had recommended him for my successor.

"Anyhow," he remarked, "let people say what they like, this Jacobus has served your turn. I must admit that this potato business has paid extremely well. Of course, if only you had——"

"Yes, Mr. Burns," I interrupted. "Quite a smile of fortune."

But I could not tell him that it was driving me out of the ship I had learned to love. And as I sat heavy-hearted at that parting, seeing all my plans destroyed, my modest future endangered—for this command was like a foot in the stirrup for a young man—he gave up completely for the first time his critical attitude.

"A wonderful piece of luck!" he said.

FREYA OF THE SEVEN ISLES:
A Story of Shallow Waters

· I ·

ONE day—and that day was many years ago now—I received a
long, chatty letter from one of my old chums and fellow-wanderers
in Eastern waters. He was still out there, but settled down, and middle-
aged; I imagined him grown portly in figure and domestic in his habits;
in short, overtaken by the fate common to all except to those who, being
specially beloved by the gods, get knocked on the head early. The letter
was of the reminiscent "do you remember" kind—a wistful letter of
backward glances. And, amongst other things, "surely you remember
old Nelson," he wrote.

Remember old Nelson! Certainly. And to begin with, his name was
not Nelson. The Englishmen in the Archipelago called him Nelson
because it was more convenient, I suppose, and he never protested. It
would have been mere pedantry. The true form of his name was Nielsen.
He had come out East long before the advent of telegraph cables, had
served English firms, had married an English girl, had been one of
us for years, trading and sailing in all directions through the Eastern
Archipelago, across and around, transversely, diagonally, perpendicu-
larly, in semi-circles, and zigzags, and figures of eights, for years and
years.

There was no nook or cranny of these tropical waters that the enterprise of old Nelson (or Nielsen) had not penetrated in an eminently
pacific way. His tracks, if plotted out, would have covered the map of
the Archipelago like a cobweb—all of it, with the sole exception of the
Philippines. He would never approach that part, from a strange dread

of Spaniards, or, to be exact, of the Spanish authorities. What he imagined they could do to him it is impossible to say. Perhaps at some time in his life he had read some stories of the Inquisition.

But he was in general afraid of what he called "authorities"; not the English authorities, which he trusted and respected, but the other two of that part of the world. He was not so horrified at the Dutch as he was at the Spaniards, but he was even more mistrustful of them. Very mistrustful indeed. The Dutch, in his view, were capable of "playing any ugly trick on a man" who had the misfortune to displease them. There were their laws and regulations, but they had no notion of fair play in applying them. It was really pitiable to see the anxious circumspection of his dealings with some official or other, and remember that this man had been known to stroll up to a village of cannibals in New Guinea in a quiet, fearless manner (and note that he was always fleshy all his life, and, if I may say so, an appetising morsel) on some matter of barter that did not amount perhaps to fifty pounds in the end.

Remember old Nelson! Rather! Truly, none of us in my generation had known him in his active days. He was "retired" in our time. He had bought, or else leased, part of a small island from the sultan of a little group called the Seven Isles, not far north from Banka. It was, I suppose, a legitimate transaction, but I have no doubt that had he been an Englishman the Dutch would have discovered a reason to fire him out without ceremony. In this connection the real form of his name stood him in good stead. In the character of an unassuming Dane whose conduct was most correct, they let him be. With all his money engaged in cultivation he was naturally careful not to give even the shadow of offence, and it was mostly for prudential reasons of that sort that he did not look with a favourable eye on Jasper Allen. But of that later. Yes! One remembered well enough old Nelson's big, hospitable bungalow erected on a shelving point of land, his portly form, costumed generally in a white shirt and trousers (he had a confirmed habit of taking off his alpaca jacket on the slightest provocation), his round blue eyes, his straggly, sandy-white moustache sticking out all ways like the quills of the fretful porcupine, his propensity to sit down suddenly and fan himself with his hat. But there's no use concealing the fact that what one remembered really was his daughter, who at that time came out to live with him—and be a sort of Lady of the Isles.

Freya Nelson (or Nielsen) was the kind of a girl one remembers. The oval of her face was perfect; and within that fascinating frame the most happy disposition of line and feature, with an admirable complexion, gave an impression of health, strength, and what I might call unconscious self-confidence—a most pleasant and, as it were, whimsical determination. I will not compare her eyes to violets, because the real shade of their colour was peculiar, not so dark and more lustrous. They were of the wide-open kind, and looked at one frankly in every mood. I never did see the long, dark eyelashes lowered—I dare say Jasper Allen did, being a privileged person—but I have no doubt that the expression must have been charming in a complex way. She could—Jasper told me once with a touchingly imbecile exultation—sit on her hair. I dare say, I dare say. It was not for me to behold these wonders; I was content to admire the neat and becoming way she used to do it up so as not to conceal the good shape of her head. And this wealth of hair was so glossy that when the screens of the west verandah were down, making a pleasant twilight there, or in the shade of the grove of fruit-trees near the house, it seemed to give out a golden light of its own.

She dressed generally in a white frock, with a skirt of walking length, showing her neat, laced, brown boots. If there was any colour about her costume it was just a bit of blue perhaps. No exertion seemed to distress her. I have seen her land from the dinghy after a long pull in the sun (she rowed herself about a good deal) with no quickened breath and not a single hair out of its place. In the morning when she came out on the verandah for the first look westward, Sumatra way, over the sea, she seemed as fresh and sparkling as a dewdrop. But a dewdrop is evanescent, and there was nothing evanescent about Freya. I remember her round, solid arms with the fine wrists, and her broad, capable hands with tapering fingers.

I don't know whether she was actually born at sea, but I do know that up to twelve years of age she sailed about with her parents in various ships. After old Nelson lost his wife it became a matter of serious concern for him what to do with the girl. A kind lady in Singapore, touched by his dumb grief and deplorable perplexity, offered to take charge of Freya. This arrangement lasted some six years, during which old Nelson (or Nielsen) "retired" and established himself on his island, and then it was settled (the kind lady going away to Europe) that his daughter should join him.

As the first and most important preparation for that event the old fellow ordered from his Singapore agent a Steyn and Ebhart's "upright grand." I was then commanding a little steamer in the island trade, and it fell to my lot to take it out to him, so I know something of Freya's "upright grand." We landed the enormous packing-case with difficulty on a flat piece of rock amongst some bushes, nearly knocking the bottom out of one of my boats in the course of that nautical operation. Then, all my crew assisting, engineers and firemen included, by the exercise of much anxious ingenuity, and by means of rollers, levers, tackles, and inclined planes of soaped planks, toiling in the sun like ancient Egyptians at the building of a pyramid, we got it as far as the house and up on to the edge of the west verandah—which was the actual drawing-room of the bungalow. There, the case being ripped off cautiously, the beautiful rosewood monster stood revealed at last. In reverent excitement we coaxed it against the wall and drew the first free breath of the day. It was certainly the heaviest movable object on that islet since the creation of the world. The volume of sound it gave out in that bungalow (which acted as a sounding-board) was really astonishing. It thundered sweetly right over the sea. Jasper Allen told me that early of a morning on the deck of the *Bonito* (his wonderfully fast and pretty brig) he could hear Freya playing her scales quite distinctly. But the fellow always anchored foolishly close to the point, as I told him more than once. Of course, these seas are almost uniformly serene, and the Seven Isles is a particularly calm and cloudless spot as a rule. But still, now and again, an afternoon thunderstorm over Banka, or even one of these vicious thick squalls, from the distant Sumatra coast, would make a sudden sally upon the group, enveloping it for a couple of hours in whirlwinds and bluish-black murk of a particularly sinister aspect. Then, with the lowered rattan-screens rattling desperately in the wind and the bungalow shaking all over, Freya would sit down to the piano and play fierce Wagner music in the flicker of blinding flashes, with thunderbolts falling all round, enough to make your hair stand on end; and Jasper would remain stock still on the verandah, adoring the back view of her supple, swaying figure, the miraculous sheen of her fair head, the rapid hands on the keys, the white nape of her neck—while the brig, down at the point there, surged at her cables within a hundred yards of nasty, shiny, black rock-heads. Ugh!

And this, if you please, for no reason but that, when he went on board at night and laid his head on the pillow, he should feel that he was as

near as he could conveniently get to his Freya slumbering in the bungalow. Did you ever! And, mind, this brig was the home to be—their
home—the floating paradise which he was gradually fitting out like a
yacht to sail his life blissfully away in with Freya. Imbecile! But the
fellow was always taking chances.

One day, I remember I watched with Freya on the verandah the brig
approaching the point from the northward. I suppose Jasper made the
girl out with his long glass. What does he do? Instead of standing on
for another mile and a half along the shoals and then tacking for the
anchorage in a proper and seaman-like manner, he spies a gap between
two disgusting old jagged reefs, puts the helm down suddenly, and
shoots the brig through, with all her sails shaking and rattling, so that
we could hear the racket on the verandah. I drew my breath through
my teeth, I can tell you, and Freya swore. Yes! She clenched her capable
fists and stamped with her pretty brown boot and said "Damn!" Then,
looking at me with a little heightened colour—not much—she remarked, "I forgot you were there," and laughed. To be sure, to be sure.
When Jasper was in sight she was not likely to remember that anybody
else in the world was there. In my concern at this mad trick I couldn't
help appealing to her sympathetic common sense.

"Isn't he a fool?" I said with feeling.

"Perfect idiot," she agreed warmly, looking at me straight with her
wide-open, earnest eyes and the dimple of a smile on her cheek.

"And that," I pointed out to her, "just to save twenty minutes or so
in meeting you."

We heard the anchor go down, and then she became very resolute
and threatening.

"Wait a bit. I'll teach him."

She went into her own room and shut the door, leaving me alone on
the verandah with my instructions. Long before the brig's sails were
furled, Jasper came up three steps at a time, forgetting to say how d'ye
do, and looking right and left eagerly.

"Where's Freya? Wasn't she here just now?"

When I explained to him that he was to be deprived of Miss Freya's
presence for a whole hour, "just to teach him," he said I had put her
up to it, no doubt, and that he feared he would have yet to shoot me
some day. She and I were getting too thick together. Then he flung
himself into a chair, and tried to talk to me about his trip. But the funny

thing was that the fellow actually suffered. I could see it. His voice failed him, and he sat there dumb, looking at the door with the face of a man in pain. Fact. . . . And the next still funnier thing was that the girl calmly walked out of her room in less than ten minutes. And then I left. I mean to say that I went away to seek old Nelson (or Nielsen) on the back verandah, which was his own special nook in the distribution of that house, with the kind purpose of engaging him in conversation lest he should start roaming about and intrude unwittingly where he was not wanted just then.

He knew that the brig had arrived, though he did not know that Jasper was already with his daughter. I suppose he didn't think it was possible in the time. A father naturally wouldn't. He suspected that Allen was sweet on his girl; the fowls of the air and the fishes of the sea, most of the traders in the Archipelago, and all sorts and conditions of men in the town of Singapore were aware of it. But he was not capable of appreciating how far the girl was gone on the fellow. He had an idea that Freya was too sensible ever to be gone on anybody—I mean to an unmanageable extent. No; it was not that which made him sit on the back verandah and worry himself in his unassuming manner during Jasper's visits. What he worried about were the Dutch "authorities." For it is a fact that the Dutch looked askance at the doings of Jasper Allen, owner and master of the brig *Bonito*. They considered him much too enterprising in his trading. I don't know that he ever did anything illegal; but it seems to me that his immense activity was repulsive to their stolid character and slow-going methods. Anyway, in old Nelson's opinion, the captain of the *Bonito* was a smart sailor, and a nice young man, but not a desirable acquaintance upon the whole. Somewhat compromising, you understand. On the other hand, he did not like to tell Jasper in so many words to keep away. Poor old Nelson himself was a nice fellow. I believe he would have shrunk from hurting the feelings even of a mop-headed cannibal, unless, perhaps, under very strong provocation. I mean the feelings, not the bodies. As against spears, knives, hatchets, clubs, or arrows, old Nelson had proved himself capable of taking his own part. In every other respect he had a timorous soul. So he sat on the back verandah with a concerned expression, and whenever the voices of his daughter and Jasper Allen reached him, he would blow out his cheeks and let the air escape with a dismal sound, like a much tried man.

Naturally I derided his fears which he, more or less, confided to me. He had a certain regard for my judgment, and a certain respect, not for my moral qualities, however, but for the good terms I was supposed to be on with the Dutch "authorities." I knew for a fact that his greatest bugbear, the Governor of Banka—a charming, peppery, hearty, retired rear-admiral—had a distinct liking for him. This consoling assurance which I used always to put forward, made old Nelson (or Nielsen) brighten up for a moment; but in the end he would shake his head doubtfully, as much as to say that this was all very well, but that there were depths in the Dutch official nature which no one but himself had ever fathomed. Perfectly ridiculous.

On this occasion I am speaking of, old Nelson was even fretty; for . while I was trying to entertain him with a very funny and somewhat scandalous adventure which happened to a certain acquaintance of ours in Saigon, he exclaimed suddenly:

"What the devil he wants to turn up here for!"

Clearly he had not heard a word of the anecdote. And this annoyed me, because the anecdote was really good. I stared at him.

"Come, come!" I cried. "Don't you know what Jasper Allen is turning up here for?"

This was the first open allusion I had ever made to the true state of affairs between Jasper and his daughter. He took it very calmly.

"Oh, Freya is a sensible girl!" he murmured absently, his mind's eye obviously fixed on the "authorities." No; Freya was no fool. He was not concerned about that. He didn't mind it in the least. The fellow was just company for her; he amused the girl; nothing more.

When the perspicacious old chap left off mumbling, all was still in the house. The other two were amusing themselves very quietly, and no doubt very heartily. What more absorbing and less noisy amusement could they have found than to plan their future? Side by side on the verandah they must have been looking at the brig, the third party in that fascinating game. Without her there would have been no future. She was the fortune and the home, and the great free world for them. Who was it that likened a ship to a prison? May I be ignominiously hanged at a yardarm if that's true. The white sails of that craft were the white wings—pinions, I believe, would be the more poetical style— well, the white pinions, of their soaring love. Soaring as regards Jasper.

Freya, being a woman, kept a better hold of the mundane connections of this affair.

But Jasper was elevated in the true sense of the word ever since the day when, after they had been gazing at the brig in one of those decisive silences that alone establish a perfect communion between creatures gifted with speech, he proposed that she should share the ownership of that treasure with him. Indeed, he presented the brig to her altogether. But then his heart was in the brig since the day he bought her in Manila from a certain middle-aged Peruvian, in a sober suit of black broadcloth, enigmatic and sententious, who, for all I know, might have stolen her on the South American coast, whence he said he had come over to the Philippines "for family reasons." This "for family reasons" was distinctly good. No true *caballero* would care to push on inquiries after such a statement.

Indeed, Jasper was quite the *caballero*. The brig herself was then all black and enigmatical, and very dirty; a tarnished gem of the sea, or, rather, a neglected work of art. For he must have been an artist, the obscure builder who had put her body together on lovely lines out of the hardest tropical timber fastened with the purest copper. Goodness only knows in what part of the world she was built. Jasper himself had not been able to ascertain much of her history from his sententious, saturnine Peruvian—if the fellow was a Peruvian, and not the devil himself in disguise, as Jasper jocularly pretended to believe. My opinion is that she was old enough to have been one of the last pirates, a slaver perhaps, or else an opium clipper of the early days, if not an opium smuggler.

However that may be, she was as sound as on the day she first took the water, sailed like a witch, steered like a little boat, and, like some fair women of adventurous life famous in history, seemed to have the secret of perpetual youth; so that there was nothing unnatural in Jasper Allen treating her like a lover. And that treatment restored the lustre of her beauty. He clothed her in many coats of the very best white paint so skilfully, carefully, artistically put on and kept clean by his badgered crew of picked Malays, that no costly enamel such as jewellers use for their work could have looked better and felt smoother to the touch. A narrow gilt moulding defined her elegant sheer as she sat on the water, eclipsing easily the professional good looks of any pleasure yacht that ever came to the East in those days. For myself, I must say I prefer a moulding of deep crimson colour on a white hull. It gives a stronger relief besides being less expensive; and I told Jasper so. But no, nothing less than the best gold-leaf would do, because no decoration could be gorgeous enough for the future abode of his Freya.

His feelings for the brig and for the girl were as indissolubly united in his heart as you may fuse two precious metals together in one crucible. And the flame was pretty hot, I can assure you. It induced in him a fierce inward restlessness both of activity and desire. Too fine in face, with a lateral wave in his chestnut hair, spare, long-limbed, with an eager glint in his steely eyes and quick, brusque movements, he made me think sometimes of a flashing sword-blade perpetually leaping out of the scabbard. It was only when he was near the girl, when he had her there to look at, that this peculiarly tense attitude was replaced by a grave devout watchfulness of her slightest movements and utterances. Her cool, resolute, capable, good-humoured self-possession seemed to steady his heart. Was it the magic of her face, of her voice, of her glances which calmed him so? Yet these were the very things one must believe which had set his imagination ablaze—if love begins in imagination. But I am no man to discuss such mysteries, and it strikes me that we have neglected poor old Nelson inflating his cheeks in a state of worry on the back verandah.

I pointed out to him that, after all, Jasper was not a very frequent visitor. He and his brig worked hard all over the Archipelago. But all old Nelson said, and he said it uneasily, was:

"I hope Heemskirk won't turn up here while the brig's about."

Getting up a scare about Heemskirk now! Heemskirk! . . . Really, one hadn't the patience——

· II ·

For, pray, who was Heemskirk? You shall see at once how unreasonable this dread of Heemskirk. . . . Certainly, his nature was malevolent enough. That was obvious, directly you heard him laugh. Nothing gives away more a man's secret disposition than the unguarded ring of his laugh. But, bless my soul! if we were to start at every evil guffaw like a hare at every sound, we shouldn't be fit for anything but the solitude of a desert, or the seclusion of a hermitage. And even there we should have to put up with the unavoidable company of the devil.

However, the devil is a considerable personage, who has known better days and has moved high up in the hierarchy of Celestial Host; but in the hierarchy of mere earthly Dutchmen, Heemskirk, whose early days could not have been very splendid, was merely a naval officer forty years of age, of no particular connections or ability to boast of. He was commanding the *Neptun,* a little gunboat employed on dreary patrol duty up and down the Archipelago, to look after the traders. Not a very exalted position truly. I tell you, just a common middle-aged lieutenant of some twenty-five years' service and sure to be retired before long— that's all.

He never bothered his head very much as to what was going on in the Seven Isles group till he learned from some talk in Mintok or Palembang, I suppose, that there was a pretty girl living there. Curiosity, I presume, caused him to go poking around that way and then, after he had once seen Freya, he made a practice of calling at the group whenever he found himself within half a day's steaming from it.

I don't mean to say that Heemskirk was a typical Dutch naval officer. I have seen enough of them not to fall into that absurd mistake. He had a big, clean-shaven face; great flat, brown cheeks, with a thin, hooked nose and a small, pursy mouth squeezed in between. There were a few silver threads in his black hair, and his unpleasant eyes were nearly black, too. He had a surly way of casting side glances without moving his head, which was set low on a short, round neck. A thick, round trunk in a dark undress jacket with gold shoulder-straps, was sustained by a straddly pair of thick, round legs, in white drill trousers. His round skull under a white cap looked as if it were immensely thick too, but there were brains enough in it to discover and take advantage maliciously of poor old Nelson's nervousness before everything that was invested with the merest shred of authority.

Heemskirk would land on the point and perambulate silently every part of the plantation as if the whole place belonged to him, before he went to the house. On the verandah he would take the best chair, and would stay for tiffin or dinner, just simply stay on, without taking the trouble to invite himself by so much as a word.

He ought to have been kicked, if only for his manner to Miss Freya.

Had he been a naked savage, armed with spears and poisoned arrows, old Nelson (or Nielsen) would have gone for him with his bare fists. But these gold shoulder-straps—Dutch shoulder-straps at that—were enough to terrify the old fellow; so he let the beggar treat him with heavy contempt, devour his daughter with his eyes, and drink the best part of his little stock of wine.

I saw something of this, and on one occasion I tried to pass a remark on the subject. It was pitiable to see the trouble in old Nelson's round eyes. At first he cried out that the lieutenant was a good friend of his; a very good fellow. I went on staring at him pretty hard, so that at last he faltered, and had to own that, of course, Heemskirk was not a very genial person outwardly, but all the same at bottom. . . .

"I haven't yet met a genial Dutchman out here," I interrupted. "Geniality, after all, is not of much consequence, but don't you see——"

Nelson looked suddenly so frightened at what I was going to say that I hadn't the heart to go on. Of course, I was going to tell him that the fellow was after his girl. That just describes it exactly. What Heemskirk might have expected or what he thought he could do, I don't know. For all I can tell, he might have imagined himself irresistible, or have taken Freya for what she was not, on account of her lively, assured, unconstrained manner. But there it is. He was after that girl. Nelson could see it well enough. Only he preferred to ignore it. He did not want to be told of it.

"All I want is to live in peace and quietness with the Dutch authorities," he mumbled shamefacedly.

He was incurable. I was sorry for him, and I really think Miss Freya was sorry for her father, too. She restrained herself for his sake, and like everything she did she did it simply, unaffectedly, and even good humouredly. No small effort that, because in Heemskirk's attentions there was an insolent touch of scorn, hard to put up with. Dutchmen of that sort are over-bearing to their inferiors, and that officer of the king looked upon old Nelson and Freya as quite beneath him in every way.

I can't say I felt sorry for Freya. She was not the sort of girl to take anything tragically. One could feel for her and sympathise with her difficulty, but she seemed equal to any situation. It was rather admiration she extorted by her competent serenity. It was only when Jasper and Heemskirk were together at the bungalow, as it happened now and

then, that she felt the strain, and even then it was not for everybody to
see. My eyes alone could detect a faint shadow on the radiance of her
personality. Once I could not help saying to her appreciatively:

"Upon my word you are wonderful."

She let it pass with a faint smile.

"The great thing is to prevent Jasper becoming unreasonable," she
said; and I could see real concern lurking in the quiet depths of her
frank eyes gazing straight at me. "You will help to keep him quiet, won't
you?"

"Of course, we must keep him quiet," I declared, understanding very
well the nature of her anxiety. "He's such a lunatic, too, when he's
roused."

"He is!" she assented, in a soft tone; for it was our joke to speak of
Jasper abusively. "But I have tamed him a bit. He's quite a good boy
now."

"He would squash Heemskirk like a blackbeetle all the same," I
remarked.

"Rather!" she murmured. "And that wouldn't do," she added
quickly. "Imagine the state poor papa would get into. Besides, I mean
to be mistress of the dear brig and sail about these seas, not go off
wandering ten thousand miles away from here."

"The sooner you are on board to look after the man and the brig the
better," I said seriously. "They need you to steady them both a bit. I
don't think Jasper will ever get sobered down till he has carried you off
from this island. You don't see him when he is away from you, as I do.
He's in a state of perpetual elation which almost frightens me."

At this she smiled again, and then looked serious. For it could not be
unpleasant to her to be told of her power, and she had some sense of
her responsibility. She slipped away from me suddenly, because Heemskirk, with old Nelson in attendance at his elbow, was coming up the
steps of the verandah. Directly his head came above the level of the
floor his ill-natured black eyes shot glances here and there.

"Where's your girl, Nelson?" he asked, in a tone as if every soul in
the world belonged to him. And then to me: "The goddess has flown,
eh?"

Nelson's Cove—as we used to call it—was crowded with shipping
that day. There was first my steamer, then the *Neptun* gunboat further
out, and the *Bonito,* brig, anchored as usual so close inshore that it

looked as if, with a little skill and judgment, one could shy a hat from the verandah on to her scrupulously holystoned quarter-deck. Her brasses flashed like gold, her white body-paint had a sheen like a satin robe. The rake of her varnished spars and the big yards, squared to a hair, gave her a sort of martial elegance. She was a beauty. No wonder that in possession of a craft like that and the promise of a girl like Freya, Jasper lived in a state of perpetual elation fit, perhaps, for the seventh heaven, but not exactly safe in a world like ours.

I remarked politely to Heemskirk that, with three guests in the house, Miss Freya had no doubt domestic matters to attend to. I knew, of course, that she had gone to meet Jasper at a certain cleared spot on the banks of the only stream on Nelson's little island. The commander of the *Neptun* gave me a dubious black look, and began to make himself at home, flinging his thick, cylindrical carcass into a rocking-chair, and unbuttoning his coat. Old Nelson sat down opposite him in a most unassuming manner, staring anxiously with his round eyes and fanning himself with his hat. I tried to make conversation to while the time away; not an easy task with a morose, enamoured Dutchman constantly looking from one door to another and answering one's advances either with a jeer or a grunt.

However, the evening passed off all right. Luckily there is a degree of bliss too intense for elation. Jasper was quiet and concentrated silently in watching Freya. As we went on board our respective ships I offered to give his brig a tow out next morning. I did it on purpose to get him away at the earliest possible moment. So in the first cold light of the dawn we passed by the gunboat lying black and still without a sound in her at the mouth of the glassy cove. But with tropical swiftness the sun had climbed twice its diameter above the horizon before we had rounded the reef and got abreast of the point. On the biggest boulder there stood Freya, all in white and, in her helmet, like a feminine and martial statue with a rosy face, as I could see very well with my glasses. She fluttered an expressive handkerchief, and Jasper, running up the main rigging of the white and warlike brig, waved his hat in response. Shortly afterwards we parted, I to the northward, and Jasper heading east with a light wind on the quarter, for Banjermassin and two other ports, I believe it was, that trip.

This peaceful occasion was the last on which I saw all these people assembled together; the charmingly fresh and resolute Freya, the innocently round-eyed old Nelson, Jasper, keen, long limbed, lean faced, admirable self-contained in his manner, because inconceivably happy under the eyes of his Freya; all three tall, fair, and blue-eyed in varied shades, and amongst them the swarthy, arrogant, black-haired Dutchman, shorter nearly by a head, and so much thicker than any of them that he seemed to be a creature capable of inflating itself, a grotesque specimen of mankind from some other planet.

The contrast struck me all at once as we stood in the lighted verandah, after rising from the dinner-table. I was fascinated by it for the rest of the evening, and I remember the impression of something funny and ill-omened at the same time in it to this day.

· III ·

A few weeks later, coming early one morning into Singapore, from a journey to the southward, I saw the brig lying at anchor in all her usual symmetry and splendour of aspect as though she had been taken out of a glass case and put delicately into the water that very moment.

She was well out in the roadstead, but I steamed in and took up my habitual berth close in front of the town. Before we had finished breakfast a quarter-master came to tell me that Captain Allen's boat was coming our way.

His smart gig dashed alongside, and in two bounds he was up our accommodation-ladder and shaking me by the hand with his nervous grip, his eyes snapping inquisitively, for he supposed I had called at the Seven Isles group on my way. I reached into my pocket for a nicely folded little note, which he grabbed out of my hand without ceremony and carried off on the bridge to read by himself. After a decent interval I followed him up there, and found him pacing to and fro; for the nature of his emotions made him restless even in his most thoughtful moments. He shook his head at me triumphantly.

"Well, my dear boy," he said, "I shall be counting the days now."

I understood what he meant. I knew that those young people had settled already on a runaway match without official preliminaries. This was really a logical decision. Old Nelson (or Nielsen) would never have agreed to give up Freya peaceably to this compromising Jasper. Heavens! What would the Dutch authorities say to such a match! It sounds too ridiculous for words. But there's nothing in the world more selfishly hard than a timorous man in a fright about his "little estate," as old Nelson used to call it in apologetic accents. A heart permeated by a particular sort of funk is proof against sense, feeling, and ridicule. It's a flint.

Jasper would have made his request all the same and then taken his own way; but it was Freya who decided that nothing should be said, on the ground that, "Papa would only worry himself to distraction." He was capable of making himself ill, and then she wouldn't have the heart to leave him. Here you have the sanity of feminine outlook and the frankness of feminine reasoning. And for the rest, Miss Freya could read "poor dear papa" in the way a woman reads a man—like an open book. His daughter once gone, old Nelson would not worry himself. He would raise a great outcry, and make no end of lamentable fuss, but that's not the same thing. The real agonies of indecision, the anguish of conflicting feelings would be spared to him. And as he was too unassuming to rage, he would, after a period of lamentation, devote himself to his "little estate," and to keeping on good terms with the authorities.

Time would do the rest. And Freya thought she could afford to wait, while ruling over her own home in the beautiful brig and over the man who loved her. This was the life for her who had learned to walk on a ship's deck. She was a ship-child, a sea-girl if ever there was one. And of course she loved Jasper and trusted him; but there was a shade of anxiety in her pride. It is very fine and romantic to possess for your very own a finely tempered and trusty sword-blade, but whether it is the best weapon to counter with the common cudgel-play of Fate—that's another question.

She knew that she had the more substance of the two—you needn't try any cheap jokes, I am not talking of their weights. She was just a little anxious while he was away, and she had me who, being a tried confidant, took the liberty to whisper frequently "The sooner the better." But there was a peculiar vein of obstinacy in Miss Freya, and her reason for delay was characteristic. "Not before my twenty-first birthday; so that there shall be no mistake in people's minds as to me being old enough to know what I am doing."

Jasper's feelings were in such subjection that he had never even remonstrated against the decree. She was just splendid, whatever she did or said, and there was an end of it for him. I believe that he was subtle enough to be even flattered at bottom—at times. And then to console him he had the brig which seemed pervaded by the spirit of Freya, since whatever he did on board was always done under the supreme sanction of his love.

"Yes. I'll soon begin to count the days," he repeated. "Eleven months more. I'll have to crowd three trips into that."

"Mind you don't come to grief trying to do too much," I admonished him. But he dismissed my caution with a laugh and an elated gesture. Pooh! Nothing, nothing could happen to the brig, he cried, as if the flame of his heart could light up the dark nights of uncharted seas, and the image of Freya serve for an unerring beacon amongst hidden shoals; as if the winds had to wait on his future, the stars fight for it in their courses; as if the magic of his passion had the power to float a ship on a drop of dew or sail her through the eye of a needle—simply because it was her magnificent lot to be the servant of a love so full of grace as to make all the ways of the earth safe, resplendent, and easy.

"I suppose," I said, after he had finished laughing at my innocent enough remark, "I suppose you will be off to-day."

That was what he meant to do. He had not gone at daylight only because he expected me to come in.

"And only fancy what has happened yesterday," he went on. "My mate left me suddenly. Had to. And as there's nobody to be found at a short notice I am going to take Schultz with me. The notorious Schultz! Why don't you jump out of your skin? I tell you I went and unearthed Schultz late last evening, after no end of trouble. 'I am your man, Captain,' he says, in that wonderful voice of his, 'but I am sorry to confess I have practically no clothes to my back. I have had to sell all my wardrobe to get a little food from day to day.' What a voice that man has got. Talk about moving stones! But people seem to get used to it. I had never seen him before, and, upon my word, I felt suddenly tears rising to my eyes. Luckily it was dusk. He was sitting very quiet under a tree in a native compound as thin as a lath, and when I peered down at him all he had on was an old cotton singlet and a pair of ragged pyjamas. I bought him six white suits and two pairs of canvas shoes. Can't clear the ship without a mate. Must have somebody. I am going on shore presently to sign him on, and I shall take him with me as I go back on board to get under way. Now, I am a lunatic—am I not? Mad, of course. Come on! Lay it on thick. Let yourself go. I like to see you get excited."

He so evidently expected me to scold that I took especial pleasure in exaggerating the calmness of my attitude.

"The worst that can be brought up against Schultz," I began, folding my arms and speaking dispassionately, "is an awkward habit of stealing the stores of every ship he has ever been in. He will do it. That's really all that's wrong. I don't credit absolutely that story Captain Robinson tells of Schultz conspiring in Chantabun with some ruffians in a Chinese junk to steal the anchor off the starboard bow of the *Bohemian Girl* schooner. Robinson's story is too ingenious altogether. That other tale of the engineers of the *Nan-Shan* finding Schultz at midnight in the engine-room busy hammering at the brass bearings to carry them off for sale on shore seems to me more authentic. Apart from this little weakness, let me tell you that Schultz is a smarter sailor than many who never took a drop of drink in their lives, and perhaps no worse morally than some men you and I know who have never stolen the value of a penny. He may not be a desirable person to have on board one's ship, but since you have no choice he may be made to do, I believe. The important thing is to understand his psychology. Don't give him any money till you have done with him. Not a cent, if he begs you ever so. For as sure as Fate the moment you give him any money he will begin to steal. Just remember that."

I enjoyed Jasper's incredulous surprise.

"The devil he will!" he cried. "What on earth for? Aren't you trying to pull my leg, old boy?"

"No. I'm not. You must understand Schultz's psychology. He's neither a loafer nor a cadger. He's not likely to wander about looking for somebody to stand him drinks. But suppose he goes on shore with five dollars, or fifty for that matter, in his pocket? After the third or fourth glass he becomes fuddled and charitable. He either drops his money all over the place, or else distributes the lot around; gives it to any one who will take it. Then it occurs to him that the night is young yet, and that he may require a good many more drinks for himself and his friends before morning. So he starts off cheerfully for his ship. His legs never get affected nor his head either in the usual way. He gets aboard and simply grabs the first thing that seems to him suitable—the cabin lamp, a coil of rope, a bag of biscuits, a drum of oil—and converts it into money without thinking twice about it. This is the process and no other. You have only to look out that he doesn't get a start. That's all."

"Confound his psychology," muttered Jasper. "But a man with a voice like his is fit to talk to the angels. Is he incurable do you think?"

I said that I thought so. Nobody had prosecuted him yet, but no one would employ him any longer. His end would be, I feared, to starve in some hole or other.

"Ah, well," reflected Jasper. "The *Bonito* isn't trading to any ports of civilisation. That'll make it easier for him to keep straight."

That was true. The brig's business was on uncivilised coasts, with obscure rajahs dwelling in nearly unknown bays; with native settlements up mysterious rivers opening their sombre, forest-lined estuaries among a welter of pale green reefs and dazzling sandbanks, in lonely straits of calm blue water all aglitter with sunshine. Alone, far from the beaten tracks, she glided, all white, round dark, frowning headlands, stole out, silent like a ghost, from behind points of land stretching out all black in the moonlight; or lay hove-to, like a sleeping sea-bird, under the shadow of some nameless mountain waiting for a signal. She would be glimpsed suddenly on misty, squally days dashing disdainfully aside the short aggressive waves of the Java Sea; or be seen far, far away, a tiny dazzling white speck flying across the brooding purple masses of thunderclouds piled up on the horizon. Sometimes, on the rare mail tracks, where civilisation brushes against wild mystery, when the naïve passengers crowding along the rail exclaimed, pointing at her with interest: "Oh, here's a yacht!" the Dutch captain, with a hostile glance, would grunt contemptuously: "Yacht! No! That's only English Jasper. A pedlar——"

"A good seaman you say," ejaculated Jasper, still in the matter of the hopeless Schultz with the wonderfully touching voice.

"First rate. Ask any one. Quite worth having—only impossible," I declared.

"He shall have his chance to reform in the brig," said Jasper, with a laugh. "There will be no temptations either to drink or steal where I am going to this time."

I didn't press him for anything more definite on that point. In fact, intimate as we were, I had a pretty clear notion of the general run of his business.

But as we are going ashore in his gig he asked suddenly: "By the way, do you know where Heemskirk is?"

I eyed him covertly, and was reassured. He had asked the question, not as a lover, but as a trader. I told him that I had heard in Palembang that the *Neptun* was on duty down about Flores and Sumbawa. Quite out of his way. He expressed his satisfaction.

"You know," he went on, "that fellow, when he gets on the Borneo coast, amuses himself by knocking down my beacons. I have had to put up a few to help me in and out of the rivers. Early this year a Celebes trader becalmed in a prau was watching him at it. He steamed the gunboat full tilt at two of them, one after another, smashing them to pieces, and then lowered a boat on purpose to pull out a third, which I had a lot of trouble six months ago to stick up in the middle of a mudflat for a tide mark. Did you ever hear of anything more provoking—eh?"

"I wouldn't quarrel with the beggar," I observed casually, yet disliking that piece of news strongly. "It isn't worth while."

"I quarrel?" cried Jasper. "I don't want to quarrel. I don't want to hurt a single hair of his ugly head. My dear fellow, when I think of Freya's twenty-first birthday, all the world's my friend, Heemskirk included. It's a nasty, spiteful amusement, all the same."

We parted rather hurriedly on the quay, each of us having his own pressing business to attend to. I would have been very much cut up had I known that this hurried grasp of the hand with "So long, old boy. Good luck to you!" was the last of our partings.

On his return to the Straits I was away, and he was gone again before I got back. He was trying to achieve three trips before Freya's twenty-first birthday. At Nelson's Cove I missed him again by only a couple of days. Freya and I talked of "that lunatic" and "perfect idiot" with great delight and infinite appreciation. She was very radiant, with a more pronounced gaiety, notwithstanding that she had just parted from Jasper. But this was to be their last separation.

"Do get aboard as soon as you can, Miss Freya," I entreated.

She looked me straight in the face, her colour a little heightened and with a sort of solemn ardour—if there was a little catch in her voice.

"The very next day."

Ah, yes! The very next day after her twenty-first birthday. I was pleased at this hint of deep feeling. It was as if she had grown impatient at last of the self-imposed delay. I supposed that Jasper's recent visit had told heavily.

"That's right," I said approvingly. "I shall be much easier in my mind when I know you have taken charge of that lunatic. Don't you lose a minute. He, of course, will be on time—unless heavens fall.''

"Yes. Unless——" she repeated in a thoughtful whisper, raising her eyes to the evening sky without a speck of cloud anywhere. Silent for a time, we let our eyes wander over the waters below, looking mysteriously still in the twilight, as if trustfully composed for a long, long dream in the warm, tropical night. And the peace all around us seemed without limits and without end.

And then we began to talk Jasper over in our usual strain. We agreed that he was too reckless in many ways. Luckily, the brig was equal to the situation. Nothing apparently was too much for her. A perfect darling of a ship, said Miss Freya. She and her father had spent an afternoon on board. Jasper had given them some tea. Papa was grumpy. . . . I had a vision of old Nelson under the brig's snowy awnings, nursing his unassuming vexation, and fanning himself with his hat. A comedy father. . . . As a new instance of Jasper's lunacy, I was told that he was distressed at his inability to have solid silver handles fitted to all the cabin doors. "As if I would have let him!" commented Miss Freya, with amused indignation. Incidentally, I learned also that Schultz, the nautical kleptomaniac with the pathetic voice, was still hanging on to his job, with Miss Freya's approval. Jasper had confided to the lady of his heart his purpose of straightening out the fellow's psychology. Yes, indeed. All the world was his friend because it breathed the same air with Freya.

Somehow or other, I brought Heemskirk's name into conversation, and, to my great surprise, startled Miss Freya. Her eyes expressed something like distress, while she bit her lip as if to contain an explosion of laughter. Oh! Yes. Heemskirk was at the bungalow at the same time with Jasper, but he arrived the day after. He left the same day as the brig, but a few hours later.

"What a nuisance he must have been to you two," I said feelingly.

Her eyes flashed at me a sort of frightened merriment, and suddenly she exploded into a clear burst of laughter. "Ha, ha, ha!"

I echoed it heartily, but not with the same charming tone: "Ha, ha, ha! . . . Isn't he grotesque? Ha, ha, ha!" And the ludicrousness of old Nelson's inanely fierce round eyes in association with his conciliatory manner to the lieutenant presenting itself to my mind brought on another fit.

"He looks," I spluttered, "he looks—Ha, ha, ha!—amongst you three
. . . like an unhappy black-beetle. Ha, ha, ha!"

She gave out another ringing peal, ran off into her own room, and
slammed the door behind her, leaving me profoundly astounded. I
stopped laughing at once.

"What's the joke?" asked Old Nelson's voice, half way down the
steps.

He came up, sat down, and blew out his cheeks, looking inexpressibly
fatuous. But I didn't want to laugh any more. "And what on earth," I
asked myself, "have we been laughing at in this uncontrollable fashion?"
I felt suddenly depressed.

Oh, yes. Freya had started it. The girl's overwrought, I thought. And
really one couldn't wonder at it.

I had no answer to old Nelson's question, but he was too aggrieved
at Jasper's visit to think of anything else. He as good as asked me
whether I wouldn't undertake to hint to Jasper that he was not wanted
at the Seven Isles group. I declared that it was not necessary. From
certain circumstances which had come to my knowledge lately, I had
reason to think that he would not be much troubled by Jasper Allen in
the future.

He emitted an earnest "Thank God!" which nearly set me laughing
again, but he did not brighten up proportionately. It seemed Heemskirk
had taken special pains to make himself disagreeable. The lieutenant
had frightened old Nelson very much by expressing a sinister wonder
at the Government permitting a white man to settle down in that part
at all. "It is against our declared policy," he had remarked. He had also
charged him with being in reality no better than an Englishman. He had
even tried to pick a quarrel with him for not learning to speak Dutch.

"I told him I was too old to learn now," sighed out old Nelson (or
Nielsen) dismally. "He said I ought to have learned Dutch long before.
I had been making my living in Dutch dependencies. It was disgraceful
of me not to speak Dutch, he said. He was as savage with me as if I had
been a Chinaman."

It was plain he had been viciously badgered. He did not mention
how many bottles of his best claret he had offered up on the altar of
conciliation. It must have been a generous libation. But old Nelson (or
Nielsen) was really hospitable. He didn't mind that; and I only regretted
that this virtue should be lavished on the lieutenant-commander of the

Neptun. I longed to tell him that in all probability he would be relieved from Heemskirk's visitations also. I did not do so only from the fear (absurd, I admit) of arousing some sort of suspicion in his mind. As if with this guileless comedy father such a thing were possible!

Strangely enough, the last words on the subject of Heemskirk were spoken by Freya, and in that very sense. The lieutenant was turning up persistently in old Nelson's conversation at dinner. At last I muttered a half audible, "Damn the lieutenant." I could see that the girl was getting exasperated, too.

"And he wasn't well at all—was he, Freya?" old Nelson went on moaning. "Perhaps it was that which made him so snappish, hey, Freya? He looked very bad when he left us so suddenly. His liver must be in a bad state, too."

"Oh, he will end by getting over it," said Freya impatiently. "And do leave off worrying about him, papa. Very likely you won't see much of him for a long time to come."

The look she gave me in exchange for my discreet smile had no hidden mirth in it. Her eyes seemed hollowed, her face gone wan in a couple of hours. We had been laughing too much. Overwrought! Overwrought by the approach of the decisive moment. After all, sincere, courageous, and self-reliant as she was, she must have felt both the passion and the compunction of her resolve. The very strength of love which had carried her up to that point must have put her under a great moral strain, in which there might have been a little simple remorse, too. For she was honest—and there, across the table, sat poor old Nelson (or Nielsen) staring at her, round-eyed and so pathetically comic in his fierce aspect as to touch the most lightsome heart.

He retired early to his room to soothe himself for a night's rest by perusing his account-books. We two remained on the verandah for another hour or so, but we exchanged only languid phrases on things without importance, as though we had been emotionally jaded by our long day's talk on the only momentous subject. And yet there was something she might have told a friend. But she didn't. We parted silently. She distrusted my masculine lack of common sense, perhaps. . . . O Freya!

Going down the precipitous path to the landing-stage, I was confronted in the shadows of boulders and bushes by a draped feminine figure whose appearance startled me at first. It glided into my way suddenly from behind a piece of rock. But in a moment it occurred to me that it could be no one else but Freya's maid, a half-caste Malacca Portuguese. One caught fleeting glimpses of her olive face and dazzling white teeth about the house. I had also observed her at times from a distance, as she sat within call under the shade of some fruit-trees, brushing and plaiting her long raven locks. It seemed to be the principal occupation of her leisure hours. We had often exchanged nods and smiles—and a few words, too. She was a pretty creature. And once I had watched her approvingly make funny and expressive grimaces behind Heemskirk's back. I understood (from Jasper) that she was in the secret, like a comedy camerista. She was to accompany Freya on her irregular way to matrimony and "ever after" happiness. Why should she be roaming by night near the cove—unless on some love affair of her own—I asked myself. But there was nobody suitable within the Seven Isles group, as far as I knew. It flashed upon me that it was myself she had been lying in wait for.

She hesitated, muffled from head to foot, shadowy and bashful. I advanced another pace, and how I felt is nobody's business.

"What is it?" I asked, very low.

"Nobody knows I am here," she whispered.

"And nobody can see us," I whispered back.

The murmur of words "I've been so frightened" reached me. Just then forty feet above our head, from the yet lighted verandah, unexpected and startling, Freya's voice rang out in a clear, imperious call:

"Antonia!"

With a stifled exclamation, the hesitating girl vanished out of the path. A bush near by rustled; then silence. I waited wondering. The lights on the verandah went out. I waited a while longer then continued down the path to my boat, wondering more than ever.

I remember the occurrences of that visit especially, because this was the last time I saw the Nelson bungalow. On arriving at the Straits I found cable messages which made it necessary for me to throw up my employment at a moment's notice and go home at once. I had a desperate scramble to catch the mailboat which was due to leave next day, but I found time to write two short notes, one to Freya, the other to Jasper. Later on I wrote at length, this time to Allen alone. I got no answer. I hunted up then his brother, or, rather, half-brother, a solicitor in the city, a sallow, calm, little man who looked at me over his spectacles thoughtfully.

Jasper was the only child of his father's second marriage, a transaction which had failed to commend itself to the first, grown-up family.

"You haven't heard for ages," I repeated, with secret annoyance. "May I ask what 'for ages' means in this connection?"

"It means that I don't care whether I ever hear from him or not," retorted the little man of law, turning nasty suddenly.

I could not blame Jasper for not wasting his time in correspondence with such an outrageous relative. But why didn't he write to me—a decent sort of friend, after all; enough of a friend to find for his silence the excuse of forgetfulness natural to a state of transcendental bliss? I waited indulgently, but nothing ever came. And the East seemed to drop out of my life without an echo, like a stone falling into a well of prodigious depth.

· IV ·

I supposed praiseworthy motives are a sufficient justification almost for anything. What could be more commendable in the abstract than a girl's determination that "poor papa" should not be worried, and her anxiety that the man of her choice should be kept by any means from every occasion of doing something rash, something which might endanger the whole scheme of their happiness?

Nothing could be more tender and more prudent. We must also remember the girl's self-reliant temperament, and the general unwillingness of women—I mean women of sense—to make a fuss over matters of that sort.

As has been said already, Heemskirk turned up some time after Jasper's arrival at Nelson's Cove. The sight of the brig lying right under the bungalow was very offensive to him. He did not fly ashore before his anchor touched the ground as Jasper used to do. On the contrary, he hung about his quarter-deck mumbling to himself; and when he ordered his boat to be manned it was in an angry voice. Freya's existence, which lifted Jasper out of himself into a blissful elation, was for Heemskirk a cause of secret torment, of hours of exasperated brooding.

While passing the brig he hailed her harshly and asked if the master was on board. Schultz, smart and neat in a spotless white suit, leaned over the taffrail, finding the question somewhat amusing. He looked humorously down into Heemskirk's boat, and answered, in the most amiable modulations of his beautiful voice: "Captain Allen is up at the house, sir." But his expression changed suddenly at the savage growl: "What the devil are you grinning at?" which acknowledged that information.

He watched Heemskirk land and, instead of going to the house, stride away by another path into the grounds.

The desire-tormented Dutchman found old Nelson (or Nielsen) at his drying-sheds, very busy superintending the manipulation of his tobacco crop, which, though small, was of excellent quality, and enjoying himself thoroughly. But Heemskirk soon put a stop to this simple happiness. He sat down by the old chap, and by the sort of talk which he knew was best calculated for the purpose, reduced him before long to a state of concealed and perspiring nervousness. It was a horrid talk of "authorities," and old Nelson tried to defend himself. If he dealt with English traders it was because he had to dispose of his produce somehow. He was as conciliatory as he knew how to be, and this very thing seemed to excite Heemskirk, who had worked himself up into a heavily breathing state of passion.

"And the worst of them all is that Allen," he growled. "Your particular friend—eh? You have let in a lot of these Englishmen into this part. You ought never to have been allowed to settle here. Never. What's he doing here now?"

Old Nelson (or Nielsen), becoming very agitated, declared that Jasper Allen was no particular friend of his. No friend at all—at all. He had bought three tons of rice from him to feed his workpeople on. What sort of evidence of friendship was that? Heemskirk burst out at last with the thought that had been gnawing at his vitals:

"Yes. Sell three tons of rice and flirt three days with that girl of yours. I am speaking to you as a friend, Nielsen. This won't do. You are only on sufferance here."

Old Nelson was taken aback at first, but recovered pretty quickly. Won't do! Certainly! Of course, it wouldn't do! The last man in the world. But his girl didn't care for the fellow, and was too sensible to fall in love with any one. He was very earnest in impressing on Heemskirk his own feeling of absolute security. And the lieutenant, casting doubting glances sideways, was yet willing to believe him.

"Much you know about it," he grunted nevertheless.

"But I do know," insisted old Nelson, with the greater desperation because he wanted to resist the doubts arising in his own mind. "My own daughter! In my own house, and I not to know! Come! It would be a good joke, lieutenant."

"They seem to be carrying on considerably," remarked Heemskirk moodily. "I suppose they are together now," he added, feeling a pang which changed what he meant for a mocking smile into a strange grimace.

The harassed Nelson shook his hand at him. He was at bottom shocked at this insistence, and was even beginning to feel annoyed at the absurdity of it.

"Pooh! Pooh! I'll tell you what, lieutenant: you go to the house and have a drop of gin-and-bitters before dinner. Ask for Freya. I must see the last of this tobacco put away for the night, but I'll be along presently."

Heemskirk was not insensible to this suggestion. It answered to his secret longing, which was not a longing for drink, however. Old Nelson shouted solicitously after his broad back a recommendation to make himself comfortable, and that there was a box of cheroots on the verandah.

It was the west verandah that old Nelson meant, the one which was the living-room of the house, and had split-rattan screens of the very finest quality. The east verandah, sacred to his own privacy, puffing out of cheeks, and other signs of perplexed thinking, was fitted with stout blinds of sailcloth. The north verandah was not a verandah at all, really. It was more like a long balcony. It did not communicate with the other two, and could only be approached by a passage inside the house. Thus it had a privacy which made it a convenient place for a maiden's meditations without words, and also for the discourses, apparently without sense, which, passing between a young man and a maid, become pregnant with a diversity of transcendental meanings.

This north verandah was embowered with climbing plants. Freya, whose room opened out on it, had furnished it as a sort of boudoir for herself, with a few cane chairs and a sofa of the same kind. On this sofa she and Jasper sat as close together as is possible in this imperfect world where neither can a body be in two places at once nor yet two bodies can be one place at the same time. They had been sitting together all the afternoon, and I won't say that their talk had been without sense. Loving him with a little judicious anxiety lest in his elation he should break his heart over some mishap, Freya naturally would talk to him soberly. He, nervous and brusque when away from her, appeared always as if overcome by her visibility, by the great wonder of being palpably loved. An old man's child, having lost his mother early, thrown out to sea out of the way while very young, he had not much experience of tenderness of any kind.

In this private, foliage-embowered verandah, and at this late hour of the afternoon, he bent down a little, and, possessing himself of Freya's hands, was kissing them one after another, while she smiled and looked down at his head with the eyes of approving compassion. At that same moment Heemskirk was approaching the house from the north.

Antonia was on the watch on that side. But she did not keep a very good watch. The sun was setting; she knew that her young mistress and the captain of the *Bonito* were about to separate. She was walking to and fro in the dusky grove with a flower in her hair, and singing softly to herself, when suddenly, within a foot of her, the lieutenant appeared from behind a tree. She bounded aside like a startled fawn, but Heemskirk, with a lucid comprehension of what she was there for, pounced upon her, and, catching her arm, clapped his other thick hand over her mouth.

"If you try to make a noise I'll twist your neck!"

This ferocious figure of speech terrified the girl sufficiently. Heemskirk had seen plainly enough on the verandah Freya's golden head with another head very close to it. He dragged the unresisting maid with him by a circuitous way into the compound, where he dismissed her with a vicious push in the direction of the cluster of bamboo huts for the servants.

She was very much like the faithful camerista of Italian comedy, but in her terror she bolted away without a sound from that thick, short, black-eyed man with a cruel grip of fingers like a vice. Quaking all over at a distance, extremely scared and half inclined to laugh, she saw him enter the house at the back.

The interior of the bungalow was divided by two passages crossing each other in the middle. At that point Heemskirk by turning his head slightly to the left as he passed, secured the evidence of "carrying on" so irreconcilable with old Nelson's assurances that it made him stagger, with a rush of blood to his head. Two white figures, distinct against the light, stood in an unmistakable attitude. Freya's arms were round Jasper's neck. Their faces were characteristically superimposed on each other, and Heemskirk went on, his throat choked with a sudden rising of curses, till on the west verandah he stumbled blindly against a chair and then dropped into another as though his legs had been swept from under him. He had indulged too long in the habit of appropriating Freya to himself in his thoughts. "Is that how you entertain your visitors—you . . ." he thought, so outraged that he could not find a sufficiently degrading epithet.

Freya struggled a little and threw her head back.

"Somebody has come in," she whispered. Jasper, holding her clasped closely to his breast, and looking down into her face, suggested casually:

"Your father."

Freya tried to disengage herself, but she had not the heart absolutely to push him away with her hands.

"I believe it's Heemskirk," she breathed out at him.

He, plunging into her eyes in a quiet rapture, was provoked to a vague smile by the sound of the name.

"The ass is always knocking down my beacons outside the river," he murmured. He attached no other meaning to Heemskirk's existence; but Freya was asking herself whether the lieutenant had seen them.

"Let me go, kid," she ordered in a peremptory whisper. Jasper obeyed, and, stepping back at once, continued his contemplation of her face under another angle. "I must go and see," she said to herself anxiously.

She instructed him hurriedly to wait a moment after she was gone and then to slip on to the back verandah and get a quiet smoke before he showed himself.

"Don't stay late this evening," was her last recommendation before she left him.

Then Freya came out on the west verandah with her light, rapid step. While going through the doorway she managed to shake down the folds of the looped-up curtains at the end of the passage so as to cover Jasper's retreat from the bower. Directly she appeared Heemskirk jumped up as if to fly at her. She paused and he made her an exaggerated low bow.

It irritated Freya.

"Oh! It's you, Mr. Heemskirk. How do you do?"

She spoke in her usual tone. Her face was not plainly visible to him in the dusk of the deep verandah. He dared not trust himself to speak, his rage at what he had seen was so great. And when she added with serenity: "Papa will be coming in before long," he called her horrid names silently, to himself, before he spoke with contorted lips.

"I have seen your father already. We had a talk in the sheds. He told me some very interesting things. Oh, very——"

Freya sat down. She thought: "He has seen us, for certain." She was not ashamed. What she was afraid of was some foolish or awkward complication. But she could not conceive how much her person had been appropriated by Heemskirk (in his thoughts). She tried to be conversational.

"You are coming now from Palembang, I suppose?"

"Eh? What? Oh, yes! I come from Palembang. Ha, ha, ha! You know what your father said? He said he was afraid you were having a very dull time of it here."

"And I suppose you are going to cruise in the Moluccas," continued Freya, who wanted to impart some useful information of Jasper if possible. At the same time she was always glad to know that those two men were a few hundred miles apart when not under her eye.

Heemskirk growled angrily.

"Yes. Moluccas," glaring in the direction of her shadowy figure. "Your father thinks it's very quiet for you here. I tell you what, Miss Freya. There isn't such a quiet spot on earth that a woman can't find an opportunity of making a fool of somebody."

Freya thought: "I mustn't let him provoke me." Presently the Tamil boy, who was Nelson's head servant, came in with the lights. She addressed him at once with voluble directions where to put the lamps, told him to bring the tray with the gin-and-bitters, and to send Antonia into the house.

"I will have to leave you to yourself, Mr. Heemskirk, for a while," she said.

And she went to her room to put on another frock. She made a quick change of it because she wished to be on the verandah before her father and the lieutenant met again. She relied on herself to regulate that evening's intercourse between these two. But Antonia, still scared and hysterical, exhibited a bruise on her arm which roused Freya's indignation.

"He jumped on me out of the bush like a tiger," said the girl, laughing nervously with frightened eyes.

"The brute!" thought Freya. "He meant to spy on us, then." She was enraged, but the recollection of the thick Dutchman in white trousers wide at the hips and narrow at the ankles, with his shoulder-straps and black bullet head, glaring at her in the light of the lamps, was so repulsively comical that she could not help a smiling grimace. Then she became anxious. The absurdities of three men were forcing this anxiety upon her: Jasper's impetuosity, her father's fears, Heemskirk's infatuation. She was very tender to the first two, and she made up her mind to display all her feminine diplomacy. All this, she said to herself, will be over and done with before very long now.

Heemskirk on the verandah, lolling in a chair, his legs extended and his white cap reposing on his stomach, was lashing himself into a fury of an atrocious character altogether incomprehensible to a girl like Freya. His chin was resting on his chest, his eyes gazed stonily at his shoes. Freya examined him from behind the curtain. He didn't stir. He was ridiculous. But this absolute stillness was impressive. She stole back along the passage to the east verandah, where Jasper was sitting quietly in the dark, doing what he was told, like a good boy.

"Psst," she hissed. He was by her side in a moment.

"Yes. What is it?" he murmured.

"It's that beetle," she whispered uneasily. Under the impression of Heemskirk's sinister immobility she had half a mind to let Jasper know that they had been seen. But she was by no means certain that Heemskirk would tell her father—and at any rate not that evening. She concluded rapidly that the safest thing would be to get Jasper out of the way as soon as possible.

"What has he been doing?" asked Jasper in a calm undertone.

"Oh, nothing! Nothing. He sits there looking cross. But you know how he's always worrying papa."

"Your father's quite unreasonable," pronounced Jasper judicially.

"I don't know," she said in a doubtful tone. Something of old Nelson's dread of the authorities had rubbed off on the girl since she had to live with it day after day. "I don't know. Papa's afraid of being reduced to beggary, as he says, in his old days. Look here, kid, you had better clear out to-morrow, first thing."

Jasper had hoped for another afternoon with Freya, an afternoon of quiet felicity with the girl by his side and his eyes on his brig, anticipating a blissful future. His silence was eloquent with disappointment, and Freya understood it very well. She, too, was disappointed. But it was her business to be sensible.

"We shan't have a moment to ourselves with that beetle creeping round the house," she argued in a low, hurried voice. "So what's the good of your staying? And he won't go while the brig's here. You know he won't."

"He ought to be reported for loitering," murmured Jasper with a vexed little laugh.

"Mind you get under way at daylight," recommended Freya under her breath.

He detained her after the manner of lovers. She expostulated without struggling because it was hard for her to repulse him. He whispered into her ear while he put his arms round her.

"Next time we two meet, next time I hold you like this, it shall be on board. You and I, in the brig—all the world, all the life——" And then he flashed out: "I wonder I can wait! I feel as if I must carry you off now, at once. I could run with you in my hands—down the path—without stumbling—without touching the earth——"

She was still. She listened to the passion in his voice. She was saying to herself that if she were to whisper the faintest yes, if she were but to sigh lightly her consent, he would do it. He was capable of doing it—without touching the earth. She closed her eyes and smiled in the dark, abandoning herself in a delightful giddiness, for an instant, to his encircling arm. But before he could be tempted to tighten his grasp she was out of it, a foot away from him and in full possession of herself.

That was the steady Freya. She was touched by the deep sigh which floated up to her from the white figure of Jasper, who did not stir.

"You are a mad kid," she said tremulously. Then with a change of tone: "No one could carry me off. Not even you. I am not the sort of girl that gets carried off." His white form seemed to shrink a little before the force of that assertion and she relented. "Isn't it enough for you to know that you have—that you have carried me away?" she added in a tender tone.

He murmured an endearing word, and she continued:

"I've promised you—I've said I would come—and I shall come of my own free will. You shall wait for me on board. I shall get up the side—by myself, and walk up to you on the deck and say: 'Here I am, kid.' And then—and then I shall be carried off. But it will be no man who will carry me off—it will be the brig, your brig—our brig. . . . I love the beauty!"

She heard an inarticulate sound, something like a moan wrung out by pain or delight, and glided away. There was that other man on the other verandah, that dark, surly Dutchman who could make trouble between Jasper and her father, bring about a quarrel, ugly words, and perhaps a physical collision. What a horrible situation! But, even putting aside that awful extremity, she shrank from having to live for some three months with a wretched, tormented, angry, distracted, absurd man. And when the day came, the day and the hour, what should she do if her father tried to detain her by main force—as was, after all, possible? Could she actually struggle with him hand to hand? But it was of lamentations and entreaties that she was really afraid. Could she withstand them? What an odious, cruel, ridiculous position would that be!

"But it won't be. He'll say nothing," she thought as she came out quickly on the west verandah, and, seeing that Heemskirk did not move, sat down on a chair near the doorway and kept her eyes on him. The outraged lieutenant had not changed his attitude; only his cap had fallen off his stomach and was lying on the floor. His thick black eyebrows were knitted by a frown, while he looked at her out of the corners of his eyes. And their sideways glance in conjunction with the hooked nose, the whole bulky, ungainly, sprawling person, struck Freya as so comically moody that, inwardly discomposed as she was, she could not help smiling. She did her best to give that smile a conciliatory character. She did not want to provoke Heemskirk needlessly.

And the lieutenant, perceiving that smile, was mollified. It never entered his head that his outward appearance, a naval officer, in uniform, could appear ridiculous to that girl of no position—the daughter of old Nielsen. The recollection of her arms round Jasper's neck still irritated and excited him. "The hussy!" he thought. "Smiling—eh? That's how you are amusing yourself. Fooling your father finely, aren't you? You have a taste for that sort of fun—have you? Well, we shall see——" He did not alter his position, but on his pursed-up lips there also appeared a smile of surly and ill-omened amusement, while his eyes returned to the contemplation of his boots.

Freya felt hot with indignation. She sat radiantly fair in the lamplight, her strong, well-shaped hands lying one on top of the other in her lap. . . . "Odious creature," she thought. Her face coloured with sudden anger. "You scared my maid out of her sense," she said aloud. "What possessed you?"

He was thinking so deeply of her that the sound of her voice, pronouncing these unexpected words, startled him extremely. He jerked up his head and looked so bewildered that Freya insisted impatiently:

"I mean Antonia. You have bruised her arm. What did you do it for?"

"Do you want to quarrel with me?" he asked thickly, with a sort of amazement. He blinked like an owl. He was funny. Freya, like all women, had a keen sense of the ridiculous in outward appearance.

"Well, no; I don't think I do." She could not help herself. She laughed outright, a clear, nervous laugh in which Heemskirk joined suddenly with a harsh "Ha, ha, ha!"

Voices and footsteps were heard in the passage, and Jasper, with old Nelson, came out. Old Nelson looked at his daughter approvingly, for he liked the lieutenant to be kept in good humour. And he also joined sympathetically in the laugh. "Now, lieutenant, we shall have some dinner," he said, rubbing his hands cheerily. Jasper had gone straight to the balustrade. The sky was full of stars, and in the blue velvety night the cove below had a denser blackness, in which the riding-lights of the brig and of the gunboat glimmered redly, like suspended sparks. "Next time this riding-light glimmers down there, I'll be waiting for her on the quarter-deck to come and say 'Here I am,' " Jasper thought; and his heart seemed to grow bigger in his chest, dilated by an oppressive happiness that nearly wrung out a cry from him. There was no wind. Not a leaf below him stirred, and even the sea was but a still uncomplaining shadow. Far away on the unclouded sky the pale lightning, the heat-lightning of the tropics, played tremulously amongst the low stars in short, faint, mysteriously consecutive flashes, like incomprehensible signals from some distant planet.

The dinner passed off quietly. Freya sat facing her father, calm but pale. Heemskirk affected to talk only to old Nelson. Jasper's behaviour was exemplary. He kept his eyes under control, basking in the sense of Freya's nearness, as people bask in the sun without looking up to heaven. And very soon after dinner was over, mindful of his instructions, he declared that it was time for him to go on board his ship.

Heemskirk did not look up. Ensconced in the rocking-chair, and puffing at a cheroot, he had the air of meditating surlily over some odious outbreak. So at least it seemed to Freya. Old Nelson said at once "I'll stroll down with you." He had begun a professional conversation about the dangers of the New Guinea coast, and wanted to relate to Jasper some experience of his own "over there." Jasper was such a good listener! Freya made as if to accompany them but her father frowned, shook his head, and nodded significantly towards the immovable Heemskirk blowing out smoke with half-closed eyes and protruded lips. The lieutenant must not be left alone. Take offence, perhaps.

Freya obeyed these signs. "Perhaps it is better for me to stay," she thought. Women are not generally prone to review their own conduct, still less to condemn it. The embarrassing masculine absurdities are in the main responsible for its ethics. But, looking at Heemskirk, Freya felt regret and even remorse. His thick bulk in repose suggested the idea of repletion, but as a matter of fact he had eaten very little. He had drunk a great deal, however. The fleshy lobes of his unpleasant big ears with deeply folded rims were crimson. They quite flamed in the neighbourhood of the flat, sallow cheeks. For a considerable time he did not raise his heavy brown eyelids. To be at the mercy of such a creature was humiliating; and Freya, who always ended by being frank with herself, thought regretfully: "If only I had been open with papa from the first! But then what an impossible life he would have led me!" Yes. Men were absurd in many ways; lovably like Jasper, impracticably like her father, odiously like that grotesque supine creature in the chair. Was it possible to talk him over? Perhaps it was not necessary? "Oh! I can't talk to him," she thought. And when Heemskirk, still without looking at her, began resolutely to crush his half-smoked cheroot on the coffee-tray, she took alarm, glided towards the piano, opened it in tremendous haste, and struck the keys before she sat down.

In an instant the verandah, the whole carpetless wooden bungalow raised on piles, became filled with an uproarious, confused resonance. But through it all she heard, she felt on the floor the heavy, prowling footsteps of the lieutenant moving to and fro at her back. He was not exactly drunk, but he was sufficiently primed to make the suggestions of his excited imagination seem perfectly feasible and even clever; beautifully, unscrupulously clever. Freya, aware that he had stopped just behind her, went on playing without turning her head. She played with spirit, brilliantly, a fierce piece of music, but when his voice reached her she went cold all over. It was the voice, not the words. The insolent familiarity of tone dismayed her to such an extent that she could not understand at first what he was saying. His utterance was thick, too.

"I suspected. . . . Of course I suspected something of your little goings on. I am not a child. But from suspecting to see—seeing, you understand—there's an enormous difference. That sort of thing. . . . Come! One isn't made of stone. And when a man has been worried by a girl as I have been worried by you, Miss Freya—sleeping and waking, then, of course. . . . But I am a man of the world. It must be dull for you here . . . I say, won't you leave off this confounded playing . . . ?"

This last was the only sentence really which she made out. She shook her head negatively, and in desperation put on the loud pedal, but she could not make the sound of the piano cover his raised voice.

"Only, I am surprised that you should. . . . An English trading skipper, a common fellow. Low, cheeky lot, infesting these islands. I would make short work of such trash! While you have here a good friend, a gentleman ready to worship at your feet—your pretty feet—an officer, a man of family. Strange, isn't it? But what of that! You are fit for a prince."

Freya did not turn her head. Her face went stiff with horror and indignation. This adventure was together beyond her conception of what was possible. It was not in her character to jump up and run away. It seemed to her, too, that if she did move there was no saying what might happen. Presently her father would be back, and then the other would have to leave off. It was best to ignore—to ignore. She went on playing loudly and correctly, as though she were alone, as if Heemskirk did not exist. That proceeding irritated him.

"Come! You may deceive your father," he bawled angrily, "but I am not to be made a fool of! Stop this infernal noise . . . Freya . . . Hey! You Scandinavian Goddess of Love! Stop! Do you hear? That's what you are—of love. But the heathen gods are only devils in disguise, and that's what you are, too—a deep little devil. Stop it, I say, or I will lift you off that stool!"

Standing behind her, he devoured her with his eyes, from the golden crown of her rigidly motionless head to the heels of her shoes, the line of her shapely shoulders, the curves of her fine figure swaying a little before the keyboard. She had on a light dress; the sleeves stopped short at the elbows in an edging of lace. A satin ribbon encircled her waist. In an access of irresistible, reckless hopefulness he clapped both his hands on that waist—and then the irritating music stopped at last. But, quick as she was in springing away from the contact (the round music-stool going over with a crash), Heemskirk's lips, aiming at her neck, landed a hungry, smacking kiss just under her ear. A deep silence reigned for a time. And then he laughed rather feebly.

He was disconcerted somewhat by her white, still face, the big light violet eyes resting on him stonily. She had not uttered a sound. She faced him, steadying herself on the corner of the piano with one extended hand. The other went on rubbing with mechanical persistency the place his lips had touched.

"What's the trouble?" he said, offended. "Startled you? Look here: don't let us have any of that nonsense. You don't mean to say a kiss frightens you so much as all that. . . . I know better? . . . I don't mean to be left out in the cold."

He had been gazing into her face with such strained intentness that he could no longer see it distinctly. Everything round him was rather misty. He forgot the overturned stool, caught his foot against it, and lurched forward slightly, saying in an ingratiating tone:

"I'm not bad fun, really. You try a few kisses to begin with——"

He said no more, because his head received a terrific concussion, accompanied by an explosive sound. Freya had swung her round, strong arm with such force that the impact of her open palm on his flat cheek turned him half round. Uttering a faint, hoarse yell, the lieutenant clapped both his hands to the left side of his face, which had taken on suddenly a dusky brick-red tinge. Freya, very erect, her violet eyes darkened, her palm still tingling from the blow, a sort of restrained determined smile showing a tiny gleam of her white teeth, heard her father's rapid, heavy tread on the path below the verandah. Her expression lost its pugnacity and became sincerely concerned. She was sorry for her father. She stooped quickly to pick up the music-stool, as if anxious to obliterate the traces.... But that was no good. She had resumed her attitude, one hand resting lightly on the piano, before old Nelson got up of the top of the stairs.

Poor father! How furious he will be—how upset! And afterwards, what tremors, what unhappiness! Why had she not been open with him from the first? His round, innocent stare of amazement cut her to the quick. But he was not looking at her. His stare was directed to Heemskirk, who, with his back to him and with his hands still up to his face, was hissing curses through his teeth, and (she saw him in profile) glaring at her balefully with one black, evil eye.

"What's the matter?" asked old Nelson, very much bewildered.

She did not answer him. She thought of Jasper on the deck of the brig, gazing up at the lighted bungalow, and she felt frightened. It was a mercy that one of them at least was on board out of the way. She only wished he were a hundred miles off. And yet she was not certain that she did. Had Jasper been mysteriously moved that moment to reappear on the verandah she would have thrown her consistency, her firmness, her self-possession, to the winds, and flown into his arms.

"What is it? What is it?" insisted the unsuspecting Nelson, getting quite excited. "Only this minute you were playing a tune, and——"

Freya, unable to speak in her apprehension of what was coming (she was also fascinated by that black, evil, glaring eye), only nodded slightly at the lieutenant, as much as to say: "Just look at him!"

"Why, yes!" exclaimed old Nelson. "I see. What on earth——"

Meantime he had cautiously approached Heemskirk, who, bursting into incoherent imprecations, was stamping with both feet where he stood. The indignity of the blow, the rage of baffled purpose, the ridicule of the exposure, and the impossibility of revenge maddened him to a point where when he simply felt he must howl with fury.

"Oh, oh, oh!" he howled, stamping across the verandah as though he meant to drive his foot through the floor at every step.

"Why, is his face hurt?" asked the astounded old Nelson. The truth dawned suddenly upon his innocent mind. "Dear me!" he cried, enlightened. "Get some brandy, quick, Freya.... You are subject to it, lieutenant? Fiendish, eh? I know, I know! Used to go crazy all of a sudden myself at the time.... And the little bottle of laudanum from the medicine-chest, too, Freya. Look sharp.... Don't you see he's got a toothache?"

And, indeed, what other explanation could have presented itself to the guileless old Nelson, beholding this cheek nursed with both hands, these wild glances, these stampings, this distracted swaying of the body? It would have demanded a preternatural acuteness to hit upon the true cause. Freya had not moved. She watched Heemskirk's savagely inquiring, black stare directed stealthily upon herself. "Aha, you would like to be let off!" she said to herself. She looked at him unflinchingly, thinking it out. The temptation of making an end of it all without further trouble was irresistible. She gave an almost imperceptible nod of assent, and glided away.

"Hurry up that brandy!" old Nelson shouted, as she disappeared in the passage.

Heemskirk relieved his deeper feelings by a sudden string of curses in Dutch and English which he sent after her. He raved to his heart's content, flinging to and fro the verandah and kicking chairs out of his way; while Nelson (or Nielsen), whose sympathy was profoundly stirred by these evidences of agonising pain, hovered round his dear (and dreaded) lieutenant, fussing like an old hen.

"Dear me, dear me! Is it so bad? I know well what it is. I used to frighten my poor wife sometimes. Do you get it often like this, lieutenant?"

Heemskirk shouldered him viciously out of his way, with a short, insane laugh. But his staggering host took it in good part; a man beside himself with excruciating toothache is not responsible.

"Go into my room, lieutenant," he suggested urgently. "Throw yourself on my bed. We will get something to ease you in a minute."

He seized the poor sufferer by the arm and forced him gently onwards to the very bed, on which Heemskirk, in a renewed access of rage, flung himself down with such force that he rebounded from the mattress to the height of quite a foot.

"Dear me!" exclaimed the scared Nelson, and incontinently ran off to hurry up the brandy and the laudanum, very angry that so little alacrity was shown in relieving the tortures of his precious guest. In the end he got these things himself.

Half an hour later he stood in the inner passage of the house, surprised by faint, spasmodic sounds of a mysterious nature, between laughter and sobs. He frowned; then went straight towards his daughter's room and knocked at the door.

Freya, her glorious fair hair framing her white face and rippling down a dark-blue dressing-gown, opened it partly.

The light in the room was dim. Antonia, crouching in a corner, rocked herself backwards and forwards, uttering feeble moans. Old Nelson had not much experience in various kinds of feminine laughter, but he was certain there had been laughter there.

"Very unfeeling, very unfeeling!" he said, with weighty displeasure. "What is there so amusing in a man being in pain? I should have thought a woman—a young girl——"

"He was so funny," murmured Freya, whose eyes glistened strangely in the semi-obscurity of the passage. "And then, you know, I don't like him," she added, in an unsteady voice.

"Funny!" repeated old Nelson, amazed at this evidence of callousness in one so young. "You don't like him! Do you mean to say that, because you don't like him, you——Why, it's simply cruel! Don't you know it's about the worst sort of pain there is? Dogs have been known to go mad with it."

"He certainly seemed to have gone mad," Freya said with an effort, as if she were struggling with some hidden feeling.

But her father was launched.

"And you know how he is. He notices everything. He is a fellow to take offence for the least little thing—regular Dutchman—and I want to keep friendly with him. It's like this, my girl: if that rajah of ours were to do something silly—and you know he is a sulky, rebellious beggar—and the authorities took into their heads that my influence over him wasn't good, you would find yourself without a roof over your head——"

She cried: "What nonsense, father!" in a not very assured tone, and discovered that he was angry, angry enough to achieve irony; yes, old Nelson (or Nielsen), irony! Just a gleam of it.

"Oh, of course, if you have means of your own—a mansion, a plantation that I know nothing of——" But he was not capable of sustained irony. "I tell you they would bundle me out of here," he whispered forcibly; "without compensation, of course. I know these Dutch. And the lieutenant's just the fellow to start the trouble going. He has the ear of influential officials. I wouldn't offend him for anything—for anything—on no consideration whatever. . . . What did you say?"

It was only an inarticulate exclamation. If she ever had a half-formed intention of telling him everything she had given it up now. It was impossible, both out of regard for his dignity and for the peace of his poor mind.

"I don't care for him myself very much," old Nelson's subdued undertone confessed in a sigh. "He's easier now," he went on, after a silence. "I've given him up my bed for the night. I shall sleep on my verandah, in the hammock. No; I can't say I like him either, but from that to laugh at a man because he's driven crazy with pain is a long way. You've surprised me, Freya. That side of his face is quite flushed."

Her shoulders shook convulsively under his hands, which he laid on her paternally. His straggly, wiry moustache brushed her forehead in a good-night kiss. She closed the door, and went away from it to the middle of the room before she allowed herself a tired-out sort of laugh, without buoyancy.

"Flushed! A little flushed!" she repeated to herself. "I hope so, indeed! A little——"

Her eyelashes were wet. Antonia, in her corner, moaned and giggled, and it was impossible to tell where the moans ended and the giggles began.

The mistress and the maid had been somewhat hysterical, for Freya, on fleeing into her room, had found Antonia there, and had told her everything.

"I have avenged you, my girl," she exclaimed.

And then they had laughingly cried and cryingly laughed with admonitions—"Ssh, not so loud! Be quiet!" on one part, and interludes of "I am so frightened. . . . He's an evil man," on the other.

Antonia was very much afraid of Heemskirk. She was afraid of him because of his personal appearance: because of his eyes and his eyebrows, and his mouth and his nose and his limbs. Nothing could be more rational. And she thought him an evil man, because, to her eyes, he looked evil. No ground for an opinion could be sounder. In the dimness of the room, with only a nightlight burning at the head of Freya's bed, the camerista crept out of her corner to crouch at the feet of her mistress, supplicating in whispers:

"There's the brig. Captain Allen. Let us run away at once—oh, let us run away! I am so frightened. Let us! Let us!"

"I! Run away!" thought Freya to herself, without looking down at the scared girl. "Never."

Both the resolute mistress under the mosquito-net and the frightened maid lying curled up on a mat at the foot of the bed did not sleep very well that night. The person that did not sleep at all was Lieutenant Heemskirk. He lay on his back staring vindictively in the darkness. Inflaming images and humiliating reflections succeeded each other in his mind, keeping up, augmenting his anger. A pretty tale this to get about! But it must not be allowed to get about. The outrage had to be swallowed in silence. A pretty affair! Fooled, led on, and struck by the girl—and probably fooled by the father, too. But no. Nielsen was but another victim of that shameless hussy, that brazen minx, that sly, laughing, kissing, lying . . .

"No; he did not deceive me on purpose," thought the tormented lieutenant. "But I should like to pay him off, all the same, for being such an imbecile——"

Well, some day, perhaps. One thing he was firmly resolved on: he had made up his mind to steal early out of the house. He did not think he could face the girl without going out of his mind with fury.

"Fire and perdition! Ten thousand devils! I shall choke here before the morning!" he muttered to himself, lying rigid on his back on old Nelson's bed, his breast heaving for air.

He arose at daylight and started cautiously to open the door. Faint sounds in the passage alarmed him, and remaining concealed he saw Freya coming out. This unexpected sight deprived him of all power to move away from the crack of the door. It was the narrowest crack possible, but commanding the view of the end of the verandah. Freya made for that end hastily to watch the brig passing the point. She wore her dark dressing-gown; her feet were bare, because, having fallen asleep towards the morning, she ran out headlong in her fear of being too late. Heemskirk had never seen her looking like this, with her hair drawn back smoothly to the shape of her head, and hanging in one heavy, fair tress down her back, and with that air of extreme youth, intensity, and eagerness. And at first he was amazed, and then he gnashed his teeth. He could not face her at all. He muttered a curse, and kept still behind the door.

With a low, deep-breathed "Ah!" when she first saw the brig already under way, she reached for Nelson's long glass reposing on brackets high up the wall. The wide sleeve of the dressing-gown slipped back, uncovering her white arm as far as the shoulder. Heemskirk gripping the door-handle, as if to crush it, felt like a man just risen to his feet from a drinking bout.

And Freya knew that he was watching her. She knew. She had seen the door move as she came out of the passage. She was aware of his eyes being on her, with scornful bitterness, with triumphant contempt.

"You are there," she thought, levelling the long glass. "Oh, well, look on, then!"

The green islets appeared like black shadows, the ashen sea was smooth as glass, the clear robe of the colourless dawn, in which even the brig appeared shadowy, had a hem of light in the east. Directly Freya had made out Jasper on deck with his own long glass directed to the bungalow, she laid hers down and raised both her beautiful white arms above her head. In that attitude of supreme cry she stood still, glowing with the consciousness of Jasper's adoration going out to her figure held in the field of his glass away there, and warmed, too, by the feeling of evil passion, the burning, covetous eyes of the other, fastened on her back. In the fervour of her love, in the caprice of her mind, and with that mysterious knowledge of masculine nature women seem to be born to, she thought:

"You are looking on—you will—you must! Then you shall see something."

She brought both her hands to her lips, then flung them out, sending a kiss over the sea, as if she wanted to throw her heart along with it on the deck of the brig. Her face was rosy, her eyes shone. Her repeated, passionate gesture seemed to fling kisses by the hundred again and again and again, while the slowly ascending sun brought the glory of colour to the world, turning the islets green, the sea blue, the brig below her white—dazzlingly white in the spread of her wings—with the red ensign streaming like a tiny flame from the peak. And each time she murmured with a rising inflexion: "Take this—and this—and this——" till suddenly her arms fell. She had seen the ensign dipped in response, and next moment the point below hid the hull of the brig from her view. Then she turned away from the balustrade, and, passing slowly before the door of her father's room with her eyelids lowered, and an enigmatic expression on her face, she disappeared behind the curtain.

But instead of going along the passage, she remained concealed and very still on the other side to watch what would happen. For some time the broad, furnished verandah remained empty. Then the door of old

Nelson's room came open suddenly, and Heemskirk staggered out. His hair was rumpled, his eyes bloodshot, his unshaven face looked very dark. He gazed wildly about, saw his cap on a table, snatched it up, and made for the stairs quietly, but with a strange, tottering gait, like the last effort of waning strength.

Shortly after his head had sunk below the level of the floor, Freya came out from behind the curtain, with compressed, scheming lips, and no softness at all in her luminous eyes. He could not be allowed to sneak off scot free. Never—never! She was excited, she tingled all over, she had tasted blood! He must be made to understand that she had been aware of having been watched; he must know that he had been seen slinking off shamefully. But to run to the front rail and shout after him would have been childish, crude—undignified. And to shout—what? What word? What phrase? No; it was impossible. Then how? . . . She frowned, discovered it, dashed at the piano, which had stood open all night, and made the rosewood monster growl savagely in an irritated bass. She struck chords as if firing shots after that straddling, broad figure in ample white trousers and a dark uniform jacket with gold shoulder-straps, and then she pursued him with the same thing she had played the evening before—a modern, fierce piece of love music which had been tried more than once against the thunderstorms of the group. She accentuated its rhythm with triumphant malice, so absorbed in her purpose that she did not notice the presence of her father, who, wearing an old threadbare ulster of a check pattern over his sleeping-suit, had run out from the back verandah to inquire the reason of this untimely performance. He stared at her.

"What on earth? . . . Freya!" . . . His voice was nearly drowned by the piano. "What's become of the lieutenant?" he shouted.

She looked up at him as if her soul were lost in her music, with unseeing eyes.

"Gone."

"What-a-t? . . . Where?"

She shook her head slightly, and went on playing louder than before. Old Nelson's innocently anxious gaze starting from the open door of his room, explored the whole place high and low, as if the lieutenant were something small which might have been crawling on the floor or clinging to a wall. But a shrill whistle coming somewhere from below pierced the ample volume of sound rolling out of the piano in great, vibrating waves. The lieutenant was down at the cove, whistling for the boat to come and take him off to his ship. And he seemed to be in a terrific hurry, too, for he whistled again almost directly, waited for a moment, and then sent out a long, interminable shrill call as distressful to hear as though he had shrieked without drawing breath. Freya ceased playing suddenly.

"Going on board," said old Nelson, perturbed by the event. "What could have made him clear out so early? Queer chap. Devilishly touchy, too! I shouldn't wonder if it was your conduct last night that hurt his feelings. I noticed you, Freya. You as well as laughed in his face, while he was suffering agonies from neuralgia. It isn't the way to get yourself liked. He's offended with you."

Freya's hands now reposed passive on the keys; she bowed her fair head, feeling a sudden discontent, a nervous lassitude, as though she had passed through some exhausting crisis. Old Nelson (or Nielsen), looking aggrieved, was revolving matters of policy in his bald head.

"I think it would be right for me to go on board just to inquire, some time this morning," he declared fussily. "Why don't they bring me my morning tea? Do you hear, Freya? You have astonished me, I must say. I didn't think a young girl could be so unfeeling. And the lieutenant thinks himself a friend of ours, too! What? No? Well, he calls himself a friend, and that's something to a person in my position. Certainly! Oh, yes, I must go on board."

"Must you?" murmured Freya listlessly; then added in her thought: "Poor man!"

· V ·

In respect of the next seven weeks, all that is necessary to say is, first, that old Nelson (or Nielsen) failed in paying his politic call. The *Neptun* gunboat of H.M. the King of the Netherlands, commanded by an outraged and infuriated lieutenant, left the cove at an unexpectedly early hour. When Freya's father came down to the shore, after seeing his precious crop of tobacco spread out properly in the sun, she was already steaming round the point. Old Nelson regretted the circumstance for many days.

"Now, I don't know in what disposition the man went away," he lamented to his hard daughter. He was amazed at her hardness. He was almost frightened by her indifference.

Next, it must be recorded that the same day the gunboat *Neptun*, steering east, passed the brig *Bonito* becalmed in sight of Carimata, with her head to the eastward, too. Her captain, Jasper Allen, giving himself up consciously to a tender, possessive reverie of his Freya, did not get out of his long chair on the poop to look at the *Neptun* which passed so close that the smoke belching out suddenly from her short black funnel rolled between the masts of the *Bonito,* obscuring for a moment the sunlit whiteness of her sails, consecrated to the service of love. Jasper did not even turn his head for a glance. But Heemskirk, on the bridge, had gazed long and earnestly at the brig from the distance, gripping hard the brass rail in front of him, till, the two ships closing, he lost all confidence in himself, and retreating to the chartroom, pulled the door to with a crash. There, his brows knitted, his mouth drawn on one side in sardonic meditation, he sat through many still hours—a sort of Prometheus in the bonds of unholy desire, having his very vitals torn by the beak and claws of humiliated passion.

That species of fowl is not to be shooed off as easily as a chicken. Fooled, cheated, deceived, led on, outraged, mocked at—beak and claws! A sinister bird! The lieutenant had no mind to become the talk of the Archipelago, as the naval officer who had had his face slapped by a girl. Was it possible that she really loved that rascally trader? He tried not to think, but worse than thoughts, definite impressions beset him in his retreat. He saw her—a vision plain, close to, detailed, plastic, coloured, lighted up—he saw her hanging round the neck of that fellow. And he shut his eyes, only to discover that this was no remedy. Then a piano began to play near by, very plainly; and he put his fingers to his ears with no better effect. It was not to be borne—not in solitude. He bolted out of the chartroom, and talked of indifferent things somewhat wildly with the officer of the watch on the bridge, to the mocking accompaniment of a ghostly piano.

The last thing to be recorded is that Lieutenant Heemskirk instead of pursuing his course towards Ternate, where he was expected, went out of his way to call at Makassar, where no one was looking for his arrival. Once there, he gave certain explanations and laid a certain proposal before the governor, or some other authority, and obtained permission to do what he thought fit in these matters. Thereupon the *Neptun,* giving up Ternate altogether, steamed north in view of the mountainous coast of Celebes, and then crossing the broad straits took up her station on the low coast of virgin forests, inviolate and mute, in waters phosphorescent at night, deep blue in daytime with gleaming green patches over the submerged reefs. For days the *Neptun* could be seen moving smoothly up and down the sombre face of the shore, or hanging about with a watchful air near the silvery breaks of broad estuaries, under the great luminous sky never softened, never veiled, and flooding the earth with the everlasting sunshine of the tropics— that sunshine which, in its unbroken splendour, oppresses the soul with an inexpressible melancholy more intimate, more penetrating, more profound than the grey sadness of the northern mists.

The trading brig *Bonito* appeared gliding round a sombre forest-clad point of land on the silvery estuary of a great river. The breath of air that gave her motion would not have fluttered the flame of a torch. She stole out into the open from behind a veil of unstirring leaves, mysteri-ously silent, ghostly white, and solemnly stealthy in her imperceptible progress; and Jasper, his elbow in the main rigging, and his head leaning against his hand, thought of Freya. Everything in the world reminded him of her. The beauty of the loved woman exists in the beauties of Nature. The swelling outlines of the hills, the curves of a coast, the free sinuosities of a river are less suave than the harmonious lines of her body, and when she moves, gliding lightly, the grace of her progress suggests the power of occult forces which rule the fascinating aspects of the visible world.

Dependent on things as all men are, Jasper loved his vessel—the house of his dreams. He lent to her something of Freya's soul. Her deck was the foothold of their love. The possession of his brig appeased his passion in a soothing certitude of happiness already conquered.

The full moon was some way up, perfect and serene, floating in air as calm and limpid as the glance of Freya's eyes. There was not a sound in the brig.

"Here she will stand, by my side, on evenings like this," he thought, with rapture.

And it was at that moment, in this peace, in this serenity, under the full, benign gaze of the moon propitious to lovers, on a sea without a wrinkle, under a sky without a cloud, as if all Nature had assumed its most clement mood in a spirit of mockery, that the gunboat *Neptun*, detaching herself from the dark coast under which she had been lying invisible, steamed out to intercept the trading brig *Bonito* standing out to sea.

Directly the gunboat had been made out emerging from her ambush, Schultz, of the fascinating voice, had given signs of strange agitation. All that day, ever since leaving the Malay town up the river, he had shown a haggard face, going about his duties like a man with something weighing on his mind. Jasper had noticed it, but the mate, turning away, as though he had not liked being looked at, had muttered shamefacedly of a headache and a touch of fever. He must have had it very badly when, dodging behind his captain, he wondered aloud: "What can that fellow want with us?" . . . A naked man standing in a freezing blast and trying not to shiver could not have spoken with a more harshly uncertain intonation. But it might have been fever—a cold fit.

"He wants to make himself disagreeable, simply," said Jasper, with perfect good humour. "He has tried it on me before. However, we shall soon see."

And, indeed, before long the two vessels lay abreast within easy hail. The brig, with her fine lines and her white sails, looked vaporous and sylph-like in the moonlight. The gunboat, short, squat, with her stumpy dark spars naked like dead trees, raised against the luminous sky of that resplendent night, threw a heavy shadow on the lane of water between the two ships.

Freya haunted them both like an ubiquitous spirit, and as if she were the only woman in the world. Jasper remembered her earnest recommendation to be guarded and cautious in all his acts and words while he was away from her. In this quite unforeseen encounter he felt on his ear the very breath of these hurried admonitions customary to the last moment of their partings, heard the half-jesting final whisper of the "Mind, kid, I'd never forgive you!" with a quick pressure on his arm, which he answered by a quiet, confident smile. Heemskirk was haunted in another fashion. There were no whispers in it; it was more like visions. He saw that girl hanging round the neck of a low vaga-bond—*that* vagabond, the vagabond who had just answered his hail.

He saw her stealing barefooted across a verandah with great, clear, wide-open, eager eyes to look at a brig—*that* brig. If she had shrieked, scolded, called names! . . . But she had simply triumphed over him. That was all. Led on (he firmly believed it), fooled, deceived, outraged, struck, mocked at. . . . Beak and claws! The two men, so differently haunted by Freya of the Seven Isles, were not equally matched.

In the intense stillness, as of sleep, which had fallen upon the two vessels, in a world that itself seemed but a delicate dream, a boat pulled by Javanese sailors crossing the dark lane of water came alongside the brig. The white warrant officer in her, perhaps the gunner, climbed aboard. He was a short man, with a rotund stomach and a wheezy voice. His immovable fat face looked lifeless in the moonlight, and he walked with his thick arms hanging away from his body as though he had been stuffed. His cunning little eyes glittered like bits of mica. He conveyed to Jasper, in broken English, a request to come on board the *Neptun.*

Jasper had not expected anything so unusual. But after a short reflection he decided to show neither annoyance, nor even surprise. The river from which he had come had been politically disturbed for a couple of years, and he was aware that his visits there were looked upon with some suspicion. But he did not mind much the displeasure of the authorities, so terrifying to old Nelson. He prepared to leave the brig, and Schultz followed him to the rail as if to say something, but in the end stood by in silence. Jasper getting over the side, noticed his ghastly face. The eyes of the man who had found salvation in the brig from the effects of his peculiar psychology looked at him with a dumb, beseeching expression.

"What's the matter?" Jasper asked.

"I wonder how this will end?" said he of the beautiful voice, which had even fascinated the steady Freya herself. But where was its charming timbre now? These words had sounded like a raven's croak.

"You are ill," said Jasper positively.

"I wish I were dead!" was the startling statement uttered by Schultz talking to himself in the extremity of some mysterious trouble. Jasper gave him a keen glance, but this was not the time to investigate the morbid outbreak of a feverish man. He did not look as though he were actually delirious, and that for the moment must suffice. Schultz made a dart forward.

"That fellow means harm!" he said desperately. "He means harm to you, Captain Allen. I feel it, and I——"

He choked with inexplicable emotion.

"All right, Schultz. I won't give him an opening." Jasper cut him short and swung himself into the boat.

On board the *Neptun* Heemskirk, standing straddle-legs in the flood of moonlight, his inky shadow falling right across the quarter-deck, made no sign at his approach, but secretly he felt something like the heave of the sea in his chest at the sight of that man. Jasper waited before him in silence.

Brought face to face in direct personal contact, they fell at once into the manner of their casual meetings in old Nelson's bungalow. They ignored each other's existence—Heemskirk moodily; Jasper, with a perfectly colourless quietness.

"What's going on in that river you've just come out of?" asked the lieutenant straight away.

"I know nothing of the troubles, if you mean that," Jasper answered. "I've landed there half a cargo of rice, for which I got nothing in exchange, and went away. There's no trade there now, but they would have been starving in another week if I hadn't turned up."

"Meddling! English meddling! And suppose the rascals don't deserve anything better than to starve, eh?"

"There are women and children there, you know," observed Jasper, in his even tone.

"Oh, yes! When an Englishman talks of women and children, you may be sure there's something fishy about the business. Your doings will have to be investigated."

They spoke in turn, as though they had been disembodied spirits—mere voices in empty air; for they looked at each other as if there had been nothing there, or, at most, with as much recognition as one gives to an inanimate object, and no more. But now a silence fell. Heemskirk had thought, all at once; "She will tell him all about it. She will tell him while she hangs round his neck laughing." And the sudden desire to annihilate Jasper on the spot almost deprived him of his senses by its vehemence. He lost the power of speech, of vision. For a moment he absolutely couldn't see Jasper. But he heard him inquiring, as of the world at large:

"Am I, then, to conclude that the brig is detained?"

Heemskirk made a recovery in a flush of malignant satisfaction.

"She is. I am going to take her to Makassar in tow."

"The courts will have to decide on the legality of this," said Jasper, aware that the matter was becoming serious, but with assumed indifference.

"Oh, yes, the courts! Certainly. And as to you, I shall keep you on board here."

Jasper's dismay at being parted from his ship was betrayed by a stony immobility. It lasted but an instant. Then he turned away and hailed the brig. Mr. Schultz answered:

"Yes, sir."

"Get ready to receive a tow-rope from the gunboat! We are going to be taken to Makassar."

"Good God! What's that for, sir?" came an anxious cry faintly.

"Kindness, I suppose," Jasper, ironical, shouted with great deliberation. "We might have been—becalmed in here—for days. And hospitality. I am invited to stay—on board here."

The answer to this information was a loud ejaculation of distress. Jasper thought anxiously: "Why, the fellow's nerve's gone to pieces;" and with an awkward uneasiness of a new sort, looked intently at the brig. The thought that he was parted from her—for the first time since they came together—shook the apparently careless fortitude of his character to its very foundations, which were deep. All that time neither Heemskirk nor even his inky shadow had stirred in the least.

"I am going to send a boat's crew and an officer on board your vessel," he announced to no one in particular. Jasper, tearing himself away from the absorbed contemplation of the brig, turned round, and, without passion, almost without expression in his voice, entered his protest against the whole of the proceedings. What he was thinking of was the delay. He counted the days. Makassar was actually on his way; and to be towed there really saved time. On the other hand, there would be some vexing formalities to go through. But the thing was too absurd. "The beetle's gone mad," he thought. "I'll be released at once. And if not, Mesman must enter into a bond for me." Mesman was a Dutch merchant with whom Jasper had had many dealings, a considerable person in Makassar.

"You protest? H'm!" Heemskirk muttered, and for a little longer remained motionless, his legs planted well apart, and his head lowered as though he were studying his own comical deeply split shadow. Then he made a sign to the rotund gunner, who had kept at hand, motionless, like a vilely stuffed specimen of a fat man, with a lifeless face and glittering little eyes. The fellow approached, and stood at attention.

"You will broad the brig with a boat's crew!"

"Ya, mynherr!"

"You will have one of your men to steer her all the time," went on Heemskirk, giving his orders in English, apparently for Jasper's edification. "You hear?"

"Ya, mynherr."

"You will remain on deck and in charge all the time."

"Ya, mynherr."

Jasper felt as if, together with the command of the brig, his very heart were being taken out of his breast. Heemskirk asked, with a change of tone:

"What weapons have you on board?"

At one time all the ships trading in the China Seas had a licence to carry a certain quantity of firearms for purposes of defence. Jasper answered:

"Eighteen rifles with their bayonets, which were on board when I bought her, four years ago. They have been declared."

"Where are they kept?"

"Fore-cabin. Mate has the key."

"You will take possession of them," said Heemskirk to the gunner.

"Ya, mynherr."

"What is this for? What do you mean to imply?" cried out Jasper; then bit his lip. "It's monstrous!" he muttered.

Heemskirk raised for a moment a heavy, as if suffering, glance.

"You may go," he said to his gunner. The fat man saluted, and departed.

During the next thirty hours the steady towing was interrupted once. At a signal from the brig, made by waving a flag on the forecastle, the gunboat was stopped. The badly stuffed specimen of a warrant-officer, getting into his boat, arrived on board the *Neptun* and hurried straight into his commander's cabin, his excitement at something he had to communicate being betrayed by the blinking of his small eyes. These two were closeted together for some time, while Jasper at the taffrail tried to make out if anything out of the common had occurred on board the brig. But nothing seemed to be amiss on board. However, he kept a look-out for the gunner; and, though he had avoided speaking to anybody since he had finished with Heemskirk, he stopped that man when he came out on deck again to ask how his mate was.

"He was feeling not very well when I left," he explained.

The fat warrant-officer, holding himself as though the effort of carrying his big stomach in front of him demanded a rigid carriage, understood with difficulty. Not a single one of his features showed the slightest animation, but his little eyes blinked rapidly at last.

"Oh, ya! The mate. Ya, ya! He is very well. But, mein Gott, he is one very funny man!"

Jasper could get no explanation of that remark, because the Dutchman got into the boat hurriedly, and went back on board the brig. But he consoled himself with the thought that very soon all this unpleasant and rather absurd experience would be over. The roadstead of Makassar was in sight already. Heemskirk passed by him going on the bridge. For the first time the lieutenant looked at Jasper with marked intention; and the strange roll of his eyes was so funny—it had been long agreed by Jasper and Freya that the lieutenant was funny—so ecstatically gratified, as though he were rolling a tasty morsel on his tongue, that Jasper could not help a broad smile. And then he turned to his brig again.

To see her, his cherished possession, animated by something of his Freya's soul, the only foothold of two lives on the wide earth, the security of his passion, the companion of adventure, the power to snatch the calm, adorable Freya to his breast, and carry her off to the end of the world; to see this beautiful thing embodying worthily his pride and his love, to see her captive at the end of a tow-rope was not indeed a pleasant experience. It had something nightmarish in it, as, for instance, the dream of a wild sea-bird loaded with chains.

Yet what else could he want to look at? Her beauty would sometimes come to his heart with the force of a spell, so that he would forget where he was. And, besides, that sense of superiority which the certitude of being loved gives to a young man, that illusion of being set above the Fates by a tender look in a woman's eyes, helped him, the first shock over, to go through these experiences with an amused self-confidence. For what evil could touch the elect of Freya?

It was now afternoon, the sun being behind the two vessels as they headed for the harbour. "The beetle's little joke will soon be over," thought Jasper, without any great animosity. As a seaman well acquainted with that part of the world, a casual glance was enough to tell him what was being done. "Hallo," he thought, "he is going through Spermonde Passage. We shall be rounding Tamissa reef presently." And again he returned to the contemplation of his brig, that mainstay of his material and emotional existence which would be soon in his hands again. On a sea, calm as a millpond, a heavy smooth ripple undulated and streamed away from her bows, for the powerful *Neptun* was towing at great speed, as if for a wager. The Dutch gunner appeared on the forecastle of the *Bonito,* and with him a couple of men. They stood looking at the coast, and Jasper lost himself in a loverlike trance.

The deep-toned blast of the gunboat's steam-whistle made him shudder by its unexpectedness. Slowly he looked about. Swift as lightning he leaped from where he stood, bounding forward along the deck.

"You will be on Tamissa reef!" he yelled.

High up on the bridge Heemskirk looked back over his shoulder heavily; two seamen were spinning the wheel round, and the *Neptun* was already swinging rapidly away from the edge of the pale water over the danger. Ha! Just in time. Jasper turned about instantly to watch his brig; and, even before he realized that—in obedience, it appears, to Heemskirk's orders given beforehand to the gunner—the tow-rope had been let go at the blast of the whistle, before he had time to cry out or to move a limb, he saw her cast adrift and shooting across the gunboat's stern with the impetus of her speed. He followed her fine, gliding form with eyes growing big with incredulity, wild with horror. The cries on board of her came to him only as a dreadful and confused murmur through the loud thumping of blood in his ears, while she held on. She ran upright in a terrible display of her gift of speed, with an incomparable air of life and grace. She ran on till the smooth level of water in front of her bows seemed to sink down suddenly as if sucked away; and, with a strange, violent tremor of her mastheads she stopped, inclined her lofty spars a little, and lay still. She lay still on the reef, while the *Neptun,* fetching a wide circle, continued at full speed up Spermonde Passage, heading for the town. She lay still, perfectly still, with something ill-omened and unnatural in her attitude. In an instant the subtle melancholy of things touched by decay had fallen on her in the sunshine; she was but a speck in the brilliant emptiness of space, already lonely, already desolate.

"Hold him!" yelled a voice from the bridge.

Jasper had started to run to his brig with a headlong impulse, as a man dashes forward to pull away with his hands a living, breathing, loved creature from the brink of destruction. "Hold him! Stick to him!" vociferated the lieutenant at the top of the bridge-ladder, while Jasper struggled madly without a word, only his head emerging from the heaving crowd of the *Neptun's* seamen, who had flung themselves upon him obediently. "Hold——I would not have that fellow drown himself for anything now!"

Jasper ceased struggling.

One by one they let go of him; they fell back gradually farther and farther, in attentive silence, leaving him standing unsupported in a widened, clear space, as if to give him plenty of room to fall after the struggle. He did not even sway perceptibly. Half an hour later, when the *Neptun* anchored in front of the town, he had not stirred yet, had moved neither head nor limb as much as a hair's breath. Directly the rumble of the gunboat's cable had ceased, Heemskirk came down heavily from the bridge.

"Call a sampan," he said, in a gloomy tone, as he passed the sentry at the gangway, and then moved on slowly towards the spot where Jasper, the object of many awed glances, stood looking at the deck, as if lost in a brown study. Heemskirk came up close, and stared at him thoughtfully, with his fingers over his lips. Here he was, the favoured vagabond, the only man to whom that infernal girl was likely to tell the story. But he would not find it funny. The story how Lieutenant Heemskirk——No, he would not laugh at it. He looked as though he would never laugh at anything in his life.

Suddenly Jasper looked up. His eyes, without any other expression but bewilderment, met those of Heemskirk, observant and sombre.

"Gone on the reef!" he said, in a low, astounded tone. "Oh—the—reef!" he repeated still lower and as if attending inwardly to the birth of some awful and amazing sensation.

"On the very top of high-water, spring tides," Heemskirk struck in, with a vindictive, exulting violence which flashed and expired. He paused, as if weary, fixing upon Jasper his arrogant eyes, over which secret disenchantment, the unavoidable shadow of all passion, seemed to pass like a saddening cloud. "On the very top," he repeated, rousing himself in fierce reaction to snatch his laced cap off his head with a horizontal, derisive flourish towards the gangway. "And now you may go ashore to the courts, you damned Englishman!" he said.

· VI ·

The affair of the brig *Bonito* was bound to cause a sensation in Makassar, the prettiest, and perhaps the cleanest-looking of all the towns in the Islands; which however knows few occasions for excitement. The "front," with its special population, was soon aware that something had happened. A steamer towing a sailing vessel had been observed far out to sea for some time, and when the steamer came in alone, leaving the other outside, attention was aroused. Why was that? Her masts only could be seen—with furled sails—remaining in the same place to the southward. And soon the rumour ran all along the crowded seashore street that there was a ship on Tamissa reef. That crowd interpreted the appearance correctly. Its cause was beyond their penetration, for who could associate a girl nine hundred miles away with the stranding of a ship on Tamissa reef, or look for the remote filiation of that event in the psychology of at least three people, even if one of them, Lieutenant Heemskirk, was at that very moment passing amongst them on his way to make his verbal report?

No; the minds on the "front" were not competent for that sort of investigation, but many hands there—brown hands, yellow hands, white hands—were raised to shade the eyes gazing out to sea. The rumour spread quickly. Chinese shopkeepers came to their doors, more than one white merchant, even, rose from his desk to go to the window. After all, a ship on Tamissa was not an everyday occurrence. And presently the rumour took a more definite shape. An English trader—detained on suspicion at sea by the *Neptun*—Heemskirk was towing him in to test a case, and by some strange accident——

Later on the name came out. "The *Bonito*—what! Impossible! Yes— yes, the *Bonito*. Look! You can see from here; only two masts. It's a brig. Didn't think that man would ever let himself be caught. Heemskirk's pretty smart, too. They say she's fitted out in her cabin like a gentleman's yacht. That Allen is a sort of gentleman too. An extravagant beggar."

A young man entered smartly Messrs. Mesman Brothers' office on the "front," bubbling with some further information.

"Oh, yes; that's the *Bonito* for certain! But you don't know the story I've heard just now. The fellow must have been feeding that river with firearms for the last year or two. Well, it seems he has grown so reckless from long impunity that he has actually dared to sell the very ship's rifles this time. It's a fact. The rifles are not on board. What impudence! Only, he didn't know that there was one of our warships on the coast. But those Englishmen are so impudent that perhaps he thought that nothing would be done to him for it. Our courts do let off these fellows too often, on some miserable excuse or other. But, at any rate, there's an end of the famous *Bonito*. I have just heard in the harbour-office that she must have gone on at the very top of high-water; and she is in ballast, too. No human power, they think, can move her from where she is. I only hope it is so. It would be fine to have the notorious *Bonito* stuck up there as a warning to others."

Mr. J. Mesman, a colonial-born Dutchman, a kind, paternal old fellow, with a clean-shaven, quiet, handsome face, and a head of fine iron-grey hair curling a little on his collar, did not say a word in defence of Jasper and the *Bonito*. He rose from his arm-chair suddenly. His face was visibly troubled. It had so happened that once, from a business talk of ways and means, island trade, money matters, and so on, Jasper had been led to open himself to him on the subject of Freya; and the excellent man, who had known old Nelson years before and even remembered something of Freya, was much astonished and amused by the unfolding of the tale.

"Well, well, well! Nelson! Yes; of course. A very honest sort of man. And a little child with very fair hair. Oh, yes! I have a distinct recollection. And so she has grown into such a fine girl, so very determined, so very——" And he laughed almost boisterously. "Mind, when you have happily eloped with your future wife, Captain Allen, you must come along this way, and we shall welcome her here. A little fair-headed child! I remember. I remember."

It was that knowledge which had brought trouble to his face at the first news of the wreck. He took up his hat.

"Where are you going, Mr. Mesman?"

"I am going to look for Allen. I think he must be ashore. Does anybody know?"

No one of those present knew. And Mr. Mesman went out on the "front" to make inquiries.

The other part of the town, the part near the church and the fort, got its information in another way. The first thing disclosed to it was Jasper himself walking rapidly, as though he were pursued. And, as a matter of fact, a Chinaman, obviously a sampan man, was following him at the same headlong pace. Suddenly, while passing Orange House, Jasper swerved and went in, or, rather, rushed in, startling Gomez, the hotel clerk, very much. But a Chinaman beginning to make an unseemly noise at the door claimed the immediate attention of Gomez. His grievance was that the white man whom he had brought on shore from the gunboat had not paid him his boat-fare. He had pursued him so far, asking for it all the way. But the white man had taken no notice whatever of his just claim. Gomez satisfied the coolie with a few coppers, and then went to look for Jasper, whom he knew very well. He found him standing stiffly by a little round table. At the other end of the verandah a few men sitting there had stopped talking, and were looking at him in silence. Two billiard-players, with cues in their hands, had come to the door of the billiard-room and stared, too.

On Gomez coming up to him, Jasper raised one hand to point at his own throat. Gomez noted the some-what soiled state of his white clothes, then took one look at his face, and fled away to order the drink for which Jasper seemed to be asking.

Where he wanted to go—for what purpose—where he, perhaps, only imagined himself to be going, when a sudden impulse or the sight of a familiar place had made him turn into Orange House—it is impossible to say. He was steadying himself lightly with the tips of his fingers on the little table. There were on that verandah two men whom he knew well personally, but his gaze roaming incessantly as though he were looking for a way of escape, passed and repassed over them without a sign of recognition. They, on their side, looking at him, doubted the evidence of their own eyes. It was not that his face was distorted. On the contrary, it was still, it was set. But its expression, somehow, was unrecognisable. Can that be him? They wondered with awe.

In his head there was a wild chaos of clear thoughts. Perfectly clear.

It was this clearness which was so terrible in conjunction with the utter inability to lay hold of any single one of them all. He was saying to himself, or to them: "Steady, steady." A China boy appeared before him with a glass on a tray. He poured the drink down his throat, and rushed out. His disappearance removed the spell of wonder from the beholders. One of the men jumped up and moved quickly to that side of the verandah from which almost the whole of the roadstead could be seen. At the very moment when Jasper, issuing from the door of the Orange House, was passing under him in the street below, he cried to the others excitedly:

"That was Allen right enough! But where is his brig?"

Jasper heard these words with extraordinary loudness. The heavens rang with them, as if calling him to account; for those were the very words Freya would have to use. It was an annihilating question; it struck his consciousness like a thunderbolt and brought a sudden night upon the chaos of his thoughts even as he walked. He did not check his pace. He went on in the darkness for another three strides, and then fell.

The good Mesman had to push on as far as the hospital before he found him. The doctor there talked of a slight heatstroke. Nothing very much. Out in three days. . . . It must be admitted that the doctor was right. In three days, Jasper Allen came out of the hospital and became visible to the town—very visible indeed—and remained so for quite a long time; long enough to become almost one of the sights of the place; long enough to become disregarded at last; long enough for the tale of his haunting visibility to be remembered in the islands to this day.

The talk on the "front" and Jasper's appearance in the Orange House stand at the beginning of the famous *Bonito* case, and give a view of its two aspects—the practical and the psychological. The case for the courts and the case for compassion; that last terribly evident and yet obscure.

It has, you must understand, remained obscure even for that friend of mine who wrote me the letter mentioned in the very first lines of this narrative. He was one of those in Mr. Mesman's office, and accompanied that gentleman in his search for Jasper. His letter described to me the two aspects and some of the episodes of the case. Heemskirk's attitude was that of deep thankfulness for not having lost his own ship, and that was all. Haze over the land was his explanation of having got so close to Tamissa reef. He saved his ship, and for the rest he did not care. As to the fat gunner, he deposed simply that he thought at the time that he was acting for the best by letting go the tow-rope, but admitted that he was greatly confused by the suddenness of the emergency.

As a matter of fact, he had acted on very precise instructions from Heemskirk, to whom through several years' service together in the East he had become a sort of devoted henchman. What was most amazing in the detention of the *Bonito* was his story how, proceeding to take possession of the firearms as ordered, he discovered that there were no firearms on board. All he found in the fore-cabin was an empty rack for the proper number of eighteen rifles, but of the rifles themselves never a single one anywhere in the ship. The mate of the brig, who looked rather ill and behaved excitedly, as though he were perhaps a lunatic, wanted him to believe that Captain Allen knew nothing of this; that it was he, the mate, who had recently sold these rifles in the dead of night to a certain person up the river. In proof of this story he produced a bag of silver dollars and pressed it on his, the gunner's, acceptance. Then, suddenly flinging it down on the deck, he beat his own head with both his fists and started heaping shocking curses upon his own soul for an ungrateful wretch not fit to live.

All this the gunner reported at once to his commanding officer.

What Heemskirk intended by taking upon himself to detain the *Bonito* it is difficult to say, except that he meant to bring some trouble into the life of the man favoured by Freya. He had been looking at Jasper with a desire to strike that man of kisses and embraces to the earth. The question was: How could he do it without giving himself away? But the report of the gunner created a serious case enough. Yet Allen had friends—and who could tell whether he wouldn't somehow succeed in wriggling out of it? The idea of simply towing the brig so much compromised on to the reef came to him while he was listening to the fat gunner in his cabin. There was but little risk of being disapproved now. And it should be made to appear an accident.

Going out on deck he had gloated upon his unconscious victim with such a sinister roll of his eyes, such a queerly pursed mouth, that Jasper could not help smiling. And the lieutenant had gone on the bridge, saying to himself:

"You wait! I shall spoil the taste of those sweet kisses for you. When you hear of Lieutenant Heemskirk in the future that name won't bring a smile on your lips, I swear. You are delivered into my hands."

And this possibility had come about without any planning, one could almost say naturally, as if events had mysteriously shaped themselves to fit the purposes of a dark passion. The most astute scheming could not have served Heemskirk better. It was given to him to taste a transcendental, an incredible perfection of vengeance; to strike a deadly blow into that hated person's heart, and to watch him afterwards walking about with the dagger in his breast.

For that is what the state of Jasper amounted to. He moved, acted, weary-eyed, keen-faced, lank and restless, with brusque movements and fierce gestures; he talked incessantly in a frenzied and fatigued voice, but within himself he knew that nothing would ever give him back the brig, just as nothing can heal a pierced heart. His soul, kept quiet in the stress of love by the unflinching Freya's influence, was like a still but overwound string. The shock had started it vibrating, and the string had snapped. He had waited for two years in a perfectly intoxicated confidence for a day that now would never come to a man disarmed for life by the loss of the brig, and, it seemed to him, made unfit for love to which he had no foothold to offer.

Day after day he would traverse the length of the town, follow the coast, and, reaching the point of land opposite that part of the reef on which his brig lay stranded, look steadily across the water at her beloved form, once the home of an exulting hope, and now, in her inclined, desolated immobility, towering above the lonely sea-horizon, a symbol of despair.

The crew had left her in due course in her own boats which directly they reached the town were sequestrated by the harbour authorities. The vessel, too, was sequestrated pending proceedings; but these same authorities did not take the trouble to set a guard on board. For, indeed, what could move her from there? Nothing, unless a miracle; nothing, unless Jasper's eyes, fastened on her tensely for hours together, as though he hoped by the mere power of vision to draw her to his breast.

All this story, read in my friend's very chatty letter, dismayed me not a little. But it was really appalling to read his relation of how Schultz, the mate, went about everywhere affirming with desperate pertinacity that it was he alone who had sold the rifles. "I stole them," he protested. Of course, no one would believe him. My friend himself did not believe him, though he, of course, admired this self-sacrifice. But a good many people thought it was going too far to make oneself out a thief for the sake of a friend. Only, it was such an obvious lie, too, that it did not matter, perhaps.

I, who, in view of Schultz's psychology, knew how true that must be, admit that I was appalled. So this was how a perfidious destiny took advantage of a generous impulse! And I felt as though I were an accomplice in this perfidy, since I did to a certain extent encourage Jasper. Yet I had warned him as well.

"The man seemed to have gone crazy on this point," wrote my friend. "He went to Mesman with his story. He says that some rascally white man living amongst the natives up that river made him drunk with some gin one evening, and then jeered at him for never having any money. Then he, protesting to us that he was an honest man and must be believed, described himself as being a thief whenever he took a drop too much, and told us that he went on board and passed the rifles one by one without the slightest compunction to a canoe which came alongside that night, receiving ten dollars apiece for them.

"Next day he was ill with shame and grief, but had not the courage to confess his lapse to his benefactor. When the gunboat stopped the brig he felt ready to die with the apprehension of the consequences, and would have died happily, if he could have been able to bring the rifles back by the sacrifice of his life. He said nothing to Jasper, hoping that the brig would be released presently. When it turned out otherwise and his captain was detained on board the gunboat, he was ready to commit suicide from despair; only he thought it his duty to live in order to let the truth be known. 'I am an honest man! I am an honest man!' he repeated, in a voice that brought tears to our eyes. 'You must believe me when I tell you that I am a thief—a vile, low, cunning, sneaking thief as soon as I've had a glass or two. Take me somewhere where I may tell the truth on oath.'

"When we had at last convinced him that his story could be of no use to Jasper—for what Dutch court, having once got hold of an English trader, would accept such an explanation; and, indeed, how, when, where could one hope to find proofs of such a tale?—he made as if to tear his hair in handfuls, but, calming down, said: 'Good-bye, then, gentlemen,' and went out of the room so crushed that he seemed hardly able to put one foot before the other. That very night he committed suicide by cutting his throat in the house of a half-caste with whom he had been lodging since he came ashore from the wreck."

That throat, I thought with a shudder, which could produce the tender, persuasive, manly, but fascinating voice which had aroused Jasper's ready compassion and had secured Freya's sympathy! Who could ever have supposed such an end in store for the impossible, gentle Schultz, with his idiosyncrasy of naïve pilfering, so absurdly straightforward that, even in the people who had suffered from it, it aroused nothing more than a sort of amused exasperation? He was really impossible. His lot evidently should have been a half-starved, mysterious, but by no means tragic existence as a mild-eyed, inoffensive beachcomber on the fringe of native life. There are occasions when the irony of fate, which some people profess to discover in the working out of our lives, wears the aspect of crude and savage jesting.

I shook my head over the manes of Schultz, and went on with my friend's letter. It told me how the brig on the reef, looted by the natives from the coast villages, acquired gradually the lamentable aspect, the grey ghostliness of a wreck; while Jasper, fading daily into a mere shadow of a man, strode brusquely all along the "front" with horribly lively eyes and a faint, fixed smile on his lips, to spend the day on a lonely spit of sand looking eagerly at her, as though he had expected some shape on board to rise up and make some sort of sign to him over the decaying bulwarks. The Mesmans were taking care of him as far as it was possible. The *Bonito* case had been referred to Batavia, where no doubt it would fade away in a fog of official papers. . . . It was heartrending to read all this. That active and zealous officer, Lieutenant Heemskirk, his air of sullen, darkly pained self-importance not lightened by the approval of his action conveyed to him unofficially, had gone on to take up his station in the Moluccas. . . .

Then, at the end of the bulky, kindly meant epistle, dealing with the island news of half a year at least, my friend wrote: "A couple of months ago old Nelson turned up here, arriving by the mail-boat from Java. Came to see Mesman, it seems. A rather mysterious visit, and extraordinarily short, after coming all that way. He stayed just four days at the Orange House with apparently nothing in particular to do, and then caught the south-going steamer for the Straits. I remember people saying at one time that Allen was rather sweet on old Nelson's daughter, the girl that was brought up by Mrs. Harley and then went to live with him at the Seven Isles group. Surely you remember old Nelson——"

Remember old Nelson! Rather!

The letter went on to inform me further that old Nelson, at least, remembered me, since some time after his flying visit to Makassar he had written to the Mesmans asking for my address in London.

That old Nelson (or Nielsen), the note of whose personality was a profound, echoless irresponsiveness to everything around him, should wish to write, or find anything to write about to anybody, was in itself a cause for no small wonder. And to me, of all people! I waited with uneasy impatience for whatever disclosure could come from that naturally benighted intelligence, but my impatience had time to wear out before my eyes beheld old Nelson's trembling, painfully formed handwriting, senile and childish at the same time, on an envelope bearing a penny stamp and the postal mark of the Notting Hill office. I delayed opening it in order to pay the tribute of astonishment due to the event by flinging my hands above my head. So he had come home to England, to be definitely Nelson; or else was on his way home to Denmark, where he would revert for ever to his original Nielsen! But old Nelson (or Nielsen) out of the tropics seemed unthinkable. And yet he was there, asking me to call.

His address was at a boarding-house in one of those Bayswater squares, once of leisure, which nowadays are reduced to earning their living. Somebody had recommended him there. I started to call on him on one of those January days in London, one of those wintry days composed of the four devilish elements, cold, wet, mud, and grime, combined with a particular stickiness of atmosphere that clings like an unclean garment to one's very soul. Yet on approaching his abode I saw, like a flicker far behind the soiled veil of the four elements, the wearisome and splendid glitter of a blue sea with the Seven Islets like minute specks swimming in my eye, the high red roof of the bungalow crowning the very smallest of them all. This visual reminiscence was profoundly disturbing. I knocked at the door with a faltering hand.

Old Nelson (or Nielsen) got up from the table at which he was sitting with a shabby pocket-book full of papers before him. He took off his spectacles before shaking hands. For a moment neither of us said a word; then, noticing me looking round somewhat expectantly, he murmured some words, of which I caught only "daughter" and "Hong-kong," cast his eyes down and sighed.

His moustache, sticking all ways out, as of yore, was quite white now. His old cheeks were softly rounded, with some colour in them; strangely enough, that something childlike always noticeable in the general contour of his physiognomy had become much more marked. Like his handwriting, he looked childish and senile. He showed his age most in his unintelligently furrowed, anxious forehead and in his round, innocent eyes, which appeared to me weak and blinking and watery; or was it that they were full of tears? . . .

To discover old Nelson fully informed upon any matter whatever was a new experience. And after the first awkwardness had worn off he talked freely, with, now and then, a question to start him going whenever he lapsed into silence, which he would do suddenly, clasping his hands on his waistcoat in an attitude which would recall to me the east verandah, where he used to sit talking quietly and puffing out his cheeks in what seemed now old, very old days. He talked in a reasonable, somewhat anxious tone.

"No, no. We did not know anything for weeks. Out of the way like that, we couldn't, of course. No mail service to the Seven Isles. But one day I ran over to Banka in my big sailing-boat to see whether there were any letters, and saw a Dutch paper. But it looked only like a bit of marine news: English brig *Bonito* gone ashore outside Makassar roads. That was all. I took the paper home with me and showed it to her. 'I will never forgive him!' she cries with her old spirit. 'My dear,' I said, 'you are a sensible girl. The best man may lose a ship. But what about your health?' I was beginning to be frightened at her looks. She would not let me talk even of going to Singapore before. But, really, such a sensible girl couldn't keep on objecting for ever. 'Do what you like, papa,' she says. Rather a job, that. Had to catch a steamer at sea, but I got her over all right. There, doctors, of course. Fever. Anæmia. Put her to bed. Two or three women very kind to her. Naturally in our papers the whole story came out before long. She reads it to the end, lying on the couch; then hands the newspaper back to me, whispers 'Heemskirk,' and goes off into a faint."

He blinked at me for quite a long time, his eyes running full of tears again.

"Next day," he began, without any emotion in his voice, "she felt stronger, and we had a long talk. She told me everything."

Here old Nelson, with his eyes cast down, gave me the whole story of the Heemskirk episode in Freya's words; then went on in his rather jerky utterance, and looking up innocently:

" 'My dear,' I said, 'you have behaved in the main like a sensible girl.' 'I have been horrid,' she cries, 'and he is breaking his heart over there.' Well, she was too sensible not to see she wasn't in a state to travel. But I went. She told me to go. She was being looked after very well. Anæmia. Getting better they said."

He paused.

"You did see him?" I murmured.

"Oh, yes; I did see him," he started again, talking in that reasonable voice as though he were arguing a point. "I did see him. I came upon him. Eyes sunk an inch into his head; nothing but skin on the bones of his face, a skeleton in dirty white clothes. That's what he looked like. How Freya . . . But she never did—not really. He was sitting there, the only live thing for miles along that coast, on a drift-log washed up on the shore. They had clipped his hair in the hospital, and it had not grown again. He stared, holding his chin in his hand, and with nothing on the sea between him and the sky but that wreck. When I came up to him he just moved his head a bit. 'Is that you, old man?' says he— like that.

"If you had seen him you would have understood at once how impossible it was for Freya to have ever loved that man. Well, well. I don't say. She might have—something. She was lonely, you know. But really to go away with him! Never! Madness. She was too sensible . . . I began to reproach him gently. And by and by he turns on me. 'Write to you! What about? Come to her! What with? If I had been a man I would have carried her off, but she made a child, a happy child, of me. Tell her that the day the only thing I had belonging to me in the world perished on this reef I discovered that I had no power over her. . . . Has she come here with you?' he shouts, blazing at me suddenly with his hollow eyes. I shook my head. Come with me, indeed! Anæmia! 'Aha! You see? Go away, then, old man, and leave me alone here with that ghost,' he says, jerking his head at the wreck of his brig.

"Mad! It was getting dusk. I did not care to stop any longer all by myself with that man in that lonely place. I was not going to tell him of Freya's illness. Anæmia! What was the good? Mad! And what sort of husband would he have made, anyhow, for a sensible girl like Freya? Why, even my little property I could not have left them. The Dutch authorities would never have allowed an Englishman to settle there. It me. Later on I let it go for a tenth of its value to a Dutch half-caste. But never mind. It was nothing to me then. Yes; I went away from him. I caught the return mail-boat. I told everything to Freya. 'He's mad,' I said; 'and, my dear, the only thing he loved was his brig.'

" 'Perhaps,' she says to herself, looking straight away—her eyes were nearly as hollow as his—'perhaps it is true. Yes! I would never allow him any power over me.' "

Old Nelson paused. I sat fascinated, and feeling a little cold in that room with a blazing fire.

"So you see," he continued, "she never really cared for him. Much too sensible. I took her away to Hongkong. Change of climate, they said. Oh, these doctors! My God! Winter time! There came ten days of cold mists and wind and rain. Pneumonia. But look here! We talked a lot together. Days and evenings. Who else had she? . . . She talked a lot to me, my own girl. Sometimes she would laugh a little. Look at me and laugh a little——"

I shuddered. He looked up vaguely, with a childish, puzzled moodiness.

"She would say: 'I did not really mean to be a bad daughter to you, papa.' And I would say: 'Of course, my dear. You could not have meant it.' She would lie quiet and then say: 'I wonder?' And sometimes, 'I've been really a coward,' she would tell me. You know, sick people they say things. And so she would say too: 'I've been conceited, headstrong, capricious. I sought my own gratification. I was selfish or afraid.' . . . But sick people, you know, they say anything. And once, after lying silent almost all day, she said: 'Yes; perhaps, when the day came I would not have gone. Perhaps! I don't know,' she cried. 'Draw the curtain, papa. Shut the sea out. It reproaches me with my folly.' " He gasped and paused.

"So you see," he went on in a murmur. "Very ill, very ill indeed. Pneumonia. Very sudden." He pointed his finger at the carpet, while the thought of the poor girl, vanquished in her struggle with three men's absurdities, and coming at last to doubt her own self, held me in a very anguish of pity.

"You see yourself," he began again in a downcast manner. "She could not have really . . . She mentioned you several times. Good friend. Sensible man. So I wanted to tell you myself—let you know the truth. A fellow like that! How could it be? She was lonely. And perhaps for a while . . . Mere nothing. There could never have been a question of love for my Freya—such a sensible girl——"

"Man!" I cried, rising upon him wrathfully, "don't you see that she died of it?"

He got up too. "No! no!" he stammered, as if angry. "The doctors! Pneumonia. Low state. The inflammation of the . . . They told me. Pneu——"

He did not finish the word. It ended in a sob. He flung his arms out in a gesture of despair, giving up his ghastly pretence with a low, heartrending cry:

"And I thought that she was so sensible!"

THE PLANTER OF
MALATA

· I ·

IN the private editorial office of the principal newspaper in a great
colonial city two men were talking. They were both young. The
stouter of the two, fair, and with more of an urban look about him, was
the editor and part-owner of the important newspaper.

The other's name was Renouard. That he was exercised in his mind
about something was evident on his fine bronzed face. He was a lean,
lounging, active man. The journalist continued the conversation.

"And so you were dining yesterday at old Dunster's."

He used the word old not in the endearing sense in which it is
sometimes applied to intimates, but as a matter of sober fact. The
Dunster in question was old. He had been an eminent colonial statesman, but had now retired from active politics after a tour in Europe
and a lengthy stay in England, during which he had had a very good
press indeed. The colony was proud of him.

"Yes. I dined there," said Renouard. "Young Dunster asked me just
as I was going out of his office. It seemed to be like a sudden thought.
And yet I can't help suspecting some purpose behind it. He was very
pressing. He swore that his uncle would be very pleased to see me. Said
his uncle had mentioned lately that the granting to me of the Malata
concession was the last act of his official life."

"Very touching. The old boy sentimentalises over the past now and
then."

"I really don't know why I accepted," continued the other. "Sentiment does not move me very easily. Old Dunster was civil to me of course, but he did not even inquire how I was getting on with my silk plants. Forgot there was such a thing probably. I must say there were more people there than I expected to meet. Quite a big party."

"I was asked," remarked the newspaper man. "Only I couldn't go. But when did you arrive from Malata?"

"I arrived yesterday at daylight. I am anchored out there in the bay—off Garden Point. I was in Dunster's office before he had finished reading his letters. Have you ever seen young Dunster reading his letters? I had a glimpse of him through the open door. He holds the paper in both hands, hunches his shoulders up to his ugly ears, and brings his long nose and his thick lips on to it like a sucking apparatus. A commercial monster."

"Here we don't consider him a monster," said the newspaper man looking at his visitor thoughtfully.

"Probably not. You are used to see his face and to see other faces. I don't know how it is that, when I come to town, the appearance of the people in the street strikes me with such force. They seem so awfully expressive."

"And not charming."

"Well—no. Not as a rule. The effect is forcible without being clear. . . . I know that you think it's because of my solitary manner of life away there."

"Yes. I do think so. It is demoralising. You don't see any one for months at a stretch. You're leading an unhealthy life."

The other hardly smiled and murmured the admission that true enough it was a good eleven months since he had been in town last.

"You see," insisted the other. "Solitude works like a sort of poison. And then you perceive suggestions in faces—mysterious and forcible, that no sound man would be bothered with. Of course you do."

Geoffrey Renouard did not tell his journalist friend that the suggestions of his own face, the face of a friend, bothered him as much as the others. He detected a degrading quality in the touches of age which every day adds to a human countenance. They moved and disturbed him, like the signs of a horrible inward travail which was frightfully apparent to the fresh eye he had brought from his isolation in Malata, where he had settled after five strenuous years of adventure and exploration.

"It's a fact," he said, "that when I am at home in Malata I see no one consciously. I take the plantation boys for granted."

"Well, and we here take the people in the streets for granted. And that's sanity."

The visitor said nothing to this for fear of engaging a discussion. What he had come to seek in the editorial office was not controversy, but information. Yet somehow he hesitated to approach the subject. Solitary life makes a man reticent in respect of anything in the nature of gossip, which those to whom chatting about their kind is an everyday exercise regard as the commonest use of speech.

"You very busy?" he asked.

The Editor making red marks on a long slip of printed paper threw the pencil down.

"No. I am done. Social paragraphs. This office is the place where everything is known about everybody—including even a great deal of nobodies. Queer fellows drift in and out of this room. Waifs and strays from home, from up-country, from the Pacific. And, by the way, last time you were here you picked up one of that sort for your assistant—didn't you?"

"I engaged an assistant only to stop your preaching about the evils of solitude," said Renouard hastily; and the pressman laughed at the half-resentful tone. His laugh was not very loud, but his plump person shook all over. He was aware that his younger friend's deference to his advice was based only on an imperfect belief in his wisdom—or his sagacity. But it was he who had first helped Renouard in his plans of exploration: the five-years' programme of scientific adventure, of work, of danger and endurance, carried out with such distinction and rewarded modestly with the lease of Malata island by the frugal colonial government. And this reward, too, had been due to the journalist's advocacy with word and pen—for he was an influential man in the community. Doubting very much if Renouard really liked him, he was himself without great sympathy for a certain side of that man which he could not quite make out. He only felt it obscurely to be his real personality—the true—and, perhaps, the absurd. As, for instance, in that case of the assistant. Renouard had given way to the arguments of his friend and backer—the argument against the unwholesome effect of solitude, the argument for the safety of companionship even if quarrelsome. Very well. In this docility he was sensible and even likeable. But what did he do next?

Instead of taking counsel as to the choice with his old backer and friend, and a man, besides, knowing everybody employed and unemployed on the pavements of the town, this extraordinary Renouard suddenly and almost surreptitiously picked up a fellow—God knows who—and sailed away with him back to Malata in a hurry; a proceeding obviously rash and at the same time not quite straight. That was the sort of thing. The secretly unforgiving journalist laughed a little longer and then ceased to shake all over.

"Oh, yes. About that assistant of yours. . . ."

"What about him?" said Renouard, after waiting a while, with a shadow of uneasiness on his face.

"Have you nothing to tell me of him?"

"Nothing except. . . ." Incipient grimness vanished out of Renouard's aspect and his voice, while he hesitated as if reflecting seriously before he changed his mind. "No. Nothing whatever."

"You haven't brought him along with you by chance—for a change?"

The Planter of Malata stared, then shook his head, and finally murmured carelessly: "I think he's very well where he is. But I wish you could tell me why young Dunster insisted so much on my dining with his uncle last night. Everybody knows I am not a society man."

The Editor exclaimed at so much modesty. Didn't his friend know that he was their one and only explorer—that he was the man experimenting with the silk plant. . . .

"Still, that doesn't tell me why I was invited yesterday. For young Dunster never thought of this civility before. . . ."

"Our Willie," said the popular journalist, "never does anything without a purpose, that's a fact."

"And to his uncle's house too!"

"He lives there."

"Yes. But he might have given me a feed somewhere else. The extraordinary part is that the old man did not seem to have anything special to say. He smiled kindly on me once or twice, and that was all. It was quite a party, sixteen people."

The Editor then, after expressing his regret that he had not been able to come, wanted to know if the party had been entertaining.

Renouard regretted that his friend had not been there. Being a man whose business or at least whose profession was to know everything that went on in this part of the globe, he could probably have told him something of some people lately arrived from home, who were amongst the guests. Young Dunster (Willie) with his large shirt front and streaks of white skin shining unpleasantly through the thin black hair plastered over the top of his head, bore down on him and introduced him to that party, as if he had been a trained dog or a child phenomenon. Decidedly, he said, he disliked Willie—one of these large oppressive men. . . .

A silence fell, and it was as if Renouard were not going to say anything more when, suddenly, he came out with the real object of his visit to the editorial room.

"They looked to me like people under a spell."

The Editor gazed at him appreciatively, thinking that, whether the effect of solitude or not, this was a proof of a sensitive perception of the expression of faces.

"You omitted to tell me their name, but I can make a guess. You mean Professor Moorsom, his daughter and sister—don't you?"

Renouard assented. Yes, a white-haired lady. But from his silence, with his eyes fixed, yet avoiding his friend, it was easy to guess that it was not in the white-haired lady that he was interested.

"Upon my word," he said, recovering his usual bearing. "It looks to me as if I had been asked there only for the daughter to talk to me."

He did not conceal that he had been greatly struck by her appearance. Nobody could have helped being impressed. She was different from everybody else in that house, and it was not only the effect of her London clothes. He did not take her down to dinner. Willie did that. It was afterwards, on the terrace. . . .

The evening was delightfully calm. He was sitting apart and alone, and wishing himself somewhere else—on board the schooner for choice, with the dinner-harness off. He hadn't exchanged forty words altogether during the evening with the other guests. He saw her suddenly all by herself coming towards him along the dimly lighted terrace, quite from a distance.

She was tall and supple, carrying nobly on her straight body a head of a character which to him appeared peculiar, something—well—pagan, crowned with a great wealth of hair. He had been about to rise, but her decided approach caused him to remain on the seat. He had not looked much at her that evening. He had not that freedom of gaze acquired by the habit of society and the frequent meetings with strangers. It was not shyness, but the reserve of a man not used to the world and

to the practice of covert staring, with careless curiosity. All he had
captured by his first, keen, instantly lowered, glance was the impression
that her hair was magnificently red and her eyes very black. It was a
troubling effect, but it had been evanescent; he had forgotten it almost
till very unexpectedly he saw her coming down the terrace slow and
eager, as if she were restraining herself, and with a rhythmic upward
undulation of her whole figure. The light from an open window fell
across her path, and suddenly all that mass of arranged hair appeared
incandescent, chiselled and fluid, with the daring suggestion of a helmet
of burnished copper and the flowing lines of molten metal. It kindled
in him an astonished admiration. But he said nothing of it to his friend
the Editor. Neither did he tell him that her approach woke up in his
brain the image of love's infinite grace and the sense of the inexhaustible
joy that lives in beauty. No! What he imparted to the Editor were no
emotions, but mere facts conveyed in a deliberate voice and in unin-
spired words.

"That young lady came and sat down by me. She said: 'Are you
French, Mr. Renouard?' "

He had breathed a whiff of perfume of which he said nothing either—
of some perfume he did not know. Her voice was low and distinct. Her
shoulders and her bare arms gleamed with an extraordinary splendour,
and when she advanced her head into the light he saw the admirable
contour of the face, the straight fine nose with delicate nostrils, the
exquisite crimson brush-stroke of the lips on this oval without colour.
The expression of the eyes was lost in a shadowy mysterious play of jet
and silver, stirring under the red coppery gold of the hair as though she
had been a being made of ivory and precious metals changed into living
tissue.

". . . . I told her my people were living in Canada, but that I was
brought up in England before coming out here. I can't imagine what
interest she could have in my history."

"And you complain of her interest?"

The accent of the all-knowing journalist seemed to jar on the Planter
of Malata.

"No!" he said, in a deadened voice that was almost sullen. But after
a short silence he went on. "Very extraordinary. I told her I came out
to wander at large in the world when I was nineteen, almost directly
after I left school. It seems that her late brother was in the same school

a couple of years before me. She wanted me to tell her what I did at first when I came out here; what other men found to do when they came out—where they went, what was likely to happen to them—as if I could guess and foretell from my experience the fates of men who come out here with a hundred different projects, for hundreds of different reasons—for no reason but restlessness—who come, and go, and disappear! Preposterous. She seemed to want to hear their histories. I told her that most of them were not worth telling."

The distinguished journalist leaning on his elbow, his head resting against the knuckles of his left hand, listened with great attention, but gave no sign of that surprise which Renouard, pausing, seemed to expect.

"You know something," the latter said brusquely. The all-knowing man moved his head slightly and said, "Yes. But go on."

"It's just this. There is no more to it. I found myself talking to her of my adventures, of my early days. It couldn't possibly have interested her. Really," he cried, "this is most extraordinary. Those people have something on their minds. We sat in the light of the window, and her father prowled about the terrace, with his hands behind his back and his head drooping. The white-haired lady came to the dining-room window twice—to look at us I am certain. The other guests began to go away—and still we sat there. Apparently these people are staying with the Dunsters. It was old Mrs. Dunster who put an end to the thing. The father and the aunt circled about as if they were afraid of interfering with the girl. Then she got up all at once, gave me her hand, and said she hoped she would see me again."

While he was speaking Renouard saw again the sway of her figure in a movement of grace and strength—felt the pressure of her hand—heard the last accents of the deep murmur that came from her throat so white in the light of the window, and remembered the black rays of her steady eyes passing off his face when she turned away. He remembered all this visually, and it was not exactly pleasurable. It was rather startling like the discovery of a new faculty in himself. There are faculties one would rather do without—such, for instance, as seeing through a stone wall or remembering a person with this uncanny vividness. And what about those two people belonging to her with their air of expectant solicitude? Really, those figures from home got in front of one. In fact, their persistence in getting between him and the solid forms of the everyday material world had driven Renouard to call on his friend at the office. He hoped that a little common, gossipy information would lay the ghost of that unexpected dinner-party. Of course the proper person to go to would have been young Dunster, but he couldn't stand Willie Dunster—not at any price.

In the pause the Editor had changed his attitude, faced his desk, and smiled a faint knowing smile.

"Striking girl—eh?" he said.

The incongruity of the word was enough to make one jump out of the chair. Striking! That girl striking! Stri . . . ! But Renouard restrained his feelings. His friend was not a person to give oneself away to. And, after all, this sort of speech was what he had come there to hear. As, however, he had made a movement he re-settled himself comfortably and said, with very creditable indifference, that yes—she was, rather. Especially amongst a lot of over-dressed frumps. There wasn't one woman under forty there.

"Is that the way to speak of the cream of our society, the 'top of the basket,' as the French say," the Editor remonstrated with mock indignation. "You aren't moderate in your expressions—you know."

"I express myself very little," interjected Renouard seriously.

"I will tell you what you are. You are a fellow that doesn't count the cost. Of course you are safe with me, but will you never learn . . . ."

"What struck me most," interrupted the other, "is that she should pick me out for such a long conversation."

"That's perhaps because you were the most remarkable of the men there."

Renouard shook his head.

"This shot doesn't seem to me to hit the mark," he said calmly. "Try again."

"Don't you believe me? Oh, you modest creature. Well, let me assure you that under ordinary circumstances it would have been a good shot. You are sufficiently remarkable. But you seem a pretty acute customer too. The circumstances are extraordinary. By Jove they are!"

He mused. After a time the planter of Malata dropped a negligent—

"And you know them."

"And I know them," assented the all-knowing Editor, soberly, as though the occasion were too special for a display of professional vanity; a vanity so well known to Renouard that its absence augmented his wonder and almost made him uneasy as if portending bad news of some sort.

"You have met those people?" he asked.

"No. I was to have met them last night, but I had to send an apology to Willie in the morning. It was then that he had the bright idea to invite you to fill the place, from a muddled notion that you could be of use. Willie is stupid sometimes. For it is clear that you are the last man able to help."

"How on earth do I come to be mixed up in this—whatever it is?" Renouard's voice was slightly altered by nervous irritation. "I only arrived here yesterday morning."

· II ·

His friend the Editor turned to him squarely.

"Willie took me into consultation, and since he seems to have let you in I may just as well tell you what is up. I shall try to be as short as I can. But in confidence—mind!"

He waited. Renouard, his uneasiness growing on him unreasonably, assented by a nod, and the other lost no time in beginning. Professor Moorsom—physicist and philosopher—fine head of white hair, to judge from the photographs—plenty of brains in the head too—all these famous books—surely even Renouard would know. . . .

Renouard muttered moodily that it wasn't his sort of reading, and his friend hastened to assure him earnestly that neither was it his sort—except as a matter of business and duty, for the literary page of that newspaper which was his property (and the pride of his life). The only literary newspaper in the Antipodes could not ignore the fashionable philosopher of the age. Not that everybody read Moorsom, at the Antipodes, but everybody had heard of him—women, children, dock laborers, cabmen. The only person (besides himself) who had read Moorsom, as far as he knew, was old Dunster, who used to call himself a Moorsomian (or was it Moorsomite) years and years ago, long before Moorsom had worked himself up into the great swell he was now, in every way. . . . Socially too. Quite the fashion in the highest world.

Renouard listened with profoundly concealed attention. "A charlatan," he muttered languidly.

"Well—no. I should say not. I shouldn't wonder though if most of his writing had been done with his tongue in his cheek. Of course. That's to be expected. I tell you what: the only really honest writing is to be found in newspapers and nowhere else—and don't you forget it."

The Editor paused with a basilisk stare till Renouard had conceded a casual: "I dare say," and only then went on to explain that old Dunster, during his European tour, had been made rather a lion of in London, where he stayed with the Moorsoms—he meant the father and the girl. The professor had been a widower for a long time.

"She doesn't look just a girl," muttered Renouard.

The other agreed. Very likely not. Had been playing the London hostess to tip-top people ever since she put her hair up, probably.

"I don't expect to see any girlish bloom on her when I do have the privilege," he continued. "Those people are staying with the Dunsters incog., in a manner, you understand—something like royalties. They don't deceive anybody, but they want to be left to themselves. We have even kept them out of the paper—to oblige old Dunster. But we shall put your arrival in—our local celebrity."

"Heavens!"

"Yes. Mr. G. Renouard, the explorer, whose indomitable energy, etc. and who is now working for the prosperity of our country in another way on his Malata plantation . . . And, by the by, how's the silk plant—flourishing?"

"Yes."

"Did you bring any fibre?"

"Schooner-full."

"I see. To be transshipped to Liverpool for experimental manufacture, eh? Eminent capitalists at home very much interested, aren't they?"

"They are."

A silence fell. Then the Editor uttered slowly—"You will be a rich man some day."

Renouard's face did not betray his opinion of that confident prophecy. He didn't say anything till his friend suggested in the same meditative voice—"You ought to interest Moorsom in the affair too—since Willie has let you in."

"A philosopher!"

"I suppose he isn't above making a bit of money. And he may be clever at it for all you know. I have a notion that he's a fairly practical old cove. . . . Anyhow," and here the tone of the speaker took on a tinge of respect, "he has made philosophy pay."

Renouard raised his eyes, repressed an impulse to jump up, and got out of the arm-chair slowly. "It isn't perhaps a bad idea," he said. "I'll have to call there in any case."

He wondered whether he had managed to keep his voice steady, its tone unconcerned enough; for his emotion was strong though it had nothing to do with the business aspect of this suggestion. He moved in the room in vague preparation for departure, when he heard a soft laugh. He spun about quickly with a frown, but the Editor was not laughing at him. He was chuckling across the big desk at the wall: a preliminary of some speech for which Renouard, recalled to himself, waited silent and mistrustful.

"No! You would never guess! No one would ever guess what these people are after. Willie's eyes bulged out when he came to me with the tale."

"They always do," remarked Renouard with disgust. "He's stupid."

"He was startled. And so was I after he told me. It's a search party. They are out looking for a man. Willie's soft heart's enlisted in the cause."

Renouard repeated: "Looking for a man." He sat down suddenly as if on purpose to stare. "Did Willie come to you to borrow the lantern?" he asked sarcastically, and got up again for no apparent reason.

"What lantern?" snapped the puzzled Editor, and his face darkened with suspicion. "You, Renouard, are always alluding to things that aren't clear to me. If you were in politics, I, as a party journalist, wouldn't trust you further than I could see you. Not an inch further. You are such a sophisticated beggar. Listen: the man is the man Miss Moorsom was engaged to for a year. He couldn't have been a nobody, anyhow. But he doesn't seem to have been very wise. Hard luck for the young lady."

He spoke with feeling. It was clear that what he had to tell appealed to his sentiment. Yet, as an experienced man of the world, he marked his amused wonder. Young man of good family and connections, going everywhere, yet not merely a man about town, but with a foot in the two big F's.

Renouard lounging aimlessly in the room turned round: "And what the devil's that?" he asked faintly.

"Why Fashion and Finance," explained the Editor. "That's how I call it. There are the three R's at the bottom of the social edifice and the two F's on the top. See?"

"Ha! Ha! Excellent! Ha! Ha!" Renouard laughed with stony eyes.

"And you proceed from one set to the other in this democratic age," the Editor went on with unperturbed complacency. "That is if you are clever enough. The only danger is in being too clever. And I think something of the sort happened here. That swell I am speaking of got himself into a mess. Apparently a very ugly mess of a financial character. You will understand that Willie did not go into details with me. They were not imparted to him with very great abundance either. But a bad mess—something of the criminal order. Of course he was innocent. But he had to quit all the same."

"Ha! Ha!" Renouard laughed again abruptly, staring as before. "So there's one more big F in the tale."

"What do you mean?" inquired the Editor quickly, with an air as if his patent were being infringed.

"I mean—Fool."

"No. I wouldn't say that. I wouldn't say that."

"Well—let him be a scoundrel then. What the devil do I care."

"But hold on! You haven't heard the end of the story."

Renouard, his hat on his head already, sat down with the disdainful smile of a man who had discounted the moral of the story. Still he sat down and the Editor swung his revolving chair right round. He was full of unction.

"Imprudent, I should say. In many ways money is as dangerous to handle as gunpowder. You can't be too careful either as to who you are working with. Anyhow there was a mighty flashy burst up, a sensation, and—his familiar haunts knew him no more. But before he vanished he went to see Miss Moorsom. That very fact argues for his innocence—don't it? What was said between them no man knows—unless the professor had the confidence from his daughter. There couldn't have been much to say. There was nothing for it but to let him go—was there?—for the affair had got into the papers. And perhaps the kindest thing would have been to forget him. Anyway the easiest. Forgiveness would have been more difficult, I fancy, for a young lady of spirit and position drawn into an ugly affair like that. Any ordinary young lady, I mean. Well, the fellow asked nothing better than to be forgotten, only he didn't find it easy to do so himself, because he would write home now and then. Not to any of his friends though. He had no near relations. The professor had been his guardian. No, the poor devil wrote now and then to an old retired butler of his late father, somewhere in the country, forbidding him at the same time to let any one know of his whereabouts. So that worthy old ass would go up and dodge about the Moorsom's town house, perhaps waylay Miss Moorsom's maid, and then would write to 'Master Arthur' that the young lady looked well and happy, or some such cheerful intelligence. I dare say he wanted to be forgotten, but I shouldn't think he was much cheered by the news. What would you say?''

Renouard, his legs stretched out and his chin on his breast, said nothing. A sensation which was not curiosity, but rather a vague nervous anxiety, distinctly unpleasant, like a mysterious symptom of some malady, prevented him from getting up and going away.

"Mixed feelings," the Editor opined. "Many fellows out here receive news from home with mixed feelings. But what will his feelings be when he hears what I am going to tell you now? For we know he has not heard yet. Six months ago a city clerk, just a common drudge of finance, gets himself convicted of a common embezzlement or something of that kind. Then seeing he's in for a long sentence he thinks of making his conscience comfortable, and makes a clean breast of an old story of tampered with, or else suppressed, documents, a story which clears altogether the honesty of our ruined gentleman. That embezzling fellow was in a position to know, having been employed by the firm before the smash. There was no doubt about the character being cleared—but where the cleared man was nobody could tell. Another sensation in society. And then Miss Moorsom says: 'He will come back to claim me, and I'll marry him.' But he didn't come back. Between you and me I don't think he was much wanted—except by Miss Moorsom. I imagine she's used to have her own way. She grew impatient, and declared that if she knew where the man was she would go to him. But all that could be got out of the old butler was that the last envelope bore the postmark of our beautiful city; and that this was the only address of 'Master Arthur' that he ever had. That and no more. In fact the fellow was at his last gasp—with a bad heart. Miss Moorsom wasn't allowed to see him. She had gone herself into the country to learn what she could, but she had to stay downstairs while the old chap's wife went up to the invalid. She brought down the scrap of intelligence I've told you of. He was already too far gone to be cross-examined on it, and that very night he died. He didn't leave behind him much to go by, did he? Our Willie hinted to me that there had been pretty stormy days in the professor's house, but—here they are. I have a notion she isn't the kind of everyday young lady who may be permitted to gallop about the world all by herself—eh? Well, I think it rather fine of her, but I quite understand that the professor needed all his philosophy under the circumstances. She is his only child now—and brilliant—what? Willie positively spluttered trying to describe her to me; and I could see directly you came in that you had an uncommon experience."

Renouard, with an irritated gesture, tilted his hat more forward on his eyes, as though he were bored. The Editor went on with the remark that to be sure neither he (Renouard) nor yet Willie was much used to meet girls of that remarkable superiority. Willie when learning business with a firm in London, years before, had seen none but boarding-house society, he guessed. As to himself in the good old days, when he trod the glorious flags of Fleet Street, he neither had access to, nor yet would have cared for the swells. Nothing interested him then but parliamentary politics and the oratory of the House of Commons.

He paid to this not very distant past the tribute of a tender, reminiscent smile, and returned to his first idea that for a society girl her action was rather fine. All the same the professor could not be very pleased. The fellow if he was as pure as a lily now was just about as devoid of the goods of the earth. And there were misfortunes, however undeserved, which damaged a man's standing permanently. On the other hand, it was difficult to oppose cynically a noble impulse—not to speak of the great love at the root of it. Ah! Love! And then the lady was quite capable of going off by herself. She was of age, she had money of her own, plenty of pluck too. Moorsom must have concluded that it was more truly paternal, more prudent too, and generally safer all round to let himself be dragged into this chase. The aunt came along for the same reasons. It was given out at home as a trip round the world of the usual kind.

Renouard had risen and remained standing with his heart beating, and strangely affected by this tale, robbed as it was of all glamour by the prosaic personality of the narrator. The Editor added: "I've been asked to help in the search—you know."

Renouard muttered something about an appointment and went out into the street. His inborn sanity could not defend him from a misty creeping jealousy. He thought that obviously no man of that sort could be worthy of such a woman's devoted fidelity. Renouard, however, had lived long enough to reflect that a man's activities, his views, and even his ideas may be very inferior to his character; and moved by a delicate consideration for that splendid girl he tried to think out for the man a character of inward excellence and outward gifts—some extraordinary seduction. But in vain. Fresh from months of solitude and from days at sea, her splendour presented itself to him absolutely unconquerable in its perfection, unless by her own folly. It was easier to suspect her of this than to imagine in the man qualities which would be worthy of her. Easier and less degrading. Because folly may be generous—could be nothing else but generosity in her; whereas to imagine her subjugated by something common was intolerable.

Because of the force of the physical impression he had received from her personality (and such impressions are the real origins of the deepest movements of our soul) this conception of her was even inconceivable. But no Prince Charming has ever lived out of a fairy tale. He doesn't walk the worlds of Fashion and Finance—and with a stumbling gait at that. Generosity. Yes. It was her generosity. But this generosity was altogether regal in its splendour, almost absurd in its lavishness—or, perhaps, divine.

In the evening, on board his schooner, sitting on the rail, his arms folded on his breast and his eyes fixed on the deck, he let the darkness catch him unawares in the midst of a meditation on the mechanism of sentiment and the springs of passion. And all the time he had an abiding consciousness of her bodily presence. The effect on his senses had been so penetrating that in the middle of the night, rousing up suddenly, wide-eyed in the darkness of his cabin, he did not create a faint mental vision of her person for himself, but, more intimately affected, he scented distinctly the faint perfume she used, and could almost have sworn that he had been awakened by the soft rustle of her dress. He even sat up listening in the dark for a time, then sighed and lay down again, not agitated but, on the contrary, oppressed by the sensation of something that had happened to him and could not be undone.

· III ·

In the afternoon he lounged into the editorial office carrying with affected nonchalance that weight of the irremediable he had felt laid on him suddenly in the small hours of the night—that consciousness of something that could no longer be helped. His patronising friend informed him at once that he had made the acquaintance of the Moorsom party last night. At the Dunsters, of course. Dinner.

"Very quiet. Nobody there. It was much better for the business. I say . . ."

Renouard, his hand grasping the back of a chair, stared down at him dumbly.

"Phew! That's a stunning girl. . . . Why do you want to sit on that chair? It's uncomfortable!"

"I wasn't going to sit on it." Renouard walked slowly to the window, glad to find in himself enough self-control to let go the chair instead of raising it on high and bringing it down on the Editor's head.

"Willie kept on gazing at her with tears in his boiled eyes. You should have seen him bending sentimentally over her at dinner."

"Don't," said Renouard in such an anguished tone that the Editor turned right round to look at his back.

"You push your dislike of young Dunster too far. It's positively morbid," he disapproved mildly. "We can't all be beautiful after thirty. . . . I talked a little, about you mostly, to the professor. He appeared to be interested in the silk plant—if only as a change from the great subject. Miss Moorsom didn't seem to mind when I confessed to her that I had taken you into the confidence of the thing. Our Willie approved too. Old Dunster with his white beard seemed to give me his blessing. All those people have a great opinion of you, simply because I told them that you've led every sort of life one can think of before you got struck on exploration. They want you to make suggestions. What do you think 'Master Arthur' is likely to have taken to?"

"Something easy," muttered Renouard without unclenching his teeth.

"Hunting man. Athlete. Don't be hard on the chap. He may be riding boundaries, or droving cattle, or humping his swag about the back-blocks away to the devil—somewhere. He may be even prospecting at the back of beyond—this very moment."

"Or lying dead drunk in a roadside pub. It's late enough in the day for that."

The Editor looked up instinctively. The clock was pointing at a quarter to five. "Yes, it is," he admitted. "But it needn't be. And he may have lit out into the Western Pacific all of a sudden—say in a trading schooner. Though I really don't see in what capacity. Still . . ."

"Or he may be passing at this very moment under this very window."

"Not he . . . and I wish you would get away from it to where one can see your face. I hate talking to a man's back. You stand there like a hermit on a seashore growling to yourself. I tell you what it is, Geoffrey, you don't like mankind."

"I don't make my living by talking about mankind's affairs," Renouard defended himself. But he came away obediently and sat down in the arm-chair. "How can you be so certain that your man isn't down there in the street?" he asked. "It's neither more nor less probable than every single one of your other suppositions."

Placated by Renouard's docility the Editor gazed at him for a while. "Aha! I'll tell you how. Learn then that we have begun the campaign. We have telegraphed his description to the police of every township up and down the land. And what's more we've ascertained definitely that he hasn't been in this town for the last three months at least. How much longer he's been away we can't tell."

"That's very curious."

"It's very simple. Miss Moorsom wrote to him, to the post office here, directly she returned to London after her excursion into the country to see the old butler. Well—her letter is still lying there. It has not been called for. Ergo, this town is not his usual abode. Personally, I never thought it was. But he cannot fail to turn up some time or other. Our main hope lies just in the certitude that he must come to town sooner or later. Remember he doesn't know that the butler is dead, and he will want to inquire for a letter. Well, he'll find a note from Miss Moorsom."

Renouard, silent, thought that it was likely enough. His profound distaste for this conversation was betrayed by an air of weariness darkening his energetic sun-tanned features, and by the augmented dreaminess of his eyes. The Editor noted it as a further proof of that immoral detachment from mankind, of that callousness of sentiment fostered by the unhealthy conditions of solitude—according to his own favourite theory. Aloud he observed that as long as a man had not given up correspondence he could not be looked upon as lost. Fugitive criminals had been tracked in that way by justice, he reminded his friend; then suddenly changed the bearing of the subject somewhat by asking if Renouard had heard from his people lately, and if every member of his large tribe was well and happy.

"Yes, thanks."

The tone was curt, as if repelling a liberty. Renouard did not like being asked about his people, for whom he had a profound and remorseful affection. He had not seen a single human being to whom he was related for many years, and he was extremely different from them all.

On the very morning of his arrival from his island he had gone to a set of pigeon-holes in Willie Dunster's outer office and had taken out from a compartment labelled "Malata" a very small accumulation of envelopes, a few addressed to himself, and one addressed to his assistant, all to the care of the firm, W. Dunster and Co. As opportunity offered, the firm used to send them on to Malata either by a man-of-war schooner going on a cruise, or by some trading craft proceeding that way. But for the last four months there had been no opportunity.

"You going to stay here some time?" asked the Editor, after a longish silence.

Renouard, perfunctorily, did see no reason why he should make a long stay. "For health, for your mental health, my boy," rejoined the newspaper man. "To get used to human faces so that they don't hit you in the eye so hard when you walk about the streets. To get friendly with your kind. I suppose that assistant of yours can be trusted to look after things?"

"There's the half-caste too. The Portuguese. He knows what's to be done."

"Aha!" The Editor looked sharply at his friend. "What's his name?"

"Whose name?"

"The assistant's you picked up on the sly behind my back."

Renouard made a slight movement of impatience.

"I met him unexpectedly one evening. I thought he would do as well as another. He had come from up country and didn't seem happy in a town. He told me his name was Walter. I did not ask him for proofs, you know."

"I don't think you get on very well with him."

"Why? What makes you think so."

"I don't know. Something reluctant in your manner when he's in question."

"Really. My manner! I don't think he's a great subject for conversation, perhaps. Why not drop him?"

"Of course! You wouldn't confess to a mistake. Not you. Nevertheless I have my suspicions about it."

Renouard got up to go, but hesitated, looking down at the seated Editor.

"How funny," he said at last with the utmost seriousness, and was making for the door, when the voice of his friend stopped him.

"You know what has been said of you? That you couldn't get on with anybody you couldn't kick. Now, confess—is there any truth in the soft impeachment?"

"No," said Renouard. "Did you print that in your paper?"

"No. I didn't quite believe it. But I will tell you what I believe. I believe that when your heart is set on some object you are a man that doesn't count the cost to yourself or others. And this shall get printed some day."

"Obituary notice?" Renouard dropped negligently.

"Certain—some day."

"Do you then regard yourself as immortal?"

"No, my boy. I am not immortal. But the voice of the press goes on for ever. . . . And it will say that this was the secret of your great success in a task where better men than you—meaning no offence—did fail repeatedly."

"Success," muttered Renouard, pulling-to the office door after him with considerable energy. And the letters of the word PRIVATE like a row of white eyes seemed to stare after his back sinking down the staircase of that temple of publicity.

Renouard had no doubt that all the means of publicity would be put at the service of love and used for the discovery of the loved man. He did not wish him dead. He did not wish him any harm. We are all equipped with a fund of humanity which is not exhausted without many and repeated provocations—and this man had done him no evil. But before Renouard had left old Dunster's house, at the conclusion of the call he made there that very afternoon, he had discovered in himself the desire that the search might last long. He never really flattered himself that it might fail. It seemed to him that there was no other course in this world for himself, for all mankind, but resignation. And he could not help thinking that Professor Moorsom had arrived at the same conclusion too.

Professor Moorsom, slight frame of middle height, a thoughtful keen head under the thick wavy hair, veiled dark eyes under straight eyebrows, and with an inward gaze which when disengaged and arriving at one seemed to issue from an obscure dream of books, from the limbo of meditation, showed himself extremely gracious to him. Renouard guessed in him a man whom an incurable habit of investigation and analysis had made gentle and indulgent; inapt for action, and more sensitive to the thoughts than to the events of existence. Withal not crushed, sub-ironic without a trace of acidity, and with a simple manner which put people at ease quickly. They had a long conversation on the terrace commanding an extended view of the town and the harbour.

The splendid immobility of the bay resting under his gaze, with its grey spurs and shining indentations, helped Renouard to regain his self-possession, which he had felt shaken, in coming out on the terrace, into the setting of the most powerful emotion of his life, when he had sat within a foot of Miss Moorsom with fire in his breast, a humming in his ears, and in a complete disorder of his mind. There was the very garden seat on which he had been enveloped in the radiant spell. And presently he was sitting on it again with the professor talking of her. Near by the patriarchal Dunster leaned forward in a wicker arm-chair, benign and a little deaf, his big hand to his ear with the innocent eagerness of his advanced age remembering the fires of life.

It was with a sort of apprehension that Renouard looked forward to seeing Miss Moorsom. And strangely enough it resembled the state of mind of a man who fears disenchantment more than sortilege. But he need not have been afraid. Directly he saw her in the distance at the other end of the terrace he shuddered to the roots of his hair. With her approach the power of speech left him for a time. Mrs. Dunster and her aunt were accompanying her. All these people sat down; it was an intimate circle into which Renouard felt himself cordially admitted; and the talk was of the great search which occupied all their minds. Discretion was expected by these people, but of reticence as to the object of the journey there could be no question. Nothing but ways and means and arrangements could be talked about.

By fixing his eyes obstinately on the ground, which gave him an air of reflective sadness, Renouard managed to recover his self-possession. He used it to keep his voice in a low key and to measure his words on the great subject. And he took care with a great inward effort to make them reasonable without giving them a discouraging complexion. For he did not want the quest to be given up, since it would mean her going away with her two attendant grey-heads to the other side of the world.

He was asked to come again, to come often and take part in the counsels of all these people captivated by the sentimental enterprise of a declared love. On taking Miss Moorsom's hand he looked up, would have liked to say something, but found himself voiceless, with his lips suddenly sealed. She returned the pressure of his fingers, and he left her with her eyes vaguely staring beyond him, an air of listening for an expected sound, and the faintest possible smile on her lips. A smile not for him, evidently, but the reflection of some deep and inscrutable thought.

· IV ·

He went on board his schooner. She lay white, and as if suspended, in the crepuscular atmosphere of sunset mingling with the ashy gleam of the vast anchorage. He tried to keep his thoughts as sober, as reasonable, as measured as his words had been, lest they should get away from him and cause some sort of moral disaster. What he was afraid of in the coming night was sleeplessness and the endless strain of that wearisome task. It had to be faced however. He lay on his back, sighing profoundly in the dark, and suddenly beheld his very own self, carrying a small bizarre lamp, reflected in a long mirror inside a room in an empty and unfurnished palace. In this startling image of himself he recognised somebody he had to follow—the frightened guide of his dream. He traversed endless galleries, no end of lofty halls, innumerable doors. He lost himself utterly—he found his way again. Room succeeded room. At last the lamp went out, and he stumbled against some object which, when he stooped for it, he found to be very cold and heavy to lift. The sickly white light of dawn showed him the head of a statue. Its marble hair was done in the bold lines of a helmet, on its lips the chisel had left a faint smile, and it resembled Miss Moorsom. While he was staring at it fixedly, the head began to grow light in his fingers, to diminish and crumble to pieces, and at last turned into a handful of dust, which was blown away by a puff of wind so chilly that he woke up with a desperate shiver and leaped headlong out of his bed-place. The day had really come. He sat down by the cabin table, and taking his head between his hands, did not stir for a very long time.

Very quiet, he set himself to review this dream. The lamp, of course, he connected with the search for a man. But on closer examination he perceived that the reflection of himself in the mirror was not really the true Renouard, but somebody else whose face he could not remember. In the deserted palace he recognised a sinister adaptation by his brain of the long corridors with many doors, in the great building in which his friend's newspaper was lodged on the first floor. The marble head with Miss Moorsom's face! Well! What other face could he have dreamed of? And her complexion was fairer than Parian marble, than the heads of angels. The wind at the end was the morning breeze entering through the open porthole and touching his face before the schooner could swing to the chilly gust.

Yes! And all this rational explanation of the fantastic made it only more mysterious and weird. There was something daemonic in that dream. It was one of those experiences which throw a man out of conformity with the established order of his kind and make him a creature of obscure suggestions.

Henceforth, without ever trying to resist, he went every afternoon to the house where she lived. He went there as passively as if in a dream. He could never make out how he had attained the footing of intimacy in the Dunster mansion above the bay—whether on the ground of personal merit or as the pioneer of the vegetable silk industry. It must have been the last, because he remembered distinctly, as distinctly as in a dream, hearing old Dunster once telling him that his next public task would be a careful survey of the Northern Districts to discover tracts suitable for the cultivation of the silk plant. The old man wagged his beard at him sagely. It was indeed as absurd as a dream.

Willie of course would be there in the evening. But he was more of a figure out of a nightmare, hovering about the circle of chairs in his dress-clothes like a gigantic, repulsive, and sentimental bat. "Do away with the beastly cocoons all over the world," he buzzed in his blurred, water-logged voice. He affected a great horror of insects of all kinds. One evening he appeared with a red flower in his button-hole. Nothing could have been more disgustingly fantastic. And he would also say to Renouard: "You may yet change the history of our country. For economic conditions do shape the history of nations. Eh? What?" And he would turn to Miss Moorsom for approval, lowering protectingly his spatulous nose and looking up with feeling from under his absurd eyebrows, which grew thin, in the manner of canebrakes, out of his spongy skin. For this large, bilious creature was an economist and a sentimentalist, facile to tears, and a member of the Cobden Club.

In order to see as little of him as possible Renouard began coming earlier so as to get away before his arrival without curtailing too much the hours of secret contemplation for which he lived. He had given up trying to deceive himself. His resignation was without bounds. He accepted the immense misfortune of being in love with a woman who was in search of another man only to throw herself into his arms. With such desperate precision he defined in his thoughts the situation, the consciousness of which traversed like a sharp arrow the sudden silences of general conversation. The only thought before which he quailed was the thought that this could not last; that it must come to an end. He feared it instinctively as a sick man may fear death. For it seemed to him that it must be the death of him followed by a lightless, bottomless pit. But his resignation was not spared the torments of jealousy: the cruel, insensate, poignant, and imbecile jealousy, when it seems that a woman betrays us simply by this that she exists, that she breathes—and when the deep movements of her nerves or her soul become a matter of distracting suspicion, of killing doubt, of mortal anxiety.

In the peculiar condition of their sojourn Miss Moorsom went out very little. She accepted this seclusion at the Dunsters' mansion as in a hermitage, and lived there, watched over by a group of old people, with the lofty endurance of a condescending and strong-headed goddess. It was impossible to say if she suffered from anything in the world, and whether this was the insensibility of a great passion concentrated on itself, or a perfect restraint of manner, or the indifference of superiority so complete as to be sufficient to itself. But it was visible to Renouard that she took some pleasure in talking to him at times. Was it because he was the only person near her age? Was this, then, the secret of his admission to the circle?

He admired her voice as well poised as her movements, as her attitudes. He himself had always been a man of tranquil tones. But the power of fascination had torn him out of his very nature so completely that to preserve his habitual calmness from going to pieces had become a terrible effort. He used to go from her on board the schooner exhausted, broken, shaken up, as though he had been put to the most exquisite torture. When he saw her approaching he always had a moment of hallucination. She was a misty and fair creature, fitted for invisible music, for the shadows of love, for the murmurs of waters. After a time (he could not always be staring at the ground) he would summon up all his resolution and look at her. There was a sparkle in the clear obscurity of her eyes; and when she turned them on him they seemed to give a new meaning to life. He would say to himself that another man would have found long before the happy release of madness, his wits burnt to cinders in that radiance. But no such luck for him. His wits had come unscathed through the furnaces of hot suns, of blazing deserts, of flaming angers against the weaknesses of men and the obstinate cruelties of hostile nature.

Being sane he had to be constantly on his guard against falling into adoring silences or breaking out into wild speeches. He had to keep watch on his eyes, his limbs, on the muscles of his face. Their conversations were such as they could be between these two people: she a young lady fresh from the thick twilight of four million people and the artificiality of several London seasons; he the man of definite conquering tasks, the familiar of wide horizons, and in his very repose holding aloof from these agglomerations of units in which one loses one's importance even to oneself. They had no common conversational small change. They had to use the great pieces of general ideas, but they exchanged them trivially. It was no serious commerce. Perhaps she had not much of that coin. Nothing significant came from her. It could not be said that she had received from the contacts of the external world impressions of a personal kind, different from other women. What was ravishing in her was her quietness and, in her grave attitudes, the unfailing brilliance of her femininity. He did not know what there was under that ivory forehead so splendidly shaped, so gloriously crowned. He could not tell what were her thoughts, her feelings. Her replies were reflective, always preceded by a short silence, while he hung on her lips anxiously. He felt himself in the presence of a mysterious being in whom spoke an unknown voice, like the voice of oracles, bringing everlasting unrest to the heart.

He was thankful enough to sit in silence with secretly clenched teeth, devoured by jealousy—and nobody could have guessed that his quiet deferential bearing to all these grey-heads was the supreme effort of stoicism, that the man was engaged in keeping a sinister watch on his tortures lest his strength should fail him. As before, when grappling with other forces of nature, he could find in himself all sorts of courage except the courage to run away.

It was perhaps from the lack of subjects they could have in common that Miss Moorsom made him so often speak of his own life. He did not shrink from talking about himself, for he was free from that exacerbated, timid vanity which seals so many vainglorious lips. He talked to her in his restrained voice, gazing at the tip of her shoe, and thinking that the time was bound to come soon when her very inattention would get weary of him. And indeed on stealing a glance he would see her dazzling and perfect, her eyes vague, staring in mournful immobility, with a drooping head that made him think of a tragic Venus arising before him, not from the foam of the sea, but from a distant, still more formless, mysterious, and potent immensity of mankind.

· V ·

One afternoon Renouard stepping out on the terrace found nobody there. It was for him, at the same time, a melancholy disappointment and a poignant relief.

The heat was great, the air was still, all the long windows of the house stood wide open. At the further end, grouped round a lady's work-table, several chairs disposed sociably suggested invisible occupants, a company of conversing shades. Renouard looked towards them with a sort of dread. A most elusive, faint sound of ghostly talk issuing from one of the rooms added to the illusion and stopped his already hesitating footsteps. He leaned over the balustrade of stone near a squat vase holding a tropical plant of a bizarre shape. Professor Moorsom coming up from the garden with a book under his arm and a white parasol held over his bare head, found him there and, closing the parasol, leaned over by his side with a remark on the increasing heat of the season. Renouard assented and changed his position a little; the other, after a short silence, administered unexpectedly a question which, like the blow of a club on the head, deprived Renouard of the power of speech and even thought, but, more cruel, left him quivering with apprehension, not of death but of everlasting torment. Yet the words were extremely simple.

"Something will have to be done soon. We can't remain in a state of suspended expectation for ever. Tell me what do you think of our chances?"

Renouard, speechless, produced a faint smile. The professor confessed in a jocular tone his impatience to complete the circuit of the globe and be done with it. It was impossible to remain quartered on the dear excellent Dunsters for an indefinite time. And then there were the lectures he had arranged to deliver in Paris. A serious matter.

That lectures by Professor Moorsom were a European event and that brilliant audiences would gather to hear them Renouard did not know. All he was aware of was the shock of this hint of departure. The menace of separation fell on his head like a thunderbolt. And he saw the absurdity of his emotion, for hadn't he lived all these days under the very cloud? The professor, his elbows spread out, looked down into the garden and went on unburdening his mind. Yes. The department of sentiment was directed by his daughter, and she had plenty of volunteered moral support, but he had to look after the practical side of life without assistance.

"I have the less hesitation in speaking to you about my anxiety, because I feel you are friendly to us and at the same time you are detached from all these sublimities—confound them."

"What do you mean?" murmured Renouard.

"I mean that you are capable of calm judgment. Here the atmosphere is simply detestable. Everybody has knuckled under to sentiment. Perhaps your deliberate opinion could influence . . ."

"You want Miss Moorsom to give it up?"

The professor turned to the young man dismally.

"Heaven only knows what I want."

Renouard, leaning his back against the balustrade, folded his arms on his breast and appeared to meditate profoundly. His face, shaded softly by the broad brim of a planter's panama hat, with the straight line of the nose level with the forehead, the eyes lost in the depth of the setting, and the chin well forward, had such a profile as may be seen amongst the bronzes of classical museums, pure under a crested helmet—recalled vaguely a Minerva's head.

"This is the most troublesome time I ever had in my life," exclaimed the professor testily.

"Surely the man must be worth it," muttered Renouard with a pang of jealousy traversing his breast like a self-inflicted stab.

Whether enervated by the heat or giving way to pent-up irritation the professor surrendered himself to the mood of sincerity.

"He began by being a pleasantly dull boy. He developed into a pointlessly clever young man, without, I suspected, ever trying to understand anything. My daughter knew him from childhood. I am a busy man, and I confess that their engagement was a complete surprise to me. I wish their reasons for that step had been more naïve. But simplicity was out of fashion in their set. From a worldly point of view he seems to have been a mere baby. Of course, now, I am assured that he is the victim of his noble confidence in the rectitude of his kind. But that's mere idealising of a sad reality. For my part I will tell you that from the very beginning I had the gravest doubts of his dishonesty. Unfortunately my clever daughter hadn't. And now we behold the reaction. No. To be earnestly dishonest one must be really poor. This was only a manifestation of his extremely refined cleverness. The complicated simpleton. He had an awful awakening though."

In such words did Professor Moorsom give his "young friend" to understand the state of his feelings towards the lost man. It was evident that the father of Miss Moorsom wished him to remain lost. Perhaps the unprecedented heat of the season made him long for the cool spaces of the Pacific, the sweep of the ocean's free wind along the promenade decks, cumbered with long chairs, of a ship steaming towards the Californian coast. To Renouard the philosopher appeared simply the most treacherous of fathers. He was amazed. But he was not at the end of his discoveries.

"He may be dead," the professor murmured.

"Why? People don't die here sooner than in Europe. If he had gone to hide in Italy, for instance, you wouldn't think of saying that."

"Well! And suppose he has become morally disintegrated. You know he was not a strong personality," the professor suggested moodily. "My daughter's future is in question here."

Renouard thought that the love of such a woman was enough to pull any broken man together—to drag a man out of his grave. And he thought this with inward despair, which kept him silent as much almost as his astonishment. At last he managed to stammer out a generous—

"Oh! Don't let us even suppose . . ."

The professor struck in with a sadder accent than before—

"It's good to be young. And then you have been a man of action, and necessarily a believer in success. But I have been looking too long at life not to distrust its surprises. Age! Age! Here I stand before you a man full of doubts and hesitation—*spe lentus, timidus futuri.*

He made a sign to Renouard not to interrupt, and in a lowered voice, as if afraid of being overheard, even there, in the solitude of the terrace—

"And the worst is that I am not even sure how far this sentimental pilgrimage is genuine. Yes. I doubt my own child. It's true that she's a woman. . . ."

Renouard detected with horror a tone of resentment, as if the professor had never forgiven his daughter for not dying instead of his son. The latter noticed the young man's stony stare.

"Ah! you don't understand. Yes, she's clever, open-minded, popular, and—well, charming. But you don't know what it is to have moved, breathed, existed, and even triumphed in the mere smother and froth of life—the brilliant froth. There thoughts, sentiments, opinions, feelings, actions too, are nothing but agitation in empty space—to amuse life— a sort of superior debauchery, exciting and fatiguing, meaning nothing, leading nowhere. She is the creature of that circle. And I ask myself if she is obeying the uneasiness of an instinct seeking its satisfaction, or is it a revulsion of feeling, or is she merely deceiving her own heart by this dangerous trifling with romantic images? And everything is possible— except sincerity, such as only stark, struggling humanity can know. No woman can stand that mode of life in which women rule, and remain a perfectly genuine, simple human being. . . . Ah! There's some people coming out."

He moved off a pace, then turning his head: "Upon my word! I would be infinitely obliged to you if you could throw a little cold water . . ."

and at a vaguely dismayed gesture of Renouard, he added: "Don't be afraid. You wouldn't be putting out a sacred fire."

Renouard could hardly find words for a protest: "I assure you that I never talk with Miss Moorsom—on—on—that. And if you, her father . . ."

"I envy you your innocence," sighed the professor. "A father is only an everyday person. Flat. Stale. Moreover, my child would naturally mistrust me. We belong to the same set. Whereas you carry with you the prestige of the unknown. You have proved yourself to be a force."

Thereupon the professor followed by Renouard joined the circle of all the inmates of the house assembled at the other end of the terrace about a tea-table; three white heads and that resplendent vision of woman's glory, the sight of which had the power to flutter his heart like a reminder of the mortality of his frame.

He avoided the seat by the side of Miss Moorsom. The others were talking together languidly. Unnoticed he looked at that woman so marvellous that centuries seemed to lie between them. He was oppressed and overcome at the thought of what she could give to some man who really would be a force. What a glorious struggle with this amazon! What noble burden for the victorious strength!

Dear old Mrs. Dunster was dispensing tea, looking from time to time with interest towards Miss Moorsom. The aged statesman having eaten a raw tomato and drunk a glass of milk (a habit of his early farming days, long before politics, when, pioneer of wheat-growing, he demonstrated the possibility of raising crops on ground looking barren enough to discourage a magician), smoothed his white beard, and struck lightly Renouard's knee with his big wrinkled hand.

"You had better come back to-night and dine with us quietly."

He liked this young man, a pioneer, too, in more than one direction. Mrs. Dunster added: "Do. It will be very quiet. I don't even know if Willie will be home for dinner." Renouard murmured his thanks, and left the terrace to go on board the schooner. While lingering in the drawing-room doorway he heard the resonant voice of old Dunster uttering oracularly—

". . . the leading man here some day. . . . Like me."

Renouard let the thin summer portière of the doorway fall behind him. The voice of Professor Moorsom said—

"I am told that he has made an enemy of almost every man who had to work with him."

"That's nothing. He did his work. . . . Like me."

"He never counted the cost they say. Not even of lives."

Renouard understood that they were talking of him. Before he could move away, Mrs. Dunster struck in placidly—

"Don't let yourself be shocked by the tales you may hear of him, my dear. Most of it is envy."

Then he heard Miss Moorsom's voice replying to the old lady—

"Oh! I am not easily deceived. I think I may say I have an instinct for truth."

He hastened away from that house with his heart full of dread.

· VI ·

On board the schooner, lying on the settee on his back with the knuckles of his hands pressed over his eyes, he made up his mind that he would not return to that house for dinner—that he would never go back there any more. He made up his mind some twenty times. The knowledge that he had only to go up on the quarter deck, utter quietly the words: "Man the windlass," and that the schooner springing into life would run a hundred miles out to sea before sunrise, deceived his struggling will. Nothing easier! Yet, in the end, this young man, almost ill-famed for his ruthless daring, the inflexible leader of two tragically successful expeditions, shrank from that act of savage energy, and began, instead, to hunt for excuses.

No! It was not for him to run away like an incurable who cuts his throat. He finished dressing and looked at his own impassive face in the saloon mirror scornfully. While being pulled on shore in the gig, he remembered suddenly the wild beauty of a waterfall seen when hardly more than a boy, years ago, in Menado. There was a legend of a governor-general of the Dutch East Indies, on official tour, committing suicide on that spot by leaping into the chasm. It was supposed that a painful disease had made him weary of life. But was there ever a visitation like his own, at the same time binding one to life and so cruelly mortal!

The dinner was indeed quiet. Willie, given half an hour's grace, failed to turn up, and his chair remained vacant by the side of Miss Moorsom. Renouard had the professor's sister on his left, dressed in an expensive gown becoming her age. That maiden lady in her wonderful preservation reminded Renouard somehow of a wax flower under glass. There were no traces of the dust of life's battles on her anywhere. She did not like him very much in the afternoons, in his white drill suit and planter's hat, which seemed to her an unduly Bohemian costume for calling in a house where there were ladies. But in the evening, lithe and elegant in his dress clothes and with his pleasant, slightly veiled voice, he always made her conquest afresh. He might have been anybody distinguished—the son of a duke. Falling under that charm probably (and also because her brother had given her a hint), she attempted to open her heart to Renouard, who was watching with all the power of his soul her niece across the table. She spoke to him as frankly as though that miserable mortal envelope, emptied of everything but hopeless passion, were indeed the son of a duke.

Inattentive, he heard her only in snatches, till the final confidential burst: "... glad if you would express an opinion. Look at her, so charming, such a great favourite, so generally admired! It would be too sad. We all hoped she would make a brilliant marriage with somebody very rich and of high position, have a house in London and in the country, and entertain us all splendidly. She's so eminently fitted for it. She has such hosts of distinguished friends! And then—this instead! ... My heart really aches."

Her well-bred if anxious whisper was covered by the voice of Professor Moorsom discoursing subtly down the short length of the dinner table on the Impermanency of the Measurable to his venerable disciple. It might have been a chapter in a new and popular book of Moorsomian philosophy. Patriarchal and delighted, old Dunster leaned forward a little, his eyes shining youthfully, two spots of colour at the roots of his white beard; and Renouard, glancing at the senile excitement, recalled the words heard on those subtle lips, adopted their scorn for his own, saw their truth before this man ready to be amused by the side of the grave. Yes! Intellectual debauchery in the froth of existence! Froth and fraud!

On the same side of the table Miss Moorsom never once looked towards her father, all her grace as if frozen, her red lips compressed, the faintest rosiness under her dazzling complexion, her black eyes burning motionless, and the very coppery gleams of light lying still on the waves and undulation of her hair. Renouard fancied himself overturning the table, smashing crystal and china, treading fruit and flowers under foot, seizing her in his arms, carrying her off in a tumult of shrieks from all these people, a silent frightened mortal, into some profound retreat as in the age of Cavern men. Suddenly everybody got up, and he hastened to rise too, finding himself out of breath and quite unsteady on his feet.

On the terrace the philosopher, after lighting a cigar, slipped his hand condescendingly under his "dear young friend's" arm. Renouard regarded him now with the profoundest mistrust. But the great man seemed really to have a liking for his young friend—one of those mysterious sympathies, disregarding the differences of age and position, which in this case might have been explained by the failure of philosophy to meet a very real worry of a practical kind.

After a turn or two and some casual talk the professor said suddenly: "My late son was in your school—do you know? I can imagine that had he lived and you had ever met you would have understood each other. He too was inclined to action."

He sighed, then, shaking off the mournful thought and with a nod at the dusky part of the terrace where the dress of his daughter made a luminous stain: "I really wish you would drop in that quarter a few sensible, discouraging words."

Renouard disengaged himself from that most perfidious of men under the pretence of astonishment, and stepping back a pace—

"Surely you are making fun of me, Professor Moorsom," he said with a low laugh, which was really a sound of rage.

"My dear young friend! It's no subject for jokes, to me. . . . You don't seem to have any notion of your prestige," he added, walking away towards the chairs.

"Humbug!" thought Renouard, standing still and looking after him. "And yet! And yet! What if it were true?"

He advanced then towards Miss Moorsom. Posed on the seat on which they had first spoken to each other, it was her turn to watch him coming on. But many of the windows were not lighted that evening. It was dark over there. She appeared to him luminous in her clear dress, a figure without shape, a face without features, awaiting his approach, till he got quite near to her, sat down, and they had exchanged a few insignificant words. Gradually she came out like a magic painting of charm, fascination, and desire, glowing mysteriously on the dark background. Something imperceptible in the lines of her attitude, in the modulations of her voice, seemed to soften that suggestion of calm unconscious pride which enveloped her always like a mantle. He, sensitive like a bond slave to the moods of the master, was moved by the subtle relenting of her grace to an infinite tenderness. He fought down the impulse to seize her by the hand, lead her down into the garden away under the big trees, and throw himself at her feet uttering words of love. His emotion was so strong that he had to cough slightly, and not knowing what to talk to her about he began to tell her of his mother and sisters. All the family were coming to London to live there, for some little time at least.

"I hope you will go and tell them something of me. Something seen," he said pressingly.

By this miserable subterfuge, like a man about to part with his life, he hoped to make her remember him a little longer.

"Certainly," she said. "I'll be glad to call when I get back. But that 'when' may be a long time."

He heard a light sigh. A cruel jealous curiosity made him ask—

"Are you growing weary, Miss Moorsom?"

A silence fell on his low-spoken question.

"Do you mean heart-weary?" sounded Miss Moorsom's voice. "You don't know me, I see."

"Ah! Never despair," he muttered.

"This, Mr. Renouard, is a work of reparation. I stand for truth here. I can't think of myself."

He could have taken her by the throat for every word seemed an insult to his passion; but he only said—

"I never doubted the—the—nobility of your purpose."

"And to hear the word weariness pronounced in this connection surprises me. And from a man too who, I understand, has never counted the cost."

"You are pleased to tease me," he said, directly he had recovered his voice and had mastered his anger. It was as if Professor Moorsom had dropped poison in his ear which was spreading now and tainting his passion, his very jealousy. He mistrusted every word that came from those lips on which his life hung. "How can you know anything of men who do not count the cost?" he asked in his gentlest tones.

"From hearsay—a little."

"Well, I assure you they are like the others, subject to suffering, victims of spells. . . ."

"One of them, at least, speaks very strangely."

She dismissed the subject after a short silence. "Mr. Renouard, I had a disappointment this morning. This mail brought me a letter from the widow of the old butler—you know. I expected to learn that she had heard from—from here. But no. No letter arrived home since we left."

Her voice was calm. His jealousy couldn't stand much more of this sort of talk; but he was glad that nothing had turned up to help the search; glad blindly, unreasonably—only because it would keep her longer in his sight—since she wouldn't give up.

"I am too near her," he thought, moving a little further on the seat. He was afraid in the revulsion of feeling of flinging himself on her hands, which were lying on her lap, and covering them with kisses. He was afraid. Nothing, nothing could shake that spell—not if she were ever so false, stupid, or degraded. She was fate itself. The extent of his misfortune plunged him in such a stupor that he failed at first to hear the sound of voices and footsteps inside the drawing-room. Willie had come home—and the Editor was with him.

They burst out on the terrace babbling noisily, and then pulling themselves together stood still, surprising—and as if themselves surprised.

· VII ·

They had been feasting a poet from the bush, the latest discovery of the Editor. Such discoveries were the business, the vocation, the pride and delight of the only apostle of letters in the hemisphere, the solitary patron of culture, the Slave of the Lamp—as he subscribed himself at the bottom of the weekly literary page of his paper. He had had no difficulty in persuading the virtuous Willie (who had festive instincts) to help in the good work, and now they had left the poet lying asleep on the hearthrug of the editorial room and had rushed to the Dunster mansion wildly. The Editor had another discovery to announce. Swaying a little where he stood he opened his mouth very wide to shout the one word "Found!" Behind him Willie flung both his hands above his head and let them fall dramatically. Renouard saw the four white-headed people at the end of the terrace rise all together from their chairs with an effect of sudden panic.

"I tell you—he—is—found," the patron of letters shouted emphatically.

"What is this!" exclaimed Renouard in a choked voice. Miss Moorsom seized his wrist suddenly, and at that contact fire ran through all his veins, a hot stillness descended upon him in which he heard the blood— or the fire—beating in his ears. He made a movement as if to rise, but was restrained by the convulsive pressure on his wrist.

"No, no." Miss Moorsom's eyes stared black as night, searching the space before her. Far away the Editor strutted forward, Willie following with his ostentatious manner of carrying his bulky and oppressive carcass which, however, did not remain exactly perpendicular for two seconds together.

"The innocent Arthur . . . Yes. We've got him," the Editor became very business-like. "Yes, this letter has done it."

He plunged into an inside pocket for it, slapped the scrap of paper with his open palm. "From that old woman. William had it in his pocket since this morning when Miss Moorsom gave it to him to show me. Forgot all about it till an hour ago. Thought it was of no importance. Well, no! Not till it was properly read."

Renouard and Miss Moorsom emerged from the shadows side by side, a well-matched couple, animated yet statuesque in their calmness and in their pallor. She had let go his wrist. On catching sight of Renouard the Editor exclaimed: "What—you here!" in a quite shrill voice.

There came a dead pause. All the faces had in them something dismayed and cruel.

"He's the very man we want," continued the Editor. "Excuse my excitement. You are the very man, Renouard. Didn't you tell me that your assistant called himself Walter? Yes? Thought so. But here's that old woman—the butler's wife—listen to this. She writes: All I can tell you, Miss, is that my poor husband directed his letters to the name of H. Walter."

Renouard's violent but repressed exclamation was lost in a general murmur and shuffle of feet. The Editor made a step forward, bowed with creditable steadiness.

"Miss Moorsom, allow me to congratulate you from the bottom of my heart on the happy—er—issue . . ."

"Wait," muttered Renouard irresolutely.

The Editor jumped on him in the manner of their old friendship. "Ah, you! You are a fine fellow too. With your solitary ways of life you will end by having no more discrimination than a savage. Fancy living with a gentleman for months and never guessing. A man, I am certain, accomplished, remarkable, out of the common, since he had been distinguished" (he bowed again) "by Miss Moorsom, whom we all admire."

She turned her back on him.

"I hope to goodness you haven't been leading him a dog's life, Geoffrey," the Editor addressed his friend in a whispered aside.

Renouard seized a chair violently, sat down, and propping his elbow on his knee leaned his head on his hand. Behind him the sister of the professor looked up to heaven and wrung her hands stealthily. Mrs. Dunster's hands were clasped forcibly under her chin, but she, dear soul, was looking sorrowfully at Willie. The model nephew! In this strange state! So very much flushed! The careful disposition of the thin hairs across Willie's bald spot was deplorably disarranged, and the spot itself was red and, as it were, steaming.

"What's the matter, Geoffrey?" The Editor seemed disconcerted by the silent attitudes round him, as though he had expected all these people to shout and dance. "You have him on the island—haven't you?"

"Oh, yes: I have him there," said Renouard, without looking up.

"Well, then!" The Editor looked helplessly around as if begging for response of some sort. But the only response that came was very unexpected. Annoyed at being left in the background, and also because very little drink made him nasty, the emotional Willie turned malignant all at once, and in a bibulous tone surprising in a man able to keep his balance so well—

"Aha! But you haven't got him here—not yet!" he sneered. "No! You haven't got him yet."

This outrageous exhibition was to the Editor like the lash to a jaded horse. He positively jumped.

"What of that? What do you mean? We—haven't—got—him—here. Of course he isn't here! But Geoffrey's schooner is here. She can be sent at once to fetch him here. No! Stay! There's a better plan. Why shouldn't you all sail over to Malata, professor? Save time! I am sure Miss Moorsom would prefer . . ."

With a gallant flourish of his arm he looked for Miss Moorsom. She had disappeared. He was taken aback somewhat.

"Ah! H'm. Yes. . . . Why not? A pleasure cruise, delightful ship, delightful season, delightful errand, del . . . No! There are no objections. Geoffrey, I understand, has indulged in a bungalow three sizes too large for him. He can put you all up. It will be a pleasure for him. It will be the greatest privilege. Any man would be proud of being an agent of this happy reunion. I am proud of the little part I've played. He will consider it the greatest honour. Geoff, my boy, you had better be stirring to-morrow bright and early about the preparations for the trip. It would be criminal to lose a single day."

He was as flushed as Willie, the excitement keeping up the effect of the festive dinner. For a time Renouard, silent, as if he had not heard a word of all that babble, did not stir. But when he got up it was to advance towards the Editor and give him such a hearty slap on the back that the plump little man reeled in his tracks and looked quite frightened for a moment.

"You are a heaven-born discoverer and a first-rate manager. . . . He's right. It's the only way. You can't resist the claim of sentiment, and you must even risk the voyage to Malata. . . ." Renouard's voice sank. "A lonely spot," he added, and fell into thought under all those eyes converging on him in the sudden silence. His slow glance passed over all the faces in succession, remaining arrested on Professor Moorsom, stony eyed, a smouldering cigar in his fingers, and with his sister standing by his side. "I shall be infinitely gratified if you consent to come. But, of course, you will. We shall sail to-morrow evening then. And now let me leave you to your happiness."

He bowed, very grave, pointed suddenly his finger at Willie who was swaying about with a sleepy frown. . . . "Look at him. He's overcome with happiness. You had better put him to bed . . ." and disappeared while every head on the terrace was turned to Willie with varied expressions.

Renouard ran through the house. Avoiding the carriage road he fled down the steep short cut to the shore, where his gig was waiting. At his loud shout the sleeping Kanakas jumped up. He leaped in. "Shove off. Give way!" and the gig darted through the water. "Give way! Give way!" She flew past the wool-clippers sleeping at their anchors each with the open unwinking eye of the lamp in the rigging; she flew past the flagship of the Pacific squadron, a great mass all dark and silent, heavy with the slumbers of five hundred men, and where the invisible sentries heard his urgent "Give way! Give way!" in the night. The Kanakas, panting, rose off the thwarts at every stroke. Nothing could be fast enough for him! And he ran up the side of his schooner shaking the ladder noisily with his rush.

On deck he stumbled and stood still.

Wherefore this haste? To what end, since he knew well before he started that he had a pursuer from whom there was no escape.

As his foot touched the deck his will, his purpose he had been hurrying to save, died out within him. It had been nothing less than getting the schooner under way, letting her vanish silently in the night from amongst these sleeping ships. And now he was certain he could not do it. It was impossible! And he reflected that whether he lived or died such an act would lay him under a dark suspicion from which he shrank. No, there was nothing to be done.

He went down into the cabin and, before even unbuttoning his overcoat, took out of the drawer the letter addressed to his assistant; that letter which he had found in the pigeon-hole labelled "Malata" in young Dunster's outer office, where it had been waiting for three months some occasion for being forwarded. From the moment of dropping it in the drawer he had utterly forgotten its existence—till now, when the man's name had come out so clamorously. He glanced at the common envelope, noted the shaky and laborious handwriting: H. Walter, Esqre. Undoubtedly the very last letter the old butler had posted before his illness, and in answer clearly to one from "Master Arthur" instructing him to address in the future: "Care of Messrs. W. Dunster and Co." Renouard made as if to open the envelope, but paused, and, instead, tore the letter deliberately in two, in four, in eight. With his hand full of pieces of paper he returned on deck and scattered them overboard on the dark water, in which they vanished instantly.

He did it slowly, without hesitation or remorse. H. Walter, Esqre, in Malata. The innocent Arthur——What was his name? The man sought for by that woman who as she went by seemed to draw all the passion of the earth to her, without effort, not deigning to notice, naturally, as other women breathed the air. But Renouard was no longer jealous of her very existence. Whatever its meaning it was not for that man he had picked up casually on obscure impulse, to get rid of the tiresome expostulations of a so-called friend; a man of whom he really knew nothing—and now a dead man. In Malata. Oh, yes! He was there secure enough, untroubled in his grave. In Malata. To bury him was the last service Renouard had rendered to his assistant before leaving the island on this trip to town.

Like many men ready enough for arduous enterprises Renouard was inclined to evade the small complications of existence. This trait of his character was composed of a little indolence, some disdain, and a shrinking from contests with certain forms of vulgarity—like a man who would face a lion and go out of his way to avoid a toad. His intercourse with the meddlesome journalist was that merely outward intimacy without sympathy some young men get drawn into easily. It had amused him rather to keep that "friend" in the dark about the fate of his assistant. Renouard had never needed other company than his own, for there was in him something of the sensitiveness of a dreamer who is easily jarred. He had said to himself that the all-knowing one would only preach again about the evils of solitude and worry his head off in favour of some forlornly useless protégé of his. Also the inquisitiveness of the Editor had irritated him and had closed his lips in sheer disgust.

And now he contemplated the noose of consequences drawing tight around him.

It was the memory of that diplomatic reticence which on the terrace had stifled his first cry which would have told them all that the man sought for was not to be met on earth any more. He shrank from the absurdity of hearing the all-knowing one, and not very sober at that, turning on him with righteous reproaches—

"You never told me. You gave me to understand that your assistant was alive, and now you say he's dead. Which is it? Were you lying then or are you lying now?" No! the thought of such a scene was not to be borne. He had sat down appalled, thinking: "What shall I do now?"

His courage had oozed out of him. Speaking the truth meant the Moorsoms going away at once—while it seemed to him that he would give the last shred of his rectitude to secure a day more of her company. He sat on—silent. Slowly, from confused sensations, from his talk with the professor, the manner of the girl herself, the intoxicating familiarity of her sudden hand-clasp, there had come to him a half glimmer of hope. The other man was dead. Then! . . . Madness, of course—but he could not give it up. He had listened to that confounded busybody arranging everything—while all these people stood around assenting, under the spell of that dead romance. He had listened scornful and silent. The glimmers of hope, of opportunity, passed before his eyes. He had only to sit still and say nothing. That and no more. And what was truth to him in the face of that great passion which had flung him prostrate in spirit at her adored feet!

And now it was done! Fatality had willed it! With the eyes of a mortal struck by the maddening thunderbolt of the gods, Renouard looked up to the sky, an immense black pall dusted over with gold, on which great shudders seemed to pass from the breath of life affirming its sway.

· VIII ·

At last, one morning, in a clear spot of a glassy horizon charged with heraldic masses of black vapours, the island grew out from the sea, showing here and there its naked members of basaltic rock through the rents of heavy foliage. Later, in the great spilling of all the riches of sunset, Malata stood out green and rosy before turning into a violet shadow in the autumnal light of the expiring day. Then came the night. In the faint airs the schooner crept on past a sturdy squat headland, and it was pitch dark when her headsails ran down, she turned short on her heel, and her anchor bit into the sandy bottom on the edge of the outer reef; for it was too dangerous then to attempt entering the little bay full of shoals. After the last solemn flutter of the mainsail the murmuring voices of the Moorsom party lingered, very frail, in the black stillness.

They were sitting aft, on chairs, and nobody made a move. Early in the day, when it had become evident that the wind was failing, Renouard, basing his advice on the shortcoming of his bachelor establishment, had urged on the ladies the advisability of not going ashore in the middle of the night. Now he approached them in a constrained manner (it was astonishing the constraint that had reigned between him and his guests all through the passage) and renewed his arguments. No one ashore would dream of his bringing any visitors with him. Nobody would even think of coming off. There was only one old canoe on the plantation. And landing in the schooner's boats would be awkward in the dark.

There was the risk of getting aground on some shallow patches. It would be best to spend the rest of the night on board.

There was really no opposition. The professor smoking a pipe, and very comfortable in an ulster buttoned over his tropical clothes, was the first to speak from his long chair.

"Most excellent advice."

Next to him Miss Moorsom assented by a long silence. Then in a voice as of one coming out of a dream—

"And so this is Malata," she said. "I have often wondered . . ."

A shiver passed through Renouard. She had wondered! What about? Malata was himself. He and Malata were one. And she had wondered! She had. . . .

The professor's sister leaned over towards Renouard. Through all these days at sea the man's—the found man's—existence had not been alluded to on board the schooner. That reticence was part of the general constraint lying upon them all. She, herself, certainly had not been exactly elated by this finding—poor Arthur, without money, without prospects. But she felt moved by the sentiment and romance of the situation.

"Isn't it wonderful," she whispered out of her white wrap, "to think of poor Arthur sleeping there, so near to our dear lovely Felicia, and not knowing the immense joy in store for him to-morrow?"

There was such artificiality in the wax-flower lady that nothing in this speech touched Renouard. It was but the simple anxiety of his heart that he was voicing when he muttered gloomily—

"No one in the world knows what to-morrow may hold in store."

The mature lady had a recoil as though he had said something impolite. What a harsh thing to say—instead of finding something nice and appropriate. On board, where she never saw him in evening clothes, Renouard's resemblance to a duke's son was not so apparent to her. Nothing but his—ah—bohemianism remained. She rose with a sort of ostentation.

"It's late—and since we are going to sleep on board to-night . . ." she said. "But it does seem so cruel."

The professor started up eagerly, knocking the ashes out of his pipe. "Infinitely more sensible, my dear Emma."

Renouard waited behind Miss Moorsom's chair.

She got up slowly, moved one step forward, and paused looking at the shore. The blackness of the island blotted out the stars with its vague mass like a low thundercloud brooding over the waters and ready to burst into flame and crashes.

"And so—this is Malata," she repeated dreamily, moving towards the cabin door. The clear cloak hanging from her shoulders, the ivory face—for the night had put out nothing of her but the gleams of her hair—made her resemble a shining dream-woman uttering words of wistful inquiry. She disappeared without a sign, leaving Renouard penetrated to the very marrow by the sounds that came from her body like a mysterious resonance of an exquisite instrument.

He stood stock still. What was this accidental touch which had evoked the strange accent of her voice? He dared not answer that question. But he had to answer the question of what was to be done now. Had the moment of confession come? The thought was enough to make one's blood run cold.

It was as if those people had a premonition of something. In the taciturn days of the passage he had noticed their reserve even amongst themselves. The professor smoked his pipe moodily in retired spots. Renouard had caught Miss Moorsom's eyes resting on himself more than once, with a peculiar and grave expression. He fancied that she avoided all opportunities of conversation. The maiden lady seemed to nurse a grievance. And now what had he to do?

The lights on the deck had gone out one after the other. The schooner slept.

About an hour after Miss Moorsom had gone below without a sign or a word for him, Renouard got out of his hammock slung in the waist under the midship awning—for he had given up all the accommodation below to his guests. He got out with a sudden swift movement, flung off his sleeping jacket, rolled his pyjamas up his thighs, and stole forward, unseen by the one Kanaka of the anchor-watch. His white torso, naked like a stripped athlete's, glimmered, ghostly, in the deep shadows of the deck. Unnoticed he got out of the ship over the knight-heads, ran along the back rope, and seizing the dolphin-striker firmly with both hands, lowered himself into the sea without a splash.

He swam away, noiseless like a fish, and then struck boldly for the land, sustained, embraced, by the tepid water. The gentle, voluptuous heave of its breast swung him up and down slightly; sometimes a wavelet murmured in his ears; from time to time, lowering his feet, he felt for the bottom on a shallow patch to rest and correct his direction. He landed at the lower end of the bungalow garden, into the dead stillness of the island. There were no lights. The plantation seemed to sleep, as profoundly as the schooner. On the path a small shell cracked under his naked heel.

The faithful half-caste foreman going his rounds cocked his ears at the sharp sound. He gave one enormous start of fear at the sight of the swift white figure flying at him out of the night. He crouched in terror, and then sprang up and clicked his tongue in amazed recognition.

"Tse! Tse! The master!"

"Be quiet, Luiz, and listen to what I say."

Yes, it was the master, the strong master who was never known to raise his voice, the man blindly obeyed and never questioned. He talked low and rapidly in the quiet night, as if every minute were precious. On learning that three guests were coming to stay Luiz clicked his tongue rapidly. These clicks were the uniform, stenographic symbols of his emotions, and he could give them an infinite variety of meaning. He listened to the rest in a deep silence hardly affected by the low, "Yes, master," whenever Renouard paused.

"You understand?" the latter insisted. "No preparations are to be made till we land in the morning. And you are to say that Mr. Walter has gone off in a trading schooner on a round of the islands."

"Yes, master."

"No mistakes—mind!"

"No, master."

Renouard walked back towards the sea. Luiz, following him, proposed to call out half a dozen boys and man the canoe.

"Imbecile!"

"Tse! Tse! Tse!"

"Don't you understand that you haven't seen me?"

"Yes, master. But what a long swim. Suppose you drown."

"Then you can say of me and of Mr. Walter what you like. The dead don't mind."

Renouard entered the sea and heard a faint Tse! Tse! Tse! of concern from the half-caste, who had already lost sight of the master's dark head on the over-shadowed water.

Renouard set his direction by a big star that, dipping on the horizon, seemed to look curiously into his face. On this swim back he felt the mournful fatigue of all that length of the traversed road, which brought him no nearer to his desire. It was as if his love had sapped the invisible supports of his strength. There came a moment when it seemed to him that he must have swum beyond the confines of life. He had a sensation of eternity close at hand, demanding no effort—offering its peace. It was easy to swim like this beyond the confines of life looking at a star. But the thought: "They will think I dared not face them and committed suicide," caused a revolt of his mind which carried him on. He returned on board, as he had left, unheard and unseen. He lay in his hammock utterly exhausted and with a confused feeling that he had been beyond the confines of life, somewhere near a star, and that it was very quiet there.

· IX ·

Sheltered by the squat headland from the first morning sparkle of the sea the little bay breathed a delicious freshness. The party from the schooner landed at the bottom of the garden. They exchanged insignificant words in studiously casual tones. The professor's sister put up a long-handled eye-glass as if to scan the novel surroundings, but in reality searching for poor Arthur anxiously. Having never seen him otherwise than in his town clothes she had no idea what he would look like. It had been left to the professor to help his ladies out of the boat because Renouard, as if intent on giving directions, had stepped forward at once to meet the half-caste Luiz hurrying down the path. In the distance, in front of the dazzlingly sunlit bungalow, a row of dark-faced house-boys unequal in stature and varied in complexion preserved the immobility of a guard of honour.

Luiz had taken off his soft felt hat before coming within earshot. Renouard bent his head to his rapid talk of domestic arrangements he meant to make for the visitors; another bed in the master's room for the ladies and a cot for the gentleman to be hung in the room opposite where—where Mr. Walter—here he gave a scared look all round—Mr. Walter—had died.

"Very good," assented Renouard in an even undertone. "And remember what you have to say of him."

"Yes, master. Only"—he wriggled slightly and put one bare foot on the other for a moment in apologetic embarrassment—"only I—I—don't like to say it."

Renouard looked at him without anger, without any sort of expression. "Frightened of the dead? Eh? Well—all right. I will say it myself—I suppose once for all? . . ." Immediately he raised his voice very much.

"Send the boys down to bring up the luggage."

"Yes, master."

Renouard turned to his distinguished guests who, like a personally conducted party of tourists, had stopped and were looking about them.

"I am sorry," he began with an impassive face. "My man has just told me that Mr. Walter . . ." he managed to smile, but didn't correct himself . . . "has gone in a trading schooner on a short tour of the islands, to the westward."

This communication was received in profound silence.

Renouard forgot himself in the thought: "It's done!" But the sight of the string of boys marching up to the house with suit-cases and dressing-bags rescued him from that appalling abstraction.

"All I can do is to beg you to make yourselves at home . . . with what patience you may."

This was so obviously the only thing to do that everybody moved on at once. The professor walked alongside Renouard, behind the two ladies.

"Rather unexpected—this absence."

"Not exactly," muttered Renouard. "A trip has to be made every year to engage labour."

"I see . . . And he . . . How vexingly elusive the poor fellow has become! I'll begin to think that some wicked fairy is favouring this love tale with unpleasant attentions."

Renouard noticed that the party did not seem weighed down by this new disappointment. On the contrary they moved with a freer step. The professor's sister dropped her eye-glass to the end of its chain. Miss Moorsom took the lead. The professor, his lips unsealed, lingered in the open: but Renouard did not listen to that man's talk. He looked after that man's daughter—if indeed that creature of irresistible seductions were a daughter of mortals. The very intensity of his desire, as if his soul were streaming after her through his eyes, defeated his object of keeping hold of her as long as possible with, at least, one of his senses. Her moving outlines dissolved into a misty coloured shimmer of a woman made of flame and shadows, crossing the threshold of his house.

The days which followed were not exactly such as Renouard had feared—yet they were not better than his fears. They were accursed in all the moods they brought him. But the general aspect of things was quiet. The professor smoked innumerable pipes with the air of a worker on his holiday, always in movement and looking at things with that mysteriously sagacious aspect of men who are admittedly wiser than the rest of the world. His white head of hair—whiter than anything within the horizon except the broken water on the reefs—was glimpsed in every part of the plantation always on the move under the white parasol. And once he climbed the headland and appeared suddenly to those below, a white speck elevated in the blue, with a diminutive but statuesque effect.

Felicia Moorsom remained near the house. Sometimes she could be seen with a despairing expression scribbling rapidly in her lock-up diary. But only for a moment. At the sound of Renouard's footsteps she would turn towards him her beautiful face, adorable in that calm which was like a wilful, like a cruel ignoring of her tremendous power. Whenever she sat on the verandah, on a chair more specially reserved for her use, Renouard would stroll up and sit on the steps near her, mostly silent, and often not trusting himself to turn his glance on her. She, very still with her eyes half-closed, looked down on his head—so that to a beholder (such as Professor Moorsom, for instance) she would appear to be turning over in her mind profound thoughts about that man sitting at her feet, his shoulders bowed a little, his hands listless—as if vanquished. And, indeed, the moral poison of falsehood has such a decomposing power that Renouard felt his old personality turn to dead dust. Often, in the evening, when they sat outside conversing languidly in the dark, he felt that he must rest his forehead on her feet and burst into tears.

The professor's sister suffered from some little strain caused by the unstability of her own feelings towards Renouard. She could not tell whether she really did dislike him or not. At times he appeared to her most fascinating; and, though he generally ended by saying something shockingly crude, she could not resist her inclination to talk with him— at least not always. One day when her niece had left them alone on the verandah she leaned forward in her chair—speckless, resplendent, and, in her way, almost as striking a personality as her niece, who did not resemble her in the least. "Dear Felicia has inherited her hair and the greatest part of her appearance from her mother," the maiden lady used to tell people.

She leaned forward then, confidentially.

"Oh! Mr. Renouard! Haven't you something comforting to say?"

He looked up, as surprised as if a voice from heaven had spoken with this perfect society intonation, and by the puzzled profundity of his blue eyes fluttered the wax-flower of refined womanhood. She continued. "For—I can speak to you openly on this tiresome subject—only think what a terrible strain this hope deferred must be for Felicia's heart—for her nerves."

"Why speak to me about it?" he muttered, feeling half choked suddenly.

"Why! As a friend—a well-wisher—the kindest of hosts. I am afraid we are really eating you out of house and home." She laughed a little. "Ah! When, when will this suspense be relieved! That poor lost Arthur! I confess that I am almost afraid of the great moment. It will be like seeing a ghost."

"Have you ever seen a ghost?" asked Renouard, in a dull voice.

She shifted her hands a little. Her pose was perfect in its ease and middle-aged grace.

"Not actually. Only in a photograph. But we have many friends who have had the experience of apparitions."

"Ah! They see ghosts in London," mumbled Renouard, not looking at her.

"Frequently—in a certain very interesting set. But all sorts of people do. We have a friend, a very famous author—his ghost is a girl. One of my brother's intimates is a very great man of science. He is friendly with a ghost . . . Of a girl too," she added in a voice as if struck for the first time by the coincidence.

"It is the photograph of that apparition which I have seen. Very sweet. Most interesting. A little cloudy naturally? . . . Mr. Renouard! I hope you are not a sceptic. It's so consoling to think . . ."

"Those plantation boys of mine see ghosts too," said Renouard grimly.

The sister of the philosopher sat up stiffly. What crudeness! It was always so with this strange young man.

"Mr. Renouard! How can you compare the superstitious fancies of your horrible savages with the manifestations . . ."

Words failed her. She broke off with a very faint primly angry smile. She was perhaps the more offended with him because of that flutter at the beginning of the conversation. And in a moment with perfect tact and dignity she got up from her chair and left him alone.

Renouard didn't even look up. It was not the displeasure of the lady which deprived him of his sleep that night. He was beginning to forget what simple, honest sleep was like. His hammock from the ship had been hung for him on a side verandah, and he spent his nights in it on his back, his hands folded on his chest, in a sort of half-conscious, oppressed stupor. In the morning he watched with unseeing eyes the headland come out a shapeless inkblot against the thin light of the false dawn, pass through all the stages of daybreak to the deep purple of its outlined mass nimbed gloriously with the gold of the rising sun. He listened to the vague sounds of waking within the house; and suddenly he became aware of Luiz standing by the hammock—obviously troubled.

"What's the matter?"

"Tse! Tse! Tse!"

"Well, what now? Trouble with the boys?"

"No, master. The gentleman when I take him his bath water he speak to me. He ask me—he ask—when, when, I think Mr. Walter, he come back."

The half-caste's teeth chattered slightly. Renouard got out of the hammock.

"And he is here all the time—eh?"

Luiz nodded a scared affirmative, but at once protested, "I no see him. I never. Not I! The ignorant wild boys say they see . . . Something! Ough!"

He clapped his teeth on another short rattle, and stood there, shrunk, blighted, like a man in a freezing blast.

"And what did you say to the gentleman?"

"I say I don't know—and I clear out. I—I don't like to speak of him."

"All right. We shall try to lay that poor ghost," said Renouard gloomily, going off to a small hut near by to dress. He was saying to himself:

"This fellow will end by giving me away. The last thing that I . . . No! That mustn't be." And feeling his hand being forced he discovered the whole extent of his cowardice.

· X ·

That morning wandering about his plantation, more like a frightened soul than its creator and master, he dodged the white parasol bobbing up here and there like a buoy adrift on a sea of dark green plants. The crop promised to be magnificent, and the fashionable philosopher of the age took other than a merely scientific interest in the experiment. His investments were judicious, but he had always some little money lying by, for experiments.

After lunch, being left alone with Renouard, he talked a little of cultivation and such matters. Then suddenly:

"By the way, is it true what my sister tells me, that your plantation boys have been disturbed by a ghost?"

Renouard, who since the ladies had left the table was not keeping such a strict watch on himself, came out of his abstraction with a start and a stiff smile.

"My foreman had some trouble with them during my absence. They funk working in a certain field on the slope of the hill."

"A ghost here!" exclaimed the amused professor. "Then our whole conception of the psychology of ghosts must be revised. This island has been uninhabited probably since the dawn of ages. How did a ghost come here? By air or water? And why did it leave its native haunts? Was it from misanthropy? Was he expelled from some community of spirits?"

Renouard essayed to respond in the same tone. The words died on his lips. Was it a man or a woman ghost, the professor inquired.

"I don't know." Renouard made an effort to appear at ease. He had, he said, a couple of Tahitian amongst his boys—a ghost-ridden race. They had started the scare. They had probably brought their ghost with them.

"Let us investigate the matter, Renouard," proposed the professor half in earnest. "We may make some interesting discoveries as to the state of primitive minds, at any rate."

This was too much. Renouard jumped up and leaving the room went out and walked about in front of the house. He would allow no one to force his hand. Presently the professor joined him outside. He carried his parasol, but had neither his book nor his pipe with him. Amiably serious he laid his hand on his "dear young friend's" arm.

"We are all of us a little strung up," he said. "For my part I have been like sister Anne in the story. But I cannot see anything coming. Anything that would be the least good for anybody—I mean."

Renouard had recovered sufficiently to murmur coldly his regret of this waste of time. For that was what, he supposed, the professor had in his mind.

"Time," mused Professor Moorsom. "I don't know that time can be wasted. But I will tell you, my dear friend, what this is: it's an awful waste of life. I mean for all of us. Even for my sister, who has got a headache and is gone to lie down."

He shook gently Renouard's arm. "Yes, for all of us! One may meditate on life endlessly, one may even have a poor opinion of it—but the fact remains that we have only one life to live. And it is short. Think of that, my young friend."

He released Renouard's arm and stepped out of the shade opening his parasol. It was clear that there was something more in his mind than mere anxiety about the date of his lectures for fashionable audiences. What did the man mean by his confounded platitudes? To Renouard, scared by Luiz in the morning (for he felt that nothing could be more fatal than to have his deception unveiled otherwise than by personal confession), this talk sounded like encouragement or a warning from that man who seemed to him to be very brazen and very subtle. It was like being bullied by the dead and cajoled by the living into a throw of dice for a supreme stake.

Renouard went away some distance from the house and threw himself down in the shade of a tree. He lay there perfectly still with his forehead resting on his folded arms, light-headed and thinking. It seemed to him that he must be on fire, then that he had fallen into a cool whirlpool, a smooth funnel of water swirling about with nauseating rapidity. And then (it must have been a reminiscence of his boyhood) he was walking on the dangerous thin ice of a river, unable to turn back. . . . Suddenly it parted from shore to shore with a loud crack like the report of a gun.

With one leap he found himself on his feet. All was peace, stillness, sunshine. He walked away from there slowly. Had he been a gambler he would have perhaps been supported in a measure by the mere excitement. But he was not a gambler. He had always disdained that artificial manner of challenging the fates. The bungalow came into view, bright and pretty, and all about everything was peace, stillness, sunshine. . . .

While he was plodding towards it he had a disagreeable sense of the dead man's company at his elbow. The ghost! He seemed to be everywhere but in his grave. Could one ever shake him off? he wondered. At that moment Miss Moorsom came out on the verandah; and at once, as if by a mystery of radiating waves, she roused a great tumult in his heart, shook earth and sky together—but he plodded on. Then like a grave song-note in the storm her voice came to him ominously.

"Ah! Mr. Renouard. . . ." He came up and smiled, but she was very serious. "I can't keep still any longer. Is there time to walk up this headland and back before dark?"

The shadows were lying lengthened on the ground; all was stillness and peace. "No," said Renouard, feeling suddenly as steady as a rock. "But I can show you a view from the central hill which your father has not seen. A view of reefs and of broken water without end, and of great wheeling clouds of sea-birds."

She came down the verandah steps at once and they moved off. "You go first," he proposed, "and I'll direct you. To the left."

She was wearing a short nankin skirt, a muslin blouse; he could see through the thin stuff the skin of her shoulders, of her arms. The noble delicacy of her neck caused him a sort of transport. "The path begins where these three palms are. The only palms on the island."

"I see."

She never turned her head. After a while she observed: "This path looks as if it had been made recently."

"Quite recently," he assented very low.

They went on climbing steadily without exchanging another word; and when they stood on the top she gazed a long time before her. The low evening mist veiled the further limit of the reefs. Above the enormous and melancholy confusion, as of a fleet of wrecked islands, the restless myriads of sea-birds rolled and unrolled dark ribbons on the sky, gathered in clouds, soared and stooped like a play of shadows, for they were too far for them to hear their cries.

Renouard broke the silence in low tones.

"They'll be settling for the night presently." She made no sound. Round them all was peace and declining sunshine. Near by, the topmost pinnacle of Malata, resembling the top of a buried tower, rose a rock, weather-worn, grey, weary of watching the monotonous centuries of the Pacific. Renouard leaned his shoulders against it. Felicia Moorsom faced him suddenly, her splendid black eyes full on his face as though she had made up her mind at last to destroy his wits once and for all. Dazzled, he lowered his eyelids slowly.

"Mr. Renouard! There is something strange in all this. Tell me where he is."

He answered deliberately.

"On the other side of this rock. I buried him there myself."

She pressed her hands to her breast, struggled for her breath for a moment, then: "Ohhh! . . . You buried him! . . . What sort of man are you? . . . You dared not tell! . . . He is another of your victims? . . . You dared not confess that evening. . . . You must have killed him. What could he have done to you? . . . You fastened on him some atrocious quarrel and . . ."

Her vengeful aspect, her poignant cries left him as unmoved as the weary rock against which he leaned. He only raised his eyelids to look at her and lowered them slowly. Nothing more. It silenced her. And as if ashamed she made a gesture with her hand, putting away from her that thought. He spoke, quietly ironic at first.

"Ha! the legendary Renouard of sensitive idiots—the ruthless adventurer—the ogre with a future. That was a parrot cry, Miss Moorsom. I don't think that the greatest fool of them all ever dared hint such a stupid thing of me that I killed men for nothing. No, I had noticed this man in a hotel. He had come from up-country I was told, and was doing nothing. I saw him sitting there lonely in a corner like a sick crow, and I went over one evening to talk to him. Just on impulse. He wasn't impressive. He was pitiful. My worst enemy could have told you he wasn't good enough to be one of Renouard's victims. It didn't take me long to judge that he was drugging himself. Not drinking. Drugs."

"Ah! It's now that you are trying to murder him," she cried.

"Really. Always the Renouard of shopkeepers' legend. Listen! I would never have been jealous of him. And yet I am jealous of the air you breathe, of the soil you tread on, of the world that sees you—moving free—not mine. But never mind. I rather liked him. For a certain reason

I proposed he should come to be my assistant here. He said he believed this would save him. It did not save him from death. It came to him as it were from nothing—just a fall. A mere slip and tumble of ten feet into a ravine. But it seems he had been hurt before up-country—by a horse. He ailed and ailed. No, he was not a steel-tipped man. And his poor soul seemed to have been damaged too. It gave way very soon."

"This is tragic!" Felicia Moorsom whispered with feeling. Renouard's lips twitched, but his level voice continued mercilessly.

"That's the story. He rallied a little one night and said he wanted to tell me something. I, being a gentleman, he said, he could confide in me. I told him that he was mistaken. That there was a good deal of a plebeian in me, that he couldn't know. He seemed disappointed. He muttered something about his innocence and something that sounded like a curse on some woman, then turned to the wall—and just grew cold."

"On a woman," cried Miss Moorsom indignantly. "What woman?"

"I wonder!" said Renouard, raising his eyes and noting the crimson of her ear-lobes against the live whiteness of her complexion, the sombre, as if secret, night-splendour of her eyes under the writhing flames of her hair. "Some woman who wouldn't believe in that poor innocence of his. . . . Yes. You probably. And now you will not believe in me—not even in me who must in truth be what I am—even to death. No! You won't. And yet, Felicia, a woman like you and a man like me do not often come together on this earth."

The flame of her glorious head scorched his face. He flung his hat far away, and his suddenly lowered eyelids brought out startlingly his resemblance to antique bronze, the profile of Pallas, still, austere, bowed a little in the shadow of the rock. "Oh! If you could only understand the truth that is in me!" he added.

She waited, as if too astounded to speak, till he looked up again, and then with unnatural force as if defending herself from some unspoken aspersion, "It's I who stand for truth here! Believe in you! In you, who by a heartless falsehood—and nothing else, nothing else, do you hear?— have brought me here, deceived, cheated, as in some abominable farce!" She sat down on a boulder, rested her chin in her hands, in the pose of simple grief—mourning for herself.

"It only wanted this. Why! Oh! Why is it that ugliness, ridicule, and baseness must fall across my path?"

On that height, alone with the sky, they spoke to each other as if the earth had fallen away from under their feet.

"Are you grieving for your dignity? He was a mediocre soul and could have given you but an unworthy existence."

She did not even smile at those words, but, superb, as if lifting a corner of the veil, she turned on him slowly.

"And do you imagine I would have devoted myself to him for such a purpose? Don't you know that reparation was due to him from me? A sacred debt—a fine duty! To redeem him would not have been in my power—I know it. But he was blameless, and it was for me to come forward. Don't you see that in the eyes of the world nothing could have rehabilitated him so completely as his marriage with me? No word of evil could be whispered of him after I had given him my hand. As to giving myself up to anything less than the shaping of a man's destiny— if I thought I could do it I would abhor myself. . . ." She spoke with authority in her deep, fascinating, unemotional voice. Renouard meditated, gloomy, as if over some sinister riddle of a beautiful sphinx met on the wild road of his life.

"Yes. Your father was right. You are one of these aristocrats . . ."

She drew herself up haughtily.

"What do you say? My father! . . . I an aristocrat."

"Oh! I don't mean that you are like the men and women of the time of armours, castles, and great deeds. Oh, no! They stood on the naked soil, had traditions to be faithful to, had their feet on this earth of passions and death which is not a hothouse. They would have been too plebeian for you since they had to lead, to suffer with, to understand the commonest humanity. No, you are merely of the topmost layer, disdainful and superior, the mere pure froth and bubble on the inscrutable depths which some day will toss you out of existence. But you are you! You are you! You are the eternal love itself—only, O Divinity, it isn't your body, it is your soul that is made of foam."

She listened as if in a dream. He had succeeded so well in his effort to drive back the flood of his passion that his life itself seemed to run with it out of his body. At that moment he felt as one dead speaking. But the headlong wave returning with tenfold force flung him on her suddenly, with open arms and blazing eyes. She found herself like a feather in his grasp, helpless, unable to struggle, with her feet off the ground. But this contact with her, maddening like too much felicity, destroyed its own end. Fire ran through his veins, turned his passion to ashes, burnt him out and left him empty, without force—almost without desire. He let her go before she could cry out. And she was so used to the forms of repression enveloping, softening the crude impulses of old humanity that she no longer believed in their existence as if it were an exploded legend. She did not recognise what had happened to her. She came safe out of his arms, without a struggle, not even having felt afraid.

"What's the meaning of this?" she said, outraged but calm in a scornful way.

He got down on his knees in silence, bent low to her very feet, while she looked down at him, a little surprised, without animosity, as if merely curious to see what he would do. Then, while he remained bowed to the ground pressing the hem of her skirt to his lips, she made a slight movement. He got up.

"No," he said. "Were you ever so much mine what could I do with you without your consent? No. You don't conquer a wraith, cold mist, stuff of dreams, illusion. It must come to you and cling to your breast. And then! Oh! And then!"

All ecstasy, all expression went out of his face.

"Mr. Renouard," she said, "though you can have no claim on my consideration after having decoyed me here for the vile purpose, apparently, of gloating over me as your possible prey, I will tell you that I am not perhaps the extraordinary being you think I am. You may believe me. Here I stand for truth itself."

"What's that to me what you are?" he answered. "At a sign from you I would climb up to the seventh heaven to bring you down to earth for my own—and if I saw you steeped to the lips in vice, in crime, in mud, I would go after you, take you to my arms—wear you for an incomparable jewel on my breast. And that's love—true love—the gift and the curse of the gods. There is no other."

The truth vibrating in his voice made her recoil slightly, for she was not fit to hear it—not even a little—not even one single time in her life. It was revolting to her; and in her trouble, perhaps prompted by the suggestion of his name or to soften the harshness of expression, for she was obscurely moved, she spoke to him in French.

"*Assez! J'ai horreur de tout cela*," she said.

He was white to his very lips, but he was trembling no more. The dice had been cast, and not even violence could alter the throw. She passed by him unbendingly, and he followed her down the path. After a time she heard him saying:

"And your dream is to influence a human destiny?"

"Yes!" she answered curtly, unabashed, with a woman's complete assurance.

"Then you may rest content. You have done it."

She shrugged her shoulders slightly. But just before reaching the end of the path she relented, stopped, and went back to him.

"I don't suppose you are very anxious for people to know how near you came to absolute turpitude. You may rest easy on that point. I shall speak to my father, of course, and we will agree to say that he has died— nothing more."

"Yes," said Renouard in a lifeless voice. "He is dead. His very ghost shall be done with presently."

She went on, but he remained standing stock still in the dusk. She had already reached the three palms when she heard behind her a loud peal of laughter, cynical and joyless, such as is heard in smoking-rooms at the end of a scandalous story. It made her feel positively faint for a moment.

· XI ·

Slowly a complete darkness enveloped Geoffrey Renouard. His resolution had failed him. Instead of following Felicia into the house, he had stopped under the three palms, and leaning against a smooth trunk had abandoned himself to a sense of an immense deception and the feeling of extreme fatigue. This walk up the hill and down again was like the supreme effort of an explorer trying to penetrate the interior of an unknown country, the secret of which is too well defended by its cruel and barren nature. Decoyed by a mirage, he had gone too far—so far that there was no going back. His strength was at an end. For the first time in his life he had to give up, and with a sort of despairing self-possession he tried to understand the cause of the defeat. He did not ascribe it to that absurd dead man.

The hesitating shadow of Luiz approached him unnoticed till it spoke timidly. Renouard started.

"Eh? What? Dinner waiting? You must say I beg to be excused. I can't come. But I shall see them to-morrow morning, at the landing place. Take your orders from the professor as to the sailing of the schooner. Go now."

Luiz, dumbfounded, retreated into the darkness. Renouard did not move, but hours afterwards, like the bitter fruit of his immobility, the words: "I had nothing to offer to her vanity," came from his lips in the silence of the island. And it was then only that he stirred, only to wear the night out in restless tramping up and down the various paths of the plantation. Luiz, whose sleep was made light by the consciousness of some impending change, heard footsteps passing by his hut, the firm tread of the master; and turning on his mats emitted a faint Tse! Tse! Tse! of deep concern.

Lights had been burning in the bungalow almost all through the night; and with the first sign of day began the bustle of departure. House-boys walked processionally carrying suit-cases and dressing-bags down to the schooner's boat, which came to the landing place at the bottom of the garden. Just as the rising sun threw its golden nimbus around the purple shape of the headland, the Planter of Malata was perceived pacing bareheaded the curve of the little bay. He exchanged a few words with the sailing-master of the schooner, then remained by the boat, standing very upright, his eyes on the ground, waiting.

He had not long to wait. Into the cool, over-shadowed garden the professor descended first, and came jauntily down the path in a lively cracking of small shells. With his closed parasol hooked on his forearm, and a book in his hand, he resembled a banal tourist more than was permissible to a man of his unique distinction. He waved the disengaged arm from a distance, but at close quarters, arrested before Renouard's immobility, he made no offer to shake hands. He seemed to appraise the aspect of the man with a sharp glance, and made up his mind.

"We are going back by Suez," he began almost boisterously. "I have been looking up the sailing lists. If the zephyrs of your Pacific are only moderately propitious I think we are sure to catch the mail boat due in Marseilles on the 18th of March. This will suit me excellently. . . ." He lowered his tone. "My dear young friend, I'm deeply grateful to you."

Renouard's set lips moved.

"Why are you grateful to me?"

"Ah! Why? In the first place you might have made us miss the next boat, mightn't you? . . . I don't thank you for your hospitality. You can't be angry with me for saying that I am truly thankful to escape from it. But I am grateful to you for what you have done, and—for being what you are."

It was difficult to define the flavour of that speech, but Renouard received it with an austerely equivocal smile. The professor stepping into the boat opened his parasol and sat down in the stern-sheets waiting for the ladies. No sound of human voice broke the fresh silence of the morning while they walked the broad path, Miss Moorsom a little in advance of her aunt.

When she came abreast of him Renouard raised his head.

"Good-bye, Mr. Renouard," she said in a low voice, meaning to pass on; but there was such a look of entreaty in the blue gleam of his sunken eyes that after an imperceptible hesitation she laid her hand, which was ungloved, in his extended palm.

"Will you condescend to remember me?" he asked while an emotion with which she was angry made her pale cheeks flush and her black eyes sparkle.

"This is a strange request for you to make," she said, exaggerating the coldness of her tone.

"Is it? Impudent perhaps. Yet I am not so guilty as you think; and bear in mind that to me you can never make reparation."

"Reparation? To you! It is you who can offer me no reparation for the offence against my feelings—and my person; for what reparation can be adequate for your odious and ridiculous plot so scornful in its implication, so humiliating to my pride? No! I don't want to remember you."

Unexpectedly, with a tightening grip, he pulled her nearer to him, and looking into her eyes with fearless despair—

"You'll have to. . . . I shall haunt you," he said firmly.

Her hand was wrenched out of his grasp before he had time to release it. Felicia Moorsom stepped into the boat, sat down by the side of her father, and breathed tenderly on her crushed fingers.

The professor gave her a sidelong look—nothing more. But the professor's sister, yet on shore, had put up her long-handled double eyeglass to look at the scene. She dropped it with a faint rattle.

"I've never in my life heard anything so crude said to a lady," she murmured, passing before Renouard with a perfectly erect head. When, a moment afterwards, softening suddenly, she turned to throw a good-bye to that young man, she saw only his back in the distance moving towards the bungalow. She watched him go in—amazed—before she too left the soil of Malata.

Nobody disturbed Renouard in that room where he had shut himself in to breathe the evanescent perfume of her who for him was no more, till late in the afternoon when the half-caste was heard on the other side of the door.

He wanted the master to know that the trader *Janet* was just entering the cove.

Renouard's strong voice on his side of the door gave him most unexpected instructions. He was to pay off the boys with the cash in the office and arrange with the captain of the *Janet* to take every worker away from Malata, returning them to their respective homes. An order on the Dunster firm would be given to him in payment.

And again the silence of the bungalow remained unbroken till, next morning, the half-caste came to report that everything was done. The plantation boys were embarking now.

Through a crack in the door a hand thrust at him a piece of paper, and the door slammed to so sharply that Luiz stepped back. Then approaching cringingly the keyhole, in a propitiatory tone he asked:

"Do I go too, master?"

"Yes. You too. Everybody."

"Master stop here alone?"

Silence. And the half-caste's eyes grew wide with wonder. But he also, like those "ignorant savages," the plantation boys, was only too glad to leave an island haunted by the ghost of a white man. He backed away noiselessly from the mysterious silence in the closed room, and only in the very doorway of the bungalow allowed himself to give vent to his feelings by a deprecatory and pained—

"Tse! Tse! Tse!"

· XII ·

The Moorsoms did manage to catch the homeward mail boat all right, but had only twenty-four hours in town. Thus the sentimental Willie could not see very much of them. This did not prevent him afterwards from relating at great length, with manly tears in his eyes, how poor Miss Moorsom—the fashionable and clever beauty—found her betrothed in

Malata only to see him die in her arms. Most people were deeply touched by the sad story. It was the talk of a good many days.

But the all-knowing Editor, Renouard's only friend and crony, wanted to know more than the rest of the world. From professional incontinence, perhaps, he thirsted for a full cup of harrowing detail. And when he noticed Renouard's schooner lying in port day after day he sought the sailing master to learn the reason. The man told him that such were his instructions. He had been ordered to lie there a month before returning to Malata. And the month was nearly up. "I will ask you to give me a passage," said the Editor.

He landed in the morning at the bottom of the garden and found peace, stillness, sunshine reigning everywhere, the doors and windows of the bungalow standing wide open, no sight of a human being anywhere, the plants growing rank and tall on the deserted fields. For hours the Editor and the schooner's crew, excited by the mystery, roamed over the island shouting Renouard's name; and at last set themselves in grim silence to explore systematically the uncleared bush and the deeper ravines in search of his corpse. What had happened? Had he been murdered by the boys? Or had he simply, capricious and secretive, abandoned his plantation taking the people with him. It was impossible to tell what had happened. At last, towards the decline of the day, the Editor and the sailing master discovered a track of sandals crossing a strip of sandy beach on the north shore of the bay. Following this track fearfully, they passed round the spur of the headland, and there on a large stone found the sandals, Renouard's white jacket, and the Malay sarong of chequered pattern which the Planter of Malata was well known to wear when going to bathe. These things made a little heap, and the sailor remarked, after gazing at it in silence—

"Birds have been hovering over this for many a day."

"He's gone bathing and got drowned," cried the Editor in dismay.

"I doubt it, sir. If he had been drowned anywhere within a mile from the shore the body would have been washed out on the reefs. And our boats have found nothing so far."

Nothing was ever found—and Renouard's disappearance remained in the main inexplicable. For to whom could it have occurred that a man would set out calmly to swim beyond the confines of life—with a steady stroke—his eyes fixed on a star?

Next evening, from the receding schooner, the Editor looked back for the last time at the deserted island. A black cloud hung listlessly over the high rock on the middle hill; and under the mysterious silence of that shadow Malata lay mournful, with an air of anguish in the wild sunset, as if remembering the heart that was broken there.

Dec., 1913.

CONRAD'S "AUTHOR'S NOTES"

IN 1919, when the first collected edition of Conrad's works was in preparation, Conrad set out to write an "Author's Note" for each volume that did not already have such a note. I have included here the three having to do principally with the tales. "Author's Notes" to the three collections containing the shorter stories will be found in *The Collected Stories of Joseph Conrad*, the companion volume to *The Tales*.

YOUTH: A NARRATIVE
Author's Note

THE three stories in this volume lay no claim to unity of artistic purpose. The only bond between them is that of the time in which they were written. They belong to the period immediately following the publication of the *Nigger of the Narcissus*, and preceding the first conception of *Nostromo*, two books which, it seems to me, stand apart and by themselves in the body of my work. It is also the period during which I contributed to *Maga*; a period dominated by *Lord Jim* and associated in my grateful memory with the late Mr. William Blackwood's encouraging and helpful kindness.

"Youth" was not my first contribution to *Maga*. It was the second. But that story marks the first appearance in the world of the man Marlow, with whom my relations have grown very intimate in the course of years. The origins of that gentleman (nobody as far as I know has ever hinted that he was anything but that)—his origins have been the subject of some literary speculation of, I am glad to say, a friendly nature.

One would think that I am the proper person to throw a light on the matter; but in truth I find that it isn't so easy. It is pleasant to remember that nobody had charged him with fraudulent purposes or looked down on him as a charlatan; but apart from that he was supposed to be all sorts of things: a clever screen, a mere device, a "personator," a familiar spirit, a whispering "dæmon." I myself have been suspected of a meditated plan for his capture.

That is not so. I made no plans. The man Marlow and I came together in the casual manner of those health-resort acquaintances which sometimes ripen into friendships. This one has ripened. For all his assertiveness in matters of opinion he is not an intrusive person. He haunts my hours of solitude, when, in silence, we lay our heads together in great comfort and harmony; but as we part at the end of a tale I am never sure that it may not be for the last time. Yet I don't think that either of us would care much to survive the other. In his case, at any rate, his occupation would be gone and he would suffer from that extinction, because I suspect him of some vanity. I don't mean vanity in the Solomonian sense. Of all my people he's the one that has never been a vexation to my spirit. A most discreet, understanding man. . . .

Even before appearing in book-form "Youth" was very well received. It lies on me to confess at last, and this is as good a place for it as another, that I have been all my life—all my two lives—the spoiled adopted child of Great Britain and even of the Empire; for it was Australia that gave me my first command. I break out into this declaration not because of a lurking tendency to megalomania, but, on the contrary, as a man who has no very notable illusions about himself. I follow the instincts of vain-glory and humility natural to all mankind. For it can hardly be denied that it is not their own deserts that men are most proud of, but rather of their prodigious luck, of their marvellous fortune: of that in their lives for which thanks and sacrifices must be offered on the altars of the inscrutable gods.

"Heart of Darkness" also received a certain amount of notice from the first; and of its origins this much may be said: it is well known that curious men go prying into all sorts of places (where they have no business) and come out of them with all kinds of spoil. This story, and one other, not in this volume, are all the spoil I brought out from the centre of Africa, where, really, I had no sort of business. More ambitious in its scope and longer in the telling, "Heart of Darkness" is quite as authentic in fundamentals as "Youth." It is, obviously, written in another mood. I won't characterize the mood precisely, but anybody can see that it is anything but the mood of wistful regret, of reminiscent tenderness.

One more remark may be added. "Youth" is a feat of memory. It is a record of experience; but that experience, in its facts, in its inwardness and in its outward colouring, begins and ends in myself. "Heart of Darkness" is experience, too; but it is experience pushed a little (and only very little) beyond the actual facts of the case for the perfectly legitimate, I believe, purpose of bringing it home to the minds and bosoms of the readers. There it was no longer a matter of sincere colouring. It was like another art altogether. That sombre theme had to be given a sinister resonance, a tonality of its own, a continued vibration that, I hoped, would hang in the air and dwell on the ear after the last note had been struck.

After saying so much there remains the last tale of the book, still untouched. "The End of the Tether" is a story of sea-life in a rather special way; and the most intimate thing I can say of it is this; that having lived that life fully, amongst its men, its thoughts and sensations, I have found it possible, without the slightest misgiving, in all sincerity of heart and peace of conscience, to conceive the existence of Captain Whalley's personality and to relate the manner of his end. This statement acquires some force from the circumstance that the pages of that story— a fair half of the book—are also the product of experience. That experience belongs (like "Youth's") to the time before I ever thought of putting pen to paper. As to its "reality," that is for the readers to determine. One had to pick up one's facts here and there. More skill would have made them more real and the whole composition more interesting. But here we are approaching the veiled region of artistic values which it would be improper and indeed dangerous for me to enter. I have looked over the proofs, have corrected a misprint or two, have changed a word or two—and that's all. It is not very likely that I shall ever read "The End of the Tether" again. No more need be said. It accords best with my feelings to part from Captain Whalley in affectionate silence.

J. C.
1917

TYPHOON
Author's Note

THE main characteristic of this volume consists in this, that all the stories composing it belong not only to the same period but have been written one after another in the order in which they appear in the book.

The period is that which follows on my connection with *Blackwood's Magazine*. I had just finished writing "The End of the Tether" and was casting about for some subject which could be developed in a shorter form than the tales in the volume of *Youth* when the instance of a steamship full of returning coolies from Singapore to some port in northern China occurred to my recollection. Years before I had heard it being talked about in the East as a recent occurrence. It was for us merely one subject of conversation amongst many others of the kind. Men earning their bread in any very specialized occupation will talk shop, not only because it is the most vital interest of their lives but also because they have not much knowledge of other subjects. They have never had the time to get acquainted with them. Life, for most of us, is not so much a hard as an exacting taskmaster.

I never met anybody personally concerned in this affair, the interest of which for us was, of course, not the bad weather but the extraordinary complication brought into the ship's life at a moment of exceptional stress by the human element below her deck. Neither was the story itself ever enlarged upon in my hearing. In that company each of us could imagine easily what the whole thing was like. The financial difficulty of it, presenting also a human problem, was solved by a mind much too simple to be perplexed by anything in the world except men's idle talk for which it was not adapted.

From the first the mere anecdote, the mere statement I might say, that such a thing had happened on the high seas, appeared to me a sufficient subject for meditation. Yet it was but a bit of a sea yarn after all. I felt that to bring out its deeper significance which was quite apparent to me, something other, something more was required; a leading motive that would harmonize all these violent noises, and a point of view that would put all that elemental fury into its proper place.

What was needed of course was Captain MacWhirr. Directly I perceived him I could see that he was the man for the situation. I don't mean to say that I ever saw Captain MacWhirr in the flesh, or had ever come in contact with his literal mind and his dauntless temperament. MacWhirr is not an acquaintance of a few hours, or a few weeks, or a few months. He is the product of twenty years of life. My own life. Conscious invention had little to do with him. If it is true that Captain MacWhirr never walked and breathed on this earth (which I find for my part extremely difficult to believe) I can also assure my readers that he is perfectly authentic. I may venture to assert the same of every aspect of the story, while I confess that the particular typhoon of the tale was not a typhoon of my actual experience.

At its first appearance "Typhoon," the story, was classed by some critics as a deliberately intended storm-piece. Others picked out Mac-Whirr, in whom they perceived a definite symbolic intention. Neither was exclusively my intention. Both the typhoon and Captain MacWhirr presented themselves to me as the necessities of the deep conviction with which I approached the subject of the story. It was their opportunity. It was also my opportunity; and it would be vain to discourse about what I made of it in a handful of pages, since the pages themselves are here, between the covers of this volume, to speak for themselves.

This is a belated reflection. If it had occurred to me before it would have perhaps done away with the existence of this Author's Note; for, indeed, the same remark applies to every story in this volume. None of them are stories of experience in the absolute sense of the word. Experience in them is but the canvas of the attempted picture. Each of them has its more than one intention. With each the question is what the writer has done with his opportunity; and each answers the question for itself in words which, if I may say so without undue solemnity, were written with a conscientious regard for the truth of my own sensations.

And each of those stories, to mean something, must justify itself in its own way to the conscience of each successive reader.

"Falk"—the second story in the volume—offended the delicacy of one critic at least by certain peculiarities of its subject. But what is the subject of "Falk"? I personally do not feel so very certain about it. He who reads must find out for himself. My intention in writing "Falk" was not to shock anybody. As in most of my writings I insist not on the events but on their effect upon the persons in the tale. But in everything I have written there is always one invariable intention, and that is to capture the reader's attention, by securing his interest and enlisting his sympathies for the matter in hand, whatever it may be, within the limits of the visible world and within the boundaries of human emotions.

I may safely say that Falk is absolutely true to my experience of certain straightforward characters combining a perfectly natural ruthlessness with a certain amount of moral delicacy. Falk obeys the law of self-preservation without the slightest misgivings as to his right, but at a crucial turn of that ruthlessly preserved life he will not condescend to dodge the truth. As he is presented as sensitive enough to be affected permanently by a certain unusual experience, that experience had to be set by me before the reader vividly; but it is not the subject of the tale. If we go by mere facts then the subject is Falk's attempt to get married; in which the narrator of the tale finds himself unexpectedly involved both on its ruthless and its delicate side.

"Falk" shares with one other of my stories ("The Return" in the *Tales of Unrest* volume) the distinction of never having been serialized. I think the copy was shown to the editor of some magazine who rejected it indignantly on the sole ground that "the girl never says anything." This is perfectly true. From first to last Hermann's niece utters no word in the tale—and it is not because she is dumb, but for the simple reason that whenever she happens to come under the observation of the narrator she has either no occasion or is too profoundly moved to speak. The editor, who obviously had read the story, might have perceived that for himself. Apparently he did not, and I refrained from pointing out the impossibility to him because, since he did not venture to say that "the girl" did not live, I felt no concern at his indignation.

All the other stories were serialized. The "Typhoon" appeared in the early numbers of the *Pall Mall Magazine*, then under the direction of the late Mr. Halkett. It was on that occasion, too, that I saw for the first time my conceptions rendered by an artist in another medium. Mr. Maurice Greiffenhagen knew how to combine in his illustrations the effect of his own most distinguished personal vision with an absolute fidelity to the inspiration of the writer. "Amy Foster" was published in *The Illustrated London News* with a fine drawing of Amy on her day out giving tea to the children at her home, in a hat with a big feather. "To-morrow" appeared first in the *Pall Mall Magazine*. Of that story I will only say that it struck many people by its adaptability to the stage and that I was induced to dramatize it under the title of "One Day More"; up to the present my only effort in that direction. I may also add that each of the four stories on their appearance in book form was picked out on various grounds as the "best of the lot" by different critics, who reviewed the volume with a warmth of appreciation and understanding, a sympathetic insight and a friendliness of expression for which I cannot be sufficiently grateful.

J. C.

1919

'TWIXT LAND AND SEA
Author's Note

THE only bond between these three stories is, so to speak, geographical, for their scene, be it land, be it sea, is situated in the same region which may be called the region of the Indian Ocean with its off-shoots and prolongations north of the equator even as far as the Gulf of Siam. In point of time they belong to the period immediately after the publication of that novel with the awkward title *Under Western Eyes* and, as far as the life of the writer is concerned, their appearance in a volume marks a definite change in the fortunes of his fiction. For there is no denying the fact that *Under Western Eyes* found no favour in the public eye, whereas the novel called *Chance* which followed *'Twixt Land and Sea* was received on its first appearance by many more readers than any other of my books.

This volume of three tales was also well received, publicly and privately and from a publisher's point of view. This little success was a most timely tonic for my enfeebled bodily frame. For this may indeed be called the book of a man's convalescence, at least as to three-fourths of it; because "The Secret Sharer," the middle story, was written much earlier than the other two.

For in truth the memories of *Under Western Eyes* are associated with the memory of a severe illness which seemed to wait like a tiger in the jungle on the turn of a path to jump on me the moment the last words of that novel were written. The memory of an illness is very much like the memory of a nightmare. On emerging from it in a much enfeebled state I was inspired to direct my tottering steps toward the Indian Ocean, a complete change of surroundings and atmosphere from the Lake of

Geneva, as nobody would deny. Begun so languidly and with such a fumbling hand that the first twenty pages or more had to be thrown into the waste-paper basket, "A Smile of Fortune," the most purely Indian Ocean story of the three, has ended by becoming what the reader will see. I will only say for myself that I have been patted on the back for it by most unexpected people, personally unknown to me, the chief of them of course being the editor of a popular illustrated magazine who published it serially in one mighty instalment. Who will dare say after this that the change of air had not been an immense success?

The origins of the middle story, "The Secret Sharer," are quite other. It was written much earlier and was published first in *Harper's Magazine*, during the early part, I think, of 1911. Or perhaps the latter part? My memory on that point is hazy. The basic fact of the tale I had in my possession for a good many years. It was in truth the common possession of the whole fleet of merchant ships trading to India, China, and Australia: a great company the last years of which coincided with my first years on the wider seas. The fact itself happened on board a very distinguished member of it, *Cutty Sark* by name and belonging to Mr. Willis, a notable ship-owner in his day, one of the kind (they are all underground now) who used personally to see his ships start on their voyages to those distant shores where they showed worthily the honoured house-flag of their owner. I am glad I was not too late to get at least one glimpse of Mr. Willis on a very wet and gloomy morning watching from the pier head of the New South Dock one of his clippers starting on a China voyage—an imposing figure of a man under the invariable white hat so well known in the Port of London, waiting till the head of his ship had swung down-stream before giving her a dignified wave of a big gloved hand. For all I know it may have been the *Cutty Sark* herself though certainly not on that fatal voyage. I do not know the date of the occurrence on which the scheme of "The Secret Sharer" is founded; it came to light and even got into newspapers about the middle eighties, though I had heard of it before, as it were privately, among the officers of the great wool fleet in which my first years in deep water were served. It came to light under circumstances dramatic enough, I think, but which have nothing to do with my story. In the more specially maritime part of my writings this bit of presentation may take its place as one of my two Calm-pieces. For, if there is to be any classification by subjects, I have done two Storm-pieces in *The Nigger of the Narcissus* and in "Typhoon"; and two Calm-pieces: this one and *The Shadow Line*, a book which belongs to a later period.

Notwithstanding their autobiographical form the above two stories are not the record of personal experience. Their quality, such as it is, depends on something larger if less precise: on the character, vision and sentiment of the first twenty independent years of my life. And the same may be said of the "Freya of the Seven Isles." I was considerably abused for writing that story on the ground of its cruelty, both in public prints and in private letters. I remember one from a man in America who was quite furiously angry. He told me with curses and imprecations that I had no right to write such an abominable thing which, he said, had gratuitously and intolerably harrowed his feelings. It was a very interesting letter to read. Impressive too. I carried it for some days in my pocket. Had I the right? The sincerity of the anger impressed me. Had I the right? Had I really sinned as he said or was it only that man's madness? Yet there was a method in his fury. . . . I composed in my mind a violent reply, a reply of mild argument, a reply of lofty detachment; but they never got on paper in the end and I have forgotten their phrasing. The very letter of the angry man has got lost somehow; and nothing remains now but the pages of the story which I cannot recall and would not recall if I could.

But I am glad to think that the two women in this book: Alice, the sullen, passive victim of her fate, and the actively individual Freya, so determined to be the mistress of her own destiny, must have evoked some sympathies because of all my volumes of short stories this was the one for which there was the greatest immediate demand.

J. C.
1920.

A NOTE ON THE TEXT

THE copy text for this volume is the Kent Edition of *Conrad's Complete Works*, published in the United States by Doubleday, Page in 1925, the year after Conrad's death. The Kent Edition was printed from corrected plates of the first collected edition, the Sun Dial Edition of 1921, which was also the source for other collected editions published before and after Conrad's death, including the Uniform Edition published in England by Dent (1923–28).

I have emended the Kent Edition in the following ways: I have corrected a few typographical errors; I have regularized Conrad's inconsistent forms of reference to the titles of his stories and books in his "Author's Notes"; and I have revised the text in the following instances, where later editing seemed to me to alter Conrad's intentions:

	This Edition	*Kent Edition*
p. 2, line 5	The Director,	The director,
p. 31, line 20	shouted 'We	shouted, 'We
p. 31, line 21	exclaiming 'No	exclaiming, 'No
p. 99, line 23	his country	his county
p. 101, line 27	meaning: No	meaning: "No
p. 101, line 28	yourself.	yourself."
p. 126, line 13	was as though	was though
p. 127, line 36	Chinamen	Chinaman
p. 217, line 11	Everything remained	Every thing remained

p. 224, line 3	temper? It	temper? it
p. 261, line 21	beginning.	beginning.—
p. 336, line 2	a seal	seal
p. 365, line 19	roar	roor,
p. 395, line 3	a historical	an historical
p. 440, line 17	hear! . . .	hear. . . .
p. 469, line 38	Who with?	Whom with?
p. 512, line 12	Why	"Why
p. 512, line 14	own—	own?"
p. 555, line 12	these	those
p. 558, line 18	strikes	strike

A BIBLIOGRAPHY OF THE TALES

Seven of Conrad's eight longer stories were first published in periodicals, five of them serialized over more than one issue. They were subsequently published in the following collections:

Youth: A Narrative; and Two Other Stories (1902)
Typhoon and Other Stories (1903)
A Set of Six (1908)
'Twixt Land and Sea (1912)
Within the Tides (1915)

Individual tales were published as follows:

"Heart of Darkness," *Blackwood's Magazine*, February–April 1899; *Youth*

"Typhoon," *Pall Mall Magazine*, January–March 1902; *Typhoon*

"The End of the Tether," *Blackwood's Magazine*, July–December 1902; *Youth*

"Falk: a Reminiscence," no periodical publication; *Typhoon*

"The Duel," *Pall Mall Magazine*, January–May 1908; *A Set of Six*

"A Smile of Fortune," *London Magazine*, February 1911; *'Twixt Land and Sea*

"Freya of the Seven Isles," *Metropolitan Magazine*, April 1912; *'Twixt Land and Sea*

"The Planter of Malata," *Metropolitan Magazine*, June–July 1914; *Within the Tides*